# THE WO
# CLUB

## Margaret Bard

**HEADLINE**

First published in Great Britain in 1992
by HEADLINE BOOK PUBLISHING PLC

Reprinted in this edition in 1992
by HEADLINE BOOK PUBLISHING PLC

10 9 8 7 6 5 4 3 2 1

British Library Cataloguing in Publication Data

Bard, Margaret
The women's club.
I. Title
823.914 [F]

ISBN 0−7472−0498−5

Typeset by Medcalf Type Ltd, Bicester, Oxon

Printed and bound in Great Britain by
Richard Clay Ltd, Bungay, Suffolk

HEADLINE BOOK PUBLISHING PLC
Headline House
79 Great Titchfield Street
London W1P 7FN

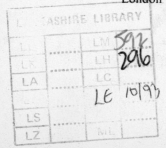

# Contents

'. . . Fire continues to rage through 37 Middlesex, New York City's prestigious club for women only. Just a few hours earlier, the newly renovated building was the scene of a glittering celebrity gala marking the tenth anniversary of the club's founding. Fire fighters and rescue workers remain on the scene. One woman and one man are known to be dead. The cause of the fire is not yet known, but apparently there was a flash explosion just before the main blaze. Police are not ruling out the possibility of arson. Known as "the world's most lavish indoor playground for women", with branches of the club scheduled to open in LA and London, the immediate future of 37 Middlesex would appear to be in jeopardy.

'This is Bodine Johnson for *Late Beat News* in downtown Manhattan.'

# Prologue

The smoked glass super-stretch limousine pulled up in front of a large, anonymous-looking building with a discreet brass plaque that read '37 Middlesex'. 'Pick me up at five, Merrick,' said the elegant, smoothly tanned blonde, slamming the limo door casually behind her. The uniformed chauffeur nodded vaguely and tipped his cap, eager to get back to the *New York Post* item he was reading, with the attention-grabbing headline: Local Entrepreneur Caught in Housewife Prostie Love Nest.

She took a final drag on her Benson & Hedges and surveyed the Manhattan street. The Club at 37 Middlesex was located in the East Sixties, one of the classiest sections of the city, but even this area had become a battleground for the forces of Donald Trump against what appeared to be rejects from *Escape from New York*. God, she found this city depressing sometimes with the noise, the dirt; all the glass and chrome in the world could not erase that constant feeling of being under siege.

In front of the building next door, a couple of Rastafarian street vendors were hawking 'genuine' Gucci bags and battery-operated plastic roses. On the other side of her, a man or woman — it was impossible to tell under that shapeless bundle of rags — was pushing a shopping cart with a life history of worldly belongings tied on to it. The acrid smell from the grilled kebabs and faintly rancid falafel was nauseating. Across the street a crowd had gathered to watch three black kids break-dancing,

1

keeping one eye on their ghetto blaster and another on their audience.

As they turned to gape at the limo, she could see a group of Japanese tourists caught between taking a picture of the break-dancers and getting a shot of her limo. It gratified her that even in jaded old New York a stretch could still command that kind of gawking attention. The gawkers assumed, no doubt, that the limo held a major movie star, a rock group or, at the very least, Mario Cuomo. Well, they weren't that far off. 37 Middlesex made her feel like a movie star. Throughout a highly select group of Manhattan society, 37 Middlesex was known simply as The Club. From the outside, The Club didn't look particularly imposing, but behind the building's simple, graceful façade lay a myriad of secrets.

She stubbed out her cigarette and gave a little wave to Merrick, sending the limo on its way. Inserting her gold Club card into the magnetized slot, she let the heavy doors swing open, admitting her into the hermetically sealed inner foyer of 37 Middlesex, the most exclusive club for women in the world.

Almost immediately she felt her mood lift. Smiling to herself, she started up the fabled pink marble staircase. No matter how many times 37 Middlesex had been renovated, the huge central staircase remained the same, a continuing symbol of the founding principles of The Club, a vast ladder of female ambition leading to the goal of ever-increasing success in a man's world.

Into the glass elevator that would shoot her straight up through the centre of the building to the top floor, the tropical roof garden with its running track and the opulently appointed health spa with the windows overlooking all of Manhattan. With its Greek columns, lush hanging plants, terrazzo-tiled jacuzzis and art deco changing rooms, the luxury spa looked like something out of *Quo Vadis*. She half expected to see Peter Ustinov

2

throw a couple of Christians to the lions. The place was truly the height of decadence, and it had seen her through an extremely messy divorce, saved her sanity, and given her a reason to go on living. Thank God for The Club. She was really looking forward to the anniversary gala tonight.

In the black and silver change-room, she examined herself in front of the artfully lit, full-length mirror. Legs great. Tummy not bad, especially when she remembered to hold it in with that crunch method detailed in *Vogue* magazine. Boobs looking damn good for a woman of forty-seven, thanks to the lift and implants she had done last spring. No visible scars. The Mariel Hemingway cut, Dr MacLeod had called it, specifically designed for Star 80. She had new tits courtesy of the divorce settlement. New tits and the limo. Lee certainly wasn't interested any more. Not in a limo and, unfortunately, not in her tits.

What a cliché her ex-husband had turned out to be. When she met the short, balding, Bronx wheeler-dealer, he thought a limousine driven by a transplanted limey was the ultimate in making it. Now, at fifty-six, and part of the Times Square Development Project, Lee had decided he wanted to return to his roots. He had dumped her to marry his nineteen-year-old secretary, whose main attraction, other than her spiked red hair and un-augmented naturally perky teenage tits, seemed to be that she came from Lee's old neighbourhood. Another cliché. Classic, in fact. Daddy had been right all along. He had told her what a liberal arts education at Mt Holyoke could not prepare her for. Never marry a wop.

Still, she hadn't come out of it too badly. The kids were pretty well grown, she looked better than she had at twenty, and she'd taken the bastard for all he was worth — the co-op, the house in the Hamptons, the Kruggerands, the limo, the cosmetic surgery, and her privacy. Which she valued above all the rest. She checked

3

her diamond-studded Piaget. Three o'clock in the afternoon. Too late for the well-heeled Westchester wives who wanted to make at least a slight effort to be home with the nanny for the kids after private school, and too early for the Wall Street women who workaholicked themselves until well after six. At three o'clock she would have the massage area virtually to herself.

Wrapping her newly streamlined body in one of the oversized pink velour bathrobes, she headed for the massage area. It surrounded her in a soft rosy pink, each tiled cubicle equipped with a pink satin day-bed. A top Broadway lighting designer had done the lights, all in surprise pink specials, designed to make even the flabbiest skin look rosy and firm. She loosened the robe and climbed on to the daybed, face down, her bare breasts and stomach pressing voluptuously against the cool satin.

'Hi there, Mrs Giordano.' She felt the robe being slipped off her and opened one eye to see Jon, the masseur, his teeth and trousers equally white and dazzling against his tanning-parlour tan. Shirtless, his strongly-muscled chest was an even expanse of brown, and the fine blond hair on his over-developed forearms gleamed like soft golden down.

'Jordan,' she corrected him, lifting her head so he could attach the Sony Walkman over her ears. For a fleeting moment, she felt slightly ridiculous as the sexy, raspy voice of Bruce Springsteen assaulted her. She knew she was too old for Springsteen (it seemed she was too old for everything these days) but the Boss was a Jersey boy with the same sweaty urgency that had once attracted her to Lee, raw and rough and ready to go.

'Oh yeah, right. I always forget that,' Jon said into the air, realizing his client was already lost in the throbbing pulse of the bass guitar line. He reached for the rose crystal bowl on the marble table by the day-bed and began to crush a peach, a couple of strawberries and half a mango into The Club's basic lotion.

She took a deep breath. The smell was overwhelmingly exotic and sensual, reminding her of that February she and Lee had taken a Club Med 'hedonism package' in Grand Cayman at a clothing-optional beach. At sunset, with the palm trees already black against the fiery orange sky, they had lain together on a silk sheet spread out on the finely powdered sand. Lee had peeled a mango and placed the slippery golden fruit between her legs, sliding the sweet stickiness back and forth until it mixed with her own, rubbing, rubbing, gently, so wet, so soft, his rough, still-calloused fingers moving within her, until she had begged him to put the mango down and replace it with himself.

The cream felt soothing and cool on her bare back. Jon's strong fingers stroked her, gently at first, lightly pressing against the pressure points at the base of her neck, erasing the tension in her shoulders, moving lower to caress her back, playing delicate tunes along each vertebra, sending the notes downward, diminuendos down her thighs, ripples along her calves. His expert fingers magically finding the right places, sticky sexy fingers, massaging rhythmically, working the muscles more insistently now, pressing firmly against the satin, warmth flowing beneath the skin, loosening the knot in her stomach, the one she just couldn't seem to rid herself of since Lee left, letting it dissolve, making her want to weep suddenly with pleasure and pain. His large, powerful hands encircled her waist, cradling her hips, kneading her buttocks, gently pulling her open to the world, prying her apart, then putting her back together again.

He was bending right over her, close to her, so close she could feel the warmth of his breath through the cool of the cream on her skin. How could he know her body

5

so well when she was a stranger to him? She shuddered involuntarily, every nerve alive, aching for release, when suddenly she was flooded with heat, running liquid to match the strawberry-scented cream, going limp, giving herself over to the sensation, oh God, it's been so long, oh please, so wonderful to feel alive again, the bubble rising within her, please, lower, just move your hand down, can't bear it, need it . . .

Jon broke away, tapping her lightly on one bare shoulder, and lifted the earphones from her head. 'Excuse me, Mrs Jordan,' he said very politely, 'but will you be wanting the usual? I can put it on your Club tab if you like.'

'Yes, Jon,' she gasped, willing him to put his fingers back where they were, 'the usual.' Like a good girl. 'Please.' And as he turned her over, sliding his wet, silky hands between her own wet silky thighs, she reached for the industrial size zipper on his white duck trousers. Thank heaven for 37 Middlesex. Thank God for The Club.

# Part I

## *The Gala*

# One

As her plane circled LaGuardia, Susie Krumins leaned back in her first-class seat and sighed. If she had even one drink she'd be bombed, she just knew it. Her stomach was a bit queasy and she felt light-headed. Hadn't they proved that drinking on a plane made you drunker faster? Better stick to ginger ale. She didn't want to be bombed before she got to the gala. If she made it to the gala. It had taken her a month of daily phone calls to get this audience with Betsy Bloomingdale to discuss a business deal. Susie had breathed a massive sigh of relief when Joan Fairfax, Bloomingdale's gourmet food buyer, finally returned her call.

'I hate talking business in my office.' Joan's clear voice bubbled mellifluously through Susie's speaker phone. 'I assume you'll be at the anniversary gala for The Club?'

'I'm catering it,' Susie said, trying to sound breezy and confident. Certainly more confident than she felt. Catering the gala was a huge undertaking.

'Marvellous! How clever of you! Of course Betsy will be there, too, and I want you to run your proposal past her, I plan to have Bloomie's special projects advisor along as well. We can all have a quick chat. Sound good?'

'It sounds fabulous.' Susie could hardly contain her excitement. A chance to sell her idea to the department store heiress in person. What more could she ask?

'But let's try and do this first thing, early on in the evening, know what I mean? It is a party, after all. More

9

than two glasses of champagne on an empty stomach —
do you believe I'm still dieting? I've got to get into that
dress — and I'll be too pissed to discuss anything more
serious than Warren Beatty's love life.'

'Oh, absolutely,' Susie agreed.

'So, early on, first thing, top priority?'

'You got it.'

'And a word to the wise, dear. Keep it casual. Betsy
simply will not be pushed.'

'Of course not,' Susie said quickly. 'High-pressure
selling is not my style.'

'I don't know, dear,' Joan laughed. 'From what I've
heard abut you, you get whatever you want.'

It was true. Susie did have almost everything she'd ever
wanted. Almost. It still seemed strange to be flying first
class, but she could afford it now, and she liked the luxury
of free booze, free earplugs, and disposable slippers. How
much her life had changed in just a few short years. And
she owed everything to The Club.

For the third time in two minutes she checked her
watch. Damn! The plane had left LAX right on time, but
they'd been circling for over an hour waiting to land.
Riffling through the magazine rack in front of her seat,
her own face suddenly jumped out at her from the cover
of *Business Woman*. 'Super Susie Is One Smart Cookie
— What Is Her Winning Recipe for Success?' *Mirabelle*
had called her the 'Catherine Deneuve of the cookie
business' and looking at this photo, all soft focus, lacy
blouse, glistening lips and cheekbones, courtesy of
Scavullo, she could almost believe it herself. Their
colouring was very similar, golden blonde hair, peaches-
and-cream skin, and surprisingly brown eyes instead of
blue. But in truth Susie lacked Deneuve's delicate bone
structure. She was of sturdy Lithuanian stock and besides,
she was at least ten years younger. Maybe Goldie Hawn?
No, she knew she resembled one of her own cookies a

10

hell of a lot more than she resembled Catherine Deneuve or Goldie Hawn. Susie's face was round and cheerful, the smile wide and welcoming, the eyes like melting chocolate chips. As sweet as one of her own cookies. Too sweet, some might say.

Turning quickly to the article inside, she discovered with a sinking heart that it was another hatchet job. 'Cookie Magnate Power-Hungry Pollyanna?' 'Two minutes with that airhead and I go into sugar overload,' was the opening statement by Sam Friedman, her arch rival and chief competitor, Sam the Cookie Man. In the three-page interview, he attacked her franchise operations, her business acumen, even the secret recipe for her famous Blondies and Brownies. Susie ripped out the article, wadded it into a little ball and stuffed it into the airline barf bag. Why should she care?

Sam was just jealous. He had a huge corporation behind him. It must bug the hell out of him that her business, Kookie Krums, which started with a sixty-thousand-dollar loan from her husband and one store in Brooklyn Heights, now generated sixty million dollars' worth of sales from her four hundred stores across the country. For Sam, it was just a business; for Susie it had become a passion. That's what she had spent the last twenty-four hours in LA trying to make one of her managers understand. Unannounced, she had walked into a Kookie Krums outlet on Wilshire Boulevard and was dismayed by a) the lack of cleanliness in the store, b) the salesman's lacklustre selling manner, and c) the taste of the frosted double-fudge brownies.

'Are you using fresh whole eggs in this, Marvin?' she asked him as sweetly as she could, knowing full well that he must be adding liquid egg yolks to the Susie's Special Batter shipped in daily from the Brooklyn Heights plant.

Marvin hung his head.

'You know I taught you better.' All of Susie's

11

managers were trained in her Brooklyn Heights school before they were allowed to go out across the country. 'I want a person who buys a Kookie Krums Brownie to stand here at this counter and say not, "This is a good brownie", not even, "This is a great brownie", but, "This is the best brownie I've ever had". Right?'

'Right,' Marvin mumbled. Her friendly brown eyes seemed to see right into him.

'And you know,' she continued in her calm, even tone, 'I don't think the shop is as clean as it used to be.'

'We passed a health inspection just last week,' Marvin said defensively.

'Oh, no doubt. But it doesn't look as, well, as appetizing as it might. Maybe a new paint job?'

'Sure. Okay.' He couldn't help answering her smile with one of his own.

'I'm not crazy about the front salesman, either. He doesn't have that off-the-wall, zany sales pitch that I really love, know what I mean? He needs a bit more pep, more personality, don't you think?'

'Jeez, Mrs Krumins, he's a cookie salesman, not a cheerleader.'

'Maybe that's the problem, Marvin. The cheerleader approach works. Really.'

Susie Krumins wasn't just the brains behind the business; she was the heart and soul of it. She wasn't selling cookies to people simply to make money. She wanted to make them feel better. In Arizona, they were actually giving chocolate to schizophrenics and people in old folks' homes because chocolate is the only thing guaranteed to lift their depression. Real chocolate, of course. Not that aerated, cardboardy-tasting stuff, but smooth creamy milk chocolate and heavy dark bittersweet.

Her catering for film business, Edible Art, was going well, too, thanks to the contacts she had made through the actress, Miriam Newman. Now she was ready to give Godiva a run for their money. She was branching out into designer chocolates to be sold in high-class department stores under the name of Susie's Sweet Sins. Chocolates made only with pure chocolate, sweet butter and real cream. No additives or apologies necessary, just wholesome goodness. She hoped to expand her line into ice-cream, too, but her pet project, the one she was aiming directly at Betsy Bloomingdale, was chocolate mousse, rich, dark chocolate mousse sold in individual stemmed glasses. Each serving would be sealed with a gold foil lid and Susie's own Sweet Sins label on it. Peel off the label, serve the mousse and then keep the glass for other things. A classy gourmet dessert for the woman too busy to make her own.

Packaging and marketing would be a snap. Susie's former commercial art training was part of what made her such a successful entrepreneur. She could design her own ad campaigns and who knew better than Susie how to sell her own product? Macy's was already interested so was Harrods in London and now Bloomingdale's. Susie had her new slogan all figured out. 'A little bite of chocolate is a little bit of love.'

Before she put her Kookie Krums business together, sitting at home at the kitchen table, she had pored over the market analyses of other successful businesses that had started in the home, especially that of Mary Kay cosmetics. Susie went to the Mary Kay seminar where the great leader herself spoke to a rapt audience of four thousand would-be Mary Kays, each of whom was eager to earn enough points to win the prized pink Cadillac. She gave a surprisingly evangelical speech: 'I want to thank God for the opportunity he has given us all. We are not just in the business of selling cosmetics. We are in the business of changing lives.'

Susie was all for that. The high priestess of pink

13

continued: 'I want you to have a dream. God didn't have time to make a nobody, just a somebody. You are a somebody, OK?'

Oh, how Susie longed to be a somebody.

Mary Kay finished her salespitch sermon with the warning: 'It's God first, husband second, job third. You may think you're a success, you may have made a pile of money, you may have earned your pink Cadillac. But if you have destroyed your husband and children in the process, honey, you have failed.'

By Mary Kay's standards, Susie had failed. It had taken her years to find the courage even to think about getting a divorce, but she'd been separated from Lokis for a year now. The baby problem she didn't even want to think about. Their life together was already lying there like a dead dog with both of them half-heartedly kicking at it.

Lokis blamed The Club for ruining their life together, but Susie knew better. Lokis was the one who had pushed her to join The Club in the first place, 'For God's sake, get out of the house, go into therapy if you have to, do something with your life. Since you obviously don't want to have a baby . . .' – that really hurt – 'when are you going to grow up and start dealing with real life?' Susie closed her eyes and remembered that moment five years ago when she knew she had reached bottom but had no idea how to get back up to the top.

Standing naked in the change room at The Club, staring into the mirror, she hadn't been able to bring herself to get dressed and go home. Lokis was right. She was just standing there, rooted to the spot, a twenty-eight-year-old – no, almost twenty-nine-year-old – woman, waiting for her real life to begin. She reached for a cigarette. She really must be going crazy, thinking things like that. Maybe she should see a psychiatrist. Her mother had been a real looney tune and Susie felt herself becoming more and more like her every day. Realizing

14

that she was holding her cigarette European-style between her thumb and forefinger exactly the way Marieke used to, she stubbed it out quickly. She didn't need a psychiatrist; she needed a vacation. On her own. Two weeks in Cozumel, away from Lokis and basal charts and thermometers. But Lokis would never agree to separate vacations.

She sure as hell needed someone to talk to. Children bring mothers together, but childless women seem to have nothing to share but their hopelessness. People kept telling her she had nothing to worry about, there was lots of time to have a family, just relax and stop thinking about getting pregnant and it was bound to happen naturally. What these people didn't realize was that she'd been trying to get pregnant for over ten years. She had married Lokis when she was eighteen.

She realized she'd been staring at the woman standing at the mirror next to her, a Diane Keaton look-alike who was blow-drying her fine, light brown hair, carefully rolling the ends under with a tortoiseshell brush. She and this woman often seemed to run into each other at The Club, usually in the pool or the sauna. Susie smiled tentatively.

'Your hair's really grown, hasn't it?'

'You think so?' the woman shouted over the noise of the hairdryer. 'I can't tell any more. It's so baby fine I can't do a thing with it, so of course I'm dying to cut it, but I can't cut it, because I promised myself I'd get it past my shoulders if it killed me,'

'Give it another month,' Susie said encouragingly. 'It looks nice and healthy. Great colour.'

'Are you kidding? I'd give anything to be a blonde like you. Natural blonde, right?'

'Right,' Susie admitted.

'Right.' The woman snapped off the dryer and hung it up in the wall slot.

Susie didn't know what else to say. She didn't want the conversation to end. She was desperate to talk to somebody, anybody.

The woman was now bending over at the waist, brushing her hair upside down. Susie wanted to tell her that with fine hair, it really wasn't such a good idea to brush it too much. 'I meet so many women here at The Club,' she suddenly found herself blurting out. 'We exchange a few words, we're always polite, but I never really learn anything about them. I see you at least twice a week. We always talk about how your hair's growing, and I don't even know your name. I don't know what I'm doing here. I don't know anything real about you . . .' She stopped abruptly, feeling totally embarrassed.

The woman straightened up and smiled at her. She had breathtaking cheekbones and an absolutely radiant smile. 'Hi,' she said, extending her hand. 'I've been spaced out on drugs, I've tried to kill myself twice, I've had two abortions, and now I'm pretty sure I'm a lesbian. Anything else you'd like to know? Oh, by the way, my name's Wilhemina van Houghton. Call me Mina.'

Susie was shocked, but she couldn't help laughing as she took Wilhemina's hand. 'Skaii Krumins, but everyone calls me Susie.'

'Former cheerleader, right?'

'Yeah, how did you know?'

'Easy. You're cute and blonde and you've got a cute blonde name.' Susie started to withdraw, but Mina kept hold of her hand. 'Hey, don't go all ice queen on me. I would have killed for a name like "Susie" in high school. Wilheminas never get to be cheerleaders.'

'Did you really want to be a cheerleader?' Susie asked. What she really wanted to ask was, do you really think you are a lesbian? but she knew it wouldn't be polite.

'Sure. Who didn't in high school? Now it seems

16

ridiculous that I would have wanted to engage in such a trivial activity, oops, sorry . . .'

'That's all right. It really was trivial. It seemed important at the time, vital even, but now . . .'

'Well, high-school hell has got to be one of the best reasons for living well.'

'What?'

'You know . . . living well is the best revenge. I think it was Gore Vidal who said that. Anyway, most of today's major politicians, actresses, and almost all of your top comedians were geeks in high school.'

'Not me,' Susie sighed. 'High school was great. It's been downhill ever since.'

'Oh, come on, grow up,' Mina snorted.

'That's what my husband says.' Susie's eyes filled with tears.

'Hey, sorry, sorry, I didn't mean to pry. You started this, you know. Can I have one of these?' Mina reached for the cigarette packet Susie had left on the counter, shook one out, and then took the lit cigarette from Susie's mouth to light her own. 'Thanks. We should both stop smoking.'

'I know. I never used to smoke. I started a year ago. When I was really depressed, the only thing that made me feel better was a glass of champagne, a dark chocolate truffle, and a cigarette. Now I can't stop.'

'First things first, OK?' Mina smiled warmly and Susie thought once again what a radiant smile she had. 'Listen,' Mina went on, 'most of the women here are just hanging on by a thread, so we might as well cling to each other. The Club is like an open hotline. You just phone in your pain.'

'But all the other women here, they seem so together.'

Mina snorted again. 'Are you kidding me? What you see around you, my dear, are women in crisis. They come to The Club to lick their wounds. Are you married?'

'Yes.'

'In pain?'

'Oh no,' Susie said 'I'm fine.' Then to her horror she burst into tears. 'Oh God, I'm falling apart!'

Mina tossed her a huge pink towel. 'Come on, dry your eyes, get dressed, and I'll take you to lunch.'

Over Greek salad and two bottles of retsina, Mina sat and listened quietly, asking a question or two, always gently, as Susie's life story spilled out. Susie hadn't even realized she was angry, but now waves of fury kept threatening to choke her. 'This isn't like me,' she insisted. 'I never lose my temper. I'm really a positive person. I believe that people are basically good at heart.'

'Yeah, you and Anne Frank,' Mina said, spearing the last black olive.

'I just don't know what to do. I feel frozen. I can't get pregnant. I know I should get a job, but I just keep thinking I'll get pregnant and that'll be my job. I can't seem to move ahead.'

'Well, what are you good at?' Mina signalled to the cute blond waiter and asked him to bring them two cappuccinos.

'I started out to be an artist, but I don't know, that's kind of in competition with my husband. He's an architect and interior designer.'

'Wait a second. Lokis Krumins? The guy that designed that new restaurant, Arena?' Susie nodded. 'Wow. He's hot. People are lining up for blocks to get into that place. I was by there last night. He's gorgeous. No wonder you've got a problem with self-image. I love that long blond hair and the way he always wears black. He's really something else.'

'Yeah. Lokis believes in living out his own fantasy.'

'He sure doesn't look like the kind of guy who would want a little stay-at-home wifey.'

'Maybe not, but that's how it is. He wants a family.'

18

'And you don't?'

'That's all I've ever wanted, but it just doesn't seem to be happening.'

'You've got tons of time. What are you, twenty-five?'

'Twenty-eight. No, almost twenty-nine. God, in a little over a year, I'll be thirty!'

'Take it from me, kid. It's not that bad. Besides, consider the alternative to finally turning thirty.'

'What is it?' Susie sniffed.

'Death,' Mina laughed. 'Hey, come on, you've got plenty of time to have babies.'

'But we've been trying for ten years!'

'And zippo? Nothing?'

Susie nodded, 'Lokis thinks that, deep down, psychologically, I don't really want kids and that's why I'm rejecting his sperm.' Mina whooped at this and suddenly, having said it out loud, even Susie realized how ridiculous it sounded. She giggled. 'I guess it doesn't make a lot of sense, does it?'

'Not really, but then most guys tend to think with their dicks. Hey, don't get hysterical, it's not that funny.' Mina leaned over to pound her on the back.

Susie stopped laughing and started to cry again. 'Sometimes I think I'll never be happy again.'

'Sure you will. What're your small pleasures?'

'My what?'

'Small pleasures. You know, the little things in life that keep you going. For me, it's breakfast. No matter how shitty things are, there's always breakfast to look forward to.'

'That's crazy, but you know, you're right. Food does make me feel better. A lot better. I'm a good cook, too. No, I'm a great cook. You know, it's funny' — Susie giggled again — 'everybody in New York seems to love restaurants. I mean, that's what keeps Lokis in business. But I'd rather cook myself.'

19

'Really? What do you cook? Gourmet, nouvelle cuisine, Americaine, any of that trendy yuppie stuff?'

'Everything. The first year we were married, I cooked a different dish every night. Three hundred and sixty-five different recipes, can you believe it? I've been through French, Italian, Middle Eastern, Cajun, Tex-Mex, everything. I do all my own baking, breads, cakes, pies; my chocolate chip cookies are to die for. Everybody loves them. I make my own pasta and my own tortillas. But you can't call that a talent. Not in this day and age. Anybody can cook.'

'I can't,' Mina said cheerfully. 'I can't eve make Jell-O.'

'Oh but it's easy. You just need to start with unflavoured gelatin . . .'

'Never mind,' Mina said, 'I don't really want to know.'

'That's just what I mean.' Susie was disappointed. 'Nobody really cares about cooking these days. Anyway, you can't make any money at it.'

'You never know,' said Mina thoughtfully.

Susie had made a fortune at it. Eventually. Her catering business had meant she could work at home, out of her own kitchen. Lokis loved that. He was even willing to lend her the money to open her first Kookie Krums store, but he quickly changed his tune. Watching Susie move from happy homemaker to America's cookie queen was more than he could handle. Especially when she started making more money than he did. She rubbed her eyes with the back of her hand. Oh well, nobody said you could have it all.

As the plane started its descent, her stomach gave a little lurch. She knew she was going to be late arriving at the gala, which was really OK, because she didn't have to be there to oversee things at this stage. She was only doing this as a favour to Gwen anyway; she didn't do much catering any more. The upper echelon of her staff were well-trained. For the first two hours they were going to be serving the tapas, assorted Spanish hors d'oeuvres. The full buffet wouldn't start until later and she'd be there in plenty of time for that.

Susie disembarked almost immediately and moved up the carpeted ramp, followed by two skycaps through the terminal and outside into the waiting limousine. She mentally corrected herself. Susie had now learned to call the chocolate brown BMW 'the car', not 'the limo'. That was supposed to be more casually classy. Sometimes it was hard being a successful big biz celebrity, as her agent, Michael Taylor, liked to call her. But it was a hell of a lot easier than being a successful wife.

In the back of the car, she pulled the curtains shut, closing herself off from the driver. There was no time to go home before the gala. The occasion was black tie, and she'd have to change into her butterscotch beaded silk jersey in the car. Luckily the dress was layered and loose fitting and relatively easy to slip into in the back seat. It was already getting dark as the car sat in a traffic jam waiting to cross the Triboro bridge. New York had experienced a fairly light winter without much snow until the first of March, which had brought a cold snap. The grey cemeteries of Queens looked bleak against the grey of the evening sky. Once on the bridge she could see the Manhattan skyline, skyscrapers lit up like Christmas trees.

God, she loved New York. It had taken her a long time to fall in love with this city where she had been so frightened at first. The city never failed to thrill her. Big city meant big time. Not bad for a former cheerleader from Minnesota. Tonight the city of Manhattan looked like a Woody Allen film, a black-and-white movie city, the buildings sharply etched against the sky. She loved the way the tall buildings drew one's eyes up. People always looked up in New York.

Over the bridge, through Harlem, and down into the affluent East side. It always amazed her that the luxury line of the upper East side snuggled so closely to the poverty line. On East 96 welfare mothers pooled their food stamps to buy Kraft dinner; on East 86 people were willing to pay two dollars for a single Kookie Krums double-fudge brownie or a triple-cream caramel blondie. New Yorkers were happy to pay well for their small pleasures.

As Susie stepped out of the car in front of The Club, a white vintage Mercedes pulled up. A handsome man in a custom-made tuxedo emerged from the front seat and dashed around to the other side of the car to help his companion out. Miriam Newman, the Tony Award-wining actress and Oscar nominee for *Paloma*, stepped forth wearing a full-length fur coat and fresh gardenias in her waist-length black hair. She looked stunning and she moved as if she knew it. Her long-time lover, Stephen Andrews, was equally magnificent at her side, A Republican senator, rumoured to be destined for the White House, he was already a legend at thirty-nine, the youngest and only remaining son of a political dynasty. On the top step, outside the main doors, he swept Miriam into his arms for a surprisingly passionate kiss as the flashbulbs popped around them. Susie mentally aimed a camera and snapped an imaginary cover for *New York Magazine*. Miriam tilted her face gracefully upwards, carefully keeping her good side out. Mina often did résumé shots for Miriam and she had told Susie how particular the actress was about her profile. Susie really liked Miriam, although they weren't close.

A wave of envy wept over her. What a perfect couple. They looked genuinely happy together. They'd been together for years, too, both of them successful in their different careers and both of them obviously still in love, just like Susie and Lokis used to be. And yet, Susie

22

thought suddenly, I wonder how much of 'them' they made up? How much of Lokis did I make up? Was he really the villain of the piece or had she simply cast him that way?

'Oh God,' Susie said aloud. 'Sometimes all this self-discovery is such a drag. It means you can never go back.'

# Two

Miriam Newman entered The Club like a queen, floating up the polished marble staircase through the glittering throng of guests and reporters toward the mirrored main ballroom. About her recent performance in the revival of *Hedda Gabler* on Broadway *The New York Times* had said: 'Miriam Newman glides through the challenging role of Hedda as though under water, effortlessly, gracefully, a powerful earth-mother goddess with an enigmatic smile.' Many people assumed that she glided through life with the same ease. With her waist-length, Botticelli-like black hair streaming behind her, the long white sable coat slung carelessly across her shoulders, she carried herself like the major star she was about to become. Halfway up the stairs, she turned to lay an elegantly manicured white hand on the banister and blow a kiss to her tall escort at the foot of the stairs.

On cue, Stephen rushed up the stairs, sweeping her into his arms (not an easy task, even with her recent weight loss on the Beverly Hills diet) and carried her all the way up to the top of the stairs, over the threshold and straight into the heart of the party. Everyone applauded the perfect couple's grand entrance. Stephen set her down and kissed her lightly, careful not to smear her make-up, and murmured, 'Take your coat, darling?'

'With pleasure.' Miriam slipped out of the fur, looking at him penetratingly, controlling her feelings with great effort. 'Are you sure you trust this in The Club's

25

cloakroom?' The fur had precipitated a violent argument earlier that evening.

'I hate this coat and I'm not going to wear it' Miriam screamed. They were arguing in the large bathroom of their Central Park West apartment, while Miriam carefully applied her make-up. Miriam was half an hour behind, which always made Stephen furious.

'Look, Miriam, you're being ridiculous. It's not as if mink is an endangered species. The coat looks marvellous on you, hon.'

'It makes me sick to think of those little animals dying in agony just so you can flaunt an image. And it's not even *you* flaunting the image. It's me flaunting it for you.' She considered her complexion attentively, reaching for a jar.

'You just hate the fact that tonight you may have to take a back seat to me for once. You can't stand sharing the spotlight with anyone, can you? Especially me.' His voice was even though cool.

'That's the pot calling the kettle beige, if ever I heard it.' Stephen's tone was really starting to irritate her. 'Believe me, wearing this oversized rug, the attention will be all on me.'

'I paid for it. I want you to wear it. This coat was custom-made for you by Pappas. He designed Sly Stallone's coat. That should make you happy.'

'I don't care if this coat was skinned and stitched by Christian Dior for Jane Fonda. The whole idea is disgusting!' Miriam could tell she was already losing the argument. No self-respecting performer would be caught dead in a fur these days. Why the hell was Stephen pressing her to make a fool of herself in public, especially right before the gala? It seemed they were constantly fighting these days, whenever they were together long enough to start a fight. She wondered whether or not she should undo another button on her silk shirt.

'How much longer are you going to be, hon?' Stephen sat on the edge of the massive bathtub, frowning at the gold-plated faucet and tapping his foot impatiently. Miriam smoothly rimmed her eyes with kohl, her trademark look.

'Don't call me "hon",' Miriam snapped again. 'It doesn't suit you and it certainly doesn't suit me. Just give me a second to finish my eyes.' With her eyes on, Miriam knew she looked like a classier version of Theda Bara; without them, she thought she looked more like a boiled potato. Properly made-up, her broad face with her wild hair, exotic colouring, and Slavic bone structure could make the most classically beautiful woman pale by comparison.

Image. Hell, she was an actress, She could understand even Stephen's need to create an image; she just wasn't sure that a mink coat created the right one. What had happened to that passionate, sensitive young liberal congressman who had once championed the cause of the poor?

Stephen sighed loudly, unzipped his fly, and started to pee in the toilet. 'Jesus, Miriam!' he yelled suddenly, losing every speck of his former irritating cool. 'Those goddamned false eyelashes of yours are floating in the john!'

'You must be mistaken, darling.' Miriam finished touching up her eyeshadow. 'I don't wear lashes any more. Even Liza Minnelli's given them up. Totally passé.'

'Then what do you call these things in the toilet?'

Miriam glanced away from her brightly lit reflection. 'I think, my love, if you will look more closely, you will find that those are a couple of very dead cockroaches.'

Stephen leapt away. 'Christ! A $900,000 co-op on Central Park West and we've got roaches in the pipes! I don't believe it!'

27

'What are you so upset about?' Miriam calmly reshaped her eyebrows so that they would stay neatly arched in a look of mild surprise for the evening. 'They're dead, aren't they?'

'That's not the point, Mim. They're revolting! I want them out of there in the next two minutes.'

'So flush them down. Stop making such a fuss.'

'I can't. I don't want five-inch cockroaches loose in our plumbing! They're the size of baby mice!'

'Oh, for God's sakes, Stephen, they're *dead*!' Miriam tore off a handful of toilet paper as she stood up, 'Get out of the way. I suppose you never saw a roach at Graceland.' Miriam had nicknamed the Andrews family home in Connecticut after Stephen's very patrician mother, Grace.

'Don't put your fingers in there! That's *really* disgusting!'

'Make up your mind.' Miriam's fingers were poised in mid-air. 'Fingers in the shit or roaches in the pipes?'

'Go ahead and flush them down, then.' He couldn't bring himself to look again. 'Just pray they don't clog the sewage.'

'You'd be great in a world crisis if you can't even get rid of a couple of roaches.'

'Well, essentially I'm a pacifist.' Suddenly Stephen was smiling again.

'You schmuck.' Miriam flushed the toilet quickly and gave him a kiss. She loved him when he smiled. She had loved him for most of her adult life, although she had been reconsidering their relationship lately. 'See, I'm even washing my hands to appease your precious puritanical sensibilities.'

'I'm sorry, hon,' he mumbled. 'You know how squeamish I am.'

'What's disgusting is this coat. I'm not going to wear it.' Miriam couldn't stop herself.

28

'You bleeding-heart liberals are all the same.'

'I recall you used to *be* one of those liberals. That's one of the reasons I fell in love with you.'

Stephen continued as if he hadn't heard her. 'You get all weepy about a few furry animals and then close your eyes to the problems of real people. What about all the men who died in Vietnam? What are their lives worth now?'

'You mean like your brother?' Miriam shot back. 'Your future would have been a lot less certain if he'd lived.' Then, as Stephen's eyes darkened with pain: 'I'm sorry, Stephen, that was a rotten thing to say. I just didn't think.'

'You don't think, that's your trouble.'

'Do you actually believe people are going to vote for you because your wife wears a fur coat?' He had changed so much in the past couple of years she felt she had to spark the few areas of the old Stephen that were still left. 'You're out of touch with most of America, Stephen. *You* can afford a coat like that, but the majority of people in this country are still struggling to make their next house payments. You think they're going to respect you for that? They'll hate you for it. Envy is the wrong criterion for vote-getting, I promise you.'

'You're the one who's out of touch. They envy my success, sure, that's American. And why shouldn't voters think that? Reagan made us realize that it's time for us to feel good about being American again. You think American women don't want fur coats? Nonsense. Every woman in this country wants one and she *should* have a mink if she wants one. Remember, the key to America is economic growth. And the key to economic growth is the private sector, the entrepreneur. And women are the true entrepreneurs of the nineties! Just look at your friend, Gwyneth Roberts.'

'This isn't you, Stephen,' Miriam insisted. 'This is not

29

the man I fell in love with all those years ago.' Sitting in the bathroom, looking at the love of her life, still feeling the heat of their argument, Miriam remembered the heat of that night. Part of Stephen's charm, with her and with the public, was the allure of what was eventually unattainable. He made you want to get close to him, to break down whatever barriers separated you from him. Underneath the wholesome, all-American boy, prep-school air of 'niceness', was an I've-been-around-the-block-and-I-can show-you-tricks-you've-never-dreamed-of quality that made him truly fascinating.

Stephen fed the media's insatiable appetite for celebrities. He made good copy. With his sandy hair, aqua eyes, and mean-cuisine body, he was the next best thing to a movie star. He conveyed a kind of 'you can trust me with your life' sincerity without being boring. The public adored him even though, or perhaps because, he seemed to be a mass of contradictions. The last in a long line of Democrat politicians, he had become a Republican. A Republican who wanted tax breaks for corporations, was in favour of much stricter censorship laws, but also a Republican who actively supported the ERA and federally subsidized daycare. He had won the support of a lot of women by focusing political attention on women's issues within the business community.

What did it really mean? Miriam had always believed she could predict Stephen's stand on all issues, but now she no longer knew where he stood on anything. It used to be that the Republicans opposed abortion while the Democrats favoured abortion rights, but even that was changing as many Republicans in the affluent suburbs favoured abortion while rural Democrats and some large city groups opposed it. What Stephen's position on that score now was, Miriam didn't know. Stephen felt about the abortion issue the way Miriam felt about Israel: he didn't want to take about it. He'd rather talk about the

30

goals of the 'corporate woman' and how she was ready to take her place in a 'new society'.

What really frightened her was that Stephen was beginning to believe his own hype. He followed the pollsters as if he were an investor watching the Dow Jones. She used to tease him that if they ever made a movie of his life, William Hurt should play Stephen Andrews. Now Stephen Andrews was playing Stephen Andrews. He kept talking about the packaging and presenting of the image as if he were a beauty product on special in a discount department store.

In the meantime Stephen was delivering his bathroom summation to his jury with typical formulaic zeal. 'Miriam, we've got to create the right kind of environment in this country for real economic growth. Women in the work force are the most vital part of that economic growth. They want . . .'

'Spare me the campaign speeches, please. Save them for the people who might vote for you.' Miriam dropped her eyebrow brush on the vanity in disgust.

'Meaning you won't?' He froze and looked at her, one hand still held dramatically aloft.

'Darling, I've never voted Republican in my life.'

'You think I'm a turncoat, don't you?'

For a moment Miriam's heart lifted. Maybe her opinion still mattered to him. 'I just can't believe you would desert the party that got you to where you are today.'

'I can't get any further with the Democrats. That's the point. They can't win and if they can't win, I can't win.'

'But you were supposed to be the candidate that would turn that around. You were their shining hope.'

Stephen's face darkened. 'The Democrats are dead in this country. Even when they have a decent candidate, they don't know how to handle him. Dukakis proved that. The party is split into factions. We've stuck with

31

the underdogs long enough. Now it's time to join forces with the winners. You're the one who was so upset when Ferraro lost. The Republicans are much more likely to get the first woman VP into government and you know it.'

'Stephen, you know I've always backed you in everything you do, but I think it was crazy of you to make the switch. Crazy and morally wrong.'

'Don't you see that our concept of morals is completely subjective?' Stephen dismissed entire value systems with a wave of his hand, and Miriam's heart sank again 'I want to accomplish something. I'm tired of waiting in the wings or standing on the sidelines. I intend to throw my hat into the presidential ring. I'm announcing my candidacy next week. I've got Gwyneth Roberts backing me. That's why tonight is so important.'

'You're crazy,' Miriam repeated.

'I know I'm not crazy. If I'd stayed a Democrat, I'd be running against a Kennedy anyway. I might as well run against him out in the open from the other side. It hasn't hurt my national profile — the polls show that. Americans love a man who makes up his mind but isn't afraid to change it.'

'You smug, self-righteous son of a bitch. Why don't you just admit you've turned into a complete and total opportunist? This whole Creative Opportunity Society movement you're involved in: all it really means is every man for himself, doesn't it?'

'I'm sorry you see it that way,' Stephen said in his maddeningly quiet tone, as though he were explaining a very simple problem to a slow six-year-old. 'It's only another indication of how far apart you and I have grown. We just don't want the same things out of life any more. We don't share the same values.'

'Or the same morals. Oh, pardon me for being subjective.'

'Don't push me, Miriam. It isn't going to work this time.'

'I can't help it. I have to. That's my role in your life, isn't it? You're the uptight WASP and I'm the pushy Jew . . .'

'Don't do this to us, hon.'

' "Hon"? "Hon"? What kind of precious little preppy endearment is that supposed to be? Since when did you start calling me "hon"? Next you'll be calling me your "better half" or "the wife".'

'I don't think so,' Stephen said carefully. He swallowed, looked away and said, 'Look, Mim, I didn't want to discuss this with you tonight, but I can't go on like this any more.'

Miriam stared at him blankly, a cold fear forming in the pit of her stomach. 'What are you talking about? Sure, we fight all the time, so I nudge you a little, you need that from me, you expect it. We make a great team. Our life is built on our partnership.'

'Our life is built on a lie. It's been expedient for us to stay together and we've had some great times . . .'

'Great times!'

'That's not enough to make a marriage, and you know it.'

'Is that what all this is about: a) I've decided to run for president, and b) I'm dumping you?'

Stephen looked slightly uncomfortable. 'What's the big deal about marriage? Neither of us really wanted it anyway.'

'I wanted it, goddamn it! You *know* I want it. And I want you. I've never really wanted anyone except you. Are you telling me that after all this time, after all we've been to each other, that you don't want to marry me?'

'Come on, Mim, you'd make a lousy political wife and you know it.'

'Try me!'

33

'Your own career is taking off. You're just about to make it really big — bigger than even you ever dreamed possible. You'd be a fool to take time out now.'

'I'll take the time. I love you. I've always loved you. I want to spend the rest of my life with you. My career isn't worth anything if it means losing you.'

'Stop sounding like a bad soap opera. Hon . . . honey, let's be really straightforward with each other. We've been together too long not to put the cards right out on the table. The logistics just wouldn't work. We're never together. I'm in Washington, you're in Spain; I'm in New York, you're in LA. That's no way to have a family.'

There was a bitter taste in her mouth that was working its way down to her heart. 'I want a family, you know I do.'

'But you're not getting any younger. I want kids. I'm going to need kids. It's a little late for you on that score, don't you think?'

Miriam could feel the tears smarting in her eyes. 'I'm only thirty-five, for God's sake! Lots of older women are having babies. Look at Glenn Close, look at Sally Field. I'm ready to do it'

'Oh, you might be able to manage one child with your current life style, but a baby would have to take a back seat to your work. You're an actress, Miriam. That's what drives you. That's what keeps you alive. You've got to be in that spotlight. There isn't room for two of us. You're on the verge of becoming a major star. You're about to win an Oscar — yes, I know you'll win — and when you do, you won't look back. You're on the fast track now, going places you've never dreamed of. You can't hang out in the east with me, you'll have to base yourself on the west coast. We're both on the verge of getting what we want out of life, don't you see that?'

'You don't give a damn what I want! You just want

34

to get rid of me, that's obvious! You pushed me to take *Paloma*, you've been pushing me to go to LA, you're pushing me out of your life. Why? I know there's something serious going on with you that you won't share with me. You've got to tell me what it is. Is there another woman? Or is it something even more serious?'

'No, nothing like that, I swear it, Miriam. I just can't live with you any more.'

'But you just finished saying we don't live together, that we never see each other!' She was screaming at him now.

'I want you out of my life for good, Miriam. I want a new life.'

'Why?'

'You're a liability Miriam.'

'Why? Tell me why?'

'I don't know. Maybe because you've been with me from the beginning.'

'And I know all your weaknesses? Is that the problem? Just when you want to feel strong? You want to start fresh without all the emotional baggage I bring to the relationship? I'll be whatever you want, Stephen. I'll help you be whoever you need to be. But you're my life. I can't be anything without you . . .'

'Cut the theatrics, Miriam. You're not on stage now.' All attempt at gentleness was gone from Stephen's voice. 'Face it, this run is over. The show has to close.'

'Don't you use that fucking theatrical metaphor bullshit with me! You have no right to do that! You were never a theatre person even when you wanted to be one!'

'It's not like that at all.'

She tried to slap his face but he caught her arms. 'Oh, what is it like then? Tell me are you afraid I'll cramp your style on the rubber-chicken circuit? Afraid of the competition from your own wife? Afraid that the people who turn out to see you will only be there to get a look

35

at me? That's why you don't want me around at all, isn't it? Isn't it?'

He held her more firmly as she tried to free herself. 'Stop it, Miriam, don't do this to yourself.'

'I'm not. You're doing it to me, you fucking bastard!'

'I'm sorry, babe.' He was starting to sound weak and desperate. 'I don't want to hurt you. I can't help it. I'm sorry.'

'Why didn't you tell me before?'

'I couldn't. I just . . . I don't know. I guess I sensed you'd react this way.'

'React this way? We're not talking about a scene here, buddy. We're talking about the rest of my life. Which I assumed, obviously wrongly, I was going to be spending with you.' She wasn't crying any longer.

'I know,' Stephen said helplessly, 'but you must have felt me slipping away. We've been leading separate lives for over a year.'

'Looks like yours was more separate than mine.'

'What's that supposed to mean?' Suddenly he looked frightened.

'Let's just say that I know more about you than the American public might care to learn. Things you're afraid to share with me.'

'I don't know what you're talking about.' But he looked worried. 'Leave it alone, Miriam. That's enough for one night. Finish your make-up and let's get to the goddamned gala.'

She stared at him incredulously. 'You actually expect me to go with you tonight as if nothing had happened?'

'Of course I do. We've never let our private lives interfere with our public life before. I need you there tonight. The press will be out in full force. I don't want them to get wind of our separation until we decide to make the announcement. So put your coat on, please.'

Released, Miriam took a step back, her eyes black and

36

flashing. 'You've got to be kidding. The great male crusader for the feminist cause and you don't know shit about women. Why should I prop you up tonight when you've just pulled the rug out from under me? Get yourself a stand-in, sweetie!'

Again that desperate look came into his eyes. 'I need you there tonight, Miriam, Gwyneth is making an informal endorsement speech. That means The Club is behind me. She's going to be one of my front-runners and I need that kind of visibility in my campaign. Gwyneth adores you. I don't want her to know about us yet. I know, I know, I'm a bastard — but I'm so close to getting what I've spent my whole life working for. And don't pretend you're any different. You'd sell me out along with your own mother for the right role and you know it.'

'Just stop right there.' Miriam could feel the cold anger in the pit of her stomach taking over. 'Next you'll be telling me, "This thing is bigger than both of us." You're a prize asshole, you really are.'

Stephen hung his head. 'I need to get my life back on the straight and narrow.'

'You can say that again.'

Again he snapped to attention. 'What do you mean by that? What are these veiled hints you keep dropping?'

'Nothing. Forget it.' Even Miriam wasn't quite sure why she had said that.

Stephen hung his head. 'I told you I'm confused.'

'You're full of shit is what you are.'

'Will you go with me tonight?'

'No. I told you, no.'

'You owe it to me, Miriam.'

She stared at him in utter amazement. 'What do you mean, I owe it to you?'

'You wouldn't have *Paloma* if it weren't for me.'

'Yes, and now I'm beginning to see why. Gets me

37

neatly out of the way and then you can accuse me of not being here.'

'It's what you've wanted more than anything in the world, isn't it? The lead in a major film.'

It was true. Miriam had waited a long time to star in a feature. As successful as she was on the stage, in spite of starring on Broadway and wining three Tonys, she had found it impossible to make the transition to film or even into television.

Stephen was right. She had what she had always wanted, but she was losing what she had always needed. Stephen.

'You owe it to me,' Stephen was repeating doggedly. 'Damnit, Miriam, it's the least you can do.'

'All right,' Miriam said slowly. 'I'll do this gig for you tonight, but don't expect me to do any more than put in an appearance.'

'That's all I ask.' Stephen kissed her gratefully. 'You're one hell of a strong woman, Mim. Thanks, baby, you're a real trouper.'

'Yeah, sure.' The pain was starting to sweep over her again.

'I'll warm up the Mercedes. Or would you rather take the Beomer?' That was his pet name for the BMW. Without waiting for her to answer, he continued, 'I think the Mercedes is right for tonight. Meet you in the lobby. And wear the coat, will you, hon? Just for me?'

'Sure.' Miriam stood rooted to the spot as he slammed out of the front door of the apartment. She could hear the elevator bell ring. As if in a trance, she moved slowly into the bedroom, over to the Art Deco dressing-table Stephen had given to her − 'my own Sarah Bernhardt' − on her last birthday. She opened the bottom right door to take out her black velvet evening bag. As she fumbled through the pile of lingerie, her fingers brushed against a padded Manila envelope. Its contents had been in the back of her mind for days, eating away at her, no matter how much she tried to ignore them. Now he was leaving her.

She heard the apartment speaker click on and Stephen's voice calling out, 'The Merc's running fine, hon. You ready?' Almost without thinking, she grabbed the envelope and stuffed it into her large evening bag. She called down to him, 'Yes, "hon". I'm ready.'

At the gala, Stephen bore the fur coat to the cloakroom like a prize kill while Miriam scanned the room, looking for a familiar face. Seeing one, she was lifting her hand to wave when she suddenly realized it was her own face reflected in the mirrored walls of the ballroom. Why don't I look ravaged under the bright light of the chandeliers? she wondered. Why doesn't the pain show on my face? Her face, so subtly expressive on camera, so mobile on stage, looked frozen in the mirror to her, embalmed and serene as people swarmed around her and glasses clinked. And why was she smiling?

Stephen bounded back, elegant in his black velvet tux, eyes gleaming. He lifted the heavy mass of her hair and kissed the back of her neck, a seemingly intimate gesture for all to see and now completely meaningless. One hand was pressed protectively into the small of her back, the other free to seize any passer-by. For all of his aloofness, Stephen had always been a toucher, a hands-on politician. 'The Senator of Sensitivity', *New York Magazine* called him: 'Keep your eye on Stephen Andrews. He's been getting the build-up for a national assault on the Oval Office. What's this guy got? Cash and charisma. Brains and balls. He's a sexy senator.'

Miriam had never really minded Stephen's physicality. What she minded was that his eyes were no longer on her. Never missing a trick, they darted around the room, sizing up all the driven men, the hungry ladies, all gleaming white teeth and bright laughter and smiles. Charming, boyish, and so attentive, Stephen would be most happy, Miriam now realized, if, like Linda Blair in *The Exorcist*, he could turn his head in a complete three-hundred-and-sixty-degree circle of the room.

With another kiss on the back of her neck, he excused himself and moved over to talk with Luigi del Bello, the flamboyant business manager of The Club. Miriam watched him take Luigi's hand and hold it just a fraction too long. My God, she thought sadly, you are such a whore.

# Three

SHE'S GORGEOUS, SHE'S BRAINY, SHE'S HOT! Sara Town, host of *In Depth*, the slick, glossy, prime-time news magazine that TV critics are calling 'a K Mart tabloid that trashes the news.' From designer drugs to the Nicaraguan contras to the AIDS epidemic, *In Depth* aims a super-charged, sensationalist, 'yup-doc' style of investigative reporting squarely at the baby boomers. The opening to *In Depth* rivals the lead-in to *Miami Vice*, all flashing video, bright colours, and pulsing rock rhythm. It's already creeping up on *60 Minutes* in the ratings. Cheap to produce, *In Depth* boasts a high-profile reporter with a conservative leaning. *In Depth* is a hit. And Sara Town is a media star.

*Rolling Stone*

Sara Town licked her lips and stared into the smoked mirror, ringed with frosted pink bulbs. With her slanted, green-gold eyes, tawny skin and sleek black hair pulled away from her face to accentuate razor-sharp cheek-bones, Sara was exotically beautiful. She was often mistaken for Eurasian or Polynesian. Her husky purring voice and her liquid velvet smile were reminiscent of a pure-bred Burmese kitten. Some people called her an opportunist, a bitch, a fascist, but most often a cat. Sara didn't mind. She had a certain admiration for cats, all sleek softness on the outside, all sharp-clawed danger on

41

the inside. Beautiful, clever, and with the ability to land on their feet.

The opulence of The Club powder-room amazed her. Gwyneth Roberts appeared to be taking her cue from Leona Helmsley: 'What do you look for in a first-class hotel? A first-class bathroom.' Now this was a first-class bathroom. Twenty-five shell-pink individual stalls with twenty-five petunia-pink porcelain johns. Rose glass-doored showers, stacks of pink plush bath towels, pink bidets, pink dressing-tables, even pink baby-changing cubicles. Although why anyone would want to cart a baby along to a spa, Sara couldn't imagine. She stuck her head inside one of the change-rooms and detected the faint smell of used Pampers. Why couldn't all these late-life pregnancy diehards leave the little buggers at home with a nanny?

A pink sweetheart rose stood in a bud vase next to the brass fixtures on each of the sinks. Sara squeezed one petal. Yep, it was real, not silk. The pink marble soap dish held a pink soap shell with The Club's ornate insignia etched on it. Next to the pink soap was the black soap. That creepy black soap and the crazy ritual of splashing your face with warm water fifty times followed by cold water fifty times. Splash, splash, splash. Ad infinitum. A far cry from the old Nivea-and-ice-cube remedy her mother used to swear by.

Leaning into the mirror, she examined her own perfectly tanned, virtually unlined skin. She didn't look anywhere near forty. Of course, this lighting had been designed to make everybody look twelve. She was no Norma Falway, the woman who had been saluted by the Cosmetic Surgeons of America for going public with her three facelifts, cheekbone implants, and saddlebag liposuction. Thank God Sara had naturally good bones. She ran some cool water over her wrists. The room reeked of Ombre Rose scent. Gwen probably had it piped through the air-conditioning ducts like legionnaires' disease.

The door opened and in floated Miriam Newman in bright blue and white silk evening pyjamas, her face frozen in its enigmatic Mona Lisa smile. She was clutching a large evening bag to her bosom. Ignoring Sara, she locked herself in a stall, forcing Sara to listen to Niagara Falls gushing out of her oversized bladder. Even with her much-touted weight loss, Miriam was still a cow.

Sara couldn't deny she was a brilliant actress. Without her, Broadway would have really died last season, instead of merely thrashing about in its final throes. However hailed as a cross between Meryl Streep and Barbra Streisand, Miriam really needed an agent for her life as well as for her career, Sara thought. Those pyjamas made her look like the flag of Israel at half mast. She could do with a boob job, too. Poor Miriam. Could she possibly have expected the American public to accept a Jewish first lady? (Look what happened to Kitty Dukakis.) An actress? And one who had been schtupping the beloved presidential hopeful in unwedded bliss for fifteen years? Come on.

She was totally the wrong mate for Stephen Andrews. At least on the surface. If Stephen Andrews made it to the White House, there'd probably be more Pop Tarts climbing the back stairs than Jack Kennedy ever dreamed of. The word 'charismatic' was so often used to describe him you'd think it was his middle name.

The toilet flushed at last and Miriam emerged, washing her hands with the movements of one born to play Lady Macbeth. She moved to leave but Sara blocked her path. She snapped her fingers under Miriam's nose: 'An Oscar for your thoughts.'

'Oh, sorry, Sara!' Miriam jumped back, startled. 'I honestly didn't recognize you. I'm afraid I'm flying a bit

43

blind tonight. I've only got one contact lens in and I can't see a thing. You know, "methinks I see these things with parted eye, when everything seems double." '

'What?' She was always quoting some damned lines from some boring play she'd been in, which made you feel illiterate and uncultured.

'*A Midsummer Night's Dream*. I didn't realize you were a member of The Club. I haven't seen you here before, have I?'

'I'm not. Are you kidding, with the initiation fee they charge for this dump?'

'You can certainly afford it with that new contract you signed for *In Depth*.'

Sara smiled modestly. 'You should never trust what you read in *NY Today*. Believe me, I know. I used to write for them. But I'd never blow it on something like The Club. Who wants to hang out with a lot of sweaty female bodies?'

'Listen, they say more business is accomplished in the sauna here than in most boardrooms.'

'Forget it. No, I'm doing an *In Depth* profile on Gwyneth Roberts.'

'Oh, of course,' Miriam murmured. 'The tenth anniversary of The Club.'

'And her involvement with Stephen. She is going to be involved in his political campaign, isn't she?'

'Yes. I'm a bit out of it tonight, I'm afraid. Sounds great. Should be a hot story.' In fact she looked as though she was about to cry.

'I'm flying blind, too. Lady Gwyneth wouldn't grant me a preliminary interview and that assistant of hers with the hominy-grits accent refused to give me a bio or press packet. It's crazy. I mean, does she want publicity or not?'

'I don't think Gwen likes being interviewed.' Miriam tried to slip past Sara to the door. She didn't want to

44

crack in front of Sara who had a reputation for moving in for the kill the minute she sensed blood.

Sara pretended to brush some lint off her svelte black mini skirt. 'A bit of a mystery woman, isn't she? She must have something to hide.'

'Who doesn't?' There had always been something about Sara Town that Miriam didn't like. Her agent had been pushing for a TV spot with her as part of the marketing campaign for *Paloma*. An *In Depth* profile by Sara Town meant you had really arrived, and the eyes of all America would be on you, at least for the fifteen minutes of programme time. Stephen said that, like Geraldo and Phil, Sara had her finger on the pulse of the yuppie public and they were going to be the major voters in this election. But it wasn't just her politics Miriam mistrusted. There was a predatory look in Sara's eyes, a hunger that really frightened her.

'I've heard she's a dyke.' Sara watched Miriam's face closely.

'I've never heard that. I think Gwen's an incredible woman,' Miriam said defensively. 'She's had to fight for everything, but look what she's achieved.'

'Yes,' Sara said sweetly. 'Her own little empire.'

'She's done a lot for women. I really admire her.'

'I'm sure we all do, but what is she like as a person?'

'Gwen's a hard woman to get to know personally. I have tremendous respect for her. Her involvement in Stephen's campaign is going to make a major difference for him. She's intelligent, concerned, hard-working. Very ambitious, a bit of a driven personality, I guess.'

'Like your Mr Andrews?' Sara struck quickly.

'Yes, I . . .' Miriam opened her mouth and then shut it again.

'Did Stephen tell you we've got a profile planned for *In Depth* to coincide with the cover of *Time*?'

'No he didn't.' A light inside Miriam switched on full

45

force, one thousand watts focused on Sara. The coveted *In Depth* spot. The timing couldn't be more perfect. Well, actually it couldn't be worse since technically she and Stephen were no longer together, but Stephen was bound to change his mind about their relationship. He couldn't manage without her. She'd be able to make him see that. If taking a back seat and shining in his reflected glory for a little while meant that she could keep him, she was willing to do that. She smiled winningly at Sara. 'It's just like Stephen not to tell me, he's been so incredibly busy lately. When are you planning to tape us? This is just marvellous. *In Depth* is top visibility at the moment. You're a wonderful interviewer. I loved your Spielberg piece with baby Max in one hand and the Oscar in the other. Terrific.'

'Thank you. Oh dear, you're really making this difficult for me.' Sara laughed in polite embarrassment.

'How do you mean?'

'Well, the profile's on Stephen. I'm afraid it doesn't include you. He doesn't want to cloud the issue of the campaign with your career and of course now . . .' She stopped and studied Miriam for a moment. 'Look, I'd love to do a spot just on you some time. Your career is really on the move. If you win the Oscar, perhaps. Or when you announce your move to LA . . .'

'Move to LA?' Miriam stared at her blankly.

'I think you and Stephen have handled this brilliantly, by the way. You've hung in together as long as you could, managed to use each other in the best possible way, and got full value out of the relationship for both your careers. Now it's time for you to move in opposite directions and you've each got a reason to do so.'

Miriam suddenly felt dizzy. Was it possible that Stephen had already told Sara Town, a woman he hardly knew, that he was planning to leave her? Her knees weakened and she tried to steady her voice as she said,

'LA does look good at the moment. I was just out there for the Golden Globe Awards. I've got a lot of offers to choose from, but I haven't made a definite decision yet.'

'Well, Stephen said once his engagement was announced, you'd probably want to get out of New York for a bit. Give the new relationship a chance to work. I must say I think it's really classy of you. Personally, I think Laura Hughes is nothing compared to you, but she is young and the fact that Senator Hughes is her father will certainly be helpful to Stephen. They don't come any better connected than Stanley Hughes.' Sara suddenly broke off. 'Are you all right?'

Miriam's knees buckled as she felt the bottom drop out. She grabbed the edge of the dressing-table to catch herself. Her head was pounding with dizziness and anger. She knew instantly that Sara was telling the truth. It took every ounce of control she had not to cry out from the injustice of it all. Laura Hughes. The very white, very Anglo-Saxon Protestant daughter of the right-wing Republican Senator Hughes from Illinois. Pale, thin, childlike Laura Hughes. Christ, she didn't even look twenty-five. But she had twenty-five years of money and breeding, twenty-five years of ponies and private schools and, most important of all, a highly influential daddy. Miriam could just imagine the three of them sitting around a roaring fireplace, drinking sherry and plotting little Stevie's path to the White House. She started to stand up, but her knees gave way again and she sank down on to the little chintz-upholstered stool again.

'Miriam, I'm truly sorry, I assumed you knew . . .' Sara reached out to steady her.

Miriam wanted to shove Sara's hand off her shoulder and smash her face in. That bastard. Now he was trying to ruin her professionally as well as personally. She was losing her cool in front of Sara Town. It would be all over the city by tomorrow morning, but she couldn't stop the rage that kept flooding her, over and over again. And the growing realization that she had been made a fool of. He had been manipulating her for months, making her feel that she was to blame for the growing distance between them when in fact he was simply carrying out his own agenda. This explained his sudden shift in politics, why he kept pressing her to relocate in LA; in fact it explained a lot of his bizarre behaviour over the past couple of months. What it didn't explain, however, was the contents of the large Manila envelope she was still clutching in her handbag. She could feel the pain gradually slipping away, leaving only cold anger.

Sara handed her a pink Kleenex. 'You know, I could do a preliminary piece on you, Miriam, just to get some background info on Stephen. I bet you have some interesting personal anecdotes. After all, you've known him longer than anyone else.'

'Except his mother.' The envelope in her bag gave her the courage to rise and face Sara. 'I'm tied up for the next couple of weeks doing a guest lead on *LA Law*. It'll keep me busy until the Academy Awards. No free time. Besides, I never talk unless I'm paid for it. But I'd like to help you out, I really would. As a matter of fact, I think I've got some material on Stephen right here that might be of interest to you.' She pulled out the padded envelope and handed it to Sara. 'I'm sure it's just what you need.'

'Thanks, love. It's really sweet of you to put yourself out this way.' Sara took the package eagerly.

'Not at all. Stephen's the one who puts out.'

Sara regarded her suspiciously, but Miriam's face remained blank. 'Well thanks. Thanks a lot. Do I have permission to use anything that's in here?'

'Use it any way you think fit. I leave that to your discretion.'

'Great. You be sure and watch the piece when it airs. I have a feeling it's going to be sensational.'

Miriam reapplied her smile as she moved to the door. 'Oh, I wouldn't miss it for the world.' She swept out, giving Sara the coolest of nods.

Snotty bitch. Sara unscrewed her mascara wand and started to give her lashes an extra coat. She was surprised to find her hand was shaking. I'm really on edge tonight, she thought. It was unusual for her to be nervous before a shoot. Must be the prospect of seeing Gwen after all these years. They had parted on somewhat less than equable terms. It was going to be strange, no doubt about it. She had no idea what to expect, but already her stomach was doing flipflops and she was actually sweating. She could feel her silk blouse sticking to her back. With the array of toiletries in this joint, you'd think they'd supply some deodorant. She took a surreptitious sniff of her armpits. Her undercover didn't seem to be working overtime. She grabbed a can of baby powder and shook it vigorously, but nothing came out. Looking down at the can she noticed that the printing was completely in Spanish. Christ! Bad enough that the subway ads were now bilingual. '*Hacienda La Cucaracha*. They check in but they don't check out.' Was this country for Americans or welfare wetbacks?

'I really admire your work, Miss Town,' said a soft, low voice. Looking up into the mirror, Sara saw a pair of huge dark eyes set in a round dark face. 'Bodine Johnson,' the black woman extended her hand with its bare, short nails. '*Late Beat News*.' She was wearing a turquoise suede suit with vaguely Indian beadwork and a loose perm modified Afro. 'Is *In Depth* doing an exposé of The Club?'

Sara laughed. 'I wish I could say that. I'm interviewing Gwyneth Roberts tonight at the gala. Then we'll be doing

49

a profile and a follow-up piece next week. But I'm sure's there's plenty to expose. I don't know how they can call this place a freehold of feminism. Looks more like the Garden of Hedon to me.'

Bodine laughed with her, a warm, throaty sound. 'I know exactly what you mean. The Club always makes me nervous, like I'm going to be lynched or something, you know? The only other black woman I've seen here is the coat-check girl.'

'Do they exclude blacks? Sara's antennae shot up immediately.

'Are you kidding? In New York? In this day and age? Legally, no; financially, sure. How many black women do you know who could afford the ten-thousand-dollar initiation fee? That's more than my mama made in a year looking after other people's kids.'

'Mm,' Sara said noncommittally, banging the can of baby powder on the edge of the sink. The last thing she wanted to do was listen to some sob story about growing up poor and black in Harlem. 'Is *Late Beat* covering the gala, Bodine?'

'Not officially. Call me Dina. My co-anchor's doing a two-minute spot. I flashed my press card at the door so of course they didn't dare turn me away. Jesus God, I'd like to get some dirt on this outfit, blow this fancy-ass place sky high, know what I mean?'

Sara looked at her, amused. 'My, my, my, do we want to be an investigative journalist instead of an anchorwoman when we grow up?'

'Damn straight. I don't have to tell you there's no future in being an anchorwoman. Not at the local level, anyway . . . When the looks go, so do I.'

'You've got quite a few years yet, I would think,' Sara said graciously.

'Thanks for the compliment, but I'm not as young as I look. I lie about my age all the time. I wasted a lot of years trying to get myself together. I do know I'm tired of bustin' my ass as a second stringer to that no-talent hack, Tom Beverage. I'm looking to write my own ticket to journalistic freedom.'

The young woman must be drunk. Sara was amazed that a newscaster from a rival network would speak so openly to her. 'Those are big words you're using there, sweetie.'

A purple blush invaded Dina's cheeks. 'I hear you. Too big for my britches? I know I haven't been out of broadcast school for very long but, like I told you, I wasted some time and now I've really got to hustle. At least I'm working in New York instead of Podunk or Baton Rouge. And, I'm going to make it, I know I am. All I need is one hot story.'

'Just one?' Sara's lips curved into a feline smile.

'Well, sure. That's all it took you. You broke that welfare scam where those pimps were using phoney names to cash welfare cheques. I mean, hot damn, the American government funding a brothel? You didn't pull any punches with that one. And look how you went after Ferraro's husband? You realize you might be single-handedly responsible for the Democrats losing in '84?'

'I doubt it.' Sara gave the lid of the can another twist. She was beginning to lose interest in this conversation.

'You know, there's something I swore I would ask you if I ever got the chance to meet you,' Bodine's tone turned a little sharper. 'Didn't it bother you at all that you were going after the first woman ever to be a VP nominee?'

'Why should it?'

'Well, hell, I mean as a woman . . .'

'Look, it's just one of life's little lessons. I don't hold her responsible for her husband's wrongdoing, but his criminal actions had to be brought to the public attention.'

'I hear what you're saying but . . .'

'The American people don't want a vice-president with Mafia connections, now do they?'

'Hey, wait a minute, there was nothing to indicate mob involvement . . .'

'He's Italian, isn't he?' Sara twisted the lid of the baby-powder can again.

'Nothing's sacred to you, is it?' Dina's voice was a mixture of admiration and resentment. 'I guess that's what it takes to really get somewhere.'

'Where do you want to get?' Sara asked idly. She really needed to get the can open and some powder under her arms.

'Right where you are. That is,' Dina tried to backtrack quickly, 'not necessarily *In Depth*. But I'd love a shot at *60 Minutes*.'

Sara put down the baby powder in amazement. 'You've got to be kidding.'

'Why not aim for the top?' Dina's smooth brown brow knit slightly.

'Honey, I'm going to give it to you straight. You don't have a hope in hell of being the next Diane Sawyer.'

'What are you talking about? You mean because I'm black? That hasn't stopped me so far. In fact, it's helped me. When I graduated from broadcast school, the courts were pushing stations to hire minorities. Women and blacks were "in". By hiring me, they could kill two birds with one stone.

Not like it was when Sara was starting out. 'Women simply don't have authoritative voices,' one station master told her. 'You girls never sound as though you're really sure of what you're talking about. There's no room for broads in broadcasting.' No, it hadn't been 'in' when Sara was starting out. 'I would like to believe I made it on my own talents,' she said coolly to Dina, 'not because I'm female.'

'You're not in favour of gender parity?'

'Equality, yes. Preferential treatment, no.'

'In other words,' there was an added edge to Dina's tone, 'you made it on your own so why shouldn't I?'

'Something like that.' Sara wanted desperately for this chat to be over. She had no time for eager little puppy dogs snapping at her heels. 'Look, my advice to you is, if you want to make it in media, stop pushing yourself as black.'

'What do you mean stop pushing myself as black?' The young woman's eyes narrowed with anger. 'I am black.'

Sara grabbed the tin of baby powder, twisting the lid once again. 'I know what you are. I've watched *Late Beat* once or twice out of curiosity. You're segregated, sweetie. They've got you ghettoized. I'm surprised you don't know that. If there's a black story, sure they give it to you, but that's about all they give you. They've got you covering tenant strikes in Harlem, interviewing Smokey Robinson at the reopening of the Apollo, and eating black-eyed peas and chittlin's at Sylvia's. But that's it. Why do you think your co-anchor's covering the gala and you had to sneak in here tonight? They've got you slotted right where they want you as the token nigger.' Dina opened her mouth to speak, but Sara rode right over her, 'I'm not trying to offend you. I'm simply stating the obvious. You shouldn't allow yourself to be pegged so easily. Be a bit more elusive. You're too specific. Being black isn't going to get you on *60 Minutes*.'

'What about Ed Bradley?'

'Perfect.' Sara snapped her fingers. 'That's exactly what I mean. I completely forget he's black.'

Bodine glared at her, the purple flush spreading further down her neck. 'Ed Bradley gave me my first job in Philadelphia at WDAS, an all-black station. I owe everything to him.'

'So?' Sara reached over and flicked a bead of sweat from the black woman's upper lip. 'I'm simply saying,

53

OK, Ed happens to be black, but it's not his *raison d'être*.'

Bodine's mouth tightened. 'What about Dahlia Lee?'

'That twinkie.' Sara's face darkened at the mention of the former Miss Kentucky who'd edged her out of her top co-anchor spot on major network news not that long ago. Fortunately lucky Sara had landed on her feet. Bigger and better than ever. She had nothing to fear from the likes of Dahlia Lee. Or Bodine Johnson. 'What about her?'

'I have great respect for Dahlia. She won the Humana Award for broadcasting last year and the NAACP Award, too.'

'She's an oreo.'

A what?'

'Isn't that the right term?' Sara said lightly 'You know, an oreo? Like the cookie. Black on the outside, white on the inside.'

'That's a cliché,' Dina said fiercely, her hands clenching.

'No, dear, you're the cliché. I mean, look what you're wearing. A turquoise suede jacket with a mini skirt. To a black-tie affair. You look like a Times Square hooker. And nobody wears an Afro any more, especially those who were born with them.'

Bodine could actually feel the heat surrounding her eyeballs and the steam coming out of her ears. A sound was torn from her, halfway between a growl and a scream. 'You listen to me, girl. I *am* a living, breathing black cliché. My daddy left when I was three. I don't remember him at all, not how tall he was, not what he smelled like, not the sound of his voice, nothin'. My sister went on the streets at thirteen, almost died of an overdose. She had three kids before she turned twenty. My brother and two, *two* of my cousins got shipped to Vietnam. They all came back in bags, every one of 'em.'

54

'Please, Ms Johnson,' Sara broke in, 'I'm really not all that interested in your rags-to-riches past—'

'Shut up and listen,' the black woman advanced on her threateningly. 'OK, so I'm a bit drunk, but you tight-ass right-wing bitch, you are gonna listen to me.' She backed Sara against the wall. 'I grew up in Harlem, East 110. It was a minefield then; it's still a war zone today. Burned-out buildings with no windows, glass all over the street, empty rum bottles in brown paper bags. And the smell: piss and blood, vomit . . . hopelessness everywhere. I remember sittin' on the john one night, I saw this black furry thing run across the room, I said to myself, "Oh, there goes our black kitten." We didn't have a black cat. It was a rat. You get on the subway, you see how quickly life changes once you get past East 96. It's another world, baby. But I survived it. My mama took in washing, scrubbed floors, played mammy-nanny to all those cute little red-headed white kids in Central Park, those kids that belong to mommies who'd never dream of puttin' their hands into their own baby's shit.' Bodine stopped, breathless, staring at her with blazing eyes. Sara remained frozen, her fingers curled around the tin of baby powder. 'My mama caught me shooting up just once. Said she wasn't gonna lose another kid to the white world. She took that needle and held it against her own chest, told me if she ever saw me doin' dope again she'd put that needle straight into her heart. I got pregnant, she held my hand through the abortion. I skipped school, she went to school with me and sat there in that classroom all day for two weeks till she knew I wouldn't ever cut class again. She saved the money to get me into Ithica. I'm the first black female to graduate from their broadcast school. I don't live in Harlem any more and neither does my mama.'

Sara came to life, applauding slowly. 'As you would say, Dina dear, "I hear you." But then, I've heard it all before. *Imitation of Life* said it better. Before your time, I know. Get with it, girl. It's the nineties. Here, put some of this on before you get sweat stains all over that godawful blue suede suit.' She tossed the baby powder to Dina and beat it out of the bathroom door.

Bodine wanted to put her head down and howl. How could she have lost her cool like that? She'd completely blown it, made a fool of herself in front of Sara Town, practically attacked the star of *In Depth*. She only hoped her station manager wouldn't hear about this. Tears streaming down her face, she stared blurrily at the large can of baby powder in her hand and blinked. Strange. It was completely in Spanish. She turned it around and around. Not even bilingual Spanish and English. Just Spanish. She gave the can a rough shake, but nothing came out. Some dipstick probably dropped it in one of the pink porcelain bidets. The little holes were clogged. She banged the can on the floor, gave the lid a sharp twist and suddenly it flew apart. The baby powder was full of lumps. Could use a few grains of rice in there. Then she looked more closely. Jesus God. She dipped her finger into the snowy white powder and gave it a tentative lick. Holy shit. If she was any authority, and God knows she had been once, this was sure as shit, shit. Sure as the driven snow, snow. Cocaine. She dropped the can into her purse and left the main bathroom by its back door.

# *Four*

'Mine, mine, this palace is mine,' Gwyneth Roberts whispered to herself, wickedly parodying what Len Cariou supposedly said when he appeared for the first time on the Broadway stage with Lauren Bacall in *Applause*. 'Happy birthday, my dear club. You are ten years old today and I wish you many happy returns.' The next day she would turn forty and she didn't mind one bit. In fact, she was looking forward to it.

She was standing at the top of the wide curving marble staircase and looked down on the foyer below, glowing with the light from the vast Orrefors crystal chandelier. Her once ginger-mouse hair glowed a rich, shiny auburn and the nondescript hazel eyes blazed emerald green. With her athletic build and fast metabolism, she rarely had to diet, and through the rigorous tortures of the personal trainer who came to stretch and pummel her every morning in the privacy of her office, her stocky body had been remoulded into something close to physical perfection, with just the right degree of muscle definition, feminine but strong. If her natural shyness kept her from being truly beautiful, that quality also gave her an air of class and an aura of mystery. Funny how forty wasn't 'old' any more. It didn't seem like the start of middle age but rather a second fling at flamboyant youth.

She had decided that both she and The Club deserved the splashiest birthday party that money could buy.

Upstairs the mirrored ballroom was already packed with wall-to-wall celebrities. The guest list read like a *Who's Who in Female America*. Men were allowed to enter The Club only if they were clinging to the arms of the most glamorous and successful women. Cher was there with another of her gorgeous younger men and Erica Jong was there with a surprisingly older man. Shirley Maclaine was 'dancing in the light' with both Ed Koch and Bella Abzug. What was it *New York* magazine had said? 'The best-kept secret in New York is Ed Koch's sex life.' Texan blonde Jerry Hall had a reluctant Mick Jagger in tow. Her flowing Xandra Rhodes robes concealed her thoroughbred model lines. Could she be pregnant again? Diane Sawyer was sticking close to Mike Nichols and Connie Chung was smiling up at Maury. She saw Jackie O arm in arm with Michael Jackson, who glittered in his black leather and gold. Would Liz show up with Larry? Would Liz show up at all? It probably depended on the state of her health. She gave a little wave to Gloria Steinem. Hearing Gloria speak at the University of Texas — my God, was it really twenty years ago? — about this amazing new revolution called the women's movement had given Gwen the direction for her own life. Peering over the balcony she spied Mimi and Jerry Rubin of Networking Inc. busily working the room and keeping an eye out for Donald Trump. The Club was fairly bursting at the seams with glittering glamorati, dazzling literati, and the top mediarati. Power, sex, and money hung in the air like expensive blended perfumes under the bright lights.

Gwen had to pinch herself mentally. All these beautiful people were coming to her house to play. What a long way she had come from the small, sturdy little tomboy who grew up in Bowness, Alberta. She remembered how that shy, frightened child-woman had arrived in the US clutching a battered suitcase and a badly bruised psyche.

Running away from scandal in her home town, she was determined to triumph over her past but never to forget it.

Like a heroine from one of her favourite childhood storybooks, Gwen had risen from poverty to power. Surveying her domain, she finally felt she had actually achieved her goal. God, the risks she had taken in the beginning. Trying to get investors to take a chance on a woman, and a Canadian woman at that. The frightening self-doubt that she and her crazy idea would never make it, the fears that came along with her hard-won success. The sudden and startling invasion of her privacy. A full-page profile in *The New York Times* and a major spread in *Forbes* magazine. Her face on the cover of *Ms.* Suddenly her opinions matter. She was quoted in *The Wall Street Journal*, *American Business*, *Time*, and *Newsweek*. *Cosmopolitan* wanted to do a makeover on her. Women, total strangers, stopped her in the street to congratulate her. And then invariably to ask her for advice. They telephoned her from across the country with their intensely private confessions and their personal problems that she, as the newly crowned champion of their rights, was supposed to be able to solve from her Park Avenue living-room.

What did she know about the division of housework, how to juggle a family and career, how to have an open marriage? She was not married and she had no children. What she did know was how hard it was for a woman to start a business on her own, how incredibly difficult it could be to get a loan without a male co-signatory, how adjectives like 'assertive', 'aggressive', 'tough', were dirty words when applied to a woman, were unfeminine. What she could say to them was, keep pushing, keep trying, and you'll get there. And when you do, it's time to reward yourself. The Club awaits you.

She was living proof of her theory of female self-determination. But sometimes she felt like a female version of Atlas, holding up half the population of America on her shoulders. Whatever maternal impulses she'd had to stifle in her private life came to the fore the minute she entered The Club building. Club members were her sisters, her cousins, her aunts, and yes, in some cases, her children. She wanted each and every Club member to make the best of herself just as she had done. The goal was to make it to the top and then enjoy the fruits of your labour.

Gwen's sense of triumph was so overwhelming that for a moment she thought she'd spoken aloud, but when she turned to the short, powerfully built man standing next to her, he simply gave her a quick hug and said, 'Happy, *cara*? The Club looks *manifico*, don't you think? Just like you, *mi bella*.' Luigi del Bello with his magnificent Roman nose and glittering, watchful eyes was Gwen's right-hand man. Almost single-handedly he had raised the funds for The Club renovations in a little over three months. Gwen was grateful to him for coming through once again, but she was starting to wonder if he was worth the trouble. He had kept The Club squarely in the black for the past couple of years, but his sexual proclivities and shady connections were beginning to make themselves known a little too publicly.

Before signing on as administrative director with Gwen, he had requested that a white Porsche be written into his contract. 'Every man should have a Porsche before he's thirty.' This year he'd demanded a chauffeur-driven Lincoln Continental, vintage, like Elvis's. And it had to be in lavender. Not a wise choice, Luigi my dear: Your slip is showing. His red brick, shuttered town-house on Christopher Street was full of art treasures and homo-erotic paintings. His Art Deco bedroom had been mirrored from floor to ceiling. When Gwen saw the mirrors, she told him they were terribly vulgar. Then she talked him into selling them all to her for The Club. Now they lined the main ballroom like a petite Versailles, a hall of mirrors in which the sparkling celebrity images of New York's *beau monde* were reflected over and over again.

'The Club looks beautiful,' Gwen agreed. 'The decorators have done a fabulous job. I couldn't be more pleased. Now on to LA and then next stop, London.' She raised her glass of Louis Roederer Cristal champagne in a toast.

Under his smooth olive skin, Lou wondered if he looked pale. As Gwen fixed him with that impenetrable gaze of hers (it was always so damned hard to know what she was thinking), he could feel the sweat trickling down the back of his Armani shirt. Didn't she suspect they were way in over their heads already? *Mamma mia*, he hoped he could still rely on Merilee.

Merilee Houston slipped her arm around Gwen's waist, giving her a quick kiss on the cheek. 'Well, sugar, you done real good. I'm so proud of you.' If Luigi was Gwen's financial support, Merilee was her emotional mainstay. Tiny, blonde, and pretty in a manufactured way, on the surface Merilee embodied everything Club women would tend to reject. Tonight, she reeked of 'Jungle Gardenia' and was wearing a Betsey Johnson bustier dress that displayed her cantilevered breasts to full advantage.

'The elevator doesn't go all the way to the top with that one,' whispered Beverley Johns, who ran the art department at Young and Rubicam during the day and the Washington Heights rape crisis centre at night. 'I bet she plans her life by the Cosmo Girl's Bedtime Astrologer.'

'Who does she think she is?' sneered Lacey Talbot, editor-in-chief of the new magazine for women over forty, *Legend*. 'The east coast's answer to Barbara Mandrell?'

'She doesn't dress for success, she dresses for easy

61

access,' giggled Liz Jordan. 'Why does a smart woman like Gwen keep that cupcake around?'

'Gwen told me, in strictest confidence,' Lacey took a slug of champagne and the women all leaned in, 'that Merilee is responsible for "saving The Club".'

'Well, what does that mean?' Liz demanded. 'Gwen's the real brains behind this operation. Merilee's just a glorified aerobics instructor.'

'No,' Lacey countered. 'She's Director of Special Services.'

'Oh.'

'Ah.'

The three women exchanged guarded looks and then Beverley burst out laughing, 'How old do you think Merilee is, anyway?'

'Who can tell? Under all that make-up, she could be twenty-eight, she could be forty.'

They underestimated Merilee, which was what made her so dangerous to them and so valuable to Gwen. Her round, heavily mascara-ed eyes were quick to ferret out staff misdemeanours and member complaints, get to the root of gossip, uncovering dissenting factions.

Gwen watched as Merilee reached into Lou's breast pocket and took out a purple silk handkerchief. She pressed it daintily to the pulse spots on her neck and forehead and then put it into her own evening bag. The intimacy of the gesture unsettled Gwen. Lately Merilee had been spending a lot of time with him, sequestered in corners, whispering. As her personal, hand-picked protégés, their first loyalty had bloody well better be to her.

Merilee noticed Gwen watching them and she urged Lou off in the direction of the bar. Goddamn, but she was tired of being a glorified secretary and sometime nursemaid. It was about time Miss Gwen got off her so-called feminist high horse and shared some of the power, not to mention some of the wealth. Merilee was fixing to be associate director of The Club by the new year. And she wouldn't mind being completely in charge of the London branch. Never mind that most British men were positively the worst in bed; she'd always wanted to live abroad. It was time for her to start moving again and if she was ever gonna make her move, she'd damn well better make it tonight. Gwen and Lou owed a lot to her.

Merilee gave Gwen another peck on the cheek. 'This place looks like the Garden of Eden, I swear it does. You probably could have waited another year before doing a complete renovation, but it's mighty pretty.'

'A face-lift before it's needed. Isn't that what the cosmetic surgeons are advising these days?' Gwen said. 'Besides, it was time for a change.'

'You are so right, honey. It looks gorgeous. And so do you. I love that evening jacket with the dragon on the back. Was I right about that Molly Parneesee dress? Was I right about cuttin' your hair?'

'You were dead right. I admit it. I feel absolutely stunning.' Impulsively Gwen gave her little southern friend a hug. Merilee might mispronounce the designer's name but she was savvy enough to talk Gwen into buying the white silk Molly Parnis gown that clung gracefully to her new leaner curves. Deceptively simple yet elegant, it was the most expensive dress she had ever owned and it looked just right with the new jacket Uncle Jack had sent her from Houston. Her auburn hair had been cropped just below her ears and sculpted back with gel to frame her heart-shaped face. The shorter hair made her look younger and more vibrant. And the emeralds in her ears matched her eyes. At Merilee's insistence, Gwen now wore only black and white, both of which set off her pale skin, dark red hair, and green eyes. Wearing only two colours made it a lot easier to organize and accessorize her wardrobe and, as Merilee had predicted, had become a sort of sartorial trademark. 'Keep it simple,' Merilee had instructed, her words being echoed by the personal shopper, 'less is more.' Looking at the hot-pink lace dress that lifted Merilee's full, cream-puff breasts and presented them on a tightly corseted shelf, Gwen smiled.

'I can't believe how wide open it all looks. The Club was just too dark before. I know y'all thought it was chic, but I like seeing the sun.' Merilee gave Gwen's hand a little squeeze. 'Isn't it heaven?'

'It is much more open now.' Gwen returned the squeeze. 'Anyway we'd better like it. We're going to have to live with it for a while.'

From a cluttered, nineteenth-century European mélange of antique styles, The Club had blossomed into a tropical setting, full of vibrant colour and life. The decorators had ripped out the centre of the building to install the solarium garden and the glass elevator that rose to the top of the building. Cool white stippled plaster walls replaced the old rosewood panelling, and the Persian carpets had been stripped away to display the jel-like mosaic tile of the main floors. The old Club had evoked an aura of quiet, understated affluence. The new Club burst forth like a passionflower.

Inside the garden, laced with creeping vines, wild orchids, and brilliant frangipani, imported tropical birds sang inside wicker cages neatly camouflaged in the squat palmettos. For city women surrounded by steel and concrete against an all-too-often grey sky, the design was brilliantly innovative. Greenhouse sauvage.

The services at The Club were constantly being upgraded. Gwen had added a computer centre and a screening room for films. The daycare nursery was a huge playroom filled with toys, games, oversized stuffed animals, a high-tech jungle gym and a Will Rogers ice-cream parlour. There was a library of the latest bestsellers in designer jackets, a billiards room, an art studio, eight meeting rooms, several sleeping rooms, and a cosmetological clinic. And then of course there were those extra special personal services, The Club's best-kept secret, the place that gold card members referred to in deep whispers as 'the private retreat'.

Gwen was particularly proud that in restaurant-fickle New York The Club was still regarded as a top spot for fine food. A different architect had designed each of the restaurants. Lokis Krumins, one of the city's hottest restaurant designers, was responsible for the golden spires and carved wood of the Thai Teak Room, renowned for its elegant service and chef from Bangkok. The red, white and blue Croissant Café was perfect for early morning breakfast meetings and the jade and white California Greenery just right for power lunches. Just added this year were the Miami Raw Bar, with a lot of neon in flamingo pink and turquoise blue, and Gwen's personal favourite, the black and silver (with touches of scarlet) Beluga Bistro, which served only caviar, vodka, and champagne. Given the strained relations between Iran and the US, Gwen offered up a silent prayer that glasnost would continue to guarantee the supply of those precious black pearls from the Caspian Sea. The new Beluga Bistro was the culinary talk of New York, thanks to Gael Green's gushing review in *New York* magazine.

Some things remained unchanged. The famous entrance to The Club, the pink marble staircase, the Orrefors chandelier, the Minton china, and the masses of fresh-cut flowers were Gwen's personal touches, a perfect combination of old and new.

'Boy, you had those contractors working right up until the last minute to complete everything.' Merilee snuck a little sip of champagne from Gwen's glass.

'I know. We just made it. The paint is barely dry.'

65

'So it's cost a bundle. It's worth it.' Merilee handed the fluted glass back to her.

'Lou talked me into taking out a whopping insurance policy. It pays to be covered.'

'You can say that again, sugar. I figure you got more than a few enemies in this town.' Then, as Gwen looked at her oddly, Merilee pointed down below. 'Look, there's Phil and Marlo. I really liked her in that thing on TV where she played the mother of a gay teenager. Did you see it?'

'When do I ever have time to watch TV?' Gwen sighed.

'Marlo looks great. She looks like a teenager herself. Phil looks real tired, though. I swear his face is almost as grey as his hair.'

'Well, I don't think he expected New York audiences to be so aggressive. They're much more polite in Chicago.'

Merilee giggled. 'You're right there. I caught a rerun of the show last week and Phil was wearing a dress. He must be trying to keep up with Oprah and Geraldo. I don't know what the topic was supposed to be but I'm tellin' you, that audience was rude. Poor Phil turned bright pink.'

'No doubt he was wishing a great hand would come down out of the sky and magically transport him back to civilized Chicago,' Gwen laughed. 'New York is so tough. The only problem is once you've lived here it spoils you for anywhere else.'

Phil and Marlo were followed by Betsy Bloomingdale, Liza with a Z, and Calvin and Kelly. Two other top fashion designers had their heads together, probably discussing their new joint line of children's clothing called Rich Kids. Merilee hung over the gallery like a wide-eyed Valley girl. Gwen suspected she was either looking for Rob Lowe or her idol, Dolly Parton.

'Do you think Ted Kennedy's going to show?' Merilee

asked. God, she was dying for a cigarette, but she knew how much Gwen hated her to smoke in public. 'Caroline and Ed are here. I just saw them.'

'I don't know,' Gwen sighed. 'His secretary RSVP'd yes, but I have a feeling the word may be out that Stephen Andrews is intending to make a try for the presidency.'

'Can we count on those two to shake hands?'

'I doubt it.' Gwen took a hasty gulp of her champagne. 'The Kennedys never forgive a turncoat.'

'Is that what you're so nervous about?'

'Do I seem nervous?' Gwen asked innocently. She'd been trying to hide it, but she couldn't stop her hands from shaking.

'Don't bullshit a bullshit artist. I know you better than anybody and you're as jumpy as an alley cat about to get herself spayed. What's the matter, Gwen? You look like you're about to turn tail and bolt the joint. It couldn't be more perfect. We got tons of press here, we got VIPs, we got BPs, we even got some good friends. Everybody's rootin' for you, honey.'

'I know. It's a terrific turnout. Much better than I expected.'

'Then what are you worried about? Everybody's here to have a good time. Don't start panicking now. This is your glory. Revel in it.'

'I'm not worried about the gala. I know we've got everything covered. You and Lou have worked your tails off to make sure of that. The party will take care of itself.'

'Then all you have to do is look gorgeous and keep smiling. That's not so hard, is it? Level with me, sweetcakes. What's wrong?'

'I can't help it, Merilee, I'm just dreading that *In Depth* interview with Sara Town. I'm OK with Suzy and I genuinely like Liz Smith. She's got class and she's always been one of my biggest supporters. I don't even mind *Entertainment Tonight* following me around from room to room. But I hate doing a formal interview. Especially with Sara Town.'

'Don't sweat it, Jenny. I promise you, you can handle her. I didn't give that bitch any ammunition when she came sniffing around here for some dirt.'

'Sara came to see you? Here at The Club?' Gwen turned the colour of her gown.

'Yeah, a few weeks ago. I think it was the day they laid the tile in the solarium. I gave her a couple of drinks, she tried to take some notes. Believe me, she didn't get very far. So no probs.'

'Don't give me that "no probs" garbage. I know that with you "no probs" always means plenty probs. Why didn't you tell me?'

'Because I knew it would only get you in a flap. You have to trust me to handle these things for you. I handled her.'

'What did she ask you?'

'Plenty. But I didn't tell her anything, I swear.' Merilee wondered if Gwen had any idea how hard she had had to work to ensure that promise. Sara Town was one wily operator and keeping her at bay was no easy task. She smiled triumphantly as she remembered that meeting.

Looking as though she'd been hand-dipped in confectioner's sugar, Merilee sat behind the desk in her own private office. Sara stood in the doorway in a black jersey dress that accentuated every line of her sinewy body. With her black hair and amber eyes, Merilee had to admit she was one hell of a sexy lady. The dress wasn't low cut or even particularly short for the fashions these days, but she managed to look provocative all the same.

'Can I offer you a drink?' Merilee asked, heading for the wet bar. 'I've got this great bourbon from Kentucky, Maker's Mark. You ever heard of it?'

'Cain't say's ah have. I'm sorry,' Sara caught herself.

68

'That's a dreadful habit I have of picking up the accent of the person I'm with. It's terribly embarrassing when I do an interview because it's not something that can be edited out. I do love your accent, though.'

Merilee smiled sweetly and handed her the bourbon. 'Oh that's OK. Everybody in New York tells me I sound like Jimmy Carter. Now I don't think that's a compliment, do you?'

'Hardly.' Sara raised an eyebrow.

Merilee smiled to herself as Sara cautiously sipped her drink. She knew Sara was wondering if she could possibly be for real. Good, she thought. You just go ahead and wonder. Stew a little, honey, while you figure out how you're gonna handle me. 'Sit down, please.'

She gestured to a small, oyster-coloured velvet armchair across from her and watched as Sara attempted to wedge herself into it. The decor of Merilee's office resembled a smoking room in a men's lounge, with the difference that every piece of furniture had been custom-built for Merilee's small size, designed to make anyone bigger — and everyone was — feel oversized and awkward. She'd read about this little business ploy in Michael Korda's book, *Power*; she had to admit that he knew his stuff. She watched in amusement as Sara shifted uneasily in the chair, trying to make her long legs comfortable.

'Now what all do you want to know about Gwen? Oh my goodness, I forgot to ask you, have you had a tour of the premises? I've always wondered why you're not a member; you're exactly the type of woman we like around here. You deserve the kind of services that we provide to our members . . . oh, listen to me rattling on! In any case would you like me to show you around? We're in kind of an upheaval at the moment, with all this construction, but it's going to be real pretty for the gala. I sure hope the decorators can make that deadline.'

'No thanks. I've been here as a guest. It's quite spectacular and I'm sure the renovations will only make it more so.' Sara opened her briefcase and produced a little tape recorder.

'Oh you're not going to use that thing, are you?' Merilee recoiled in horror. 'I can't stand the sound of my own voice and I sure don't want it preserved for posterity.'

'Of course. Whatever you say.' Sara put away the recorder and took out a notebook and pen, shifting in the chair again. 'Now, it must have cost a bomb to redo this place.'

'Honey, you can say that again.' Merilee refilled their two small glasses. 'Ice?'

'No thanks. This will be fine.'

'Smart girl. This here's fine sippin' whisky.'

'It's lovely. Thanks. Tell me,' Sara said briskly, uncapping her gold fountain pen. 'How did you raise the money for these renovations?'

'Well, our members take good care of us. They love The Club and they want it to be the best it can be.'

'Of course, but it all seemed to happen awfully quickly. Once the building-fund campaign was announced, you seemed to reach that goal within a matter of months.'

'Now that's Lou's department. Mr del Bello, I mean. He's in charge of the fundraisin' around here and I declare he could get blood out of a turnip and water out of a stone. He's a real go-getter.'

'Mm, so I've heard,' Sara said, taking another cautious sip of her bourbon. 'He and Ms Roberts are pretty close, aren't they? Are they an item?'

'No. What makes you think that,' Merilee took a sip of her own bourbon.

'Well, they are seen together a lot. Elaine's, The Four Seasons, Lutece, even The White Horse. He's her most frequent escort. Except for you, of course.'

70

'They work together,' Merilee said shortly. 'Sometimes they play together.'

'But neither of them is married,' Sara said smoothly, 'so naturally we all assume . . .'

'Believe me,' Merilee interjected with a smile, 'there's nothin' goin' on between those two.'

'Has Gwyneth ever been married?'

Merilee immediately noticed the shift from 'Ms Roberts' to 'Gwyneth'. 'Not since I've known her. I guess you could say she's wedded to her work. The Club's not simply a job to her; it's her family. Her whole life in fact. She doesn't have time for anything else. You want another shot?' Merilee reached for the little bottle with the distinctive red wax around the cap.

'Sure.' Sara drained her glass. 'Wow. That stuff has quite a kick to it.'

Merilee chuckled. 'Now I told you it was for sippin'. You can't knock back Maker's Mark like that. It'll rot your insides for sure.'

'Damned right!' Sara laughed with her. 'Do you think Gwen has something against marriage?'

Now it was 'Gwen'. 'No, no, I wouldn't rule out that possibility, but you don't have to be married these days. Look at Gloria Steinem. Look at you, for that matter. You got your own financial security. What do you need a man for except for sex, and there's always plenty of that around, right?'

'Right. But that old biological clock must be ticking away.'

'Gwen's got a pretty full plate right now as it is. That girl — excuse me, I know I should say *woman* around here — she just never stops working. First one here in the morning and the last one to leave at night. She chooses the daily special menus in the dining-room; she schedules the film showings and contacts the speakers and all; I mean she takes a real personal interest in the day-to-day

71

workings of The Club. It's a hands-on operation for her. She ain't no figurehead. Have you seen that screening room? That place is somethin' else. Come on, let me give you the grand tour.'

Sara pretended to study her notebook. 'Does she date anyone that you know of? She's not linked to any man except Luigi del Bello.'

Merilee set her drink down and regarded Sara with outright suspicion. 'Now why are you askin' me all this? *In Depth* isn't supposed to be tabloid television. You sound like one of those sleazy reporters from the *National Enquirer*.'

'Only one step removed, I'm afraid,' Sara laughed lightly. 'A major portion of our audience does have a *People* magazine mentality. They're always dying to know if there are wedding bells in the future.'

'Sure, sure, but you usually don't mess with that stuff. I read *People* magazine, too, and it was right there in Star Chatter that you told the network you'd only sign on for *In Depth* if they guaranteed you wouldn't have to waste your time with society gossip. That newspaper column you used to write had "I take myself seriously" written all over it. What is it they used to call you? "The Caustic Crusader"?'

'Oh come now, you've got to admit that her personal life remains a mystery to the general public. Gwyneth Roberts is a modern-day female equivalent of Howard Hughes.'

'And that's how she wants it to stay.'

'But she's a public figure and naturally her public is curious. Does she simply not like men?'

'You better watch your step, sister,' Merilee said sharply. 'Gwen doesn't have to give you this interview, you know.'

'Oh but she does. You couldn't buy the kind of publicity *In Depth* will give The Club with this eight-minute segment. We're in the top ten; we reach a huge, nationwide audience. She'd be a fool to turn that down.'

Merilee ploughed ahead. 'She will turn it down if she thinks for one minute it's going to be a hatchet job. I can make sure she turns it down. She listens to what I say, and if I tell her not to go with you she won't go.'

'I'm sorry if I've overstepped the bounds,' Sara said hastily. 'Just trying to find a personal hook for the piece, that's all. Let's stick to the more obvious questions then. How did she come to start The Club? An exclusive club for women. It's such a marvellous idea; I wonder why no one thought of it before?'

'You'd be surprised what great ideas are out there floatin' around just waitin' for someone to think of them. Gwen says she woke up in the middle of the night with a vision of opening a women's club and once she got hold of it there was no stopping her.'

'How did she finance it originally?'

'Well, right from the beginning she wanted to sell shares in The Club to women, but none of them wanted to buy.'

'Why not? You'd think they'd be eager to get in on the action.'

'Well, that was ten years ago. A lot has changed since then. Mostly due to Gwen and this Club. Even gettin' women to join was hard in those days, much less put up any capital.'

Sara made a few quick notes. 'Where did she get the capital then?'

'I think she had to take out a personal loan to get the ball rollin'. I don't really know. I wasn't in on the beginning.'

'That is strange. Unless some businesswomen thought there was something odd in the proposal, something not quite above board?' Sara frowned slightly, tapping her Cross pen against her teeth.

Merilee slammed her drink down on the oak desk. 'Just what are you drivin' at?'

'I'll tell you what I'm driving at, Ms Houston. There's a rumour around town that The Club was built with laundered money, that The Club is on shaky financial ground and that the shit may be about to hit the fan.'

'And you think you're gonna be the one to make it all come out in the wash? On national television? You gotta be out of your cotton-pickin' mind. The women of this city are behind The Club one hundred per cent. The women of this country need to believe that The Club is waiting for them if they ever get the chance to live in New York. Hell, most of them would like to see a branch of The Club in their home town. You try and stir up a hornet's nest and you are gonna be one sorry little girl. You'll be about as popular as Henry Morgentaler at a Right-to-Life convention. We'll slap a libel suit on you so fast it'll make your head swim.'

'I don't make accusations that I can't back up, Ms Houston. With facts and figures.'

Merilee rose from behind her desk, pulling herself up to her full height of five feet nothing. 'I wouldn't do that if I were you. You go pokin' about in too many dark cupboards and you're bound to pull out a couple of skeletons you hadn't counted on, know what I mean, sugar?'

Sara continued to smile with what was now undisguised contempt, relieved to rise from her own chair. 'Is this kiss-my-grits, honey-chile act for real?'

'Let's just say it's realer than that phoney British crap you like to throw around like so much stale crumpet. I know you, sister. I know you real well.'

'Are you trying to threaten me?' Sara closed her notebook with a snap, one eyebrow arched.

'You got it. Right on the button, Ms Town. Or should

I say Ms Washington?' Merilee sat down again to watch Sara's immediate reaction. 'Well, hush my mouth, I think I just scored a bull's-eye.'

'I don't know what you mean.' Sara had seized her briefcase and was edging towards the door.

'Just tryin' to protect my own,' Merilee drawled. 'Course I know all that happened a long time ago, but you think your fans would like to learn you're not everything you claim to be? Think they want to hear you're not quite the third-generation blue-blood right-wing WASP you pretend to be? I don't think they'd understand. Not at all. In fact I think you might be right out on your ass before you could say House Un-American Activities Committee.'

'You little bitch,' Sara fairly spat at her.

'How do you know the proof of what you really are isn't just floatin' around out there ready to confront you at some point?' Sara opened her mouth to speak but Merilee glanced at her little pink fingernails and went on comfortably. 'I'm just tryin' to warn you. You mess my Ms Gwen about and I guarantee I'll mess you about. I don't know what your motives are for wantin' to destroy her, and for the life of me I can't see why she still cares about you, but you're not gonna hurt her if I'm around, y'hear me?'

'I hear you.' Sara's hand was trembling on the doorknob.

'You keep your mouth shut; I'll keep mine shut. Is it a deal?'

'It's a deal,' Sara mumbled.

'Oh and by the way, I just want you to know, honey' — Merilee aimed her parting shot after her — 'in my opinion, your father was a saint.'

Remembering how quickly Sara Town had got out of that door, Merilee started to laugh. 'Don't worry,' she said to Gwen. 'I think I fixed her wagon. It's my job to keep you away from that kind of hassle.'

'I know and I love you for it.' Gwen gave her a grateful hug. 'But I still wish there was some way I could get out of the interview. Let Lou do it. Or you.'

'Are you kidding? Much as I would love to be on national TV they don't want to see me or Lou. You think they want to see Jon Peters on *60 Minutes*? No, they want to see Barbra Streisand. Or Lesley Ann Warren. Or Kim Basinger. Or whoever's his latest. You're the star of this show. They're gonna want you. Gwen, you have to do it. If you want to open in London, not to mention LA, we need all the publicity we can get.'

Gwen put her hand to her forehead and absent-mindedly rubbed the frown line between her eyes. 'You're right. Of course you're right. I just hope I can handle it.'

'Trust me, you can handle it. You're all grown up now.'

'Let's hope I am.' But her stomach turned over at the thought of facing Sara Town anyway.

Merilee squeezed her hand encouragingly. 'Hey, don't think about that now. It's all blood under the bridge. Get yourself another glass of bubbly and do some circulating. They all want a piece of you tonight, honey.'

Balancing the fluted glass of champagne in one hand, Gwen moved gracefully through the crowd, greeting guests and accepting the accolades they all were ready to heap upon her: 'You really did it, Gwen baby, the place is dynamite Great stuff You'll be able to up the dues this year.' 'You look fantastic What have you done to your hair?' 'Are we going to hear anything from Stephen Andrews tonight? Is it true if he decides to run, you'll be heading up his campaign?' 'Great dress!' 'Great hair!' 'Great food!' 'Great party!'

The cameras snapped discreetly as a couple of photographers from UP and API followed her from room to room. They weren't even giving her a chance to eat at her own party. Passing the buffet, she took a quick swipe at the table laden with shiny red lobsters brushed with garlic olive oil, artichoke truffle salad, angel hair pasta with baby mussels and quail eggs stuffed with caviar. The Miami Raw Bar was serving fat Blue Point oysters and cherrystone clams. The Teak Room was offering satay kebabs, grilled tamari shark, and steamed dumplings filled with tea-smoked duck. The Will Rogers ice-cream parlour was featuring a brand new flavour of Häagen-Dazs created especially for The Club's gala, wild strawberry with fresh ground pepper (it sounded bizarre but Gwen had tasted it and she knew it was exquisite).

She smiled wryly. It used to be you could get away with serving wine and several kinds of cheese. Now food had replaced sex in the hearts of many New Yorkers. A new restaurant was discovered, shared among the women of The Club the way a really fantastic lover used to be, and dropped just as quickly as a stud who could no longer perform. As she listened to the rippling conversation, the talk was of food, face-lifts, money and sex, in that order.

'Have you tried that chocolate cognac cannoli? It's to die.'

'Are you kidding? I'm on the Diamond Diet. I eat so much fruit I oughta be stamped Sunkist.'

'Darling, she's had her *entire* body lifted. Her navel is practically up to her double chin.'

'Don't waste your time investing in oil. Everyone I know is moving into fibre optics.'

'So I said to Bill, "Look, I'm not something to be passed around." And he said, "Oh yes you are." So I was.'

'Aren't you worried about mussel poisoning? I mean, some people have become paralysed and lost their memory from eating mussels.'

'What are a few brain cells compared to the taste of these?'

'I'm having the fat from my thighs liposuctioned and injected into my cheeks.'

'Great. I knew those thighs would come in handy.'

'This housing market is unbelievable. I bought my condo three months ago and already it's appreciated close to half a mil.'

'Now that I'm thirty, I'm dismayed to find just the teeniest flicker in my idealism.'

'Really? I thought your love affair with yourself would last for ever.'

'Man, there's nothing but dykes at this gig. The ratio of broads must be three to one. I should be cleaning up here, but so help me I can't even get arrested.'

'Yeah, I know what you mean. All I can say is, when women discovered their sisters, they forgot their brothers. Why in hell is that something to celebrate?'

A CELEBRATION OF WOMEN. The huge banner across the ballroom proclaimed the theme of the gala. The entire evening was a tribute by and for women. The food was catered by Susie Krumins of the Kookie Krums gourmet empire. Meryl Streep and Roseanne Barr had agreed to co-host the entertainment for the evening. Lily Tomlin had promised to do her bad lady routine and Dolly and Linda and Emmy Lou were going to reprise 'To Know Him Is to Love Him.' At the moment, Whitney Houston was belting out her latest love cry so loudly that Gwen had trouble catching all the conversations. She wished she knew who half these people were. There were also a lot of people here tonight she wished she didn't know.

A major Broadway producer grabbed her arm as she went by and started to cry into his kir royale about his wife's death. Gwen was expressing her sympathy over his loss when he interrupted her to say, 'Nobody would fuck

78

me when Caroline was alive. They said they loved her too much. Now she's dead and they still won't fuck me. They say they love her memory too much. Can you beat it?' An independent film maker lay down on the floor and announced he wouldn't get up until Madonna lay on top of him. One guest had already thrown up in the passionflower centrepiece in the library. Cheryl Tops had (once again) tried to commit suicide in the shower, but she was back now, slugging the champagne and giggling.

A fat, fiftyish literary agent from CAA, who definitely should not have been wearing a red neoprene mini skirt and sequined halter top, leaned heavily on the bar, discussing her current lover with the bartender, Toto.

'I think I should pass him on to you, Toto. He's got this absolutely immense thing. My dear, it's like giving birth. When we're, you now, *doing it*, I keep worrying he's going to have a stroke. All the blood rushes from his head to his crotch.' Then, describing the third husband she was currently in the process of divorcing: 'Suddenly, at the age of fifty-five, Taggert discovers he likes little boys. I mean, it's really bizarre. My shrink calls it late-onset homosexuality. You know, like diabetes?'

Toto fixed her an extra-strong Harvey Wallbanger and shrugged philosophically. 'Well, don't give up hope. Look at Carlos La Jolla, the most notorious queen in Queens. He's been taking it up the rear since he was ten years old. Now he's fifty-two and he just got married.'

'Oh!' screamed the agent with delight. 'You mean we can make them go the other way, too?'

The party was in full swing.

# *Five*

Michael Taylor was standing outside the main bathroom waiting for Sara. Wearing the Wall Street uniform of blue suit and red tie, he leaned against the wall and drank a weak Scotch while reading a political analysis of Libya. Michael never went anywhere without a good book and a miniature fully stocked bar in his briefcase. Michael was Sara Town's personal manager and one of the top agents at the most powerful agency in New York, the Creative Talent Agency. He hated parties. He claimed he was in the business of selling and why should he have to sell past regular hours, but despite his complaining he knew, as everyone knows, that in the entertainment industry, evening deals are the most concrete. There are more contracts written in Chivas Regal than there are forged in ink.

Creative Talent Agency had been founded on the principles of Japanese business management, all for one and one for all, where the client is God. CTA agents were expected to maintain low visibility and shun the press, leaving temperament and eccentricity to their star clients, of which they had the biggest roster in town. Michael Taylor fitted the profile perfectly. He had been called the Zen master of talent agents. Inscrutable to the point of appearing dull (*Spy* magazine referred to him as 'personality free'), his impassive surface concealed a hidden agenda: to screw every woman in New York City. Michael was arguably the best agent in the business, and he was indisputably the best lay. Of course that was hardly saying much these days. These days it seemed the whole world was going gay, a massive stampede to the powder-room. In New York, there are one hundred and twenty-four eligible women to eighty-two men. Take away the maimed, the married, and the gay, make that six men. Michael Taylor was providing a valuable service. Clients and friends of clients. Mothers of clients. Even barely pubescent daughters of clients. Passed from hand to hand and mouth to mouth, Michael was the best-kept secret in New York.

Business is business and sex is sex and never the twain should meet, Sara's ex-mentor and ex-lover, Victor, used to say. That's why he was her ex. Victor had a good head for business but he wasn't terribly good at the business of giving head, which was why Sara eventually had to give him up and sign with Michael Taylor at CTA. She recognized immediately that Michael had a passion for pussy. Every time she thought of leaving Michael's representation, which was often (many celebrities go though agents like Kleenex), she remembered his sexual talents and put off the decision.

Jay Bernstein was ready and willing to take her on. He'd done a fabulous job for Farrah and for Mary Hart. Hadn't Jay B. been the force behind the 'Sexy Over Forty' campaign that kept Linda Evans in Krystle perfume? He had made a fortune for his ladies – who could ask for anything more?

Sara could. Money and power were important to her, but even more important was the satisfying of her libido. Sara was a sex junkie and Michael was her most constant supplier.

As she came barrelling out of the main bathroom, Sara grabbed him by the ear. 'Come with me,' she hissed, dragging him along the corridor to a smaller powder-room, slamming the door behind them and locking it.

'What's with you, lady?' Michael attempted to disentangle himself from her grip.

'I've just had the most bizarre encounter with that black tart from *Late Beat News*, Nadine or Charlene or some hopelessly coloured name.'

'Bodine Johnson. I'd like to represent her. I think she's quite good. The network never gives her much to do, though.' Michael opened his briefcase and poured himself another shot of Johnnie Walker Red.

'With good reason. That woman makes Cleopatra's asp look like a household pet. She literally shoved me up against the wall and nailed me with her life story.'

'You're probably her role model, dear.'

'Thanks a lot. That makes me feel about a hundred and two years old.' Sara let go of his arm and started to rummage in her shoulder bag for her make-up kit.

'What have you got there?' Michael pointed to the large padded envelope under Sara's arm.

'Oh, just some background stuff on Stephen Andrews for the *In Depth* profile.' She handed it to him. 'Miriam Newman practically shoved it down my throat. Boy, is she pissed at him for dumping her after all these years! She must have been the only person around who didn't know it was coming. She looked as if she were ready to open a vein all over that pink marble floor.'

'Can you blame her?'

'No, but I don't blame Stephen either. He's not exactly my favourite person these days, but Miriam is such a cow. OK, OK, I know she's one of your top clients, but I simply can't stand her. I don't know why you continue to represent her.'

'She's the best actress in the country today,' Michael said staunchly.

'That's definitely a matter of opinion.' Sara quickly and expertly began applying a brownish blush under her chiselled cheekbones.

'What do you care? She's no competition for you.'

'All women are competition for me. So tell me, do you really like Miriam?'

'I don't discuss one client with another. You know that.'

'Oh, don't give me that CTA party-line crap. Sometimes I think the agency is run by Moonies.'

Michael refused to bite. 'What do you want me to do with this?' He waved the envelope at her.

'Just stick it in my shoulder bag. It's probably some baby pics of Senator Andrews on a bearskin rug. I don't have time to deal with it now. I'm on camera in less than twenty minutes and I haven't finished my make-up yet.'

'Didn't the station send your make-up girl with you?' Michael was always checking to see that his clients were treated properly.

'Oh, sure, Diane's here. She's already done her work. Now I have to do mine. Only I know best how to disguise my imperfections. I've got these grotesque bags under my eyes, thanks to you.' Sara had spent all last night and much of the morning in bed with Michael. 'Don't you ever give it a rest? At the rate you're going, you'll be dead by the time you hit thirty.'

Michael gave her a charmingly lustful leer. 'Great. That gives me four years still to go.' At twenty-six, he was still considered a young hotshot whizz kid in the biz.

'You knew I had a shoot today. Why didn't you tie me down?' Acknowledging Michael's smile: 'Get your mind out from between my legs. God, this lip rouge makes me look like a half-baked tea biscuit.' She scrubbed at her lips and reapplied a darker gloss. 'Michael, I don't know what's wrong with me tonight. I feel so out of it. It's not like me to be nervous. We're supposed to roll in fifteen minutes and I'm just not together.'

'Do you want a hit?' Michael's eyes were dark brown, opaque.

Sara looked around quickly. 'Yeah, right, OK.' He loosened his red silk tie and undid the top two buttons of his striped shirt to reveal the silver vial on a chain that glinted against his smooth, honey-coloured chest. A mixture of Irish, Welsh, and Spanish ancestry, Michael played his Byronic good looks to the hilt. He unscrewed the mother-of-pearl lid and dipped the tiny silver spoon into the vial.

'Close your right side, Sara.' She placed a finger against her nose, closing off the right passage and inhaled deeply. 'Now the other side.'

'How pure is this stuff? I know I'm going to be winging the interview, but I don't want to be flying.'

'Hey, don't get your knickers in a twist.' Both Michael and Sara loved borrowing British phrases. 'It's good stuff. I got it off Luigi del Bello.'

'You're kidding! The business manager of The Club is supplying you with drugs?'

'Hardly. I ran into him in the hall and he laid it on me. It was a present, not a business transaction. Come on now, lick the spoon.'

'Like a good girl?' Sara smiled her cream-fed smile at him.

'Sure. Don't I always know what's best for you?'

'Yes!'

'All right then. More?' Michael was generous with his coke.

Michael had a hit and Sara took another one. She was feeling better already. A quick look in the mirror. Looking better, too. She unbuttoned a couple of buttons on her Anne Klein blouse. It was boring to have to dress so straight on-camera when her off-camera taste ran to the more exotic. She squirted a shot of Poison into her cleavage and, hiking up her skirt, aimed the atomizer between her legs.

'Michael, darling,' she purred seductively, 'while I've

got my skirt up, would you like a bit of an appetizer?'
Michael looked bewildered. 'Come on, don't be so dense.
I realize you pigged out last night, but the buffet won't
be served until much later. We've got a long and tedious
evening ahead of us. So how about it?' She moved her
hand suggestively along one silky thigh.

'What now?'

'Don't be so fucking paranoid. The door's locked and
there's nobody in here but us "perverts". They're all in
the ballroom looking at themselves in those endless
bloody mirrors.'

'But you're on camera in' — checking his watch
hurriedly — 'less than ten minutes.'

'Michael love, I'm not wearing any knickers and I'm
not wearing any pantyhose. We've got ten free minutes.
Let's not waste them.'

'Look, Sara . . .'

She put her hands on his shoulders. 'Down, boy.'

'I don't really think . . .'

'Get down.' She loved to give those commands and,
God, how he loved to be ordered about.

'All right, but you owe me one.'

'Down.'

Michael got down. Down on his knees, between her
legs. His practised hands sliding along her slim, tanned
legs, moulding the muscles of her calves, gently caressing
the backs of her knees, stroking the soft tissue inside that
made her jump with surprise and pleasure. Good reflexes,
had Sara. He brought his mouth to the inside of her thigh,
biting gently, tiny careful bites, licking along the inner
flesh, tiny tongues of fire, liquid flames, cupping her bare
buttocks, pulling her crotch close to his face. He could
feel her legs flexing and unflexing, like a marathon
swimmer or a dancer on pointe.

'Lovely, lovely,' she whispered, her head rolling from
side to side, her eyes closed, fingers winding blindly

86

through his thick, black hair, digging her fingernails into his scalp.

The quivering starts before he has even found the goal of desire, the involuntary shuddering as she slams against his face, a response that startled him the first time they made love but that now arouses him almost as much as it does her. This frenzied greed for what he has the power to give and to withhold from her. Even when she think she's in control, her body betrays her, reduced to asking, begging, pleading; and her wildness drives him wild. Holding her away from him for a moment, he kisses her mouth, letting her taste herself on his tongue, and then gently he moves down to part her again, tongue slipping in and out, in and out, a kitten delicately lapping cream.

Her breathing is jagged, sighing, panting, pelvis pushing forward, rotating, straining for the release. A high-pitched moan escapes her, she clutches his head in a vice, reaching for him, writhing, snake-like, her thighs lock, trembling and then rigid, reaching for the ultimate, exquisite sensation.

He lets go of her ass, slipping one hand under her blouse, reaching for her breast, grabbing the nipple, pressing, pinching, skirting that fine line between pleasure and pain, rolling the nipple like a plump brown raisin between his long fingers. With his other hand he reaches inside her, fingers vibrating quickly as if reading in Braille, finding the most sensitive spot, thrumming surely, as the inner walls ring with primordial song. She twists his ears with her fists, then clamps her legs around his head again, cutting off all sound, all thought. The breath explodes from her raggedly and he puts his hand over her mouth to stifle the scream . . .

'Miss Town? Sara Are you in there?' Someone knocked at the door. Michael could barely hear the sound, but he tried to pull away. Sara's hands clawed tighter into his hair. The knocking resumed, louder.

'Sara, are you all right? We'll be going in two minutes.' Michael shoved her knees apart. She arched her back and pulled his head to her one final time. The knocking grew louder. 'Sara, are you coming?'

She drew up her knees, rocking from side to side, and screamed over Michael's head at the top of her voice, 'Yes!'

# *Six*

'This must be an exciting and rewarding night for you, Gwyneth Roberts,' said Sara Town, as one of her camera crew clipped a miniature microphone to the front of Gwen's white silk dress. They were standing in a corner of the main ballroom as the gala swirled around them. 'The most glamorous celebrities in New York City are here tonight to celebrate the tenth anniversary of The Club with you. Is it fair to say "you've come a long way, baby"?'

We both have, Gwen thought, blinking against the harsh television lights as she looked into the slanted, amber eyes of the woman who had once been her closest friend. The delicate features had sharpened with time and the creamy skin stretched more tautly over the high cheekbones. Sara looked harder, as if everything said about her over the years had gradually become part of her physical appearance. Still, she was so beautiful that it made Gwen's throat ache to see her. Suddenly she was afraid she was going to cry. It frightened her that Sara could still arouse such strong feelings in her.

She took a deep breath and smiled at her, but there was no answering emotion or even recognition in Sara's veiled gaze. 'Yes, the gala is a real celebration. It was exactly ten years ago today that The Club first opened its doors to the women of New York. I had a vision. I wanted to build a showcase for the new American woman. Ten years later we're still here and going strong.

I think that's a cause for celebration, don't you?'

Sara's eyes flickered with detached amusement. 'That almost sounds like one of your own press releases, Gwen – may I call you Gwen?'

A wave of emotion threatened to engulf her. So many memories came flooding back to her. 'Of course, Sara.'

'Your life reads like a Harlequin romance. Tell me, can a little girl from an oil town in Alberta find happiness as the wealthy owner of an exclusive women's club?' Fast-talking Sara took the soft approach with her interviewees before moving in for the kill.

'I'm pleased that so many women are able to share the wealth with me,' Gwen said. 'It's time for men to make room for us because we're definitely moving up in the world.' Damn, she sounded stiff and preachy; she mentally ordered herself to relax.

'Everyone knows how committed you are to advancing the cause of women, but more than that, you are a very shrewd businesswoman with a keen eye on the market. How could you predict ten years ago that women would be willing to pay big bucks for aerobics and acupuncture? What makes The Club anything more than a glorified YWCA?' She coloured the words just enough to conjure up images of dingy lockers and sweaty socks.

Gwen nervously smoothed a lock of wayward red hair. She knew this interview was a mistake, whatever Merilee believed. Wrong, she corrected herself. You didn't agree to do this interview because of the publicity. You wanted to see your old friend face to face and here she is. What are you so afraid of? Maybe Sara hasn't changed but you have. She's still on the attack but you have no reason to be on the defensive. She cleared her throat and smiled into the camera, 'The Club offers a great deal more in the way of special services. I saw a need and filled it. Ten years ago, I looked around and saw society discriminating against women . . .'

Sara cut her off with, 'Then why not open a crisis centre in midtown Manhattan? Why an exclusive super-posh pleasure palace?'

'I'm a businesswoman,' Gwen said, 'and I'm interested in the very specific methods by which women can get ahead in business. Ten years ago, I was at the top of my own profession, earning good money, and yet none of the men's clubs would allow me to join. As Richard Nixon said, "A woman has more chance of becoming President of the United States than President of the Bohemian Club." Private clubs symbolized the upper echelons of business in a male-dominated society. I felt it was time for us to get in on the action.'

'But by creating a club exclusively for women, aren't you merely duplicating the old boys' networking system you're supposedly rebelling against?'

Gwen paused for a second as if reflecting. 'Perhaps, but I see that as a necessary phase. I'm not saying women's needs are more important than men's, but we deserve the focus we are finally getting. Men have had that focus for centuries.'

'Is it true that a man has actually filed a discrimination suit against The Club? He applied to join but you won't let him because he is a man.'

'Men are allowed to avail themselves of The Club's services so long as they are guests of a member.'

'Surely you don't allow them to swim in the famous nude pool we've all heard so much about?'

'No, of course not.' She smiled. 'But there are certain hours when the pool is open to them, provided they are accompanied by members. We are a private club, an intimate social entity and, as such, we may choose our own membership.'

Sara's tone grew sharper. 'The Club has over ten thousand members. Do you really call that an intimate social entity? I think most people would call it a business

91

and as such the law does not allow discrimination.'

'There is no racial, religious, or social discrimination here. Any woman can join The Club.'

'Any woman with ten thousand dollars for the initiation fee and four thousand for annual dues. How many women can afford that?'

'Well, we started with just under one hundred members,' Gwen said mildly, 'and as you yourself just pointed out, we now have over ten thousand. The truth is that a lot of women are able to afford our services. Why shouldn't they have them?'

'And just what is the extent of those services? Is it true that The Club is at this moment under investigation?'

'Not that I'm aware of.' Gwen fought to contain her surprise.

'Do you still call yourself a feminist?' Sara said suddenly, openly searching for Gwen's weak spot.

'Yes I do.'

'How does an expensive health spa like The Club advance the cause of women?'

'I . . .' Gwen felt herself flush and stop. How could Sara know that she herself was beginning to feel uncomfortable with her own personal success and to question the value of The Club? She forced herself to continue. 'We're not here tonight to debate the progress of the women's movement. We're here tonight for a party.'

Coiled, cobra-like, Sara struck out again. 'Where did you get the money to start The Club, Ms Roberts?'

'Originally I tried to finance The Club by selling shares to women. When I found many were afraid to take a risk, I had to find the money on my own.'

'And how did you find the money?' Sara repeated sharply. 'Do you come from a wealthy family?'

'I come from the wrong side of the tracks, Ms Town, just like you.' Gwen felt the heat flooding her face.

Stung, Sara lashed out again, 'How do you respond to allegations linking The Club to organized crime?'

Now Gwen was really stunned. She had no idea what Sara meant. What was she talking about?

'Are you going to answer the question?' Sara pressed her.

Gwen held her head high and looked straight into the camera. 'I hold myself accountable to my bank and to my creditors. I am not accountable to you.'

Sara smiled triumphantly. 'And there you have it, folks. New York's most successful businesswoman just told me to mind my own business. This is Sara Town reporting from the main ballroom at New York's fabulous The Club.'

The cameras stopped rolling. The VTR technicians were winding up the cable and pushing equipment to the back of the hall. Michael Taylor and the unit manager advanced on the two women, but Sara had not moved away from Gwen. 'Why did you resist me so much? I gave you a chance to defend yourself in a national interview. Coast-to-coast coverage.'

'Being interviewed by you, Sara, isn't worth the coverage. It's like starting out the day by eating a live toad. It does make the rest of the day seem better, but only by comparison. Now if you'll excuse me, I have guests to attend to.'

Gwen turned on her heel and ran straight into an angular, good-looking young man, dressed completely in black, his long blond hair pulled back from his face into a long tail. 'Gwyneth Roberts,' he said, 'I'd like a word with you.'

'Lokis,' she greeted him with enthusiasm and relief. 'I'm so glad you could be here tonight. As one of the original architects of The Club, you deserve to share in this glorious celebration.' She reached out to take his hand, but the look on his face stopped her.

93

'I've got nothing to celebrate.' The bitterness in his voice was unmistakable 'I've lost my wife, I've lost my child, and it's all because of you. You and The Club.'

'I don't follow you,' Gwen said, keeping her voice low and reasonable.

'Susie was happy being a housewife. I know that's a dirty word to you, Ms Roberts' — he fairly hissed the name — 'but she liked it. You're going against nature, meddling in people's lives . . .'

Gwen was very much aware of Sara still hovering in the background, taking it all in. 'Lokis, this is neither the time nor place to discuss this,' she began, but he cut her off.

'I busted my ass to make that marriage work and you know it. Ten years, everything's great, everything's fine, then she joins The Club and, thanks to you, she's up and gone, walks right out on me. The Club' — he spat the words out at her — 'goddamn The Club!'

A trickle of sweat ran down the back of Gwen's neck. Lokis Krumins was one of the top designers in New York, a talented, artistic young man. Usually gentle and soft-spoken, he stood in front of her, so angry that the veins stood out in his neck, his hands trembling at his sides. Poor Susie.

As if reading her mind, Lokis said roughly, 'I'm not crazy. I know exactly what I'm saying. I love my wife and I want her back. The way she was before.'

'We're having a celebration here.' Gwen was keenly aware that Sara was behind her, hanging on every word. 'Can't this wait until after the party'

'Don't patronize me, lady! God, you all stick together, don't you, you bitches!' He was clenching and unclenching his hands.

'Hey, Lokis!' Merilee Houston had joined them, with Lokis's wife, Susie, standing behind her. 'You're just a bit wazooed, honey. Why don't you come on outside and get some air . . .'

Lokis wheeled on her, eyes blazing. 'Get away from me, you slut! You seduced me! Grabbing at me, shoving your tits in my face! You're no better than Gwen is. The two of you planned this together. You set out to ruin my marriage. Why? That's all I want to know, why?'

Feeling Gwen's gaze on her, Merilee backed away. 'I don't know what he's talkin' about, Jenny, I swear I don't. He's crazy.'

'Crazy?' Lokis laughed loudly. 'Yeah, I'm crazy, all right. Crazy to invest in The Club in the first place, crazy to let my wife ever set foot in here. Fucking up her head, telling her what to think, what to do.' He turned back to Gwen, 'You told her you would help her kill our baby. I'd like to kill you.' He was still speaking quietly, but his eyes were glittering and his face was flushed.

Gwen looked at Merilee, who had backed against the wall. She shook her frizzy blonde head wordlessly, silently willing Lokis to shut up and get the hell out.

Gwen's heart was pounding. Surely, she wasn't in any real danger. The man in front of her did not seem crazy. He was acting crazy but he knew what he wanted. Their eyes met and she was startled to see the genuine pain there. 'Lokis,' she said gently, 'why don't you come into my office and I'll try and tell you what you want to know. Susie, will you come with us?' Angry and embarrassed, Susie nodded. 'Lovely. Come on, Lokis, what do you say?'

'No,' Lokis said, moving backwards. 'I don't trust you.'

'Really, this has gone far enough.' Frightened as she was, Gwen was losing patience. 'Then I suggest you leave quietly. Unless you want me to ask security to make you leave.'

Turning in Susie's direction, Lokis pleaded, 'I love you, baby. Please come home with me.'

Susie refused to look at him, staring instead at her beaded beige handbag. 'If you love me, then leave me alone. Just leave me alone. It's over.'

'I can't,' Lokis was shaking. 'You're my wife and I need you at home with me. I'm not leaving here unless you come with me.'

'All right,' Susie sighed and started to move forward.

'You don't have to go with him, Susie,' Gwen said warningly. 'I can get Joe Garcia to put him in a cab and send him home.'

'It's all right. I'll go with him if that's what he wants. I guess I owe him that much. Look, if you need to find me, I'll be at this address for the next couple of hours.' She scribbled on the back of a Club matchbook and turned to Lokis.

Lokis began to cry. 'Susie, I've made such a mess of things! I'm sorry, baby, but I miss you so much. I just don't want to go on living without you.'

'Sure you do.' Susie put her arms around his shoulders. 'You've just had too much to drink, that's all.' She gently steered him towards the steps and they made their way down the marble staircase and out of the front door.

Gwen leaned gratefully against the balcony, looking down into the foyer as the pounding of her heart slowed.

'Gwen, I need to talk to you. Let me explain.' Merilee was clutching at her sleeve.

'Later,' Gwen said curtly. Her palms were sweating; right now she needed to get away from everybody and be by herself in the privacy of her own office. After the events of the evening, she wanted nothing more than to have a stiff drink from her private bar, run her wrists under cold water, and try to pull herself together enough to return to the party. She headed for her office, high heels clicking on the mosaic tiled floor. She was almost through the door and home free when she felt a sharp tap on her shoulder and turned around to face Sara Town again.

'I wish I'd got that little scene on tape,' Sara purred, smiling her cream-fed smile. 'That would be a choice piece of inside dirt to show the viewers across the country. Are you often threatened by irate husbands? Still trying to fix other people's lives, aren't you? You simply can't stop meddling. You haven't learned anything at all, have you?'

Gwen looked into Sara's golden eyes and the memories washed over her. Why can't we forgive each other? she thought. Why can't you ask me how I am? Or tell me if you've ever thought of me? When will enough be enough?

# Part II

*The Club*

# *One*

Bowness, Alberta. 1959. 'I've got to get out of here. I won't end up here. I've got to find a way out.' Growing up in Bowness, Alberta, those words kept running through Gwen's head like the refrain of a song. Bowness was a poor relation to Calgary — across the Bow River, to the west of the city, yet not part of it, living in its shadow. Coming from Bowness branded you; it was like having 'working class' stamped across your hockey jersey.

Ice-hockey was big in Bowness, for girls as well as for boys. All you needed was a pair of skates. Ice-hockey was rough and dirty and cold, just like the town of Bowness. The Bow River was the dividing line between city and country. As close as it was to Calgary, once you crossed the Schouldice Bridge into Bowness, you were in a small town, with small-town attitudes and small-town goals. Gwen learned early not to end up pregnant at seventeen. By the time she was eleven, she could tell which girls were going to make it and which ones were destined to be lost. There was a hopelessness in the eyes of the losers although they weren't yet into their teens.

'Out, I've got to get out,' Gwen, often called Jenny, would mutter to herself, trudging home from school through the snow along the frozen river bank, her knitted toque barely covering her ears and her toes dangerously numb in her fleece-lined winter boots. Wearing her blue Woods parka with ski pants on under her skirt, she passed the low, squat little houses of grey stucco or cheap brown

101

board with their tiny windows and tar-paper garages, the laundry hanging on the line in the back yards. All the streets had Bow in their names – Bow Crescent, Bow Green, Bow Wood – which made them sound like a fancy housing development, one with curved asphalt lanes, large brick houses and white picket fences, a Canadian dream suburb. But most of the streets were just gravel and potholes, and no house had more than a thousand square feet. Every dingy little house was graced with either a pick-up truck or a camper parked in the back. Gwen's house did not even have an indoor toilet. In the dead of winter, having to pull on her ski pants, grab a handful of rough toilet paper and stamp over the hard packed snow to the outhouse, she considered life in Bowness particularly bleak.

The natural environment of Bowness was anything but bleak. Nestled in the valley of the foothills by the river, it was actually quite pretty, especially in the spring when the warmer weather softened everything with fresh green and the run-off from the mountains swelled the river. In this almost jewel-like setting lived a large immigrant – mostly German and Dutch – community. Everybody was poor. 'Rich' to them was Mr Erlich, who owned the variety store, or Mr Koenig, who owned the auto bodyparts shop. Like a lot of the kids in Calgary, Gwen's father worked in the oil business. But there were no presidents of oil companies, no geologists, not even engineers; if they were in oil, they were roughnecks and rigworkers.

Gwen's father was a tool push. Bill Roberts was a Scot, a huge bear of a man, six-foot-six, with a shock of fiery red hair and a bushy red beard. From him she got her own red hair, although hers was closer to a ginger-mouse red. She was sturdy, too, like her dad, but on the short side. Her mother, on the other hand, was French Canadian, pretty and small-featured, delicate and petite.

Why couldn't she be tall and imposing like her dad? Or tiny and cute like her mum? Looking in the mirror, Gwen decided that she had got stuck with the worst features from each of her parents. A short, sturdy, boyish girl with a Scottish stubbornness and a French temper.

Years later, when Gwen had become friends with Sara, Sara loved to ask her, 'Is your mother's name really Jeanne d'Arc Roberts?'

'Jeanne d'Arc Marie-Claire Hélène Bernadette Grenier before she married my dad.'

'God, what a combination, French Catholic and Scots Presbyterian!'

'You don't now the half of it,' Gwen said grimly. Jeanne was such a strong Catholic that before she would marry Bill she had him sign a paper that their children would be brought up in the faith. She enclosed the document in glass and put it on the sideboard in the house Bill had built for her, an ever-present reminder to him. For her fifth birthday, Gwen's Little Gramma had given her her very own rosary. Gwen called her mother's mother Little Gramma because she was four-foot-eleven, while her Big Gramma, Bill's mother, was nearly six feet tall. Little Gramma spoke almost no English; she was lively and quick and she loved to dance. Big Gramma was a stern, no-nonsense plain-faced woman, who, along with her husband, had been sent from Scotland to Canada to work on the farms. Little Gramma usually took Gwen to mass but once when she was sick and Jeanne was spending the day with her, Gwen had to go to the Presbyterian Church with Big Gramma. She toddled along, one little hand holding Big Gramma's big one, the other clutching her rosary. Big Gramma had snatched the rosary away from her, thrown it on the ground, and stamped on it, calling it 'papist trash', and 'a sign of the devil', and Gwen had cried to see her favourite necklace lying broken in the dirt.

103

But she loved both Big Gramma and Little Gramma and she knew she was lucky to have them to look after her. Usually both parents in Bowness had to work so the children were on their own a lot. Gwen couldn't remember a time when her mum had been there when she got home from school.

'Sounds grim,' Sara said, when Gwen told her about being an original 'latchkey kid' before the term was invented.

'I don't know. We had a lot more freedom than most kids. You learned to take care of yourself in Bownesia.'

'Bownesia?'

'That's what we called it. Because there was such a danger of losing your mind and getting totally lost. Some of us were tough. There was nothing we couldn't do, nothing we wouldn't try. Of course there was a lot of abuse, a lot of alcoholism. What Dad said went. His word was law, depending on how hard he could hit or how loud he could scream.'

'It's like something out of Charles Dickens.'

'Not really. Compared to most kids, I was lucky. My mum wasn't out every night at bingo and my dad didn't spend his entire paycheque at the Bowness Hotel Beverage room, playing shuffleboard and drinking Winnipeg red-eyes.'

'What's a Winnipeg red-eye?'

'Beer and tomato juice. My friend Brenda's dad, always smelled like beer. He promised her and promised her that he would stay sober for her thirteenth birthday party. She had just made her wish and blown out the candles when he came staggering into the house, drunk as a skunk, and threw up in the middle of the living-room floor, right on top of the gift we'd brought for her. She was mortified, but the rest of us weren't particularly surprised. We knew Brenda's dad was a drunk. We accepted it. That was the law of Bowness. No whining.

It happened, that's all. I was lucky with my dad. In my eyes, there was nothing he could do or say that was wrong.'

Gwen loved her dad with a shy, awkward passion; she wished desperately that he could be home with them all the time. Until the end of the dirty thirties, oil riggers worked on the rigs twelve hours a day, seven days a week, with only Christmas Day off. In the fifties, when Gwen was growing up, the hours hadn't much improved. Turner Valley was still going strong and Bill Roberts was away a lot, but when he came home, she rarely left his side, following him around like a puppy. She knew he had really wanted a son. Jeanne had had four miscarriages and two stillborns, all boys, before Gwen came along. 'Funny that you, a slip of a girl, should be the one to make it,' her father said. 'That proves you're tough, Jenny. Peasant stock. A survivor, like me.' But the pride in his voice couldn't completely dispel the disappointment in his eyes, and she was always afraid he would send her back where he got her to exchange her for a boy. She threw her arms around him and hugged him hard, vowing to do everything she could to make him proud of her.

'Daddy, I can run faster than any boy,' she said. 'I can climb higher and I can hit harder. You just watch me.'

'And by the time she was ten years old, it was true. He took her fishing in the summer; they camped out in Banff and she learned to hike for miles in the wilderness. In the winter, he took her tobogganning and skiing down Paskapoo. He showed her how to tell when the Chinooks, the warm winds, were coming from the west by the arch of colour in the sky. He taught her how to hunt; she learned to load a .22 and how to skin the deer she had shot herself.

And of course there was hockey. If her dad was in

town, the minute her homework was finished, they'd grab their skates and head for the rink. 'Best hockey coaches in Canada come from Alberta,' Bill used to say. 'Albertans take their hockey seriously.' Her dad took it even more seriously. He was a Maple Leafs fan; her mum supported the Canadiens. Sometimes when the Leafs lost, he wouldn't speak to her mother for a whole week. To Bill, hockey was a metaphor for life. Gwen knew her dad believed that you could live your whole life based on the concepts that he drilled into her over and over again: Always be the best you can be. Aim for number one. Give it your best shot, shoot to score, and you'll make your goal.

In the barely light early morning hours on a Saturday, tying on her skates with fingers already frozen from the cold, a cold so raw she could see her breath in front of her as she skated out on to the rink, the underlying subtext of her dad's message rang out loud and clear: 'You're no good to me unless you're a winner.' Gwen was fiercely determined to be a winner, no matter what.

'You're turning her into a tomboy,' her mother said, raising an eyebrow at her daughter's scraped elbows, bruised shins, and scabby knees.

'So?' Bill snorted. 'She's gotta learn how to take care of herself. The best school there is is the school of hard knocks.'

Next to hockey, her dad loved the oil business. In the summer, if he was drilling nearby, he would take Gwen with him out to the site to see the rigs. The battered old pick-up truck, which always needed new shocks, rattled along the prairies and Gwen stared out of the window at the rocking-horse pumps moving gently up and down against the brilliant western skies. 'The skies out here are really special. I guess it's something to do with the light. You don't get skies like this back east,' Bill said. 'And the prairies are like the ocean. You can see for a hundred miles. Stand on a matchbox and see for two hundred miles. I couldn't live without the prairies; they make me feel free.'

Gwen, sitting close to him on the front seat, felt a shiver of delight that he would share these private adult feelings with her as they headed out to Longview or Black Diamond or wherever the newest drill site was. She watched with pride as the drilling crew 'made a trip' to 'change the bit' under the watchful eye of her father. He was the boss of the rig.

In the early boom days of the fifties and sixties, Alberta was oil mad. Calgary smelled like oil; you could feel the get-rich fever in the air. The Palliser Hotel was full of Americans who had come up to Canada to get in on the action. Her father's best friend was Jack Brand, a Texas oil man from Houston. Black Jack, they called him, but Gwen called him 'Uncle' Jack. The second son of a rancher, Jack was determined to get out of cattle and into oil: 'I know the oil business is a crapshoot, but I've always had a luck dragon on my back. I can take a risk. I'm gonna let my big brother, Jimmie Ray, carry on the family tradition and run the ranch. Me, I'm fixing to be an entrepreneur.' Entrepreneur. Gwen loved the sound of that word, and she loved Uncle Jack's southern accent, which made him sound like a riverboat gambler. Texas sounded so exotic she wished she could go there right now and see his ranch outside Houston and the family mansion in River Oaks. She loved to hear him talk about his family. In fact, she loved everything about Jack. He was tall, almost as tall as her dad, with curly black hair and bright blue eyes and a really nice smile. When Uncle Jack reached down and ruffled her red hair, it made her squirm with delight.

'You ain't no bigger'n a nickel candy bar,' he would say affectionately, crouching down to look directly into her eyes. 'But you're a tough little nut, aren't you, sugar?'

'Peasant stock,' her dad said, as he always did, 'like me.'

'Shoot, Bill, don't flatter yourself. This little honey's a lot prettier than you.' Gwen blushed. She knew Uncle Jack was just sweet-talking her, trying to make her feel better. She wasn't pretty at all. In fact she was so homely that every once in a while she would catch her mother looking at her with a worried frown. Usually she didn't care because she fully intended to get out of Bowness on her own steam anyway, but she wished she could be just a little bit better-looking for Uncle Jack. 'Yep, Gwenny-Penny,' Jack went on in that slow, soft-spoken way of his, 'you make me want to hurry up and find me a girl to marry just so that I can have a great kid like you.' And Gwen blushed again and ducked her head because she hoped he wouldn't find anyone too quickly. She planned to marry him herself when she grew up.

Uncle Jack had studied both geology and engineering, which he claimed made him schizophrenic. 'Engineers and geologists are like oil and water. The geologist finds the oil; the engineer figures how to get it out of the ground. Engineers see the oil field as just so many feet of drill stem, so many bits. Geologists are even crazier. They think about rocks. An engineer thinks vertically; a geologist thinks horizontally.'

'So how do you think, Uncle Jack?'

'Well, I guess being both, maybe I think diagonally.'

'I'm going to be a geologist when I grow up,' Gwen said firmly. 'I like rocks.'

Both men laughed. 'Well, it's a man's business,' her dad said, 'but if any woman can make it in oil, I bet you can. You're smart as a whip — she's top of her class, Jack — and you're not afraid to get your hands dirty: that'll take you far in oil.'

'You got to have a sense of adventure and romance,' Jack agreed. 'You need to have that luck dragon on your back in order to be able to smell that oil in the ground.'

Gwen had thrown herself on to the ground and buried her nose in the prairie dirt. 'I can smell it,' she declared. 'I can smell oil.' They all laughed and Uncle Jack picked her up and swung her on to his shoulders as the three of them headed back to the pick-up.

Uncle Jack was part of the family. He took her to the Stampede parade along Ninth Avenue where they saw the Stampede Queen and her princesses, a troop of Mounties, plus a lot of real cowboys and Indians on horseback. When he took her to the Stampede rodeo he always let her eat as much cotton candy and caramel popcorn as she wanted. He took her and her best friend Brenda to the top of the Calgary Tower for breakfast and they looked out of the revolving window at the city spread out beneath them. The best times were when all of them piled into the pick-up truck and drove to Claresholm to the Flying N Ranch for a steak; Jack and her dad would argue about which place had better beef, Texas or Alberta. 'You're talking to a rancher son,' Jack would say. 'Don't tell me I don't know my beef.'

Uncle Jack came back to Alberta three summers in a row and at the end of each summer, Gwen had to fight back the tears when it was time to say goodbye. Her dad usually gave Jack a white Stetson hat, the symbol of Calgary, and Gwen gave him a new Stampede belt buckle. Uncle Jack always gave her the same thing, a big box of stationery so that she would write to him during the winter. She wrote to him faithfully and he sent her presents from Houston: a fringed leather jacket and a pair of red cowboy boots, and a Longhorn sweatshirt from his old alma mater, the University of Texas, in Austin. But the best present he sent her was a little bomber jacket with a hand-embroidered dragon on the back. The accompanying note read, 'Now you have your own luck dragon.'

'Dad, is Uncle Jack rich?' Gwen wanted to know. The boots were hand-tooled and the jacket looked expensive.

'Looks like he's getting that way. He's pretty close to starting up his own oil company down there.'

'So how come he's still friends with us? 'Cause I know we're poor.'

For a moment her dad looked angrier than she'd ever seen him. 'Don't you ever say that, Jenny. We're not poor. And if you're going to value your friends in terms of money, you're going to be a very miserable little girl. Uncle Jack is plain folks. He comes from the school of hard knocks, just like us.'

Gwen knew the only way out of Bowness was through education. Education offered her hope, and knowing that the teachers pushed their students to study hard and accomplish something. Gwen worked hard and got the best grades in her class, but in her heart she believed there must be another secret to success that everyone else knew. When she went to a friend's house, she would look behind things, under things, searching for clues. Books offered her some clues. For her, the printed word was magic, a wonderful vision of a different way of life. She became a voracious reader, going through every book in the children's section of the Bowness Library. The books were divided into girls' and boys' sections. Gwen started with *The Five Little Peppers and How They Grew*, *The Secret Garden*, *The Little Princess*, *Little Women*. She loved stories about large, close-knit families who rallied around each other in time of need. Her own family was small; when her dad was away, it was hard on her mum. Often it was just she and her mother sitting alone at the Formica table in the kitchen, her mother finishing a dress for one of her customers who lived in the ritzy Mount Royal section of Calgary, and Gwen finishing her library book. But the girls in these books were such wimps. She liked Jo in *Little Women*, but Meg was a goody-goody and Beth was so perfect that God took her to heaven. She soon discovered the books in the boys' section, books like *The Hardy Boys* and *Kidnapped*, and liked them much better, identifying more with their heroes than with Cherry Ames or Sue Barton.

When she finished the last book in the children's section, she went to the head librarian, Miss Green, and asked her what to read next. 'Usually I have to entice children to read a book, but you're turning into a regular little bookworm,' and she drew up a reading list for Gwen. When Gwen had gone through all the books on the list, she went back to Miss Green for a new list. 'You are a young lady in search of a soul,' said Miss Green, fancying herself a literary oasis in a prairie desert. 'We will expand your horizons.' She doubled Gwen's reading list, and Gwen ploughed straight through that one, too, until soon the Yorkshire moors of *Wuthering Heights* were as familiar to her as the gently rolling foothills of southern Alberta. Miss Green invited her to join her Sunday afternoon book club, the only child in a group of middle-aged immigrant women trying to improve their English and the Dalhousie twins, the two weird bachelor brothers, who were not really twins at all and who ran the only movie theatre in town.

Movies were even better than books. Twenty-five cents would get you in to the Saturday matinee and that included popcorn and a soft drink. The movie was usually a double feature so Gwen left the house at noon and often didn't get home until six. What wonderful adventures she saw up on the silver screen: *Tarzan, Zorro, The Cisco Kid, Gunfight at the OK Corral*, and *The Vikings*, with Kirk Douglas and Tony Curtis. She and Brenda agreed that the men seemed to have all the fun in these pictures; the women basically packed their socks, sent them off, and stayed at home wringing their hands and worrying about their brave heroes who never seemed to give them a moment's thought as they swung through the jungle or squared off for a fight to the finish. Women were weak; men were strong. It was such a drag being female.

Her attitude started to change when her dad was laid off just after her sixteenth birthday. He fell from the rig and hurt his back. The oil business was in a slump anyway, but that didn't make him feel any better about what he imagined he was missing. He was laid up for almost a year, lying in bed or on the sofa, eating peanut butter out of the jar and stuffing saltine crackers into his mouth, while he watched *The Price Is Right* and *The Tommy Hunter Show* with angry eyes. Pretty soon his workman's comp would run out and then where would they be? They had already missed three mortgage payments and were in danger of losing the house. Gwen's mum could hardly support the family with the work she got as a seamstress. And what made everything worse was that, after all these years, she was pregnant again.

Little Gramma and Big Gramma came over often and helped out as much as they could. Little Gramma took one look at Gwen's father slumped in front of the TV, empty Coke cans and cracker crumbs all over the floor and said with a tight-lipped smile, '*Vraiment*, men are so much weaker than women, but we have to pretend they are stronger. When things are breaking down, it is the women, *les femmes de la famille*, who hold it all together.'

'The paycheque is the power,' said Big Gramma. 'Never forget that. Money means independence.'

Watching her mother grow paler and heavier with each month, Gwen applied for a cashier's job with Safeway. At first the Safeway training school over in Calgary was fun, like playing store. There were mock groceries stacked on the shelves and the trainees had to walk up and down the aisles memorizing the prices. It was stupid and boring, but Gwen had a good head for figures. She passed and was immediately hired by the Safeway on Seventeenth Avenue in south-west Calgary. Every afternoon after school, she caught the bus over the bridge to the Safeway store, put on the white uniform with her name embroidered over the breast pocket and crammed her unruly hair into the heavy hairnet that all food services workers had to wear. At night she caught the bus home again, ate some cold leftovers standing up at the kitchen counter, and started on her homework. Sometimes she was so tired after work that she just fell into bed, setting the alarm clock for 4 a.m. so that she could get up early to do her homework before school. She couldn't let her grades drop; she was counting on a Queen Elizabeth scholarship to get her through her first year at the University of Calgary. She hated the long hours at Safeway, the rude customers, and the fact that she was exhausted all the time.

'It's not fair. You're missing the best part of being a teenager,' Brenda said. It was true if she wanted to work at Safeway and keep her grades up, there was no way she could go out with friends. Brenda said that was the worst part about her dad getting laid off — missing the hockey games and school dances and, most important of all, the boys. Gwen complained to Brenda that she was right, it really wasn't fair; but secretly she didn't mind all that much. What could possibly be romantic about a bunch of sour-smelling boys in work boots and down-filled parkas? She didn't like any of them the way she used to like Uncle Jack.

She was grown up enough now to realize that Uncle Jack wasn't going to wait for her. In fact, he'd gotten married last year. She had a couple of wedding snapshots taped on to her dresser mirror in the bedroom. His wife was a blonde with big hair and a small mouth. He must be pretty happy; they were expecting their first baby in June.

In some ways she felt so much more mature than her peers, already supporting herself, but in other ways she knew she was hopelessly naïve. Kevin Donohue, one of the baggers at Safeway, kept asking her out, but she always turned him down. His idea of a big night on the town was probably taking her into the Ladies and Escorts entrance at the Hotel Bowness and popping a few brews for which he was bound to expect something from her at the end of the evening.

Sex was still a mystery to her; she hadn't sorted out her desires. But at least it meant there was no chance of her ending up pregnant at seventeen. Brenda had given in and was sleeping with her boyfriend, Chuck. She'd already had one pregnancy scare, so maybe Gwen wasn't missing so much after all. And at the end of the week when she signed the payform and took home a cheque for one hundred and five dollars, exactly fifteen dollars more than the monthly mortgage payment, when she placed her hard-earned money in her grateful mother's hands, her heart swelled with pride. The look in her mum's tired eyes made it all worth while. Gwen and Mum were managing to hold things together.

Lots of women held it all together in Bowness's families. Donna Berger and Katya Oostend were single mums raising three and four kids on their own. Patty Kruger and Linda Schultz were women going out to work whole days at Kmart and Woolco and then coming home to do the housework and look after the kids at night. Brenda's mum's husband, the drunk, regularly beat her up, although everybody in Bowness tried to ignore the occasional bruised face or black eye, pretending to believe her stories of walking into a door or slipping on the ice. And there was her own mum, pregnant at forty-one, almost fainting every morning from nausea, trying to help her dad get back on his feet again when he seemed to have given up all desire to go on living. What was wrong with him? He was bigger and stronger than both of them put together; he was supposed to protect them, instead of lying there like a beached whale. Little Gramma was right.

Big Gramma was right, too: money did mean independence. Her mother wouldn't be in this position if she had a real job and some decent education. Gwen swore to herself that she would never, never depend on anyone else to support her financially. Emotionally, physically, spiritually, maybe, but she would make her own money and she would make it on her own. When I get out of Bowness. And I'm going to get out of Bowness. She repeated the familiar litany over and over to herself.

'I think you should give this a try. I know you can win.' Miss Green waved a sheet of paper under her nose. Gwen was returning *Catch-22* to the library; she had almost no time to read any more, but she'd managed to finish the book during her coffee breaks at work. 'This should be right up your alley, Jenny,' the librarian repeated.

Gwen read the paper. The United Nations Pilgrimage for Youth were sponsoring a speaking competition through the Odd Fellow and Rebekkahs Lodges. You had to prepare a speech on some topic that had to do with the UN, present it at the various lodges around town, and whichever student was judged the best speaker would win a summer trip, not only across Canada, but down into the States, ending up in New York City. All thirty-six Canadian winners there would have lunch with U Thant, the secretary of the UN. A chance to see all the places that she had only read about!

With Miss Green's research assistance, Gwen wrote a piece on the value of UNESCO and how vital it was to develop it for the world's future. She practised the speech for Little Gramma, who had trouble following the

115

English, and for Big Gramma, who said that she had always thought that UNESCO was one of those cooking oils made from rapeseed, and for her mum, who told her the speech was great but she needed to stand up straighter and put her shoulders back. When she tried it out on her dad, he waved her away, telling her she made a better window than a door, because she was blocking his view of the TV set while he was watching *Juliette*. Standing in front of the entire school, giving her speech for assembly, Gwen was so nervous she had to cough several times and clear her throat over and over again, but after that she was over the worst and by the time she faced the two judges at the Rebekkahs Lodge, she was starting to feel more confident. The judges loved her speech and so did the judge at the Oddfellows who sent her on to the finals in Calgary. Then it was the last night of the contest and her mum and her two grammas were clapping for her along with Brenda and her mum and when they called out, 'The winner is Gwyneth Roberts of Bowness!' she thought she would die of joy. Here she had never even been out of Alberta, and now she was on her way to the city of her dreams, New York.

'Out. I'm finally getting out of Bowness.' She hugged herself with excitement as the chartered bus carrying her and thirty-five other contest winners sped east across the country. The Oddfellows were putting them up along the way and the Rebekkahs were providing their meals as they stopped in each major city to see the sights. They saw the provincial legislatures in both Regina and Winnipeg; Maple Leaf Gardens and the University of Toronto, and a weird new housing complex on Bloor Street called Rochdale where long-haired students planned to manage their own building through committee; the Houses of Parliament in Ottawa, and Vieille Montreal, Eglise Notre Dame, and the new underground Metro system Montreal was building for Expo '67. Gwen saw a stuffed forty-

116

pound frog in Fredericton, ate her first lobster in Halifax, and attended the musical of *Anne of Green Gables* in Charlottetown. She visited Harvard and Filene's basement in Boston, saw the Lincoln Memorial in Washington and the Liberty Bell in Philadelphia, but nothing came close to the thrill of New York.

New York was big and dirty and scary and absolutely wonderful. Her first night in the city, she took a walk on her own and when she got back the bus driver gave her hell: 'What were you doing out on the streets by yourself like that? Are you crazy? Where are you from, some jerkwater town like Moose Jaw, Saskatchewan?'

'Bowness, Alberta,' Gwen admitted, wishing he wouldn't shout so loud in the middle of the hotel lobby. Nobody was paying any attention, however; everybody seemed to talk loud in New York.

'Yeah, right. Well this is the big city, little lady. You gotta watch your pocketbook and watch your ass.'

Gwen knew he was really angry, otherwise he never would have used a word like 'ass' in front of her, but she didn't care. She had fallen in love with New York City. This was where she intended to live some day.

The UN was magnificent and U Thant spent more than two hours with the students over lunch, answering their questions. A small, dark man with glasses, darker than the Indians who hung out around the Bowness Hotel beverage room, he was poised and confident, with twinkling eyes and a wry sense of humour. He had read a draft of her UNESCO speech and seemed eager to compliment her: 'You have an excellent understanding of the burgeoning third-world problems. You are going into politics perhaps?'

'No, the oil business,' Gwen answered with pride.

'Ah, I see.' U Thant raised his eyebrows above his gold-rimmed glasses. 'You are opting for money instead of public service.'

117

'The way I see it, the oil business is a public service industry,' Gwen said stoutly.

'Interesting concept,' he murmured, shaking her hand again and moving away. She didn't wash her hand for three days after that. The other students were impressed that U Thant had talked with her. She noticed that some of them seemed to defer to her for the rest of the trip; whatever activity Gwen suggested they pursue in their unscheduled time, they all voted to go along with her. Maybe U Thant was right, maybe she should go into politics. It was all pretty heady stuff.

It had been absolutely the best summer of her whole life and she could hardly wait to tell her parents all about it, but the minute she walked through the front door she sensed that everything had changed. There was a new energy in the house, a sense of new life. Her mum had had the baby and, miracle of miracles, it was a boy. Her dad had recovered from his back injury, and he was starting a new business, selling drill bits and other rig machinery, so he wouldn't be going away any more. And he was obviously besotted with his baby son. He must be, Gwen thought, to allow a son of his to be christened Sebastien Raymond, a French name and the name of a saint all in one.

Her mum took her aside to tell her, 'We are going to send you to school in Calgary this year, a Catholic girls' school. I want you to have one solid year of good Catholic education before you go to U of C.'

Gwen was stunned. 'But, why? I'm just about to start grade twelve, this is my last year, and I want to graduate with Brenda and the rest of my friends . . .'

Her mother stopped her firmly: 'I want you to have one solid year of Catholic education before you start university.'

'You can't do this to me,' Gwen said as the panic welled up inside her. 'It's not fair. What does Dad think?

118

I bet he doesn't want me to go to Catholic school.'

Her mother bit her lip. 'It was your dad's idea for you to go to St Mary's. He thinks it'll do you good to get away.'

The betrayal ripped through Gwen. 'You just want me out of the way, that's all! You want to be able to pretend you're newlyweds with a brand new baby!'

Her mother's eyes held a mixture of guilt and pain. 'We need to be on our own,' she admitted. 'Your father believes he's been given a second chance, and he must have that to feel like a man. But I promise you, Jenny, that's not why we're sending you away. I want you to have the chance I never had. You're smarter than I am. You've got more ambition. You already know what you want. Now go out and get it.'

'What I want is to stay here with you and Dad,' Gwen said stubbornly.

Her mother shook her head slowly. 'St Mary's is an excellent school. You will be getting the best education in Alberta. When you are there you will feel what we feel.'

But all Gwen could feel was the pain, the pain of being kicked out of her own house, the house that she had worked so hard to help them to keep.

After the freedom and independence of her life in Bowness, it was like being slammed into jail. Her day now was almost entirely regimented. First thing in the morning, the girls gathered to hear the news of the world delivered by the Mother Superior over the loudspeaker in the auditorium. Of course this was limited to the religious news of the world, which country the Pope happened to be visiting or which people Mother Teresa happened to be saving.

Gwen had been accustomed to seeing nuns at mass, of course, long before she entered St Mary's. Here they surrounded her and her classmates all the time, all in full

119

habit, constantly playing with their rosaries. If they were not able to lure you into the convent by the time you graduated from high school, it would be too late: a girl's enrolment at St Mary's was their last chance to get her.

The first class of the day was religion. Some of that was interesting, particularly when they studied the saints and martyrs who had sacrificed their lives for God. Gwen became fascinated by Pope Joan, the woman who disguised herself as a man to be ordained as a priest, a cardinal, eventually becoming Pope in 855. The worst part was having to learn the catechism word for word. With her photographic memory she could memorize anything, but learning by rote bored her. It didn't teach a person how to think or analyse. How could her parents possibly believe that this would prepare her for entrance into the University of Calgary as a geology major?

The girls in her class weren't that much different from her class mates at R.B. Bennett, except maybe a little less self-reliant and maybe a little more boy-crazy because there were no boys around. How was she ever going to get through the year?

'Hi, I'm Lucy Bainborough.' A stunningly pretty redhead held out her hand. 'I was amazed at what you said about Pope Joan in class today'

'Thanks, but I don't think Sister Agatha appreciated it too much.' Gwen shook her hand. It felt odd because she couldn't remember ever shaking hands with a girl her own age before and, stranger still, she could feel the imprint of Lucy's hand in her own long after it had been withdrawn.

'Is that stuff really true? All that about her having a lover who made her pregnant and that's how they found out she was a woman?'

'Supposedly yes. She gave birth to her child right there in the street in the middle of a papal procession and the crowd stoned her to death.'

'Wow. What happened to the baby?'

'Oh, they killed the baby, too. They thought it was the Antichrist.'

'God,' Lucy said. 'It sure didn't pay to have sex in those days, did it? Can you imagine Saint Bernadette having sex?'

'Not the way Jennifer Jones played her in the movie.'

Lucy laughed. 'How about Joan of Arc?'

'Not with the Dauphin. But with all those foot soldiers, maybe.'

'Well anyway, I thought Sister Agatha was going to lose her drawers when you brought up Pope Joan having a baby. You've got some guts, kid.'

Lucy was looking at her with respect — no, awe — as if she wanted to be her friend for life, which Gwen found hard to believe. After all, she was the daughter of a roughneck; everyone knew that Lucy's father was one of the famous Burns family who had been part of Calgary since the beginning and had made most of their money in meat. Gwen was a jock; Lucy was the ultimate in femininity. Her hair was a true strawberry blonde, not gingery like Gwen's, a real gold shot through with streaks of fire. She had round, china-blue eyes and creamy, translucent skin that flushed a warm pink at the slightest provocation. She looked truly luscious, like a slowly ripening peach. Lucy had a book called *The Measure of Beauty*, which detailed the perfect classical ideal of proportion and balance. It sounded crazy to Gwen, but when Lucy made her measure her, Lucy's waist was exactly ten inches smaller than her bust and hips and her eyes exactly the right distance apart. Then they measured Gwen and discovered what she had suspected all along, that none of her proportions were right and that none of her features matched.

Lucy looked like an angel, acted like the devil and got away with murder. She cut classes to sneak into the movies in town. She smoked in the washrooms and slugged the Scotch that she cleverly kept in a Listerine bottle. It was Lucy who slipped a copy of *Fanny Hill* between the pages of her Latin text. It was Lucy who made up the most horrendous sins to shock the priest at confession and it was Lucy who always asked the most embarrassing questions at retreats.

A priest was always brought in to lead these weekend sessions, which was practically the only good thing about them. For the three days, you weren't allowed to speak. You were supposed to be quiet, think of God and contemplate your life. Then at the end of the three days, the girls filed into the auditorium where a wooden box had been placed on the small stage. Inside the box were slips of paper with questions. They were unsigned; anonymity was supposed to free you to ask deeply personal, soul-searching questions. But of course most of them concerned sex, and the priest would do his best to answer them directly. The depth of the sin of masturbation was a favourite. The priest usually answered, 'This is not a healthy act. God is testing you. Redirect your energies.' But Lucy's questions were so raw that poor Father Thomas would blush, and clear his throat and say in a choked voice, 'I think the writer of this question needs further counselling. See me later in Mother Superior's private office.' And Lucy would snort and elbow Gwen in the ribs to let her know that of course the question was hers.

During the week the nuns had complete power. Here was a group of women surviving just fine without men. They made the rules and strictly enforced them. St Mary's was their own private domain, until the priest showed up. Then the deferring and kowtowing, the bowing and scraping, reminded Gwen of the way her mother behaved around her father or her old friend Brenda gave way to her boyfriend, Chuck.

122

No make-up was allowed at St Mary's. Gwen imagined Brenda and her other friends back in Bowness drawing little Twiggy lashes below their eyes and wearing their mini skirts and ribbed sweaters. She wore a uniform: blue serge dress with white cuffs and a white Peter Pan collar, black Oxfords, and black lisle stockings. Like some old lady! The only time she didn't have to wear the uniform was during gym class when she was allowed to wear a short tunic. Lucy thought the gym tunic was sexy enough to pass for a mini skirt; she would put her gym tunic on to go past the boys' school on their way to field-hockey practice.

In Gwen's opinion, field-hockey was a game invented by men to keep women off the real playing field, the ice rink. But she was good at the game and captain of her field-hockey team.

'You're a natural born leader,' Sister Agatha told her. And Gwen was beginning to sense that maybe it was true. Not that Sister Agatha was any expert. Lucy called her Sister Bessie and said she looked like a cow. Her description was devastatingly accurate. Sister Agatha was dark and hefty with round, sad eyes and damp palms. Her mournful eyes seemed to follow the two girls wherever they went.

Lucy's leadership was of another kind. She was wild, and she made Gwen want to go crazy with her. When they sat next to each other on the bus, heading into town to sneak off to a movie, the pressure of Lucy's knee against hers sent shock waves through her body. She couldn't stop thinking about Lucy. Lying in bed at night, trying to go to sleep, she saw Lucy's heart-shaped face swim behind her closed eyes, and it was Lucy she saw in her mind when she woke up the next morning.

She wished now that she'd gone out with Kevin Donohue back in Bowness when he'd asked her, gone out with him and gone to bed with him. Here she was stuck in a girls' school just when her libido was finally beginning to wake up. And fixating on the wrong person. Well, what could they expect? The school was a hotbed of barely repressed sexuality. They actually had dances in the gym where the girls danced with each other. How could they not get turned on? Was she falling in love with Lucy? No, that was ridiculous. She was just inexperienced, had missed some steps along the way, was suffering from a major case of arrested development. She'd read all about it.

She and Lucy were sitting on the floor of the washroom. They had skipped trig. class, gone through almost a whole pack of cigarettes and half the Listerine bottle. They knew it was dangerous but Gwen was keeping her eye on her watch; they had another fifteen minutes to go before school was out for the day. They had slid down the wall on to the floor towards the end of the stall. Lucy's arm was around Gwen, Gwen's head was on Lucy's breast, and Gwen could feel herself letting go, letting go of everything when the door swung open and Sister Agatha burst into the room. For a moment all of them froze. Every particle of Sister Agatha was quivering. Looking shocked and furious she yanked them both to their feet. Grabbing Lucy, she hustled her out of the door, saying over her shoulder to Gwen, who cowered in the corner, 'I'll see you in my office. In fifteen minutes.'

Trembling, Gwen faced the wrath of the formidable Sister Agatha across the desk. She could hardly breathe. Her entire future was at stake. 'This is a major blot in your spiritual copybook, Jenny,' the nun said quietly. She paused and looked at her hands, folded peacefully on the edge of the desk. 'You've got a strong academic record and you're headed for college. Surely you don't want to do anything foolish that might jeopardize that.'

Gwen shook her head mutely.

'Surely you don't want to hurt your parents.' Gwen started to breathe in little gasps: her father would kill her if he knew about this, and her mother — what would her mother think? Gwen couldn't begin to imagine. It was too frightening to comprehend.

'Now Jenny, I want you to kneel down here and ask God's forgiveness. Let's pray together. We'll put our arms around each other and we'll pray together.' Sister Agatha held out her arms and, still trembling, Gwen went into them and the two of them sank down on to their knees.

Weeks went by and Gwen kept waiting for the other shoe to drop. She and Lucy avoided each other assiduously, both too frightened and ashamed to talk it through. She continued to go to Sister Agatha three times a week for spiritual counselling. They would get down on their knees and Sister Agatha would hold her tight and stroke her hair, which made Gwen very uncomfortable. What was expected of her? Where was all this leading? Finally one day she couldn't stand it any longer and the words flew out of her: 'Look, I can't do this any more. I don't know what you want from me, but whatever it is, it's not making me feel any better. I'm not going to do this any more.'

'I'm sorry you feel that way,' Sister Agatha said quietly, her expression odd. 'You're making a mistake. I'm only trying to help you.'

'I'm sorry,' Gwen whispered miserably and she turned and fled.

Her father and mother were waiting for her as she walked into the house. 'How could you do this to me?' her father greeted her angrily. 'Kissing another woman! Just the thought of it makes me sick'

'No,' Gwen started to say, hurt and confused. 'That's not what happened!'

'Don't lie to me, Sister Agatha just telephoned us!'

'I'm *not* lying, Sister Agatha is lying.'

Her mother's face turned ashen, 'How dare you accuse a nun of . . . not telling the truth.'

'But it's true, she *is* lying! I've never kissed anyone, boy or girl! Sister Agatha's been touching me, she's the one who's been doing it, she's the one who wants . . .'

Crack! Her father's hand came down across her face. 'Don't you dare say something as disgusting as that!'

'But it's true, Daddy, it's true!' She was crying now, holding her cheek.

'Stop it!' He raised his hand to hit her again, but her mother grabbed hold of his wrist.

'Bill, please, don't! You let her grow up like a boy! She's sick! She can't help it! It's not her fault.'

'Are you saying it's my fault? Are you blaming me for the fact that my daughter is a queer?'

'God will punish her!' Her mother was sobbing.

'Nothing happened' Gwen cried, 'I swear nothing happened!'

'Get out of my sight!' he screamed at her. 'I don't want you in this house any more.'

Gwen stopped crying instantly. 'No, what you're saying is you don't need me here any more. Not now that you have Sebastien, your son.'

'Get out!' He advanced towards her again. 'Get out of my house!'

'Oh, I'm going, Dad. But it's not *your* house. If I hadn't made the rest of your payments, you would have lost it. This is my house. You're standing on my money.' She knew she had scored a fatal hit when she saw him falter slightly at that. But it didn't make her feel any better. Because now she could never go home again.

# *Two*

Hibbing, Minnesota. 1968. Susie (nee Skaii) Jacobaitis pulled the pillow down over her ears and tried to shut out the sound of her parents' angry voices arguing in the next room. She had grown up listening to her parents fight about the small, snow-bound town, a Scandinavian outpost of northern Minnesota.

'I hate this Hibbing,' she heard her mother, Marieke, say, for what had to be the five-hundredth time. 'How could you bring me to this godforsaken place?' Skaii could just imagine how her mother looked in the heat of the argument, her face all red and shiny, her silvery blonde hair slipping out of its hastily skewered French braid. It frightened and disgusted her to think of her mother like that, like some crazy woman who couldn't keep her emotions under control.

'Jesus, Mary and Joseph,' her father's voice was raised and that frightened her, too. 'What are you remembering that was so wonderful about the old country?' Skaii's father was Lithuanian but had lived in Brussels throughout the Second World War. Now, in the frozen landscape of the northern United States, they continued their own private war over Hibbing. For Jacob, their arrival in this country meant a new start in life, with hope for a real future. For Marieke, it symbolized the beginning of the end of her life and no future. She hated the desolateness of the place, the long winters, the cold, the snow, and the lack of culture and sophistication.

127

Hibbing was so remote that Skaii's teachers, most of whom came from other parts of the US, received something called isolation pay to help them cope. There was no art gallery in town, no theatre or ballet, no boutiques or serious bookstores, no bistros or coffee bars, only snow-covered spruce trees, jagged rock formations and the icy silver beauty of Lake Superior.

'And what was so terrific about Brussels, Marieke? The place was full of Nazis! Collaborators! We are lucky to be alive. No money we had, not enough space for an animal, dirt there was everywhere. The war made everything and everyone dirty. Here it's all clean and new.'

'And empty and stupid,' her mother shouted right back. 'There isn't even any decent bread here. What wouldn't I give for just a simple baguette?' Skaii couldn't understand what her mother was complaining about. What could be better than Wonder Bread? It was truly wonderful, all soft and white and spongy, perfect for moulding into animal sculptures.

'Keep your voice down you'll wake the child!' Didn't they know she was already awake? How could she sleep with this kind of shouting going on? She wondered how many other eleven-year-old girls in Hibbing had to listen to a nightly parental battle. The muffled, furious whispers that grew into loud confrontation, and then the long silences in between that were almost worse than the angry words. 'Your friends, Marieke I know you miss,' her father was attempting to mollify the situation, 'but you know you are not really trying to make friends here. The other women, they invite you to their koffee klatches, but somehow you make them feel they are not good enough for you.'

'They are not good enough for me. Stupid bovine hausfraus with not a thought in their heads except for cooking and cleaning.'

'Well then, you say you like to be by yourself, so what is it precisely you are missing?'

'My work, you fool! I want my work, Jacob. My work is my life.' In Brussels she had been an economist, her work translated into five languages. Here, her English was good, much better than Jacob's, but her outlook remained solidly European.

'It's not necessary for you to work. Why work if you don't have to? There is more money here when just I work than what we had at home.'

'Some work,' she spat. 'In Brussels, you were honoured, your job meant something. There you were a scientist, a research chemist. Here you are just a small-town druggist dispensing liver pills to the village idiots.' Her command of the English language was the one weapon she had over her stolid, squarely built husband; with her tongue she could beat Jacob into the ground.

'What means honour when you are starving?'

'I'm starving here. My soul is starved. It's so ugly here, the winters are so long, so cold, so bare. I want New York, I want San Francisco. Even the twin deaths, the Twin Cities, St Paul and Minneapolis, would be better than this.'

Even with a pillow over her ears, Skaii could hear the ice in her father's tone, as thick as the ice on Lake Superior, as he said, 'You live with your heart, not your head. You do not see what beauty there is here.'

Skaii could see it, flung out by nature, still relatively unspoiled by humans. She loved the power of the stark landscape and the changes the weather brought to it. In the winter, she loved the black and white birches arched through the steel-grey sky, the fairy-like icicles hanging from the fir trees, and the broad expanse of snow dotted with the brightly coloured red roofs of the Finnish houses. It was like finding a violet under the ice, the one touch

129

of colour that made everything else so beautiful. Her mother was right, the winters were terribly long and hard, but that made the summers, gold and green, all the more intense for being so brief.

Skaii's father claimed the grandeur of nature only increased his belief in the power of the Creator. Her mother swore the bleakness of this place went a long way to proving there was no God. 'No one could create a land like this on purpose. He meant it to be purgatory,' Marieke would say. Religion was another battleground between them. Marieke, who had escaped the camps because of her blonde hair and blue eyes, was actually partly Jewish. She had met Jacob through the Belgian Resistance. Jacob, dark and Semitic-looking, was devoutly Russian Orthodox. The existence of any God was something Marieke had long doubted, but, from the moment she had laid eyes on Jacob, she was wildly attracted to him. He wouldn't sleep with her unless she married him, and she wasn't therefore going to let religion stand in the way of her marrying him. Once they were married, however, the war began.

'How can you still believe?' Marieke cried. 'How can you possibly believe in God after the holocaust?'

'A test it was,' Jacob would say, 'a tragic test. Those who suffered will not be forgotten. They will be rewarded later. The power of God, it is truly almighty.'

'If God is all-powerful, why does he allow evil in the world?'

'Ah, the age-old question. This world is not important. The reward, the true joy, is in the next.'

'Yes, but I am living now,' Marieke would sigh. 'Here, in this world.' And the argument would start all over again.

Why argue, Skaii thought, when it was so much easier to give in? Her father had his rules. Hibbing had its rules. Why did her mother continually want to flout them? Skaii

130

loved her mother but sometimes she was afraid that deep inside she really hated her. Hated having a mother who dressed in black silk as if she were in mourning for her life. Why couldn't she wear pastels and polyester like everybody else's mother? And that braided hair made her look like a refugee milkmaid! At her age, she should cut it and have a perm. Both her parents were old enough to be her grandparents. They'd been married a long time before Skaii came along. It was bad enough having a mother who smoked, but Marieke rolled her own cigarettes and held the cigarette between her thumb and forefinger, European style, as she smoked. Why did she have to look so weird?

She refused to do her grocery shopping at the A and P on Saturday mornings with all the other mothers. She was forever running out to the corner store to pick something up for supper. 'I miss the boulangeries and the boucheries we had in Brussels,' she complained. 'I want things to be fresh.'

'Yeah, but you wait till the end of the day. Why can't you plan ahead?' Skaii whined. 'Cindy's mother has a different dish for every night of the week, you know, like meat loaf on Monday, tuna casserole on Tuesday . . .'

'Roast beef for Sunday dinner?' Marieke interrupted and made a little face. 'How bourgeois. I don't like ritual. I hate routine.'

'Well, face it, Mom. You're just not organized. You never know what we're having for dinner.

'I'm guilty I admit it,' Marieke smiled. 'It rarely crosses my mind.'

'But it's not as though you had anything else to do. I mean, what do you do all day?' Skaii demanded. 'What are you doing with your life?'

'My dear, I really don't know,' Marieke said, cutting the ties off her flowered apron and tossing it into the old-rag hamper.

131

'Why can't you be more like Aunt Bea?' Skaii pleaded. Aunt Bea was her father's sister who married a Scandinavian doctor and lived in a big Tudor house in Minneapolis. She had six children and every time Skaii went to visit, the family fulfilled every one of her *Partridge Family* fantasies. Her English was excellent and she and her husband, Eric, prided themselves on being Americanized.

'First you cream the butter with the sugar,' Aunt Bea instructed, as Skaii surveyed a vast array of ingredients and cooking utensils laid out in perfect order on the white Formica kitchen counter. Like Jacob, Bea was short and stocky and dark, with a round face, warm brown eyes and a melting smile. When she put her arms around Skaii, her ample bosom provided a comfortable shelf for both crying and cuddling. Skaii had even seen her aunt rest the saucer of her teacup on that bosom shelf when the two of them shared cambric tea in the late afternoon.

The kitchen was enormous, as big as the whole first floor of Skaii's house back in Hibbing. The walls were lined with knotty pine cabinets and the cabinets were always full of food, as was the avocado-green fridge and matching freezer. Aunt Bea canned her own vegetables, put up her own preserves, ground her own meat, and made all her own baked goods. Store-bought bread and cookies were not allowed in the house. Of course, Skaii's cousins were always trading their home-made meatloaf on rye for peanut butter and jelly, and sneaking off after school to Burger King for a quarter pounder and chips with gravy, but Skaii knew just how lucky they were to have Beatrice for a mom.

Aunt Bea was a prize-winning cook. In the living-room, on top of the grand piano which smelled of fresh flowers and furniture polish, sat a big glass case with over one hundred carefully pressed ribbons from the

Minnesota state farm fair cooking competitions. Most of the ribbons were blue first-prize winners for things like lemon meringue pie or red devil's food cake, but there were one or two yellow second-place ribbons for the few times Bea had strayed into the exotic with Chinese dumplings or Mexican flan. What she did best was good old middle-American cooking, plain and simple, but with just that extra ingredient that took a dessert out of the ordinary and into the sublime. Her giant chocolate-chip cookies had actually won the Pillsbury bake-off. Right next to the ribbon case was a large, gilt-framed, black and white photograph of Aunt Bea jumping up in the air, clutching a cheque for two thousand dollars in her hand. The Pillsbury judges had flown her all the way from Minneapolis, Minnesota, to San Bernadino, California, for the final bake-off, where Aunt Bea had managed to beat out the forty-seven other finalists (one from each state) with her chocolate-chip cookie recipe. Now she was about to impart the secret of her success to Skaii.

'Use only fresh, unsalted butter, no margarine or Crisco,' she cautioned. 'You're going to let the fat stand in the mixing bowl in a warm place until soft. Not too warm. You do not want it to melt, you just want it creamy. Then you add in one cup of white sugar and one cup of brown.'

'Why two kinds of sugar?' Skaii watched, fascinated, as the mixture in the big pottery bowl turned a bubbly golden colour under the expert touch of her aunt's wooden spoon.

'The white sugar is lighter, but the brown, it has more flavour.' She deftly cracked two eggs with one hand and dropped them into the bowl. Skaii watched the bright yellow yolk disappear into the batter. 'Never use artificial flavouring. You want real vanilla extract if not the bean itself. And I like to add a touch of brandy. Now you make yourself useful. Sift the flour and the salt and the baking powder together.' She passed the hand sifter to Skaii as if it were a rare icon. 'Now you do not want to use packaged chocolate chips; bigger chunks of bittersweet chocolate melt better. Most Toll House recipes call for chopped walnuts, but I prefer pecans. They're hard to get up here, but the taste is worth it. And, the *pièce de résistance*, my top secret ingredient . . .' she looked at her niece sharply and whispered conspiratorially, 'you're sure I can trust you with this?' Skaii nodded. 'All right then . . . just at that last minute I add grated mandarin orange peel to cut the sweetness. Now,' she handed Skaii a great big spoon, 'you drop the batter on to the greased cookie sheet. And don't skimp. "Nothin' says lovin' like something from the oven, and a big cookie says it best." '

Together they slid the aluminium pan into the oven and, as the sweet smell of chocolate and butter and sugar filled the kitchen, Skaii threw her arms around her aunt and hugged her hard. Within the circle of her aunt's embrace, she felt safe. This was what family life should be.

Marieke began to wander off, sometimes for days at a time, sometimes leaving them a note, sometimes not. Once Skaii and her father had to go all the way to St Paul to fetch her where the police had found her in Dayton's department store, sitting in a lazy-boy chair among the room settings for sale on the second floor. Every once in a while she would run away to the bush, saying it was time for her to join the land, not reject it. She wanted Skaii to run away with her, but Skaii refused. She liked Hibbing. All she wanted was for her mother to accept it as home.

'Why can't you be more like Aunt Bea?' Skaii persisted.

'You would prefer to have Aunt Bea for your mother,

is that it?' Marieke asked with a wry smile. 'Well, I can't say as I blame you.'

'No, of course not,' Skaii said guiltily. 'It's just that Aunt Bea seems so . . . happy.'

'Happy?' Her mother fairly spat the word. 'What is the relevance of that?'

# *Three*

For Miriam Newman growing up in Fresno, California, being Jewish was one of the two most important things in her life, that and food. She had been painfully skinny until she was four years old and had her tonsils out. Wheeled into the recovery room and given a bowl of vanilla ice-cream, little Miriam set out to make up for lost time. At thirteen, she had a forty-inch bust, a thirty-three-inch waist, and she was only five-foot-two. At her cousin Sheila's wedding, she weighed one hundred and sixty-five pounds. Everybody thought she was the mother of the bride. From that point on, her life was defined by her weight.

Reading her first Philip Roth novel, she wished she could blame her adolescent angst on having a classic Jewish mother, but Reva Newman didn't come close to fitting Roth's stereotype. A tiny redhead with a trim figure and a button nose, she watched Miriam like a hawk at meal-time, dropping the choicest tidbits into the mouths of her two younger — and skinnier — daughters. Although she cooked kosher, Reva rarely made the traditional heavier dishes like kugel or latkes. She packed Miriam special lunches of cottage cheese and pineapple, carrot sticks, and small bananas. Miriam knew how to get around that. She ate two lunches. Cottage cheese and carrot stick at recess. Salmon timbales, mashed potatoes, and chocolate pudding at noon in the cafeteria.

When the Newman family gathered in the rumpus

room to watch TV, Barbara and Valerie gorged themselves on caramel popcorn or sweet almond knishbrot while Miriam chastely sipped a glass of diet soda and nibbled on raw vegetables. Halfway through *Laugh-In*, Miriam would excuse herself to fetch more celery. Then, her heart pounding with guilty excitement, she would stuff her face with boiled beef, cold baked potatoes, and chunks of challah dipped in congealed gravy. Standing there in the darkened kitchen she ate quickly and stealthily, hardly tasting the food she crammed into her mouth.

'What are you doing in there?' her mother would call.

'Nothing, Mom. Just slicing a green pepper.'

'Well, hurry up. You're going to miss Ruth Buzzi.'

By the time Miriam felt full, she also felt ill. Into the bathroom, drink a glass of salt water, stick her finger down her throat.

'Are you still in there?'

'Yes, Mom.'

'Are you all right?'

'Yes.'

'Have you got your period?'

'No, Mom. And please keep your voice down. A little louder and we can dance to it.'

Sticking her finger down her throat rarely made her throw up. She seemed to have a cast-iron stomach. Sometimes she would plan her binges weeks in advance, always with the idea that she would throw it all up, but when it came to the point, there she'd be, crouching on the fuzzy pink bathmat with its matching toilet-seat cover, her finger down her throat, gagging away without success. She ate Ex-Lax as if it were the chocolate candy it pretended to be and guzzled Milk of Magnesia. Then she had to slug back Kaopectate to counteract the laxatives.

In desperation she tried wrapping herself in Saran Wrap, her thighs rustling guiltily under her clothes as she moved through their split-level house on Van Ness.

'What's that funny noise?' her mother asked suspiciously. 'What have you got on under there?'

'It's an experiment for science class. I'm supposed to do a report on it at the end of the week.'

'Some experiment. My daughter, the shower curtain.'

The plastic made her sweat like a pig, but she didn't lose any weight. Where did all this soft white flesh come from? Everybody else in her family was thin. It wasn't fair.

Despite her weight problems, Miriam was smart. She started school at five and then she skipped fourth grade, too. She was bright, talented and funny, the class clown. She would have traded it all to be thin and have a perfect nose like Twiggy.

The Newmans shared a Christmas tree with the neighbours next door, but they sprayed it white with fake snow and decorated it with blue baubles. Miriam called it a Chanukah bush. Christmas was not their holiday. At school all her friends were Jewish; in the neighbourhood very few of them were. Two sets of friends, like the two sets of dishes in her mother's kosher kitchen. She felt lucky to be getting off school for the high holidays when the kids next door had to go to class. Her father tried to explain just how special it was to be Jewish, and sometimes dangerous. His parents had fled Kiev, victims of the pogroms. 'It will happen again,' he warned. 'To be a Jew is often be a victim. But there are compensations. You can be glad you are Jewish.'

When she was eight, a group of boys from the nearby Catholic school threw a rock at her. 'Dirty Christ killer!' She ran home in tears. The priest at Holy Redeemer had been so horrified that he had made all the boys come to the Newman house and apologize to the entire family.

Miriam's father could see that world Jewry was

changing. Although he had grown up orthodox, he switched to reform when his own children were old enough to go with him to synagogue. 'I don't want to sit separate from you,' he explained. 'Religion should bring the family together, not keep us apart.' They would pass Grandfather Newman on the street on his way to temple, going in the opposite direction, and the two men would bow to one another like polite strangers.

Miriam went to Hebrew school every day and, shortly before her thirteenth birthday, she had a Bar Mitzvah. Her mornings were spent learning math, English, and science; the afternoon was devoted to Hebrew. Her sister Barbara refused even to take the night classes, and by the time it was Valerie's turn, she wasn't having any of it, but Talmud Torah was important to Miriam.

'What happened in school today?' her father asked, carving the pot roast into wafer-thin slices for Miriam's plate.

'The principal threw the book at us.'

'What do you mean?' Even Valerie looked interested.

'I mean he literally threw the book at us. He threw a siddur. He aimed it at Tommy Gundelfinger but he hit Sandy Levine instead. Boy, was she p.o.'d.'

'Don't use that kind of language at the dinner table, please. Your mother doesn't like it.'

'Well, I didn't say pissed off, did I? I said p.o.'d P.o.'d is OK, isn't it?'

'Don't they teach you anything at all in school?' Her father's voice rose in frustration as her mother's hand came down over Miriam's own as it reached for the mashed potatoes.

'Of course. I learned that Arabs are bad and Jews are good.'

The family said in union, 'We could have told you that.'

Entering Roosevelt High meant culture shock,

trespassing in the kingdom of the WASP. She was two years younger than everybody else, so she felt socially retarded, but her brain was exploding with challenging new ideas. Did she really believe in God? What did Judaism have to do with life in the modern world today? Why couldn't she eat pork now that it was properly processed, and what was wrong with having a lobster tail with her steak? What was so great about being Jewish anyway?

'You're turning into quite a nasty little anti-Semite,' Reva said with growing exasperation following a barrage of Miriam's questions one evening. 'Get your feet off the upholstery.'

'I feel smothered, OK?' Miriam draped herself over the chintz couch in the living-room and toyed with a cushion the way she'd seen Katharine Ross do in *The Graduate*. 'This whole ambience of Yiddishkite is too much for me. I'm drowning in schmaltz. I can't breathe.'

'I don't know what to do with you. You're either surly or you're crying, one or the other. You better straighten up and fly right, miss, that's all I have to say.'

'Oh, Mother, you don't understand. I can't live by your rules. They're archaic. Can't you see I'd rather die than end up like you?' Miriam knew she was destined to be a star. She had an inner light. Ricky Battlestein had told her so.

'You'll live by my rules while you're living in this house, young lady. If you have a house of your own some day and if I am privileged enough to be allowed in it, then I'll live by your rules, but you better decide what they are.'

'Leave her alone, Reva,' her father said with a chuckle, shaking his newspaper as he turned a page. 'She's not a baby any more. We're lucky she's not on the streets; we're lucky she's not taking drugs in this horrible time.

141

She's just going through adolescence. Let her flex her rebellion muscles a little.'

'Well, if she's not careful, she's going to rebel herself right out of a decent home and loving family.'

To Miriam, family meant a sticky honeycomb of demands, little syrupy pockets of mistrust waiting to suck her under.

In the meantime high school was an escape, although she had to work hard to find her niche. She joined a club called Hell, made up of the brains, the artistic 'weirdos', and a couple of teachers. It was 1969. Woodstock was happening. There were men on the moon. The sexual revolution was in full swing. But the members of Hell didn't do drugs or sex. They met in a little room in the basement where they read Ayn Rand novels, did silk screening, played chess, and brewed their own beer. They were the intelligentsia, their meetings were of the mind. Miriam was beyond sex. She was an artist.

As a little girl, she had worshipped Natalie Wood. In fact she had fully intended to grow up to be Natalie Wood until she found out you couldn't become another person already living. Then she planned to be a prima ballerina assoluta and she practised in her back yard, taking thirty-six curtain calls, the way she had seen Alicia Alonso do when she came to the San Francisco Civic Center. Pirouetting in her mother's vegetable garden, Miriam threw kisses to the neighbours. Three times a week she took ballet lessons with Theodora Lee, a former ballerina from Louisville, Kentucky. Theodora Lee was blonde and even more beautiful than Natalie Wood. Why couldn't Miriam have been born blonde with a southern accent?

Every Saturday morning, Miriam and the girls in her ballet class would go to Miss Lee's flat above the dance academy for a private 'salon', as she called it. They filed into her bedroom where they received them in her velvet-draped, four-poster bed. Climbing on to the foot of the bed, they tumbled over each other like young puppies, each one eager to get close to her muse. Miss Lee predicted their individual futures. One day she took Miriam's chubby hand in her own long slender one and said seriously in her educated drawl, 'I do not believe that Mimi is going to be a dancer.'

Miriam's heart stopped. Why else had she given up eight years of her life? Why had she forced herself to up-chuck after eating Sonemores if not to be a dancer? Why had she turned down Tommy Gundelfinger's offer to take her to the roller rink if not to be a dancer?

'No, Miriam is not going to be a dancer,' Theodora Lee repeated and Miriam wanted to die. 'Miriam is going to be an actress. A great actress. And we will start today.'

She made her lie down on the floor with a book on her stomach while she taught her how to breathe with her diaphragm and to 'speak from the centre'. It was a bit of a disappointment not to be heading for a career as a dancer, but secretly Miriam felt relieved. Ballet dancers were practically all anorexic. You could be fat and still be an actress.

Nonetheless she continued to hate her body. At Roosevelt High, she managed to get out of PE by taking lots of showers and claiming to have her period twice a month. She preferred not to deal with her body, not to recognize the billowing breasts, swollen belly, and pale doughy thighs that belonged to her. She couldn't imagine any boy wanting to touch it; she didn't like touching it herself. Even when she danced, she never looked at herself in the mirror but at some idealized image of herself dancing in front of her. Her body was a shell, something she had borrowed for a time and would eventually cast off, caterpillar-style, when the right skin came along to slip into.

Her parents sent her to the B'nai Brith fat girls camp on Huntington Lake. The routine was rigorous: up at six-

143

thirty for a cup of hot lemon water, torturous calisthenics, an early morning ride through the *manzanita*, swimming, water-skiing, tennis. Miriam hated it. Standing at the end of the diving board, shivering with cold, exposed and humiliated in the regulation red tank suit that made her look like a giant beach ball, she could no longer escape the reality of her body. With her glasses off, she couldn't even see the water she was supposed to dive into. She might hit her head on a rock, go into a coma, and never wake up again. She might be paralysed from the neck down. Was it worth it? On a hiking expedition up to Big Falls, she conveniently broke her ankle. There was no point sitting around all summer with a cast on her leg at a fat girls camp, so Miriam was sent home.

In high school, Theodora Lee's breathing exercises started to pay off. Miriam got the lead in all the class plays. In her senior year, when she was sixteen, she played Annie Sullivan in *The Miracle Worker* and got a standing ovation every night of the four-day run. Watching Tammy Lockwood play Helen Keller (Tammy only got the part because she weighed all of eight pounds and could be schlepped about easily by the rest of the cast), groping around, pretending to be blind, Miriam thought to herself, I should play Helen Keller. All I'd have to do would be to take off my glasses. It's so unfair. Why do I have to be fat and near-sighted?

Reva and Mark couldn't see why Miriam needed contact lenses, but Miriam couldn't wait. She worked after school typing term papers for Fresno State College students and earned the money for her contacts.

'You have a serious astigmatism,' the ophthalmologist observed as he asked her to point to the edge of the wing of the oversized red and green fly on the card. 'Contact lenses won't correct that. In fact, you won't see as well. Soft lenses won't give you the correction you need and

144

the gas permeable are a lot of hassle. I can't really recommend them for you.'

Miriam didn't care. Her Coke-bottle glasses were gone.

In the meantime contact lenses were a pain. They felt like boulders in her eyes and if she left them in too long, she'd wake up the next morning and not be able to open her swollen burning eyes until her mother put ice on them. And they were a major investment. How many lenses had she lost in one year, down the drain, on stage, at the movies, in dance class? Once Ticker the family poodle swallowed one and she had to wait two days to dig through the dog doodoo to find it. Even that was worth it. Anything was better than looking like Golda Meir.

Convincing her parents to let her have a nose job was even tougher.

'You're too young. Wait at least until you're eighteen.'

'I'm not too young. I want it now.'

'It's not going to change your life, you know.'

'I don't want to change my life. I want to change my nose.'

'You want to look like everybody else? To be homogenized like the rest of the world into one big quart of milk? Having a nose job is like having an abortion, God forbid you should ever know what that's like; it's like killing a part of yourself.'

'Oh Mother, you don't understand.'

'Look at Barbra Streisand. Where would she be with a shikse nose? Maybe she couldn't even sing? You say you want to be an actress. This could change your voice, then where would you be?'

'Mother, my nose is just a piece of flesh. It's not me. What's me is what's inside.'

'Honey, I think I know what your mother means,' her father broke in. 'Go ahead with this, I'll pay for it, if it's what you really want, but not because you feel you

145

have to alter yourself physically to meet someone else's standards. You know we love you just the way you are.'

'They're my standards. I hate this nose.'

'Someday you'll realize the limitations of other people's perceptions,' her mother said darkly, but Miriam would not be deterred. She had sat through high school with her hands cupped around her nose to hide it. She had held her head up in the air to give it a more patrician angle. She had shadowed and highlighted it with so much make-up that it looked like a muddy, streaked blob in the centre of her face.

Her father didn't trust the plastic surgeons in Fresno, so they drove to LA. In the doctor's office, six other teenagers were waiting to get their noses done. One was a Catholic boy who had fallen on his face; the other five were Jewish girls.

'Look towards the window.' The doctor examined her face from all angles, studying it carefully to work out the proper dimensions. Miriam held her breath, terrified he was going to say no. Finally he said, 'I'm not going to give you a small nose, so don't count on that.'

'But I want a small nose. I want a tiny nose. Like Marlo Thomas.'

'I don't do noses *like* somebody else,' the doctor said sternly. 'Do you want to end up like Nanette Fabray? No-nose Nanette? Look, you have a strong face, Miss Newman. I am an artist. Leave it to me.'

She spent the next two days after the operation in Mt Sinai Hospital with a cast on her nose and two very black eyes. When the bandages came off, she was a little disappointed. Her nose wasn't that much smaller, but she had to admit it was truly a beautiful nose. She no longer looked like Golda Meir; she looked like Ingrid Bergman playing Golda Meir.

In the fall, she went off to UCLA to pursue a double major in drama and English (something to fall back on, dear, if the acting doesn't work out). Her parents refused to let her go east to university. At seventeen they wanted her to stay close to them and Miriam was secretly frightened of being on her own in New York. LA was a big centre for actors, too, especially for film. Her heart belonged to the theatre but she was willing to give movies a try if any famous producers came knocking at her door.

UCLA was still a hotbed of student activism, although not as radical as Berkeley. The Vietnam war had already changed their lives and the shooting of the students at Kent State made them realize that their world closer to home was a dangerous place. Charles Manson and three of his followers were found guilty of killing Sharon Tate, and a court martial jury convicted Lt William Calley of the premeditated murder of twenty-two South Vietnamese men, women, and children.

Miriam tried to block it all out and focus on what she was there for, to make it in the theatre. She knew it was going to take every ounce of energy, determination, and discipline she had to become an actress. Freshmen were never cast in leading roles but, to her amazement, she landed the lead in *A Taste of Honey*, playing Jo, a working-class girl from Liverpool who falls in love with a black sailor and has his baby. Miriam worked day and night using a tape recorder to master the difficult northern British dialect, and she spent hours in the library researching Liverpool. She lived on brown rice and steamed vegetables, although her weight didn't matter because she was supposed to be pregnant for most of the play. Her friends thought she was better than Rita Tushingham had been in the movie and the LA *Times*, which hardly ever reviewed university productions, said she was 'a talent to be watched'.

Even in the free-wheeling early seventies. A *Taste of Honey* was considered hot stuff. There was an ideological battle going on on campus between the SDS and the black

147

power factions. When Miriam kissed a black actor on stage, half the audience got up and left. There were obscene phone calls and threats on her life. Miriam was surprised. She hadn't realized theatre could be political. At university, she was still the youngest person in her classes, but the other students seemed like irresponsible children to her, undedicated and undisciplined. All they wanted to do was get stoned and demonstrate. All she wanted to do was act. A *Taste of Honey* made her a campus celebrity and she revelled in the attention.

Clayton Norman Brown, a local television producer, came to see the show and took her out for Mexican food. They went to Mehico Typico and Miriam sat quietly as Brown drank a number of margaritas in very quick succession. He lit a strange black cigarette, which he told her was a Sobrani, inhaled deeply and looked at her with bleary alcoholic eyes. 'You're wasting your time in a university drama programme. You need to be out in the real world. Four years is a long time to wait.'

'UCLA's got one of the best theatre departments in the country. I have the chance to explore the boundaries of my talent here and to stretch my dramatic capabilities within a controlled environment,' Miriam said primly, quoting not the blurb in a university brochure, but the words of her father as he drove her up from Fresno.

'Yeah? Well, this production of *Taste of Honey* is a piece of shit,' Clayton said bluntly. 'The other members of the cast aren't up to your standard. Besides, you're miscast. You should be playing Jo's mother.'

'I'm only seventeen.'

'You're kidding!' He looked at her in surprise. 'You look a lot older. Anyway, that's beside the point. What I mean is, you're not right for Jo. You're not an ingénue.'

'You mean I'm too fat.' Miriam guiltily pushed away her chili relleno and mole enchilada late-night special.

'No, no. I mean you're an emotional heavyweight.

148

You're a potential powerhouse of an actress, honey. Sure, you could lose some weight — you'll have to if you want to do film or television — but basically you're a Rubens. Accept it.'

Miriam winced. All those pink fleshy girls with thick red lips and snaky hair. 'Don't say that. You really think I'm ready for the profession?' The idea both excited and terrified her.

'Mm, seventeen, I don't know . . .' Clayton looked at her thoughtfully. 'You're good enough but, as I said, you're not an ingénue. I'd think about a professional training school if I were you. Julliard in New York. There's a good school in Canada, too. It depends on what you want. You intend to stick with stage or you want to get into movies?'

'Do I have to decide right now? I'd like to leave myself open, weigh the options . . .'

'Of course you need to decide now! God, what are they teaching you here?' Clayton pounded the table with his fist. 'What do you think life is — a dress rehearsal?'

It was the first time Miriam had ever heard the analogy and it struck her as brilliant. 'All right, all right, I'll think about what you've said.'

'Yeah, you think about it. Get out of this cocoon as fast as you can. You got a lot of growing up to do, but I don't think you're going to get that here.'

'I'm going to work harder to lose weight.'

'Sure, if you want to. And, for God's sakes, do something about your hair. It looks like a Brillo pad.' Miriam's hand went protectively to the cap of tight waves that she kept short because her hair was naturally curly. She could never get it into the long, straight hippie look so she had opted for a modified Afro instead. 'Grow it out. Let it go its own wild way and loosen up. You could stand to loosen up yourself, honey. You need some life experience to draw from. The world is upside down right

149

now. It's wild, it's crazy. Ya gotta go with the flow.'

Then he made a grab at her left breast and asked her
to go to bed with him: 'I'd like to explore the inner
workings of your talent.'

Miriam was shocked, but Brown had given her
something to think about. Life experience she could only
get as it came to her, but she would definitely allow her
hair to grow.

Her hair grew like a weed and was past her shoulders
by spring, long black hair, thick, untamed, and gloriously
curly. She put herself on the Stillman diet — high protein,
low carbohydrate, and lots of water. And then a miracle
happened: she suddenly grew four inches. At five six, she
could, she supposed, still be termed somewhat
Rubenesque, but she could no longer be called fat. She
had grown into herself. Cast as Ellida in Ibsen's *Lady
from the Sea*, she looked stunning for the first time in
her life and she knew it. *Lady* was an avant-garde, semi-
professional production (she played opposite Kyle
Jackson, the TV star) with a set completely surrounded
by real water. Miriam made her entrance practically nude,
wrapped in a sheet, soaked to the skin, running through
the water. On opening night she came on stage and the
audience rose en masse to applaud her entrance. This time
the LA *Times* deemed her 'ravishing and riveting . . . here
we have a major classical actress in the making . . . a
promising young star.' Of course she was meant to be
a classical actress. Her voice, her weight, her presence
were perfect for Ibsen and Shaw and Shakespeare. Why
was she wasting her time in sunny southern California?
She needed to go somewhere where they took art
seriously. Without telling anyone she flew to Montreal
to audition for the National Theatre School of Canada.

150

# *Four*

Austin, Texas. 1967. Sara Town came out of the gymnasium where registration was being held and looked across the University of Texas campus with its towering oak trees and Spanish colonial brick buildings. The heat of the blinding Texas summer had given way to the relief of a cooler, less sultry fall, but there was still an underlying unease on campus, a sense of a powder keg about to be set on fire. In the fall of 1967, the United States was in social and political turmoil, and nowhere was that more in evidence than on university campuses throughout the country. 'Student power' was the cry. Questions were being shouted from the rooftops and the answers were no longer merely 'blowin' in the wind'. Martin Luther King had just published *And Where Do We Go from Here, The Future of Civil Rights*. Bobby Kennedy was beating incumbent president, Lyndon Johnson, in all the polls. Sex and drugs and rock and roll were everywhere and the times, 'they were a changin' '.

At Berkeley, students were protesting. In Chicago, students were rioting. New York was full of strikes and sit-ins and, even as far away as Paris, students were gearing up for a revolt that would tear up the streets of the city in the spring, leaving parts of it as bombed out in appearance as they had looked following the Second World War. But the south is always a little behind fashion, and for the moment there were only the

151

beginnings of unrest, an overlay of false calm before the storm. Sara decided that the University of Texas at Austin would be the perfect place in which to rewrite her own personal history.

For Gwyneth Roberts, Texas offered the promise of a new life too. The brochure for UT made the setting look almost Mediterranean with its graceful yellow brick and red-tiled Spanish architecture — a far cry from the concrete and stucco of Bowness — and the prospect of no snow and balmy temperatures even in January sounded good after the harsh Alberta winters. Tuition at UT was cheap, and with the money from her Queen Elizabeth scholarship, she ought to be able to get through at least one year. She liked the fact that she would be studying at Uncle Jack's alma mater. Most important of all, Texas was a long way away from Canada. Nobody would know who she was or where she had come from.

She was majoring in petroleum geology. The list of associated courses in the university catalogue read like a series of foreign languages. Most of her first year would be given over to basic freshman courses, but after that the real fun would begin. Of course she would be taking basic geology, studying the age of the earth from fossils to crystals, but there was also geomorphology, the study of glaciers and the types of structures they left behind, sedimentary petrology, where she would be looking at soft rocks under a microscope, and mineralogy and crystallography. Maybe she would take a few business courses, too. If she got her BSC in geology, she could work toward becoming an explorations manager with an oil company, maybe even Uncle Jack's own company in Houston, Treasure Resources. Her goal in life was to find oil and gas and get paid for it.

As she walked across Guadalupe Street, called the Drag by the UT students, she was filled with exhilaration. The September sun bathed her face with its warm rays and

152

she could feel the comforting heat flowing through her veins, giving her a new lease of life. She stopped at the foot of the tower, the famous tower where Charles Whitman, an ex-Marine, had shot thirty people, killing sixteen of them on the grounds, right in front of the library and even as far away as the Co-op bookstore on the Drag. News of that event had even reached Bowness. Gwen remembered feeling vaguely threatened, even thousands of miles away, at the undercurrent of violence that existed in the American south. Gazing up at the observation deck at the top of the tower, feeling the breeze ruffle her short, reddish curls, it was hard to believe anything dangerous had ever happened here. It all seemed so peaceful, but she sensed that peace was deceptive. On northern campuses, the battle lines were more clearly drawn. Beatniks had been replaced by hippies and yippies. The world was divided into the 'straights' and the 'long hairs', the clipped and the shaggy. Here, in Austin, the counter-culture was just beginning to take a tenuous hold, a harbinger of the time when the town would become a centre for radical politics and the rebirth of country music.

Gwen walked past neatly dressed young men and women sitting on the grass, bent over open textbooks, making careful notes in their three-ring binders, flashing their slide-rules and absent-mindedly fingering their drawing pencils as they charted on blue-lined paper the stresses in frame buildings and voltage against time. Engineering students definitely belonged in the category of straights. Right around the corner, in front of the fountain, waited a group of scruffy, loudly vocal demonstrators, protesting against the war in Vietnam. 'What do we want?' 'Peace!' 'When do we want it?' 'Now!' This group sounded aggressive, a look of commitment mixed with fanaticism in their eyes. Part of Gwen wanted to stop and talk with them, but part of her

153

hung back. Certainly she was against the war in Vietnam, but could a motley crew like this really have any effect on LBJ far away in Washington? The protestors raised their fingers in the V sign for peace and Gwen timidly gave them an answering V.

She hurried up the steps of Carruthers, a red brick residence for freshmen women and one of the oldest buildings on campus. Unbuttoning her navy-blue blazer, much too formal and hot for a Texas fall, she ran up the three flights of stairs to her room. Originally intended for three students, it was large but sparsely furnished. Three oversized desks took up most of the space, but there were only two beds. Each was tiny, not much bigger than a cot, with a thin, flat mattress and a pillow the shape and consistency of a soggy saltine cracker. Facing north, the room was dark most of the day, lit only by a couple of weak bulbs in the crook-necked lamps bolted to the desks.

'It's a bit like the Bastille, isn't it, love?'

Gwen whirled around to face the most beautiful girl she'd ever seen. Slender and sinewy, with sharply defined cheekbones and thick, shiny, dark hair, she was a dead ringer for that exotic dark actress in the new James Bond film, Barbara Carrera. Her large, almond-shaped eyes were brown with shooting flecks of gold and green.

'You sound English,' Gwen stammered, trying not to stare at the glamorous creature in the doorway.

'No,' the girl replied, 'just phoney.' She laughed, a sexy, throaty laugh. 'As a matter of fact, you're the one that sounds English to me.'

'I'm from Canada,' Gwen hated to seem shy and awkward in front of this self-possessed serenely cool beauty, who exuded confidence from every pore.

'Oh, no, does that mean you're going to be saying "out" and "about" all the time?' She gave them the strange vowel sound that Americans think characterizes a Canadian accent. 'And "eh"?'

'I'll try not to,' Gwen said stiffly.

'Hey, I'm only kidding,' Sara laughed again. Her voice really was a lot like Suzanne Pleschette's. Or maybe Lauren Bacall. Gwen had read in *Cosmopolitan* magazine that Lauren Bacall had practised screaming every day to lower her voice. She knew that cigarettes and whisky could make a voice deeper, too. She hoped she wasn't going to have to room with somebody who was a heavy smoker.

'You've got an amazing voice,' Gwen said.

'Glad you like it. Since it looks like you're going to be stuck with it for at least this semester. I'm Sara Town.'

'Gwyneth Roberts.' She couldn't take her eyes off her new roommate. Her long black hair was parted in the middle and fell halfway down her back. She was wearing an Indian print skirt and a gauze blouse so thin Gwen was amazed to see her nipples. Nobody in Bowness or Calgary would be caught dead on the street like that. She looked wild. She looked sexy. She's perfect, Gwen thought with a sinking heart. How am I ever going to able to live with her?

She's perfect, Sara thought with relief. Look at that tasteful blue blazer and grey skirt. Two inches above the knee exactly, That's class. She shy and reserved, even sort of mysterious. But what on earth is she doing all the way down here in Texas? 'Aren't you a long way from home? What made you pick UT? I mean it's hardly one of the top schools in America?'

Gwen flushed as she took off her blazer and hung it up neatly in the closet. 'Oil. And I wanted to get out of Canada. See something else of the world. I guess I don't really have the guts to try Europe.'

'Europe's dead, honeychile. Don't you know that? The good old US of A is where it's at, where it's happenin', man.'

'I hope you're right. Texas seems very . . . exciting. Different from Canada, that's for sure. Anyway, UT 's great for geology. That's what I'm majoring in. I think. Looks like we're all taking pretty much the same thing this year.'

'Yep. Introduction to just about everything.' Sara dropped her shoulder bag on to one of the beds. 'We must be the only white girls in this building.' She bounced tentatively on the bed. 'You can practically hear the fucking halls echo, this place is so empty.'

'It'll probably fill up. All students have to live in approved housing for the first two years.'

'Are you kidding me?' Sara looked at her in amazement.

'No. It says so in the catalogue.'

'You must have been sent a pretty old catalogue. The university dropped approved housing a couple of years ago.'

'You mean we don't have to live in the dorm?'

'Well, to be honest. I can't afford anything else. I worked my ass off to get here.'

'Me, too.' Gwen was a little shocked at the coarse language that seemed to fly out of Sara's mouth. 'Why did they drop the approval?'

'Integration.'

'Integration?'

'Yeah, UT was the first university in the south to integrate.'

'That's great.'

'You really think so?' Sara raised an eyebrow.

'Of course,' Gwen said stoutly. 'Coloureds are just the same as everybody else.'

'Coloureds? Coloureds?' Sara almost choked on the word. 'Where have you been, child? Don't you know we call them black now?'

'Well, in Canada we call them coloured people. Or Negroes. Of course they're mostly from Jamaica so they're not really all that black.'

Sara laughed. 'It hardly matters. It was a useless victory

156

anyway. Most of them don't go to UT, they go to the black college in town, Huston Tillotson. For the moment, they seem pretty subdued. I guess you heard about the riots in Newark and Detroit?' Gwen nodded. 'But did you hear what happened at San Francisco State?' She chewed on one stubby fingernail. At least her nails weren't perfect, Gwen noted with some relief. Most of them were bitten to the quick.

'No.'

'CORE and SNCC practically held the faculty hostage until they agreed to add a black studies course to the curriculum, taught by Eldridge Cleaver, no less. And California taxpayers are expected to support that? It's crazy.'

'Well, I don't know,' Gwen said carefully. She really wanted to like Sara, but she couldn't be friends with a racist. 'I can see their point.'

Sara gave her a sharp look. 'You may be right. Anyway, as I was saying, we don't have many on campus yet, but the feds forced government officials to issue a statement that landlords who discriminated racially would lose the university approval. So the good ole boy landlords said fine, we'll rent to juniors and seniors who don't have to live in approved housing, we'll rent to non-students, we don't give a shit, but we'll die before we integrate. That's the south for you.' She took off her leather sandals and flung them across the room, lying back on the bed. 'Jesus, this thing is lumpy. It's not going to work at all. Do you mind if I confiscate the third desk?'

'What for?'

'I want to use it as a bed. At least for now anyway.'

'You're going to sleep on a desk?'

'Sure, why not? I can put a slab of foam on it. It'll be great for my back.'

'You could sleep on the floor, couldn't you?' Gwen said shyly. 'I mean on the foam on the floor. They had

157

some photos of that in *Cosmo* last month. It looked pretty comfortable.'

'*Cosmo*? Really . . .' Sara drawled. 'No, I'm afraid I'm not up to sleeping on a Texas floor.' She gave an exaggerated shudder. 'Nobody, not even po' white trash sleeps on the floor. You got to be as far off the ground as possible to git away from them nasty June bugs and big ole roaches.'

'Are you from the south?' Gwen asked. Sara seemed to switch accents with lightning speed.

'No.' Sara sat up quickly. 'Say, listen. What did you put on the registration form in the space for sex?'

'Well, F for female, of course. What else would you put?'

Sara laughed, that husky, sexy laugh. 'I put "yes — as often as I can get it." '

'You didn't.' Gwen watched, fascinated, as Sara spread a tie-dyed silk scarf on the bed in front of her. On the scarf she placed a box of matches, an English toffee tin, a packet of rolling papers and what looked like a silver paper clip. She opened the tin, took out something that looked like dried herbs and placed a pinch in the middle of the cigarette paper. She licked the edge of the paper, rolled it up neatly and twisted the end. Licking one end of the cigarette, she placed the other end in her mouth and then lit the end she had licked. Gwen knew she must be smoking marijuana. At St Mary's the nuns had shown a film on the evils of marijuana right after the hygiene film that showed you how to attach a Kotex to a sanitary belt. 'Sara, what are you doing?' She ran to shut the door to their room.

Sara took a long drag and held her breath, her words coming out in tight little gasps. 'What does it look like? Here, have a hit.' She held the joint out.

'Sara, is that . . .' Gwen searched for the right word, 'is that pot?'

158

'We call it grass now, dear heart.' Sara stretched out languorously on the bed, her black hair gleaming against the white pillow. 'Pure Peruvian. Try it.'

'No thank you.' Under her starched collar, Gwen was sweating. What if the dorm mother came upstairs to check on them? What if the girls next door discovered they were sharing the wing corner with a couple of drug addicts? As the sweet smell of burning leaves filled the room, Gwen rushed to the window and flung it open.

'Why don't you stuff a towel at the base of the door? Like John Barrymore in *Dinner at Eight*.' Sara sounded as if she could hardly breathe. 'What are you so paranoid for? Everybody does grass. It's completely harmless.'

'They haven't proved that for sure,' Gwen snapped. 'Look, I just don't want to get thrown out of university on the first day, do you mind? What you choose to do is your own business, just don't involve me in your . . . vices, that's all.' Even to her own ears she sounded like a total prig, but she just couldn't afford to jeopardize her record.

'I didn't ask for a lecture, thanks very much. Silly, they're not going to throw us out. We haven't even paid our first semester's tuition. Believe me, they want our bucks. Pay now, get dropped later. All right, all right, I'll put it out.' She hastily stubbed out the joint, placed it in the little silver clip, put it in the plastic bag and dropped it into her purse. 'Are you satisfied, Miss Legree?'

Gwen felt foolish. It was Sara's room just as much as it was hers. A year was a long time to be closeted with someone you didn't get along with. And she had to admit she found Sara intriguing. 'Look, I'm sorry, Sara. I overreacted. Where I come from they've practically never heard of grass. Bowness, Alberta, well it's a pretty straight place. It's called the buckle of the Bible belt. Of course they all drink themselves into oblivion at the local hotel beverage room and trash everybody behind each other's back. If you're not exactly like everybody else, they want to ride you out of town on a rail.'

For the first time Sara's guard seemed to slip and she smiled warmly. 'Believe me, I know what you mean. Hey, listen, forget it.' Rummaging through her shoulder bag, she brought out a small white card. 'Did you have to sign this? A pre-registration oath?'

'Sure. You have to sign it before you can register.'

'I don't believe this thing. I mean, a loyalty oath. It's like something out of the dark ages.' Sara read from the card: ' "I am not now nor ever have been a member of any organization that is on the US Attorney General's list of subversive organizations." I've never heard of half these organizations, have you?' She read aloud. ' "The Friends of Italia, the Friends of Poland, the Friends of Roumania, the Communist Party, IWU and the United Klans of America.' Sara signed the card, turned it over and then wrote something on the back.

'What did you write?'

Sara handed the card over to Gwen. She had written, 'Signed in protest.'

'Are you a Marxist?'

'Definitely not. Couldn't be further from it.'

'Lots of people back home vote New Democrat. That's Socialist. You can even vote Communist if you want.'

'Not here. It's illegal. I'm an anarchist. I don't believe in any form of government. I've never been a member of any of those organizations but I protest at the unconstitutionality of having to sign a piece of paper saying so. It's wrong, it's morally wrong, just one more example of Big Brother is watching you.' Her eyes flashing with sudden anger, she grabbed the card out of Gwen's hand and ripped it in half.

'Sara, don't. They won't let you register if you don't sign the oath.'

160

'I'm not completing registration,' Sara said coolly.
'What?'

'You heard me.' She tucked her legs up under her on
the bed. 'I'm not going to register. Not yet.'

'What do you mean? You have to register.'

'No I don't. The deadline is September twenty-five.
That's three weeks away. I'm just going to shop around
a bit, sit in on some classes, audit a few seminars. Once
you get enroled in a course, it's hard to change.'

'But that's against the rules.'

'No it isn't. Not any written rule. Once you've paid
your fees you're a member of the university and you can
enrol in any course at any time.'

'I don't see the point.'

'Look, Gwen,' Sara said impatiently. 'A university is
supposed to be a place for self-discovery. I just got here.
How can I make an informed choice between courses and
professors when I don't know anything about them? I'd
like to hang out here for a bit without any academic
pressure.'

'But you're here to learn something, aren't you?'

'Sure I'm here to learn how to think critically and
independently. UT is here to safeguard society's values.
We're going to be in conflict, but that's life.'

'What makes you think you know more than the
professors do? I thought the whole purpose of a
university is to put you in competition with other
academics.' Sara's ideas seemed radical to her, but it was
exhilarating to be taken into her confidence like this.

'I'm not in competition with other students here. I'm
competing within myself, against myself. I'll set my own
academic standards. I don't need teachers or exams to
do that for me.'

'Then why bother going to university at all? Why don't
you just go back to wherever it is you came from, sit in
a room and educate yourself.'

161

Sara swung her legs off the bed and got to her feet. 'Because I want to get to the top, sweetie. I intend to set this university on its ear.'

'But is that right?'

Sara looked at her with real interest for the first time. 'Very perceptive of you. What I want and what I think is right are always getting mixed up.'

'What do you mean?'

'Nothing,' Sara gave her a quick smile. 'Forget it. What I want right now is food, but what I think is right for us is to avoid ptomaine poison in the dining-hall. Let's go out and celebrate, OK. We're roommates. I think we're going to be great friends. What do you say? Dinner's on me.'

'Sounds good.' This beautiful, strong-minded woman liked her. For the first time, the pain of her family's rejection began to recede.

'Want to hit the San Jack?'

'Sure. What is it?'

'San Jacinto Café. Best food bargain in Austin. Chicken fried steak, biscuits with cream gravy, okra, Texas-style chilli, you name it. Most expensive thing on the menu is two bucks.'

'What's chicken fried steak?'

'Something that should never be done to decent meat. You take a piece of steak, dip it in batter and fry it in heavy duty grease. Supposed to be Elvis Presley's favourite food. It's really revolting but you should try it once. It's practically the official state dish down here.'

'Well, since you're buying . . .' Gwen reached for the orange and white armband that was on the rickety night table by the bed.

'It's an experience, I guarantee it.' She started for the door. 'What are you doing?'

'We've got to wear our frosh bands.'

'Forget it, I'm not wearing that crap. This is not Nazi

162

Germany for Christ's sake. Don't be so chickenshit.'

'I'm not chickenshit.'

'I think you are, but my guess is it's really not your fault. You're obviously bright, but somebody or something has been trying to keep you in line and scared you half to death.' As Gwen opened her mouth to protest, 'Don't tell me about it if you don't want to. Come on, let's go get a brew.'

As they walked across the mall, Gwen fingered the armband over her white blouse. How could Sara have figured her out so quickly? She was still scared, and angry with herself for being scared. More than anything, Gwen wanted to put her past behind her and get on with her new life.

Huge hands suddenly grasped her shoulders, lifted her up into the air and swung her on to the sidewalk. She looked up into the meaty red face of a Texas Longhorn lineman wearing the orange and white scrimmage uniform. 'You're standing on the grass, freshette.'

'There's no sign,' Gwen trembled.

'The grass is off limits to you until next week, freshette.' His piggy little eyes flicked over to Sara and assessed her with interest. He reached for her with his great ham-hock arms.

'Hands off, meatloaf,' said Sara, stepping daintily and purposefully into the centre of the sidewalk.

'You a freshie, too?' Flushed and sweating, the big guy looked as if he were mentally licking his lips. He towered over her.

'Yes,' Sara said. 'So what?'

'So you ain't dressed properly, that's what. Like your friend here. Where's your armband, freshette?'

'You don't like what I'm wearing?' Sara smiled seductively up at him through fringed eyelashes.

'Yeah, now that you mention it, I do, baby. You got a nice pair on you,' he said appreciatively.

163

'Sweet of you to point that out,' Sara purred.

'Yeah, you're a right little kitten mitten. I'd like to wrap myself up in you.'

'Fuck off, beef head,' Sara said simply. 'Wrap it up and send it special delivery to CARE.'

His face seemed to inflate like a frog's, turning from red to purple. 'Watch your mouth, you little smartass bitch. You don't tell a sophomore to f---, I don't even want to repeat it. You don't talk to an upper classman like that, not if you want to stay on this campus. You better get yourself straight, girl, or you're gonna get kicked outta here before the leaves are off the trees.'

'Look, fart face,' Sara smiled sweetly up at him, 'don't hassle me. The university may turn its head and look the other way when it comes to hazing, but they sure as hell aren't going to throw me out of school for disobeying a pig like you. And don't give me any of that class structure freshman channelling bullshit. You couldn't find your asshole if your head was up it.'

Cowering behind an oak tree with a Stokely Carmichael poster tacked on it, Gwen waited for the quarterback to pummel them both into the ground, but instead his little piggy eyes narrowed into his fat cheeks and he started to laugh. 'I like a woman who can talk tough and dirty. You'd make a great cheerleader, honey. Longhorns are shootin' for number one again this season.'

'No thanks,' Sara slung her purse back over her shoulder.

'They only take one freshie on the squad. I think you could make it. It's an honour, baby.'

'Not interested. You ready, Gwen?'

'I'm right here.' Gwen crept out from behind the tree. He followed after them, calling out, 'Well, hey, don't go away mad, sweet thing. You want to go get a beer at Scholtz's?'

164

'No thanks.'

'Hey, you can't walk away from me like this!'

Sara didn't pause for a second. 'Watch me.' She grabbed Gwen's hand and the two of them took off running towards the coloured lights of the San Jacinto Café. Once inside, they both dissolved in laughter.

'Did you see the look on his face?' Sara shrieked, collapsing on to one of the orange vinyl booths in the dimly lit restaurant.

'I'll never forget it,' Gwen was out of breath from the running.

'I don't think he'll ever forget it either,' Sara said, reaching down under her long skirt to tighten the straps on her sandals. She grabbed the waitress going by and ordered two draught beers.

'He just melted into a little puddle at your feet like the Wicked Witch of the West. You were amazing.' They both laughed.

'What a pig,' Sara said. 'Sometimes I think men and women should be kept apart. Except for sex, of course. In fact, I'm not so sure that most men shouldn't be kept locked up most of the time and just let out every now and then to service us, to do their duty.'

'Well, that's sort of the way it was for me my last year in high school,' Gwen said shyly.

'That sounds mysterious. Tell me more.'

'No, all I mean is, I went to a girls' school back in Alberta. We used to get together with guys every couple of months; the rest of the time we were kept apart, like enemies. I think Canadian men still have a lot of the British influence in them. You know, they're raised to believe that women are like a foreign continent, dark and mysterious, waiting to suck them in.'

'And we are, darling, we are,' Sara said, taking a slug of her ice-cold draught. 'So you went to an exclusive girls' school?'

'Yes,' Gwen sipped hers tentatively. American beer seemed a lot thinner than Canadian.

'Aha, I knew it. You're a genuine upper-class Canadian.'

'Sorry to disappoint you. My father works in oil.'

'Right.' Sara's eyes lit up.

'On the rigs. Well, he used to. Now he sells machinery.'

'Oh.'

'It's going to be strange going to classes with guys and sitting right next to them. I'm kind of nervous about it. I mean, when that football player picked me up off the ground, I didn't know what to do . . .'

'You're OK, Gwen, just a bit naïve.' Sara downed the last of her beer in one gulp.

Gwen wondered if Sara was really as tough as she acted. She seemed quick to categorize everyone and so sure of the validity of the categories. 'Well, I thought you were wonderful.'

'He's a pig.' She wiped the foam off her mouth and ordered another draught.

'But aren't you worried?'

'About what?'

'He'll have it in for you now.'

'Great,' Sara said smoothly. 'I told you, I'm a shit disturber.'

'For the next month, Gwen watched while Sara went to work on the restructuring of the university. Within a week she had formed 'liber-action'. 'What does that mean?' Gwen wanted to know.

Sara took a deep breath, 'We're a group of students dedicated to academic experimentation with the sole purpose of bringing together students and faculty for an intellectual exchange of ideas . . .'

'Yeah, but what does it really mean?'

'Less emphasis on grades and exams. We learn what

166

we want to learn and we move on when we decide we're ready to move on. Did you hear that almost a quarter of the new freshmen at UT have refused to register? It's working already.' Sara laughed in triumph.

Little by little, Gwen found herself drawn into Sara's plan of action. With Jeff Bernstein and his girlfriend Linda Ackerman, Terry Kramer and John Scott, they formed a core group of student activists, which grew in numbers as the semester went on. They helped to set up people-generated classes, groups of students who wanted to study one particular topic in a field with teachers to be used only as resource persons. They held sit-ins and strikes until the university began to listen to their demands. Sara was in the forefront of the movement, with Gwen following her right into the middle of the controversy. It was exciting for her to be involved with Sara in a mutual cause.

By mid-term, they were fast friends and would stay up until the early hours of the morning planning their strategy, getting only a couple of hours of sleep. The university administration had not yet agreed to their demands for an across-the-board policy on grades, so Gwen continued to study hard for all her regular courses. Sara seemed to do well without even trying or at least she liked to give that appearance. They went to movies together and listened to music together. They listened to 'Sgt. Pepper' and 'Let It Bleed'. They agreed that the Beatles were basically clean, even if 'Lucy in the Sky with Diamonds' was really about LSD, but the Stones were truly down and dirty. Mick Jagger was telling an entire generation, 'You can't always get what you want', Grace Slick was singing 'One pill makes you larger the other makes you small', and Jim Morrison was urging, 'Come on baby, light my fire'. Gwen still refused to smoke any dope, but being with Sara made her feel high. Sara seemed to love being with her, too. Yet as close as they

167

got, Sara remained an enigma to Gwen. What was her family like? 'I consider myself an orphan. I won't be able to get anywhere if I'm bound to tradition or family. We have to exist in the now.' Did she believe in God? 'I'm a heretic in the truest sense of the word.' What were her genuine political beliefs? 'Consider me a freelance,' was really all Gwen could get out of her.

The University of Texas campus was a Pandora's box of activist groups, all of them screaming out at full voice. New buzz words were everywhere: establishment, flower power, love-in, subculture, druggie. Fucking was called balling. The police were pigs. When students stole shampoo from Tower Drugs and canned goods from the Piggly Wiggly, they called it 'liberating the goods' and joked about how they were 'ripping off the establishment'.

Gwen traded in skirt and blazer for jeans and beaded cotton tops. Sara was beautiful whatever she wore. Beautiful, outspoken, controversial, provocative, but above all, fast and wild. Sometimes she felt as though they both needed to stop to catch their breath, but Sara was constantly moving on. To Gwen her roommate was like the Red Queen in *Alice through the Looking Glass*, running, running until she was out of breath, just to stay in one place. She kept pushing Gwen to live as she did.

'You know, Gwenny, you're a stack rat,' Sara said, referring to her long hours in the library. Gwen loved the building where the shelves descended six floors underground. She liked to pretend she was in a sci-fi fantasy, living in a futuristic world.

'That's better than being a slut.' Outwardly she condemned Sara's success with men, but inwardly she was envious of it. 'Speaking of which, I wish you'd do your dirty work on alien soil.' Sara was always sneaking her latest conquest into their room.

'Why don't you open your eyes and ears? You might

168

learn something. It's not going to go away, you know. You have to deal with it some time.'

'What?'

'S-E-X.'

'Oh, that.' But she wasn't up to dealing with it. She bought a set of earplugs and a sleep mask. Sara went to Texas tea parties, which were held in the FIJI frat house, the wildest fraternity on campus. Texas tea was a lethal combination of iced tea and over-proof alcohol mixed up in garbage cans. The object of those who attended was to get as bombed as possible as quickly as possible, and not to leave the party until they got laid. Attending a Texas tea party was considered the ultimate in trash. Sara rarely missed one.

'How can you do it?' Gwen was sleepy and angry at the same time. 'It's three o'clock in the morning and you look like you just crawled out of bed.'

'I did,' Sara smiled happily, her dark hair a wild tangle, her make-up softly smeared.

'You're getting a bad reputation.'

Sara gave a little shrug. 'If it feels right, do it. For God's sakes, Gwenny-penny, this isn't the Middle Ages. There's a sexual revolution going on or hadn't you heard?'

'Sure, and you're the one who's revolting.' She was starting to wake up.

'You're right, kiddo, you are so right,' Sara giggled, still tipsy. For Sara, the sex available all around her was like so much free candy. How could you turn it down?

'But what if you get pregnant?'

'Can't. I'm on the pill.'

'You didn't get the pill from the health centre?'

'Sure. I told them I was engaged. They'll give it to you if say you're getting married.'

'But what if . . .?'

'Oh, Gwenny, Jenny, Gwen, Jen,' Sara jumped on to

her bed and tickled her mercilessly. 'What if? What if? Do you know how often you say that? It should be emblazoned on your forehead, what if? Look, I like sex. I can't help it. And I don't see any reason to keep the guys waiting. Not like old Mary Jane. Old Sniffles.' Both of them started to laugh. Mary Jane Snurf, alias Sniffles, was a home ec. major down the hall who came in every day in tears over some new culinary crisis. 'Mah mayonnaise separated. It did worse than separate, it actually curdled. What am ah gonna do?' Once Sniffles went downstairs, saw the date waiting for her in the lobby and came straight back up again. 'A cain't go out with him,' she sniffed. 'He's not wearin' any socks.' She waited fifteen minutes until she was sure he had left. Then she went down into the common room, ran into another date, and they disappeared into the night. That date had been waiting for Sara and she never forgave Sniffles for it.

'I forgot to tell you I got even with Sniffles,' Sara said, stripping off her rumpled skirt and blouse, flashing her perfect breasts at Gwen, and climbing, nude, into her own bed.

'You never told me that. How?' Gwen yawned and got under the covers.

'Well, you know the guy she's pinned to now, that pre-law student who's related to coach Darryl Royal?'

'Oh, yes.' Gwen vaguely recalled a tall, skinny, balding blond who looked fairly ridiculous in his Nehru jacket.

'Well, a couple of weeks ago, I ran into him at the Galbraith-Buckley debate.'

'And?'

'And I took him to bed and ruined him.' Sara laughed her husky laugh which always made Gwen's throat tickle. She wondered what that meant. How could you ruin a man? She was afraid to ask.

170

# Five

'And what are you going to do for us?'

Miriam faced the panel of eight judges at the National Theatre School auditions. The faces of the other seven blurred as she focused on the man who had asked the question, Morgan Llewellyn, the school's director.

In the late sixties, people talked about having an aura. You were supposed to close your eyes, rub them hard, and then when you opened them, look straight into a mirror. Supposedly you would see the halo around your head and you could distinguish its colour. That was your aura. One's personality and future could be determined by its colour, one's potential by its brilliance. Miriam had thought it was all a lot of garbage until she met Morgan. Silvery and shimmering, his aura enclosed him in a magic circle.

The minute she saw Morgan she wanted him to put his arms around her. And that is exactly what he did. She'd been waiting to audition for over an hour; the judges were way behind. In the bathroom, theatre school candidates were toking up, throwing up, and giving up. Each knew that there were eight hundred other applicants for the sixteen places and out of those sixteen places, ten went to male applicants and only six to female. This was to get them used to the realities of the classical theatre where there are six times as many roles for men as there are for women.

Miriam was nervous, too, but she was determined that

the competition would not see her sweat. She found herself a corner and worked on her monologues, one classical and one modern, as the school had requested. Every fifteen minutes she would check her red lipstick and freshen her green eyeshadow.

Morgan Llewellyn was a massive man with long greying hair, remarkably blue eyes and a nose that belonged on a Roman coin. His face had a ravaged look that Miriam found disturbing and compelling, a cross between Merlin the magician and Fagin.

'And what are you going to do for us?' Morgan patiently repeated the question.

'Helena from *All's Well* and Helen from *A Taste of Honey*. Two Helens, is that OK?' She laughed nervously.

'Good contrast.' His voice betrayed no emotion. 'Go ahead. In your own time. Take all the time you need to prepare.'

Miriam wasn't quite sure what he meant by 'prepare'. She had learned her lines and so she got on with it. She swallowed, took a deep breath, and raced through both speeches, giving them a force and energy fuelled partly by emotion and partly by nerves. There was a brief silence when she had finished. Morgan rose from behind the table and walked over to her slowly. Then he took her hand and looked directly into her eyes, as though he saw something there that no one else had ever seen. She expected him to say marvellous or well done or even lousy, terrible, but instead he merely said, 'That wasn't you. Do Helena again and this time do it in your own voice, using your own words if you wish. Forget the text. Just speak to me. Reach me.' He stood back a few paces, arms folded. She started again, faltering, but he stopped her before she was even halfway through. 'No, that's not it.'

'Tell me what you want,' Miriam said, trying to keep the pleading out of her voice. 'I take direction very well.

Tell me what you want me to do and I'll do it.'

'That's the point. I don't want you to do anything. Just let go. Stop listening to yourself, judging yourself. Don't perform.' Then, noticing she was shivering: 'What's the matter? Are you cold, lovely?'

'No,' she whispered, unable to stop shaking, unable to turn away from those piercing blue eyes. 'I guess I'm just a little nervous.'

He smiled and reached out to her, enclosing her in a great bear hug. 'So am I,' he said softly, 'so am I.' He slipped off his brown cardigan sweater and wrapped it around her. Almost instantly her trembling stopped. 'Now try the speech again,' he urged her. 'Start from the other end of the room and come to me. Affect me. Scream, cry, hit me, whatever you feel like doing, but make me feel the pain that Helena feels, the pain of loving someone who will never really love you. Reach out. Touch me with your soul.' The other judges in the huge, draughty rehearsal hall seemed to melt away. Haltingly she moved towards him, concentrated on the lean, intense figure on the other side of the room. Helena's words eased out of her, then gradually her feeling of loss and the power of the speech overwhelmed her and carried her along. By the time she reached Morgan they were both in tears. 'How did that feel?' he asked her gently.

'Strange. Frightening, I guess. I forgot where I was and just focused on you.'

'A very good place to start.' They both laughed and their eyes locked together again. For a moment, Miriam thought she felt Morgan reach up and brush the tears from her eyes, but she knew his hand had never left his side. Then, suddenly all brisk business again, Morgan said, 'Thank you very much. We'll let you know.' Miriam found her way out of the door and was back in her room at the hotel before she realized she was still wearing his sweater.

The telegram informing Miriam that she had been accepted by the National Theatre School of Canada provoked an uproar in the Newman household. 'I don't want you leaving the country,' her father said, 'You're too young.'

'I'm eighteen. I can do what I want.'

'Not as long as I'm paying for it.'

'I'll get a summer job. I'll cash in one of my bonds if you'll let me. I've got to try this. This is one of the top acting schools in the whole world. Eight hundred actors were trying to get in and they took *me*. That means I've got talent.'

'Maybe they took you because you're from the US and thy need those American bucks, did you ever think of that?' her father asked.

'I'm an actress, Daddy. I've got to take risks. I've got to go where my creative urges take me.'

'But to Montreal?' her mother interrupted. 'To a foreign country? They don't even speak English there, it's all French.'

'The school is half French, half English. All my classes will be in English.'

'There's nothing but sex and drugs in a city like Montreal.'

'There's nothing but sex and drugs at UCLA. I should think you would want me out of there.'

'I'll foot the bill for one year,' her father said sternly. 'If you make a success of it, more power to you. But if it doesn't work out, I want you back on American soil.'

Climbing the steps of the Theatre Monument National where her first class would be held, Miriam was filled with a sense of becoming a part of theatrical history. The Monument was over a hundred years old. Sarah Bernhardt herself had trodden these boards. She hugged

174

herself with excitement. The students for the French and English sections met together in the theatre. Miriam sat in a velvet seat and stared up at the roped-off balcony, the private boxes, and the high painted ceiling. Morgan Llewellyn gave the opening address, switching effortlessly from French to English. The boys in the French section looked intriguing in their tight pants and black turtlenecks. The boys from the English section looked boring, not a leading man among them, Miriam thought, although there was a guy across the room from her with twinkling eyes and a rather sardonic smile who looked at least bright. The French girls were petite and skinny with carefully made-up faces and a studied air of worldliness and sophistication. One of them was wearing a strange sort of Greek toga shift that was so short that when she sat down you could see the string of her Tampax. Miriam was shocked and fascinated. Most of the English girls were overweight with long stringy hair and large breasts.

'You have all been chosen to be part of a very special experiment,' Morgan was saying. 'The National is a relatively new thing in this country. Up until now to train as an actor you had to go to Britain or maybe to the US, although in my opinion there are no decent classical schools in the States.' Miriam beamed at him, hanging on every word. She knew she had come to the right place. 'Acting is growing. Think of yourself as a child again. Develop at your own rate and take the next step only when and if you are ready. All we ask is that you remain open to any and all stimuli.'

Montreal was a city full of stimuli. Canada was a lot like the US, but Montreal seemed to be a country in and of itself. Miriam instantly fell in love with it, the elegant old buildings combined with the modern chrome and glass of the new shopping and office complexes and the underground centres connected by tunnels to each other beneath a city that could be snowbound in the long Canadian winters. She loved the Metro built for Expo '67 and the glittering crystal opulence of the Places des Arts where visiting opera and ballet companies played. Fresno and LA seemed like a series of endless shopping malls compared to the sophistication of a real city like Montreal. She loved the French spoken all around her, the *joual*, with its fast rhythm, strong nasal accent, and strange mixture of English and French idioms. On Saturdays, she explored the Main, St Laurent Boulevard, which divided the French and English sections of her city right down the middle. The smells and sights and sounds of the place assaulted her senses. And everywhere she looked there was a United Nations array of fabulous food, from the exquisite boulangeries and patisseries to the Greek, Indian, Hungarian, and Chinese restaurants, to the expensive gourmet dinners of Old Montreal. However, Miriam wasn't so sure about the school, now.

'Some of you feel that you are ready to fly when in fact you are just beginning to learn how to crawl,' Morgan had said to them on the first day. Miriam, who had more stage experience than anyone else in the class, was frustrated to find herself stuck in the crawling stage. Why weren't they allowed to do any real acting? Why were they spending all their time pretending to be flowers or animals?

Morgan drew most of his images from nature. 'That's all acting is,' he told them, 'that sense of discovery. Open to any and all stimuli. Let's play. Like children. It should be fun. Even when it's most painful, it should be fun.'

Miriam didn't think it was fun; she found it incredibly hard. They did trust exercises in which you had to run across the room with your eyes closed and 'trust' that someone else would catch you before you hit the wall. Miriam always opened her eyes just at the last minute.

The focus on self was starting to bother Miriam, but it was hard to get away from it, Acting was all about how you look, how you sound, how you feel. You had to discover yourself, motivate yourself, sell yourself, exploit yourself.

Once a week an acting student had to sit in the 'hot seat' and be badgered by his fellow classmates until he broke down and cried. It reminded Miriam of the truth game she had played in the Hell Club back at Roosevelt High. Sitting in the hot seat, she refused to cry and then she couldn't cry. She would sit in the seat for hours on end while the others chanted at her, screamed at her, alternating between praise and abuse. Everybody else cracked in the seat. Miriam remained a stone.

Yet Morgan could make her cry. Not directly. Not since the day of her audition. But sometimes she would look at him, wearing that old brown sweater, holding a Gitane in one hand and gesturing grandly with the other, telling tales about his boyhood in Wales, how a gypsy had told him he would be dead by the time he was fifty and now time was running out — but how he couldn't die until he had played Lear, and Miriam's eyes would unexpectedly fill with tears. When he spoke in Welsh, she was moved by the grandeur of the words, even though she had no idea what they meant. She was drawn to his passion, even though she couldn't understand his obsession with childhood. Childhood had been the unhappiest time in her life. Morgan said he adored the childlike quality in his actors, particularly in the women. Once when he telephoned Miriam at home to tell her a movement class was cancelled, he woke her up and upon hearing the sleep in her voice, cried with delight, 'You sound just like a six-year-old!'

Morgan's wife, Bambi, taught movement at the school. As much as the students idolized Morgan, they ridiculed her. She had a wispy, doe-like voice that matched her name, but there was nothing timid about her. Bambi wore mini skirts, and although she was almost as tall as Morgan she wore net stockings and white boots up to her crotch. The students labelled her style, 'Early sixties Lolita hooker.' She had bleached-blonde eggbeater hair like a chrysanthemum gone wrong. She allowed Morgan a very loose leash which allowed her the freedom to pursue the male students. Arriving early before class, she went straight to the green room, taking of her hip-length fun fur coat and fuzzy purple tam. Then, putting her leg up on the table, she would ask in her baby hustler voice, 'Could one of you boys undo my boots for me?' She never wore any panties and, as Christopher Albright used to say, 'That's not a sight you want to see before you've had your morning coffee.'

To the Llewellyns, having sex was like having a drink or a toke — harmless, satisfying and, if you kept yourself open to the experience, mind-expanding.

'I bet you two dollars I can grab your zipper without touching your weeny,' Bambi said, reaching directly for Christopher Albright's crotch.

'Sorry, Bambi, I don't have two dollars on me . . .

'*Oops*!' Bambi giggled. 'Uh, guess I owe you two dollars.'

Morgan never came right out and said Miriam would be a better actress if she were to have sex as often as possible, but he implied it. As he was with all his students, he was physical with her, hugging and touching her often. He was big, robust, full of joy. Did sex make him that way?

Miriam's big secret was that she was still a virgin. She'd planned to rid herself of that little encumbrance at UCLA, but she'd been too busy keeping up with the demands of a double major, classes during the day, performances at night, studying in the wee hours of the morning. Now she had to admit her parents were right about Montreal. Sex and drugs were all around her. The school was a free-flowing paradise of the let-it-be philosophy. She practised saying 'fuck' in front of the mirror so that she could pepper her conversation with the correct four-letter words. The weight of her virginity was something she could confess to no one.

With Gary Stoddard, Miriam began working on a scene from Shaw's *St Joan*. An Australian actor, short of stature, with a wily, monkeyish face, Gary was a true comic with a zany, off-the-wall sense of humour. She could always count on him to make her laugh. Miriam found him surprisingly sexy. When they rehearsed their scene together, there was always an underlying hum of sexual tension, but Gary never made a move towards her. She wondered if he might be gay like Christopher Albright, but he didn't seem to be. Often she caught him looking at her and when she returned his glance, he would wink at her as if to say, 'You and I are above all this nonsense, aren't we?' He called the hot seat exercise, 'getting fried', and the ensemble sensitivity sessions, 'group grope'.

The sensitivity sessions involved sitting opposite a partner, taking his hand and staring into his eyes until 'contact' was established. Once contact was made, you were supposed to 'explore' each other, 'moment by moment', to reach the 'centre' of your partner and get in touch with 'gut feelings'. Most of the guys seemed to carry their centres below the belt as far as Miriam could see. To find a partner, you had to close your eyes and move about the room until you came into physical contact with someone. Most of the guys closed their eyes and stuck their arms out in front of them, hands cupped, until they came in contact with tits. Sometimes Morgan would turn the lights out and 'moment to moment' really became a free-for-all. 'Getting to know you, getting to know all about you,' Gary sang under his breath, sliding around the room, peering around through half-closed lids

for Miriam — then as his hands closed around her —
'Oh, no, not you again.'

'This is a spiritual rather than a physical exercise,'
Morgan assured them. 'You should feel nothing sexual
from moment to moment. Don't try to send any specific
messages to your partner. Just be open.'

'Excuse me, Morgan, but I thought acting was reacting.
If I'm touching the female anatomy, my reaction is
bloody well going to be sexual. Does this mean I'm
flunking sensitivity?'

'If you have trouble with this exercise, Gary,' Morgan
focused on him serenely, 'if you're getting turned on by
it, then the difficulty lies with you. Perhaps you can only
channel physicality into sexuality. That's wrong . . . well,
not wrong — he hastily corrected himself — 'but it's not
the object of moment to moment.'

Miriam was definitely flunking sensitivity. Exploring
Tom Ellis's mouth with her fingertips sent shivers down
to the depths of her. Tracing the outside edge of Ronald
Ruttan's earlobe made her inner thighs quiver.
'Discovering' Brian Manton's thigh made her tremble
with desire. She must be doing it wrong because she was
definitely getting turned on. And when Tom, Ron, and
Brian 'discovered' her mouth, earlobe and thigh, she was
sure they could feel the heat rising from her body. I've
got to be more detached, she thought, pulling away
slightly.

'You're holding back, Mim lovely,' Morgan called out
from the front of the room where he was exploring Sandy
Madison moment to moment. 'Don't make a judgement,
just go with the feeling.'

'I don't understand,' she wailed to Gary over coffee.
'I'm sure I'm feeling the wrong things.'

'What you're feeling is what you're feeling. You can't
control that. I thought that was supposed to be the whole
point of this stupid exercise, but if you ask me, the real

point of moment to moment is for Morgan to get his kicks watching all of us. He is the ultimate voyeur.'

'No, he's not. He's right. I'm an uptight JAP bound by my repressions.'

'What's a Jap, something oriental?'

'Jewish American Princess.'

Gary laughed. 'Ah, now I see. If Philip Roth and Lenny Cohen say you're hung up, why then it must be so.'

'Well, we are. At least I am. I wish I could lay myself open emotionally.'

'What you're laying yourself open for is a heavy pass. Morgan's a lech. Keep an eye on that one, m'dear.'

Miriam laughed. Gary was funny and witty and growing more attractive to her daily.

Two weeks later came the end of first year crits. Out of sixteen students, only ten would be kept on. Miriam sat outside Morgan's office as several of her friends came out in tears. Her stomach was turning over and she had trouble catching her breath. She didn't know if she'd made any progress with 'the process', but she couldn't give up at this point and go back to California. There was too much at stake. As Gary came out of the room he looked shell-shocked, but he gave her hand an encouraging squeeze and she got up to go in. Morgan was staring out of the window with his back to her when she entered the room. She stood and waited, fingers resting on the back of the chair facing his desk. For a long time he said nothing, toying with the rope on the venetian blinds, idly opening and closing them, letting the light in and then shutting it out.

'Miriam,' he said finally, 'I had great hopes for you. I thought you were really special. There's no doubt you've got the talent, you've got a beautiful voice, good presence, but' — her heart caught in her mouth — 'your emotions are locked away somewhere. You analyse when

181

you should be responding; you think when you should be feeling. I don't know how to reach you.' He stopped and turned his magnetic blue eyes on her. 'I don't know if you can be reached.'

Miriam felt a tingling start at the base of her scalp and flash through her body like a high-voltage current. 'Are you trying to tell me I'm not going to be asked back for next year?'

'I don't know. I haven't made up my mind yet.'

'I'm going to be an actress,' she said fiercely. 'Kick me out if you want to but you won't keep me from acting.'

Morgan spun around. 'Of course not. You were already competent when you came to us and you will certainly be competent when you leave. But you will not be great.' Miriam swallowed hard as he continued: 'You just can't seem to open up to the experience. I think part of the problem is this friendship between you and Gary. He's an odd man, very locked up, very protective. Are you involved with him?'

'No . . . I don't know . . . not yet. What has that got to do with it?'

'The depth of your talent is different from his. He's funny, I'm not denying that, but good comedy demands that you stand outside the situation. Gary's a master at that. As a dramatic actress, you have to be in the situation. Satire can reduce any emotion, no matter how powerful, to a joke, making it meaningless and instantly dismissable. I'd hate to see you settle for that when you have so much more in you. I think that you and Gary are impeding each other's progress.'

'I don't really see why.' She thought this remark unfair. 'He's a good friend, a lot of fun. We share the same outlook on life.'

'You can't, that's my point. Gary is outside the mainstream. He's closed himself off. And he's making

182

you close yourself off, too. If you close yourself off from life how can you possibly portray it with truth?'

'I think Gary and I are good for each other. There's so much pressure here: who's going to stay, who's going to go. No matter how often you tell us we're not in competition with each other, we are. We're all in competition to please you.'

'What have I got to do with it?' He was watching her closely, standing very still.

'I don't know. I wish I did.'

'You bewilder me, you really do. I'm only a catalyst. I'm not the result, lovely.' Miriam's eyes filled with abrupt tears at his use of the endearment. 'Look, Mim, Gary feels it, too. He asked that if you do come back to the school that you stay clear of him. He's very fond of you but he doesn't want to work with you for a while.'

'What?'

'Well, you see, lovely, you reach parts of Gary that he's not ready to explore. He needs to hold you apart. You simply aren't giving him enough room to grow.'

Miriam found she was sweating violently. 'He said that?'

'Yes.' Morgan's eyes were full of gentle pity. 'He asked me to talk to you, to try to explain how he feels. The last thing he wants to do is to hurt you.'

The rejection stabbed her sharply. 'I see.' She gripped the back of the chair, fingers white. 'It looks as though everyone wants me to go, doesn't it?'

'Does it?' Morgan's voice was like a caress. 'What do you want? To go or to stay?' She couldn't answer, just stood there silently, the tears rolling unheeded now down her cheeks and gripping on to the chair. And then his arms were around her, her face crushed against his chest, the familiar smell of the brown cardigan filling her nostrils, and she was crying, great wracking sobs that

183

shook them both. She could feel a heart pounding and she didn't know whether it was her own or his. She couldn't stop shaking and she couldn't stop crying. He stood there holding her close for a long time. Gradually she became aware of the warmth of the afternoon sunlight slanting through the blinds and the street sounds from below. He moved away from her at last and rolled open the bottom drawer of his filing cabinet, taking out a bottle of Scotch and a pack of Gitanes. He offered her a cigarette but she shook her head. He lit one for himself and the strong, acrid smell made her cry again.

'God, I'm sorry, Morgan. It all seems to be coming out at once. I think I better have some Scotch.' She sat down. The shock of the liquor burned her throat and the trembling and crying began to subside. She put the mug down, wiped her eyes with his sweater, and turned to leave. With her hand on the doorknob she asked him, 'Tell me something. Why did you take me in the first place? What did you want from me?'

That drew a wry smile that crinkled his sharp blue eyes. 'Well, first of all, I wanted my sweater back. You walked off with it and I knew the only way I'd get it back was to accept you into the school.'

'Fuck that bullshit,' she said, proud of the way the words rolled off her tongue. 'The least you can do is be honest with me. Do you have faith in my talent? Would it be worth my while to come back next year?'

He hesitated before answering, taking a long draw of his cigarette. 'You're free to make that choice. It's your decision entirely.' His cobalt eyes fixed her, well-aimed pins piercing a butterfly.

'I can't handle this freedom. Help me. Tell me what to do.'

'All right,' he said slowly. 'If you really think you're willing to make a true commitment to the process, come back to Montreal a month early next semester, around the end of August. Do a special in-depth sensitivity session. With me. Alone. It will be completely private. No pressure to perform. We'll just work for a couple of hours each day.' His hand touched her face. 'Such an open face. You really can't hide a thing, you know.' There was a fluttering in her stomach and she was suddenly wet between the legs. 'What is it, lovely? You look frightened.'

For the first time that year she met his gaze head on. 'I am.'

'I know, my lovely. I am too.' They smiled at the *déjà vu* of the words. He paused for a few moments more, then: 'Forget about it for the summer. Don't think, don't analyse. I know I'm always telling you that but it's so important. Have a wonderful summer and I'll see you in the fall.' He kissed her lightly on the forehead and she carried the burning imprint of that kiss out of the door.

She went back to Fresno for the summer, home to her parents and the security of being a child in the warmth of her family, perhaps an innocent for the last time. She taught creative drama to children in the park during the day and waited on tables at a seafood restaurant at night. Her parents saw she was determined to go back to Montreal and they didn't put up a fight. She avoided professional theatre, hardly saw a movie, resolved to keep her mind clear. Throughout the summer a motor was running inside her, as she wondered what would happen when she returned to Montreal.

Tommy Gundelfinger, home from med school, asked her out a couple of times and she went. He was six feet tall now, his acne had disappeared, he was a devotee of D.H. Lawrence and an excellent kisser. Miriam knew he would make a comfortable first lover and part of her longed to get it over with, but part of her realized she had waited this long, she could wait a little longer.

185

They sat crosslegged, facing each other, in the darkened rehearsal hall at the Monument National. The room was still, blinds drawn, windows shut tight. The strangely mirrored blue eyes were alert in the artificial gloom, fixed on her. She forced herself to return his gaze, her heart slamming wildly against the door of her chest, the sound of the sea rushing strangely through her head.

'Now,' Morgan said, touching the points of her collarbone lightly with his fingers, 'begin in your own time. Just take it slowly. Moment to moment.' As always, she felt the tremor start within her at the sound of those words. 'This is a new moment. Take it in. Experience it fully.' She ran her hands over the planes of his face quickly, superficially. Gently he put her hands aside. She took a deep breath to calm herself and started again, slowly, carefully, trying to read his features like the characters of Braille. She sketched the outline of his face, his smooth forehead, the strong curve of his jaw, tracing his eyebrows delicately, circling the bony structure of the eye sockets, then down along the hawklike nose, the curve of each nostril. When she came to his mouth she hesitated, then with a fingertip drew the outline, moving across the lips like a silent kiss; stroking his neck, feeling the powerful, thickly knotted muscles of his shoulders relaxing under her touch; the strength of his upper arms; the broad forearms corded with veins; the wide palms with their gracefully tapering fingers. She moved along his chest, kneading the muscles tapering down to his waist, the slightly soft belly, gripping the strong thighs beneath the faded jeans. She tried to keep her breathing measured . . . in for five seconds, out for five seconds. She felt no reaction from him. He continued to look at her, into her, through her. She drew her hands away with a sigh.

'Am I on the right track?' she asked in a whisper,

aching to know and yet frightened of breaking the concentration. 'Is this what . . .?' He stopped her mouth with his fingers and let the silence of the room smother them again. He picked up a strand of her hair, running his fingers through it, over and over again, then pressing it against his own face. Lightly he followed the structure of her face, returning again and again to each feature of it, with a little more pressure each time, like reading a Ouija board with a secret message hidden just below the surface of her skin. He brushed his hand back and forth across her mouth until her lips parted of her own accord and he slipped his fingers inside her mouth, sliding them in and out, in and out. She felt her cheeks go hot and dropped her glance, but he lifted her hair off her neck and turned her face up to him. He rubbed the back of her neck slowly, steadily, working one vertebra at a time, circling the hollow of her throat, feeling her pulse beat wildly at his touch. His hand grazed her breast and she caught her breath as the nipple immediately hardened, clearly outlined under her leotard. She flushed with embarrassment; she wasn't wearing a bra. His hand moved down to her waist and she fought the urge to grab it and pull it back up to her breast. She felt herself incline toward him, muscles rigid, breath rattling in her throat. She curled her hands into tight little fists and bit down on the inside of her mouth. When his hands cupped the heavy weight of her breasts a low moan escaped her. She pulled back instantly, shielding herself with her arms.

'Oh, God, Morgan, I'm so sorry! I know I'm doing this wrong. I keep getting my impulses confused.' Her throat was thick and she coughed, trying to clear it, laughing at her own discomfort. And then her eyes filled with tears.

In one smooth move he slipped the leotard off her shoulder. She gasped as the cool air hit her naked breast and then groaned as the warmth of his mouth surrounded her. Involuntarily she arched her back, thrusting to him. Her hand shot out, under his blue work shirt, grabbing at his chest, squeezing and pulling at it. He bit her nipple gently, then sucked hard, making her scream with pleasure. She tried to control herself, frightened at her own abandonment. She pulled his face up to hers, kissing him open-mouthed, taking his tongue and drawing it into hers as though she had been doing it all her life. His tongue felt large, alive and wet and demanding. She wanted to take him in at every orifice. Morgan lifted himself away from her and she reached for him instinctively, dragging him back, pressing him hard against her, but he held her apart from him for a moment, her arms behind her back. 'Oh, please,' she whispered, 'please,' unsure what she was pleading for.

'Miriam, look at me,' he commanded, his normally gentle voice like thunder in her ears. 'This is truly a new moment. Do you want this? Are you sure? I don't want us to hurt each other.'

'Yes,' she whispered, almost choking on the word. 'I want it.'

He undressed her with great care, kissing each part of her as she was revealed, licking along her thighs, parting them gently at first and then more insistently, spreading them wide, holding her up, sliding a finger, then his tongue, in and out, as she opened herself to him, the heat of her clutching at him. Back and forth he moved over her, stroking, rubbing, the rhythm of her own breathing increasing as she raised her knees and with her own hands clutched at her breasts, lifting herself up, moving against his hand and mouth. Suddenly she felt a great light inside, an increase of excitement that was almost painful in its exquisiteness and then a series of inner contractions. She could actually feel her muscles clenching and then letting go of his fingers, and she screamed with pleasure. Her breathing slowed and she opened her eyes to see him looking down at her lovingly. Once again he asked her, 'Do you want this?'

'Yes,' she said. 'Oh yes, I want you inside me.'

He unsnapped the buttons of his work shirt and threw it on the floor. He unbuckled his belt and slid off his jeans, revealing himself erect. The sight of him was so beautiful, so overpowering, that Miriam had to turn away. His cock was long and thin and uncircumcised, as beautifully tapering as his hands. She was fascinated by its exotic hood, the sensitive foreskin folded like the petals of a delicate flower pulled back to reveal the bud. But the length of it frightened her. She wanted to tell him that she was a virgin but she was afraid. So she opened her legs wide and braced herself. But he took her hand and placed it around the base, sliding it up and down, teaching her how to touch him. He slid her fingers to the head, rubbing them in the sticky liquid there and then placing her fingers in her mouth. It tasted salty, like sea water, the essence of sea. She touched him lightly, encircling him with her fingers, but he closed her fingers more forcefully around him. He moved himself over her, supporting himself on his elbows and placed himself between her legs, sliding his cock slowly back and forth. Just the head inside, then a quick thrust to the hilt. Miriam winced. He drew out immediately and looked at her questioningly. She smiled and, taking him in her hand, guided him in again, tightening against him. She cried out. But as he moved to withdraw again, she held on to him and relaxed, moving against him, meeting his thrust, forcing him to thrust into her. She locked her arms and legs around him and hung on for dear life as they rocked back and forth. Once he went too far and she tensed again. He withdraw at once and, looking down, saw that he was covered with blood.

'Oh, my darling, my little lovely, why didn't you tell me?' he crooned. She shook her head wordlessly and

189

brought him back into her. 'What a gift, my love, I'm sorry, I can't stop' — and he plunged into her again, gripping her buttocks, digging his fingers into her soft flesh, driving into her until he came with a roar. He rested on her for a moment and then she rolled away from under him, exhausted. He grabbed her and kissed her, little kisses all over her face and eyelids. 'Oh bless you, my darling, bless you for that, you clever girl. Such a wealth of love. I have never made love to anyone for the first time. You've broken through, my lovely, crossed the barriers of trust. We're on our way.' He kissed her deeply and she felt herself flutter again. 'Now I know I was too fast for you, my darling,' he said, drawing her close to him again. 'This one's for you.'

By the time the rest of the class returned to school, their affair was in full swing. The first thing Morgan did was to gather them all together in the green room for a sharing session, to fill each other in on progress made during the summer months away from Montreal.

'Any breakthroughs?' Morgan wanted to know. 'Even faltering steps?' Everyone had something to share. Gary had returned to Australia and realized he now felt more like a Canadian than an Aussie. 'It's saner here,' he told them. 'They're doing some interesting film projects back home but I really think there's more opportunity here.'

'Did you take any work?' Morgan asked. 'You know that's against the rules.'

'Yes I did.' Gary was defiant. 'It's a stupid rule and I don't see why it should matter to you what I do with my free time.' Miriam had a terrible feeling that he had picked up on the vibrations between her and Morgan. How could he not?

Christopher Albright shared the fact that he'd had his first heterosexual experience, 'Just to see what it was like.

190

An actor has to be open to any and all stimuli but frankly, kids, I prefer the boys to the girls.' R.D. Grainger talked about working on the geriatric ward of a hospital for the insane in Thunder Bay. 'How does that Neil Young song go? "Hopeless, hopeless, hopeless" or is it "helpless"? I don't know but believe me that's exactly what it was like.' Miriam sat quietly, viewing the whole exercise as a variation on the old how I spent my summer vacation routine, until Sandy Madison made the startling confession that she'd actually been pregnant last year and over the summer vacation had had a baby and given it up for adoption so she could come back to school in the fall.

'A brave choice,' Morgan said proudly, and the class was respectfully quiet.

Then Morgan raised his hand and all heads turned towards the master. 'Miriam and I have something from the summer that we want to share with you.' Miriam looked up instantly, lifting the heavy curtain of hair back from her face. 'We have been drawn together into a love relationship. We've touched each other in a very special way.' Another profound silence greeted this announcement. Miriam looked down at her hands, staring at the blue spot where a piece of pencil lead had bedded itself two years ago during a final exam. 'It places a huge burden of trust on you people,' Morgan went on, 'but one that I know you can handle. Miriam and I want you to share in our happiness. We will lay ourselves completely open to you.' Gary snorted. Morgan fixed him with a glance and continued, 'What Miriam and I have found has nothing to do with my relationship with Bambi and it will not have anything to do with the process, the work that all of us in our own magic circle will be doing this year.'

'Except that Miriam will get to play all the best parts,' Sandy Madison muttered.

'It's disconcerting to be around the two of you,' Chris Albright said. 'I feel as if I want to run home and take a cold shower every hour on the hour.'

'You've got some nerve, Llewellyn,' Gary said, but his eyes were burning into Miriam, with a look that said how could you betray me like this?

'Is that how you feel?' Morgan pinned him down. 'Tell me how you really feel.'

'Oh, skip it,' Gary said and walked out.

Miriam wanted the earth to open up and swallow her on the spot. How could Morgan do this to her? To remove her from the ranks and elevate her to a special pedestal. The smug, self-satisfied pride in his face almost made her want to hit him. What right had he to make their private passion public? Then his cobalt blue-eyed gaze turned its love on her and she felt enveloped in its warmth and privilege.

'It won't affect my relationship with any of you,' Morgan promised them. 'There is plenty of me to go around. Nothing is going to be different.'

Outwardly Morgan was true to his promise. He gave Miriam no extra time during class hours. If anything he treated her with more reserve than before. She was consumed with jealousy watching him with the other students, unable to stop watching him as he lingered in the green room to talk to Christopher or when he drew Sandy aside to whisper a note of direction in her ear. She knew he was often unfaithful, to her and to Bambi. To him fidelity was a ridiculous concept and she knew she couldn't demand it. He didn't demand it of her either, but she was faithful. She couldn't look at or think of anyone else.

It was obvious that even Bambi felt threatened. In movement class she would drive Miriam to the point of exhaustion and ride her mercilessly about her weight. 'I know you don't intend to be a dancer, sweetie,' she said, her Jackie Kennedy wispy little-girl voice turning waspish, 'but I doubt if you intend to be an elephant either.' Once she slammed Miriam up against a locker in the changing room and screamed at her to 'let my marriage breathe.' The next day, pale and tight-lipped, she apologized to her and begged for her forgiveness. It was clear she found it hard to follow her own rules. And when Miriam had dinner with Bambi and Morgan, as she sometimes unwillingly did (Morgan loved to see the two women together, his blonde and his brunette, ebony and ivory, Snow White and Rose Red), Bambi seemed to thrust Morgan at her. 'Drive Miriam home, won't you, love? Now you take good care of that sweet lady, you hear?'

Her other classmates kept their distance. Fucking the teachers was standard practice at theatre school and, although Miriam's involvement was heavier than most, the other women in the class knew it was probably a fair representation of what the theatrical profession would offer them once they left school.

Gary continued to avoid her, but that was to be expected. It had never been established that Gary was gay (unlike Christopher Albright who had come out of the closet with full fanfare, practically accompanied by the *Aida* chorus), but Morgan kept making sly little digs about his sexuality and trashing homosexuality into the bargain, especially when he got drunk with some of the students in the pub. 'The faggots run the theatre in this country,' he said. 'If you're a guy and want to get anywhere, you'll have to learn to suck cock, right, Gary? Become an expert at it. That's the way to get to the Shaw Festival. That's the way to get to Stratford. Put it on your résumé. Special abilities: dance, mime, give the best head in town.' He was particularly angry that, having played leads for the RSC in London, he was relegated to character support roles at Stratford. 'That bloody King Tut,' he said, referring to one of the stars at Stratford, 'what could that faggot know about *Henry IV*? Bloody poofter. It's a man's play. About what real men do.'

He had quit Stratford to teach at the National because he could 'no longer learn from my contemporaries. Now I learn from you students. I can learn from you and you can learn from me, give and take, that's what acting is all about. Bloody Stratford. Brains in the bum; talent up the arsehole.'

His bitterness frightened her and so did his drinking. Drinking transformed him Jekyll/Hyde style in a startlingly short time. Warm, affectionate, and basically optimistic when he was sober; with only a couple of drinks under his belt, he sank into Welsh gloom and doom. Sometimes he would turn nasty, attacking anyone who happened to be out of the room at the moment (and some who were in the room). At a BYOB party at Sandy's communal flat on rue S. Andre, he tore off all his clothes and threw them out of the window. 'Let's all go naked!' he shouted. 'Come on, all of you Let's strip!' None of them followed his example. Miriam knew his body so well, but it looked new to her in this light, pale and vulnerable, his cock shrunken and swinging sadly between his legs. He was too drunk to have an erection. She felt shame for him and for himself. It was like seeing God naked. The disciples shielded their eyes.

But loving him was worth any pain and embarrassment. When it was working well for them, being in love with Morgan was like falling in love with the whole world. It spilled over into class. During the sensitivity sessions, Miriam finally felt the all-encompassing closeness with the rest of the group, as though she could make love to them all and give them what he had brought to her. But of course she never would. Loving Morgan, making love with Morgan was plenty, more than enough for her. He delighted in the womanliness of her body, her full breasts and wide hips.

Although he claimed to be attracted to her sexual innocence and was constantly striving to find the child within her, Miriam felt like a mother to him, his strength, his refuge, his hiding place. He called her his baby, his big doll, and he loved it when she trailed round the apartment wearing one of his T-shirts or sat in text analysis class with her legs apart, wearing no underwear. He pushed her to be erotic as long as the eroticism seemed unstudied, an unknowing sexuality.

In the spring, Miriam began to realize that Morgan was involved with someone else. 'I told you,' he said, with a dismissive wave of the hand. 'Casual sex means nothing to me. It's drinking water.' However, Miriam suspected this was no casual drink of water but full-scale hydrotherapy. She tried not to confine him or press him but she was desperate to know who it was. 'If you must know, it's Sandy Madison. There's nothing to be jealous about. We go back a long time.' And Miriam knew instantly that Morgan was the father of the baby Sandy had given up for adoption. She was devastated. She tried to be objective, to tell herself that it *was* only a drink of water, a casual affair, but she knew that nothing Morgan did was really casual, not at the centre.

At the end of their second year, the class presented their first full-scale production in front of a paying audience. Miriam was cast as Masha in Chekhov's *The Three Sisters*. She identified completely with the character's loss; it paralleled what was happening to her in real life. She was brilliant in the role and she knew it. At least her unhappiness could fuel her work on stage. Morgan continued to participate in moment-to-moment sensitivity sessions every Friday, the purpose being that the emotion-freeing work should now be carried over into performance. He invited Dr Edmund Harris — whose many books Morgan credited with playing an important part in what was becoming known as the Sexual

Revolution — to come to Montreal for a marathon sensitivity session. The group encounter would take place in Morgan and Bambi's apartment. The students would be locked in for three days straight, the culmination of two years of sensitivity work.

As the jeans and leotard group tripped happily into Morgan's tiny flat and the safety lock was bolted behind them, Miriam felt twinges of unease. What could happen to them all in the next three days? Who was going to get hurt? She was pretty positive it was going to be her. And wasn't it a waste of Canada Council money to sit around and feel each other up? But Morgan's eyes glowed with missionary zeal and there was no way she could leave the room now. Edmund Harris was a bespectacled, mild-mannered Clark Kent of a man with an impressive list of degrees which gave credence to his reputation as a psycho-sexual guru.

He started them off with a general warm-up, bending stretching, freeing their bodies to illuminate their minds, and then moved on to space, trust and status exercises; claiming a space, standing in the centre of it for twenty minutes straight. Then he had each of them come forward in turn and sit in a chair to be asked questions about childhood, life, and most important of all, sex. Miriam was petrified he would ask her to recount her first sexual experience. But she wasn't asked that. Dr Edmund Harris opened her session to questions from the floor and, sitting in the hot seat, keeping a tight hold on herself, Miriam was startled by a full frontal attack from Gary.

'Why did you drop me so completely, so suddenly?' he asked as if he'd been storing the question for many months.

'What do you mean?' Miriam felt the colour flood into her face.

'Well, one day we're the best of friends, couldn't be

196

better. Say goodbye for the summer, see you in the fall and all and then, bang, not a word. Not a look, a touch, a whisper. All of a sudden I'm poisona non grata. I don't get it. What were you doing? Using me for your own nefarious purposes?' Miriam started to speak but he held up a hand to stop her. 'Hear me out. You'll get your turn. I've been waiting a year to confront you with this. I'm leaving NTS. I'm not coming back for third year. But I want to know before I leave — the class was riveted on Gary — 'in the immortal words of Tennessee Williams, "why did we come close enough and no closer?"'

She was truly bewildered. 'Look, Gary, I don't know what you're talking about. If there has been a barrier between us, you're the one who put it there.'

'Oh sure, right, blame someone else and turn it to your own advantage. You're an expert at doing that. Getting involved with the prize student is one step, getting involved with the teacher is the next step, getting involved with your director, etc, etc, etc. You'll get to the top all right, baby, and you don't care how many people you step on along the way. Ever heard of upwardly mobile fucking, m'dear? You win the prize for it.'

'Gary, you don't have to do this . . .'

'Yes, I do. I have to do this. I don't mind you fucking Morgan, if that's the way you want to climb the stairs, but I sure as hell resented you kicking me down those stairs. Why? That's all I want to know. I keep telling myself you must have a reason for it, but what? Why?'

'I . . . Morgan said you . . . he told me . . .' she faltered, knowledge growing with fear and anger. She looked at Morgan and he raised his arms helplessly.

'Oh yes, Morgan, the miraculous mordant Morgan. Now that was a pretty chickenshit thing to do, getting Morgan to tell me you thought I was encroaching on your territory, invading your space, impeding your development as an artist, the only real fear that any of us have in this dump . . . damage to our precious little talents. Who could defend himself against that?' His face was red and he was blinking in angry bursts.

'Gary, you are wrong, so wrong I never said that I wouldn't do that to you!'

'I was in love with you,' he declared. 'I didn't know how to tell you. That was my fault. But I was moving towards it. I held out my hand to you and you not only didn't take it, you cut the bloody thing off.' The tears streamed down his face. Miriam wanted to run to him and hold him, but before she could move, Morgan was across the room, his arms around Gary.

'Let it all out, Gary. This is a breakthrough. You've got to let it all out. I love you, we all love you. It's love.'

Dr Harris and the others followed suit, clutching at him, stroking him, declaring their love for him, sharing their tears with him, while Miriam stood rooted to the spot. With almost manic strength, Gary pulled away from them. Grabbing Morgan's prized glass coffee table, he hoisted it high over his head.

'You bastard!' he shouted at Morgan. 'You fuckers! All of you, fucking wankers! Let go of me! Let me out of here!' He threw the table across the room, out of the open window and on to the street eight storeys below. For a moment, nobody moved. Then they all rushed to the window. Gary unbolted the door and ran out of the apartment with Morgan following after him. Miriam looked down at the mass of broken glass on the street. A crowd had gathered, looking up at the window, but nobody seemed to be hurt. She saw Gary push his way through the crowd and run towards the Bleury metro station. Morgan stopped to explain to a cop what had happened. She watched his hands wave expressively in the air, a story theatre version, like watching a movie without sound. Then the street

198

cleaners came and cleared the glass away and slowly the crowd began to disperse.

Dr Edmund Harris drew the students back into the room as Morgan came pounding up the stairs. Everyone wanted to talk about what had just happened but Morgan stopped them with, 'Don't think. Don't talk. Just feel. It's like riding a horse. Get back on. Grab the experience. Use the emotion. Lie down on the floor and, moment to moment, get in touch with what you personally, on your own, are feeling.' One by one the students dropped to the floor, stretching out on their backs in the ritualistic relaxing position. 'Now get in touch with your breathing. Find your centre and when you feel comfortable with that, reach out and touch the person next to you. Moment to moment. Make the contact.'

Quiet. Except for the sound of breathing. The room focused in on itself. Slowly, tentatively, as if they were one being, hands reached out, flesh came in contact, cheek next to thigh, face on belly, bodies moving against anything that moved. As the pitch of eroticism increased, clothes slipped away and the room was alive with writhing flesh, a tangle of naked bodies, hand on thigh, mouth on breast, it didn't matter whose or where.

Miriam went limp, her mind shutting off completely, allowing herself to be kissed and fondled and passed from one to another. What did it matter? It was all a lie, just one big lie. The sounds of lovemaking surrounded her, filling the room. She opened her eyes to find another woman pinned under Morgan. Not two feet away from her, he was making love to Sandy Madison, the white globes of his buttocks gleaming as he pounded into her over and over again.

Like the breaking string of the harp at the end of *The Cherry Orchard*, something inside Miriam snapped. She extricated herself from the living growth on the floor, quietly pulled on her clothes, unfastened the dead bolt

199

and slipped out of Morgan's apartment. She had had enough. So apparently had the parents of the students of the National Theatre School of Canada. A month later there was an inquiry into the teaching practices of Morgan Llewellyn and he was fired as the head of the English acting section.

By that time Miriam was on her way back to the United States. She was still aiming for New York. But first there would be a side trip to Yale.

# *Six*

Liber-action occupied the Student Union building. They burned a baby doll. Dressed in black pyjamas and covered with stage blood from the drama department, they piled themselves in the middle of the cafeteria in a pool of water surrounded by a circle of lighter fluid. The lighter fluid was set ablaze and burned a circle around the pile of 'bodies' while other students chanted, 'Hey, hey, LBJ, how many kids did you burn today?' The campus police arrived and everybody went limp. Passive resistance. More buzz words. The security guards carried them out one by one and put them in the orange and white paddy wagon.

Liber-action grew in number as other political activist groups joined with them until it seemed to become one big all-encompassing movement with civil rights marches and anti-war demonstrations and academic freedom rolled into one. But as the group moved away from demonstrating against the repression of the university and into a broader political arena, Sara started pulling away from it. 'I don't understand you,' Gwen said. 'You were so gung ho when we were working to overturn the grading system. But when it comes to an issue like civil rights or the war in Vietnam, you don't seem to give a damn.'

'What does some black in a Detroit ghetto or some slant in the Mekong delta have to do with me? I'm a white, middle-class student. I can only fight my own battles.'

201

'That sounds pretty selfish. You don't want to be part of the effort to stop the war?'

'Rich kids,' Sara sneered. 'Playing at being revolutionaries. What do they know about the real world?'

'But, Sara, you founded liber-action. It's your organization.'

'I know, but it's going in the wrong direction now. We've become fragmented. Too many causes. There are blacks in the movement now. And gays. Everybody's got his own axe to grind. Jeff keeps talking about the will of society but what is society except a group of individuals? And some of those individuals are simply more dynamic and powerful than others.'

'Thank you, Ayn Rand,' Gwen snapped, but she was worried about the changes in Sara. She'd virtually stopped eating; she was drinking heavily and popping all kinds of pills. On the surface, she looked as perfect as ever, but something was gnawing away at her. 'What's happened to you, Sara? You got me into this in the first place and now you don't believe in it any more? I don't know who you are. I never know what accent you're going to come up with next or how you're going to be dressed. First it was hippy freak, then radical chic, now you're going middle America on me. You're either ironing your hair or perming it.'

'What's that got to do with who I am?' Sara's fingernails drummed nervously on the desk.

'Nothing, but I don't think you believe that. It's like you're trying on all these different images to help you decide who you're going to be and what you're going to think. It's as if you're constantly playing character, somebody, anybody, other than yourself.'

'People stare at me,' Sara said suddenly. 'All the time they are staring at me.'

'So? You're gorgeous. You expect people not to look at you?'

'I want them to look at me. I just don't want them to stare. Look and then look away.'

'In other words don't get to close. That's exactly how you make me feel, Sara. You're my best friend but I'm afraid to dig too deep with you. I've told you about my problems back in Bowness. You know all about me. But I don't know you at all. You've done a one-hundred-and-eighty-degree turn since September. Is this all due to Trayne's influence?' Trayne Barnett was the drop-dead-gorgeous medical student Sara had begun dating seriously. He came from a wealthy Galveston family and was very conservative.

'No. It's got nothing to do with Trayne. I'm just starting to think for myself, that's all.'

'No, you're just thinking *about* yourself.' As Sara opened her mouth, 'Look, forget it. I don't want to get into this right now.' Gwen turned away and rolled a sheet of paper into her typewriter. 'Leave me alone so I can finish this essay.' She furiously attacked the keys of her typewriter, then paused and looked at Sara, troubled. 'I don't understand where your mind is, not to mention your heart. What we're doing in the movement is important. We're involved in a war that we have no business being in.'

'What's all this "we" crap? You're a Canadian. It's got nothing to do with you.'

'It does. It has. I can't help myself. It really upsets me to hear you talk like this. Sometimes you sound like a racist. I know you don't mean to, but that's how it comes out. Now you're saying you think I'm wrong in protesting against a war that not only is totally unjustified but also one we, excuse me, the American government, can't win.'

'We could if we really committed the right money and troops to it. Johnson's just pussyfooting around. He doesn't really want to get his paws wet.'

'It's a morally unjust war,' Gwen repeated quietly. 'I

203

don't see how we can go on rooming together, let alone stay friends, if we don't agree on this.' But even as she said it, she felt her throat tighten up. She couldn't possibly carry such a threat through. Sara had become too important in her life. She could see the fear come into Sara's eyes, too.

'Don't be silly. Friendship shouldn't be based on politics. Who cares whether or not we'll vote the same way once we're old enough to vote? What matters is that we're loyal to each other, that we're always there for each other.'

'I know.' Gwen's eyes unexpectedly filled with tears. 'I'll always stand up for you, Sara. But do you know what they're starting to call you? Fascist . . . I can't even say the word.'

'Cunt,' Sara finished for her. 'I know.'

'How can anyone be right-wing in the sixties? You're going against the flow.'

'Believe me,' Sara said softly. 'I know.'


Martin Luther King was killed in April and Bobby Kennedy in June. The summer blazed hotter than ever. Sara left Austin to 'earn her keep', she said, and presumably to see her family. Gwen had still not learned much about them. She gathered that Sara had lived all over the US, that her father had moved the family from place to place, apparently finding it difficult to hold a job. Her brother, Miles, two years older than Sara, was a second lieutenant stationed in Vietnam. She wrote to him occasionally, but they weren't close, she said.

'How did he get drafted?' Gwen asked.

'He wasn't drafted. He enlisted. He chose to go.' Then, sensing Gwen's embarrassment, Sara went on. 'That's what I mean. You really don't know what you're talking about. You have some vague idea of moral right and wrong, but Miles is there. Living it every day. He believes in what he's fighting for, he believes in doing his duty

204

to his country. With him, it's a personal commitment.'

'I'm sorry, Sara. I didn't know.'

'It's OK. He's tough. He can handle it.' But it was clear Sara wasn't handling it all that well.

'Your mother must be worried sick.'

'My mother's dead,' Sara said flatly. 'End of subject. Listen, what do you say we get out of the dorm next year and take a place in town on our own? I'm going to work all summer, save some rent money. Want to go in with me?'

'Yes, I do,' Gwen said quickly. Despite their differences, there was a lot of feeling between them and each was trying hard not to be judgemental about the other. There was no way Gwen wanted to give up her friendship with Sara.

Gwen went to Houston to visit Uncle Jack and his family. He offered her a place to stay for the summer and a job with Treasure Resources. The fledgling oil company was now a roaring success and he was revelling in it. 'Exploratory drilling is a crapshoot,' he told her. 'You can pour your money into it, drill for months and still come up with a dry hole. But when you strike oil, there's no feeling like it. You feel you've mastered nature.' As a beginning geology student, Gwen was given the task of working on drawing up the prospect maps, which mapped the formations underneath the Treasure Resources' prime properties. She coloured in the different contour areas and drew in the prospect arrows. She'd been afraid that if Uncle Jack learned about the family scandal, he might not want to take her on, but when she screwed up her courage enough to tell him about it, he said it didn't make any difference to him whatsoever. He was sorry that she'd had a falling out with her dad, but he still loved her and would do anything to help her keep that 'lucky dragon on her back.' She still had the jacket

205

he'd given her years ago and she carried it with her as a good luck charm . . . Living with Uncle Jack and his wife, Diana, and their little girl, Paige, gave her a chance at some semblance of family life, although she sensed that Diana had reservations about the nature of Uncle Jack's feelings for her. She did her best to stay on Diana's good side and she had a ball with Paige. It was one of the happiest summers of her whole life, and she could hardly wait to see Sara again to tell her all about it.

In the fall, she and Sara went house hunting and found a cute little white cottage on Blanco Street which was furnished, with separate bedrooms and a fully equipped kitchen for only one hundred dollars a month. They both fell in love with it. There was a huge pecan tree in the back yard and they bought a Hibachi for barbecuing and an ice-cream freezer. They made butter pecan ice-cream and took turns cranking the freezer. It stayed hot right through to the end of September. Sometimes they took a picnic out to Barton springs and had a swim right after classes. When they could borrow a car, they went to Pearl's oyster bar to listen to blues or to the all-night drive-in movie at the Longhorn. Sara knew all the best places to eat. Sara knew wine. Sara knew what movies were hot and what books were on the best-seller list. Gwen was content to let her lead. The friendship seemed firmly cemented.

Over the next couple of years, an uneasy truce existed between them about Vietnam. They still stayed up all night talking, but they argued less about politics and more about sex.

'I've got to stop screwing around,' Sara said.

'I can't believe my ears,' Gwen looked up from the book she was reading. 'You giving up sex? Your favourite drug?'

'Well, I really want to marry Trayne. I think I'm in love with him.'

' "Love between a man and a woman can be

counterproductive and debilitating," ' Gwen quoted a passage from the book. ' "Sex is just a commodity." '

'Give me that book,' Sara grabbed the book Gwen was reading out of her hands. '*The Feminine Mystique* by Betty Friedan. Give me a break. This is anti-male hate literature.'

'No, it's not.' Gwen tried to grab the book back. 'Give it back.'

'Not until you promise to get out of this house and have some fun. Come on. Let me fix you up. Trayne and I are renting a car and driving to San Antonio next weekend. Come with us. We can have lunch at La Louisianne. Go the zoo. See a movie. *Bonnie and Clyde*.'

'Too violent.'

'OK, OK, Camelot. I'm always telling you how much you look like Vanessa Redgrave.'

'Thanks a lot. She's got shoulders like a truck driver.'

'No she doesn't. I think she's stunning. In Camelot they've got her in these incredible long red wigs. She looks beautiful. She can't sing but she looks great. And I read that she's having an affair with Franco Nero.'

'You've already seen it?'

'Yeah, but I'll see it again. If you'll come. Trayne's got a friend. OK, I admit he's a little conservative, probably too far to the right for you now that you've become Red Emma, but he's really good-looking. You don't have to marry him.'

Gwen was tempted. Trayne was sloe-eyed and handsome and much more civilized than most of Sara's conquests. A friend of his might not be politically correct but he probably would be cute. 'No, I don't think so.'

'Fine. You want to sit home and watch re-runs of *The Flying Nun*, it's OK by me.'

'Give me some credit for taste. I'm going to the lecture at Hogg Auditorium. Gloria Steinem and Florence Kennedy are going to speak. Why don't you and Trayne and his friend come with me? We can go to Pearl's afterwards.'

'Are you out of your tree? That's no way to get laid. Why would any man want to spend an evening listening to a lot of dykey woman complain about how they're being used and abused by men? I don't define myself as a woman, I define myself as a human being.'

'But don't you find you need a female support group?'

'Other than you? No. Women aren't meant to get along with each other. Women are the competition. Men are the prize.'

'That's not true with us. You and I don't compete with each other.'

'That's because you're not all that interested in men.'

'Maybe it's because I prefer to open my mind, instead of my legs.'

'Picky, picky. OK, OK, do what you want, but come Monday you're going to be sorry you missed San Antonio.'


The lecture opened Gwen's eyes to a completely new outlook on life. This new women's liberation movement seemed to be speaking directly to her. Florence Kennedy, a tall, thin black lawyer, spoke first with passion and eloquence. Gwen listened intently as she talked about 'woman as nigger', explaining how sex and race discrimination were linked together. Betty Frieden compared suburban housewives to the inmates of Nazi concentration camps. Gloria Steinem talked about the woman as slave image that was reinforced by television and through advertising and she told the group about her plans for a magazine where the emphasis would not be on how to make yourself more attractive to catch a man or what to serve your husband for dinner. 'Stop thinking of yourselves as second-class citizens.' Gwen joined the others in a standing ovation.

She started wearing her hair long and straight like Gloria and she traded in her round granny glasses for the new aviator frames. Sara said she looked like a pilot for Alaskan Airlines, but why should she listen to Sara? Sara's looks could stop traffic in downtown Dallas. Now it wasn't so important to look pretty; it was important to look smart and capable. She had stopped wearing a bra and reading *Cosmo*.

'Gloria's right. Women and blacks are second-class citizens in America, so I'm screwed on two counts,' said her new friend, Barbara Williams. Sara was never around any more, and the two of them couldn't seem to agree on anything these days. She had met Barbara at the Steinem-Kennedy lecture. Maybe it was seeing Gloria and Flo on stage together, one white and one black, and the high energy and warmth that flowed between them and out to the audience. Maybe it was simply wanting to venture further into unknown American territory, but she saw Barbara sitting across the aisle from her and she set out to become her friend.

Barbara was as sharp and sophisticated in her way as Sara. She wore expensive-looking clothes and a modified Afro. Her mother used to pick up a special blusher and lip gloss for her from Biba's boutique in London. Barbara's mother was head of the English department at the black college, Huston Tillotson, but she sent her daughter to boarding school in Switzerland.

'Why did you come back to Texas to go to university?' Gwen wanted to know. 'You could have stayed in France.'

'I hate the snow,' Barbara laughed. 'I missed my friends. I missed peanut butter. I need my Skippy.'

'But isn't it easier for a black person to live in the northern US?' Gwen never knew when she was treading on delicate ground in pressing Barbara to 'share the black experience' with her. 'Isn't there less racial prejudice?'

209

'Under the surface, it's really no different. Believe me, up north they're plenty prejudiced. They're just more polite about it.'

Gwen was absolutely fascinated with Barbara. Back in Bowness there were lots of Germans, Dutch, and Ukrainians, but nobody really thought of them as ethnic.

The restaurants in Austin were integrated but Barbara and Gwen sharing a meal could still evoke stares. 'It would be worse if I were a black man,' Barbara said. 'Southerners really hate that. You know, protecting the virtue of white southern womanhood and all? In Alabama, a black man can go to jail if a white woman accuses him of rape, on the flimsiest of evidence.'

'That's awful.' Gwen was horrified.

'The mystique of the black male.'

'What do you mean?'

'They've heard that black men are well hung and they're afraid that secretly, down deep, all white women avidly crave big black dicks.'

'Are they?'

'What?'

'Well hung?'

'Don't ask me,' Barbara laughed. 'My limited experience has only been with Jackson. He looks pretty big to me, but he claims he's just average. I see white women staring at him, though. They don't have any manners at all. They look right at his crotch. Jackson says sometimes he's tempted to unzip his fly, take it out and show it to them if they want to see it that bad.'

'They're probably just curious. Like I was.'

'Hell, no, they want it. And a lot of black men want them right back.

'Where the hell have you been?' Sara snapped. 'You were supposed to defrost the fridge this afternoon.'

'Out with Barbara. Went to Two-Jays for a hamburger.'

'I never see you any more.'

'That's hardly my fault. You spend most of your time with Trayne anyway.' At Christmas Trayne had given Sara a disgustingly ostentatious ring, which Sara flashed at every opportunity. They were supposed to be announcing their engagement at the next official party of the Young Americans for Freedom but, given Sara's fidelity track record, Gwen would believe that when she saw it.

'We're going to catch the seven o'clock show at the Varsity. *Teorama*. You love Terence Stamp. Come with us.'

'With you and Barbara? No thanks.' Sara stuck her nose into the copy of Vonnegut's *Cat's Cradle* which she had been reading.

'Why don't you like her?' Gwen persisted. 'Because she's black? Or because her grade point average for last semester was half a point higher than yours?'

'No, because she's boring.' Sara slammed the book shut, went into the bathroom and slammed the door behind her.

The one thing Barbara was not was boring. She and Gwen were becoming passionately involved in the feminist cause. It called on some deep reserve of anger that Gwen had kept hidden for a long time. Even more than the early days with Sara, she felt like part of a significant whole, a new and still slightly squeaking machine that was moving gradually forwards. It was a heady feeling. She wanted Sara to share it with her.

'Come to my women's group with me,' she urged. 'Just come and rap.'

'Come and rap? Rap? I never thought I would hear the little girl from the oil fields of Alberta say "rap". The last thing I want to do is sit around with a bunch of women who never wear make-up and don't shave their legs. It's got nothing to do with me.'

'It's got everything to do with you. Don't you care about the liberation of women?'

'Do you actually believe there's some sort of male conspiracy to hold us all back?' Sara rummaged through her purse for her packet of cigarettes. She'd started smoking now, probably, Gwen thought gloomily, because holding a cigarette in her hand gave her a chance to show off her engagement rock.

'Yes I do. History proves it. Is it fair for men to have the best jobs, to be paid more?'

Sara lit a cigarette and waved the smoke away with her diamond-studded left hand. 'What, you think there should be quotas? Your pal Barbara telling you that blacks should be hired whether they're qualified or not?'

'It's a necessary stage.'

'Huh uh. Reverse discrimination.'

'Do you really intend to get married, stay home and have babies? Don't you realize that' — here she quoted Gloria Steinem — 'the role of wife is inhuman — marriage makes you legally half a person?'

'Oh, me.' Sara waved her hand in the air carelessly. 'We're not talking about me, we're talking about the average woman.'

'The women's movement is going to change the world as we know it. Do you have any idea how sexist our vocabulary is?' Gwen could feel her face getting red with the exertion of the argument but she had to make Sara understand how important this was to her.

'Jenny,' Sara said seriously. 'I think you're getting just a little wiped out on this thing.'

'Come to group with me, Sara,' she urged again. 'It'll change your life.'

'You woke me up, goddamnit,' Sara hissed late one night

212

as Gwen crept into the house after a group session.

'I'm sorry. We went to Scholtz's for a beer.'

'Who's we?'

'You know, Barbara, the group.'

'Christ, spare me!' Sara sprang out of bed and paced the room like a restless panther. 'Oh shit, you really woke me up. Now I won't be able to get to sleep. I was all mellowed out when I came home and now I'm revved up again.'

'I'm sorry,' Gwen whispered. 'At least tomorrow's Sunday.'

'So what? I've got a shitload to do. I'm going to have to take a pill.' She reached for the blue quilted jewellery box that she now called her bedtime pharmacy.

'I wish you wouldn't.'

'Who cares what you wish?'

'Have you had anything to drink?' Gwen was at the table before Sara could get there, blocking her.

'Trayne and I had a couple of bottles of wine at the Driscoll, but I'm not drunk if that's what you're worried about.'

'Goddamnit it, Sara, it's dangerous.'

'What the hell do you know about it?' Sara snatched up the little white vial and shook two yellow Valium into the palm of her hand. As she moved her hand to her mouth, Gwen caught her wrist.

'Sara, don't. You can't mix tranquillizers with alcohol.'

Sara wrinkled her nose. 'It's only a couple of baby Vals. I haven't had much to drink. I'm mostly stoned and I can't come down.'

'Come on, Sara, that's even worse.'

Sara popped the two small pills into her mouth and swallowed them dry. 'Shut up. I know what I'm doing. I've done it before. Now go to bed and get some sleep.' She climbed into bed and wrapped a pillow around her ears.

213

Gwen lay rigid in the next room. What was going on with Sara? Obviously she had been avoiding all the signs. She'd had a scare a couple of months ago. Being awakened by the sound of rattled snoring, Sara choking on her own tongue, Gwen rushing her to the health centre to have her stomach pumped. 'A mistake,' Sara said. 'Believe me.' And Gwen had believed her. What a fool she had been not to realize what was going on. Why didn't Trayne know about any of this? Had he been avoiding the signs or was he just too stupid to notice them?

Waking up Sunday morning, groggy from lack of sleep — she always needed more than Sara did — for a moment she didn't know where she was. Standing at the foot of her bed, like a Christmas tree angel, was a golden-haired vision in white. 'Sara?' she asked tentatively.

'Well, what do you think?' Sara ran her fingers through her newly blonde hair.

'What happened?' Gwen asked fuzzily, rubbing her eyes and then looking again towards the foot of the bed.

'Like it?'

'This happened during the night?' Gwen was disoriented.

'Jesus, no. I got up early and bleached my hair. I've been thinking about it for a couple of weeks now, I wanted a change, so I just went ahead and did it.'

'That's your own hair?' Gwen said stupidly.

'Yes, I just told you,' Sara answered impatiently, plugging in the curling iron. 'Maybe it doesn't look so great because I haven't curled it yet. I'm going for that Julie Christie look.'

'I guess it'll take some getting used to.'

'I'm used to it already. Sara seemed nervous, moving and talking quickly even for her. 'Only problem is what should I do about my bush? I can't have blonde hair and a black bush. Or maybe I can. Might make an interesting contrast, what do you think?'

214

'I think you're crazy.'

'Oh don't be so boring, Jenny. Actually, I don't think it's safe to put bleach on your pubic hair. Maybe I should henna it instead. That would lighten it and it's much safer.'

'How could you change yourself like this?'

'Don't be so dramatic. People change their hair all the time. Don't you think I look pretty?'

'Yes, but you were pretty before. I don't understand.'

'There's no big mystery. Trayne told me he prefers blondes, so I thought I would try it.'

Gwen didn't know what to say. Oh great, you're marrying a man who wants to change everything about you, even your pubic hair? She sat in bed as Sara finished curling her hair, unplugged the curling iron, and began pulling on her pantyhose. She kept looking at Sara, wishing she could remember all the things she had wanted to tell her in the middle of the night.

'For God's sake, Gwen,' Sara snapped her fingers under her nose. It's no big deal. It'll grow out.'

'I know . . .'

'And if I don't like it, I can always change it back. But I have a feeling I'm going to like it. Maybe blonde is the real me.'

Gwen let her legs drop over the side of the bed. She wanted to say, 'And who is the real you? Do you have any idea?' But she really didn't have the energy to pursue this conversation any further. 'Did you get the letter from your brother? I forgot to tell you, it came in yesterday's mail. They even censored part of the address. Maybe that's why it took so long to get here. I put it on the phone table.'

'OK, thanks,' Sara said. 'I'll read it later. I'm going to walk down the block and meet Trayne halfway. He gets so antsy if he thinks I'm not ready to go.'

'Sara, how come your brother's name is different from yours?'

'What do you mean?' Sara's hand was already on the door when she stopped and turned back to look at her.

'I just wondered. It says Miles Washington on the return address.'

'So?'

'Washington, not Town. Did your dad remarry or something?'

'Why are you asking me this now? I'm late already. Trayne's probably sitting at Tower Drugs drinking endless cups of coffee and burning me in effigy.'

'I just wondered.' Gwen started to get up.

'I changed my name, OK?'

'What?'

'Legally. When I turned eighteen I changed my name to Town.'

'What's wrong with Washington?'

'Nothing's wrong with it. I just didn't like it. It wasn't me. Town's classier.'

'I don't get it.'

'There's nothing to get. Who the hell cares? It's none of your business anyway. What the fuck were you doing going through my mail?'

Gwen got out of bed and faced her. 'I wasn't going through your mail. I took it out of the box, sorted it, and put the only one that was addressed to you on the phone table, OK. What are you getting so uptight about?'

'Don't pry into my mail and don't pry into my mind,' Sara said, her words like icy daggers aimed directly at Gwen's heart. She picked up her gloves and left the house without saying another word.

Sara was now writing for the daily paper in Austin, *The Austin American Statesman*. Her column was called 'One Student's Point of View', and of course that point of view was a conservative one that reassured all the citizens of Austin who were terrified they were going to be torched

216

in their beds by radical hippies. Two of her editorials had won the International Students' Prize. Sara said she represented the voice of reason in a world gone crazy, but Gwen's friends saw her as an establishment tool and accused her of selling out. Gwen had given up trying to defend Sara and her actions to anyone.

Now that she was well and truly engaged, Sara's extra affairs had decreased, but she didn't really seem happier. Gwen decided that she was battling within herself the fear of becoming dependent on Trayne. He was undeniably sexy in his cool way, but somehow manipulative. Sara behaved differently when she was with him, adoring and coy, nothing like the real Sara as Gwen knew her. Had known.

'Well, we're coming up to the end of four years here, Gwen. How long are you going to sit on it?' Sara asked one night as she lay on the sofa, flipping through *Bride* magazine. Trayne's family was pushing for a June wedding.

'What do you mean?' Gwen wondered if Sara would want her to be a bridesmaid at the wedding. So far Sara hadn't said anything about it and Gwen was afraid to ask.

'You're going to be the oldest virgin graduating from UT, maybe the only virgin to graduate from UT.' Sara took a deep drag on her cigarette. 'You know what's really wrong with you? You're afraid. Afraid of making any kind of personal commitment.'

Gwen had found it was better not to respond to this. Sara's teasing had taken on an edge over the last few months. Gwen assumed that she felt that at least it kept the two of them together and that it came out of Sara's jealousy of Gwen's involvement with Barbara and the group. She was still estranged from her family back in Bowness, but Alberta seemed a long way away now. She believed that finally she was putting all of that behind her.

\* \* \*

217

Head down, bracing herself against the surprisingly bitter March wind, Gwen walked across the mall and down the hill towards Waller Creek. A hurricane in Galveston had sent the central Texas temperatures plummeting to thirteen degrees Fahrenheit and no one in Texas was prepared for such cold. Both the top and bottom buttons were missing from her Afghan jacket and the heel on her right shoe was starting to loosen. Her summer savings were running low and she still had a couple of months left in the semester to go. She crossed the bridge over the creek and turned left on San Jacinto, heading for home. Up ahead she saw Sara in her new mink coat. The coat was only strips of fur interspersed with leather, but it was real mink. 'Goes with the diamond,' Sara said, but Trayne hadn't bought her the coat. She'd bought it herself with her salary from the newspaper. Gwen waved at Sara but she seemed to be deep in an intense conversation with a slight, stooped black man wearing a shabby brown hat and an ill-fitting grey suit.

As Gwen came nearer to them, she saw that the black man was gesticulating and clutching at Sara's sleeve, but she kept shrugging him off as if trying to get away from him. It looked as though one or both of them were crying. The man put his arms around Sara, and for a moment, she let him hold her in the embrace. Then she tore herself away and yelled at him, 'Get away from me. Get out of my life. Haven't you done enough already? Leave me alone.' A car pulled up beside them just as the man reached out for her again. Sara shook herself free and ran towards the house. Gwen heard the man call after her, 'I expect you to be there, Sara. It's the least you can do for me.' Then he disappeared into Tower Drugs.

Gwen ran all the way home. The door to the little white house was locked and by the time she had scrambled in her purse for the key and managed to get it unlocked, Sara had her luggage spread out on the bed. She was carefully and methodically packing, so intent on her task that she didn't turn around when Gwen came in.

'Sara, what's wrong? What's happened? Where are you going?'

'Away for the weekend. I should be back on Monday.' Sara continued to roll each pair of pantyhose into a neat little ball, shoving them into the corners of her suitcase.

'Is it something to do with that man?'

'What man?' She folded her black sweater dress neatly and inserted layers of tissue paper between the folds. 'This dress always wrinkles so badly. You wouldn't think that would happen with a knit, would you?'

'I saw you talking to that man. What did he want? Did he hurt you?'

Sara stared at her blankly. 'He just stopped to ask me directions. I don't know him.'

'Sara, he called you by name.'

'I don't know him,' she repeated, as if in a fog.

'Sara, tell me what's happened.' Gwen grabbed her by the shoulders.

'My brother's dead.' The tears streamed down her face, but she seemed unaware of them.

'Oh, God, Sara, no.' Gwen let go of her. 'In Vietnam?' Sara nodded. 'Was he killed in action?'

'That's what they're saying, yes. They say it was an accident. They say he got caught in enemy fire, but we think . . .' she stopped for a minute and flicked away the tears with her fingers, carefully, automatically, so as not to destroy her make-up, an idiosyncrasy that Gwen had always found fascinating. 'He was killed in heavy fighting near the Cambodian border north-west of Saigon. There were eight US deaths and Miles is one of them.'

'Oh, Sara, I'm so very sorry,' Gwen reached out to take her hand.

'They've shipped his body back from Saigon. There's going to be some sort of investigation.'

'Investigation? But why?'

'They think he was fragged.' The words came out of her mouth with no emotion, no colour to them at all.

'Fragged?'

'They think his own men turned on him and killed him and then made it look like an accident.'

'But I don't understand, why would they do that?'

'I told you, Miles believed in this war. Some of his platoon didn't. He wrote me about it. They were fighting the war but then they turned against it, after they'd been over there for a while. So maybe they just offed him. Anyway,' she shook her head wearily, 'we think it's possible. Oh God, I wish I hadn't encouraged him to go. I talked him into enlisting. It's my fault.'

'No, you mustn't believe that,' Gwen put her arms around Sara. 'You did what you thought he wanted. You did what you thought was right.'

'No, I didn't,' Sara said flatly. 'I did it to punish my father. I knew it would hurt him to see Miles in the service so when Miles said he wanted to go, I didn't discourage him. Oh, God, he'll never forgive me.'

Suddenly the pieces fell into place. 'The man you were talking with . . .' Gwen said slowly.

'Yes, that black man is my father. And I wish he were dead.'

# Seven

Hibbing. 1970. Skaii knew something was wrong when she came home from school one day and found her father waiting for her. Jacob was never home from the pharmacy before six o'clock and it was only three-thirty in the afternoon. He was sitting at the dining-room table, the remains of their breakfast spread out in front of him.

'Your mother's had a nervous breakdown,' he told her as he folded his napkin carefully and covered a half-eaten piece of toast and a fried egg that had congealed on the white china plate.

'What do you mean?' Skaii felt the fear start in the pit of her stomach and rise all the way up into a lump in her throat.

'It's only for a month or two.' He reached out and took her hand. 'Then she will be fine, I promise you. It's not serious.'

'What's wrong with her?' Skaii could tell he was lying about it not being serious because he didn't want her to worry. It was obvious that Jacob had been crying. His mouth was a thin, white line, and every time their eyes met, he looked away, as though just the very sight of her would make him cry again.

'Rest she needs. A little time away from us, perhaps. Not long. She said to give you a big hug and to tell you she misses you already.'

'Did she go crazy?' Skaii's stomach was churning and she was finding it hard to swallow. Her father's sturdy

221

frame seemed to have shrunk in the chair. For the first time, he looked like an old man.

'Of course not,' her father said. 'Rest she needs, that's all. Things got too much for her. She's not crazy.'

But Skaii knew he was just trying to protect her. She'd been afraid all along that her mother was crazy and now she was afraid for herself because maybe insanity was inherited, and everybody said she looked so much like her mother.

Skaii was sent to Minneapolis to stay with Aunt Bea and Uncle Eric. She'd always loved being with Aunt Bea, but visiting was one thing, living there was another. The cousins were all older than she was. They had their own lives. What made her father think they would welcome her into theirs? And Uncle Eric had never really given her the time of day. How could he replace her father? Uncle Eric smiled a lot but he always looked tired. Slightly balding, he combed three long strands of pale blond hair forwards, but he was really dumb if he thought that fooled anybody. He was over six feet tall and rail thin. 'Jack Sprat,' Bea joked wryly, grabbing a handful of loose flesh on either side of her thickening waist just above her padded hips and then patting her husband's flat belly. 'How can a man who eats my cooking stay so thin?' 'I never get a chance to eat your cooking,' was the ritualistic teasing reply. And it was true. Eric was a GP who seemed to be on call twenty-four hours a day. He rarely made it through a meal without being called away to the hospital. Skaii didn't know what to think about Uncle Eric and she couldn't really figure out how Bea felt about him herself. He was the man who wasn't there. The best that could be said about Uncle Eric was that he never got in anybody's way and of course it was his money from his extensive practice that enabled Bea to run the huge house and the six huge kids so smoothly.

Sandy-haired and ruddy-faced, the cousins were all tall,

strapping kids who fairly exploded with good health. The house was always full of their friends. Alan and Rob, who were junior and senior in high school, had formed a rock group and spent most of the time jamming in the basement rec room. Nona and Neva, identical twins, were sophomores and active in Future Homemakers of America. They were almost as tall as their father, pretty in a statuesque way and frighteningly self-confident. Skaii found them intimidating. With a bunch of equally confident girls, they took over the living-room where they usually had bolts of fabric draped over the backs of the chairs and patterns spread out all over the floor as they listened to Carole King on the stereo and worked on their latest sewing projects. On the weekends, Evan, the oldest son, who was majoring in animal husbandry at the agricultural college, would bring his friends home (along with his laundry) and they would hole up in the den, 'popping a few brews and watching the game.' And in the kitchen, Bea would hold court, percolating coffee and baking butter tarts for all the housewives that were her neighbours in the suburban complex. Sitting around the heavy wooden kitchen table, they exchanged recipes and talked kids and even shared intimacies about their husbands, their ribald laughter floating up to the top of the staircase where Skaii crouched, eavesdropping. It seemed strange to her to think about Uncle Eric and Aunt Bea 'doing it', although obviously they had because there were the six kids to prove it. Her mother never mentioned sex and somehow Skaii had assumed that once you were in your forties and had all your kids, sex stopped. Yet these large, plain, raw-boned women — bovine, Marieke would have called them — whispered secrets to each other and giggled like schoolgirls.

Bea's oldest daughter, Karen, had gone off to the University of Wisconsin in Madison, so Skaii inherited her room with its four-poster bed and a big closet that was divided into shelves that were just for sweaters, and drawers that were just for scarves and a special box unit that pigeon-holed each pair of shoes. Karen was outdoorsy and athletic (she was studying forestry) and the room was decorated in greens and browns, much more right for a boy than a girl, Skaii thought. Bea must have sensed that she didn't feel comfortable among all the corduroy and the track and field trophies, so she gave Skaii carte blanche to choose how she would like to redecorate the room completely. Eric agreed to pay for the paint and the fabric, Bea would do the necessary sewing and the cousins were strong-armed into helping with the repainting. As she saw the entire family going all out to welcome her, Skaii gradually began to feel at home.

The house continually smelled of fresh baking: sour rye bread, blueberry muffins, buttery pound cake, and double-fudge brownies. Helping Aunt Bea in the kitchen, she began to relax, to feel comfortable inside her own skin again. Maybe if she held on to herself very tightly, she could keep the craziness from slipping out. Cooking seemed to calm her. Creaming the hard chunk of butter with the brown sugar until it became a golden bubbly mixture, sifting the flour, greasing the long cookie sheets, cutting the cookies into replicas of birds and stars and, at Christmas time, snowmen and Santas, Skaii began to find a new peace. Her aunt was always there when Skaii came home from school. Sometimes Skaii would sit in class and imagine her at home in the kitchen planning the evening meal like a general preparing for battle.

Her aunt was a strict disciplinarian, but that was fine with her. She didn't have to worry about what was expected of her when the house rules, the circles of order, were so clearly laid out for her to follow. Aunt Bea never asked her what she thought or felt, only what she had managed to accomplish that day. Marieke was forever asking Skaii what she thought about this, what she felt about that, when all Skaii wanted was to be left alone to figure out exactly what she did think and feel. Aunt Bea had one set of rules, school had another, church had another. Skaii followed them all to the letter and never got them mixed up. She wanted to please everybody so that she wouldn't be sent back home to her father. She wanted to stay right here in Minneapolis, in the refuge of this close-knit and exuberant family, in this dream house full of food and love. If she was absolutely perfect, maybe Aunt Bea would let her stay.

Once a month she went to visit her mother in the state hospital. The grey stone hospital, with its institutional green walls and scuffed tiled floors seemed austere and strange. A smell of antiseptic mixed with fear permeated the place and Skaii was convinced that behind every door lay a myriad of guilty secrets, each as embarrassing as her own. The sun-room, where her mother usually received her, had been painted a cheery shade of yellow in an attempt to brighten it up. There was a Christmas tree, indoor/outdoor carpet, some posters and a calendar on the wall, but the decorations were perfunctory, the lights blinked on and off sporadically, and the calendar was three years out of date. There were large windows all across one end of the room, but in the middle of winter, the windows were obscured with a grimy frost and the view they offered was on to the slush-filled parking lot. It all seemed sad and scary and kind of hopeless. How could her mother get over a depression in such a depressing place? Skaii began to dread her visits. And they didn't seem to make much difference anyway.

In the beginning, her mother didn't even acknowledge Skaii was there. She sat and stared out of the window, picking at the skin around her fingernails, and shrugging her shoulders in a nervous, repetitive gesture that both frightened and irritated Skaii. Why didn't she just get herself together, stop acting so weird? Just six months ago, her mother had been fine. A little crazy, OK, but fine. How could everything have fallen apart so quickly? Every once in a while she would turn and look at Skaii with dazed, watery eyes as if she were a stranger, someone she couldn't quite recognize but thought she should know. And Skaii felt just as strange. She saw the same body sitting there, maybe a little thinner and a lot paler from being indoors all the time, but still a familiar body. But where was the person inside it? As hard as she looked, she couldn't find her mother in there at all.

Her father said her mother was on anti-depressant drugs to 'calm her down', but she didn't seem calm, she just seemed out of it. Her father told her the doctors were trying a lot of different drugs to see which side-effects she could tolerate the best, but as far as Skaii could see, the side-effects were all the same. Her mother was gone. Back home in Minneapolis (and she felt guilty that she did think of it now as home), she heard her aunt and uncle whispering that if the drugs didn't work, the doctors might have to resort to ECT. When she went to the library to look it up, she discovered that the letters stood for electroconvulsive therapy: electric shock treatment. The description of the process was horrifying. Now she was really scared. Her father hadn't mentioned the possibility of shock treatments. He must be just as scared as she was. And if her aunt and uncle were whispering about it, that must mean that it was something both dangerous and shameful. The article in the mental health journal seemed to be saying that it wasn't dangerous and that it really worked in some cases, but it still sounded awful.

That night she dreamed about her mother, strapped to a table with a tongue depressor in her mouth and great silver pincers on either side of her forehead as she convulsed in agony. Then her mother faded away and in her place, lying on the table, was Skaii herself. She

226

woke up, screaming and crying. What if she went crazy, too? Aunt Bea came running in and put her arms around her, holding her tight and rocking her back and forth. 'It's not your fault, lovey,' she said, as if she could see right into Skaii's guilty heart. 'Your mother will get better. You have to put your trust in God.'

But Skaii knew that God could see even deeper than Aunt Bea and she was riddled with guilt. He had looked into her soul and seen that she didn't love her own mother as much as she loved Aunt Bea and now he was punishing her. She would have to try even harder to be perfect, to follow all the rules. She would have to become a different person.

The next year she started high school and the rules changed again. You had to be pretty, you had to be popular, you had to be fun. The kids had stopped trying to change the world and had started looking out for themselves. Disco was in. Being a cheerleader was back in. Skaii took a long hard look at herself. Her grades were OK, she looked terrific in short skirts and, most important of all, she was a natural blonde. She should be perfect cheerleader material, but she knew her inside didn't match her outside. Her breasts were perkier than her personality, she wasn't popular with the girls, and the world of boys was foreign territory waiting to be conquered if only she could learn the language. She had to learn how to be fun.

Skaii knew how to please her teachers (you just listened and did what you were told), but she wanted to please her peers. Her name was all wrong, that was the first thing. The girls in her class were Debbie, Cathy, Tracy. Skaii decided to become Susie. On her eighteenth birthday she would have her name legally changed, but for now she insisted that everybody call her Susie. She cut her blonde hair in bangs, she cultivated a chirpy little voice, and she smiled until her jaws ached. She was always willing to lend any of her stuff to the other girls. She developed an infectious little giggle. Skaii took life seriously; Susie didn't have a care in the world. Not athletically inclined, she practised jumps and cartwheels on Aunt Bea's front lawn until she could land neatly on her feet every time, her blonde hair falling in a smooth curtain to her shoulders. When she made head cheerleader, she knew that her new persona was finally starting to work for her. Skaii was shy, Susie was a good listener. Skaii was terrified of boys, Susie could flirt. Skaii was smart, Susie was a lot of fun.

Bouncing down the locker-lined high school halls, she spread good feelings as thick as the cream-cheese icing on Aunt Bea's carrot cake, melting male and female hearts alike. Sometimes Susie felt like Clark Kent. Underneath the bubbly Susie happy face lurked a timid, troubled Skaii, predisposed to Icelandic Bergmanesque melancholy of the 'losing at chess to the devil' variety. But the minute she put on her bulky white cheerleading sweater and blue and gold pleated skirt, energy shot through her like dye injected into a major artery. She became Super Susie, bouncy cheerleader and teen queen. She made Aunt Bea's double-fudge brownies for the boys on the football team and helped them with their homework, and she dated her first true love, Lokis Krumins, star quarterback. Lokis was a farm boy, shy and laconic to the point of muteness most of the time. He rarely spoke in complete sentences and Susie had to work hard to draw him out, using *Teen Talk*'s one hundred and fifty questions to keep a boy talking, but it was worth it. She knew she looked best next to Lokis. He was even blonder than she was, with deep blue eyes.

She was ashamed to admit she hardly even thought about her mother. She wrote to her frequently, but her mother rarely answered. She didn't feel like she was Marieke's and Jacob's daughter any more. She belonged to Bea's family and she was safe. Gradually she felt Susie replacing Skaii, her new life engulfing her as comfortably as the letter sweater and the blue skirt. All she wanted was to like everybody and to be liked by everybody. What was so great about setting yourself apart from other people and feeling smarter or superior? What was so wrong with wanting to be happy? Susie was elected Homecoming Queen and as she rode around the football field in the white convertible with Lokis at her side, she truly believed she'd never been happier.

At Christmas, her mother wrote that she was out of the hospital. Susie was going to go home for Christmas but then she and Lokis were elected king and queen of the winter carnival. There were so many parties and outings over the holiday weeks that she just couldn't get away. Beside she'd be graduating at the end of this year and she'd be home then, did her mother understand? Marieke wrote back that of course she understood and she'd see her in the spring. After graduation, Susie went back to Hibbing where she found her father in the throes of divorcing her mother. It was wrong. After all, he was almost fifty-five years old. Her parents should stay together. But part of her blamed her mother. Marieke's craziness had lost her her husband. Her mother seemed quite cheerful about the divorce, saying that now she was finally free of the rotten old bastard and could live the way she'd always wanted to live. Susie could understand that, but Skaii was riddled with guilt. She knew that God was punishing her for the happy time in Minneapolis. She sat her parents down and tried to talk them into staying together, but the divorce went through. Jacob married the baker's daughter, Edith Willman of Willman's Bread, a woman as bland and simple as one of her father's dinner rolls.

Her father wanted Skaii to live with him and Edith until they moved to Minneapolis. (Like Marieke, Edith wanted

229

get out of Hibbing and, for her, he was willing to do it.

'Oh, Dad, I just couldn't bear it,' Susie cried. 'I don't want a new mother. I mean Edith's fine, but she's only five years older than I am. It wouldn't feel right.'

'No, it is not possible, I know. But your real mother, maybe she needs you closer to her?'

'I'm going to stay in Minneapolis, Dad. I want to go to university.'

Marieke bought a trailer and moved to a town just across the Canadian border called Thunder Bay, a place even bleaker than Hibbing. One spring, when the ice-breaker moved into the harbour and the whole town was rejoicing, Marieke made one of her forays into the woods. She knew she was dying of cancer and she wanted to be alone to think and write. She composed a long letter to her daughter, telling her how much she loved her and how sorry she was for failing her. She ended with, 'My darling daughter, I'm sorry you lost faith in me, but I have never lost faith in you. Know that you are much, much stronger than I am. Although you could never really count on me, believe me, you will be able to count on yourself.'

To Jacob she wrote a brief note to be opened after her death: 'Dear Jacob, I was wrong about this world. Hope you are right about the next.'

# *Eight*

Gwen had never seen Sara cry. It was a matter of principle with her never to reveal any vulnerability. But now she covered her face with her hands and wept, harsh gut-wrenching sobs that seemed to come from some place deep inside her, some place Gwen hadn't been aware even existed. They sat on Sara's bed and Gwen put her arms around her friend, hugging her until the crying eventually stopped in a series of long shuddering sighs. Finally Sara pulled away, grabbed a Kleenex from the night table and blew her nose.

'Oh shit,' she said in a voice still thick with tears, 'I hate it when I do that.'

'You never do that,' Gwen said.

'I know, because I hate it.'

'You want a drink?'

'There's nothing in the house. Believe me, I know. I split the last Lone Star beer with Trayne when he brought me home last night.'

'You must have been desperate. I know how you hate that pissant stuff.'

Sara managed a small laugh. 'What have you got hiding away in this place that I don't know about? A hip flask of brandy strictly for medicinal purposes?'

'Yes, for cramps.' Gwen went out of the room and returned with two mugs and a Whitman's Sampler chocolate box out of which she took a fifth of cheap cognac.

'How come I didn't know you had that?'

'Because you would have drunk it all long ago.' She poured a hefty shot and handed it to her. Sara immediately downed it and held the mug out again. 'Look, do you want to talk about your brother?'

Sara shook her head. 'No, not just yet.'

'OK, then why didn't you tell me about your father?'

Sara rolled the mug back and forth between her hands to warm the brandy. 'Isn't that obvious? Because I didn't want you or anyone else to think I was black.'

'Is he your real father?'

'Oh yes, he's my real father all right. My mother was white. I feel white. I don't feel black.'

'It's funny but I always thought you were sort of racist.'

'You've got to admit I had a pretty good cover,' Sara smiled shakily.

'But why? Why would you want to deny what you are?'

'You really are naïve. You don't, you can't know what it's like to live as a black in a white-dominated society. You have no idea. I had no idea myself. I wasn't brought up in the South. We moved back there when I was ten. I was born in Paris and then we lived in a suburb of London.'

'England?'

'Yes. There were a lot of mixed families and nobody paid much attention at all to what colour you were. My dad had been stationed in Europe in the Second World War and after the war ended he just stayed there for a while.'

'I didn't know the army was integrated in the Second World War.'

'It wasn't. But Paris was. My father was a chaplain there. What he saw there really opened his eyes. Black and white living together. No problem. At least that's how it seemed to him. For the first time in his life he was treated like a human being.'

232

'Why would he want to come back to the US then?'

'Good question,' Sara said with more than a touch of bitterness. 'He is, was, an AME minister. Afro-Methodist-Episcopal. It's this strange combination of denominations wrapped up in one organization. The bishop in his diocese asked him to come home, back to Columbia, South Carolina.

'All the civil rights thing was just starting to happen, he felt he was needed, and he decided to put himself back into that struggle, regardless of whether or not he was putting the lives of his wife and kids in jeopardy. I don't expect you to understand what that means. You're Canadian.'

'Look, I know that being black in America is a lousy experience. And to be thrust into a hostile situation when you're not prepared for it . . .'

'It was like walking into hell. My mother had some idea of what we were getting into, but Miles and I, we didn't have a clue.'

'And your dad?'

'Oh he knew, all right. But I don't think it mattered all that much to him. We were just sacrificial lambs on the altar of social progress.'

'Sara, that doesn't sound fair.'

'I've told you, you can't understand,' she said fiercely. 'You don't know anything about it. We flew by jet from London to New York and then took a DC4 to Atlanta, Georgia. Miles and I were so excited; it was the first time we'd ever flown. The bishop had a car waiting for us and we drove, can you believe it, we drove from Georgia to South Carolina, a black man and a white woman with two kids who knew what they were, driving together through the heart of Dixie. It was a crazy thing to do. For the first time in my life I stopped trusting my father, stopped believing that he would put us first and protect us at all costs. When we could we stayed with people that he knew along the way in black ghettos, shantytowns full of rats and roaches and blatant poverty like nothing we'd ever seen. People stared at us everywhere. It was almost impossible to go to the bathroom because most bathrooms were for whites only, even in gas stations. There were separate drinking fountains labelled "white" and "coloured". If we had to stop at a motel, one of my parents had to stay in the car. They'd take my mother in a white hotel but never my father, if they saw him. They'd take my father in a black motel and sometimes my mother but not always. And they never knew what to do with us kids. We could pass for white, me easier than Miles although he could have been Jewish or Portuguese. If I was with my mama, we were treated one way. That gracious Southern hospitality you read about really does exist. If I was with my dad, people looked at us with such hate — that's the only word for it, genuine hate. That trip was a real eye-opener. In the fields of Georgia, I saw my first chain gang, a group of men stripped naked to the waist, black men like my own father, chained to each other and guarded by a white man with a rifle.'

'Oh God, Sara, how awful!' Gwen shuddered. 'Did your parents try to explain all this to you, make you understand what was going on and how wrong it was?'

Sara sighed. 'My mama was in shock, I think. My dad tried to tie it all in with God and a good Christian way of life and some future reward in the promised land if we could all learn to live together in harmony on this earth. It didn't make much sense to me or Miles; we just knew we were in danger. We thought once we reached Columbia, which wasn't that far from North Carolina where things were supposed to be more enlightened, once we were in our own home, everything would at least be better, if not OK.'

'And what happened?' Gwen asked, already dreading the answer.

'It was worse, far worse than anything we could have imagined. The house the church had ready for us was in a black neighbourhood. I hadn't expected that, I don't know why, and nobody bothered to tell me that's where we were going to be living or what it would be like for me. Right away we were looked upon with great suspicion. People resented my father bringing a white woman into the neighbourhood when they thought he should have married black, so we were pretty well ostracized by everybody. They started us off in a black school but that didn't work out so they switched us to white. That meant we couldn't bring friends home from school or tell anybody where we lived. Miles and I found that out the hard way. In my father's church, we were the only white people there. The services were long and kind of scary with a lot of responses from the congregation, a lot of crying out and answering back. But the church was just a cover for what we were really doing in South Carolina, which was to get the state desegregated as soon as possible.'

'It sounds kind of exciting to me, Sara. Important. I mean, I guess you had to be there.' She refilled Sara's mug with brandy. 'It sounds like you and your parents were real revolutionaries doing something really important.'

Sara's eyes clouded over as she remembered. She shook her head, to see Gwen staring at her. 'It wasn't exciting. We were terrified,' she said flatly. 'We were outlaws, accused of trying to overthrow the government. They called us "Reds" as if we were the same as communists. They threw water bombs at us. Slogans were painted on our house. We had abusive phone calls night and day.'

'Couldn't the police do anything about all this? Couldn't they protect you?'

'Protect us?' Sara gave a sharp little laugh. '*They* were harassing us! We were under investigation. They burned

235

a cross on our front lawn. My father's church was torched. They wanted us out of there real bad and they finally did it.'

Gwen had to ask the question but she was afraid to hear the answer. 'What happened?'

Sara turned her head away, staring out of the bedroom window for a minute before she spoke, her voice low. 'My mother was killed in a car accident. The brakes were probably tampered with. I know they meant to get my father. They got my mother instead.'

A cold horror crept through her veins. She could suddenly see Sara's mother, a young woman probably just as beautiful as Sara, stepping on the brake pedal, feeling it give way beneath her foot, looking up in terror as she crashed headlong into death, leaving two small children and a husband. Sara was right. Gwen had no understanding of this kind of evil. It was not in her experience. Even so she knew that Sara's father had been through far more.

'You blame your father for this, don't you, Sara?' she said quietly.

'Who else? You going to give me that white liberal bullshit line of how the system's at fault and I should work to change it? Like you and Jeff and Barbara and all your other little so-called radical pals playing at revolution?'

'I'm not saying you personally have to work to change it if you can't find the strength. Your family's already fought hard enough. But it's morally wrong of you to support it, to actively join it. That's what you've been trying to do here, isn't it?'

'You think I should be out there helping "my people" in the struggle against the white oppressors? Forget it. "My people" never did anything for me but cause me pain. And anyway, the fight's over. Everything's integrated now. Legally anyway. And I told you, I don't

236

see myself as black. I don't accept it. I didn't choose it. I don't want it. I've got a chance at a totally different kind of life now . . .'

'Does Trayne know about any of this?'

'Are you kidding? Of course not. I figured if I could fool him and his family, I could fool anybody. That's why I came to Texas in the first place. No way I'd go back to South Carolina, but Texas is still the South. And I did fool them. I fooled everybody. I've got a new family now. Trayne's dad is crazy about me and his mother, well, she's possessive and protective of her baby boy but she's got nothing against me personally. There's nothing from my past holding on to me now that Miles is gone. Oh God, it's not fair! How can he be dead and my father still alive?' She started to cry again and Gwen put a hand on her shoulder.

'Sara, listen to me. You've got to come to terms with your father. Maybe after the funeral, you'll have a chance to . . .'

Sara shrugged her aside. 'I'm not going to the funeral.'

'What?'

'I'm going to Dallas for a media convention. I'll be back Sunday night.'

'Sara you've got to go. Your father flew all this way to get you. He needs you with him right now.'

'Too bad. Too late. I'm not going.'

'Sara, please. I'll go with you. You shouldn't make the trip alone. Let me come with you.'

'No.'

'You owe it to Miles.'

'Miles doesn't need me now. He won't know I'm not there. He can't know anything. Because he's dead. Oh God . . .' Sara grabbed hold of the headboard and began to slam herself against it, crying in great racking sobs.

'You mustn't blame yourself. It's not your fault.'

237

Suddenly Sara turned and pushed her halfway across the room.

'Get your dykey hands off me!' Sara hissed like a caged cat. 'Let go of me! You're always clutching at me, clinging to me like some goddamned parasite! Find your own life! Leave mine alone!'

'What are you talking about?' She backed off, stunned.

'You're obsessed with me, you're in love with me, and you're too pathetic to even realize what that is.'

'What do you mean?' Gwen whispered, fearful that Sara might actually strike her. 'I'm just trying to help. I care about you. I love you.'

'You don't just love me, sweetie, you're in love with me, you want to make love to me . . .'

'Don't,' Gwen said hoarsely.

'Face it, you're a lesbian, you can't help yourself. No wonder your parents threw you out. You're a disgrace to your family. And you're a threat to me.'

'Why are you doing this? You're upset. You don't know what you're saying.'

'You got too close to me. I hate you for that.'

'Sara, please . . .'

'Get away from me don't touch me! Don't you ever touch me again! You make me sick, do you understand? I'm getting on that plane and don't you dare try to stop me.' She grabbed her suitcase and ran out of the door, slamming it behind her.

Gwen sat numbly on her bed, listening to the sound of Sara's footsteps racing down the stairs. She wrapped her arms around herself and held on tight. She could hardly breathe and her stomach hurt, as if she'd been kicked in the gut. How could Sara turn on her this way? She rocked back and forth on the bed, too stunned even to cry.

'Hey, there, Miss Gwenny-Penny. You OK?' She

238

looked up to see Trayne Barnett standing in the doorway, wearing a full tux and carrying a small white florist's box in his hand. 'You look like you just lost your best friend.'

'If you want Sara, she's gone away for the weekend,' she said shakily.

'Yeah, I know, the cold-hearted bitch. I passed her as I was coming in. She's stopped just long enough to tell me that she's standin' me up for tonight.'

'Sorry, Trayne.' Gwen managed to get up off the bed.

'She just happened to forget to tell me she's flyin' to Dallas for the weekend. Can you believe it? I mean, tonight's the med school ball. It's the biggest bash of the whole year. We've had the tickets for weeks. And she stands me up for it. Can you believe it?'

'Look, Trayne, I'm sorry,' Gwen tried to put a note of finality in her voice. If he would just get out of here, just leave her alone so she could cry or scream or something. But he stood there staring at her, tossing the little white box in his hand like a juggler with one orange.

'Hey, why don't you go with me? You know, in Sara's place.'

'What?' Gwen looked at him uncomprehendingly.

'Be my date for the ball.'

'Are you crazy?'

'No. Come on, it'll be a hoot. The banquet's at Green Pastures and the dance is in the ballroom afterwards. It's a great place, you ever been there? It's this old mansion, you know, real plantation style, it's great, the food's great . . .'

'No.'

'Shoot, why not? You'd be doin' me a favour. I mean, I have to go. It's practically a graduation requirement. And look, I shelled out the bucks for the monkey suit and the corsage. It'd be a shame to waste them.'

'No, really, thanks, Trayne.'

'Hey, Sara won't mind. You're her best friend. She'd

239

want you to use the ticket. Have a great evening. You'd be doin' us both a favour.'

The mention of Sara's name shocked Gwen into focus. Why the hell shouldn't she go with Trayne? She had nothing else to do except sit at home and cry. Besides, it was a free meal and free booze. What she needed tonight was to get really plastered so she could get through the weekend and talk things over with Sara when she got back from Dallas. 'OK, you're on,' she said. 'Give me fifteen minutes to change and I'll meet you downstairs.'

'Hey, great.' Trayne's eyes lit up. 'I'll get the car. You're a real pal, Gwen. We'll have a hell of an evening, I promise you.'

Green Pastures looked like Tara revisited, a big white mansion set among huge oak trees with a lily pond out in the back. Trayne kept her well supplied with bourbon and branch water as they wandered through the high ceilinged rooms of the banquet halls, stopping to chat with his classmates. Trayne told everyone they talked to that his fiancée had stood him up and that Gwen had stepped in to take her place, and didn't she look great in that white gauzy dress. Everyone oohed and aahed over her and her dress and said wasn't it real bad of Sara to run off like that and miss the best party the med school had to offer. Soon the warmth of the bourbon dissolved the stone in her stomach and she found she was actually enjoying herself. Trayne made her laugh with his descriptions of pre-med pranks he'd pulled in his undergraduate years, stories of what went on in the operating room, and how just as soon as he graduated from UT he was heading back to Galveston to join his daddy's practice. Did she think Sara would like living in Galveston?

Gwen nodded and smiled a lot. She was glad she didn't have to talk much. Trayne was a master of the art of

240

polite bullshit and as long as she kept nodding and smiling he seemed satisfied with her company.

The sit-down dinner was wonderful and Gwen was surprised to find she was really hungry. She stuffed herself with the crab soup and fresh shrimp and pecan chicken and chocolate profiteroles, all washed down with great quantities of icy Pouilly-Fuissé. She was feeling better and better and the argument with Sara was moving further and further into the back of her brain. It didn't even matter that she was a lousy dancer. Trayne was good at leading on the slow numbers and surprisingly uninhibited on the free form stuff. She happily helped herself to champagne as it came swinging past her.

Trayne watched her with amusement. Maybe the weekend wasn't going to be a total washout after all. So typical of Sara just to fly the coop like that. She was probably shacked up in the Dallas Hilton right now with some limp dick journalist from the *Dallas Herald Times*. He had no illusions about Sara's fidelity; as long as she realized that once they were married all that crap was going to have to stop. He didn't expect her to be a nun, but he didn't want a wife who messed around on him either. He studied Gwen gyrating on the dance floor to the band's version of 'Satisfaction', her red hair swinging wildly from side to side. Funny, he'd always had her pegged as one of those man-hating ball-busters. She never paid much attention to him when he came to pick Sara up and didn't seem to go out much herself with guys. But get some booze into her and she really loosened up a lot. She even listened to him, which was a hell of a lot more than Sara did. Dinner with Sara was like a continual *Meet the Press*. Just because Sara was smart was no reason to make him feel stupid. It was nice to meet a shy woman for a change. Gwen sort of blushed every time he looked into her eyes. And he was feeling as horny as hell. He wondered how Gwen would respond. Could he trust her not to tell Sara?

In the car, Gwen realized that she was totally bombed, which was just as well because Trayne was obviously heading towards his place and not hers. They staggered up the stairs to his apartment, but as he turned the key in the lock, she suddenly felt terribly nervous. They both knew why she was there. At this point, she wasn't exactly sure what she would do. He fixed her another bourbon and water and put on Laura Nyro, an album she particularly liked. At least he had good taste in music to fuck by. He lay down on the floor with his head in her lap, which she found sort of comfortable. It was nice just to be close to someone. She wanted to go ahead with it, give it a try, and see what it felt like. Maybe everything would work out all right after all.

But when he began to make love to her, it was all terribly wrong. As angry as she was with Sara, she felt guilty when Trayne touched her the same way she knew he must have touched Sara. How did he feel about this? She couldn't tell; his face was all red and he was breathing very hard. Did he really want her or was he trying to settle the score with Sara? In fact, was that what *she* was trying to do? He had slid her dress off and then folded it neatly on the chair by the sofa. He was probably going to make a great doctor, she thought. She looked down at her naked breasts. They seemed like foreign objects to her now. What was she doing here? As he moved to take one in his mouth, she felt oddly detached, watching herself like a character in a play. With his tongue, he traced a line from her breasts to her waist and, as he moved lower, she began to stiffen. His mouth still on her, he removed her slip with professional ease. She felt cold and a little silly lying there in her silk stockings and garter belt. She bent over to detach them, but he stopped her saying, 'No, no, baby, that's wild. Kinky. I've never made love to a woman in a garter belt before. I love it. No pantyhose.'

He put his hand on her leg and she jumped about a mile. 'What's the matter, are my hands cold? I can warm them up under the hot water.'

'No, no,' she reassured him as she lay back on the rug and tried to relax, but when he parted her thighs and put his mouth there, she froze with embarrassment. She dug her fingers into the carpet and held herself rigid as he lapped at her carefully. Would he be able to tell she was a virgin? Should she hope he wouldn't notice? Why was he wasting all this time? Very gently she knocked on his head. He looked up, startled.

'Excuse me, Trayne,' she said as politely as she could manage, 'Could you take your clothes off, too? It feels a bit weird, you know? I mean, you're doing all the work.'

That's the way it should be,' he laughed. 'Your job is just to respond, OK? You just lie back and let me do you.'

'No, please . . .'

'Hey OK, darlin', you don't want to wait, we won't wait.'

He stood up somewhat unsteadily and took off his clothes, folding them neatly and placing them on another chair. She flung one arm across her face, to keep from seeing him. She hoped she looked seductive. When she peeked, she found he looked all right. His body was slim and muscular, with a smooth, hairless chest, strong legs — she remembered Sara telling her he was a swimmer — and a nice neat behind. Sara raved about his body but as far as she could see he was just OK. Neatly put together but nothing compared to Sara. His 'thing' — she didn't know what to call it, and tried to remember all Sara's pet names for it: dick, stick, wang — was pink and kind of jaunty, a nice size, not as huge and red and threatening as she'd feared. But when he entered her, it hurt. Where was the pleasure she was supposed to feel? It was sort

243

of like putting a Tampax in over and over again. Not hideous, but hardly exciting. She closed her eyes and tried to meet his thrusts. She was missing the beat somehow. Trayne was really working hard, kissing her gently and then fiercely, arranging her body into every conceivable configuration without success. Gwen remained one step behind him all the way.

'You're sweet, baby doll, you're so sweet,' he kept murmuring, but she didn't feel sweet, she felt exposed and sort of silly. At least she didn't feel repulsed, that was reassuring. Finally he gasped, 'Sorry, babe, gotta go for it,' and there was a clutching and a groaning and suddenly a deep thrust that left her newly wet and desperately embarrassed. He rolled off on to his back and lay there breathing heavily. Sara described making love with Trayne as some sort of transcendental experience, exalted, passionate, almost beyond description. Could this be the same man? Could it even be the same act? She could feel the wetness trickling out of her and she sat up abruptly to examine the carpet. She couldn't tell if she was bleeding or not. There was a large round wet spot in the chocolate brown shag.

'Hey, don't worry about the carpet, baby doll, I'll go get some Kleenex.' He got up and returned in a minute with a box of Kleenex which he placed on the floor beside her. She thanked him but she really didn't know what to do with it so she just lay there quietly. Trayne lit a cigarette and looked at her kindly. 'Boy, I just don't turn your crank, do I? I give it my best shot and you're not at all impressed. I don't usually strike out like this.'

'No, no, it's not you, it's . . .' Gwen didn't know how to explain. It had to be her fault. Everything Sara had said was true. She was repressed, she was frigid, she was . . . oh God . . .

'Are you worried about Sara, is that it?'

'No,' Gwen said sharply. 'Right at this moment, I don't give a shit about her.'

'Hey, OK, right on. I'll drink to that.' He toasted her with his bourbon. And in that moment, Gwen realized exactly what they were both doing here. They were trying to prove something to Sara. 'Don't take it so hard,' Trayne kissed her lightly on the mouth. 'It's just a roll in the hay. Give me ten minutes and I'll be ready to try again. I swear to you, you won't walk out of this room unsatisfied. I got a reputation to live up to here.'

Oh no, Gwen thought with a sinking heart. She couldn't go through that again. The whole thing had been so neat, so methodical, like a visit to the gynaecologist. And suddenly, remembering that Trayne was a med student, she burst out laughing.

'What's so funny?'

Gwen couldn't stop laughing, gasping for breath. 'You're a doctor! You're going to be a doctor!'

'So what?' She was whooping now, trying to hold it in as it burst out of her in gasps and snorts. 'You're not, by any chance, going to be a gynaecologist, are you?'

Trayne jumped up immediately. 'What are you accusing me of? You think I'm too clinical? You think I go by the book is that what you're, saying? That I'm predictable and boring?'

'No! No!' Gwen tried to suppress the giggles but they exploded out of her again. 'You're what they call a probing internist! Get it?'

'Oh yeah, real funny.' Trayne's face was dark. 'You want to go wild, we'll go wild.' Scooping her up in his arms, he strode into the spotless bathroom with its tasteful navy-blue shower curtain and chocolate-brown towels. Holding her on one hip like a baby, Trayne turned on the water in the shower stall. 'We'll fuck in the shower, how does that grab you?' He was shouting at the top of his lungs while carefully testing the temperature of the

245

water against his wrist. Weak with laughter, Gwen
pounded on his back with her fists to be put down.
Instead he sat down on the closed toilet lid, holding her
firmly on his lap, while he rummaged through his
medicine chest under the sink. What was he looking for,
a magic combination of bath oil and shower gel to fuck
by? Catching sight of the two of them in the full-length
mirror on the bathroom door, two naked people sitting
on the john, Gwen got the giggles again.

'No good?' Trayne demanded. 'This is not what you
want? OK, on to the next stop.' Holding her aloft, he
bore her back into the living-room like a prize suckling
pig. Plunking her down unceremoniously on the corduroy
sectional sofa, he said, 'Look, darlin', you just gotta relax
and enjoy this. You're too uptight. You gotta go with
the flow.' The sixties hippie jargon sounded strange
coming from him and Gwen started to giggle all over
again. 'Hey, hey, hey, I said stop that! Come on now.
Let's give it another try. We can smoke up. That ought
to do the trick. Stay the night, OK? Darryl and Race are
away for the whole weekend. You have to give me
another chance. My honour's at stake here, you know.
I'm gonna make you come if it kills me.'

Why the hell not? Gwen thought. The thought of going
back to the empty house depressed her and although the
thought of a repeat performance with Trayne didn't
exactly turn her on, she figured it wasn't fair to judge
him — or herself — the first time around. Besides, she
loved the thought of getting stoned, really stoned, for the
first time. After two years of university, she might as well
blow everything in one evening, including Trayne if only
he'd show her how to do it. 'Sure, why not?' she agreed.

'Great' Trayne bounded away and back with a first-
aid kit containing all the head shop paraphernalia, and
expertly began to roll a joint. He lit it with his gold lighter,
took a drag, and politely passed it to her. Bravely she

246

drew the smoke into her mouth but before she could direct it into her lungs, most of it escaped. 'No, no, baby doll, you ain't gettin' the good stuff. You're just making the air high. You got to take it all the way in and hold it in real good.'

'As the actress said to the bishop.'

'What?'

'Nothing, skip it. Just a joke. Let me try again.' Deep breath, sucking it in, choking on the smoke, a lot of coughing and splattering.

'Oh, honey, you can hold your liquor but you don't know nothin' about smokin' dope.' Trayne's Gulf Coast accent was becoming as thick as the smoke in the room. 'You don't know how to inhale, little darlin'. I think I'm gonna have to help you out there.' He took the joint out of her hand, drew in a couple of mouthfuls of smoke, leaned over and, parting her lips with his, blew the smoke into the back of her throat. 'Great, huh?'

Gwen managed to nod without releasing the smoke. She felt light-headed and daring and much more excited than she had an hour ago when they were making love. Her breathing deepened and she found herself timing it to coincide with Trayne's. What a weird feeling being so completely in tune with another living being. Her neck was dissolving into her shoulders her head was revolving, rotating three-hundred-and-sixty degrees like those snow owls at the zoo. Her hair was separating into millions of fine strands, tiny flames of fire, lifting her up off the sofa. She was at one end of the room and then she saw herself at the other with no idea how she got there. And she opened up to Trayne and he was kissing her, one kiss, one long soul kiss, tongue like a giant sea anemone filling her mouth, choking her, teeth scraping teeth, chalk across the blackboard. And he was crying out to her, 'Come, baby, come! You gotta come! Come with me!'

And she was praying out loud, 'The body of our Lord,

247

Jesus Christ, which was given for thee, preserve the body and soul into everlasting life.' Melt, dissolve into the sea, the walls of the room folding in on her like the many-sided boxes in the college board exams, shapes changing, solidity bending, glass fragmenting. Her teeth were floating free, flying out of her mouth, along with words, too many words. She told Trayne everything, talked about it all, everything that came to mind.

Trayne's face appeared to her in 3-D, lunging forward, then receding, his body diminishing in the distance, his head enlarging, features distorted, a hydrocephalic baby with a twisted grin. His features melted into her father's face, her father's head on Trayne's body, with the sad eyes, full of shock and disappointment: 'You've let me down, Gwen, you're no longer my daughter.' Human heads grotesquing into animals, a wolf, a lion, half male, half . . .

He brought her a cup of coffee and she threw it in his face. She tried to hit him and when he grabbed her hands and held them behind her back, she sank her teeth into his shoulder. It took him a minute to wrap her up in a sheet and she twisted and turned the whole time, flailing at her bonds, ripping the cotton with her toenails, screaming. Every once in a while the room would stop spinning and she would think she was coming out of it, coming down to land on earth, but then the blades would whirl again, propelling her back up, up on to the ceiling, looking down on the room, on the floor, on Trayne's anxious face as his features dissolved and regrouped themselves like shifting plasticine images. Crying, shaking, she tried to run out of the room but, as in a dream, her legs wouldn't move, caught in tendrils of seaweed, as she reached for the doorknob that always remained just out of her grasp.

She didn't come down until the following day. Trayne was with her all through the night, bringing her coffee,

248

putting wet towels on her head, covering her with blankets when she started to shiver and removing them as the sweat poured off her. She clung to him as he told her she was going to be perfectly OK, it was just a bad trip; it was only grass, not to panic. After she'd taken a shower and borrowed a pair of jeans and a sweatshirt from him — the sight of her gauzy white dress almost nauseated her — she felt well enough to go home.

Trayne came into the house with her, just to make sure she was really all right. He was being very careful with her, very quiet and polite, as if she might break at any moment and fly into a thousand pieces right in front of him. They were both having trouble looking at each other, both of them wondering how they could have allowed themselves to get so close. Clearly a gulf had to exist between them now.

Gwen didn't know what to say. Don't tell Sara? She was sure he wouldn't. And he must be sure she wouldn't.

Trayne cleared his throat awkwardly. She wanted to stop him before they both made further fools of themselves, but the blood in her veins turned to ice when she heard him say, 'Gwen, when you were high, you told me something real bizarre about Sara. I don't know, I think you were feeling pretty crazy, but you told me the weirdest story about her father being black, about Sara being part black.' He started to laugh and then he stopped when he saw her face. She quickly turned away. 'Shit, it's not *true*, is it?'

Gwen couldn't say anything. The panic enveloped her. She had told him everything. Never mind everything, she had told this well-bred Southern boy — whose manners she knew just barely covered a hundred-year history of lynchings and burnings — the one thing Sara would not possibly want him to know.

Studying her face, his eyes widened. 'Oh, sweet Jesus,' he breathed. He started to cry: 'I don't want to know this. I can't handle this! My family won't tolerate this. My dad will kill me.'

'They don't have to know, Trayne,' Gwen said desperately. He wasn't listening. 'Who cares? It doesn't matter anyway. If you don't want them to, your folks will never know. I mean, you didn't know. You didn't even suspect, did you?'

'I know *now*. That's the point. Can you understand that, you stupid bitch? Now *I* know. That changes everything.'

'Why? Nobody cares about it these days!'

'Are you crazy? Where do you think you're living, girl? New York City.'

'It doesn't mean anything to Sara. If that's how she sees it you should be able to see it that way, too.' She was pleading now. This marriage meant too much to Sara. She was pinning all her hopes on being Mrs Trayne Barnett III. But Trayne was looking at her as if he'd just leaned that his fiancée was a leper. 'If you really love her, Trayne, it shouldn't make any difference to you! You must see that!'

All politeness was gone from him now. 'But it does make a difference. It makes me *sick*.' He looked at her with tears in his eyes. 'God, how could you tell me this? I hate her for not telling me.'

'I'm sorry.'

'Not as sorry as I am.'

Her heart was slamming against her chest. 'Trayne, please, you can't call off the marriage! It'll kill Sara. She loves you so much.'

He slapped her, hard. 'Don't you goddamn tell me what to do goddamn with my own goddamned life! You're no longer in it! And neither is she!' And he slammed out of the front door.

Getting through the rest of the weekend was a nightmare. Gwen crept around the house, trying to hold

250

on to her sanity, going over and over the events of the last thirty-six hours, trying to find some sort of meaning to it all. She must formulate a plan. How to tell Sara? What to tell Sara? But the minute Sara walked through the door that night, Gwen saw that she already knew. Her face was bruised and swollen, with the beginnings of a black eye. She dropped her suitcase on the floor and her handbag on a chair.'

'Who did that to your face?' Gwen whispered.

'Who do you think?'

'He hit you?'

'Yes.'

'Oh, God, Sara, I'm sorry.'

'For what? For fucking my fiancé? Or breaking off my engagement? Or getting me a beating? Or making it impossible for me to stay at UT?'

'Everything.' Gwen's voice was thick in her throat.

'I see. Just for ruining my life in general.'

'Sara, please, I didn't mean . . .'

'Oh spare me. You *meant*. There's no doubt you meant to destroy everything I've worked so hard to build up here.'

'I never meant to hurt you. I love you. If Trayne doesn't love you, if he can't love who you really are, then you wouldn't want to be married to him anyway. I can't believe he would hit you.' But then she remembered that he had slapped her, too. 'You don't want to be married to someone like that.'

'I'd have liked to have made that decision for myself. I didn't expect to be helped right out of it by my best friend.' Sara spat the words at her.

'Don't, please.'

'You slept with Trayne because I accused you of being gay. You wanted to get back at me for that.'

'I know, I know that's why I went to bed with him. But not to get back at you. I just wanted you to be wrong.'

251

'Then why would you tell him about my father? How could you do that?' Sara's eyes were full of tears.

'I didn't mean to, I swear I didn't. He got me high and it just came out. I didn't know what I was saying. I didn't even know where I was. I was out of control.'

'You're jealous of me. I'm not really surprised at your treachery. But I am surprised at the depth of it.' She went to the closet and grabbed Gwen's suitcase and held it out to her. 'Now pack your things. I want you out of here.'

'Please, you've got to listen to me.'

'No, you listen to *me*, dear friend, and you listen good. You're a loser, Gwen. You'll never amount to anything. I don't want to see you again. Stay out of my way. Completely. And if you think this little episode is over, it's not. If I'm going down, I'm taking you along with me. I've told a number of people about your little escapade in Canada. By tomorrow morning it should be all over the campus. If I were you I'd get right out of town, now.'

# Nine

'I love you, Susie Sunshine. You have brought such light into my life.' Lokis was so excited that he almost choked on the words. He wondered if Susie knew how hard it was for him to express his emotions. They were having a special candlelight dinner in his bachelor digs just off campus in Minneapolis. Every bit of the dinner was homemade. Susie had even baked a huge loaf of sourdough bread, better than the sourdough bread he'd tasted at Fisherman's Wharf on vacation in San Francisco with his parents last summer. She looked so beautiful in the candlelight with her long blonde hair and that fuzzy white angora sweater and a soft blue skirt she'd designed and made herself. They were listening to Abba, a rock group that everybody had thought might be the Beatles getting back together but which turned out to be a group from Sweden who knew only a few words of English.

'I love you, too, honey,' Susie whispered, quite overcome. It was the first time he'd ever told her he loved her. For two years she'd been waiting to hear those words. Soft-spoken and a little shy, he looked so sexy in his black jeans and a black turtleneck. Tonight, in honour of their special dinner, he'd added a loose jacket. She loved the way his straight blond hair fell across his forehead and his graceful hands that were constantly in motion. She loved him. Farm boy turned artist.

'There's a surprise for you.' Lokis reached across the table, took her hand and kissed it. He seemed nervous.

'What is it? Where?' Instantly Susie was bouncing out of her chair.

'No, no, you have to eat your dessert first.' Lokis grinned with delight.

'Why can't you tell me now?' Susie started to giggle, which always made Lokis laugh, too.

'Come on, eat your dessert.' Lokis sipped his coffee and watched her carefully dip her silver spoon into a great mound of chocolate mousse, slide it slowly into her mouth, and then lick every morsel of it off the spoon, giving a little sigh of ecstasy before plunging the spoon back into the bowl again. 'I love those sounds that you make when you eat.'

'What sounds?' Susie turned bright pink.

'Those little orgiastic sounds of delight. You really enjoy your food. They're the same sounds you make when you . . .'

'Stop!' Susie turned even pinker. 'Anyway, it's really good. I love all that whipped cream you added on top at the last minute. It's really disgusting but it's great. How come you're not eating any?'

'I'll eat mine when you've finished every bite of yours.'

'OK,' Susie said suspiciously, and then struck something hard in the bottom of the dish. 'What's this?' She dug around with her spoon and found a lump. 'Oh no, there's something in my mousse! I must not have whipped it enough. Honey, don't eat yours yet.' She dabbed at the gooey chocolate with her spoon until she had the lump captured. When she had rubbed it off, it emerged, a white gold engagement ring. 'Oh, Lokis, oh it's beautiful, oh wow . . .'

'Susie Sunshine,' Lokis said very seriously. 'Will you marry me?'

'Yes, yes, oh yes!' She was out of her chair and into his lap in a flash, kissing his face all over and rubbing her hands all over his chest while she breathed in his ear.

And then his mouth was on hers and his hand was inside her fuzzy sweater, where she wasn't wearing a bra — God, it felt good. When her hand went between his legs, she could feel him already hard under the heavy denim of his jeans, and she reached for the zipper. Suddenly he stopped her. 'Why did you do that?' she asked almost in pain. Why do you always do that?'

'Because you're not ready.'

'I'm ready! Believe me, I'm ready!' They were both breathing hard.

'I want to wait until we're married.'

'But we're *going* to get married! You just asked me to marry you and I said yes!' She reached again for his zipper, but he took her hand away gently and held on to it.

'Let's wait until we're married,' Lokis repeated stubbornly.

'Wait a minute. Shouldn't I be saying that? Shouldn't you be begging me to make love to you while I'm telling you we have to wait until we're married?'

He flushed and looked down at the floor. 'Yeah, I know, so I'm old-fashioned, OK? Everybody we know is sleeping together so why don't we go ahead and do it right. I want it to be perfect.'

Susie threw her arms around him. 'And that's why I love you. Because basically I'm old-fashioned, too. I want a big wedding and a whole bunch of kids and I guess I want to be a virgin on my wedding night.'

Lokis kissed her lightly on the lips and gently disentangled himself from her embrace. 'I'll make it worth the wait, I promise.'

'Yeah, I bet you will. So what do you want to do now? Everything but? There's lots of chocolate mousse left. We could take off all our clothes and borrow a couple of your paintbrushes and do a little body painting. There's one part of your body I'd like to cover in chocolate mousse and then I'd like to lick it all off.'

'Stop! Stop!' Lokis groaned. 'You're driving me crazy, wench! For someone who's supposed to be naïve and innocent, you've got a pretty wild imagination.'

'OK,' she sighed. 'I won't tempt you further. Come over here and put your arms around me and tell me about our house.'

Lokis grabbed his drafting pen and a huge pad of paper and, putting one arm around Susie and leaving the other one free, they began to play their favourite game. 'It's going to have a solarium-type living-room, PK? With huge windows reaching from floor to ceiling so the sun can pour in first thing in the morning. We'll have masses of plants — you get to choose the plants — and you get to decorate the kitchen, except that we've got to have an island in the middle, with inlaid tiles and lots of copper pots hanging all the way around . . . so you can do all the cooking you want . . .'

'Skip the kitchen,' Susie said, snuggling into his shoulder. 'Tell me about the bedroom.'

'Ah, the bedroom. Well, we'll start with a big brass bed. King-size. And we'll end with a big brass bed. Nothing else in that room. Just the bed.'

'And the sheets will be one hundred per cent percale. Soft, real soft, because they'll get washed a lot because we'll use them a lot. . .'

'Oh, God, baby,' Lokis whispered. 'I can't wait to marry you.'

'I can't wait to marry Lokis.' Susie wanted her best friend, Tracy, to be the first to know. She flashed the engagement ring at her and both of them squealed.

'You're a living breathing cliché, do you know that?' Tracy teased. 'You're marrying your high-school sweetheart. I mean, come on! Captain of the football team meets head cheerleader. Instant romance. You've known him since you were fourteen, been dating since

256

you were sixteen. How can you let yourself fall into that stereotype?'

'You have to admit he's gorgeous.'

'I admit it. Just give me one night with him so he can show me how gorgeous. Forget it, forget it, I'm only kidding. Anyway you're both gorgeous. You're perfect together. Didn't you tell me he cried just as much at *Love Story* as you did? Now there is a sensitive man. And all that blond hair! You're a golden couple.'

'Will you be my maid of honour? I'm going to have six attendants but I want you to be the main one.'

'Sure. What are you going to make me wear? Some Laura Ashley thing that makes me look like a chubby milkmaid while you look like a fairy princess?' Tracy was always complaining about her fat hips and thunder thighs.

'OK, I'm making the dresses myself, and yes, the pattern is Laura Ashley, but they're really nice. A good long line. Romantic. Elegant. Sort of Victorian with a high neck and a lot of lace. I've already picked out the material. It's a very fine blue gingham.'

'What did I tell you? Milkmaid. Oh boy, I can hardly wait,' Tracy snorted. 'But I'm telling you, Susie, you are just not with it. Nobody's getting married these days. Why don't you just live together? Why do you have to marry him?'

'Because,' Susie said simply. 'I want to sleep with him so bad I can hardly stand it.'

'I repeat, why do you have to marry him?'

'Why do you have to marry him?' her father said. 'You're just a baby yourself, you're not even nineteen. Why do you have to get married?'

'I thought you liked Lokis, Dad.'

'I do, yes. But as a boyfriend, not yet a son-in-law. Does he have a real profession ahead of him? Drawing

257

little pictures, what does this mean? Is it dollars and cents; is it money in the bank?' Jacob loved all the North American expressions.

'Lokis is an architect and a designer, Dad,' she explained patiently. 'He draws little pictures of houses. He's not a fly-by-night.'

'What means this, fly-at-night?'

'I mean that he knows how to build houses as well as design them. He's a carpenter, like you.'

'I am a druggist.'

'I know, but you built our house in Hibbing. You work with your hands so does Lokis. People will hire him to tell them how to build their houses. He knows structure from the inside out. He'll make a lot of money.'

'Do you think your mother would be happy to see you married so young? If she were alive?'

Susie's face darkened. 'Mama wasn't happy about much of anything. You know that, Dad. But I think she would like Lokis, yes. After all, he is an artist. He's not your average Minnesota farm boy. I mean, he grew up on a farm but he wants more than that.'

'You are marrying a Latvian. A communist. Latvia is a tool of the Soviet bloc.'

'So is Lithuania,' Susie argued. 'Lithuania is still part of the Soviet Union, too.'

'That is why I left it. War is over, do I leave Brussels and go back to Kaunas? No, I come here. Where it is free.'

'It's the same with Lokis's family.'

'No, it is not. Lithuania was taken by force by the Russians. We resisted,' he said proudly. 'Latvia asks to be in the Soviet Union. It is different. Says much about the people who live there. Lithuanians are resisters; Latvians are accepters.'

'Anyway, he's American now, right?'

'Sure, he's American,' Jacob conceded. 'But what about school? You only have one year of art school and

258

already you want to quit? You've got talent. It's a sin against God not to use it.'

'I can draw, Dad. And I'm good at math. But I'm sick of school. I just want to help Lokis get through university and have a baby as soon as I can.'

Instantly her father looked worried. 'You are pregnant? Is that what this is all about? You have to get married?'

'No, no, I promise. It's nothing like that. But I wish I were. I just want to be married. I want my own home. I know it sounds hopelessly middle class but that's all I've ever really wanted.'

'You're too young to get married,' her father grumbled.

'OK, but if I'm going to marry anybody, it might as well be Lokis, right? I mean, basically you like him,' Susie persisted.

'Basically I like him, yes. What's not to like? He loves you. I love you. That much we agree on for sure.'

'And I love you, Daddy!' Susie threw her arms around him. 'It's going to be a beautiful wedding and a perfect marriage, you just wait!' Her father hugged her back. Susie's enthusiasm was hard to resist. She was so fiercely determined to be genuinely happy and to make others around her happy. And after all, what else was life for?

The wedding was held out of doors and the weather was perfect. Susie carried a parasol, trimmed with white ribbon and antique lace, to ward off the sun, and her attendants wore big, wide-brimmed straw hats. Tracy and all the other five attendants were brunettes. Susie had designed and made her own wedding dress, an ivory silk cloud of Italian satin with a V front and back, wedding-band collar and bonnet sleeves, just the tiniest hint of a bustle and froths of antique lace at the neck and wrists. Her blonde hair was curled into long ringlets that fell halfway down her back and she carried fresh gardenias. Aunt Bea had tried in vain to talk her into silk flowers. Lokis and his six groomsmen were all in powder-blue tuxedos and the bridesmaids were in blue gingham. Tracy's fear were completely unfounded. She and her fellow attendants looked fresh and natural and softly nostalgic. There was plenty of blue gingham left over, so she had lined her cedar hope chest with it. No point in letting it go to waste and, besides, every time she opened the chest, the lining would remind her how perfect her wedding had been. They had a harpist and a flautist and Susie's cousin, Raasa, sang, 'There Is Love'. Raasa's daughter Tiffany was flower girl, daintily strewing rose petals down the garden path, and Lokis's nephew Peter carried the two rings on a blue velvet pillow up to the rose-covered arch. And, most wonderful to her, was Lokis, waiting for her at the altar, proud and handsome, his eyes glowing with love.

Susie had wanted Aunt Bea to cater the reception but Bea said no, they should both take a day off cooking and hold the reception at the Radisson Hotel in downtown Minneapolis, where she knew the chef and could personally oversee the buffet. Everybody pigged out and danced the night away until Susie changed into her going-away outfit and she and her husband climbed into their powder-blue Toyota, which was covered with Kleenex pompoms and crêpe paper streamers. They were going to spend their honeymoon night in a real log cabin in the woods at Chippewa Park.

It had been surprisingly hot for an early September day, but the night cooled off and the stars came out. Lokis picked her up and carried her over the threshold into the little cabin they had rented for the night, she was suddenly glad they had waited. Now her honeymoon would truly be a momentous event. Lokis laid kindling and logs in the real fireplace and lit the fire while Susie undressed in the tiny bathroom. She felt a thrill at the thought of 'her man' providing warmth for their little home for the night. She knew it was corny in 1979 but she didn't care.

Shyly she pushed the door of the bathroom open and peeked around the corner. As her trousseau negligée, she was wearing her mother's wedding dress from the forties, a sheer chiffon affair meant to be worn with a satin underslip. Without the slip, the chiffon dress was almost completely transparent, the lace appliqué slightly masking her breasts. From the high embroidered collar down to the base of the hemline ran a row of exactly one hundred tiny hand-stitched covered buttons. Susie had counted them all. She intended to make him unbutton each and every one, one at a time. There was something eerie about wearing her dead mother's wedding dress on her wedding night — but, at the same time, life-affirming.

Slowly she moved toward the four-poster pine bed where Lokis lay under a heavy down comforter. He smiled at her and held out his hand. 'What's that you're wearing?'

'My mother's old wedding dress. Do you like it?'

'I love it. I've never seen anything or anyone more beautiful in all my life,' he said softly. He got out of bed and pulled back the comforter to show her that the bed was completely strewn with fresh rose petals. Susie started to cry and Lokis had tears in his eyes, too, as he pulled her down on to the sweet smelling bed. 'I love you so much, Susie, my sweet, sweet Susie,' he murmured, burying his face in her chiffon-covered breasts, 'You're all that matters to me and I want us to be together for ever.' He was breathing softly in her ear, his fingers gently stroking her neck, his mouth moving over hers. It had been so long since they had touched; with the excitement of planning for the wedding, they'd hardly seen each other. It felt so good to be in his arms again. Slowly, carefully, just as she had fantasized, he unbuttoned each

261

delicate little button, one at a time, his fingers clumsy with excitement, kissing each inch of her bare skin as it was slowly revealed to him. As the dress fell away from her body, he kissed and licked and sucked his way down her, painting her body with his tongue, feeling her tremble beneath him, making her strain upwards to him, making her reach out for him. Exploring every bit of her with his hands and his tongue, he was different and new and even more exciting. He had made her come before, but this was on a new level of erotic joy. With his mouth, he parted the soft downy hair, opening her up, letting her widen under his fingers and mouth, asking her to give herself over to him. She arched up to him, letting herself dissolve into the exquisite sensation. And then, slowly and carefully, he moved into her, he was actually inside her, gently moving within her and it felt so right, so wonderful, so perfect.

To Susie marriage was like the ultimate in playing 'house'. Lokis went off to school every day and she stayed home, cooking and cleaning. Just like Aunt Bea. She had never felt so safe, so protected, so happy to be sharing her life with someone else.

They were living on a little farm just outside Minneapolis. Lokis's parents were away in Europe for the year and they had suggested that the young couple move on to the farm. It was a hobby farm of about sixteen acres with a few horses and cows and a sizable vegetable garden. Susie was up early every morning to milk the two cows and gather some fresh eggs in time to make a huge breakfast for Lokis and send him off to the university. He told her she didn't have to get up for him, but she insisted on it. She liked sitting across the breakfast table sharing a meal with her husband. So what if she was totally out of step with the times? Were her girlfriends having as much fun as she was?

The routine of the days held a magic for her. Once the house was in order and she'd baked the bread and done whatever she was going to do in preparation for the evening's meal, she would have her own special time. Turn on the radio and dance naked around the living-room. Nobody could see her; there were no neighbours close by. Write a little poetry. Do a little sketching. Play with the tortoiseshell barn cat and her new kittens. Iron some shirts for Lokis. They had both agreed that some household tasks were 'girls' jobs' and others were 'boys' jobs'. Ironing a shirt was a girl's job. Ironing made Susie feel peaceful, seeing the wrinkles come out of the cloth, leaving the surface smooth. If only life could be controlled as easily.

Ironing a blue denim shirt for Lokis and imagining how it would look against the blue of his eyes when he put it on, or better yet how great it would look lying in a heap on the floor after he'd taken it off to make love to her, filled her with real pleasure. She had just finished reading *The Female Eunuch* in which Germaine Greer talked about the fairy-tale syndrome, how women were brought up to believe that the prince would kiss them and it would all be perfect when in fact the first time usually was horrible. Well, she had news for Ms Greer. The first time had been perfect, but the second time was even better and the third and the fourth were better still and, God, she could hardly wait for Lokis to get home.

When he walked through the door, she ran to him and jumped into his arms, kissing him all over, and he'd say, 'Come here, wench. Let's go make a baby.' And he'd carry her off into the bedroom with its huge brass bed and percale sheets. She loved it when he called her 'wench'. It made her feel sexy and slightly slutty. And she intended to sleep with only one man for the rest of her life. That's what was so great about marriage. She could be bad and do outrageously sexy things and it was

263

all legal. She'd been so afraid that once they were married, they wouldn't have anything to say to each other, that all her conversation would be used up over a couple of dinners and then what would they do for the rest of their lives? But she and Lokis couldn't seem to stop talking. They told each other everything and they even agreed on just about everything. She had always wanted a man who would be a lover and a father and a friend. Being married was like having a new best friend and getting to sleep with him, too. Lokis's parents decided to stay in Europe even longer so they had two whole glorious years of their heaven. Then one day Lokis told her they were moving to New York.

'I hate New York,' Susie said.

'This is not New York. It's Brooklyn Heights.'

'I don't care,' she said defiantly. 'I still hate it.'

'Look out the window. It's an exciting world out there. Look at all the people.'

'That's exactly what I hate. It's so crowded. I feel claustrophobic. Everywhere you turn there's somebody standing right where you want to be.'

'That's what I love about it,' Lokis crowed 'There's such a feeling of power there. We'll be at the centre of the action. The nightlife, the restaurants, the parties. I love the parties we've been giving. You're a fabulous hostess, Suse. Nobody cooks the way you do. And I love the way you've decorated the apartment.'

'But I hate this apartment. I miss the farm. I miss the country. I miss good food. I think the restaurants are terrible.' She knew she was whining but she couldn't help it.

'Damnit, Susie, I'm an artist. I'm studying to be an architect. I can't live on a farm in Minnesota, for God's sake. I have to be in New York. New York is where it's happening. One year at Pratt and look where I am. I'm already getting contracts. I'd be nowhere if we were still stuck up north.'

'I know, honey, I'm sorry. I'm just so bored and lonely. I want to have a baby. What's wrong with me? I'm young, I'm only twenty-four, I'm healthy and we fuck all the time. So why isn't it happening?'

Lokis winced at her use of the profanity. He was an artist but he wasn't that New York yet. 'I don't know, sweetheart. We're certainly trying. Maybe we're trying too hard.'

'Do you want to stop trying?'

'Hell, no.' He made a lunge for her and had her T-shirt dress off before they made it to the bedroom.

# *Ten*

The director of the Yale School of Drama and the Yale Repertory Theater was hoping to discover another Meryl Streep or Sigourney Weaver. The entire school was obsessed with Streep, looking for anyone who possessed the quality 'Streepesque' or, as Miriam liked to call it, 'creeping Streepism'. Miriam knew she didn't have that actress's classical blonde good looks and flashy technique, nor did she have Weaver's height, ironic style, or off-the-wall sense of humour. But she had something neither of the school's famous graduates possessed – passion, a deep, fiery, gut-wrenching passion, and she had it in spades. 'Volatile', 'emotional', 'extreme', 'tempestuous', 'powerful': these were the words used in years to come to describe how Miriam differed from all the others.

Despite Yale's hefty tuition, her father had caved in once again, 'OK, honey, I'll cough up the money for your first year, but you gotta make this one work. Otherwise, enough of this acting stuff, you get yourself a real job, OK?'

'OK,' Miriam agreed with only a twinge of guilt and trepidation. In addition to the acting training, Yale offered her a unique opportunity to perform in full-scale productions attended and reviewed by the New York critics. It meant an amazing opportunity to learn more about her craft and Miriam promised herself that she would give herself over to it completely. They warned her she would be worked to death. She was ready for that.

They told her the pressure would be intense. She swore she could handle it. She was going to make them forget all about Streep and Weaver. By the time she graduated from Yale, there would be a new legend, the legend of Miriam Newman. She wouldn't allow herself to be sidetracked the way she had been at NTS. Morgan was becoming a distant memory.

At Yale each director set himself up as a guru. Each drama teacher had his own brand of acting technique. It seemed to Miriam that each guru that came along would be shot down only to be replaced by another guru just as Miriam was beginning to catch on to his method. Her artistic psyche seemed to be being buffeted about even more than it had been in Montreal but, at the end of the first year, suddenly, miraculously, her vision cleared and she found her own style of acting. Everyone in the class was outstanding, a much higher calibre of actors than at NTS, but Miriam came to realize that she was the best. She was truly unique, a genuine original of her own making.

If the credo at NTS had been 'don't think − be', then the motto at Yale was 'don't be − think'. Miriam's acting combined the best of both. She loved researching character. All her good-student urges came out as she pored over seventeenth-century French painters and listened to Couperin in preparation for her role as Elmire in *Tartuffe*. When she was cast as Blanche in *Streetcar*, she spent her spring break in the French quarter of New Orleans, walking the streets, drinking Southern Comfort and listening to the blues, soaking up the atmosphere to ground her performances in reality. She was a master of preparation, but once on stage, she gave herself over to the moment and took extraordinary risks.

For years to come, the Yale instructors talked about that breathtaking moment in Chekhov's *Cherry Orchard* where, as Madame Ranevskya, forced to leave her family home for ever, she had made a wide, slow circle of the stage, arms outstretched as if to embrace every stick of furniture, and then removed her outer clothes, in bits and pieces, circling faster and faster, as if to divest herself of every particle of her former life. It was the total antithesis of the way the moment was usually played, not nostalgic and sentimental, but wild to the point of hysteria, the anguish of being forced out of the past and the joy of a greatly longed for and now suddenly possible hope of freedom.

In three years at Yale, she played over forty leads of incredible versatility and range. She played Blanche and Antigone and Desdemona. She sang the lead in *Threepenny Opera* and she played a very bizarre Dorothy in an experimental version of *The Wizard of Oz*. She was Yale's leading lady and she intended to be starring on Broadway within the next three years. Nothing and nobody could get in her way. Until *Cat on a Hot Tin Roof* and Stephen Andrews.

Miriam is in one of her rare slim periods. Stephen Andrews. Six-foot-five, so tall and powerful he makes her feel small and delicate. Sandy hair, aquamarine eyes, an athlete's body with a scholar's intellect and a certain kind of aloof charm guaranteed to inflame Miriam. The clawing, crotch-acting, sexual frustration of Maggie the Cat for Brick has become her own desire for Stephen Andrews. Like an animal in heat, she longs for him to notice her, desperate for his touch to free the passions he evokes in her. He never really looks at her, only plays a scene to her. He doesn't seem to know she exists. Her emotions spilling out all over the stage, all over him, don't seem to interest him. She wonders what does?

'I've got a lot to live up to,' he tells her one night after rehearsal, sitting in Joe's Pizza Parlor at a corner table under an autographed picture of Frank Sinatra who refers to Joe as his *paesano* and testifies to the delights of his pizza. The sign in the window said A PIZZ which Stephen explains is the authentic Italian term for pizza. He is so obviously upper middle-class WASP preppie.

How does he know so much about New Haven's underground? There's a lot she wants to ask him but she senses she will get further with him if she lets him do the talking.

'I come from a long line of New England Democrats,' he continues. 'True blue Yankee lawyers. I mean, we're talking Plymouth Rock, ancestors on the *Mayflower* here. But don't let the blue blood fool you. I'm against nuclear power and I'm for social change. I intend to make a difference in this world. Otherwise, what's the point?'

Miriam watches the smoke from his cigarette curl lazily up and join the rest of the smoke in the room. She loves the bars in the eastern US, all dark and smoke, with the neon Pabst and Coors signs advertising draught beer on tap. No California-style hanging plants and wicker furniture for Joe's Pizza Parlor. Joe knows that a bar should look like a bar, crowded and dim and slightly sinful.

'It must be difficult being the son of a congresswoman,' she says tentatively, hoping to keep him talking. Up until now they have communicated solely through the words of Tennessee Williams. When Stephen suggested they go out for a drink to talk about the show, Miriam jumped at the chance. 'I mean I guess she's quite famous, pretty outspoken. How does your father deal with that?'

'Dad's dead,' Stephen says abruptly, pouring each of them a glass of wine from the bottle he ordered personally from Joe. 'That's why Grace has his seat. When he died, she ran in his place on a platform promising to fulfil his mandate.'

'She sounds like a pretty gutsy lady.' Miriam stares at the huge thick-crust pizza. Pizza is death to her hips.

270

'Gutsy? I don't know. Obsessed is more like it. I think Grace sees herself as a cross between Rose Kennedy and Cornelia Wallace.' Stephen allows himself a small secret mile.

In repose, his face is strangely passive, as if he is withholding his blessing from people, which makes the occasional smile seem all the more valuable. I know it's a cliché, Miriam thinks to herself, but when he smiles, it's like the sun breaking through the clouds. He really is a beautiful man. She takes a sip of the acrid Italian wine and involuntarily makes a face.

'Too sour for you? Valpolicella's better than true Chianti. That stuff's pure vinegar. What do you think of this? Smooth, isn't it?'

'Oh, it's great.' Miriam doesn't want to tell him that the only wine she grew up with was Camel Concord grape, which has a sugar content six times that of what they're drinking tonight. She allows herself a tiny corner of pizza to counteract the wine's acidity. Pizza is the last thing she needs now that Zasie, the costume designer, has announced his decision to keep her in a thin, peach-coloured satin slip for most of the show. If she eats this pizza, she'll have to fast for twenty-four hours to make up for the damage of twenty minutes. She decides it's worth it as Stephen goes on.

'The duchess is very stubborn.' Stephen downs his wine in one gulp and refills his glass.

'Why do you call your mother the duchess? Is it a family joke?'

'No,' Stephen says with a laugh, but it is not a real one. It has a choked sound to it. 'Believe me, if you met Grace, you'd know. She's a dictatorial, domineering old bitch.'

Miriam is shocked, almost titillated, that he would refer to a parent so casually and harshly. In her world, parents are sacred. 'Do you call her that to her face? The duchess?'

271

'Sure. She is the kind of woman who assumes that it's a compliment. Grace may represent the common people but she hardly has what I would call the common touch.'

'Do you call her Grace in real life, too?'

'In real life?' He lifts an eyebrow mockingly. 'Of course. Why not?'

'Miriam's eyes widen. 'I can't imagine calling my mother by her first name, even now. I'm almost old enough to vote, but I'm sure she still thinks of me as her fat little girl.'

'You're not fat,' Stephen says quickly. 'You've got a beautiful body.' Miriam flushes and lets her fingers move nervously to the candle in the centre of the table. 'What's the matter, you don't like the way you look?'

'I've got a great look for a character actress, I know that. But, God, I hope I don't have to wait till I'm thirty-five to make it. They keep telling me I'll grow into my look, but this profession is so cut-throat. I wasted a year and a half in Canada at theatre school before I even got to Yale so I feel like I'm already behind.'

'You're going to be a brilliant Maggie,' Stephen says seriously.

'You really think so?' Miriam begins to pick at the ball of multicoloured waxes that have melted together from the various candles stuck into the bottle on the red and white checked tablecloth.

'You've got the kind of face that changes from moment to moment. I read so much in your face. You can go from being quite plain' — Miriam winces — 'no, no, it's wonderful, really it is . . . to being truly radiant. Your emotions are right up front. I really envy that. You're absolutely gorgeous and what makes you even more intriguing is that you really don't know how gorgeous you are.' He stops suddenly. 'What's the matter, am I embarrassing you?'

'Not at all,' Miriam says tartly. 'It's just that you sound

like you're describing an *objet d'art*, not a living, breathing person sitting across from you.' Who happens to be more than a little in love with you, she finishes silently.

'You're a terrific actress, you know.'

Now she is blushing. 'Well, Maggie is a bit of a stretch for me. I mean, physically, I know I'm not right for the part. But I do think I understand her emotionally. That incredible frustration of wanting something you can't have.'

'Do you?' Stephen is looking at her curiously. 'Funny. I had you pegged as a typical Jewish American Princess, stuck-up, spoiled and self-protective.'

'Oh really?' Instantly she hates him. 'Isn't that interesting. That's exactly my assessment of you. Old money. More than a bit of a snob. In fact, a pseudo-intellectual, pseudo-liberal snot. Not to mention a racist.'

'Hey, hey, take it easy!' His voice is softer now, gentler. 'I said it was only my first impression. And calling you a JAP is not a racist remark. We're talking culture here, not race.'

'Boy, do you have a lot to learn,' Miriam says hotly.

'I love it when you get angry. Let those sparks fly!'

'And you're a sexist. I bet the famous Grace would not be pleased to hear you talking like a male chauvinist porker.'

Stephen nods. 'You're right there. Believe me, I wasn't being sexist. I admire your passion. When we do that last scene together, you literally eat up the stage. I don't have a chance, I know it. What I'd like to find out is where all that passion in the scene is coming from. You've got the power to play Maggie, no doubt about it, but do you really understand her crazy need to hold on to a lost cause? You don't seem the type to give yourself over to unrequited love.'

If you only knew, Miriam thinks, smiling wryly. 'Don't

273

slot me into the "repressed Jewish bourgeois Hausfrau looking for the perfect husband" pigeon-hole. I'm too big to fit into it.'

Stephen is laughing genuinely for the first time. 'Back off, please. I don't know what I meant. Believe me, you don't fit any stereotype. I wouldn't dream of slotting you into any hole. You're genuinely singular and unique, one of a kind, a first edition, they broke the mould when they made you . . .'

Miriam is laughing now, too. 'OK, OK, I believe you! What about you? If we're really going to research these roles, let's put you in the hot seat. Have you ever loved someone who didn't love you?'

'Other than family? I doubt it.'

'Family? What do you mean? Of course your family loves you. Parental love is a given.'

'Sure. Maybe for you . . .' Then hastily as he sees she's about to jump in with a question, he adds, 'Look, love isn't at the top of my list right now. Let's forget it. I don't want to analyse any more. I really only wanted to take you out tonight to tell you how marvellous you are on stage and how much I envy you. The character takes you over. I can see it happening. You stop being Miriam. You *become* Maggie. It's an amazing process to watch.

'That doesn't happen to me. I've got the looks and the presence, and sometimes that's enough to fool the people at least part of the time, but basically I'm just playing myself. Grace says my personality is too strong for me to lose it in a character. She thinks I'm not cut out to be an actor. Hell, I don't know, maybe she's right. But I'm not ready to give up yet. The head of the drama department here is encouraging me to switch from law to drama. If he thinks I can make it in the business, why should I care what my mother believes?'

'Is she pushing you to go into politics?'

'Of course. Fortunately, my brother Richard is first

in line to inherit the throne, so as far as I'm concerned, I'm off the hook. The duchess packed me off to Yale to study law. I love acting, but if I ever decided to go into the theatre full-time, it would mean a battle royal at home.'

'But isn't it your choice? What do you want, Stephen?' Miriam demands, finally giving in to temptation, grabbing a hunk of pizza and taking a big bite of sausage and cheese. Impassioned discussion always made her hungry.

'I suppose,' Stephen says carefully, giving her another one of his slowly growing thousand-watt smiles, 'if I looked into the depths of my own ego, what I'd really like to be is a star.'

He's certainly gorgeous enough. His extreme height gives him a commanding presence, like a tall, golden god. Stephen doesn't even have to try, but the fact that he does try makes him all the more persuasive. Something behind those piercing blue-green eyes, something enigmatic and brooding, draws people to him like a magnet. He can walk into the student union, sit alone at a table, and within fifteen minutes have everybody else in the room gathered around him.

He seems to be totally unaware of the sexual frenzy he arouses in Miriam. She alternates between being glad he hasn't picked up on it and wanting to blurt out her undying passion. Since the night at Joe's Pizza Parlor, he has remained pleasant and polite, but if anything, even more distant.

When they get together to run lines for *Cat*, Miriam can't concentrate on the cues. She finds herself doing little mind fucks. What if I reached out and took Stephen's hand and licked between each finger? What if I took that fourth finger, the one with the ring from Phillips Exeter, what if I put that finger into my mouth and sucked on it, would that wake him up? What if I sank my teeth right into that point just inside the open collar of his shirt, that point on his shoulder where I can see a tiny blue vein pulsing? What if I slid my hand down behind his belt, beneath his pants, and grabbed that perfect ass? The pure rawness of her fantasies startles her. She rationalizes them by reminding herself that she is, after all, playing one of Tennessee Williams' lustiest characters on stage.

A Maggie, in another fantasy world, breathless with love, dripping with lust, wearing a peach silk slip that makes her look almost nude, she sprawls on the huge brass bed, begging for Brick to take her and impregnate her. The line between Stephen and Brick blurs as she loses herself night after night in theatrical sexual ecstasy. The more she hooks into the lust of the character, the more she feels the lust, the more she pursues him; the more Brick/Stephen resists, the more she pursues. She loses all concept of time. She ceases to exist except for the three hours that she spends every night at the theatre on stage on the bed. Miriam is on the brass bed, she's completely wet, inside and out, thick tendrils of her long, curly black hair, sticking to her neck and forehead, the sweat dripping off her shoulders and barely covered breasts, while he sits there in his white silk pyjamas, drinking stage bourbon and looking right through her, so removed and so enviably cool. If only the torture would end soon, if only it would never end.

On closing night of the show, the last performance, in the last scene of the last act, Miriam cradles him in her arms, looking down at him with her own subtext of infinite love and tenderness. She speaks the last lines of the play: 'Oh, you weak, beautiful people who give up with such grace. What you need is someone to take hold of you . . . gently, with love . . .' A cloud seems to lift from Stephen's eyes, those incredible blue-green eyes staring up at her, suddenly full of genuine tears and a look of such real need that Miriam loses her breath, stumbles, and improvises the final words of the play. An absolutely real moment on stage, so rare that it completely catches her off guard and she remains frozen on the bed.

As the curtain comes down, they both remain in their final positions, looking at each other, at Stephen and Miriam, looking into each other for the first time. Slowly Stephen moves away from her and off the bed, still holding her with his gaze. He stands by the bed, searching her face, and she wants to hold him there for ever. Suddenly he bends down and swoops her up off the bed, carrying her off stage, behind the wings, down the winding steel staircase, past wardrobe and make-up, the props shop, the green room and straight into his dressing room. He carefully sets her down and pauses just long enough to lock the door. With tumultuous applause and shouts of bravo ringing over the loudspeaker, Miriam starts to pull away from him, but he shoves her up against the wall and begins kissing her hard, feverishly, as if he wants to bruise her with his mouth, to leave his mark on her. His breath is hot and heavy, he is panting and sweating. Lifting her up, light as a piece of delicate glass she has never felt so small and fragile, he wraps her legs around his waist. Tears streaming down his face, one hand holding her wet, slippery body against the wall, the other searching frantically, almost roughly, between her legs, finding the wetness that is already there, the melting that betrays her need, begging for it, fingers thrusting into it. 'I love her, I love you,' he whispers fiercely, biting at her, pulling at her. 'Please, Miriam, love me, I need you to love me, love me now, oh God, please, love, love . . .' His mouth moving urgently against her neck, licking her, sliding down, wet and demanding, to her breast, until he finds the nipple hardened through the satin of her thin slip, sucking on it as though he will never let her go.

On stage, the curtain opens for the curtain call,

revealing a bare stage with an empty bed. The audience gasps at the brilliant symbolism of the moment. A symbol of the sterility and lack of communication for which this playwright is famous. No need for a curtain call. The audience goes wild.

In the dressing room, Miriam and Stephen also go wild, fucking furiously on the make-up table, on the floor, in the shower, and on the Equity-approved couch. She is clinging to him as he moves her around the room, thrusting against him again and again. He is moaning, sounds torn out of him that she has never heard, never expected to hear. She is opening up to him, pulling him inside her, grabbing on to his hardness, feeling him pulse within her as the orgasm overtakes him, but in minutes he is hard again, inside her, without leaving her, they are both crying now, licking each other's tears, and crying out their love to each other.

He was so different from Morgan that Miriam couldn't believe she was attracted to him, but maybe it was because he was so different. Morgan had not been a small man but Stephen would dwarf him. And he was a genuine, blue-blooded WASP. He loved the fact that she was Jewish. He thought that guaranteed she would be 'hot-blooded', the opposite of him. It was true that he was cool and contained, elegant and classy, more in control of his emotions and (seemingly) of every situation than she was. Again and again, he brought her to her knees with desire, but once she was there, he joined her with equal passion. She loved looking at him, couldn't get enough of his sandy hair and intense eyes, the gentle, slow burning smile, and the Greek statue's body. Once he caught her staring at him and he said, 'You know, Mim I do have a brain. Sometimes I think you only love me because I'm good-looking.'

'That's not the only reason,' she said, 'but it is at the

278

top of my list.' She hated to admit it, but sleeping with Morgan had not prepared her for the beauty that was Stephen.

He was very good at making her wait, at teasing her in just the right way, holding her away from him, doing magical things with his tongue and his fingers. And he loved her body, he genuinely loved it. With Morgan, no matter how much he praised her, no matter how gently he touched her, in her heart she felt he preferred the slender, flat-chested pre-pubescent type, the type Miriam would never be and hadn't been even when she was pre-pubescent. But Stephen revelled in her flesh, in the fullness of her breasts, in the curve of her hips, even the expanse of her thighs, as he kissed and licked and sucked and bit every inch of her in adoration. 'I haven't kissed you here,' he would whisper, kissing the back of her knee and then working his way up to the curve of her buttocks. 'I need to taste you here' − sliding his tongue into the curve of her armpit and tasting the drops of sweat there. 'I want to touch you here. . . now' − and his hand moved between her thighs. He made her believe she was gorgeous, and he made her come. A lot. She was hooked.

At first she was frightened, afraid that giving so much to Stephen would take away from what she had to give on stage. But, surprisingly, her passion for him off stage only served to fuel her passion on stage for her work. She felt she could do anything. She was getting by on five hours of sleep a night, her scholastic average had risen a point, and the energy just kept flowing through her.

He was reserved and cool, but once that reserve came down, all defences came down with it, at least physically. 'Your mother must have brought you up right,' she told him.

'No, actually I'm the family rebel,' Stephen laughed almost shyly. 'Getting dirty was a sin in my family.

Technically we're Episcopalian but there's a strong Puritan streak in the family. Grace insisted that we kids be scrupulously clean. If my brother Richard or I got a speck of dirt on us while playing, our clothes had to be changed immediately. Dirt must be avoided at all costs.'

'Maybe that's why you're secretly drawn to my darker places. You want to throw yourself in the mud and roll around it.' Miriam let her hand slide along his thigh.

'You got it, babe. Come here' − he pulled her head down to him − 'Let's do dirty things. Make me dirty.'

He told her that his mother, while being an ardent feminist, was straitlaced when it came to sex. 'Once she caught me masturbating and she tied my hands together behind my back and made me stand naked in the corner. When Dad came home and found out what she had done, he was appalled. He said something like that could screw me up for life.'

'You seem pretty healthy in that department. But Grace Andrews, feminist champion of birth control and unlimited access to abortion? I would have thought she'd regard the sexual impulse as natural and normal.'

'Oh, sure, bodily appetites are natural and normal, but they must be controlled. "Put your energy into what will accomplish the most, do the most good," she would say. "The most important thing in life is to do what you set out to do and not get sidetracked along the way. Use the looks and the power given you to make people believe in you. Don't fritter them away for momentary pleasure. You are part of a very special family. You were born with a responsibility and you mustn't abdicate your responsibility just for a bit of fun." Grace can make the word fun sound ominous and sinful,' Stephen said wryly. Miriam hadn't even met his mother yet but she imagined a formidable matriarch.

'She's not a gorgon, but she is one hell of a strong lady. Second best was never tolerated in our house. We were

280

brought up to be winners. Grace believes that some people are born to lead and others to follow.'

'And I take it you're not meant to be a follower?'

'Hardly. I come from a long line of domination and authoritarianism. I'm doing my best to break the tradition and the family is doing its best to hold me to it.' Bit by bit, Miriam learned about his past, what it was like for him to grow up as a member of the richest family in Wallingford, Connecticut. 'It was confusing, you know? We're supposed to be liberal Democrats but we've got enough money to buy and sell the whole town. Roosevelt Democrats, my mother calls us.'

'I assume she means Franklin, not Teddy.'

'Right. My grandfather was actually a friend of FDR. Grandad is really quite something. He's a self-made man who created this journalism empire . . .'

Miriam had heard of Andrews Enterprises. She knew the saga of the small-town family newspaper that had grown up to stick its fingers into a lot of different corporate pies.

'A scion of the town, the backbone of the community, and what a rigid backbone he is. We're talking about a family wiped out on politics. Prime dinner-table topic of my formative years was the state of international affairs. He pushed my father into politics, got him elected governor of the state and then, when Dad died, he pushed my mother to run in his place and got her elected, too.'

'Come on Stephen, I'm sure the voting public had something to do with it. Everybody agrees Grace made a terrific governor.'

'Oh, sure. Better than my father. Now she's retired and she's pinning all her hopes on Richard.'

'He seems to be doing fine.'

'Richard is doing OK.' Stephen's face shadowed slightly at the mention of his brother, who was a United States senator. 'I think he pushes himself too hard, but

I know he feels he's in some sort of battle with time.'
Richard had been confined to a wheelchair for the past
three years.

'He was wounded in Vietnam, wasn't he?'

'Yeah, but the crazy part is he wasn't even fighting in
the war. He was already a senator and he was over there
on a Congressional fact-finding mission. There were
rumours of our guys committing various atrocities and
they were sent over to check them out. Nixon's president
— we're talking a mostly Republican committee — so they
don't want to look too hard or too deep. They mostly
want to sit around the hotel pool in Saigon drinking rum-
and-Coke and availing themselves of all the cheap nooky.
But Richard's a shit disturber; he wants to jump right into
the fray and go where the action is. ''We're not finding
any facts,'' he says. ''We're basically getting wasted and
waiting to be flown out of here.'' He was really pissed
off because he wasn't getting any help from Washington
and no support from the troops based in Saigon. They
were telling him, ''Go back to Washington. Keep your
nose out of it. We've got a war to fight.'' Richard was
having none of that. He got himself a ride on an evac
copter that was not well armed. They were flying straight
into the war zone when they were shot down.'

'Oh no.'

'It gets worse. In the area in which he was shot down,
there were no Charlies around . . .'

'What does that mean?'

'It means just what you think it means. If there were
no Charlies, he must have been shot down by Yankee
troops.'

'Oh Stephen!'

'Well there were certainly a lot of people who didn't
want him around. People saw him leaving by chopper
and he was shot down where there were no Cong.'

'I thought they were everywhere.'

282

'No. It took two years before the Cong got that close to Saigon.'

'Oh God, Stephen,' Miriam whispered.

'When the chopper came down the pilot was dead and Richard was badly inured. A young black corpsman patched him up and radioed for help. They came and airlifted him out without any flak at all.'

'But there must have been an inquiry into the whole thing? I mean . . .'

'Oh sure, there was a full-scale congressional investigation, but it never came to much. Nobody knew anything. If they did they weren't saying anything.'

'But the black medic he must have seen what happened.'

'No, he was killed shortly after. Richard doesn't really know what happened. He has his theories. Anyway, the medic's dead and Richard's alive, but he's paralysed. There's a lot of damage to the spinal cord and it may be deteriorating. We just don't know. I don't think Richard wants to know. He's got a lot to do and he's just going to keep on doing it.'

'So I guess you feel you've got a lot to live up to?'

'Well, expectations always ran high in our family. It was always "be the best you can be." Both Richard and I were sent to military school. We both hated it, although I handled it better than he did. Grandfather was a pretty tough disciplinarian, even tougher than Dad, and he imposed strict curfews on us. I mean, the other side of "be the best you can be" was "I'm very disappointed in you. Perhaps you're not going to amount to anything after all." '

'Jesus. So you tried to be perfect.'

'No, I abdicated. I left that responsibility to Richard. He's the perfect one in the family. Let him carry the torch. He's the talker. He's the brains. He's the guiding light and the great white hope.'

'But I bet you're everybody's favourite.'

'Why?'

'Because you're the prettiest.'

Stephen laughed. 'How do you know?'

'Listen, I've seen that picture of the two of you on your desk. Richard's cute, OK, and the wheelchair makes him romantic in a tragic sort of way . . .'

'Don't joke about it.' He was suddenly very angry.

'Come on, babe, you've got to find a way to laugh. You're just as good as Richard and none of you Andrews are that much better than everybody else, I don't care what Grace tells you.'

'Oh really?' Stephen gave her a little, slightly superior smile. 'We have an image to maintain. Grace says we're the closest thing to royalty this country has. To Grace, you're either vile or perfect. There's no in-between.'

'Oh, great,' Miriam said, 'I can hardly wait to meet her. Which category do Jews fit into?'

'I told you we're liberal Democrats,' Stephen said stiffly. 'Nobody in our family is anti-Semitic.'

'Yeah, I'll just bet, Miriam thought. She had taken Stephen home to Fresno to meet the folks over spring break. Her mom and Valerie and Barb thought Stephen was as handsome as a movie star, 'even sexier than Robert Redford.' Her dad, after circling warily around him for a day or two, ended up shooting baskets with him in the back yard and eventually decided he was 'pretty bright and an OK guy.' Of course she knew that her parents would prefer that he be Jewish, but nobody was talking marriage yet and it was obvious that Stephen really cared about her. She knew they liked him far better than they would have liked Morgan if they had ever met him. All in all his visit had gone pretty well. She did not have equal expectations for her own presentation to the Andrews family in Wallingford.

The house was a huge stone restored farmhouse on

284

what appeared to be a vast acreage nestled in the rolling hills of Connecticut. It couldn't quite be termed palatial, but when a butler met them at the door, Miriam knew she was definitely entering another world. Thanks a lot, babe, she thought, you might have prepared me a little better for this. The butler took Miriam's overnight case with a great deal of show, glancing at it with just a flicker of disdain, and ushered her upstairs to the guest room. It was full of early American antiques, much maple and brightly flowered chintz, a four-poster bed with an appliqué quilt, hooked rug, chamber pot, marble washstand with pitcher and basin — obviously for decoration only — and a lot of very old family photographs hanging on the walls. There was even a plate rail lined with a multitude of blue and white china plates just over her head. It looked like something out of a movie about George Washington and the battle of Valley Forge.

'I'll send the maid up to unpack your things,' the butler said.

'No thanks,' Miriam said quickly, 'I can do that myself.' No way was she going to let some stranger paw through her socks and undies. She took a deep breath, knowing that she would have to draw on all her research for the Henry James play she had done in her first year at Yale.

The redoubtable Grace looked much younger and tinier than Miriam had expected, even though she had seen pictures of her. She was maybe a little over five feet tall, blonde and razor-thin, with a strong jaw and sharp eyes. The quintessential WASP queen. Instantly Miriam felt fat and swarthy. George Andrews, Grandad, was exactly as she'd pictured him, tall, craggy, formidable, a handsome figure of an old man with a shock of white hair, reminding her of Ralph Bellamy. He hardly said two words to her the entire weekend.

But Richard was, well, just as wonderful as Stephen had described him. He looked a lot like Stephen, with the same sandy hair, although his was curlier and fell down over his forehead in almost a rakish way, with the same intelligent eyes and level gaze, and more of a twinkle. His legs were twisted in the chair and had obviously atrophied, but Miriam only noticed them on first meeting. After that she was drawn to his eyes, the way he looked at her, into her, as though he was sharing a secret with her.

'Brains, beauty and talent,' he said, giving her the once-over. The heavy lines around his eyes and mouth betrayed the pain he must constantly be in. 'That's what I call a triple threat. You done good, little brother. Oops, sorry, Grace, I hope you don't consider that a sexist remark. I'm just stating the facts.' He shrugged charmingly.

'You haven't offended me,' Miriam said, taking his outstretched hand. There was such genuine warmth in the way he spoke to her that she felt more comfortable already. He made her feel his attention was completely focused on her. No wonder he was such a successful politician.

'Stop that, Richard. Behave yourself. Hello, I'm Grace and I insist you call me Grace. I feel as though I already know you, Stephen's told us so much about you.' Grace drew her away. 'It's a delight to meet you, Miriam. What a lovely Old Testament name. Miriam.' She let her lips roll around it as though she had a small marble of shit in her mouth.

'And a very popular old family name here in New England, too, I gather,' Miriam countered smoothly. She wasn't going to let this sharp-edged little woman push her around, even if she had been governor of Connecticut for two consecutive terms. She looked at Stephen who couldn't seem to make up his mind whether to be embarrassed or proud that Miriam was meeting his mother head on. She hoped she'd never be placed in the position of having to say to Stephen, 'It's between your mother and me; now choose.' She wondered if Grace would ever put him in that position.

Richard laughed and she could see a glimmer of respect in George Andrews' eyes as he led the way into the dining-room. Dinner progressed fairly smoothly. The five of them sat at an enormous walnut dinner table and worked their way through eight courses of an indifferent meal of pot roast, acorn squash, creamed onions, and something called Indian pudding for dessert. It tasted like corn meal mush. The conversation bubbled along on a superficial level.

Miriam thought she was acquitting herself well. Luckily she had played Tracy Lord in *The Philadelphia Story* at the beginning of the season. Actually she would have known which fork to use and what to do with a finger bowl even if she hadn't played Tracy, but she liked to believe that each part she played enriched her, made her a more well-rounded person. Stephen was seated on her right and she couldn't easily catch his eye and assess how he thought she was doing, but halfway through the meal she felt his hand slide over on to her knee and slip up under her dress so she figured she was doing fine.

After dinner, they moved into the sitting-room, another room furnished in chintz and maple and hooked rugs, to sip coffee and brandy. In front of the fire, the conversation heated up as Richard began berating Nixon and Watergate and talking about how difficult it was to be a Democrat in this regime and how a lot was going to come out about Nixon eventually, much more than anyone could possibly guess. Miriam sat quietly sipping her Calvados and watching and listening. This was an old actor's trick of hers, to sit back and observe, to try to determine the power balance, and to study the other characters. It was a show in itself to watch the Andrews family in action, sparking off each other as the argument escalated in intensity with Grandad and Grace often playing devil's advocate to whatever line Richard took. At first Miriam couldn't understand what she was watching, but then she realized that to them it was a game, an exercise, a sort of verbal political scrimmage in which there were no clear-cut winners. The debate was all. She was pleased to see that Stephen held his own well. He jumped right into the fray with Richard. Then, just as suddenly as it had started, the discussion was over and everyone went upstairs to go to bed – Stephen and Miriam to their separate rooms.

The next morning Miriam discovered that Grandad and Stephen had gone out to look at the horses and maybe take an early morning ride. That left her shoved into a cosy breakfast nook surrounded by more blue and white wallpaper and blue and white china, sitting across from Grace. She figured that Grace had set up the little scene herself. Miriam took a deep breath and braced herself for the challenge.

'I like you, Miriam, I really do,' Grace said, taking half a teaspoon of brown sugar out of the sugar bowl and dropping it on to the hot oatmeal in her bowl. 'You're obviously intelligent, you've lovely to look at, and you seem very independent. I admire that.' She stopped to remove a few grains of brown sugar and place them neatly on the side of the plate under her bowl. Miriam waited impatiently, fingering her teacup. 'I'm sure you know that I have high hopes for my son, for both my sons in fact. Richard's doing remarkably well.'

'He's amazing,' Miriam murmured. 'I have tremendous respect for him. And for you. You accomplished a lot as governor of this state. I wish you were willing to run again. We need strong women in government.'

'Thank you, dear.' Grace gave her a slightly surprised

smile. 'But my days in politics are definitely over. Richard's definitely on his way and Stephen . . . I've got plans for Stephen. I hope . . .' She stopped again.

Miriam kept silent, finishing the sentence in her own mind: I hope you're not going to stand in his way or hang on to him. I hope this is just a college romance.

'I have my own career and my own plans,' Miriam volunteered politely after a few seconds, firmly stirring two heaping spoonfuls of brown sugar into her own oatmeal.

'I'm sure you do, but . . .'

'Look, Mrs Andrews . . .'

'Grace.'

'Mrs Andrews. Stephen and I are serious about each other, if that's what you want to know, but we do not have any serious intent beyond that. I am serious about becoming a professional actress. Stephen is serious about becoming a lawyer. I don't think his goals include politics.'

'Not now.'

'In that case, you may be disappointed. But that's something between you and him, of course. At the moment he and I intend to enjoy each other's company for as long as that enjoyment lasts. I am going to be an actress. That's where my heart really lies and Stephen understands that.'

Grace relaxed, perceptibly relieved. 'Stephen tells me you're very talented and you certainly have dramatic presence. You should do very well. There have been a number of famous Jewish actresses. Sarah Bernhardt. And of course Barbra Streisand.'

Miriam watched the brown sugar melt into a puddle of golden syrup in the middle of the lumpy cereal. 'Your Jewish voters must find the way you categorize people quite interesting. I hope I have more to recommend me as an actress.'

'Indeed you do.' Richard wheeled cheerfully and noisily into the kitchen. 'Sorry to break up the hen party, but I need a favour of you, Miriam. Can you come and give a listen to the presentation I have to make before the House Ways and Means Committee on Monday? I could use some professional pointers on my delivery. Sometimes my thoughts get ahead of my mouth and I trip over my tongue just at the most crucial point in my address.'

'Excuse me, Mrs Andrews.' Miriam slid out of the breakfast nook and followed Richard into the library where she grabbed a fat chintz pillow from the Victorian sofa and muffled a scream in it.

'Aw, Mim' — Richard fell comfortably into the diminutive of her name that Stephen was now using — 'Don't let her get to you. Grace is so used to having everything go her own way that she can't stop trying to manipulate everyone she meets on what she sees as her own personal chessboard.'

'She doesn't have to keep on hitting me even after I've told her exactly what she wanted to hear. I said that I don't have long-range designs on her precious baby son! What more does she want from me?' Miriam took a deep breath and made a concerted effort to lower her voice. The last thing she wanted was for Grace to know she'd scored a palpable hit. 'I'm sorry, I know she's your mother.'

'You're a threat. Don't underestimate your own strength here. And I personally hope that you *do* have long-range designs on Stephen. It would be very good for him. He's in love with you, in a way that he's never loved any other woman before. That's threatening to a mother, especially one as possessive as Grace.'

'Yeah, but she's supposed to be a great champion of women's rights.'

Richard grinned, pushing the wayward lock of hair

back from his forehead. 'All that goes by the boards when it comes to her own sons. Grace is a tigress where Stephen and I are concerned. You're competition. But that doesn't mean you should bow out of the game. You're wonderful for Stephen. I've never seen him so happy, so confident within himself. You make him open up and trust the world. He needs that. He needs you, Mim. I don't think you have any idea how much.'

'No.'

'Believe me. I think you could be his salvation.'

Before Miriam graduated from Yale, the New Haven arts critics wrote a paean to her talent which ended wistfully: 'And we are blessed for having had her on our stages for the past three years. We wish her well. We will miss her.'

She knew that the comfort and security of the Yale Repertory Theater would be hers for as long as she wanted it, but for her and Stephen there was only one place to be: New York.

She had an audition with Joseph Papp of the New York Shakespeare Festival at the Public Theater. Stephen had an offer from one of the biggest and best law firms in Manhattan. He had been president of the student senate and made the *Yale Law Review*. He didn't need Grace to pull strings to get him into the top law firm in New York, but of course she did pull and he had to admit her influence didn't hurt. He started at a high salary. He was already near the top and there was little or no question of it being necessary for him to work his way up.

Their first fight concerned where they were going to live. Miriam wanted to live in a loft in Bohemian Soho or at the very least on the upper West Side with the other theatrical people. Stephen was opting for the East Side, on Park Avenue. 'What are you trying to do, buy into that romantic mythology of suffering for your art? You

291

want a place with a mattress on the floor, a hanging bare bulb, and a Greek chorus of roaches?'

'No, I just want to be where the action is.'

'You are where the action is. You're in New York. Who cares whether we live on the East or West Side? If you want to feel like the proverbial starving artist, you can take the subway to auditions.'

'I know we're not starving artists. You've got a job that pays enough to support half my graduating class. But I've got to arm myself for the big struggle.'

'So, that's exactly my point. The acting profession is enough of a struggle in itself. There's no particular good-luck mantra, no hidden merit in living the struggle if you don't have to.'

As it turned out, Miriam faced no struggle at all, professionally or personally. Within two week of arriving in New York, Joe Papp hired her to play her old favourite, Helena, in a multi-racial production of *All's Well That Ends Well*. She didn't have to make the rounds, suffer the indignities of cattle-call auditions, do TV commercials or work as a waitress. She started out as a fully fledged actress and she never looked back. The role of Helena led to that of Isabella in *Measure for Measure* and Isabella led to the chance to play Mark Antony in an all-female production of Julius Caesar — 'Julie Cheshire' — as Stephen teasingly called it.

Her performances were attracting attention from the critics and from the New York theatre-going public as well. Shopping at Zabar's for Nova Scotia lox, fresh cream cheese, and bagels for their Sunday morning lie-ins together, Miriam was recognized by a customer standing in line at the check-out. 'Oh, Miss Newman, I think you're great!' exclaimed the short balding man in the tight white sailor pants and purple tank top. 'I just loved your Isabella. You were so sexy. Usually that role is played like Greer Garson and you think, ''So what's

292

the big deal about Isabella's virginity anyway, why would Angelo want to go to bed with a cold stick like that?'' But you were hot. Donny and I used to spend all our culture bucks at the Met but now we go to the theatre to see you, isn't that right, Donny?' he elbowed the guy next to him, a powerfully built curly-haired man wearing a lumberjack shirt and fatigues with a bandana in his back pocket.

Donny nodded. 'You're going to be a star, Miss Newman, and when your name's in lights on Broadway I'll be able to say I knew you when.'

Outside Zabar's, Miriam and Stephen exploded into giggles. 'You're going to be a star, babe! Take it from Donny!'

'Oh sure. I'm supposed to believe two opera queens who probably think or wish I were a man in drag!'

'Fat chance.' Stephen gave her a big sloppy kiss.

'I'm not on Broadway yet. I haven't made it yet.'

'Well, the Public is kind of considered Broadway.'

'Yeah, but it's not the *real* Broadway. I want to be on real Broadway.'

'You will be, babe. I guarantee you will be!' And he picked her up in his arms and whirled her around right there in the street in front of everybody.

The many and varied joys of Manhattan were theirs to explore as young lovers. All the museums and art galleries, the ballet and the opera. Even though Donny and his pal had stopped going to the Met, Miriam and Stephen loved it. They tried to see as many plays on and off Broadway as could be fitted into Miriam's own schedule. The Public was a rep theatre so she sometimes had nights off. They walked in Central Park and even took a horse and buggy ride, although Stephen told her that only tourists from Iowa ever did that. 'Well, I'm a tourist from Fresno,' Miriam said.

They both did a lot of cooking and shopped for special

293

ingredients at the ethnic delis and the Korean vegetable and fruit stands and the bakeries for fresh raisin pumpernickel and garlic cheese loaves and olive-oil pepper baguettes. Miriam had never seen so many different kinds of bread. And they ate out a lot. At the theatrical hangouts like Joe Allen's and Charlie's and Sardi's. At the famous old restaurants like La Cirque and La Côte Basque and The Russian Tea Room. And at the new trendy in-spots like The Quilted Giraffe and The Amsterdam Café. On the nights when they didn't go out and didn't feel like cooking, they ordered in, while Miriam waded through a pile of scripts and Stephen ploughed through a stack of briefs. On Sunday mornings, like all New York lovers, they lay in bed and did the *Times* crossword puzzle and each other.

Everything was entirely perfect. Stephen was made a partner even sooner than he and Miriam had expected. They had the apartment in New York, the run of the family house in Wallingford (although Miriam never felt really comfortable there unless Richard was in for the weekend), and were thinking about buying some property in upstate New York.

They had discussed how difficult it would be to keep two major careers going at the same time. They had agreed to trade off years, one year being Miriam's to concentrate on her career, then the next year for Stephen's career. The first year had been Miriam's and it looked like the second year had been Stephen's. Suddenly it was Stephen's year all over again when they least expected it.

They'd been out on the town, dining in a Greek restaurant with much retsina and ouzo, stopped in at the Improve to catch a new comedy act before, as Miriam put it, it turned into coke-and-fuck jokes, and then finished up at a blues club, listening to Miles Davis and drinking generous amounts of Jack Daniels. Stephen closed and locked the door to their apartment with one hand and began unbuttoning her blouse with the other. 'I've been wanting to do this all evening,' he whispered hoarsely, his fingers fumbling with the buttons. 'I could see your breasts all evening, watch your nipples getting hard. You've been driving me crazy.' Miriam immediately went to work on the buttons of his shirt, getting it off him as fast as she could manage in her drunken state. Blouse and shirt slid to the floor in heaps. He was breathing in her ear, and her hair, which had been pinned up for the evening, tumbled down over both of them. He kissed her deeply, unhooking the front clasp of her bra and tossing it away as she tugged at his belt buckle, trying clumsily to free him. His hands cupped her breasts, moving softly around her nipples until she thought she would faint if he didn't touch them. When she unbuttoned her skirt and let it fall on the floor, both of them nearly tripped over it. Heading for the bedroom, they only got as far as the sofa, leaving the trail of clothes on the floor behind them. Stephen picked her up and put her on the sofa, pulled his pants down and then he was in her. 'Beautiful, Mim, my beautiful darling, I need . . . so much, please, please . . .' and she held him, praying that this was exactly what she was giving him at that moment.

The phone shattered the moment. Miriam started to pull away, but Stephen said, 'No, no, let it ring.' They were both breathing heavily, and then they started to giggle like naughty children. Stephen said, 'No, no' again, but Miriam looked at the clock, and it was three a.m.

Something made her say, 'Answer it, Stephen.' Stephen pulled away but they were both still giggling guiltily when he finally picked up the receiver on the eleventh ring. Miriam held her skirt against her as she looked at the clock again. She could hear Stephen talking as her heart still pounded and the blood rushed in her ears. When she looked back at him she could see he had suddenly gone white. She tried to ask what was wrong but he wouldn't look at her, so she got up and went into the bedroom to put on her bathrobe. When she came out again, he had hung up and was sitting by the phone staring out into space. His hands were still shaking and he looked deathly ill.

'What's the matter?' she asked, her heart in her mouth.

'It's Richard,' he said. 'Richard's dead.'

'My God! What happened?'

'They don't know. They're not really sure. He was home, he had dinner with Grace and Grandad, they talked a bit, he went to bed. Grandad went to bed, too, but Grace was still up and she heard a crash, so she ran upstairs and into his room. He'd fallen out of bed and he didn't seem to be breathing. He's been having a lot of trouble breathing lately, you know, but she thought he was just in shock.' Stephen was speaking in a very measured tone as if explaining by rote to a child what had happened. 'Grace screamed and got the whole house up but by the time the paramedics got there he was gone.'

'Did they take him to the hospital?'

'Yes, but there was nothing they could do. He's gone. He's definitely gone.' He put his face in his hands and started to weep.

'This is so hard to take in,' Miriam said, but already the alcoholic fuzziness was gone from her brain and the objects in their living-room were coming into sharp focus. 'I mean, he's up for re-election, he's in the middle of the campaign.'

Stephen lifted his face and looked at her with streaming eyes. 'Yeah,' he said. 'Richard's only been dead two hours and Grace already wants me to run in his place.'

The funeral was big and showy, standing room only. Many people had loved and respected Richard and they

296

all wanted to pay tribute to the young politician cut down in his prime. Ted Kennedy spoke at the service and Tip O'Neill — strong, white-haired, massive Tip O'Neill — actually broke down and cried. The funeral was a long and drawn-out affair, with eulogies, military honours, and hymns. The family conference about Stephen's future that evening in the sitting-room at Wallingford was short and tense, the family members surrounded by massive arrangements of bright flowers.

'You can win, I know you can win,' Grace said. 'You've already got credibility through the family name, through my name. You're Richard's brother, for God's sake.'

'I always intended ours to be a family of kingmakers,' Grandad said. 'You can't let us down, son.'

'You owe it to Richard,' said Grace, with a half-crazed gleam in her eye. Now that she had borne up well through the funeral service she looked ready to fall apart.

'Yes, you owe it to Richard,' Grandad said. 'And to the voters of Connecticut who have put their faith in him.'

Miriam looked down at her hands and said nothing. She kept expecting Richard to say something that would make it all right as he always had done, but of course he was no longer there. Stephen said very little. He listened to his mother and his grandfather and nodded his head but it was a nod to let them know he had heard what they were saying, not that he agreed to do it.

In the car on the drive back to New York, they were both lost in their own thoughts. They sat in silence watching the windshield wipers slice through the pouring rain. Neither knew quite what to say. Finally Stephen spoke. 'I feel like Robert Redford in *The Candidate*. I don't feel ready for this. I've been avoiding this all my life and I thought the pressure was off because of Richard.'

'The pressure would never really have been off,'

Miriam said. 'Not for Grace. She's had her own game plan for you all along. It's just happened sooner than she thought it would.' She was thinking, we'll have to move to Washington. I guess we'll have to live there. Can an actress be based in Washington? No, that's selfish. How can you think about your own career at a time like this? What's more important, getting up on a stage and making a fool of yourself, pretending to be somebody who doesn't exist, or being part of the body that governs this nation? But I've just started on my way. This isn't fair.

'I don't feel ready for this,' Stephen repeated. 'But what if I can really do some good? Wouldn't it be wrong not to try?'

'I don't know the answer to that.'

'Is it what you want for me?'

'I want what you want. You know that.' One of the wipers scraped as it dragged across the windshield. It was giving her a headache.

'I know it's what Grace wants for me.'

'What do you want for you? In your heart. In your gut. Don't take any time to think about it. Just tell me. What do you want?'

Stephen took a quick, shaky breath. 'I want to go for it.'

Miriam took a deep breath herself: 'Then I'll do my best to help you get it.'


What was left of the Andrews family sprang into action. They hired a pollster. They hired a media strategist. They hired political packagers. Stephen Andrews was an image-maker's dream. Son of one of Connecticut's most wealthy and prominent families. Heir to a political dynasty. Younger brother to a hero and senatorial legend. Honest, intelligent, thoughtful, while at the same time impressing people as decisive. Not a whisper of scandal in his background. He was tall, charismatic, and very, very

298

electable. Less of a renegade than his older brother. The team sold him as a combination of old money and young ideas. Women were crazy about him. Too bad he wasn't married, but he probably would be fairly soon. He was only just thirty. Grace had the money and the profile to make him electable almost immediately.

Miriam made her own contribution to the campaign. She worked with Stephen on his speeches, instructing him on which words to stress and where to breathe, where to take a small beat for effect and where to pause a little longer to keep his audience waiting breathlessly for what he had to say next. With his height and his look Stephen could always get people to look at him; Miriam taught him to be direct, sincere, and focused so that they would continue to pay attention once he opened his mouth. She provided him with the technique that was to set him apart from other politicians, how to make a prepared text that he'd delivered many times seem fresh and spontaneous, as if the thoughts had just occurred to him and he couldn't wait to share them with his listeners.

On the campaign trail with him, on the rubber-chicken circuit, Miriam spoke to women's groups and stood at his side giving him the support he needed. She read all the newspapers she could get her hands on and cut out any articles that might be helpful to his platform, which was basically borrowed from Richard. And even Grace had to agree, she brought him a lot of Jewish votes. After several months and the help of over $1 million of family money, Stephen Joseph Andrews was elected Democratic senator for the state of Connecticut in a landslide victory.

On her own, Miriam drove to Washington and found them a place to live in a tree-lined cul-de-sac in the Georgetown area. It was an elegant little townhouse with a garden patio and wonderful antique gas lamps. Stephen took to the house immediately and to the political life almost as quickly. They kept the apartment in New York for appearances' sake. After all, they weren't married. Grace was in seventh heaven, coming to Washington as often as Stephen would allow her, to sit with Miriam at the hearings and watch him perform. Whatever path Richard had been set upon, the way was infinitely clearer for Stephen and Grace knew he was destined to go much further.

God, Washington was dull. It was such a tightly closed circle, like a highly specialized theatre company, a repertory company in which there was a hierarchy of leads, supporting actors, and bit parts, where all the players had been acting together for years. There were the usual trade secrets and company affairs that nobody was supposed to know about but which were, of course, common knowledge. Miriam told herself that she was just playing another role in her career. At all the political functions with Stephen she felt like a fish out of water with the other political wives, perhaps because she wasn't really a wife.

'Let's wait and see how all of this turns out,' Stephen had said, 'before we talk about marriage. I'm going to be doing a lot of commuting between Washington and Wallingford. You're doing a lot of commuting between Washington and New York. When do we have time to get married?' He didn't mention her spending a lot of time in Wallingford. As hard as Miriam tried, she couldn't seem to win Grace over and now she no longer had Richard to back her. She understood Grace's possessiveness but she still found it difficult to accept. She wasn't even sure she wanted to get married; she only wished that Stephen would at least ask her what she wanted.

The funny thing was, she wasn't commuting between Washington and New York. A year had gone by and she'd only been back to the city once or twice. Her acting career had come to a standstill. For a while her agent had kept calling with offers and she kept turning them down. Eventually she stopped calling. Probably they'd all forgotten about her by now, even Donny and friend. Then she got a call from Joe Papp to play Josie in Eugene O'Neill's *A Moon for the Misbegotten* opposite an incredible Irish actor from the Abbey Theatre in Dublin. The show was scheduled for a limited run at the Public, but if the reviews were good the production would definitely be headed for Broadway.

Miriam knew she was perfect casting for Josie, the outsized Irish tavern-keeper's daughter who falls in love with a tiny man. Nobody had come close to topping Colleen Dewhurst's performance opposite Jason Robards, not even Kate Nelligan. She salivated at the thought of getting her tongue around the poetry of the piece, mastering the Irish dialect, and giving herself over to the larger-than-life emotions of Eugene O'Neill.

Part of her wanted Stephen to beg her to stay in Washington, to swear he couldn't live without her, never mind how Grace felt. Miriam believed the most wonderful thing she could do now would be to marry Stephen and become an official part of the Andrews family. But instead he said, 'Go. Take the show. You'll hate yourself if you don't. And eventually you'll hate me. You've got to do it.'

He was right and she knew it. She wanted a crack at Josie. It could be her breakthrough. She had to go back to New York.

# *Eleven*

When she and Sara had come to a parting of the ways, it seemed like a kind of death to Gwen. Staying in Austin at the university was not an option; she wanted to get out of Texas altogether and she couldn't face going back to Canada. With Sara's accusations still ringing in her ears, she boarded a Greyhound and headed north. It hadn't been easy telling Uncle Jack that she wouldn't be coming into the business with him in Houston.

'I'm heading for New York,' she said, 'transferring to Columbia to get my BA. I'm thinking about becoming an oil analyst. I already know the oil side of the oil business; now I want to learn the business side.'

'Well, you're going to the right place,' Uncle Jack told her. 'If you want to be a top oil analyst, you have to be near the people who pay you. New York's the financial centre for everything, even the oil industry. But hell, I'm going to miss you, honey.' He knew something must have gone wrong for her in Austin, but he didn't press her. Instead he gave her a kiss and a letter of introduction to a contact he had at a New York brokerage firm, saying, 'If it doesn't work out, you know you've always got a place here with me.'

Fear sat like a stone in the pit of her stomach. Once again she was running away from her problems, once again she was starting all over. As the bus rolled over the Texas state line, she stared out of the window at the changing landscape of Arkansas, Tennessee, Virginia, West Virginia, Maryland, Pennsylvania, and New Jersey. The closer she got to New York, the more she felt the stone of fear dissolve and a new resolve seep in. This time was different. She was no longer a frightened girl of seventeen, overwhelmed by life and other people's expectations of her. She had done well in Texas, graduating with honours from the university and gaining a knowledge of the oil business from Uncle Jack's company. He had faith in her and that should give her the courage to find faith in herself. And this time she wasn't really running away — it was time to move on, that was all, time to start building her future. When the bus pulled into Port Authority three dusty and depressing days later, she walked out of the station into the teeming throngs on Eighth Avenue and immediately felt better.

By rights she should have been scared out of her mind. She had never heard so much noise coming at her from all sides or seen such filthy streets, full of people pushing and jostling each other. There was an energy to this adrenaline-charged city; she could feel it coming up through the sidewalk under her feet. The people all looked like Central Casting's idea of pimps, hookers and drug dealers, except that probably, Gwen suspected, they actually *were* pimps, hookers and drug dealers. Even the anonymity this huge city provided buoyed her up, a quality she recognized instantly. Nobody cared where she had come from; they were only interested in where she was going. If she worked really hard, she could probably get her Master's in eighteen months. Uncle Jack's contact turned out to be Ian McFadden, president of McFadden, Earps, Lennox, and Klein, one of the major brokerage firms in New York. Ian McFadden looked like the ideal CEO, silver-haired and strong-jawed, with just a touch of Scots brogue in his voice.

He loved the fact that Gwen was also Scottish and had a background in the oil business; he hired her as an executive assistant to their top oil and gas analyst, Jonathan Long.

Jonathan was tall and sandy haired, with a genial, relaxed manner that hid a driving, cut-throat ambition. 'I set out to make my first million by the time I was thirty and I've done it,' he said. 'It'll be tougher for you. There are virtually no female oil and gas analysts in the business at all; if you make it, you'll be one of the first. You come from the oil business and that's good. The geology degree may prove helpful, but you'll need more than that. You've got to have an analytical mind, and you've also got to have good judgement, especially in those areas that don't lend themselves to analysis. You've got to be able to call the broad trends in the industry. If you want to be the best, you've got to be plugged into the industry and gain access to privileged information.

'If you're reading about it in the newspaper, it's old news, it's already happened. It's up to you to learn to predict what's going to happen. Management, company strategy, business planning: you'll be able to get those from your courses at Columbia, and they are very important, but if you don't call the sector right, you could lose everything. The investment business is basically a crapshoot. The psychology of the stock market is based on fear and greed. So, you're getting into the business at just the right time; there's no hotter market than oil.'

Jonathan's advice was good and she knew he was right about the oil business. In the mid-seventies, oil prices were booming, quadrupling from three dollars a barrel to twelve and from twelve to thirty with no slowdown expected. Getting in on the ground floor, like the oil prices, she had nowhere to go but up. After the sunny southern hospitality of Texas, New Yorkers seemed brusque and rude, but Gwen decided she preferred that. At least the New Yorkers were up front about their feelings; if you weren't clear about what those feelings were they were usually happy to tell you about them, whether you asked or not. Eccentricity was in; conformity was out. Gwen could hardly wait to join the hurrying throngs, borne aloft by the addictive energy of the city. With the right attitude and a lot of hard work, it just might happen for her, although what might happen she didn't yet know.

In the beginning at least, her weekends were free. She spent them exploring all the landmarks she'd dreamed about as a little girl back in Bowness, Alberta. Not the tourist icons like the Empire State Building and the Statue of Liberty, but the Chrysler Building and the towers of Wall Street. Not the Plaza Hotel and Sardi's, but the Algonquin, home of the famed Round Table literary set, and the Chelsea Hotel where Brendan Behan and Dylan Thomas had lived, written about, and then died. There was so much history here; dare she think she would ever be able to carve out a place for herself? She walked everywhere, feeling the pulse of the city, and within a couple of weeks, she knew she wanted to live there the rest of her life. The first thing she bought for her room was a blow-up of the famous *New Yorker* cartoon that depicted the US according to New Yorkers. It showed the streets of New York and the Hudson River. New Jersey was just a little brown smudge, an even smaller smudge represented the mid-west and, way off in the distance, a couple of hills to represent California. I'm at the centre of the world, she thought. New York is the heartbeat. And she settled into her demanding course work and put in long hours at the firm with gusto.

\*　　\*　　\*

Like Gwen, Sara left Texas headed for the one place where she could count on losing herself in the crowd — New York City. She knew the city was going to be tough, but so was she. After all, she was a survivor. Trayne Barnett III and his whole rotten family could go to hell. Who wanted to be stuck in a backwater town like Galveston, Texas, anyway? Besides, she wasn't really cut out to be a doctor's wife. She wanted a career and she wanted to make it big. The most likely place for that to happen was New York. She had some excellent letters of reference from her journalism professors at UT and she hoped that they, along with her International Students award, would guarantee her easy entry into the print media. She'd make the rounds and then, within a year, she hoped, she'd be working for one of the New York dailies. At the end of her first three months in the city, she began to realize just how tough it was going to be. University was one thing; real life was another.

Trotting her portfolio of clippings from *The Austin American Statesman* and the university paper was getting her nowhere with any of the more established papers in New York. The *Times* gave her an interview as a token courtesy to all UT graduates. *The Post* and *The News* wouldn't even see her. Nobody seemed to be impressed at all with her credentials until she got to Joe Arpeggio of *New York Today*.

*NY Today* was a fairly new paper that had recently gone tabloid with a decidedly right-wing slant. Its style was slightly less sensational than the *Post*'s and its format of short, densely packed articles, and the name, *Today*, enhanced the impression that readers were getting a fastbreaking news bulletin instead of warmed-over stories. Sara knew that both her style and her point of view were perfect for the paper and by the time she got to Joe she would have screwed him any which way to get a job. They settled on her blowing him twice a week between six and seven p.m. in his office while the cleaning lady washed the frosted glass window on his wood-panelled door.

From the exalted possibility of being Mrs Trayne Barnett III to crouching under Joe's oak desk and taking his big cock in her mouth until he came all over her face seemed to Sara to be a spiral descent into a personal hell. She felt she didn't have a choice. The percentage of women working in print journalism was minuscule and she knew she was lucky to have a job at all. And was it really that much different from the unspoken deal she'd had with Trayne? Besides, Joe told her it was cooperate or die and for all she knew he meant it literally. He was known to have mob connections.

There was a standard three-month probation period at the paper, shortened in Sara's case to three weeks. Every time she made it through a three-week period, her stay of execution was extended for another three. Which of her talents this was due to she wasn't quite sure, but she came to realize that she had a certain power over him. He was ready to give her anything she wanted. 'I like to think of myself as your mentor,' he told her. 'Stick with me, baby, and you'll go far.' Joe was from South Philly and talked like he'd seen *The Godfather* just once too often, but the more she swallowed her pride — and Joe — the more he raised her weekly salary.

She worked in the composing room at night, surrounded by much older men, most of them Irish, who all seemed to have taken Jimmy Breslin as their role model. They were sexist and racist and alcoholic. Whenever one of the hard-bitten, ink-stained, gin-reeking geezers swore, he immediately apologized to Sara. 'I don't give a shit,' she usually countered, which kept them on their toes. Unaccustomed to having any women around, especially one who could match them profanity for profanity, they didn't know how to deal with her. Tom O'Brien, who had been in print journalism for over thirty years, liked to make a great show of scratching his balls, saying, 'Oh dear, I forgot. We're in the presence of a lady.' To which Sara simply responded with, 'How are they hanging, Tommy?' The composing room was always sweltering and one mid-July night the heat was so oppressive that Tommy and the other guys stripped off their shirts and pants and did the layout in their undershorts. Not to be outdone, Sara stripped down to her half-slip and her no-bra bra. Joe let her do some writing and reporting, but always in the area of 'soft news', people-oriented pieces on social events, human interest stories, what Joe called 'women's stuff' (even though there was no official women's page in *New York Today*), as opposed to hard news, which dealt with murder, war, and politics, what Sara considered the 'good stuff'. Much as she hated to admit it, it was looking as though she was stuck in a dead-end job.

It was three years since Gwen had come to New York. After gettin her MBA from Columbia, McFadden, Earps, Lennox, and Klein had taken her on as an oil analyst in a junior capacity to work with Jonathan Long. Uncle Jack had prepared her well for the oil side of the business, and Jonathan had trained her in the economics of the industry; she was anxious to show them and the head of the firm, Ian McFadden, that their faith in her was well deserved. The work load was incredible. She had to be up early to connect with stock exchanges all over the world, working twelve-, fourteen- and sixteen-hour days, but the excitement of the business made it all worthwhile. It was exciting being on the phone every

309

day with London, Toronto, and Tokyo as she became part of a huge communication machine, advising brokers and their clients to buy company A and sell company B.

The stock business remained one of the last bastions of male chauvinism and at first she tried to be as butch as all the males in the office. Gradually she came to realize that her own feminine characteristics — intuition, sensitivity, and more than a little power of persuasion — were working for her, not against her. She could be just as lethal when it came to closing a deal, but her polished negotiating skills and ability to listen and analyse enabled her to jump off into the deep end with a clear focus. She often left the rest of the partners dead in the water. She was learning to work hard and pace herself, to keep something in reserve.

Jonathan was now her partner instead of her boss and they grew closer and closer every day. It was very important that they keep their relationship strictly business, he told her. Of course they would continue to be friends, but any deeper involvement could jeopardize their productivity as an investment team. Gwen suspected that she simply wasn't glamorous enough for him. He was constantly showing up at company functions with one stunning long-stemmed beauty after another hanging off his arm, but Gwen wasn't really jealous. She knew she wasn't ready yet to face that side of her life. And he was right; together they made one hell of an investment team. He was an expert on management strategy and she was proving to have an unerring instinct for oil industry trends. It thrilled her to be able to walk into a room full of PhDs in math and find them sitting there with their notebooks open, waiting for her to fill them in, waiting for her to say, 'I think OPEC's just about to cut production. That means oil prices will be going up ten dollars a barrel. Buy the following three companies and buy them now.' She, a working-class girl from Bowness, Alberta, had them hanging on her every word.

Jonathan had told her, 'If you're right, you'll rarely get the credit. If you're wrong, you'll have to take the fall. Sometimes you'll be wrong and that's OK, but you better be right more often than you are wrong.' Realizing she tended to agonize over a wrong deal longer than her male colleagues, she quickly learned to cut her losses and bounce back. The unwritten rule of Bowness stood her in good stead: No whining about any mistakes you make; you were wrong, now deal with it. But she was right more often than she was wrong. The tough world of high finance was forcing her to develop the thicker emotional skin she'd been badly in need of, and with success or failure often only a phone call away, she discovered there was more than a little of the gambler inside her, urging her to go for it, egging her on to take that extra risk. So far she was winning.

The women's movement was thriving in New York City; it was much more active and vocal than it had been in Texas and she wanted to stay involved. One of the first things she had done upon arriving in New York was to walk in the Woman's March for Equality. Only two months in New York and there she was marching down Fifth Avenue with Gloria Steinem, Kate Millett, and Ti-Grace Atkinson. She joined the National Organization for Women, which was working to prove that women could effect social change and alter the course of history. She was at the Town Hall for the famous Germaine Greer-Norman Mailer debate. The Supreme Court had ruled that the constitutional right to privacy protected a woman's choice regarding abortion. The United Nations declared that 1975 would be the official International Year of the Woman. Gwen was lobbying for the ERA and campaigning for Bella

Abzug, the first woman from New York to run for the United States Senate.

She was also dating — well not exactly dating, but going out with a man at least twice a week. Luigi del Bello ran her favourite restaurant in Little Italy, Carpaccio's, a sprawling (for New York), cheerful spaghetti joint, a neighbourhood tradition for over thirty years. Half Italian, half French, Lou was shorter than she was, handsome and sexy in a rough, working-class way; his glittering eyes flicked her up and down, silently promising that if anyone could rouse her sexually, it would be Luigi del Bello. She ate there often and he was always so attentive that she more than half expected him to ask her out and when he finally did, she thought, Why not?

New York City born and bred, he loved it with a passion that equalled hers, and he knew the city like the back of his hand. To Gwen, a lot of what was going on in New York in the seventies was the height of decadence. Lou seemed to have access to widely varied strata of New York society, claiming to know everyone from dock workers to upper East Side art and antique dealers, from Andy Warhol and Halston to Bianca Jagger, Dennis Hopper, and Margaret Trudeau. With him she went to poetry readings at St Mark's Church and the White Horse tavern. He knew all about shopping in The Village and Soho and the specialty food stores on West Broadway, as well as Bloomingdale's and Bendel's. They celebrated Thanksgiving Day with Macy's parade and prepared for Christmas by watching the lighting of the giant tree in Rockefeller Plaza. Lou was funny and smart with a quick wit that could always make her laugh, just what she needed after a brain-tortured day at the investment firm. He told her all about growing up in a tightly controlled Italian neighbourhood and took her to meet his father, who was a cardiac invalid and

312

spoke almost no English. Lou enthralled her with explanations of the differences between the Sicilian Mafia and the Neapolitan Mafia. 'The Sicilians are civilized; the Neapolitans are loud, flashy.'

'And which branch do you come from?' Gwen asked.

'My mama was Neapolitan and my papa is Sicilian. Like oil and water, they never mixed. That's why I've got such a split personality.'

He took her to Carnegie Hall to hear Stephan Grapelli and Madison Square Garden to hear The Grateful Dead. They went to the Palm Tree, a Latin discotheque, and to Roseland where, at midnight, the ballroom dancing turned into the throbbing pulse of disco too. He knew when Studio 54 and Regine's were on the way out and the Paradise Garage was on the way in; he knew all the after-hours sex clubs, both gay and straight, Plato's Retreat, the Spike, the Anvil, and the Mineshaft. Lou was a font of information with a wealth of ideas about what they could do with a Saturday night in the Big Apple. About the only place he didn't take her was the gay baths, but he told her all about them.

At first his sexual preferences were unclear to her; it was fine with her that he didn't make a pass because she was still unsure how she would respond. The signs were all there, she'd just been too naïve to read them; but somehow once she knew he leaned towards a heavy preference on the homosexual side of bisexual, it made him all the more attractive. A lot of women were sleeping with gays these days; maybe he'd be the one to break the spell over her and unravel the mystery. For Lou, sex was a power game. At the moment, however, they were equals and she didn't want to tip the balance.

But what about her needs? She had set them aside for too long; it was time to find out for herself. Lou had told her about a bar down in Alphabet City, a sushi bar run by a Japanese woman. Gwen gathered her courage and walked in. She ordered a steaming porcelain jug of sake and nigiri sushi. The sushi was excellent, but then it was good almost everywhere in New York. The decor was typical Japanese restaurant chic, lots of bamboo and scrubbed wood and lacquer work. There were lots of men sitting around and she wondered if she was in the right place.

After she'd eaten the last bite of tekka maki, a hostess in a kimono tapped her on the shoulder and said, 'Come with me.' Gwen followed her out of the main part of the restaurant, through a heavy beaded bamboo curtain and down a narrow hallway into a darkened bar. The music was loud and the lights were dim, but she could see couples dancing together, and sure enough they were all women.

Gwen stayed shyly on the sidelines, the way she used to all those years ago at St Mary's, waiting for someone to ask her to dance. And then someone did ask her, someone who was wiling to lead so that Gwen could follow. She opened her arms and Gwen moved into them. They spent the night together and it was surprisingly easy, familiar and at the same time strange, smooth yet passionate. Now that the unthinkable had finally happened, she felt neither frightened nor guilty, not wrong but, for the first time in her life, right. It wasn't her father's fault, or Lucy Bainborough's fault, or Sara's. It wasn't anybody's fault. It was just the way things were. So she might as well accept it.

She flew down to Texas for the first National Woman's Conference. It was difficult for her to set foot in the state but the conference promised to be a thrilling event, and it was. Fifteen thousand women from all over North America gathered in Houston, along with observers from countries all around the world. On the other side of the city, Phyllis Schafly led an anti-equality protest rally that was endorsed by the Ku Klux Klan and other right-wing factions who feared their power base was being threatened. There Gwen listened and talked and learned and came away more determined than ever to work to change the position of women, both legally and socially.

Being in Houston also gave her a chance to get together with Uncle Jack. She hadn't seen him for a long time. He had divorced Diana, and was embroiled in a nasty custody battle over his daughter. The business was going well. He was greyer and maybe a pound or two thicker around the middle, but as devilishly handsome as ever.

'Honey, I'm so proud of what you've done with your life,' he said, giving her a hug and then holding her out at arms' length to take a good look at her. 'You're so sophisticated, I just don't believe what I'm seeing. I like those high heels. Why, you're a real New York woman now.'

'I love my work. I can't thank you enough for putting me in touch with Jonathan Long.'

'Well, he thinks the world of you. I hear you make a pretty terrific team. Is it strictly business with you two?'

'I'm afraid so,' Gwen laughed. 'I'm not really Jonathan's type, but we're great friends.'

'So have you got anybody else on the romantic scene? Another guy waiting in the wings? You're planning to get married, have kids?'

'I don't think that's on the cards for me, Uncle Jack,' Gwen said carefully, studying his reaction.

He nodded slowly. 'Well, if you ever change your mind, you just let me know.'

'I will.' She hugged him hard. 'You know I'll always love you, Uncle Jack.'

'And I love you, honey.'

At McFadden, Earps, Lennox, and Klein, she was rising quickly within the firm, building a high profile for herself and earning the respect of her colleagues. 'You work as hard as any man,' Jonathan Long said. 'You're always in the office when I arrive and you're still here when I leave at night.' The admiration in his tone was clear, almost as clear as the subtext that somehow that made her less of a woman.

Well, that was his problem. It was her work that saved her from falling apart, her work that had given her financial security and a new sense of self-worth. She had found she was good at making money. Her personal portfolio was growing, too, as she invested her money carefully. She'd moved from 82nd and Amsterdam to a co-op on West End Avenue and she was saving money for a small summer place in Sag Harbor.

These days when she looked in the mirror, she hardly recognized herself. What she saw was a surprisingly attractive, capable young woman, expensively dressed in an understated way, a woman who radiated poise and confidence. Everything about this woman said, 'You can trust me.' The image in the mirror in no way resembled the frightened little ginger mouse from Bowness, Alberta. She had a purpose and a future. She had become part of the driving rhythm of the city.

On her way home from work, she picked up a copy of the brand new tabloid, *New York Today*, and there on the cover was a photograph of Sara Town and the headline, 'Turn to page six for Tell It Like It Is.' Quickly she leafed through the front section and there was Sara's byline on an editorial about a demonstration in front of an abortion clinic. Eagerly she scanned the article and realized it was Sara all right, the same old Sara, taking a right-wing approach when everybody else was leaning to the left. They called her 'the Caustic Crusader'; here she was advising the women of New

316

York that 'abortion is murder' and that 'reproductive rights do not justify the convenience of ending someone's life.'

She remembered when abortion was illegal in Texas, flying to Mexico with Sara, holding her hand while Sara's insides were scraped out with no anaesthetic, then taking her home to Austin to nurse her back to health. Sara had sworn it meant nothing to her, just a bit of tissue she didn't want or need. And now here she was claiming to be a Right-to-Lifer. Maybe she really couldn't see the truth about herself. No, there was no way Gwen was ready to come face to face with Sara again. She folded the newspaper neatly in two and tossed it into the garbage can.

The interview that finally catapulted Sara into the public eye started out as 'women's stuff'. It was presented to her on a silver platter quite unexpectedly. In the lobby of the St Regis Hotel, wearing dark glasses and holding a dragon-headed cane, sat Salvador Dali. Sara had gone in to pick up a copy of *NY Today* at the St Regis news stand to check out a piece she'd written on the opening of a new disoththeque down on Spring Street the day before. She had walked past Dali and out of the door, did a fast doubletake and walked back into the lobby and right up to him to introduce herself. Struck by her unique beauty, most particularly her golden eyes which, as he pointed out, matched the topazes set on the head of his cane, he invited her to tea in the St Regis salon the next afternoon.

When she arrived at the bar at four-thirty the next day, the door appeared to be locked and the room was dark. Trying to peek through the frosted glass, she couldn't see anything, but when she leaned heavily on the door it gave way. A waiter burst through behind her, wheeling a silver tea trolley on which sat a

317

candelabra and a samovar. By the candlelight she could just make out Dali sitting at a small round table in one corner. He had removed his dark glasses to reveal eyes made up to look like a Pierrot mask. He was dressed completely in white. He motioned to her to sit beside him and sample the English muffins with ginger marmalade and the perfectly cut potted shrimp sandwiches. Under the guise of making pleasant tea-party conversation, Sara was able to ask America's most flamboyant artist some highly personal questions.

'How did you meet Mrs Dali?'

'I opened the door to my studio one day and there she was, standing on her head, naked. How could I refuse to love someone who presented herself to me in such a manner? I found her instantly irresistible. As I have found you.' He kissed her hand.

'Do you love animals?'

'On the contrary. I hate all animals.'

'But you travel with two ocelots.'

'For effect only. They attract attention and I adore attracting attention. The ocelots have become symbols of what people see in me, but I don't like them. Stupid beasts. Smelly, highly strung, and innately nasty. Perhaps that is like me.' He laughed a wheezing laugh.

'Why don't you ever paint children?'

'Oh, but I have. Once I painted Shirley Temple as a child with a dead rat in her mouth. Needless to say, it remains in my private collection. If you come to visit with me again, perhaps I shall let you see it.' Dali took a pinch of snuff and sneezed loudly into a white silk handkerchief.

At five o'clock, an Israeli model arrived, bearing a string bag of withered oranges from a kibbutz. At five-thirty a man in a gorilla suit appeared. He was a ventriloquist who sat a dummy on his hairy knee. The dummy did all the talking. At six Rudolf Nureyev arrived

318

and sat on the floor and darned his tights, drinking his tea out of a glass and sucking on a lump of sugar, Russian-style. At six-thirty a Broadway producer turned up with a tiny Japanese geisha girl. Staring at the carefully make-up pink and white face, Sara detected the stubble of a beard under the heavy rice powder of the midget.

Having tea with Salvador Dali was like being in one of the artist's own paintings, a surrealistic Mad Hatter's tea party. Each guest spoke in a different language and Dali answered in that language. Sara did her best to keep up; if she could interview Dali she could interview anybody. When she asked him what it was like to be a celebrity in his profession, he smiled and said, 'Celebrity is a profession. It is its own profession.'

In a cab on her way home, careering uptown to her Riverside Drive apartment, the cab driver, a wiry Greek with milky blue eyes and stringy hair, ranted and raved at her for the entire trip. Sara clung to the door handle with her left hand and made rapid notes with her right while the driver leaned on his horn whenever the traffic stopped moving, which was every three or four blocks. He had a lot to say about the US and its politics and he pounded on the steering wheel to punctuate his rapid-fire delivery.

'America is the number one needle-pusher,' he declaimed as they swung wide around the corner of Fifty-Sixth and Third. 'We put the needle in the arm of every other country. We make them dependent on us and then we kick them in the nuts for it. Ya know, we assassinate our own CIA men in other countries, did ya know that?'

'Really?'

'Yeah, we have to kill them.'

'Why?'

'Because they know too much.'

'About political scams in other countries you mean?'

'No, about corruptions in our country, this country. They know too much so they have to be snuffed out.' He made the sound of a fire extinguisher. 'Look at this city. You see that pretty skyline? It's a fake. False front for a slum heart, you know what I'm talkin'?' He twisted his head completely around to look at Sara through the bullet-proof glass that separated the front from the back seat. She nodded quickly and he turned his attention back to the traffic in front of him. 'But I love this city. You give me a choice between New York and paradise, I take New York' — as if he made the choice daily — 'every time. No president can make it without New York.

'Those Kennedys. They talked a great game but they're shysters. Lace-curtain Irish, ya know what I mean? JFK? I believe he's still alive today. Somewhere. He's a vegetable but they're keepin' him alive. Him and Marilyn. Bobby's for sure dead, though. I know the guy who killed him — had him in the cab once — so I know for sure he's dead.

'Lyndon Johnson, he took his clothes off in the back seat of my cab. Don't ask me why. I'm drivin' him through Central Park, I look back and he's naked as a jaybird, scratching his gall bladder scar. You think I lie?' He glared at her in the rear-view mirror, narrowly missing another car. 'If I'm lyin' may I have an accident right now and, God forbid, I die, you walk away from the crash without a mark on you, I swear it's the truth.'

'Mm mm.' Sara was scribbling like mad.

'I'm a gambler by nature. There ain't a cow in the New York State area that hasn't eaten grass from my farm. You know what that means?'

'No,' Sara tried to shield her notebook from his eye as he glanced over his shoulder again. 'What does it mean?'

320

'It means there ain't a gambling joint in New York that hasn't made money off me. They know me, I'm famous. You give me fifty bucks, I show you where the real dirt is. You want dogs, I can get you dogs. Not just any dog, but the specific breed, whatever you want.'

'No thanks.'

'Mohammed Ali? I take him everywhere. I'm drivin' by Madison Square Garden one night. It's pissin' rain, 'scuse my language, you a nice lady . . . Ali comes out . . . so I open my window and I yell out to him, "Hey, you may float like a butterfly, sting like a bee, but if you don't sign my visor, your name's not Ali." Well he looks up real surprised, just like he's been stung by a bee, so I yell the same thing again. He makes his way through the crowd to the cab, my cab, opens the door and hops in. I drove him around for eight hours straight. He signed my visor. See up there? Just look under the mug shot.'

Sara looked and indeed it did say 'Cassius Clay alias Mohammed Ali', a scrawling flamboyant signature.

'That's great!'

'Yeah, great. Once this lady in my cab, she come right through the barrier, crawled into the front seat, this seat here' — he patted the seat beside him — 'told me to take her to the George Washington Bridge. So I did. Parked the cab under the bridge and we went at it, right here in the front seat.' He looked hopefully at Sara who stared fixedly out of the window at the Hudson River whizzing by. 'Then I drove her home and she paid me.'

'She paid you?' Sara dropped her pencil.

'Yeah, for sure. I left the meter running. Man, that was some tab we ran up. I could tell you some stories, believe you me. You should write a book about me.'

Believe me, I will, Sara thought, closing her notebook with a snap as the cab pulled up in front of the door of her four-flight walkup. 'Thanks for an interesting ride.'

'You know what I'd do if I had a hundred thousand dollars?' the cabby asked wistfully, his hand closing over the generous five-dollar tip she handed him.

'What?' Sara asked, genuinely interested.

'I'd get it in one-dollar bills and I'd climb to the top of the Empire State Building and throw them all down, one at a time, to the people below. I just want to make everybody happy, ya know?'

The ultimate American dream. Sara's comparison interview with Salvador Dali and the New York cabby was picked up by the *LA Times* and the London *Observer*. Headlined 'The Real Surreal New York', it gave her new credentials as a hotshot journalist and won her a Peabody. The *New York Times* started sniffing around and Joe got scared he was going to lose her. The twice-a-week blow jobs had ceased. They had become wary colleagues. If she moved to *The Times* or even to the *Post* it would mean starting all over again. No, she would hang in with Joe. She had a feeling he was ready to give her whatever she might want.

*New York Today* subtitled itself *The Paper of Opinion*. Even factual, supposedly straightforward news reporting read like an editorial, so Sara's new personal column fitted right in. Joe had given her carte blanche to lambaste all sacred cows with equal impunity. Grabbing *NY Today* from a news stand on the street, running down into the subway, jumping on the Bank Street or Brooklyn Line, young executives, autoparts workers, and secretaries alike thumbed through the tabloid, first to find the daily 'Reporter's Choice Girl' (some dental assistant in a fairly tame cheesecake pose) and then to Sara's controversial column, 'The Caustic Crusader'. The upper right-hand corner had a head shot of Sara, which changed with the seasons. Living in the bastion of eastern liberalism, plenty of people in New York City identified strongly with Sara's right-wing views. Because she was female they expected her to be a liberal. Beyond all this, Sara was different. Her outspoken, highly opinionated style made her worshipped by some readers and detested by others, but the more outrageous her opinions became, the more the circulation for the paper increased.

Somehow it wasn't enough for Sara herself. She was itching for more, nagged by the feeling that print journalism wasn't really where it was at any more. Newspapers were dying as their owners decided to invest in cable TV. Journalism-school graduates across the country, inspired by the Watergate team of Woodward and Bernstein to save the world, were switching to TV. Newspapers were losing money; TV was making money. Reviewing her own options, Sara decided she was in the wrong part of the business. NOW and the FCC were pressuring stations to hire women in profile positions. She'd be great on TV.

At a party at the Tavern on the Green, she had met Victor Marshall, an expatriate Czech who was head of local Channel 7 News. Met him and slept with him. Once. Sara got out her little black book, called him up and told him she just couldn't stop thinking about him, his smell, his touch, the way he'd licked her ear and called her his little sugar pancake, his little cabbage roll. Hadn't he told her to telephone him at any time of the night or day? Well, she was calling him at two o'clock in the morning because she was just desperate to see him. She needed him to come over and lick her ear right now.

Victor got her an audition for an open spot as anchor on the early morning news. In addition to Victor and a couple of station execs, the sportscaster and the weatherman also watched her audition. The make-up girl slapped some heavy pancake on her, a copy editor handed her some sample copy and by the end of the audition, it was obvious that Sara was right. The camera adored her. It was also patently obvious that if she didn't go along with the auditioners' thinly veiled requests for sexual favours, she wasn't going to get the job. She said yes to everything.

Joe was pissed off that she was leaving. 'You're giving up a great newspaper job to go on TV?' he said. 'I thought you wanted to be in journalism, not show biz. You're a reporter, not an actor.'

'That's why I'm perfect for the job,' Sara said calmly. 'They're looking for both.'

'They're looking for someone with a pretty face and a great body. What's more important? The news or the sexpot who's reading it? We're talking about style over substance. It's shit.'

'But I've got the substance. I've got the background in print and I've paid my dues.'

'And what are you going to have to show for it? With TV there ain't no bylines, no clippings, nothing you can hold in your hand. TV is all hype, all image. Now you see it, now you don't, blink and it's gone.'

'That's exactly what I love about it. There's nothing to hold on to, no way to pin me down. I'm not just going to be anchoring the news you know. I'm going to be writing and reporting and interviewing as well. I like what little interviewing I've done so far. I like getting inside other people's lives, learning their secrets . . .'

'Without having to share any of your own.'

'It's over, Joe. You're history,' Sara said bluntly, standing up to go. She gave him the finger. 'Thanks for everything. See you around.'

Gwen was fuming. She was lying in bed in her sparsely furnished apartment. Now she had tons of space but no time to shop for furniture to help fill it. She ran through the events of the day until her frustration reached boiling point. She'd been trying for months to join the New York Athletic Club, but it was 'restricted' – i.e. exclusively male. Of course she hadn't been able to get her hands on a genuine membership list because it was confidential. 'We are an intimate and personal entity,' stated the letter sent in reply to her inquiry, 'with a right to exclude others.'

That made her blood boil. What that letter told her was not only, 'we don't want you, you can't belong', but even worse, 'you're not big enough to play in this ballgame and you'll never be big enough if we have anything to say about it.' Exclusive men's clubs were a symbol of the upper echelons of business at the top of a male-dominated society. Power, it was all about power. It was just another variation on a little boy's secret treehouse policy: 'Keep out. No girls allowed!'

Did they think she would ruin the tone of their precious club just because she had a higher voice and shaved her legs instead of her chin? Ian McFadden was a member and she'd asked him to get her a membership application but after dicking around for over a month, he finally confessed he couldn't back her on this one.

'You're a great gal, Gwen,' he said. 'Nobody works harder for this firm than you do, but you should find a women's group where you can feel at home and free to talk about female things.'

'You mean like disposable diapers and menstrual cramps?' Gwen immediately shot back.

Ian flinched. 'Now I didn't mean that. Listen, I'm a man who loves women, you know that. I have the greatest respect for you and what you've managed to achieve here. But men have to have a chance to get together sometimes without having any women around. Surely you can understand that. We've got a lot of club activities where a woman wouldn't feel. . .well, comfortable. I like to go hiking on the weekends with a bunch of the guys, for example. We want to be able to take a pee in the wilderness. I hardly think you'd appreciate that.'

Damnit, it burned her ass to think she had worked twice as hard to get equal pay only to discover she didn't have equal access to the privileges that money could buy. If they had earned it, why hadn't she? All those MBAs she saw every day on the streets of Manhattan, wearing business suits and sneakers, rushing to and fro, from home to office and back home again without a break, trying to be top executive, wonder wife and super mom all rolled into one, didn't they need a break from all the pressure? Didn't they deserve a reward? Didn't she?

And then it hit her. Excited, she got up, slipping into her green silk kimono, and padded out to her living-room.

Why wasn't there an exclusive club for professional women? With more and more of them managing to reach the upper levels of business right here in this city, such a club could be successful. A sanctuary and support system. She paced the floor as the ideas tumbled over one another in her excited mind. A health spa with full athletic facilities and all the latest equipment. An Olympic-size pool. A weight-training clinic. Daycare facilities. Yoga, aerobics, karate. And to exercise the mind as well as the body, classes in business and workshops in the arts. A library. A gallery featuring women artists. Meeting-rooms. Lecture series. A gourmet restaurant and wine bar. Wouldn't it be great to have a bar a woman could go into on her own without being hassled? A swimming pool where women wouldn't have to share the lanes with men, or worry about how they looked in bathing suits. Hell, they could swim without any bathing suits if they wanted to.

The more she thought about it, the more excited she got. It needed to be luxurious, beautiful, even opulent. And it must allow for complete privacy, a cocoon for self-improvement, a haven of self-indulgence sealed away from the frenetic pace and demands of the city life outside its walls.

She couldn't sleep. She had to share her idea with someone. Throwing on her sweats, she ran out of the door, hailed a cab straight to Lou's restaurant. He had recently split the building in half, expanding into a nightclub and renovating the main body of the restaurant. She hadn't seen it for a while and, when she walked in, it had literally been transformed. After so many years in the same location with the same old food in surroundings that could only be described as early Italian kitsch, Lou had hired a female chef from California to revamp the food and Lokis Krumins, the top restaurant designer, to redo the decor. Gone were the red chequered tablecloths, wine-bottle lamps, and posters of Napoli and Verona, replaced by high-tech glass and chrome and fresh flowers on every table.

She picked up a menu. Gone were the veal and pasta dishes, too, the sausage-grinder subs and the cheap Chianti at $8.50 a bottle, replaced by designer pizza with sun-dried tomatoes and buffalo mozzarella, semolina-dipped red and white onion rings, roasted eggplant salad, and Montepulciano d'Abruzzo at six bucks a glass. Gone also were the 's from the restaurant's name. Lokis had made that artistic decision. If tonight was any indication, the decision was a good one; the place was packed on a Tuesday at eleven o'clock at night. The adjacent nightclub had a big neon sign flashing the word 'Environment' in alternating colours and there seemed to be a line-up of young trendies waiting to get in.

As soon as he saw her enter the restaurant, Lou

signalled to her to sit at a table near the fireplace. Within seconds he joined her.

'So what you think, *cara*?' he asked. 'Lokis did a fabulous job, no? We got lineups round the block for the nightclub. I've had to hire two bouncers just to deal with the crowds. For the moment, Environment is the 'in' place to be and I intend to keep it that way. These kids are so fickle, you know? One week a club is hot, the next week they've moved on to somewhere else. But Lokis has come up with a great marketing ploy. He's going to be continually changing the decor of the club; it'll be a completely different environment. The restaurant's doing great, too. This new cuisine, you've got to try it. We're calling it Cal-Italian.'

'I know,' Gwen chimed in. 'You got a terrific review in *New York Magazine*.' A waiter appeared and placed a flaming Sambucca in front of her. The warm anisette liquor with its floating coffee beans was one of Gwen's favourites and she downed most of it quickly before taking a deep breath and saying, 'Lou, I've got what I think is an amazing idea and it involves you, so hear me out before you jump in and say anything, OK? I'm on a roll.' Lou leaned one elbow on the table, one finger to his lips and Gwen explained.

Lou nodded his head all the way through, exploding in little exclamations of approval; slapping the table with the palm of his hand at appropriate points. When she finally finished, flushed and breathless, he said, 'You're right. It is a terrific idea. I take it you want me to set up the restaurant part of the operation for you?'

'Of course.' Gwen nodded and looked at him, waiting to hear what he would say next.

'I'm interested. In fact, I'm very interested. For an operation of the scope you're envisioning, the food services will have to include the very best. That's what the members will expect and that's what they're going to get.'

'You are the best!'

Lou took her hand and kissed it. 'I know,' he said modestly. 'I've got contacts all over the world in the food industry. Imported semolina from Italy for the pasta — the pasta will be homemade, of course — Nova Scotia lox, lobster from Maine, stone crab claws from Florida . . .'

'And prime Alberta beef,' Gwen broke in.

'You think Alberta beef's better?'

'I know it is. No steroids. We used to go to this place just outside Calgary. The Flying N Ranch. Best steaks you've ever tasted.' Momentarily Gwen's eyes clouded over.

'OK, Alberta beef it is,' Lou said. He hated what happened to her when she spoke of her home. He knew he would never be able to reach the pain or guilt that she carried from those years. 'We'll have the best coffee in town. I import my beans directly from Colombia. They think we Americans don't appreciate good coffee so the top grades go to Europe. But I get mine directly from Colombia.'

'Lou, I really love you!' Gwen's excitement was escalating along with his. 'We can make this happen, I know we can!'

'Listen, Gwen.' Lou looked suddenly very serious. 'This club idea is more than just a hot money-making proposition. It could be a wave of the future. Particularly here in New York. And I want to be part of it.'

'What are you saying?'

'I'm saying I want to do more than run the restaurant for you. I want to be your business partner. I am willing to invest in such a club right now. I want in on the whole deal.'

329

Gwen studied him carefully for a long moment. Then she leaned across the table, her hand extended. As they shook on it, she said, 'You've got yourself a deal, partner.'

For the next three months they spent all their free time scouting properties. Real estate anywhere in Manhattan was always at a premium, particularly in the East Sixties which was where they both agreed would be the ideal location for The Club. Already there were harbingers of the gentrification, new regulations governing the commercial use of property, and escalating prices that would characterize the building boom of the 1980s. Finally, when they were just at the point of giving up, they found a property, a small old hotel on Middlesex Lane, a tiny, block-long street near Lexington and Third. It was up for sale and, miracle of miracles, they might, they just might, be able to afford it. Technically The Middlesex could not be termed a true brownstone because it had more than four storeys, but it had been built around the turn of the century and it had the high front step and the floor to ceiling windows so characteristic of a brownstone. The marble staircase in the lower lobby and the magnificent ballroom were obviously part of the original design, but the hotel owners had added a greenhouse on top of the building, all of which Gwen immediately fell in love with. There was even a small courtyard surrounded by a wrought-iron railing. Middlesex Lane seemed somehow removed from the hustle and bustle which existed only a block away, and the building itself had the air of old money, class and privilege. The Middlesex Hotel was absolutely perfect.

'We'll call it 37 Middlesex,' Gwen said. 'Just the address, that's all. It sounds vaguely English and you know what Anglophiles New Yorkers are

'37 Middlesex,' Lou repeated, savouring the words.

330

'That's good. Keep it classy, keep it mysterious, keep it discreet.'

'The kind of place people might walk right by without giving it a second glance,' Gwen continued with growing excitement, 'but once inside, what you find is heaven.'

They put together a proposal for investors that included location, the market they were aiming for, how soon they expected 37 Middlesex to turn a profit, and other salient points of business. They approached friends, business contacts, Lou's customers at the restaurant, anyone they could think of who might be interested. Because Gwen didn't want to tell her boss she was leaving the firm, she couldn't approach her clients about investing, but she did drop some hints that her situation might be changing soon and they should definitely stay in touch. And of course she felt honour bound to tell her partner, Jonathan, about her plans for 37 Middlesex.

'I don't know what I'll do without you, Gwen,' Jonathan said worriedly. 'We're a team. That's what's made us so hot. This is like blowing a hole in a 737 at five thousand feet. How can you do this to me?'

'Jonathan, you'll be fine. You'll find another partner. The scuttle butt is that Milton Hayden at Mayfair Investments is about ready to make a move.'

'No way I'll consider a male partner. You've convinced me of that. I want to work with another woman. You've really blazed a trail in this business, Gwen. I wish you luck with this club venture. The potential is there for it to really fly. But God, Gwen, I'm going to miss you.' For the first time he gave her a hug, and Gwen hugged him back tearfully.

Because she wanted women to be actively involved in the running of The Club along with her, she offered shares to women at five thousand dollars a share. Shareholders would be able to elect four of the seven members of the board of directors. Jonathan, whom she and Lou had decided to let in on the deal, helped her put together a list of the five hundred most prominent women in New York State. Carefully, methodically, she went after them one by one.

'I don't know,' she confessed to Lou, 'What if we don't get the money we need? I'm putting myself at financial risk here and so are you. What if the club doesn't go? What if it's too soon? Are we really ready to do this thing? I've still got so much to learn. Maybe we should give it a year or two.'

'No.' Lou was firm. 'Risk now — learn later. You're in the right place at the right time. You've got to seize this opportunity. 37 Middlesex is your baby; do it before someone else does.'

She and Lou drafted a glitzy prospectus. The deal looked wonderful on paper. They held investors' meetings at Carpaccio, with Lou supplying free wine and fancy finger food, while Gwen made the promotional pitch. They didn't get all the investors they needed, but they decided they were close enough to give it a go.

Gwen had $1 million in her savings and another million in her portfolio. They took out a mortgage on the land and made a down payment on the building. Her building. It excited her just to say it, even more to walk by and see it, her property, the future site of her club. 37 Middlesex.

Sara was an instant hit on Channel 7 *Eyewitness News*. At the end of just three weeks, the viewers were writing in to say they loved her as much as the camera did. Her husky voice was seductive enough to get viewers to pay attention to her and authoritative enough to make them believe every word she said. They not only listened to her, they trusted her. Soon she was up to three broadcasts a day and within one year Channel 7 went from number three to number one.

Almost all the anchorwomen on television were Diane Sawyer clones, blonde, crisp, energetic to the point of being perky. Sara's delivery was just that little bit slower, as if she were weighing every word carefully before she shared it with her audience. She studied every move of the still relatively few female anchors. From Sawyer she learned to be charming. From Savitch she stole the technique of holding the microphone out for a few seconds after the subject finished talking because that was often when he would suddenly open up. She studied them carefully but she was different from all the ice-princess blondes, and not just because she was the 'token brunette'. At first they had wanted her to bleach her hair; she refused. Then they suggested she cut it into the sculpted, stiffly sprayed helmet worn by Woodruff and Walters, and she refused. Her softly sensuous shoulder-length hair was part of her appeal and, once it became her trademark, other anchors began to copy her. She wore the regulation tailored suits and dresses, but she'd unbutton the top button or wear a lacy camisole, nothing too blatantly sexual but just enough to remind the viewers that a woman was bringing them the news and not a man. She was cool and classy with a hint of something darker and smouldering. The sparks usually ignited when she did an actual interview. An interview with Sara Town was like stepping into a comfortable warm bath only to find that the water became suddenly painfully hot. Once, she reduced Elton John to tears and he finally hit her over the head with his latest album cover.

But to her viewers Sara Town was never lethal, only lovable. They sent her gifts at the station, flowers and stuffed animals and chocolates. Many people remembered her from her newspaper column. She came into their living-rooms every night and they felt as if they knew her, as if she were speaking directly, personally to each and every one of them. She had become a local broadcasting star.

Thanks to Victor, she was also moving in a faster circle of people. They were living together, which had its advantages and its disadvantages. Now the disadvantages were gradually outweighing the advantages. Victor, the dark, brooding, suffering Czech who had fought along with Alexander Dubček in 1968, was beginning to get on her nerves with his never-ending angst, his running political commentary, and his deeply ingrained European chauvinism. Victor the romantic refugee was becoming Victor the bore. Since she was a Texas refugee, Victor insisted on teaching her 'all about New York', which restaurants were in and which were now *déclassé*, which books to read, which art exhibits to see, and what she should know and say about the painters whose work they saw. He told her how to dress, act, work, feel, and think, and she was getting sick of it. On the surface, Victor couldn't differ more from Trayne Barnett, but scratch that surface and they were brothers under the skin. Do this, do that, don't do this, never do that. What it always came down to with both of these men was 'You're not good enough for my world, you're not good enough for me, you have to be fixed.'

What it really came down to for Sara, however, was that Victor wasn't good enough in bed. The novelty of having her ear licked was starting to wear thin, particularly since he was no good at licking anywhere else. He was lousy at giving head, had no taste for it at all. Sometimes she literally had to grab him and put his head between her legs and hold it there until he got her off. He was continually asking her if it was 'working', which she knew meant 'haven't you had

334

enough?' And she always had the feeling he was holding his breath because when she'd finished — and she loved to drag it out because that really pissed him off — he always came up gasping for air. No, no, it definitely was time for Victor to go.

Out of the blue she got a call from a guy named Ted Turner who told her he'd seen her on *Eyewitness* and thought she was ready to go national. Turner was starting a brand new network of his own, CNN. Round-the-clock, twenty-four-hour news on cable.

'It's little more than a gleam in my eye right now,' he said, 'but I'm giving you a chance to get in on the ground floor. I think you're ready to make the move to network.'

'Oh yes!' Sara agreed.

'If you're really set on staying here in New York, I can start you off with Mary Alice Williams. But I'd rather see you in Washington. With the election coming up, the conventions set for this summer, and the campaign coverage, there's going to be a lot of action in Washington. What do you think?'

'I'd be willing to consider a move.' Sara's heart was beating a mile a minute but she tried to sound cool.

'Great. That's just great. You'll be taking a risk, but then I've heard you're a lady who likes to live dangerously.'

Oh shit, thought Sara, here it comes. Who do I have to fuck to get this one? 'Any strings attached?' she asked.

'No, no strings. Other than the fact that, as I said, I'd prefer to start you in Washington.'

Sara breathed a sigh of relief. 'Mr Turner, you've got yourself a deal.'

She hung up the phone and practically whooped out loud. National. She was going national. With the biggest event of 1980, the upcoming presidential election.

335

Probably it was only some sort of affirmative action. Turner was seeking out women in the same way that Channel 7 had. Part of her rebelled at this. She'd prefer to get the job on her own merits.

But wait a minute. Her own merits were damned good and would stack up well against just about any man. Certainly her current co-anchor here in New York, Roger Stilton, was no match for her. Talk about a limp dick. Sara mopped up the screen with him and everybody knew it. She was dying to get away from him; she was dying to get away from Victor; in fact, she was dying to get away from New York. Maybe the politics were dirtier in Washington, but at least the streets would be clean. She was ready for Washington. But was Washington ready for her?

Gwen and Lou had intended to have a low-key elegant opening for 37 Middlesex in keeping with the mystique surrounding their new venture, but the party for which The Club opened its big brass doors to the public for the first time turned out to be a major social event of the season. A prestigious club exclusively for women seemed part of the tidal wave of expectancy that signalled the end of a safe and boring decade with hope for an exciting new one. The eighties promised to be much more active and 37 Middlesex seemed destined to be at the centre of the action.

The party started at the cocktail hour, right after work, and it went on until the wee hours of the morning. Guests were given a grand tour of the luxurious surroundings and encouraged to avail themselves of all the splendid facilities the new club had to offer; try a workout in the gleaming new weight-room, take a swim in the Roman-style terrazzo-tiled pool, follow it with a sauna and a massage, then change into evening clothes for cocktails and hors d'oeuvres in the waterfall lounge

336

or stop in for a special screening of *Kramer versus Kramer* in The Club's private screening-room. There was something to please every jaded New Yorker and most guests stayed a lot longer than they had intended in order to move from one pleasure to another.

Lou had outdone himself with the food. Each course featured the cuisine of a different country, and the guests moved from room to room to sample each of them. The hors d'oeuvres offered at one end of the lounge were miniature dim sum, and assorted sushi were provided at the other; the salad course was served in the health bar, and the main course — Cal-Italian — catered by Lou's female chef at Carpaggio, was served in the dining-room, mesquite-grilled pompano, roasted goat, risotto fritters, baby artichokes, and a flat, herb-flecked bread called foccacia. Dessert consisted of fresh fruit to be dipped in Belgian chocolate fondue, with six different types of imported Colombian coffee served on the rooftop garden. Champagne and dancing followed in the main ballroom.

Three rotating bands provided a variety of musical entertainment throughout the evening, but the real star of the show was 37 Middlesex, The Club itself. There were also representatives — 'spies', Lou called them — from male professional clubs in San Francisco, LA, Boston, and Toronto.

That night 37 Middlesex outdid them all. Gwen and Lou moved through the crowd hardly daring to believe that their dream had actually come true. Suzy Knickerbocker and Liz Smith would have plenty to say in their columns the next day. For the next six months, The Club at 37 Middlesex would be the talk of the town.

# *Twelve*

Everywhere Susie went there seemed to be babies. Even in Manhattan, there was an abundance of baby chic. Babies in restaurants, at the museums, at gallery openings, and in Central Park on Sunday afternoons. Babies in designer sleepers and Snugglies out for a stroll on Columbus Avenue in their high-tech strollers, snoozing while their mummies and daddies shopped at Only Hearts and The Last Wound Up. Babies were in and childless couples were out. Susie looked at all the babies longingly. The world of New York was big and scary; she wanted to get lost in a baby. It went from a wish to a need to a tremendous craving.

She searched her body for signs of change, the slightly enlarged nipples, the swollen tummy, but every month when that depressingly familiar reddish brown stain appeared in her underpants, she thought she would die of disappointment. She knew she'd make a great mother. And Lokis would make a great father. So why wasn't it happening? Tremendous expectations every month and then that overwhelming feeling of failure. Failure and emptiness. Lokis was trying not to mention it too much but she knew he was looking at her differently. At her age, she should be a baby-making machine. Her full breasts and round hips seemed to mock her every time she looked in the mirror.

She'd taken her basal temperature over one thousand times, first thing in the morning, without moving a muscle, while she was still lying in bed. She'd had an endometrial biopsy to determine her hormone levels and a postcoital mucus test to analyse Lokis's sperm count and activity. Dr Christine Carter, the specialist they were seeing, could find nothing wrong. She diagnosed it as unexplained infertility and told them both to go home and try to relax while having sex. But it was ruining their sex life. Now Dr Carter told them they had to do it at very specific times and in very specific ways. Susie hated taking her temperature. Lokis hated having to wear boxer shorts instead of jockeys. They were using ice packs and doing it doggie-style, which had never been her favourite position. She was lying on her back with her legs up in the air for half an hour. The minute her temperature went up she called him at the studio and he would rush home — to 'plug the bitch.'

She tried hard to keep the magic going. She took all the plants off the balcony and put them in the living-room. She bought a cassette tape of jungle sounds. She put on her leopard bikini and fed Lokis grapes one by one and they made it on the living-room floor under the aspidistra. She transformed the kitchen into a Parisian bistro with a red and white checked tablecloth and wine bottles and Toulouse Lautrec posters. When Lokis came home from work, she greeted him at the door wearing only a little red apron and black patent pumps. She filled the tub with bubble bath, lit the bathroom with candles, and put on a cassette of Vivaldi's *Four Seasons*. They drank champagne and did it in the tub.

But it didn't work. Nothing worked. She was barren. What a melodramatic word. Sounded like something out of a Victorian novel.

Oddly, with so many babies around, infertility seemed to be a nationwide epidemic at the same time. The Dalways, their neighbours in the next apartment, had been trying to get pregnant for a long time, too. When they finally succeeded, they did so in a big way. Beverly Dalway had given birth to twins and of course Lokis and Susie had celebrated their good fortune with them. After that, with the babies actually there, the two couples didn't have much in common any more. All Beverly could talk about was how cute Brian was or how precocious Bartley was, which depressed Susie more than ever. It just wasn't fair.

Lokis's career had really taken off. He had quit studying architecture because he was getting a lot of work designing restaurants. He and a fellow student from the Pratt Institute had found an old barber shop complete with some of the old fixtures, carved oak pedestal chairs, a carved oak bar, and a brass cash register. The rent was incredibly affordable, particularly for New York. Along with another friend, they turned it into a coffee bar that they named Shave and Haircut. Lokis now spent most of his Sundays haunting antique stores for more brass fittings and oak furniture. In the front of the café he had a shop with retro fashion and *objets d'art* from the 1920s and 193Os.

'I'm seduced by space,' he said to Susie. 'Creating spaces, transforming spaces: I love to have people walk in the door and be drawn into a whole new world that I've created for them.'

Shave and Haircut became immensely popular as a hangout for young upscale artists and, on the basis of that, Lokis was offered a contract to do Manna from Heaven, a wholefood restaurant which he did in natural stone, brick and wood with his own touch of sophistication, making it more than the usual granola-head health bar. He did a fifties-style diner called Gas Works in the Village. He was fast becoming the hottest young designer in town. He did a brasserie on Amsterdam, a California-style bar and grill on Columbia Avenue, and a Japanese teahouse on the upper east side.

341

He did his first club down in Tribeca, a wine bar in Soho, and a Tex-Mex bar in the West Forties. Lizardo's, as the Tex-Mex place was called, was all in black and silver, with a stuffed monitor lizard hanging like a chandelier from the ceiling over the bar in the middle of the room.

By this time he'd moved away from the natural materials into a more futuristic look. He relied heavily on black and silver, glass and chrome tubing in his work. He was still wearing all black himself, now with his hair cut short in front and long in the back. He obviously thought he looked artsy but to Susie he just looked weird.

She wondered if she should get a job. It seemed to be a full-time job taking care of Lokis. An artist needed an emotional and social support system, he kept telling her, and she was doing her best to provide it. Part of that support seemed to be club-hopping until four in the morning with all the trendoids, as Susie liked to call them. They all wore strange hairdos and a lot of make-up and black clothes. OK, so the black made sense, given the dirt and grime of Manhattan street life, but it was so depressing. They were all reading trendy novels about New York and talking in an odd stream-of-consciousness style that was just pretentious, Susie thought, but she didn't dare say any of this to Lokis. He was having the time of his life.

While he had been at Pratt, she had helped him with all his design projects, and now that he had incorporated himself into his own business, she continued to work with him. She was a quick, concise sketcher with strong technique. Lokis, on the other hand, was a great ideas man, who didn't like to finish anything. He was always on to the next project, leaving Susie to complete the current one. 'These cretins can't visualize anything,' he would say. 'Make it look pretty, Suse. Otherwise they won't buy it.' The accounting course she'd taken in high school was proving useful, too, because she could keep his books, which saved them a lot of money.

Working with him was fine but he didn't really want her to get a job outside their home or his studio. Maybe she should go back to school? At first he tried to veto that, too. 'I know you're feeling insecure, honey. This baby thing's got you twisted into knots. You're looking around for something that you can do without me. But, hey, I don't want to lose my best draughtsman. Your lines are so much better than mine. You're more precise. I need to be able to count on that.'

' You're not going to lose that if I go back to school. I love helping you. You're brilliant, I've known that all along, and I want to be a real part of your success . . .'

His face hardened. 'Look, baby, let's get one thing straight. People are not buying you, they're buying me. You're the craftsman; I'm the artist. All you do is photocopy my mind. You want to translate me, that's fine, but it's my language, not yours.'

That really hurt. Taking a deep breath, Susie tried to steady her voice. 'I'm happy to go on translating for you, as you put it. I just want to take a couple of classes. I need to upgrade my technique. It could make all the difference in our — your presentations.'

Lokis's face relaxed and he had the good grace to look a bit sheepish. 'I'm sorry. You've got to understand. There isn't room for two artists in this family. You're talented but I am, I think you'll agree, maybe a bit more talented. If the two of us take a separate course of action we might never make it, but if one of us gets behind the other, one of us has a chance of making it really big. It sounds selfish but I don't think you're a trailblazer. You're one hell of a follower and I'm glad of it. If you want to go back to school, go back to school. I won't stand in your way.'

*     *     *

343

It was a long subway ride in from Brooklyn Heights to the New School at Seventh Avenue and Thirteenth. At night she took the same long subway ride back home to make dinner, work on her drawings for class plus her renderings for Lokis, and try to study. When Lokis got home at night he didn't feel like studying. He felt like partying. He began to host all-night drinking sessions with his buddies in black.

'They're not party animals,' he said defensively when Susie complained about the noise and the mess and the cigarette smoke and, she feared, some drugs. 'They're good business contacts, honey. It's all for business.'

When she finally climbed up into the loft bed and put on her headphones so that she could sleep, Lokis followed her upstairs, saying everyone was leaving, he was going to bed now, too. They had both kind of put sex on hold for a while but now Lokis wanted to make love all the time. As soon as she came in the door, hot and sweaty from the subway, he would yank down her pantyhose and want to go at it on the kitchen table. 'Isn't it great to break old patterns?' he asked, enthusiastically pumping away while Susie surreptitiously checked her watch to see if she could manage to squeeze in a shower before she laid out the Greek salad and cold cuts she had picked up at the deli. Lokis was really unhappy that she wasn't cooking any more, but she just couldn't find the time. Once she was in the shower, he would suddenly join her, miraculously erect again, clutching her from behind, soaping her between the legs, getting her hair wet. 'Wow, terrific, eh, baby? I thought I was turning into an old man there for a while but now it's like starting all over again, isn't it?' She'd manage to get away from him, go up to the loft, lay out her drawing materials and then, suddenly, there he'd be. The sight of Susie with a piece of paper and a draughting pen in her hand seemed to inflame him. 'I love you all rumpled and ink-stained,'

344

he said, fondling her breasts and breathing garlic sausage all over her. 'You look so cute with those glasses on, like a French schoolgirl or maybe a brainy Brooke Shields. Mmm. Sexy. I like it.'

'Come on, Lokis, leave me alone. I've got to study,' she begged.

'Give me some heavy-duty private lessees, OK?'

'No. I've got an exam next week and I'm way behind. Will you give me a break, please?'

'What do you need to study for? You're brilliant already, my beautiful, talented Susie Sunshine. My gorgeous, smart, super-talented, multi-faceted wife. You can handle the courses without all this studying. You're the oldest person in the class anyway.'

'Don't remind me. Everybody else still has zits.'

'You're already smarter than the rest of them. You know life. The exam will be a snap.'

He actually followed her to the exam. She couldn't believe it. He actually hung around outside the classroom, waiting for her to take her exam. Every time she looked up from the page, he winked at her and gave her a thumbs-up sign. Once he unzipped his pants and started to expose himself trying to get her attention, and then laughed when she flushed and tried to wave him away.

'Whatever possessed you to do something like that?' she asked him on the subway ride home. 'If anybody else had seen you, you could have been charged with exhibitionism'

'Oh, don't be so straight, Suse. Jesus, I thought you'd get a kick out of it! I was cheering you on. Your own personal mascot. Just making sure you pass with flying colours!'

She passed. Now what? She didn't know what to do. If she couldn't have a child she was terrified that Lokis might leave her. Even though they were having major problems, the thought of life without Lokis petrified her. What if he stopped loving her?

Lokis came home one night and announced that he was working with an absolutely incredible woman. 'She's amazing,' he said, his voice more alive than she'd heard it in a long time. 'So together. A really hard-headed businesswoman. Knows just what she wants and goes after it. Her brain runs a mile a minute.'

'Oh yeah?' Susie said, feeling the jealousy in her expand and swamp her.

'Yeah. It's exciting just sitting and having a conversation with her.'

'What does she look like?'

'Short, attractive, red-haired.'

'Oh.' Now she was experiencing major waves of panic. 'Does she have kids?'

'No, she's not married' – Oh God – 'I think she's gay.'

Great relief and new interest. 'You're kidding? What's her name?'

'Gwyneth Roberts.'

'Didn't you already design something for her?'

'Yeah. A house in Sag Harbor. Now she's sold it. That's the point. She's selling off everything and investing in a professional club for women. She's bought a building on a great piece of property, prime downtown real estate and she wants me to do the rebuilding. It'll be a long contract.'

'A club exclusively for women?'

'Yeah, like the New York Athletic Club. That kind of thing.'

'Sounds like a glorified coffee klatch.'

'Not with the plans Gwen's got in mind. She wants it to be a showpiece for women. I'm going to invest in the project. I have a feeling it's an idea that will sell.'

'Can you afford a personal investment like that?'

'Don't be a nag.' Lokis was always annoyed when she questioned his financial decisions. 'The plans are spectacular. Do you want to help me out on the design?'

'No, I don't think so. Actually, I want to go back to Minnesota for a visit. I'm worried about Dad. Can you get along without me for a while?'

'Sure, honey, if that's what you want.' He looked none too pleased. 'I'm going to miss my favourite draughtsman. Not to mention my favourite accountant.'

Susie desperately needed a break from the noise and the grime of Manhattan. And she needed a break from Lokis. He was busy, and as it turned out, her father really needed her. His second wife Edith had divorced him and moved to Salt Lake City. Her father had had a stroke three months earlier and hadn't told her or Susie. Now Susie was concerned about him rattling around in that big old house all by himself. Of course he didn't want to go into a home, so Susie found him an apartment in a senior citizens' complex where he could have someone look in on him every day and still be on his own. It took a couple of months to find the place and get him settled in. By the time she returned to New York, The Club was open and Lokis was already on to another project. She told him she was sorry she'd missed the opening, but secretly she was relieved. A professional club for women only made her more aware that she didn't really have a profession. She had already failed at the only profession she had ever wanted.

Once again she thought maybe she should take her portfolio around and see what she could pick up in terms of commercial artwork. Lokis wanted her to stick with him even though both of them knew she wasn't functioning all that well in that area. Once she had left the drawings for one of their most important projects in the washroom at Macy's. It was in the Lost and Found, thank God, when she went back to get it the next day,

347

but Lokis had missed a deadline and he was as mad as hell.

'What is the matter with you?' he demanded angrily, snatching the portfolio from under her arm. He blasted her royally.

'I'm sorry,' she mumbled.

'Get with it, Suse. You want to go away this Christmas? It's our turn to use the time-share condo. You want to spend New Year in Grand Cayman? Or do you want to risk getting AIDS kissing everybody in Times Square?'

In the last few years they had really moved up in the world financially. No more subways. No more deli food. Their place in Brooklyn Heights had gone co-op and they had bought it outright. Lokis had also invested in a loft-cum-studio in Tribeca in lower Manhattan. Lokis practically screamed at her: 'Or do you just want to sit here and rot?' Stonily Susie stared out of the window of the co-op at the street below as the wind pulled two yellowing leaves off the large maple tree and dropped them neatly on top of the raked pile at the foot of the tree. 'Jesus, come on, Susie, you don't have to help me with the Rubell project! If you don't have the time, you don't have the time. Just let me know.'

Susie turned and forced herself to focus on him. 'Oh, I've got time,' she said with a smile that infuriated him. 'I've got all the time in the world.'

'I've had just about enough of this,' he said angrily. 'You've got to grow up and join the real world.' He grabbed his chequebook from the desk and scribbled a cheque, tore it out, and handed it to her.

'What's this for?'

'It's five thousand dollars for your first year's membership. I want you to join The Club.'

# *Thirteen*

'Thank you all so much. This award means everything to me.' Miriam clutched the Tony in her sweaty right hand and fought to maintain her poise and control. The funny-shaped little gold-plated figure named after Antoinette Perry was the most prestigious award given in New York theatre. It meant that her peers believed that her performance as Lady in Tennessee Williams's *Orpheus Descending* was the best performance given by an actress that season.

Since returning to New York four years ago, she literally hadn't stopped working. *A Moon for the Misbegotten* had moved from the Public to Broadway, receiving massive critical acclaim and enjoying a good long run. In fact, she'd been nominated for a Tony for the role of Josie, but she hadn't won, probably because everybody was waiting to see if she was really was as good as she seemed to be or just a flash in the theatrical pan. Starring in quick succession as Sarah Bernhardt in the short-lived musical version, *Sarah*, Lady Macbeth in another Papp production that had made it to Broadway for a limited run, and now Lady, Miriam was on her way to becoming a major star of the Broadway stage.

All of her idols were in the audience tonight. Streep, Nelligan, Susan Sarandon, and Sigourney Weaver — they were all here to see her receive the coveted award. Her role models had now become her competition.

She and Stephen made their way through the crowd

of well-wishers at the post-awards party, accepting congratulations on her performance on stage and Stephen's performance in the Senate. His critical reappraisal of the Vietnam War. *Look How Far We've Come*, had been number three on the bestseller list for the past eight months, and was still getting a lot of media hype. They were maintaining separate bases now and seeing each other whenever they could, on weekends, after a show had closed and before she started rehearsal on the next a few weeks later, or when Congress was not in session. She missed him terribly. Part of her wished he would just demand that she give up the business, marry him and move to Washington, but the other part of her knew how lucky she was to have a man like Stephen, because he was so supportive of her career and understood her drive to make it to the top of her profession. As if reading her thoughts, he put his arm around her and whispered in her ear, 'I'm so proud of you, darling. We're in high-powered company here, but I know that I'm with the most beautiful, talented and sexy lady in this room. You're a wonder, my love.'

'Congratulations, Miriam!' Gwyneth Roberts enveloped her in a big hug. 'You've deserved this award for three years in a row now. They finally had the sense to give it to you.'

'This is going to make a big difference to your career, *mi bella*,' Luigi del Bello kissed her hand. Miriam never knew quite what to make of Gwen's associate, but Stephen loved his flamboyant manner, and found his camp behaviour a welcome change from the reserve of political life. They often spent time together when Stephen was in New York. There was something about him that made Miriam uneasy, not because he was homosexual — gay men were her male colleagues for the most part — there was just something shifty in the way he looked at her, as though he knew a secret that she didn't. However, she really enjoyed Gwen's company. The four of them 'double dated' on the town when they could. Gwen was always either with Lou or alone; Miriam never saw her with any other man. It made her wonder about her a little, but although she and Gwen were becoming friends, she sensed there were barriers she couldn't cross.

Joining The Club a year ago had helped Miriam's career and now that Gwen had invited her to join the advisory board of directors, it was giving her a reputation in the city of being more than 'just an actress'. She had originally joined because her agent at the time, Maggie Reilly, said it was a great place to network for television and film.

'Theatre's no prob for you, hon.' Maggie was a short, squat tank of a woman with a heavy New Jersey accent. 'But we gotta crack that media market if you're ever gonna be worth more to me than a cup of cawfee. These network guys, they don't know Shakespeare from Shaw. To them, it's what you look like, how successful you are, what your TV Q is. We're talkin' image here, hon. You walk in there looking hungry, you won't get the job. These guys are sharks. They can smell "need" and nothing turns 'em off quicker. Wear a fur coat to a commercial audition and let it drop on the floor. Get Stephen to buy you some heavy-duty rock to wear on your fingers or in your ears.

'And I think you should join The Club. Posh new joint for women. All the top casting directors for soaps are members. I hear they do more casting in the sauna than they do in the offices of ABC. It costs an arm and a leg to join but I think you better spring for it. Image, hon. It's all image.'

Maggie should have gone to work for Stephen. Lately he was talking less and less about political issues and more and more about image. She watched him put one arm

351

around Gwen and another around Lou as he said, 'Mim, darling, I'm going to let you work the room alone for a bit. I need to spirit Gwen and Lou away to talk about politics and Washington and all that stuff I know you find boring.' Miriam opened her mouth to protest that she didn't find it boring at all as he leaned over and stopped her with a kiss, 'This is your night. Take it. Enjoy it. You've worked hard for it. And you deserve to bask in the glory all by yourself. I'll be watching out for you. I love you.' He blew her a kiss and the three of them moved away, talking and laughing, Lou gesticulating wildly in the air.

For a moment, Miriam felt bereft. She liked having Stephen on her arm at occasions like these, because he made her feel protected and confident as if just being with him somehow validated her own worth. She liked being part of a team, and when he was away from her she felt as if a major part of her identity was missing. For the zillionth time she wondered if he could possibly love her the way she loved him.

Feeling gentle tap on her arm she turned to see a short, slightly overweight young man with a round face and intensely dark eyes. 'M-M-Ms N-newman,' he said politely, 'could I have a m-moment of your time?' He looked awestruck to be in her company, something that would have embarrassed her even a year ago but to which she was now becoming accustomed and even, much as she hated to admit it, enjoying. 'You're a brilliant actress . . . my absolute all-t-time favourite star . . . God, this is coming out sounding like I'm some s-sort of groupie . . . could I walk away and start this over again, p-please?'

'Why don't you do that?' Miriam laughed as she watched him literally walk to the other end of the room, turn on his heel, take a deep breath, and walk back to her.

'OK. What I meant to say is that I think you are an

extraordinary talent. You create a life on stage that is very specific and you draw the audience right into it. You never impose anything on the character, you're not looking to find yourself in the character. You create something totally new, not yourself, not the character, but a third entity, something you and the playwright have given birth to together. It's truly amazing to watch you work because when you act we never see you working, just being. Am I making any sense at all?' He didn't stop for her answer but finished up in a rush with, 'I guess what I'm trying to say is that it's not just a Tony you're holding in your hand, but the future of American theatre.'

'Whew, that's quite a speech!' Miriam was laughing again. 'OK, OK, what do you want from me? I have a feeling it's not an autograph.'

'I want you to read my play. I'm a playwright and I've written a play specifically for you. There's no one else who can play this role. It is you.'

'You're a playwright?' Miriam was already starting to back away.'

'Oh, shit, I forgot to introduce myself. I'm David Arlen Love. I've got a show running right now off-Broadway at the Manhattan Theatre Club. *Devil's Kiss*.'

Miriam stopped to take a closer look at the intense young man. 'I've heard of you. But I expected you to be much older. You look like a baby.'

'I'm about the same age you are. OK, maybe a little younger, although I'm not as young as I look. I'm not as short as I look either. There's a lot more to me than meets the eye.'

'I can see that.' Miriam was surprised at how much David was making her laugh. 'You've had a couple of things done in the regionals, right? This is your first New York gig.'

'Yeah, I'm from Detroit.'

353

'Detroit? You can't be in the theatre and come from Detroit!'

'Why not? You can be in the theatre and come from Fresno,' he shot back.

'You seem to know a lot about me. Not many people know about my Fresno connection.'

'I've been following your career for a long time.' David's eyes fairly glowed with admiration. 'Look, I don't want to tie you up too long and keep you from circulating. I just want you to read my play and promise you'll meet with me to talk about it.' He reached into his briefcase and drew out a loosely bound manuscript. 'Let me take you to lunch. Please.'

'I don't know,' Miriam was starting to demur when Stephen broke in on them.

'Listen, darling, I hate to do this to you, especially tonight, but I've got to fly back to Washington. Something's come up. I'm taking the red-eye and I want you to drive me to the airport.' Stephen already had his coat over his arm and was holding hers out for her. A sudden burst of anger flooded her. Why was he asking her to leave a party that was in her honour on one of the most important nights of her life? He'd said it was her night, so why was he spoiling it? He hadn't even asked if she was willing to drive him to the airport; he just assumed she would do it.

Miriam turned back to David. 'OK, I'll read your play and I'll meet with you to discuss it. Only let *me* buy the lunch. Shall we say the day after tomorrow, one o'clock at The Club?'

'The Club? You mean "The Club"?' David looked impressed.

'Yes. I'm a privileged member. Let's meet in the main dining-room. It's not as glitzy as the waterfall lounge, but the food is great. I'll make the reservation and get you clearance.'

'Clearance? What is this, the CIA?'

'You can't get into The Club at all without a programmed membership card. So when you arrive on Wednesday, just push the buzzer, announce who you are, the doors will open, and an attendant will bring you up to the restaurant.'

'Mim, are you coming, love?' Stephen was tapping his foot impatiently.

Impulsively Miriam gave David a quick kiss on the cheek. 'See you Wednesday,' she said.

'See you Wednesday.'

'Boy, this place is really something else.' David Arlen Love polished off the last of his dozen fresh oysters, set the little fork down, and looked around the high-ceilinged dining-room. 'It's like an oasis in the middle of New York. Although I have to admit, I feel a little out of place here, though, rather like the time I saw *For Colored Girls . . .*'

'*Who Have Considered Suicide When the Rainbow Is Not Enuf.*' Miriam finished the title of the play for him.

'Yes. I was sitting among all these black women in the audience. Not only was I the only male, I am also Jewish. I felt like the ultimate enemy. I wanted to yell out, "Hey, wait a minute I'm not a red-necked macho male chauvinist racist pig! I'm a sensitive playwright! I don't write about the white urban male mythology. I write about ethnics. And I write great roles for women."'

'How Jewish are you?' Miriam asked.

'What?'

'Well, you're eating traif.' She pointed to the row of empty oyster shells on the plate resting on a bed of ice in front of him.

'Traif? You call superb oysters like these traif?'

'They are good, aren't they? Luigi del Bello has them brought in from Maritime Canada. Usually they're

355

Malpecques but at this time of the year, apparently the Bras d'or are better. Sweeter and less salty than the Malpecque, Lou says.'

'*Ostreidae virginica*,' David said, looking lovingly at the empty shells.

'A man who knows the Latin for oyster. How exotic,' Miriam said with a smile, 'but obviously you don't keep kosher.'

'I was raised religious, but I've kind of gotten away from it.'

'Me too.'

'But Judaism keeps drawing me back, I don't know.' His eyes were thoughtful.

Miriam changed the subject. 'Don't think of yourself as the enemy here at The Club. You're not completely alone. At least the waiters are male.'

'Quite a bunch of stellar studs you've got here, haven't you?' David glanced admiringly at a green-eyed blond surfer type who had been solicitously hovering around them.

'Are you gay?' Miriam asked David directly. Somehow, when you worked in theatre, it was natural to ask.

'Me? Are you kidding? No. I think you already know that I'm at least halfway in love with you now. Of course I don't expect you to do anything about it. You seem very well taken care of in that department.' He spoke seriously, but his brown eyes were merry. 'So,' he said suddenly. 'I've been good all through the soup and the appetizer, but I can't make it though to dessert without asking. What do you think of the play?'

Miriam took a bite of her salad. 'I think it's wonderful, David, I really do. You've obviously got great respect for actors.'

'I started out as an actor. Of course I respect them. You're the ones putting yourselves on the line.'

356

'And I've got respect for the text. You started out as an actor?'

'Yeah, I've done everything: drive a cab, worked with emotionally disturbed children. I was even a strip-o-gram delivery boy for a while.' His cheeks flushed slightly. 'I always believe it's better to take a straight job in the real world than to do bad work in theatre.'

'Well, you've found the right niche now. Your writing is beautiful, David. This play reads like a film script. Very cinematic. Plot less important than emotions. No direct throughline, but you don't need one. What's really interesting is that you had me fooled completely. I was hoping it would end up with Malka and Barak getting together but I just couldn't see how they possibly could. When they did, I burst into tears. You have an incredible facility with language. It's like music or poetry. The dialogue sounds like everyday speech − I believe the characters talk the way real people do − but somehow it all adds up to poetry.'

'Lyric realism. That's what the *Times* critic calls it.' David was blushing again.

'I think you're right up there with David Mamet and Chris Durang.'

'Durang is great, but I find his humour pretty cynical. Can't really empathize with his characters. Mamet I love, but his approach is to demystify the American Dream. God, this food is terrific.' The blond beach-boy waiter whipped away their oyster plates, replacing them with a platter of mixed grilled seafood brushed with olive oil, garlic, and fresh basil.

'But don't you agree that mindless greed and the pursuit of wealth has turned us Americans into the enemies not only of the Third World but of each other?' It felt good to talk about theatre in terms of politics with someone other than Stephen, sharing ideas instead of listening to a lecture. David was hanging on her every

357

word just the way she used to do with Stephen.

'Sure, but that's not what I'm writing about. Granted, Americans are users and destroyers, but we're also hopeless romantics, always questing, reaching for the stars. Always believing that the right person is out there waiting for us somewhere.'

They attended to the platter for a few moments.

'It's a terrific play, David. But I'm not right for this role,' she interposed gently. Seeing his face fall, she added, 'I'm a classical actress mainly. I'm not good at this modern stuff. I'm not good at passing for normal.'

'What's not normal?'

'My size, for one thing.'

'What are you talking about? You're beautiful. You're womanly.'

Miriam smiled wryly. They all eventually ended up calling her fat. Even Stephen was beginning to bug her abut her weight even though she was thinner than she'd been in a long time. 'I'm a classical actress,' she repeated.

'But I'm giving you a chance to break out of that mould. You've played enough of those heavy-duty ball-busters. I know there's vulnerability in you. I can see it, feel it, when I talk to you. I don't often get it from you on stage. And how about doing an American play for a change instead of all this French and Scandinavian stuff?'

'Tennessee Williams and Eugene O'Neill are American.'

'Still period stuff. You need to do something modern,' he insisted.

'It's a comedy. I'm not funny.'

'You can be funny. I know you can.'

'This character you've written for me . . . Malka . . . she's supposed to be a young librarian who falls in love with a bagelmaker. I don't read as young. And she has

358

to be transformed at the end. She has to suddenly become beautiful.'

David reached across the table and pulled out the pins that held her chignon in place. Her thick dark hair spilled down around her shoulders. 'Why, Miss Newman,' he said. 'You are beautiful. OK, an old trick from *The Rainmaker*, but seriously, Miriam, I know you can do this part. You can be young, you can be beautiful, you can be whatever you want to be, whatever I see you to be. The theatre is a place for magic.'

'You talk a great game.' Miriam could feel herself weakening. Off-Broadway? For a six-week run? For scale? Her agent would kill her. 'And I have to admit what attracts me to the script is not just the text, but the subtext. You saw an awful lot between the lines.'

'As we do in real life. We hardly ever say what we mean. We often say, "Get away from me, leave me alone," when what we mean is, "Stay with me. Love me. Please love me." '

Unexpectedly her eyes filled with tears. 'You're a wise man, David Love. Wise and very, very sweet.'

'Then you'll do the play?'

'I'll do the play.'


She bloomed in the role of Malka. Never before had she been so enthralled by a character, she who 'lost herself' in all her roles. Her partnership with David was that rare and priceless synthesis of writer and actor perfectly attuned to one another's art, drawing inspiration from the combination and fuelling new creations.

Perhaps just as important to Miriam was their non-professional partnership as it grew and strengthened. They talked about everything, about their books, plays, acting reviews and reviewers, their early years in the business over lengthy post-rehearsal and -performance dinners and on the phone. They discussed David's new play ideas, and they shared dreams and insecurities together.

Miriam could admit her fears to him, that her success was only temporary, that she was not really all that good as an actress at all. She told him how much she missed Stephen, how she missed discussing her work with him, quickly adding how tremendously proud she was of him and of his own career and buoyed by his often unspoken support of her work. Thank God David wasn't her type. For one thing, he looked so much like her. Same dark hair, deep brown eyes, strong nose, sensual mouth. It would be like making love to her brother. She knew he would never push it and she knew he valued the strong friendship between them as much as their professional partnership. The bond between them continued to develop as she starred in more new plays as he wrote them.

Stephen was away more and more. She was afraid she was losing him. How could she possibly expect to hold on to him if she wasn't there with him? How did she know Stephen wasn't right in the middle of Washington's hotbed of scandal? The thought of him even touching another woman made her want to kill, but she knew that was crazy. Hadn't he told her that he loved her and only her. She tried to keep her fears under control, but every once in a while she would break down and cry on David's shoulder. He always told her exactly what she needed to hear: 'Stephen would be a fool to lose you. Political life is even more of a fantasy world than show business. You're not a conventional couple so you've chosen not to live by conventional rules. Marriage wouldn't necessarily bind him to you anyway. He'll keep coming back to you because you're the only one who loves the real Stephen. The rest of the world is in love with some idealized vision of Stephen Andrews. You keep him grounded in reality.'

Grateful to David, Miriam tried to guide him in his turn through the trials and tribulations of his own rapidly increasing love life. 'Now that I'm becoming the toast of literary New York,' he confided to her, 'women who wouldn't have looked twice at me on the street are banging down my door to get me into their beds. It's terribly flattering but more than a little scary, sort of an embarrassment of riches.'

She was standing on the stage again, holding another Tony in her hand, this time for her role as Malka in *For Love of a Bagelmaker*. This time she wasn't nervous. As the audience rose to applaud her and she gazed out at all the familiar friendly faces of her peers, her heart swelled with joy and pride. She acknowledged the applause and the cheering gracefully, knowing they were applauding not only her performance but her creative relationship with David. His work had shaken the New York theatre establishment. He was well on his way to creating a completely new theatrical form. Broadway lived again and she and David were largely responsible for making it happen. In the last month he had been contracted to write his first screenplay and Miriam hoped this would be her ticket to make the crossover into film. She had rarely been happier.

Except for one thing. Stephen wasn't there to share it with her.

# Fourteen

New York. 'I've lost the restaurant. The bank is foreclosing on Carpaccio.' Luigi looked like death; this face was drawn and he was sweating heavily. Even his custom-made clothes sagged on him. He and Gwen were sitting in his office, a mound of budget spreadsheets laid out in front of them on his enormous mahogany desk. They had gone over them three times now and The Club's financial situation still looked bleak.

Gwen had been aware that the restaurant was in trouble for over six months now. To secure the money to buy into The Club as a partner, Lou had taken out a massive loan, guaranteeing it by pledging the restaurant and the land it was on as security. He'd ended up defaulting on a number of payments when he didn't have enough money from other sources and what he had had gone straight back into The Club. When he'd received a letter demanding payment from him as guarantor, he had freaked right out. Jonathan Long had come to his aid that time, and then Lou missed four more payments. He was called before a judge to plead his case.

'What happened?' Gwen asked worriedly. 'I thought the board's lawyer thought you had a really good case. Did he tell the judge the property had been in the family for years, that Carpaccio's a family business?'

'Of course. It didn't make any difference. The bank doesn't see me as a family man, I'm afraid. After all, I'm not married. I don't have any kids. As far as they're

363

concerned, I'm a tough businessman who knew exactly what he was getting into. The judge actually said that.'

'Did you tell them it looks as though The Club is about to turn around?' Gwen couldn't believe he would give up so easily.

'That means nothing to them. The bank isn't even interested in taking over my shares. They have no interest in a company that's not making it yet.'

'I really believe we're just about to turn the corner. If we can only hang on . . .'

'Yeah Tell that to Papa. The restaurant was his soul, his pride and joy. When he signed it over to me, it was like signing over his life. He's not taking it well. I feel so guilty.'

Gwen was fighting with her own guilt. They had nearly lost The Club the first year. Lou had taken out a second mortgage on it. And she had allowed him to do it. She'd been so sure of her vision.

As if reading her mind, Lou hastened to reassure her. 'Don't blame yourself. I wanted The Club every bit as much as you did. I begged you to let me be a partner, remember? I knew it was a risk, taking out another loan, but what else could we do? Our backs were against the wall. We wouldn't have been able to open otherwise. Everything cost twice what we expected. Lokis's renovations led us into cost over-runs that meant we were over-extended before we'd even got off the ground.'

'We both trusted him because he'd done a good job for us before.'

'Look, we had faith in him because he had faith in us. He invested his own money in The Club. It's not his fault there was a builders' strike. Never announce an opening date in New York,' Luigi said grimly. 'That gives the unions perfect reason to go on strike.'

'I've failed,' Gwen said softly. 'We've been in business for two years now and it's just not paying off. I figured if we made it through that first year, we'd be fine, and we did make it, though barely.'

'Well, we're in deep shit now. We were under-capitalized from the beginning. We shouldn't have expected The Club to be running at full capacity by the end of the first year. That was crazy. I just expected more women would be willing to jump on the bandwagon sooner. They didn't come through for us.'

'I know and I don't understand why.' Gwen was fighting the urge to break down and cry. 'That hurt; I can't tell you how much it hurt. They weren't buying me.'

'They still will. I can feel it in my gut. We're so close to achieving everything we've worked for, if we can just hang on for another six months, a year. It'll pay off and when it does, *cara*, it will be worth any sacrifice we've made so far . . .' The phone interrupted him. He barked hello into the receiver, listened for a few moments, and then slowly replaced it.

'What now? What's the matter?' Gwen's heart jumped into her throat at the look on his face.

'It's Papa. He's had a stroke. He's in intensive care at Roosevelt Hospital. He's not expected to last the night. *Madre de Dio*, this is all my fault!' He was pulling on his cashmere coat, his fingers fumbling with the buttons. 'I have to get over there right away, I need him to forgive me, he must forgive me.'

'I'm coming with you,' Gwen said, following him out the door.

'No, please, this is a family matter. Please let me go alone.' And he was gone.

She wandered back into her own office, picked up a file folder of bills from her desk, and tried in vain to focus on the papers in front of her. A voice inside her head was berating her, mocking her: 'You use people up and then you throw them away. You're a failure. You'll never amount to anything.' Absent-mindedly she snapped on the television to distract her and was in the middle of pouring herself a stiff drink when she heard a familiar voice say, 'And this is Sara Town, reporting from the nation's capital.' Looking up she saw Sara standing in front of the White House. Angrily, she snapped off the set, taking pleasure in seeing Sara's face vanish from the screen. Goddamnit, she wouldn't let Sara be proved right. She would keep The Club alive. She would make it pay, no matter what the cost.

Washington. Sara was covering the presidential race. She had followed Reagan's campaign all the way through to the White House and now she was a White House correspondent. Nixon she was leery of, had been from the very beginning. She would leave him to Diane Sawyer, but Ronald Reagan was another kind of man altogether. She idolized him, supported him with every ounce of her being and although she kept her politics to herself because as a journalist she couldn't be seen to be linked to either party, Regan must know where her political heart lay. The one time they had met face to face, he told her that he had never missed reading her 'Caustic Crusader' editorials in *NY Today* and that he had, in fact, saved several that she'd written on Carter and the hostage crisis.

'Sound editorialism,' he said, smiling his benevolent movie-star smile, 'a good, clear analysis of the big political picture. The American people are lucky to have you.'

He shook her hand and Sara felt her entire life had been validated in that single moment. At press conferences, he reserved his choicest quotes for her, fitting them around whatever question she asked him, giving her a perfect sound bite and a memorable headline which only served to raise her national profile further. He loved to call the correspondents by their first names and he usually had a bit of extra praise for Sara. 'I can always count on you, Sara, to ask an intelligent question. I guess that means you expect an intelligent answer,' he would say in his rich voice with a jovial twinkle in his eye.

'That's right, Mr President,' she would reply, only the slightest bit flirtatiously, 'and I know I can count on you to give me one.' More than a few people noticed the mutual admiration between them. She would have to be very careful where Nancy was concerned. The President's wife guarded her mate like a jealous tigress. If Nancy didn't like you, you were out.

It was an exciting time to be in Washington as it moved from the casual Georgia style of Jimmy Carter to a fresh uptown elegance. This was where the real news happened. She loved the glitter and the glamour and she didn't begrudge the Reagans one bit of it. What was the point of being the country's highest elected official if you were only going to pretend to be plain folk? Surely part of the fun of being President of the United States of America was in being treated like royalty. Picked up and carried along on the tidal wave of Reagan's popularity, Sara was becoming part of the inner circle of Washington society, out on the town almost every night with a different man. She was making more money than she'd ever made in her life and dating some of the city's most powerful men. What more could she want?

New York. 'I'm sorry, Ms Houston,' Gwen said, still reeling from the apparition that faced her across the desk, 'your credentials certainly look good, but I'm not sure you have the right image for this job.'

On Luigi's recommendation, she had agreed to interview Merilee Houston, but it was proving to be a complete waste of her time. What could Lou have been thinking of? This tiny blonde with the kewpie-doll body and meringue hairdo couldn't possibly function as programme director for an exclusive women's club.

367

Maybe, just maybe, as an aerobics instructor, but even that was doubtful. This woman was a joke. She looked like one of those inflatable dolls from the back of a men's magazine. As Merilee leaned over the desk to point out an item on her résumé, Gwen found it difficult not to stare down the front of her peasant blouse at the cleavage so amply displayed there. Did Lou honestly believe a nice pair of breasts could sway her? She felt her irritation rising.

'Completely the wrong image,' she repeated firmly.

'Maybe I don't look New York enough for you, but you sure liked the letter of application I sent you. Image is an easy thing to change if you really feel it's all that important, but don't judge a book by its cover. Sometimes lookin' dumb lets you be twice as smart. I've got a good head for business and I know people. Back home we prize that. Don't you feel the same here in New York? Look, I came all the way from Texas to see you. I think you owe me some serious consideration.'

Texas. Just the name sent ripples of long-buried pain running through her. 'I know, and you do seem to have accomplished a lot there.' The résumé in front of her did look impressive and Lou assured her the references had checked out. Merilee had run her own real estate agency in Austin, which had grown into a state-wide firm. She had been publicity manager for the Alley Theater in Houston and creative director for an ad agency. She had trained as a dancer and was a certified aerobics instructor. Gwen could fill two positions with one person if she hired Merilee Houston.

'I really think I could accomplish a lot here,' the petite blonde continued earnestly. 'You know I'm more than qualified for the job. I've also got shorthand, typing, and I'm computer-literate. Not that I'm offering myself as a secretary, but there might be projects you and I would want to discuss privately, in which case you could avail yourself of my secretarial skills.

'I want to work alongside you more than anything else in the world. You're my role model. I've been following your career for a long time, Ms Roberts. You're smart, you're tough, and you're a real lady. I admire that. You've accomplished a lot, startin' a business like this on your own and all, but I think you've kind of missed the boat here.'

'What do you mean?' Gwen was amazed that this Pop Tart had the audacity to tell her how to run her own business.

'Look, The Club is spectacular to look at, I'll grant you that. But it's no secret that it's in trouble. You're havin' financial problems and I think I can tell you why. Take away the glitz, get rid of the waterfall, the marble staircase, the glass elevator, and what have you got?'

'What do you think?' In spite of herself, Gwen was interested.

'A glorified YWCA, that's all. You got your daycare, you got your swimming pool, your library, your gym, your computer centre, and all that's great. But the underlyin' message here is, "work harder, be better, be stronger". Your members are already running as fast as they can just to stay in one place. You're just applyin' more pressure when you should be helpin' them to relax.'

Gwen leaned forward. 'Go on.'

'You should be making them feel that they are already successful, not that they're still not good enough. We fought hard to get where we are. But we're here. We made it! The Club should be a place where women come to be pampered, to have their every whim satisfied. There should be a beauty salon, a full-time masseur, a screening room for movies, fashion shows . . .'

'Fashion shows?' Gwen could hardly conceal her disdain.

369

'Now see, that's what I mean. You want everything to be real serious, big business, making deals, making contacts, and that's real important, I agree. But all work and no play makes Jill just as dull as Jack. Get some good-lookin' guys around here – OK, not in the pool area if the members want to skinny-dip – but at least the waiters in the lounge should be real men and easy on the eyes. Give us something to look at besides each other. We want these men to be at our beck and call. Tell Luigi they gotta be gorgeous and straight. Give women something they can't get anywhere else and I promise you, they'll be lining up around the block to get in. You want The Club to be more than a gymnasium. You want it to be paradise.'

Washington. The racing-green Jaguar pulled up in front of the red brick high-rise. Sara leaned over and quickly kissed the man in the navy three-piece suit. 'It's been a lovely evening. Thank you so much. Call me.'

'Aren't you going to invite me up?' The former White House aide, now one of Washington's top financiers, looked surprised and more than a little hurt.

'Not tonight, love. Sorry. I've got an excruciatingly early call at the studio tomorrow and I need to get some sleep. But we'll get together soon, I promise. Maybe this weekend in Connecticut? Keep your tennis arm in practice.' And she was out of the door before he could stop her.

He watched the doorman come out into the cold Washington winter night, moving slowly and painfully, to tip his hat and open the lobby door for her. Damnit to hell, he'd just blown four hundred bucks on dinner at Sans Souci with not a thing to show for it except a hard-on. Cursing her under his breath, he gunned his motor and roared off into the night.

Hurry, Sara urged silently, as the elevator shot to the

top of the high-rise, depositing her on the thirtieth floor. Fingers trembling, she unlocked the door to her penthouse apartment and ran towards the bedroom, stripping off her clothes as she ran, the tailored overcoat and the red wool faille dress, off came the full white slip and pantyhose. Nude, she pawed through the clothes in her closet, past the Calvin Klein, the Carolyn Roehm, the Liz Claiborne sportswear, until she found what she was looking for. Zipping herself into the soft red suede mini skirt, which just barely covered her hips, she leaned over to let her breasts fall into the lacy black bustier. She pulled on a red suede jacket and a pair of high black boots. Breathing heavily, she stopped to glimpse herself in the full-length mirror. What she saw pleased her enough to allow a small, cat-like smile to curl the ends of her lips. More slowly she watched herself reapply her crimson lipstick. Now she was ready to go hunting.

It took some doing to find a bar like this in Washington – dimly lit, smoke-filled, slightly seedy. Washington taste ran more to brass-and-wood cocktail lounges or white walls with masses of greenery and wine glasses on display. But the minute she walked in, Sara knew this was the right pace. Happy Hour at The Back Room started at four o'clock in the afternoon and went on until well after midnight. The staff served free peanuts in the shell, and the floor was ankle deep in discarded shells. Sara ordered a double Tequila Gold, straight up, with two pieces of lime, hold the salt. She leaned against the bar, slowly sucking on a piece of lime, surveying the dark, smoky room.

Then she saw him. Straddling a tall stool at the other end of the bar, drinking a long-necked bottle of beer. On the short side, dark hair, black jeans, leather jacket, the muscles of his chest standing out like bas relief under the thin white T-shirt. He was wearing custom-designed snakeskin boots. She liked the boots. Maybe, just maybe, she would like the voice as well. She made eye contact with him. Shit, he was too young. He wouldn't be interested in her. But no, he was definitely looking her way. Sara lifted her shot glass in his direction silently. Draining his bottle, he set it down on the bar, and made his way through the crowd and over to her, slowly, casually. Good. Watching him move made her mouth water. Her heart was already pounding with guilty excitement. He put one heavy boot up on the chair beside her and leaned down over her. She could smell the slightly sour beer on his breath, mixed with cigarettes and the musky odour of leather and sweat; it made her feel faint. 'Mind if I join you?' he asked quietly. He had a slight southern accent and her heart leaped at the sound. Exactly what she needed. She said nothing but kept on sucking on a piece of lime, staring at him boldly.

Giving her a small, twisted smile, he sat down beside her and calmly took the piece of lime out of her mouth and into his own. Picking up her tequila from the table, he knocked back what was left in the glass and signalled the waiter to bring them another round. Up close, he was not as young as he had first seemed. There were heavy lines around his mouth and eyes. For the next hour, they sat there, smoking and drinking shots of tequila. They said very little; Sara preferred it that way. As far as she was concerned, he existed only in this moment, here and now. His eyes never left her, like a snake watching its prey. He thought he had her under his control. She smiled inwardly; he was in for a surprise.

She took his hand and slid it up her skirt, along her bare leg, up her thigh. His narrowed eyes widened fully when he realized she wasn't wearing any underwear. Her hand was on his as she guided it between her legs, to the centre of her, the very core, moving it slowly, teasingly, knowing he could feel how wet she was, how soft and open.

Suddenly he thrust one finger inside her and she gasped. He smiled again, amused, triumphant that he'd been able to get a reaction out of her. 'Shh,' he said, leaning closer. 'Let's not attract any more attention than we have to.' She looked around the bar. Nobody was watching; they were all drinking and talking. Then her head whipped back to him and she gasped again as he thrust more fingers into her. Slowly, he began to fuck her with his whole hand, leaving his thumb to play with her, moving her into liquid fire. Her head dropped on to her chest but he slipped his other hand up under her hair to the nape of her neck and pulled her head up, forcing her to look into his eyes. 'Keep talking,' he ordered quietly. 'Just act normal or I'll have to stop. You don't want me to stop, do you?'

'No,' she whispered, barely able to get the word out, concentrating on his other fingers, focusing all her being on that pulse point, and then her eyes closed and she came in a long shuddering silent scream.

When her breathing had returned to normal and she opened her eyes again, she was cold with anger. Bastard. He had won that round. He had made her lose control. It was time to even the score She opened her red leather jacket a little wider and leaned across the table to him, allowing her breasts to spill out over the black lace. 'Come home with me,' she whispered huskily. 'It's your turn.'

In the taxi, she was all over him, tongue down his throat, hands sliding inside his shirt and down the back of his jeans, breathing heavily in his ear. She could feel his mounting excitement as they pulled up in front of her building. The doorman came out, slowly, to open the door for them.

'Evening, miss,' he said.

'Evening, Henry,' Sara replied, and the two of them watched as he moved slowly back around the corner to his post by the front door. The man from the bar reached

for the elevator button, but Sara put out her hand to stop
him. 'Don't,' she said. He looked at her in surprise. 'Over
here,' she whispered, pulling him into a little alcove beside
the elevators.

'Are you crazy?' he asked softly. 'Anyone could come
along. The security guy, he's right over there,'

'So?' Sara taunted, lifting her arms and freeing her
breasts from the top of their restraint.

'Oh Jesus,' he moaned, and backed her up against the
wall, his mouth coming down over one nipple.

She unzipped him quickly, lifted her skirt, and took
him into her. He was groaning quietly, his breath in her
ear, as he thrust at her frantically.

'Oh yes, baby, yes, come inside me, do it,' she
crooned, and then, just as she felt him nearing the
climax she suddenly pushed him out of her and away.
'Henry,' she called breathlessly. 'Could you come here
a minute?'

'What the hell are you doing?' The man was panting,
stuffing himself back into his jeans, his fingers shaking.
Sara turned away to button her jacket.

'You bitch!' the man hissed, bent over and struggling
with his zipper. 'What seems to be the trouble, miss?'
The doorman rounded the corner.

'No trouble, Henry. This gentleman was just leaving.
Would you escort him to the door, please?'

'Of course, miss. You have a good night, you hear.'

'Good night.' Sara watched the two of them go. As
the man turned back to look at her, she gave him the
finger. 'Fuck you, Trayne,' she whispered to herself, and
then she threw her head back and laughed.

New York. The Club was growing by leaps and bounds.
Gwen had to admit that a lot of The Club's new success
was owing to Merilee Houston's suggestions. When she
joined the staff of The Club, it lifted some of the work

load off Gwen's shoulders and gave her the first friend she'd had since Sara. Merilee was an odd choice for Gwen, she knew, but the little Texan had an earthy sense of humour and a straightforward manner that belied her frothy appearance.

'People tend to let their guard down around me because they think I'm safe. They trust me right away. That could be real useful to you around here.'

'Merilee' — Gwen laughed — 'are you offering to spy for me?'

'Well, why not? You got a big operation here. You got to be sure you're gettin' the best value for your money out of everybody who's workin' for you. You sit up here in your office all day, on the phone, makin' deals, talkin' with suppliers; how can you be sure what's goin' on downstairs? Maybe people are rippin' you off left, right, and centre. I'm not sayin' they are, mind you, I'm just sayin' they could be. I'm loyal. You can trust me not to trust anybody except you.'

Gwen found herself laughing. She knew she should find this idea offensive, but what Merilee was saying made a lot of sense. She couldn't keep her eye on everything all the time. Her homestyle way of talking often made Gwen cringe, but it also made her laugh. She was used to keeping her protective shell intact, but Merilee kept pecking away at it, trying to get her to relax. She called her a driven personality: 'You just don't know when to quit, do you, honey? You're what I call "wiped out on your job." ' For her birthday, Merilee had given her Dr Maclowitz's book, *Workaholics*, which had a questionnaire in the front

Do you find it difficult to 'do nothing'?

Do you work on weekends and holidays?

Do you find it hard to take a vacation?

Do people tell you 'you live for your work'?

Gwen had to answer 'yes' to every question with a triple

'yes' for the last one. She found her work endlessly fascinating, so fascinating that she had to stop herself from working twenty-four hours a day. Away from The Club, she felt lost. The Club defined her.

'You need to have some fun,' Merilee said, dragging her on to Fifth Avenue for an enforced shopping spree. 'Don't you ever get lonely?' A long time ago, yes, but not any more. Now thousands of women paid ten thousand dollars apiece to join her Club and become her friends. Except, if she was honest with herself, she had to admit they weren't really friends at all but clients, customers. Maybe Merilee was right.

The two of them flew to London on a theatre tour package to catch the West End shows. They flew to Vegas where Gwen learned how to work the slot machines and won at blackjack. They went to Aspen to ski and to New Orleans for Mardi Gras, never taking off more than a few days at a time, but it was more than Gwen had ever done before. 'You've got to learn to delegate authority,' Merilee advised. 'Let Lou run things for a while; that's what you hired him for.'

Merilee was responsible for changing Gwen's ginger hair to auburn — 'just to liven it up a little' — and putting her into designer clothes: 'You've got a great body. Why not show it off?' They stayed up all night talking and drinking Maker's Mark. Merilee was affectionate and demonstrative. Once when they were walking up Fifth Avenue, she took Gwen's hand while they window-shopped. Gwen involuntarily pulled away, explaining that just wasn't done in New York.

'Why ever not?' Merilee exclaimed. 'If you like someone, it's natural enough to want to touch them. Why, back home, people do it all the time. Even guys. It doesn't mean anything.'

Having Merilee for a friend was like having an odd little sister, one who looked up to her and maybe even had a bit of a crush on her. Gwen felt flattered, although she was afraid of getting too involved.

She was now virtually cut off from her family. Jeanne and Bill had not contacted her for years. They had called once to let her know there was a profile of her in the *Calgary Herald* Sunday Magazine, describing her career in New York and the growth of The Club.

Jeanne sounded far away on the long-distance line, her voice crackling with the same old resentment. 'With all your success, Jenny, it breaks my heart that you're not married.'

And her father said, 'Sebastien's graduating from high school. He just squeaked by grade-wise, but he's got a hockey scholarship to go to university. Takes after his old man, eh? Chip off the old block, eh?'

Gwen could feel the long-buried resentment welling up in her. She should be able to handle this, but damnit, it hurt, it really hurt. Immediately after she sat down and dictated a letter to them on Club letterhead. She congratulated Sebastien on his hockey scholarship. She enclosed a money order for $5,000 US and signed it. It was petty of her, she knew, but if they couldn't really be in her life it was better that she keep them out of it completely.

She saw Uncle Jack every time he came to New York on business. There had been a steady parade of younger and younger women in and out of his bed and his life as he grew greyer and fatter. He always brought her a present with the dragon motif: a gold-embroidered evening bag, a hand painted screen with a fire-breathing dragon, and a pair of Oriental statues that she kept at the entrance to her apartment. She would always love him even though he wasn't really in her life any more either.

She was good to the staff at The Club, buying them little presents, sending them on trips, remembering their children's birthdays and graduations, always careful to keep her distance. She was afraid that any close relationship would undermine the structure of The Club organization and impede her career progress; that they would make her feel things, things that she never wanted to feel again. When people told her how lucky she was to have made it so far, Gwen outwardly always agreed with them, but in her heart she knew her seemingly sudden success was owing to years of hard work and sacrifice, not to luck. She had never won anything free and clear. Whatever happened to her she made happen.

On a plane bound for Manzanillo, Mexico, with Merilee, for a week of sand and sun, Gwen flipped through a magazine and stopped at an article about a daytime soap star who had decided to have a facelift right on the TV show. 'This cometic surgery stuff is big business,' she said, passing the magazine over to Merilee.

'Yeah, I know. They're startin' younger and younger. I bet you half our members have had somethin' done. Hey!' Merilee slammed the magazine shut so quickly that Gwen almost spilled her Bloody Caesar all over her white linen suit. 'We should have a facility for plastic surgery right at The Club. You know, like those health spas in the Caribbean where you check in for a facelift and then spend two weeks relaxing by the pool so that when you come home your friends think you're looking great just because you've had a nice long rest. A discreet service for our very special members.'

'A clinic right on The Club premises?'

'Sure, Why not?'

'OK. Look into it.' Gwen patted her friend's hand approvingly. Merilee was always coming up with extra services they should provide at The Club.

Lying on the beach at Las Hadas, Gwen sighed as she surveyed the array of human flesh spread out in front of them, baking in the sun. 'There are some incredible bodies here, especially after New York. Makes me feel

378

sort of white and flabby, too long a winter, too much sitting behind a desk.'

'Yeah, you are too right about that.' Merilee took a noisy slurp of her margarita. 'Give us a couple of days in the sun and we'll put these beached whales to shame. I think you have a beautiful figure, one nice long elegant line. My line is just ruined by these two big ole watermelons sticking out here.' She looked down in disgust at the pillowy breasts fighting for control within her black string bikini top. 'You're not tall but somehow you don't look short like me. I guess it's the way you carry yourself.' She wriggled her little pink toenails in the powdery white sand. 'You know I can never make up my mind which I prefer naked, men or women. I think I like women's bodies better. Kind of round and soft and smooth. I think they're more graceful somehow, don't you agree?' She ran her hand down Gwen's bare back, 'I mean this line here, this is artistically beautiful, physical perfection, you know what I'm talkin'?'

Gwen pulled away and rolled over. She could never quite figure Merilee out. There was no way she would take that kind of risk, not even on vacation, far away from The Club. She took a slug of her own margarita and quickly changed the subject.

'Take a look at that couple over there. He's got to be at least fifteen years younger than she is. How did she manage to get a guy like that?' She indicated a handsome dark-haired man with drop-dead pectorals and a dazzling white smile who was solicitously rubbing suntan oil over the back of a stringy blonde who, although well-toned, looked far too old to be wearing a thong bathing suit.

Merilee rolled over on the sand to take a look. 'I swear, Gwen, for somebody who's lived in New York City for fifteen years, you are plenty naïve. He's her escort. Her companion.' Giggling at Gwen's blank expression, she added, 'Honey, she's *payin'* him.'

'You mean he's a gigolo?'

'Too right. Lots of women don't mind payin' for sex. Why, you think there's somethin' wrong with it?'

'Actually I don't,' Gwen said thoughtfully. 'Men have been doing it for years. As long as it's safe, why not?'

'I think it should be a service. Like gettin' a facial or a massage or havin' your legs waxed. Nothin' makes a woman's skin look better than gettin' laid. Sort of groomin' for the inner body.' They both giggled and then stopped and looked at one another. 'Are you thinkin' what I'm thinkin'?'

Gwen said it very quietly, 'I don't know, Merilee. Isn't that illegal?'

'There are ways around it, I know there are.'

'But would our members really pay for sex?' Gwen looked sceptical.

'Not all. A select few would. Those who are smart enough to know what they really want and successful enough to be able to pay for it.'

'In other words, those who can afford it, in every sense of the word.'

They were both silent for a moment. 'We'd have to create an area that was off-limits to regular members,' Gwen said, 'a kind of . . . private retreat. We'd have to regulate that somehow.'

'Easy,' Merilee snapped her fingers. 'Their membership cards that get them into The Club. Certain ones could be further programmed to admit them into the special private area. If your card isn't programmed, you can't get in. Lou can handle that. He can run it all from the computer in his office.'

'Specially privileged members. I like that. We'd need an escalating fee structure: the more freedom you buy into, the more you have to pay. Oh, I don't know.' She frowned. 'This is a crazy idea. It's so far from what I had in mind when I started The Club.'

'Gwen, listen to me. You're still caught in the bra-burning seventies. Equal pay, abortion on demand, protection from abuse, sure, those are all important issues. But face it, honey, those battles have been won. Now women just want to enjoy themselves, take advantage of their freedom. Why shouldn't we do what men have been doing for years? The Club has got to go full service. In every sense of the word.'

'What about Lou? you think he'll go along with all this?'

Merilee stretched her kewpie-doll body to its full height. 'Oh, I don't think we'll have any problem with Lou. You just leave him to me.'

Merilee's wise mama used to tell her, 'Fairies got those beautiful wings, honey, so's they can fly. Their feet ain't made to touch the ground for long.' Mama must have known Luigi del Bello in another life. As far as Merilee was concerned, Lou's feet needed to be nailed down. Bisexuals make great one-night stands, but to keep Lou on her side of the border for very long was going to take every page in Merilee's erotic bag of tricks.

And the tricks were getting used up pretty damn fast. She had put on men's boxer shorts and blown Lou in the locker room at The Club. (A male locker room would have excited him more, but the smell of expensive female sweat was almost as stimulating.) She'd tied him up with silk scarves and tickled him all over-with her hot-pink Mae West boa. She'd poured chocolate syrup all over his dick and licked it off. She'd singed her fluffy yellow pubic hair down to nothing, spread apricot brandy all over and stuck clung peaches up her twat, telling him to 'Git 'em all out whichever way you can, sugar pie.' Keeping Luigi del Bello entertained was exhausting and her food bills at the all-night gourmet deli were astronomical.

Getting Lou into her bed the first time had been no

381

mean feat and keeping him there was twice as difficult. He was the closest person in the world to Gwen and therefore afraid of crossing her. Even though he'd recommended Merilee for the job in the beginning, once he saw the friendship developing between them, he was afraid she would ease him out of his prize position as Gwen's favourite pet. But he was attracted to her, too — what man in his right mind wouldn't be? — and she'd flattered him and cajoled him and eventually won him over.

The difficulty now was that she was hooked on him. She hadn't planned on that and she sure as hell hoped it wouldn't throw her game off. Sleazy sex was OK but getting involved was a definite no-no for her. She liked to be seduced and that was as far as it had usually gone.

Merilee had lost her virginity at age thirteen and screwed around royally until she was twenty-five; she'd gone through a lot of hamburger to acquire her taste for steak. She no longer panicked over men like so many of The Club members did. Late-blooming thirty-plus teenagers, fighting over the few available men in New York, growling over sexual scraps, wondering where their next fuck was coming from. The irony was that with all their emphasis on the so-called 'sisterhood' she'd rarely seen a more competitive bunch of backbiting bitches when it came to men. What a laugh. She knew The Club members regarded her as some sort of victim of the male conspiracy, which was fine. Sexual equality was an economic issue, not a social or political one. In her opinion, the women of The Club weren't getting used enough. They were just a bunch of horny rich bitches. Which is why her plans for The Club were going to work so well.

Merilee had never even come close to getting married; well, not after she'd turned eighteen and counted herself safely out of the Dime Box, Texas, high-school wedding

382

sweepstakes. Merilee thrived on intrigue and mystery. Why shop at the same grocery store every week for the same product? Lovers were so much easier to throw away than husbands. Men were easily recycled, with most of the brands pretty much interchangeable; but Luigi del Bello had thrown her for a loop. Was it because he was a hot-blooded Italian? Or the fact that he was her first bisexual that made him so fascinating?

'I am defined by my sexuality,' Lou told her, after a bout of marathon sex in his waterbed.

'I guess that means you're ambisexual,' she quipped.

'No, I call myself bisessuale but, except for a few lapses in taste,' he said, sticking his tongue in her ear, 'I'm basically queer. Or in Italian, "*finocchio*".'

She was used to a certain amount of latent homosexuality in the South − men feeling each other up football-style − but the fact that Lou could actually prefer fucking another man to fucking her really annoyed her. Her trump card was her femininity and Lou wanted to play that one himself. OK, there was nothing effeminate about him on the surface, she had to admit, and he had the biggest cock she'd ever seen. She couldn't reach all the way around it with her tiny hand. Lou swore it wasn't really that big, that because he was so short it only looked humungous by contrast, but Merilee wasn't convinced. Being a confirmed basket-watcher, she knew he was something pretty special in that department. Merilee usually preferred tall men who could pick her up and fling her around. Lou was kind of scary, maybe even a little creepy, but, lordy, she just couldn't keep her hands off him. Was it simply because she knew that ultimately he was unattainable?

Whenever he seemed to be dozing off or fantasizing about one of his waiters, she pinched his nipples sharply or scratched the hell out of his ass with her acrylic nails. That always brought him back to her. On the odd occasion when he asked her to take a little whip and humiliate him, she was surprised at how eager she was to do so. Did that mean that, deep down, she really hated men, as Gwen said a lot of women did these days? Oh well, anything to keep him interested.

At the moment, he seemed to be pretty well under her spell, too. But how long would it last? And how long would it be before Gwen began to suspect something? The most delicious danger of their affair was that Gwen might discover it. The way Gwen looked upon her staff, Merilee figured her involvement with Lou was tantamount to incest. No, they would have to proceed very, very carefully. She was walking a thin line here, playing Lou along just enough to keep him interested and on her side, but she couldn't afford to let herself get completely hooked. It was time to look for another distraction. It was time for her and Lou to take The Club to new heights of satisfaction.

# *Fifteen*

The short plump brunette stood hesitantly at the brass-plated reception desk, clutching her purse as if it were her life. Flipping through a vast Roladex, her blood-red nails clicking against the cards, the smartly dressed Asian receptionist seemed to be ignoring her on purpose. Andrea coughed politely.

The receptionist made a careful notation with her gold pen, looked up languidly, and then slammed the pen down on the desk. 'Yes?' she asked, her eyes sweeping Andrea from head to toe. Her thick black hair revealed subtle aubergine highlights as it swung and framed a face like that of a porcelain doll.

'I'm on a visitor's pass. I'm from out of town, Evanston, Illinois, actually, just in town for one day, and I'm wondering . . .'

'Sorry,' — the china doll cut her off in a bored voice — 'we don't have temporary membership, and you are not allowed in here if you are not a member of The Club.'

'I know that,' Andrea said defensively, 'but as I already told you, I'm the guest of a member.'

'So what's your friend's name?' The receptionist examined one of her long crimson nails and tapped it tentatively against the desk. A bit loose.

'Lacey. Lacey Talbot.'

'Really? Oh wow!' Instantly the young woman came to life. Andrea couldn't get over how people in New York reacted to Lacey. She was editor-in-chief of the new magazine for women over forty, *Legend*, and currently married to one of TV's top producers. Andrea would have been jealous of her if she weren't positive that Lacey would give it all up in a flash for a terrific husband and a couple of great kids like she had. Andrea had been married for twenty-five years and she and Greg had managed to send all four kids to college.

The receptionist punched a couple of keys on her computer terminal. 'Mrs Talbot is in the rooftop salon having a bikini wax,' she said. Andrea stared respectfully at the tiny machine. 'She'll be done at one-fifteen, in about ten minutes.'

'Should I go on up?' Andrea asked hopefully. She had read about the rooftop salon in a recent issue of *Vogue* magazine.

'I'm sorry, that's not allowed,' the receptionist said apologetically. 'A member has to escort you to any of the upper floors. But I'll page Mrs Talbot. She shouldn't be too long. Why don't you have a seat in the waterfall lounge?' She waved to a cluster of tables around a magnificent waterfall shooting great jets of water straight up into the air. Each table had its own blue and white umbrella. Andrea thought it was what a sidewalk café on the Champs-Elysées would probably look like.

She settled herself in one of the wrought-iron chairs and opened her *New York Times* to the arts section, hoping she looked like a native New Yorker, all the while stealing surreptitious glances from behind her newspaper. She never ceased to be awed by the sybaritic splendour of The Club. There was certainly nothing like this back in Evanston, the peach sherbet walls, gilt sconces and lofty cream ceilings. A waiter, a dead ringer for Tom Selleck, put a tall, frosted, fluted glass in front of her and turned away.

'Excuse me, what is this? I didn't order a drink.'

The waiter turned and bowed slightly. 'It's a glass of

Dom Perignon. Would Madam prefer Moët & Chandon?' Seeing her confused expression, he added, 'It's on the house.'

'Oh, no, no, Dom Perignon is fine. It's great.' Complimentary champagne! How decadent. She sipped it slowly as she looked around, wishing she were wearing something more elegant. Her Ports corduroy suit was the best outfit she owned but it fairly screamed suburbia in the midst of all these streamlined professional women who carried their MBAs as comfortably as they did their three-tiered briefcases. Anybody can look good with a hundred-and-fifty-dollar haircut, Andrea thought a bit resentfully, nervously tucking a loose tendril of naturally curly hair back into the unsweep she had been sure would make her look more New York. She hadn't been to the city in a couple of years; obviously sleek bobs were in. She took another slug of champagne.

She looked up to see a glass elevator descending through the centre of the building, right through the middle of the waterfall. As the elevator touched bottom, the water magically cut off and the door opened, depositing its passengers on dry ground. A tall woman with straight shoulder-length blonde hair in a trim black suit came towards her, and Andrea stood up to meet her. The two embraced.

'It's so good to see you! You look great! And The Club is just as fabulous as it was the last time I was here.'

'No, now it's even better. They've just added a bunch of "special services". It's the only place in New York where I can get absolutely anything I want. I've just become a lifetime member. It cost me a fortune, but it's worth it.'

'There are so many celebrities here! I don't remember that from before.'

'Yeah, 37 Middlesex has definitely taken a step up in terms of clientele. We won't be swimming with my secretary this time. She couldn't afford the hike in dues. The Club's strictly for the élite now. Company presidents, society matrons and the occasional movie star.'

'I feel like a groupie.'

'Well just make sure you don't hassle the celebrities in any way — no asking for autographs. One of the privileges of Club membership is guaranteed privacy.'

'I won't forget,' Andrea agreed. 'You know, you still look like Mary Travers.'

'And you still look like Connie Francis. That husband of yours must be keeping you pretty happy . . .' Andrea burst into tears. 'Hey, what's the matter? What's wrong?'

'Greg's having an affair.' Andrea sobbed. 'At least I think he is.'

'Well, that's not really anything to cry over,' Lacey said, trying to comfort her. 'It's not as though you've been Miss Fidelity yourself.'

'Yes, I have, I've only slipped once or twice. I'd hardly call that having an affair. This has been going on for months and don't know what to do.' She sobbed even harder.

'I know just the thing,' Lacey soothed. 'Since I'm now a privileged member, I'm going to take you "where the boys are." '

'The movie?' Andrea rooted for a Kleenex in her purse.

'No, no. There's a special event for charity this week, a male fashion show.' Seeing Andrea's doubtful face, she added, 'This one is different. Trust me. You'll love it.'

'OK.' Andrea could hardly hide her disappointment. She hadn't come all the way to New York to watch a bunch of fags model clothes. She obediently followed Lacey into the elevator and the glass cage lifted off as the water came on again. As they moved swiftly upwards through sheets of torrential water, Andrea giggled to herself. It was kind of exciting, although not all that different from letting the kids stay in the station wagon when it went through Krazy Kelly's Kar Wash.

'Where's the fashion show?'

'It's in the privileged members' very private lounge. My card has now been programmed for some of the areas that are off-limits to regular members. I'll have to get you clearance. I love the private lounge. It's like stepping into Fantasyland. Well, my own personal fantasy, anyway. It always reminds me of a New Orleans brothel. Did you ever see *Pretty Baby*?'

'Yeah, but I don't remember much besides Brooke Shields. And Susan Sarandon's tits.'

'Well, it's all red velvet, brass fixtures, beaded curtains, soft lighting. It's sexy. You'll love it, you'll see.'

The elevator stopped in front of a double-panelled door. Lacey inserted her card and punched in a code and the door swung open. The private lounge. It *was* pretty sexy, Andrea had to admit, sinking into a plush red velvet chair and accepting another glass of champagne. Damnit, a girl could get used to this kind of luxury. She wondered if there would ever be a branch of The Club in Evanston. She picked up the heavily embossed card on the table in front of her and read it aloud: ' "Specials of the day. Derek, Leroy, Kevin, Tad, and Gino." What's that mean?'

'Those are the names of the models. They show here quite frequently. Tad's a real hunk.'

A waiter put a plate in front of her. 'What's this?'

'Fresh angel hair pasta with smoked salmon, capered cream sauce, and caviar. Try it,' Lacey urged. 'It's divine.'

'I shouldn't. I've been cellulite city ever since Michelle was born. However . . .' Andrea attacked the food with gusto.

'Andrea Kaplan, that was thirteen years ago. Are you planning to do anything about it?' Lacey snapped a breadstick in two.

'Like what? You should talk, skinny Minnie. You eat

389

like this every day and your body makes Jane Fonda look positively piggy.'

'I work at it. The classes here are terrific. The aerobics instructor looks like a Barbie doll but she's tough. I've completely recontoured my upper body. Of course, running helps, too.'

'So when do you have time to get out a national magazine?'

'I work later hours. I've always been a night owl, you know that.'

'How does Eric like it?'

Lacey tossed the breadstick back into the wicker basket and took a hefty swig of her champagne. 'Well, actually, we're getting a divorce.'

'Oh, no! You two seemed to get on so well.'

I know. Sometimes I think my role model in life is Elizabeth Taylor. I must be addicted to serial monogamy. I mean, this will be number five. But' — she brightened visibly — 'I'm having a scintillating affair.'

'Who with? Do I know him? Is it a younger man?'

'I doubt if you know him, but your kids will. He's younger, yeah.' It's Damon Lee. I interviewed him for the magazine and we ended up in the sack.'

Andrea's chin practically dropped on to the table. 'The rock star? Omigod! Michelle used to listen to him all the time! He's gorgeous, but how old can he be? Nineteen?'

'Not really. He look younger than he is. I mean, he's got three kids by his first wife. Of course, they start a lot younger in Britain. Publicly he's twenty-seven but he's really closer to thirty-four.'

'Still . . . does Eric know?'

'Who cares? He couldn't keep up with me sexually and it was such a drag having to stroke his ego all the time to make him feel he wasn't Mr Lacey Talbot instead of Eric Strong. What a bore.'

'But Eric's famous in his own right.'

'Sure, but nobody knows what he looks like. Did you have any idea what Grant Tinker looks like? No, of course not, but you'd recognize Mary Tyler Moore anywhere, right? I'm hardly a movie star but with those appearances on Carson I completely lost my privacy. Eric couldn't take it.'

'Are you going to marry him?'

'Who, Damon? Are you kidding? He pays more to support his coke habit than he does to support his kids, but he's good for a few laughs, oh, shh . . . there's Merilee Houston, the aerobics teacher I was telling you about, actually she's been promoted to executive associate of The Club. I have to admit The Club's a helluva lot more fun since Miss Merilee came on the scene. Look at her. Isn't she a hoot?'

Andrea looked at the tiny blonde pastry making her entrance on to the runway at the end of the lounge. She was wearing a low-cut black leotard cut high on the legs, revealing a pair of black and yellow striped tights. If I wore those, I'd look like a demented bumblebee, Andrea thought bleakly, squeezing her own less-than-rock-like thighs under the table.

'Hi, y'all,' Merilee drawled into the mike, giving a friendly wave to her audience. 'We've got some great outfits for you this afternoon and a cute bunch o' guys to show them to you, haven't we, Lou?'

Andrea saw a short, well-built swarthy man with a big nose and glittering eyes stand up and give a little wave, too. 'Right you are, Merilee,' he said jovially. 'They sure turn my crank.'

'What does he mean?' Andrea whispered.

'He's a fruit,' Lacey answered, 'and everybody knows it. He handpicks the models and he's got great taste.'

'Terrific,' Andrea muttered. 'All gay for sure.'

'Shh.' Lacey elbowed her in the ribs. 'Wait and see.'

'The proceeds from this afternoon's fashion show will

go to the Earthquake Relief Fund for Soviet Georgia,'
Merilee announced, 'and that's a real good cause, so y'all
dig deep into your pocketbooks and let's come up with
some big bucks here this afternoon.' The sweet, languid
strains of Pachelbel's 'Canon' filled the room.

'Who's the designer?' Andrea asked.

'Oh.' Lacey dismissed the question with a wave of her
hand. 'They're all different, I guess.' She stopped talking
as Merilee picked up the microphone again.

'Now the first outfit we're going to see this afternoon
would be just right for your husband's boardroom. This
is a Giorgio Armani design. We're talking style, we're
talking class here.' A wildly handsome Michael Douglas
look-alike in a conservative three-piece suit sauntered
down the runway. He paused to take off the jacket and
sling it over his shoulder. The women clapped politely
and the music changed to 'Just a Gigolo'. The model
tossed the jacket to Merilee and slowly began to unbutton
his pale-blue silk shirt, exposing a smooth, lightly tanned
chest.

'What's he doing?' Andrea gasped.

'I told you this was different.'

The man reached for the buckle on his alligator belt
and stepped out of his Armani slacks. These too he threw
neatly to Merilee and proceeded to parade around in the
briefest of bikini briefs.

'Omigod,' Andrea whispered as the man undulated out
of the red silk bikinis to reveal a long, thin, gracefully
shaped cock just barely tumescent. 'I don't believe this!'
She put her head down on the table.

'Andrea, don't be an ostrich. There's more.' Lacey
poked her.

Andrea peeked between her fingers. The man was
standing there, proud, relaxed in front of the room full
of admiring women. Then he threw that last garment to
a woman in the audience.

'Help,' Andrea whimpered. She put her head back down.

'OK, ladies. What am I bid for this incredible Armani suit?' The room was very quiet as if each woman were holding her breath. Slowly one hand went up. 'Eight hundred dollars. I have a bid of eight hundred dollars.' Merilee's amplified voice was breathless. Another hand went up: 'We're moving up to one thousand. Do I see twelve hundred?'

'What are they bidding on?' Andrea asked in a tiny voice.

'Ostensibly the suit,' Lacey answered.

'Now, c'mon, ladies, this is all going to earthquake relief.' Merilee saw another hand go up. 'Sold for fifteen hundred dollars.'

'But no suit is worth fifteen hundred bucks!'

Andrea opened her eyes to see the naked Adonis climb off the stage and disappear behind the red velvet curtains, followed almost instantly by an aristocratic grey-haired woman of about sixty. 'Is this what I think it is?' Andrea said almost in shock. 'Is this some kind of a slave auction?'

'It's just fun,' Lacey assured her.

'But isn't it prostitution? I mean, wasn't some place closed down in LA for doing this kind of thing?'

'That was a real brothel. This is more like an escort service. What you do with the guy is up to you. And The Club doesn't make anything on the deal. The proceeds all go to charity.'

'But how about. . .well, disease, safety, you know . . .'

'The guys are safe. They're all checked out by Dr MacLeod, The Club's doctor. But these days you can't be too careful. That's why I always carry a raincoat with me.'

'A raincoat?'

'These,' Lacey reached into her purse and removed

what looked like a solid-gold business card case. She opened it up to reveal an assortment of condoms.

'That's disgusting!'

'What's disgusting? Men hire escorts all the time. And what do you think those massage parlours were all about? Grow up, Andrea. This is the nineties.'

'But isn't it illegal?'

'This is a private club. All the entrances are specially carded, but if the police were to get in here it really wouldn't look like much more than a bachelorette party that had gone a bit far. Nobody really cares what you do, as long as you keep it quiet. Besides, who's going to blow the whistle on a deal like this? It's just another service. The Club provides everything else to keep the body fit. Why not a little recreational sex?'

Andrea giggled in spite of herself. 'Where do they go to . . . do it?'

'There are rooms at the back. They look like individual saunas. In fact, they *are* individual saunas. But they also have daybeds. A small fridge with juice and booze. Music. Body oils. You bring your own sexual aids, although' – Lacey wrinkled her nose – 'with a body like Derek's there, who needs aid? I'm only looking for relief.' She gave Andrea's arm a friendly squeeze and Andrea managed another laugh. 'So, do you want to try it?'

'What? You mean pay for a guy to make love to me? I couldn't, oh no I couldn't.'

'OK. We'll see how long you hold out.' Lacey eyed her speculatively and took another slug of champagne. 'I wonder.'

Andrea was beginning to wonder, too. In spite of her initial revulsion, the champagne, or something, was beginning to get to her. She could feel her nipples stiffening just at the thought of touching a naked stranger. She crossed her legs and watched the next model, a sinewy black man wearing a soft leather jacket and leather pants, dance on to a heavy rock beat. He was bare-chested and his muscles rippled as he performed a gracefully restrained break-dance at the edge of the stage. He struggled a bit getting out of his leather pants and the women watched him breathlessly as he slid them down his legs inch by inch. Despite all she had read about black men — and all the jokes Greg had told, with a lampshade on his head, at parties — his cock was not enormous. But it was fascinating, a fiery, purplish thing with a large vein that seemed to throb in time to the music. Maybe Lacey was right. She'd seen things almost as graphic as this on 'Donahue'. Of course they didn't strip completely the way these men were doing. Merilee was extolling the virtues of the leather outfit and all around her women's hands were going up in the air to bid.

Lacey regarded her with amusement. 'Having second thoughts? Ever done it with a black guy?'

'You know I haven't,' Andrea said indignantly. 'I've told you about every guy I've ever made it with and you can count them on the fingers of one hand. I guess the closest to black would be that Brazilian tennis pro at the country club and we only did it twice.'

'I could go for this guy. There's something dangerous about him.'

'I know. That's just the trouble. He looks like he'd rather mug me than make love to me.'

'That's the point. Controlled danger.'

'Lacey, you're sick!' Andrea was genuinely shocked.

'I know. I used to feel really guilty about it. It's against everything my magazine preaches, but I just love the idea of being tied to the bedpost and fucked out of my mind.'

'That's awful!'

'I know. I think I'm going to spring for this guy.' The bidding was up to twenty-two hundred.

'Lacey, that's ridiculously expensive!'

'So what? I can drop close to that taking a bunch of writers out to Ma Maison and have less to show for it. Hey, I've got an idea. Let's go in together on a guy. We can share one.'

'Oh, no, Lacey, I couldn't . . .' But she already knew that she could.

'Come on, it'll be fun. This will be one New York experience you'll never forget!'

'OK,' Andrea said suddenly, her blood pounding. 'But not the black guy. He scares me.'

'OK,' Lacey agreed, and they watched him go off hand-in-hand with an overly tanned blonde with a beauty mark by her lower lip.

'And now, straight from hot, juicy, funky Hawaii comes the ultimate hunky outfit,' Merilee breathed into the microphone and, to the strains of the theme from *Magnum PI*, a tall man with dark hair, a moustache, and bright blue eyes sauntered forward, his hands jammed into the pockets of his sweatpants. He was also wearing a soft blue flowered shirt. Andrea gasped. It was her waiter from the waterfall lounge.

He moved up and down the runway like an athlete, his broad shoulders tapering to a small waist and spectacularly firm buns beneath the cotton drawstring pants. Andrea suddenly wanted to take that drawstring between her teeth and worry it the way their dog Maxie did with his bacon-flavoured rubber bone. She wanted to pull those pants down over those slim tanned hips, sliding them off the tanned hairy legs, revealing – oh God, now it was out, the biggest cock she had ever seen in her life. Long and thick, it hung like a cub between his muscular legs.

'Him. I want him,' Andrea whispered to Lacey, her breath coming in short little gasps. 'The outfit is nothing but cotton so it can't be too expensive. Isn't he gorgeous?'

'But he looks like Tom Selleck,' Lacey said in dismay.

'I know,' Andrea said with reverence. 'Just like him.'

'Isn't he a little plastic?'

'No, no, he's perfect.' Andrea shot her hand into the air, signalling five hundred dollars.

'Wait a second. I'm not sure'

'I'm being outbid here.' Andrea shook Lacey's hand off her arm. The bidding was now up to eight hundred. The waiter moved down the runway until he was standing right in front of Andrea, towering over her. She stared up at his cock, and as she looked at it, it began to grow. Omigod, he was getting an erection from just looking at her. She raised her trembling hand for nine hundred dollars.

'Hold it, girl! I mean, are you sure this is the one we want?'

Andrea had never been surer of anything in her life. 'I want that one.' She wanted it in her hand, in her mouth, inside of her. 'Remember I'm on vacation. You live here all the time.'

'OK, OK.' Lacey reached for her purse.

'Going, going, for nine hundred dollars,' Merilee said quietly into the microphone.

Andrea waved her hand wildly in the air and gave a little yelp as she realized that she had just signalled a thousand bucks. In her confusion and lust she had just outbid herself.

# *Sixteen*

Joining The Club was the best thing that had happened to Susie Krumins since she had come to New York. Little by little, the city, which had originally seemed so overwhelming to her, was starting to feel less threatening. The Club became her home away from home. Now she had something to do every day and a place to go, a place where Lokis couldn't follow her and look over her shoulder to see if she was properly 'translating his genius.' Being surrounded by all these glamorous, high-powered women, who seemed so together, with their lives and loves in order, wasn't as intimidating as she had feared. Maybe some of that drive and glamour might rub off on her. Besides, they weren't all beautiful, they weren't all rich; some of them weren't so very different from her. The Club fees were steep, but Susie had met several women who were actually moonlighting with an extra job to be able to afford what The Club could offer them.

Just walking into the building made her feel special; when she emerged after having lunch or doing a workout, people on the street looked at her with interest. It seemed that everybody in New York City wanted to know what went on behind those hallowed doors.

The minute she went through those doors, she left all her problems behind and entered a world where time was suspended. The membership Lokis had bought her didn't include a card to the limited area called the private retreat where supposedly all sorts of special services and amazing activities were arranged, but for now she was quite happy to explore the main areas of The Club. Each floor was more spectacular than the next, like climbing a circular staircase of fantasy where each step led to new delights. No wonder Lokis was proud to be one of the original designers. Just being in such beautiful surroundings made Susie feel beautiful herself.

It gave her a special little thrill when Gwyneth personally welcomed her into The Club by buying her a drink in the waterfall lounge. She did that for all new members, and it made Susie feel that her joining The Club was actually important to the founder of this magic place. Gwen toasted her with champagne and interviewed her about her life, asking her what her future plans were, and whether or not she had any suggestions for how The Club could be improved. All this in the space of fifteen minutes. It was exhilarating just being in Gwen's company. And she looked just exactly as Susie imagined a female executive should look: a smallish woman, with spike heels and her red hair piled on top of her head to make her look much taller. She was a striking-looking woman, with strong, open features, direct, and very, very confident. Susie couldn't imagine her letting any man take advantage of her.

She could hardly keep from blurting out, 'I want to be just like you. Will you be my mentor?' Gwen listened to what Susie had to say as if every word was a new thought and one worth considering, sometimes jotting down notes in a little leather-bound book that she carried in her briefcase, interrupting Susie's continual flow of conversation only to say things like 'good point,' or 'I think I'll pass those concerns on to Merilee.' The time they spent together went so quickly that Susie hardly realized that Gwen had unfolded her elegant frame out of the chair, given her a firm handshake, and moved fluidly out of the room. The interview was suddenly over.

Susie really envied her her poise and timing. That was exactly the kind of self-improvement she hoped The Club would give her. She was tired of being fresh and innocent; she wanted to be worldly. She was tired of being supportive of others; she wanted to create a support system for herself. She vowed to herself that she would learn the secret that these superwomen all seemed to possess so easily.

As the days went by, her time at The Club became more and more important to her, as she built a little ritual around the hours she spent there. At nine o'clock in the morning the workout facilities were usually empty. The female executives who had to be at the office by eight-thirty had already done their workouts and the young moms were still getting their kids off to school. Sometimes she worked out on her own; sometimes Merilee Houston joined her. Then they would have lunch together, either in the health bar of the waterfall lounge, depending on Merilee's schedule. For all of Merilee's positive obsession with sex, and her eccentric appearance, she was gossipy and fun, with a surprisingly good head for business. And in the gym she was like a drill sergeant. After years of basically sitting at home, Susie was ready to explore her physical potential and get into training for her own personal Olympics. Merilee helped her establish a rigorous regimen, followed by a quick run around the jogging track to get the kinks out and then a swim and a sauna. She liked the privacy of the morning swim, thirty laps if she could manage it, and then the reward, a nice long sauna and a needle-cold shower. Exercising on her own made her feel virtuous and working out in the empty room made her feel like she owned the place, her own private luxury gymnasium.

The visible changes in her body pleased her. Working out in the weight-room was strengthening her leg muscles and her arm muscles. Her stomach was flatter. She laughed out loud as she realized what working out reminded her of: ironing. You could actually see the results happening. She sensed that she was getting ready to fly, but how and where?

Forming a tentative bond with some of the other women was making a difference, too. One morning as she was doing her run, she saw a woman sitting alone by the side of the track. Before she knew it she was stopping to ask her, 'Do you want to talk?' Surprisingly they had talked for an hour about this and that, nothing really important, just exchanging a few recipes, but at the end of it she could tell the woman felt better and so did she. For many years her best friend, really her only friend, had been Lokis. She hadn't had a close girlfriend since Tracy, her maid-of-honour back in Minneapolis. She missed that kind of closeness with another woman. Merilee was lots of fun when it came to talking about food or sex, but she wasn't exactly bright. Susie was really feeling a need for some intellectual stimulation and heart-to-heart emotional analysis.

The day she opened up to Mina in the changing-room was a landmark for her. She really opened up. It was as if the floodgates had finally burst open and all the feelings that had been dammed up inside her for the past five years — no, for the past twenty-eight years — came pouring out to this warm, sympathetic woman with the understanding eyes and bright smile. Susie stood there naked, sobbing her heart out, Mina calmly handing her one Kleenex after another and asking her questions that she knew had needed to be asked for a long time.

'You're in a lot of pain,' Mina said, matter-of-factly but kindly, taking each soggy Kleenex from Susie's hand, balling it up neatly and throwing it away.

'I know.' Susie made an attempt to pull herself together, feeling embarrassed. 'And I'm just not used to it. I've had twenty-seven years of happiness and one year of incredible pain. That's really a pretty good track record.'

Mina whistled, 'Twenty-seven years of happiness. That's a long high to come down from. No wonder you're crashing.'

'No, you don't understand. I'm usually pretty good at programming myself to be happy. I mean, I don't mind being unhappy for a couple of days, but this . . . I can't handle it. I don't know what to do.'

'What are you talking about? You can't make a conscious decision to be happy. You either are or you aren't. Unless you mean that you've been going through life seeing things the way you want to.'

'You mean that because I didn't see the shit, I didn't realize it was all around me?'

'Something like that. Maybe you're just beginning to wake up and see the real world.'

'That's what my husband says.' She could feel the tears welling up again.

'Sure, but from what you've told me, he meant it as an insult. I'm telling you it's a good thing. You've got a lot going for you, Susie. Everybody who meets you here at The Club likes you.'

'They do?' Susie snuffled in disbelief.

'Yeah, and not just because you give great recipes. You're open, you're honest, and just plain nice. In the best sense of the word. For us jaded old New Yorkers, you're a breath of fresh air.'

'You mean I'm dumb. Typical blonde bubblehead. Because I don't have three degrees and a six-figure income.'

'No, not at all. It's just that innocence, real genuine innocence, is in rather short supply around here. But there's such a thing a awareness. There's nothing wrong with choosing to step around the shit. You just have to acknowledge that it's there and know that eventually you'll have to deal with it.'

403

Susie burst into tears again, 'I think I just reached that point.'

Mina put her arms around her. 'So that's not such a bad thing either. The real world can be pretty tough but it can also offer a lot on its own terms.'

'But I feel as if my life is over.'

'Come on! You're not even thirty! OK, maybe *one* life is over. But I'll bet you've got another one right in front of you. I think you haven't really gotten started yet and, when you do, you're going to surprise yourself.'

'You don't even know me and you seem to have a lot of faith in me.'

'I have faith in women. We're a pretty amazing group of people.'

Cooking for Mina was almost as much fun as cooking for Lokis. Maybe even more so because Lokis knew all her tricks while they were new to Mina. Mina, who admitted she was a lousy cook herself, greeted each dish with such ecstatic praise that it embarrassed her.

'Come on, it's only cooking. We're not talking about brain surgery here,' Susie protested.

'It's as much of a mystery as brain surgery if you don't know how to do it. As a matter of fact, I know more about brain surgery than I do about cooking!'

Mina had been a medical photographer at Roosevelt Hospital before becoming a freelance photographic artist. The walls of her loft were covered with huge blow-ups of babies being born and heart-lung transplants being performed. Susie was surprised at how beautiful the photographs were. In fact she found them just as artistic as Mina's later work.

She cooked for Mina once a week. She gave her a shopping list, and Mina did all the shopping and paid for the ingredients. At first it had been just the two of them. Then they had expanded it to include Merilee,

404

although Mina wasn't crazy about her. As word got around that Susie Krumins was a spectacular cook, other women from The Club began to approach Susie and Mina asking to be invited to one of the 'gourmet evenings'. As a result Susie was gaining a whole new circle of friends. Then Liz Giordino asked her to make her famous chocolate-chip pound cake for her daughter's graduation party and paid Susie for not only the cake, but something extra for the time it took her to make it. Sally Traynor paid Susie to come to her law firm, use the company kitchen, and whip up a lunch for the partners. Susie made crabmeat mousse, baked brie, artichoke hearts with raspberry vinaigrette, and fresh fruit compote laced with Cointreau. She served it in the boardroom and pretty soon she was receiving calls to cater whole dinner parties. Even Gwen asked her to do an afternoon high tea at The Club. She didn't know what to charge, so at first she just doubled the cost of the food. Soon she discovered that she could actually charge outrageously high prices and people would still pay them if they liked the food.

Of course she didn't really see her new pastime as catering, but Sally Traynor told her that what she had here was what was technically a small business and that she had better get herself registered. Even though she was working out of her own home, she needed to be incorporated for tax purposes, so she and Mina registered a name: Supper's on Susie. Susie designed her own flyer, had them printed up, and delivered them by hand in her Brooklyn Heights neighbourhood and placed them in the racks at The Club. Supper's on Susie guaranteed intimate little picnics à deux, dinner parties for fifteen, and cocktail parties for up to fifty, all from recipes perfected in Susie's kitchen. Through word of mouth alone, Susie's culinary reputation continued to grow.

Lokis seemed delighted for her. It was great to have his Susie Sunshine back, full of her old optimism, cheerful and smiling. Her natural high energy returned and she was able to keep the business going and still help him out with the occasional design project. The house smelled the way it used to smell when they were first married, full of fresh bread and warm chocolate and melting cheese. Seeing Susie covered in flour, up to her elbows in sourdough, shoving pans in and out of the oven, really turned him on. And it seemed to turn her on, too. They were back to making love again and his world was the way it had been before.

The Club offered a night course in accounting and Susie jumped at the chance to take it. It was a basic course, meeting only a couple of nights a week, that wouldn't certify her as an accountant, but she didn't really need that. She wanted to expand her business skills now that she was doing Lokis's books and her own as well. Whenever she could she met with Gwen to pick her brain for business advice. Once the accounting course was finished, Gwen advised her to learn how to use a computer. Susie talked Mina into taking The Club's introduction to computer training, which Lou taught. The two of them spent three nights a week at The Club working away at the computer banks, listening to the friendly hum of the other machines around them, and delighting in the new technological lingo they were both learning.

'I love all these terms like "main menu", "drive", "diskette",' Susie said as she sat in front of the terminal and watched the numbers come up as if by magic on the screen in front of her. Computerizing her books was making budgeting much easier and faster. 'It's like some weird secret foreign language.'

'Don't you find all this terminology rather sexual?' Mina asked.

'Are you kidding? What could be more cut-and-dried than computers?' Susie answered, her fingers flying over the keys.

'Well, things like "hardware" and "software". Doesn't that make you think of sex?'

Susie giggled her throaty giggle. 'Yeah, now that you mention it, it does. How about floppy disc?'

'No, no,' said Mina. 'I prefer "hard drive", don't you?'

'Mm, yes. Always. How about "personal installation"?'

'Or "full-range equipment"? "With extra attachment"?'

'Can't you just imagine saying to some guy, "I'd like you to park your hard drive in my soft options"?' Susie said. And they both giggled like schoolgirls. But learning the computer made Susie feel very capable and mature.

'What are you making?' Mina burst into Susie's kitchen one wintry day and flopped down in a chair to pull off her snowy boots. 'It smells great in here!'

'Hors d'oeuvres for Lacey Talbot. She's having a midnight buffet for her magazine staff. Supposed to be limited to one hundred of her nearest and dearest, but now that she's seeing Damon Lee, I bet you closer to five hundred will show up. And even for one hundred people you've got to plan on five hundred hors d'oeuvres. I'm getting really sick of rolling up these little buggers.' She held up a piece of Mexican chorizo wrapped in Jack cheese and jalapeno pepper. 'It's going to be a drag getting these to melt just the right amount at just the right time.'

'Don't ask for my help. I'll screw it up for sure.' Mina padded over to the gas range in her stockinged feet and lit a cigarette from the flame. 'What do you enjoy most about all this catering stuff anyway?'

'Oh, the desserts. Definitely.' Susie had now moved on to the miniature pie shells and was filling each one with a dollop of egg and smoked salmon. 'I love working with chocolate and sugar. It's a real art, you know. If you make a soup and it doesn't turn out, you can always add something to fix it. With pastry, if it's too sweet or a little bitter, you have to throw the whole thing away. Desserts are tricky but I love the challenge.'

'Yeah, your desserts are great. Especially your cookies. I'm not a dessert person but I can never pass up one of your double-fudge brownies.' Mina reached for one of the several dozen cooling on a rack near by.

'You know what my dream is?' Susie deftly slid the tray of quiches into the oven. 'I'd like to have my own store. One that just sells cookies. Brownies, blondies, and those huge chocolate-chip cookies like Aunt Bea used to make.'

'That's a great idea!' Mina slammed her hand down on the table, making Susie jump a mile and the brownie rack tremble. 'Do it! Why don't you do it?'

'You can't have a business that's just cookies. Desserts maybe, but not just cookies.'

'Why not? I bet you could charge a dollar a cookie!'

'A buck for one cookie? You're crazy! Nobody would pay that.'

'Sure they would if it tastes as good as this. New Yorkers will. Everybody's into "quality" right now. You use real butter, brown sugar, the best Belgian chocolate. They'll pay the right price for the right product. Especially here.'

'I wouldn't have any idea how to start a business like that.'

'Then find out. The Club's got a whole library full of books about entrepreneurship. That's the new "in" word you know, "entrepreneur". I think Gwyneth even gives a course in how to start your own business. I know she's hired a couple of management consultants. If you really want someone to be your mentor, ask her advice. She's a businesswoman.'

'No, I couldn't. She's already given me too much help already. Besides she's out of my league. This catering thing's a fluke. I'm just an ordinary housewife who happens to be a better than average cook. Gwen's a real entrepreneur.'

Mina put her finger in her mouth and mimed gagging. 'I love you, Susie, but sometimes you're too straight to be true. Listen to yourself. You sound like a commercial for fabric softener. The Club has lots of resources. That's what Gwen's there for. And have some faith in yourself. You can do this, I know it. Come on, you've got to give it a try.'

Susie waited until she'd found just the right spot in a nearby mall for her storefront. With each new step she went back to Gwen, reported her progress, and got her advice about the next step to take. She got a vendor's licence from Brooklyn. She ordered her counters and her showcase and her cash register. With the money from Supper's on Susie, she installed the ovens. She registered the new business's name with the state. She was going to call her shop Aunt Bea's Homemade Cookies, but Mina said, 'Forget that, it's boring. And it doesn't say anything about you.' By this time they were meeting in Gwen's office once a week. 'So they're Aunt Bea's recipes. The business is *your* idea.'

Gwen agreed. 'I think it should be your business completely. Besides, you don't want your Aunt Bea suing you for using her name and image.'

'She would never do that.'

'You never know,' Gwen said. 'Money does strange things to people. You've got to protect your investment.'

'Yeah, she's right,' Mina said. 'Go for it, Susie. You can do it.' And they both toasted her with champagne.

So Susie abbreviated her last name from Krumins to Krums, and the store became Kookie Krums. Supper's on Susie had expanded her own bank account sufficiently to cover her bulk orders of cookie ingredients and install her counters and shelving. Lokis wrote her a cheque for $65,000 to cover the first six months of her lease, the hiring of two students to help her sell, and daily operations.

'Put your own stamp on it,' Gwen said. 'Make it personal,' Mina added. 'Give it that old Susie Sunshine style.' So Susie went about making sure that everything about the company began and ended with her. The failure or success of the company would be entirely hers. She designed the chocolate-brown and white aprons and caps that she and her sales people wore. She painted the big cookie-house mural on the main wall and put tracer lights all around the little brown and white storefront. For the first two weeks, she stood out in the mall, handing out free chocolate-chip cookies to shoppers, telling them, 'Get 'em while they're hot, right out of the oven.' Once she even led the crowd in a cheer, spelling out 'cookie'. Afterwards the excited crowd had mobbed the shop and bought every cookie the store had.

Her cookies were terrific, big and warm and chewy, with lots of chocolate chips and extra nuts. When she designed her happy face cookies, using chocolate chips for the eyes and to make a huge grinning mouth, they sold out immediately. Susie loved it. She loved the surprised smile when the customer realized the cookie in his hand was still warm, the moan of pleasure when he bit into it, and the smile of delight at its moist, chewy texture. As far as she was concerned, she wasn't just selling cookies, she was selling happiness.

Kookie Krums was almost an instant success. Before she knew it she had three stores in Brooklyn and she was so busy she hardly had time to turn round. The next step was opening a store across the river in Manhattan and that really scared her.

'Why?' Mina demanded. 'What are you so afraid of? You've got more than a going concern here, you're doing raging business. You've got to expand into a bigger market.'

'All I know is making cookies. I don't know how to *sell* them. I don't know anything about marketing.'

'So learn. You seem to be doing pretty well just on instinct. If it ain't broke, don't fix it.'

'Everybody I've talked to is telling me it won't work, that Brooklyn is one kind of market, Manhattan another. It's a big risk.'

'So, if you listen to them, you'll never do anything.'

'Yeah, but maybe they're right. I don't really have the background or training for business. I've only had a couple of courses. It's a tough market. Other people out there have lots more experience than I do.'

'There are always going to be people smarter than you and prettier than you and richer than you, but the way you're making money, you're catching up with the competition fast. Don't let other people stop you. Don't start doubting yourself now.'

'But I feel so guilty. I'm letting Lokis down just when he needs me the most. He's been really supportive about this whole thing. You know he's had to hire two new assistants at the studio?'

'It's about time. He's been getting you as slave labour for free long enough! Look, your priorities are going to have to shift for a bit and he'll just have to understand that. You can't give Lokis one hundred per cent and Kookie Krums one hundred per cent too. You've got more energy than anyone I know but even you have limits. Just tell him that fifty per cent of you is worth more than one hundred per cent of 'most any other woman, and see how he responds.'

'Good argument,' Susie said, 'but I don't think he'll buy it.'

Lokis didn't buy it. As long as Susie was working out
of their home, everything was fine. Even the first Kookie
Krums store seemed to be just an extension of what she
was doing before, but three stores? And now Manhattan?
He'd tried to be understanding and supportive, but damnit, now that she was moving into his arena, he didn't like
it one bit. He didn't like the fact that while he had a small
studio in Soho, Susie had leased corporate office space
that was three times the size of his. He didn't like the
fact that she was hardly ever home now. When she wasn't
at one of her stores, she was at the office and when she
wasn't at the office, she was at The Club. Worst of all,
she was now making more money than he was.

What had happened to the sweet little girl who just
wanted to be married and have a family and help him
get where he was going? She'd turned into a one-woman
conglomerate with a cash register for a brain and a
spreadsheet for a cunt. She hardly ever giggled any more
because she wanted to be 'taken seriously' and not
'dismissed', whatever the hell that meant. She even
answered her phones in a deep voice, barking, 'Yes?'
instead of 'Hello'. What had happened to that sweet
girlish, flirty voice he used to love so much? And she was
smoking now, too. It was all The Club's fault. He blamed
it completely for turning her head around. What really
went on inside those doors anyway? He desperately
wanted to know. If he could just see the secret interior
of the enemy camp, then maybe he'd know how to plan
his attack.

Susie wanted him to join the new co-ed aerobics class
at The Club. 'Come on, this is something we can do
together. We really need that right now. It's for members
and their spouses or "significant others". Co-ed aerobics
was Merilee Houston's idea. You'll love her, she's a great
teacher; she's really cute and a lot of fun. Next to Mina,

412

she's my best friend there.' Lokis said yes. This was exactly the opportunity he'd been waiting for.

'Isn't Merilee just fabulous?' Susie asked him after their first session.

'Fabulous doesn't come close to describing her,' Lokis agreed.

Watching the delectable little blonde bouncing up and down in her hot-pink spandex tights with fuzzy blue leg-warmers, Lokis fell instantly and deeply in lust. Susie claimed she still loved him, but she was rarely home and, when she was, she was too tired to have sex. When he pointed this little lack out to his charming wife, she had actually whipped out a leather-bound date book and riffled through the pages to find her next available opening. It was depressing to realize that 'sex with Lokis' now had to be scheduled, sandwiched in between 'marketing session with Mary Ann' and 'buying trip with Sondra'.

Merilee Houston was a sight for Lokis's starving eyes. He wanted to lick her all over, take tiny bites out of her, rest his head between those beautiful little legs. While her body was in obviously great shape and well toned, she was still round and curvy; Susie in her quest for 'muscle definition' was losing all pliancy and had become firm to the point of resistance. Merilee took them through a fiercely gruelling workout but, as far as Lokis was concerned, the pain was worth it just to watch her delicious little form contort itself into every conceivable suggestive position. As the loud rock music throbbed from the speakers, Merilee tightened and released her neat little buttocks, encouraging them all to 'squeeze, squeeze'.

'When you work the body, you work the mind as well,' Merilee said breathlessly, her eyes sparkling. 'You've got to find an image and go with it. Now when y'all do a big stretch, you've got to reach out for all those goals in life you hope to achieve. Now, come on, y'all, reach for the stars!' She lifted one shapely little leg straight over

413

her head at a one-hundred-and-eighty-degree angle. As Lokis watched her tiny leg brush her little pink ear before she lowered it to the ground, he moaned involuntarily. 'You've got to hook into your own special fantasy. When you do a pushaway exercise, a lunge or something, just think 'bout pushin' away all the bad things around you. All the nasty things you've been havin' trouble dealin' with, just push them out of your space. Come on, *push*!' Lokis pushed Susie so hard that she lost her balance and fell headlong on to the tatami mat and he had to help her up. Legs spread wide, her narrow Danskin stretched perilously tight across her pubic bone, Merilee arched backwards in an effortless backbend and brought her head between her knees to peek out at the class from beneath her crotch. 'Symbolize physically what you are seeing mentally.' Lokis felt faint. 'Now just pick your favourite fantasy and indulge.' Lokis closed his eyes in ecstasy. He was way ahead of her.

Or so he thought. Merilee noticed him watching her. She knew what he wanted and she had just about decided she was going to let him have it. He was a perfect contrast to Luigi and she needed a little variety in her sexual menu. Merilee always wanted what somebody else had. When she was a little girl and Cathy Lynn next door had a blue velvet dress made to look just like the blue velvet riding outfit that Scarlett O'Hara's Bonnie Blue Butler had in *Gone with the Wind*, Merilee had screamed and hollered until her mama sat up all night and made one for her. If her best friend had a new man, she wanted him right away, not for who he was but for what he was, another woman's guy. And it gave her a perfect excuse when, as they inevitably did, her entanglements came untangled. What was the point of reaching for a prize if you could actually get your hands on it and keep it? It was the ultimately unattainable that attracted her.

Lokis was almost too easy a mark. She knew he felt

stranded. Generally she liked a little more uncertainty, a chase, a pursuit. So she let Lokis chase her until she caught him, as her mama would have put it. After a couple of months she invited him over to help her install some new kitchen cabinets. She was redoing her kitchen and she knew he was a big restaurant designer and probably booked up for like weeks to come, but would he just do her this one little favour? When he turned up one Saturday afternoon when Susie was driving down to Maryland to see about expanding her business there, Merilee met him at the door wearing a fuzzy white sweater, just like the ones Susie used to wear. He could just see the outline of her brassiere through the light angora. Merilee always wore a bra, an intricate lace confection, even when it was no longer fashionable. What was the fun in ripping off the wrapping when you already knew what the present looked like? The sweater was low-cut and when Merilee bent over Lokis caught a glimpse of those tantalizing, teasing, tasty tits and he didn't see how he was going to hold on to his sanity much less his fidelity much longer, She was so tiny, so perfectly made, it would be like fucking a china doll. He quickly moved away from her and opened the box of tools he'd brought with him, throwing wrenches, screwdrivers, and pliers on to the floor. He climbed the stepladder to take a look at the cabinets while Merilee sat on the floor, took off her socks and proceeded to paint her toenails.

'I bet you think this is real silly,' she said, bending over again to dip her little brush into the bottle of pink frosted polish. Lokis dropped his hammer and Merilee had to hand it up to him, reaching high on her tippy-toes. 'I mean, here it is the middle of winter and I'm mostly wearin' my boots and my knee socks anyway. Who's gonna see my bare toes?'

'Ah wouldn't know.' Lokis found himself slipping into the easy rhythm of her accent.

'Are you makin' fun of me?'

'Why, no, honeychile.' Lokis put the last screw into place with his electric screwdriver and started to sand down the top shelf.

'You *are* makin' fun of me but I don't care. It's just so great to have a man around the house. I love watchin' you work, the smell of a man's sweat when he's doin' manual labour. It's so sexy, you know what I mean?'

'Can't say as I do.' Lokis was sweating buckets. He couldn't believe he was actually falling for this woman's so obvious approach.

'Don't forget to use the bathroom before you go. And be sure to leave the seat up.'

'Why?'

' 'Cause I like to know a man's been in the house. Hey, what do you think?' Merilee stretched out her baby legs and wiggled her little toes invitingly, letting him see right up her skirt, 'You like the colour?'

'Well, now, I don't know. I think I better just come on down there and take a closer look.'

'Why don't you just do that?'

Lokis was down the ladder in a flash, had her sweater off and her bra unhooked. Merilee made a great show of resisting, swearing she'd never meant this to happen, Susie was her best friend in the whole world, and she just couldn't think of him that way, all the while arching her back and wiggling her pelvis and lifting her heaving breasts up and straight into his hungry mouth. His lips closed around her rosebud nipple, Merilee made little mewing noises, her hands weaving through the long curls of his hair, massaging the muscles in his neck and sliding up his back under his shirt. She was holding her legs tightly together and Lokis tried desperately to wedge his knee between them, sliding his hand under her skirt, moving his fingers around her silky French knickers. She was wearing — oh God, garter belts, wispy bits of things

416

that slid right into his hands and down her legs. She must have been wearing stockings and taken them off just before he arrived. The image made his blood boil. Her silky half-slip slid away just as easily but as he moved to slip the kickers off, she pulled away again, saying, 'No, no, you mustn't. It's wrong. Let's just sit here and talk. I can't think when you're touching me like that.' But the minute he let go of her she was all over him again, grabbing at his thighs, running her hand down the back of his black 501s to cup his ass, her tongue halfway down his throat, panting and thrashing. He seized her hands and held them over her head, and while she sighed, 'I can't help myself, I don't know what's come over me', he was able to get her pants off. Then she pushed him away again, crying, 'No, no, we would never forgive ourselves!' She whipped her head from side to side, her blonde hair catching him cross the face like a silken curtain. He placed his hands around her throat and held her still as her wide eyes stared up at him like a startled fawn. Then slowly, inch by inch, she drew her skirt up, until it was gathered about her waist and, spreading her legs wide, with her long fingernails traced the inside of her thighs up and down. Lokis watched fascinated as she gently explored herself, stroking, back and forth, and then thrusting deep inside, drawing her finger out and then pushing it in again ever so slowly so that he could watch the muscles contract and expand inside her. His eyes were glued to her, his cock rock-hard, straining against the zipper of his jeans. With agonizing slowness, Merilee withdrew her finger and, just as gradually, inserted it into her mouth, her mouth sucking it in like a vacuum. He had never seen anything so openly erotic in his life. He could already feel himself inside her, inside the wetness of her. She slowly extracted her finger from her mouth and slipped it between her legs again, but he caught her hand and set it aside. Rising to his knees, he

417

tugged at his belt buckle, frantically unzipping his fly and letting his swollen cock spring free. Merilee flung her arm over her eyes, 'Oh God, you're huge!' she cried. 'You're never going to fit inside me!'

He started to pull his black jeans off over his boots, but she clutched his naked buttocks and breathed into his crotch. 'No, leave them on. It's easier that way. I love your boots. They're so hard, so rough.' Thoroughly inflamed, he flung himself on her. 'Be careful,' she whispered as he plunged into her. But he did fit. Perfectly.

# Seventeen

Miriam had hit a lull. After the steady success of her theatrical work in David Arlen Love's plays, her agent couldn't seem to find her any new projects. He kept coming up with all sorts of excuses. Maybe it was her weight. Maybe she just wasn't conventionally pretty enough for film. Maybe her talent and personality (not to mention her ass) were too big for the screen. She refused to accept his excuses.

She tried to break into television. Pilot season in LA never found her being considered for a series lead. She was always up for the friend of the lead, the sympathetic doctor, the concerned civil rights lawyer. And most of the time she didn't even get those supporting roles. The one pilot she had managed to land had never become a series. When they filmed *Dinner at the Diner*, for which she won her second Tony playing a waitress who has a religious experience in the middle of the Arizona desert, even then Robert Altman had replaced her with Cher. It was so humiliating. After nearly a year of fruitless attempts she had almost given up.

Then Stephen was appointed to the Senate Subcommittee on Censorship and Pornography. He was delighted. This would be his chance to raise the nation's consciousness about the squalid conditions of urban America's sex industry. He broached his plan with Miriam first, and then presented it to the Subcommittee, who were not as easily persuaded to support it. Ever stubborn and encouraged by Miriam's own enthusiastic endorsement, however, Stephen raised the money to produce *Love Unveiled*, a docudrama on the Times Square sex shops. Miriam narrated the chilling, eighty-minute film and helped research the seamy side of Manhattan for material. She interviewed a number of hookers on the street. They all told her that if she really wanted to learn the 'tricks of the trade', she would have to dress like a hooker herself and try her luck on Eighth Avenue.

So she put a red wig on and climbed into a black leather jump suit and hit the streets. Within ten minutes of standing in front of the X-rated cinema at Eighth and Forty-Second, she had picked up a huge, bald-headed, pasty-faced man in a three-piece suit and a lot of gold jewellery. Ignoring Stephen's desperate hand signals not to go any further, she gave the high sign to the hidden camera and led her nervous, sweating client straight into a nearby cheap hotel, complete with neon sign flashing outside the window. The hidden camera followed them right to the door of the hotel bedroom. The john had his clothes off and his money and his cock out before Miriam told him the truth.

Shocking, sensational stuff. The message was clear. Massage parlours, telephone sex, live sex acts, kiddie porn — Stephen and his task force exposed it all and presented it in a powerful, fast-paced eighty minutes of sordid sexuality. The film was initially shown only at special cinemas and by invitation only, but because it was intended to be a serious sociological statement, *Love Unveiled* received a wider distribution and ended up winning a special prize at the Cannes Film Festival. The porn scenes, designed to show the Times Square sexual underworld at its very worst, were so hot that kinky men in raincoats lined up for blocks.

Suddenly Miriam Newman had a new public image.

And nobody could have been more surprised than she was. Suddenly in her thirties, she was sexy, she was hot. On the screen, she seemed open and vulnerable, ready to embrace, dazed and dreamy. She'd been determined to carry through on her research, but the thought of hanging out, barely clothed, on Eighth Avenue had so terrified her that she'd fortified herself with several horse-sized Valium. During her famous encounter with the john, she was so sedated that by the time the man tried to kiss her, she had almost fallen asleep. The resulting reviews for *Love Unveiled* were some of the best of her career.

Miriam and Stephen came back from Cannes to political and artistic acclaim. *Love Unveiled* had won a special jury prize. Miriam was so convincing on screen as a hooker that the Europeans were touting her as a new sex symbol. The European reviewers raved about her and the American critics were equally ecstatic. Vincent Canby was struck by the 'dreamy, trance-like quality' of her performance, Pauline Kael raved about her 'quiet stillness' and Janet Maslin called it 'a nitty gritty characterization that steams up the screen, guaranteed not to leave a dry seat in the house.'

But despite the rave reviews, she still wasn't getting any film offers. 'When it comes to film, I can't even get arrested,' she grumbled to Stephen. 'There's nowhere else I can go in theatre. Television is all right but it's not where I really want to be; I've got to take that next step on to the big screen. But how?'

'You need a property,' said Stephen. 'Something created just for you.'

'I thought I had that with David Arlen Love's work. David's in LA right now finishing the screenplay for *For Love of a Bagelmaker*. But will I get to recreate my starring role No. David wants me but he doesn't have casting approval. The director says I'm on the short list, but I know he'll end up going with Sally Field or Cher, whether David is happy or not. I don't want to pressure him when he's trying to make a go of it in LA. And he's getting married. Did I tell you that?'

Stephen shook his head. Miriam knew he didn't like to talk about David because he was a little jealous of their friendship. Fine. It was good to let him think that, while he was surrounded by political groupies in Washington, she had someone else in her life, too, even if he was just a friend. 'Yeah, he's marrying a woman he met in LA. She's Japanese. A make-up artist. One of the best in the business, apparently. She's pregnant so David's going to become a husband and a daddy at the same time. He sounds deliriously happy with all of it and I'm delighted for him. But I don't think I'm going to get to play Malka in the movie.'

'Then you've got to find something else. Something that is so perfect for you that only you can play it. There has to be something like that.'

'There is,' said Miriam. 'It's *Paloma*.'

Like Vivien Leigh and Scarlett O'Hara, Miriam knew she was born to play *Paloma*. It was a bestselling novel about a peasant woman in the Spanish Civil War who was executed by Franco's troops for arranging the escape of her children to Canada. Miriam read the novel over and over again and each time she read it she saw the movie version in her head:

March 1939. Southeastern Spain. The little town of Albacete between Madrid and Cartagena. It's the end of three years of bitter fighting between the republicans and the nationalists. The nationalists are headed by El Caudillo, the leader, Franco. The republicans are a disparate group of peasants fighting for their freedom.

Paloma Galera is a young peasant woman, mother of two small children, Luis and Concha. Her husband is away fighting with the republican forces, but it has become a losing battle. Albacete is the headquarters of the International Brigade, sympathetic leftists who have come from all over the world, including a group of Canadians called the Mackenzie Papineaus. Recruited by the Canadian Communist Party after the abortive march on Ottawa demanding jobs, the Mac-Paps have come to Spain to fight for freedom. It has been a long hard struggle and the Mac-Paps are brave and idealistic.

Now Madrid has been taken.

Cartagena has fallen.

And, finally, Albacete.

The cause is lost and the Canadians find themselves trapped in Spain. Paloma, who has fallen in love with one of them, a Captain James Duncan, agrees to get them out. She knows the Costa de la Luz, coast of light, like the back of her hand. She commits herself to the cause of saving James and five other members of the International Brigades. She promises to lead them over the mountains to the town of Almeria where the British Navy is sending a sub into the sheltered waters off the coast to pick them up. Of course those waters are constantly patrolled by German boats. And the mountains are full of the Falanges, Spanish Fascists, mopping up the area, looking for any republicans or International Brigade members who may be hiding in the hills. Paloma knows that she will be risking her life and the lives of her children by taking them on this dangerous trek.

Paloma bundles up the children. Seven-year-old Luis is strong enough to walk but Concha, who is not quite four, will have to be carried a good deal of the way. Captain James Duncan and his fellow soldiers follow close behind, hiding in the bushes when there are any signs of danger. When the Falanges stop Paloma, she tells them that her husband has been killed fighting for Franco and that she is taking her children to their grandmother in Almeria. In a tense race against time they move through the Sierra de Segura and Sierra de los Filabres, the mountain ranges they must cross to reach their destination. The British Navy sub sent from Gibraltar is to pick them up at an appointed spot, at an appointed hour, under the cover of night. If the Canadians miss it, they will be lost, and so will be Paloma and her children.

In a battered rowboat, with the five men hidden under a tarpaulin, Paloma rows with her children out into the ocean to meet the submarine. All along she has promised James that she and the children will go with him to Canada, but at the last moment she puts the children on board with him and climbs back alone into the rowboat. Tearfully she tells him she cannot leave Spain. 'I can't go with you until I have found my husband and told him face to face that I love another man. Take my children. Keep them safe. I will join you as soon as I can. I love you.' She blows kisses at the bewildered children and she resolutely rows back to shore in a blinding storm, her face wet with both rain and tears. She never sees her children or her lover again. Back on shore, she is immediately seized by the Falanges and held for seven days before being shot.

Miriam cried every time she came to the end of the book. *Paloma* had all the ingredients to make a major motion picture, not to mention the kind of role that only comes along once in a lifetime. The actress who portrayed the heroine would have to convey the kind of indomitable spirit that makes others follow her willingly into possible death. Miriam believed she was the only actress who could give Paloma the strength, spirituality, and firm practicality, the passion and complexity, that the role and the real woman on whom the story was based required. Stephen read the book and instantly agreed that this was the one they'd been looking for. But how in hell, even with their money and contacts, were they going to get their hands on such a hot property?

First she had to convince the author of the book, Luis Galera, not only to give her the rights but to agree to Miriam, a virtual unknown, playing the title role. Luis had grown up in Canada, eventually returning to Spain to live and write in Madrid. The character was based on his mother, he was one of the children she had managed to save, so he had grave reservations about an American actress being right for the role. First of all, Miriam was Jewish, not Spanish. And she was tall where his mother had been tiny. There was the problem of mastering the necessary authentic Spanish accent, but even more important than that, Luis felt very strongly about the kind of voice Paloma should have, and it was not Miriam's. She would have to work very hard to make him believe she was the embodiment of his creation, much less the reincarnation of his mother. Finally Stephen flew to Madrid and persuaded Luis to come to New York to see Miriam in her current show, a Broadway revival of *The Rose Tattoo*.

Overwhelmed by Miriam's power on stage, Luis sold the rights to *Paloma* to Stephen for $300,000. David Arlen Jones agreed to write the screenplay with the author, which was important because David would bring a much-needed light touch to what was essentially a grim story. Then Miriam flew to Greece to meet with Costa Gavras, the director she managed to talk into taking on the film. With him on board, they knew they had a very attractive package, one that the studios would be dying to get their hands on.

Bidding was tough, but eventually they brought in Touchstone, the new division of Disney that specialized in adult projects. *Paloma* would be shot on location in Spain in the hopes of being edited and in the can, ready to be shown at Cannes in May. Miriam's dream was about to come true, but she would be away from Stephen for at least four months.

The night before she was to fly to Spain, she set out to seduce Stephen anew. It had been wonderful to have him home for a couple of weeks during the pre-production period on the film, to be able to get his opinion on the costume designs Susan Becker was finalizing and to discuss the original music John Williams was writing. But personally there seemed to be a huge gulf between them. When they did see each other, they hardly made love at all. Maybe it was just because they'd both been drinking a lot the night before she left, but once they were in bed, Stephen lost his erection. In a breathless voice, he had begged her to pinch his nipples, hard, and stick her finger up his ass. She had done it and it had worked, but it left her confused. Was she no longer able to satisfy him? What was going on with him in Washington that she didn't know about?

In the morning he said nothing more abut it and Miriam didn't want to bring it up. She wanted their last few moments together to be loving ones that she could remember while she was far away on location, but as her plane took off for Madrid, she felt that he was the one leaving her, rather than the other way around.

Washington. Sara Town stood face to face with the charismatic Stephen Andrews, the Democratic senator from Connecticut. He photographed like a dream, but in person his appeal was stronger. No wonder every woman in North America wanted to support the new movement he was calling the Creative Opportunity Society, something that sounded like the less-government-more-free-enterprise line that the Republicans subscribed to. Reagan was trying to maintain his ideals, but even so the parties were starting to look interchangeable.

Stephen took her hand on meeting and held it for an extra second, just long enough to let the electric current flash between them, long enough for Sara to experience a little frisson of sexual delight. She looked into his eyes trying to read the message there. Usually she kept her professional life separated from her sex life, and she preferred a slightly rougher trade than an upper-class eastern prep-school product offered, but holding Stephen's hand, she felt there was more to him than his good looks and bland charm alone. There was a tiny hint of darkness that was most intriguing. Yes, she was definitely interested and she knew she'd piqued his interest, too.

The question was, did this clean-cut but oh-so-sexy senator play around at all? Other than living with an actress he was not yet married to (and Jerry Brown and Linda Ronstadt had made that seem less than shocking), Stephen Andrews had a reputation for being squeaky clean. Mind you, anyone who went out of his way to explore the sex shops of Times Square and film them, not to mention casting his own wife as a hooker and letting her come close to turning a trick with a real john, probably had somewhat more of an axe to grind than just being anti-porn.

She'd have to be careful, very careful, but then so would he. One could never tell with these preppie types. For all she knew, he might like to be tied to the bedpost and have seedless grapes stuffed up his ass. At the very least, it would be fun to find out.

Madrid. For Miriam, it was torture being away from Stephen, and she was nervous about her first starring role. She'd never had more than a few days on any film and now here she was, on set every day and in almost every scene. Although R.D. Patterson, a Canadian star, had been cast to sweeten the marquee, his role was smaller.

427

Miriam knew she had to carry the picture; the success or failure of *Paloma* lay on her shoulders.

Robert Patterson, or Bobby as he was called, had a reputation for being highly temperamental, difficult, and a real bastard to his leading ladies: if he didn't like her or felt she wasn't up to his artistic standard, he could make her life miserable. Miriam won him over in a day. After all she was a serious actor. Gavras insisted on several weeks of rehearsal before they even started shooting and by then it was clear from the first dailies that Miriam and Bobby generated a unique chemistry that would make the picture work on a romantic level. Off the set there was a lot of chemistry between Bobby and Miriam, too, but Miriam wasn't going to do anything to jeopardize the success of the film, and she really didn't want to be number 1,553 in Bobby Patterson's love life anyway. They had a wonderful time together, but Bobby was on the picture for only three weeks before he headed back to the States.

David was around for the first two weeks and it was wonderful having him there for support and re-establishing their own bond. The pictures of his wife and baby daughter were beautiful and on the surface at least all was well, but Miriam sensed pain behind David's usual wacky sense of humour; there was something he wasn't telling her, something deeply troubling to him. When the call came for David to fly back to LA within twenty-four hours, she wasn't surprised. 'Kyoko's ill,' he said. 'She has leukaemia.'

'Oh God, David, no!'

'We knew it when we got married. She was in remission but her pregnancy reactivated the disease and, damnit, she wouldn't go back on chemotherapy because she was afraid it would damage the foetus. I begged her to have an abortion. At the time, her life meant more me to me than something that wasn't yet, as far as I was concerned, a living human being. Now, I don't know. I'm so glad we have Tammy, we both cherish her . . . but, oh God, I can't give up one life for another!'

'She'll pull through, David.'

'She's got to,' he said grimly, his eyes glistening. 'I don't want to cry. I'm flying straight to her and I don't want there to be any tears.'

'Miriam held out her arms. 'Then cry with me so that you can be strong with her.'

And he came into her arms and they both wept.

David left for LA and didn't come back for the entire shooting period. Miriam was really on her own. Halfway through, she begged Costa Gavras to let her fly to Washington for a little break with Stephen.

Grudgingly he gave her a five-day pass while they did some second-unit shooting. Being with Stephen didn't relax Miriam the way she hoped it would. He seemed surprised, even irritated that she was there. His announcement that he intended to switch to the Republican party immediately touched off a big argument over what Miriam called basic human values and what Stephen referred to as warmed-over sixties idealistic bullshit.

They were hardly ever alone; it was hard to get him away from his aides, advisors and speech writers, the ever-growing entourage of people that seemed to surround him these days. When she did see him, he was usually in the company of Senator Stanley Hughes from Illinois and his daughter, Laura. Miriam had never liked the retired Air Force colonel with the steel-grey hair and iron jaw, who was head of the Armed Services Committee: he was too right-wing (she referred to him as that warmonger) and he seemed to have an ever-increasing influence over Stephen's thinking. It was obvious that Stanley Hughes was behind Stephen's sudden desire to become a Republican.

She liked his daughter, Laura, even less, a pale, rabbity daddy's girl who seemed to echo her father's opinions on everything from the MX missile to the ERA. Now Stephen had hired her as his press aide, to help him effect the change in just the right way through the media, to ensure that public opinion (and the voters) would shift with him. Apparently she was doing a good job. All Washington was buzzing about the switch and the feeling seemed to be that it was not only the right move for Stephen Andrews to make in terms of his political career, but that it came from a sincere shift in his thinking.

Miriam was glad that Stephen's mother had not lived to see him jump the Democratic ship. Nothing she could say would make him budge from his position; his mind was made up. She got on the plane for Madrid, feeling once again that they were growing further and further apart. Where would this season of change for them end? What did he want from her? What did he so desperately need that she could no longer give him?

Washington. Sara sighed with deep satisfaction and, raising her arms above her head, stretched voluptuously, displaying her lithe body to full advantage against the peach satin sheets. 'Well, that was a pleasant surprise,' she said to the man lying spread-eagled next to her. ' I must say I like being swept off my feet and seduced. You have an amazing amount of energy, Mr Andrews. That bodes well for your political future.'

'If anyone was seduced, lady, it was me. Don't tell me you didn't plan this. I can't believe you sleep on these sheets every day.'

'A woman never knows when she might get lucky.'

'Here I am thinking I'm meeting you to discuss my party switch, and I wind up in bed with America's favourite interviewer.' Stephen gave her one of his slow-burning smiles.

430

'I find sex is a great little icebreaker, don't you? There's always something unspoken, that awkwardness between a man and a woman before they've made love that makes it hard to concentrate. I like to remove that barrier right away. Much more comfortable, don't you agree?'

Stephen laughed admiringly. 'No wonder you get such great interviews. Your approach – and I mean this as a compliment – is very masculine.'

'Thank you. I accept it as a compliment.'

'How did you know I'd be interested?'

'Let's just say that I knew a part of you was interested. You revealed that early on.' Sara reached over and placed her hand on him. 'In fact, I'd say you have a hard time hiding your interest. I've never had a man your size before.'

'I'm not all that big,' Stephen said, watching himself grow again under her touch.

'I couldn't imagine you would match your height, but you do. Miriam doesn't know how lucky she is to have this at her beck and call.' The mention of Miriam's name made Stephen wilt under her hand so she quickly went on, 'Don't worry. Discretion is my middle name. It has to be in this business.'

Stephen looked relieved. 'We're not married. I shouldn't feel guilty about this, but I guess I do. There's a reporter around every corner in Washington just waiting to catch you out. Hell, you're press yourself, but you were just too good to pass up.'

'Your secret's safe with me,' Sara opened the drawer of the bedside table 'if mine is safe with you.' She took out several silk scarves, a thin whip and a small white envelope. She poured the contents of the envelope into a line on the mirror, rolled the envelope into a sphere and inhaled deeply. Stephen watched as the entire line of white powder was sucked up and into Sara's nose. He couldn't believe what he was seeing. This was one of America's top anchors, the woman who had so calmly covered Irangate and guided a shaken nation though the trauma of the Challenger, doing cocaine right in front of him, a US senator. They both must be crazy.

Sara shook her head, letting her dark hair sweep forward, hiding her face and then looked up at him, her eyes narrowing to contented slits. 'You want to try it?' She held the envelope out to Stephen, who stared in fascination. She licked her lips. Oh, this was going to be easy. 'And then if you're very, very good,' she purred, letting her fingers trail lightly over the whip and catch in a jade green silk scarf, 'we'll see if we can't find something to do with these.'

Madrid. Miriam focused all her attention on her work. She was hungry to work, willing to work twenty hours a day. Her days became a series of getting up early, into make-up, on set for a full day's shooting often going into overtime, and then falling into bed at night. Every minute was costing thousands of dollars; there was no time to be wasted. Because the film was a series of flashbacks and Miriam played not only Paloma but Paloma's mother as well, she had to age up and down, from twenty to sixty-five, depending upon the day's schedule. Maintaining that high level of intensity day after day was exhausting, made worthwhile only by David and Luis's magnificent script and the superb rushes they were getting every day. Miriam insisted on seeing the dailies and checking her performance, knowing that she couldn't possibly go back to the hotel and sleep without knowing how her work was progressing. Scratchy and out of sequence as the dailies always were, even without the underscoring music that would eventually pull it all together, what was actually up there even now was stunning. The depth of her performance pleased Costa Gavras and even amazed

432

herself. She could look heartbreakingly plain in one scene and in the next, wildly sensual, even beautiful. One minute she was a ravishing young girl of twenty, the next an ageing sage, full of wisdom and pain. If it was clear that *Paloma* would make or break her film career, it was equally clear that her performance was one that the critics would undoubtedly call 'a triumph of the human spirit.' Even the crew, the jaded grips and gaffers, were impressed. On the last day of shooting, when Costa finally declared, 'It's a wrap,' the crew broke into loud applause and cheers for everyone involved in the project, but especially for Miriam. It warmed her heart to know she'd done a good job. Now all she wanted was to get home to Stephen.

Washington. Stephen knew he had to get out of this relationship. Sara was exciting − God, she was exciting − but he knew she was also dangerous. Kinky sex was one thing but drugs were another matter entirely. What was the matter with him? Was he going through some mid-life crisis, some major battle within himself, some urge to self-destruct? He was living a lie that was forcing him to work even harder to cover his tracks. Part of the excitement was keeping it from Miriam; part of it was the possibility of her discovering it. What would Stanley Hughes think if he knew about the seamy underbelly of his clean-cut protégé, Stephen Andrews? What would Laura think? Or his mother or grandfather?

But goddamnit, didn't he deserve a little fun? The pressure of political life was monstrous; he needed something to help him relax. He'd gotten into politics to help others, of course, but where was the fun of power without enjoying a few of its perks? The devil in Stephen was driving him to do this, but God, that devil was deliciously, decadently seductive.

The pressure was getting to him, that was all. Any

closer to the edge and he might fall into the abyss. Maybe he was truly invincible.

Christ, he must be losing his mind. He needed to get back to New York for a bit. Miriam was there. Miriam was safety. He had to get back to Miriam.

# *Eighteen*

What the hell was going on? Lokis hadn't been home in forty-eight hours. Returning from her trip to Louisville, Kentucky, to check out a couple of sites for new stores, Susie had been so tired she had flopped into bed without waiting up for Lokis to get home. This morning, she barely noticed he wasn't in bed beside her. She was in such a hurry to get down to the offices, she didn't bother to check to see if he was up early and working in the back room. Coming home tonight, there were no signs that he'd been in the apartment at all in the past two days. It was now midnight and she still had no idea where her husband was. She was starting to worry.

Nervously she dialled the number of his studio and managed to get hold of Lindy, his design assistant, working late. Lindy said Lokis had been late getting in to work this morning and had left early for a dinner meeting with a client. Who that client was, she didn't know. Susie started to get angry. He'd been acting strange lately: instead of pushing her to have sex in the hopes of her getting pregnant, he was suggesting they give it a rest. That wasn't like him.

She picked up the phone and gave Mina a call. Sometimes she was up after midnight and willing to talk, but all Susie got was a recorded message, so she left a message for her to call back if she got in within the next couple of hours. She was too restless to sleep and besides she wanted to talk with him, to see if they couldn't get things straightened out between them.

Maybe she should try Merilee? They hadn't been spending as much time together lately, mainly because Mina didn't like her, but if Merilee wasn't with one of her hot dates, she'd probably be willing to get together even at this late hour. They could get drunk together and really have a high old time of it. Merilee took a long time to answer the phone and when she did she said she'd love to meet Susie tomorrow for lunch at The Club but tonight she had cramps so she was taking some Valium to knock herself out. Susie slammed the phone down in disgust.

Merilee hung up the phone and turned to Lokis who was stretched out on her Peruvian alpaca wool rug in front of the TV eating taco chips and guacamole dip. Sick of anything that even came close to the kind of gourmet stuff that Susie created, Lokis was now addicted to the Tex-Mex junk food Merilee served him, along with her complying, pliant little body, wicked mouth, and facile fingers. 'She knows,' Merilee said, 'She's testing us.'

'No, she's not,' Lokis assured her, his mouth full of corn chips and jalepeno peppers. 'She doesn't have a clue.'

He was right. Susie didn't know. But she had begun to suspect. Something. Picking up Lokis's black leather jacket to put it away (he was always leaving his clothes all over the apartment and Susie refused to hire a full-time maid even though they could afford one), a note fell out of the pocket. 'It's so good to feel your big ole arms around me. You're my favourite bull and I can hardly wait to ride you again. XOXO.' The note blurred in front of her eyes. Susie picked up the phone, dialled Merilee's number, but before Merilee could answer she hung up. It had to be her, who else could it be? She phoned Mina again, praying that she would answer this time and, when she did, Susie said, 'Get over here right away.'

Susie was desperate. For the last two hours Mina had been trying to calm her down. 'I mean, who else is going to actually write a note in a Texas accent, for God's sake? I thought it was going to be a real battle to get Lokis to The Club to take that aerobics class. Now he loves it! He loves her! I know it!' She was practically shrieking.

'Look, you don't even know if it's true. I'll admit it looks pretty suspicious. That's the main reason I've never liked Merilee.'

'You knew she was after Lokis? And you didn't tell me?'

'No, no. But she's always after something. She can't be trusted. And she's not nearly as dumb as she acts.'

'Yeah, and right now she's after my husband. How could she do this to me? I feel so betrayed. She's supposed to be one of my best friends. What's wrong with me? Do I look like the quintessential victim? Am I still that naïve and stupid?'

'Stop blaming yourself. Merilee is a well-known husband-hunter who just happened to set her trap for Lokis. She's a joke. Really. It's nothing to do with you. Lokis is feeling vulnerable right now; he's jealous of your success. It's his problem, not yours.'

'Great analysis, thanks, Mina, but what am I going to do?'

'Well, you've got to make up your mind. You can either confront him and try and make it work. Or say nothing and try and make it work. Or you can leave him. It's up to you.'

The Club. Susie cancelled her appointments for the morning and went there for an early workout. The problems at home and the problems at work would join forces for one terrific migraine if she couldn't relax

437

somehow. She dove into the pool and did her thirty laps but today it just felt like so much thrashing about. Today her legs felt heavy and she felt the water dragging her down to the depths of depression. No, not that again, please. She hadn't been depressed since she started Kookie Krums. With the business thriving she was richer than she'd ever dreamed. How stupid to be rich and depressed. She pulled herself up over the edge of the pool and towelled off, scrunching her permed hair with her fingers. Lokis hated her short hair, but it was so much easier to handle. She didn't feel up to rinsing the chlorine out of it. She'd only have to get her hair wet again when she took her shower later anyway.

Grabbing her scented body lotion, she headed for the sauna, just as Miriam Newman came out of the dressing-room and descended the marble steps into the pool. She walked as regally as if she were striding up to the podium to accept an Academy Award. Actually, she might be getting one. *Paloma* hadn't even been released yet, but Susie had read it was predicted to be a blockbuster. Wearing nothing but a red bathing cap and a smile, Miriam stepped gingerly into the water. What can she possibly have to smile about at seven-thirty in the morning? Susie wondered as she disappeared into the heat of the sauna.

As it turned out, quite a lot. The rough cut for *Paloma* had looked good enough to show it at Cannes in May and enter it in competition before its United States release. Miriam and Stephen had flown to Cannes and the whole twelve-day experience had been like a second honeymoon. This time she was there with every possibility of coming back a star. Situated on the Cote d'Azur, right on the beach, the vivid blue of the sea matching the sky, and surrounded by palm trees, the biggest film festival in the world, and Stephen was with her. Miriam loved everything about Cannes, from the clapping, cheery, whistling screenings to the pickpockets on the boardwalk and the inflated prices in the seaside cafés. It had been a constant round of cocktail parties and black-tie suppers, breakfast meetings and business luncheons, plus numerous screenings, culminating in *Paloma* winning the coveted Palm d'Or and Miriam splitting the Best Actress award with Barbara Hershey.

*Paloma* also won a prize at the Festival of Festivals in Toronto and in Montreal. At the special screenings, the critics went wild for Miriam's performance and her agent, Michael Taylor, was besieged with phone calls from the press asking for advance stories on her before the film even opened. Once the studio got word that the critics were touting Miriam as a potential Oscar winner, they began to give her the star treatment. A limo arrived to take her to every interview, make-up and hair were arranged, and she was given first-class accommodation in the best hotels in Boston, Chicago, and San Francisco as the marketing campaign for *Paloma* began to heat up.

Michael Taylor had talked her into hiring Tabitha Rhymer as her personal publicist. Miriam had assumed that the publicist assigned to her by the studio, Shelley Arnstein, would be enough to handle the publicity junkets, but Michael said, 'The studio publicist will be scheduling up to eight or ten interviews a day for you; she won't possibly have time to devote herself to the details that you are going to need. A personal publicist will make sure your clothes are clean and that you have time to eat. She'll act as a buffer and help smooth the way. I wish that I could come with you, but with the hype surrounding the start-up of *In Depth*, Sara Town needs me here in New York.'

'I can manage just fine on my own,' Miriam assured him.

'You're not grasping the enormity of the task, Mim. The studio publicist will be making you work in the service of the film. A personal publicist will help you work in the service of yourself. You're involved in a build-up heading straight for the Academy Awards. Believe me, you're not going to have time to turn around. Hire a personal publicist.'

Tabitha Rhymer, a short, stocky black woman, was expecting her first child in a few months, but she seemed to have tons of energy. Vivacious and charming, she was a pit bull protecting 'her star', fielding delicate questions about Miriam's relationship with Senator Stephen Andrews, and making sure that the interview focused on her career instead of on Stephen's hopes for the White House. Before each interview she carefully briefed her, e.g. 'Now, you remember, Jay Scott is from the Toronto *Globe and Mail*. Dislikes political films if they're polemic. Has a background in theatre so he knows where you're coming from. Has an acid pen, but good taste. Watch your step.'

The campaign started out slowly with appearances on *Live at Five* and the Regis Philbin and Kathie Lee Gifford morning show, worked up to *Good Morning America* and *The Today Show* and by the end of two months their schedule was so full that if Miriam hadn't had Tabby around to remind her, she literally would have forgotten to go to the bathroom.

The studio decided to premiere the film, a black-tie affair followed by dinner at Sardi's, a fabulous Spanish feast in honour of Paloma's birthplace. Miriam was delighted it would be in New York because it meant that Stephen could at least make the dinner even if he had to miss the eight o'clock screening. The press had a field day. Flanked by Tabitha and Shelley Arnstein, Miriam worked the room, trailed by a crew from *Entertainment Tonight*. Shelley was careful always to have Miriam photographed between two celebrities to ensure that she herself could not be cropped out of the final published photo. AP and UPI were there along with the electronic media to cover the star-studded event, and the reviews next day were ecstatic.

'At last, a political film that doesn't preach or proselytize . . . *Paloma* is terrific entertainment.'

'A love affair in the grand style where the parties involved are willing to die for each other and we, the audience, believe it . . . Bobby Patterson and Miriam Newman steam up the screen . . . tremendous sexual chemistry.'

'A film so perfect it gives us a reason to believe in movie-making again.'

'An amazingly powerful performance . . . unforgettable heroine.'

'A tour de force for Miriam Newman . . . worthy of an Academy Award.'

The early critical response meant that Miriam was nominated for every award going: the New York Critics Awards, the LA Critics Awards, and the Golden Globe Awards. There was no doubt about it her career was on a roll.

Feeling beads of sweat sliding down her forehead from the blasting heat of the sauna, Miriam spread her towel out on the wooden bench of the second level and sat down cautiously, a prescribed distance away from Susie, who sat cross-legged, sweating profusely herself. The sharp pine smell of the overheated wood was soothing; it was somehow comfortable to be sitting naked next to someone she didn't know, sharing a sensual experience with a stranger. Each recognized the other from the press attention they had both been getting lately and each felt she should say something to the other, but the effort seemed too great and the warmth of the sauna lulled them into a pleasant, companionable lethargy. Surreptitiously they studied each other's bodies. Each would have changed places with the other in a minute. Susie looked at Miriam and sighed. Her own body was now trim and strong, but she felt almost boyish next to the overpowering femaleness of Miriam. The large round breasts with their peony nipples curving into a surprisingly narrow waist and full hips looked lush in the dim light.

Miriam viewed Susie's trim athleticism with envy. She was so thin that she knew that if you touched her, the flesh would be firm, without any give. Touching Miriam was like sinking into an overstuffed sofa cushion. She sighed herself and got up to pour more water over the dry, hot rocks, filling the room with a thick cloud of steam.

The door opened and Merilee Houston came into the sauna. Instantly Miriam stiffened; she disliked the tiny Texan. This was one area of Gwen's judgement that was definitely cloudy. Gwen claimed it was Merilee's programme of special services that had put The Club back on track and Miriam could see that membership had increased, but her actor's instincts told her that this woman was nothing but trouble. She moved back to sit on the wooden slats of the next level up.

Susie could hardly control herself. She hadn't yet confronted Merilee and the sauna was hardly the place to do so, especially in front of Miriam Newman. Merilee's little body, dressed or undressed, bounced as merrily as her name implied. Perfect little upturned breasts, wasp waist, and neatly sculpted legs culminating in a golden blonde fluffy bush of pubic hair. Bleached, Susie thought viciously. At least I'm a natural blonde. Three little maids from school are we, thought Miriam, something for every taste right here in this room.

'Merilee giggled and patted her meringue hair. 'Hi, y'all,' she said. 'You girls been pourin' too much water on those rocks again, I just know it.' Susie wondered how she could have trusted this woman. 'Now y'all know how

Gwen feels about that,' Merilee went on. 'It upsets the balance of the sauna. You want steam, y'all should use the steam-room.'

'The steam-room is too enervating,' Miriam said abruptly, wishing that Merilee would just get out. She could feel the tension in the room and she had no idea what it was all about. It was certainly ruining her good mood.

'Now what does that mean, "enervatin'"?' Merilee queried in her soft slur. 'I know it was on the *Reader's Digest* word list last week, but I forget. I think it's the opposite of what it sounds like. I've learned a lot from the *Reader's Digest*.'

'I'll just bet you have,' Susie said sharply, and the overpowering heat of the sauna was suddenly thicker. Merilee shifted her attention to Susie. 'You and I should have lunch together sometime soon, honey.' Susie busied herself with pouring pine-scented body oil over her legs and rubbing it in fiercely. Merilee giggled nervously and patted her hair again. 'Well, I guess I better get out of here before this steam makes my hair fall, sure as you're lookin' at it.'

'We'd rather not, Merilee,' Miriam said the minute the sauna door was safely shut. 'Oh please don't make us look at that hair! Is she for real or what?' Miriam started to laugh and suddenly Susie joined in, she couldn't help herself, and soon the two of them were giggling helplessly. 'I'm Miriam Newman,' She held out her hand.

Susie took it. 'Susie Krumins.' And then the two of them started to laugh again at the idea of shaking hands, nude, in a sauna.

'I'm sorry,' Miriam said when they were both finally able to control themselves, 'I just can't stand that woman. Gwen really values her but she just makes my skin crawl. I don't know why I hate her but I do.'

Suddenly Susie blurted out, 'I hate her because she's

fucking my husband.' She covered her mouth with her hand. 'Oh God, I don't know why I told you that. I don't even know you. I guess it's because this is the first time I've admitted to myself that it's really true.'

'And now that you know,' Miriam said gently, 'what are you going to do?'

Avoiding the sympathy in Miriam's eyes, Susie snatched up her towel and marched to the door. 'I'm going to dump the bastard.'

# Nineteen

Liz Jordan sat in the waiting room of the cosmetic surgery centre at The Club, listening to a muted Muzak version of 'Yesterday' and chain-smoking Benson and Hedges. As always, she marvelled at how tastefully the room was decorated. With its dove-grey carpets, hand-painted silk screens, Japanese prints, and Hokkaido vases full of cherry blossoms, it resembled a private salon in a top Tokyo hotel more than a doctor's office. She half-expected some kimono-clad geisha girl to tritz in and perform the tea ceremony any moment.

Not like the same-day surgery centre on East 71st with their fluorescent lighting, ten-year-old copies of *Today's Health* and plastic folders full of such comforting little pamphlets as 'Liposuction and You' and 'Learning to Live with a Chin Implant'. Liz refused to have a facelift in a place like that, opting instead for the discreet and serene surgical chambers of Dr Robert MacLeod, The Club's own private resident plastic surgeon.

Liz had had her first lift at thirty-nine, a bit early, but the results were certainly worth it. She liked the idea that her looks would be frozen in time and thirty-nine still marked the best year of her life to date. Dressed in a butterscotch suede pantsuit, her expensively streaked blonde bob neatly framed her tanned and flawless (thanks to Gorgette Klinger) complexion and scalpel-smooth jawline. Dr MacLeod was truly a genius. Even at forty-seven, she knew she looked pretty fabulous . . .

445

The same could not be said for her youngest daughter. Mindy, just fourteen, sat next to her mother, idly kicking her legs against the mauve and white patterned sofa. With her long dishwater blonde bangs virtually hiding her round, button brown eyes and her snub-nosed face wearing its usual sulky expression, the plump teenager resembled an overfed Sealyham puppy. Too bad she'd inherited her father's short, squat, doggy build instead of her mother's racehorse elegance.

'Don't bang your heels on the furniture, Min,' Liz said sharply. 'If you're nervous, get up, move around. And keep your mouth closed if you're going to chew gum.'

'Can I have a coffee?' Mindy whined, looking yearningly in the direction of the Mr Coffee maker which offered four different gourmet blends of coffee next to a tempting array of petits fours and miniature Danish.

'It's "may I have some coffee" and no, you may not. You *may* have some freshly squeezed juice or some mineral water. You'll find it in the little fridge in the corner. And don't even think about touching those cakes.'

Mindy slowly clambered to her feet and wandered over to the fridge, opened the door, and took out a mango and passion fruit drink that was a particularly lethal looking magenta colour. She drank it down in one gulp and then drifted towards the magazine racks that rivalled those of the Gotham Book Mart. She rifled through *Vanity Fair, Town and Country*, and *Harpers* until she found a dog-eared copy of *Teen Beat*. She stood in the corner, flipping through the pages, blowing and popping pink bubbles loudly.

'Remove that gum,' Liz ordered, and with a look of great pain Mindy did so. Liz sighed, stubbed out her Benson and Hedges and immediately lit another one. She really was at her wit's end. Lee would be furious if he found out about this . . . She was supposed to be in

446

charge of raising the girls. That's why he'd agreed to such hefty alimony and child support, leaving her on her own with the kids while he blithely went his own way, running the business and screwing his secretary. The man had no class and his values were Neanderthal, but one whiff of this latest trouble with Mindy and he'd be back in court in a flash renegotiating his payments. If she could just get Mindy through this bad patch to the end of ninth grade, she could pack her off to boarding school in Rhode Island in the fall. Her grades weren't bad considering the time the child obviously spent screwing around.

Last time Liz had taken Mindy to the Center for Reproductive and Sexual Health down on East 21st. As they crossed the Right-to-Life picket line in front of the clinic, demonstrators had shoved brochures at them illustrated with still photos from *The Silent Scream* as they shouted 'Murderess!' 'Baby-killer!' and 'The soul is alive at six weeks!' Mindy had burst into tears and Liz had had a hell of a time getting her into the building at all.

Once inside they had had to sit with all the thirteen-year old black prostitutes, repeats for third and fourth abortions, who didn't know how to keep their asses much less their noses clean. The whole procedure had been dreadfully humiliating. And the questions the nurse had asked Mindy about 'the physical side' of her life! As if she were some victim of urban blight instead of a pampered, privileged Park Avenue princess. Here, at The Club, Liz was on home territory. She felt safe. No one need ever know.

'Liz, my love, how's my favourite Giordano girl?' Dr MacLeod came to greet them.

'Jordan,' she corrected him for what had to be the hundredth time and put out her half-smoked cigarette.

'You're looking gorgeous, my love.' A tall, good-looking man in a terribly WASP-jock fashion, Dr MacLeod treated all The Club ladies like lovers and, in fact, many of them, including Liz at one time, were. 'What are you doing in here? You're not going to need my magic fingers for another two years or so.' He kissed her on the cheek. He smelled of soap and spicy, lemony aftershave.

'It's not me this time,' Liz said grimly. 'It's my daughter. Mindy, sit,' she snapped, as if to a small dog and Mindy obediently sat on the chaise longue next to her mother.

'Her nose looks just about perfect to me and she's a bit young for a lift, although Brooke S., know who I mean? — nudge nudge, wink, wink — was already been hounding me to do her upper and lower lids before she graduated from Yale.' Dr MacLeod laughed loudly at all his own jokes. He took a personal and professional look at Mindy. She does look rather like a dog, Robert MacLeod thought. He reached out to inspect her face, as she pulled away from his probing hands. Like an overgrown, bad-tempered pup, she appeared ready to bite any alien finger that came her way with that tight little mouth.

'It's not facial work we need done, Robbie. I'm afraid the problem is a bit . . . lower. I'm wondering if you might be able to . . . help us out here. Of course I know you don't usually do this sort of thing, but a friend of mine . . .' — Liz faltered, her mouth suddenly dry — 'well, Trudy McCamus actually, said you had helped her out when she was in trouble and . . .' She stopped again.

Robbie MacLeod stopped smiling. Turning to Mindy, he addressed her directly, 'How far along are you, love?'

'Huh?' Mindy looked bewildered.

'How many periods have you missed?'

The girl turned bright red. 'I dunno,' she mumbled.

'Don't mumble, Min. Just two,' her mother cut in firmly. 'She's exactly ten weeks' pregnant.'

448

Now Robbie looked surprised. 'How can you be so sure?'

'Because I keep a chart on her. It's not the first time, you know. She got pregnant eighteen months ago, right after her first period and since that little slip-up, I've been watching her pretty closely.'

'Not closely enough, eh, Mindy?' The doctor chuckled and winked conspiratorially at Mindy, who turned a deeper shade of red and looked down at the floor 'Why aren't you on the pill?'

'She is, goddamnit, she is! But she's been skipping days and then taking two or three pills at one time. Stupid girl!'

'I just forgot,' Mindy whined. 'I can't remember everything, you know?'

'How about remembering the word "no",' Liz snapped. 'Her father will kill her. He just can't handle the idea that his baby girl is . . .' God, how to put it — 'sexually active, not to mention stupid enough to get knocked up.'

Mindy glowered. 'Why can't I just have the baby and quit school? I don't want to go to Bryn Mawr. I don't even want to finish high school. I want to be a hairdresser.'

'You are not going to end up a hairdresser, not with the money I've spent on your education. Goddamnit, why can't you be a normal acquisitive, right-wing, consumer child like all your other little Yuppie friends?'

'Yeah, well, why can't you stay married? Daddy left you for a nineteen-year-old popsie,' Mindy taunted.

'The divorce was not my fault and you damn well know it!' Liz was steaming. 'You're lucky that I stuck with you. Go and live with your father if that's what you want. *If* he'll take you. See how you like that . . .'

'Girls, girls!' Dr MacLeod raised a placating hand. 'Let's solve Mindy's immediate problem and then the two of you can fight out her future between you. Now Mindy, you go through that door on the right and ask my nurse, Chloe, to give you 12 mg. of Valium to relax you. I promise you it won't hurt a bit and we'll clear this little situation up right away. It'll be over before you know it and you'll be good as new.' Mindy's lower lip trembled but obediently she trotted off down the hall, clutching her copy of *Teen Beat*.

'Can you call it a D-and-C?' Liz pleaded. 'Lee is still paying my Club bill and I don't want him to get suspicious. If he gets wind of this, he'll cut his payments.

'I can credit the surgery to you and, tell you what?' — Dr MacLeod chuckled and then, glancing quickly towards where Mindy had exited, he reached out and drew her into his arms. 'You know I'd do anything for you,' he whispered. 'How's about I just call it a tummy tuck?'

'Oh thank you, Robbie.' For a moment, she allowed herself to relax within his embrace. It felt so good and it had been such a long time. His hand reached under her jacket and found the silk of her camisole top . . .

'Mom, are you coming? Or do you expect me to go through major surgery all by myself?' The sound of Mindy's voice pulled them apart quickly.

'I'll be right there.' Liz hastily buttoned up her suede jacket and headed down the hall, then turned back to whisper gratefully, 'Thanks, Robbie. You're a lifesaver.'

'No problem.' The doctor favoured her with one of his conspiratorial winks. 'Always glad to help a lady in distress.'

450

# Twenty

'I want a divorce,' Susie said.

'You mean you're leaving me?' Lokis looked totally amazed, although Susie couldn't imagine why. He must have been expecting this.

'I've got to be on my own to sort things out. I've never really been on my own. I went straight from my father's house to Aunt Bea's to living with Tracy and going to art school in Minneapolis. I know it sounds selfish, but I just can't be part of a "we" any more. I need to be "me".'

'Are you telling me you're losing your identity? Don't make me laugh,' Lokis said bitterly. 'I'm the one who's become Mr Susie Krumins. I'm the one who's Prince Consort to the Cookie Queen.' He was trying to sound sarcastic, but Susie could see his lower lip quivering.

'I know, and that's not fair, either to you or to me. It put a real strain on the relationship, but that's not reason enough to break a trust. I can't live with you now, not after this.'

'Don't divorce me, Susie, please.' His eyes were really welling up with tears. 'I'm not ready for that, not yet!'

'All right, then, a trial separation,' Susie amended and instantly was angry with herself. 'You're the one who's been unfaithful,' she said as firmly as she could.

'Susie, please, give me a break. Merilee means nothing to me. I was just lonely and horny. I won't see her again, I promise. Please give me — us — another chance. It was

451

only once in ten years. A guy can make a mistake once, can't he?'

'It wasn't only once. From what I understand it was once on the kitchen floor, once in the kitchen sink, probably on the kitchen table, in the sauna at The Club, numerous times in her bed and at least once — and for this I really can't forgive you — in my bed.' Susie was amazed to discover how angry she was. Not just hurt and embarrassed, but downright furious with him.

'But it's only one woman! In all the years we've been together I've slept with only one other woman besides you.'

'And I've slept with no other man besides you.'

'Oh, so that's what this is all about. You're feeling cheated because you were a nineteen-year-old virgin when you married me and you never had a chance to screw around. If that's what you really want then go ahead, do it, have an affair. I give you permission.'

'That's disgusting! You don't understand me at all, do you? And let me remind you I don't need your permission to do anything.'

'Jesus, you've become so hard, so tough! The Club has really changed you. Can't we go back to the way we were? Whatever happened to my little Susie Sunshine?'

'She died,' Susie snapped. 'I made her up. And then I killed her. She wasn't me in the first place. I created her in high school because I was afraid I was going to go crazy like my mother so I simply became someone else.' The minute the words were out of her mouth, she knew they were true. 'What can I tell you? You fell in love with a fake. And, no, we can't go back because I wouldn't even know how to start over. I loved the idea of Susie *Sunshine*, too, and I tried to hold on to her as long as I could, but she slipped through my fingers. I'm not that person any more and neither are you. You're a New Yorker now and so am I. Susie *Sunshine*'s gone

452

and I don't know who or what is going to take her place.'

'So what do we do now? Are you kicking me out of the house?'

'No.' Susie took a deep breath. 'I'm moving in with Mina. You can keep the house.'

'You're moving in with that lesbian? She's going to jump you within two minutes! Maybe that's what you want. The Club is full of dykes and now you want to be one, too. Oh well, that explains everything,' he sneered. 'This has got nothing to do with me, does it? Or with Merilee. That's just an excuse so you can get rid of me. She's got you completely brainwashed, hasn't she? You're going to spend the rest of our life licking pussy.'

She made no attempt to argue further with Lokis. Once he realized her mind was made up it seemed that he was going to stay out of her way. Susie instructed her lawyer to start divorce proceedings while she turned her attention back to her business, which was demanding every single minute of her time. There were now over two hundred Kookie Krums stores throughout the US and the company was planning to move into Europe. Susie was exploring the idea of expanding into Japan as well.

Sweet Susie Enterprises had three vice-presidents in charge of operations, eight regional operations managers, a number of store managers, team leaders, and on down to the hourly employees. Right at the top of the pyramid was Susie herself, maintaining personal quality control over the entire operation. All the Kookie Krums stores were company-owned and -operated. No franchises for her. Each store was a member of the Kookie Krums family and responsible for keeping the product up to standard. The batter was made in Brooklyn Heights from Susie's own secret recipe and shipped to each store. Whole eggs and chocolate chips were added at each site. No automatic ovens were used either. The employees put the cookies into the ovens and pulled them out when they were done.

'No automatic ovens means no automatic pilot,' Susie told her trainees at the Kookie Krums training school in Brooklyn Heights. 'Each of you has a vested interest in the success of our product, the flavour and texture of each cookie you make and sell. That's why everyone at Kookie Krums, from the top executives to the cleaning staff, has to go through the experience of making and selling our cookies. You have to know what it feels like to put a cookie into a customer's hand. It's a wonderful feeing to make someone happy.' Susie no longer had to cheer on her customers but she continued to cheer on her staff and management teams. 'The money you earn is just part of it. This is a family business. Think of the employees of your outlet as your family. Remember, food is love.'

By the time Susie finished with them, they were champing at the bit to get out there and flog those cookies. Of course they were all in love with Susie Sunshine, too. What would they think of the real Susie if she ever found out what that was? Now was certainly not the time to explore it, not when she was getting extraordinary results out of her employees and fierce loyalty from her management teams. Which was just as well since they were now pretty much all the family she had. Except for Mina.

Was she making the right decision? Leaving Lokis, OK, but sharing a flat with another woman, wasn't that a step backwards? Shouldn't she be trying to make a go of it on her own? But she loved Mina's loft with its high ceilings and the broad expanse of white walls with the occasional photograph.

And she really did love Mina. Next to Lokis, Mina was the best friend she'd ever had. Living with her was turning out to be fun. She had both security and privacy. Little more was demanded of her than half the rent and a willing ear to listen to the continuing saga of Mina, the string of women who trooped through her bed and her life. She was always falling in love with married women, who would inevitably go back to their husbands, leaving her heartbroken, at least for a time.

'They look upon me as dessert while a man is the main meal,' Mina complained bitterly. 'I'm just a fling for them, something to be toyed with and enjoyed, then tossed aside while they go back to real life. For me it's true love. It's not fair.'

'You seem to fall in love an awful lot,' Susie observed wryly. 'I always thought that lesbians were the most faithful of all the sexual groups. Isn't it your theory that male homosexuality reinforces the male sexual impulse that is driven so strongly towards instant gratification? A man and a woman balance each other out in a system of checks and balances. Didn't you tell me that gay men are the most promiscuous?'

'Did I?' Mina sounded surprised, sipping her steaming coffee. 'Well, if I did, please don't repeat it. It's not considered politically correct. And it's probably not even true any more, given how AIDS has affected the homosexuality community. All the gay men I know are monogamous now. Getting married in unofficial ceremonies. Adopting children. It's all rather hopelessly middle-class. We were supposed to be sexual revolutionaries together and now they've sold out. Maybe it is a sudden need for fidelity, but I think more likely it's fear.'

'Didn't you tell me that gay women are the most faithful, that they get involved in long relationships?'

'We have the same vision you do: finding that one perfect mate, living happily ever after in a little house with a white picket fence, 2.3 children, and a dog.'

'So the relationship is more important than the sex.'

455

'That's not exactly true of me,' Mina grinned.

'No, I can see that. What's it like . . .' — Susie stopped, suddenly embarrassed — 'what's it like having sex with another woman?'

'You mean do we flip for who gets to be on top? No, it's not like that. For some women, it's an extension of self, you know, like touching yourself? But I think of it as more of a circular thing. When you make love with a man, and, yes, I have done that, the end result is almost always his orgasm. He warms you up, you do it, he comes, hopefully you come, and that's it.'

'You must have been sleeping with the wrong men!' Susie giggled.

'No, you know what I mean. No matter how great it is, how often he makes you come, once it's over, it's over. At least for a little while. It has to be. He scores a goal and then there's a rest period. Listen, I know it can be very intense and very exciting, but basically it's a direct line. Result-oriented. With a woman, it's like the sea, a continuous ebb and flow, waves washing over you, lifting you up and then gently letting you down. It's endless; you don't know where it begins or where it stops. It just keeps flowing, and you both keep riding the waves, circles within circles of desire.'

'It sounds wonderful.'

'It's different. I mean, desire is desire, sex is sex, but somehow it's different.'

'Do you feel normal?' Susie asked hesitantly.

'I know I'm not the norm, but, yes, I feel normal. The decision is not whether to be gay or straight. The decision is when and how you are going to accept what you are.'

Susie cleared her throat uncomfortably as she tried to formulate what she wanted to know next. 'When I told people I was moving in with you they, some of them, warned me you . . . well, you might try to seduce me.'

Mina nodded thoughtfully. 'Lokis, right? Men always think that gays are out to convert straights. I admit I've fallen in love with a lot of straight women but it wasn't because they were straight. That kind of challenge I don't need.'

'It wasn't just Lokis. A couple of women warned me as well.'

'And now you're disappointed that I haven't made a pass at you?' Mina looked amused.

'No. I don't now. Maybe.' Susie was suddenly flustered.

'Are you attracted to every guy who happens to have a piece of meat between his legs? No. Some guys you enjoy being with; some guys you just have to have. I love you, Susie, I really do. But what can I tell you? You're just not my type.'

'Oh.' What did she feel, disappointed, relieved, rejected? 'What is your type?'

'Slim, athletic, kind of rangy. Attractive, not necessarily beautiful. Super bright. Compassionate. And I'm a sucker for red hair.'

'Gwyneth Roberts,' Susie said suddenly. 'You're in love with Gwen.'

'Yep,' Mina said. 'And I'm not even sure if she's that way inclined. She's a mystery to me. Such a private person.'

Susie agreed. 'But you've been friends for a long time. Don't you talk about sex at all to her the way you do to me? I mean, she must know you're gay.'

'Well, we've never talked about it, but I suppose she must.'

'You don't exactly make a secret of it!' Susie snorted. 'Why don't you just tell her how you feel?'

'God, no, I couldn't,' Mina turned three shades of red and hid her face in her hands. 'What if I'm wrong about her? I've got this awful fear of making a complete and utter fool of myself. And once something like that is said, it can never be unsaid.'

'Well, sure, but if you don't say it, you'll never know. Are you really in love with her?'

'Yes,' Mina said in a low voice, ducking her head. 'There's no doubt about that, Gwyneth Roberts could have whatever she wanted from me. If she wanted it.'

In the weeks that followed Lokis wouldn't leave Susie alone. He couldn't accept the fact that she was gone for good. Whenever she walked into the loft the phone started ringing. If she didn't answer it, he often jumped in his car and drove over to pound on the door. He raced his car up and down the street late at night, early in the morning. Even before she was up and out of the house and down at The Club. Mina told her to call the police, but she couldn't do that, not to the man who had been her husband, her first love.

'He's chasing me harder now than he did before we got married,' she confessed to Mina.

'Why should that surprise you?' Mina was sitting cross-legged on the floor of the living-room. On the weekends they liked to clear out the liquor cabinet, polishing off the remains of the near-empty bottles before opening new ones. 'He misses your steady drawing hand and the way you used to match his socks for him.'

'He says now that I'm gone he realizes how much he loves me.'

'Sure. With men love equals need.' Mina finished the crème de menthe and started in on the Drambuie. 'Yuck. This stuff is awful. What a way to ruin good Scotch!'

Susie reached for the peach brandy. 'Since when are you an expert on long-term relationships? You go through lovers like Kleenex.'

'And I've always got an extra one up my sleeve in case I need to blow my nose. Oops, sorry. But you've shot

458

your wad on one measly J-cloth. You've got a million-dollar business to run. You can't let Lokis become an energy drain on your psyche.'

'I've left him physically. Why can't I leave him psychically, to use your word?'

'I think you surprised yourself by being the one to leave. I think all along you felt you weren't good enough for him and that eventually he would leave you. But he didn't, so you left him. Only you don't quite believe it. You're not used to being in a position of strength.'

'Then why do I feel so weak and worthless? Why do I feel he's won?'

'Guilt maybe? Good old-fashioned Minnesota middle-class guilt, the least productive emotion going.'

'But I'm making a fortune and feel like a failure.'

'That's crazy. When I met you you were crying because you were afraid you'd never accomplish anything. Now you've accomplished it and you're afraid you don't deserve it. Part of the impostor syndrome. "I don't know how I got here and if anybody finds out how worthless I am, I'll lose everything." It takes a tremendous amount of energy to hold on to that feeling of worthlessness. Any negative belief takes a lot more energy to uphold than a positive one.'

'Seth speaks?' Susie said cynically.

'No, as a matter of fact, Susie speaks. You were the one who told me that you can manipulate your circumstances the way you want them to be, that you can actually choose to be happy. I thought you were totally Pollyanna, but you've shown me that you're right. It's all in how you look at it. You now own a top-grossing business and you do a great job of running it.'

'No, I don't.'

'You must or it wouldn't be a success. In order to keep it going you have to at least pretend you're competent. It takes twice as much energy to pretend you're competent while believing inside you're a loser! Why don't you accept the fact that you *are* competent, more than competent, and just devote one hundred per cent of your energies to that?'

'But I keep making mistakes.'

'Well, sure. If you keep a bird blindfolded for years and suddenly take the blindfold off to let it fly free, it's bound to run into a few walls. But it is still flying. And so are you.'

Susie smiled. 'You know, that's the first time you've admitted that I've made a difference in the way you think.'

'That's exactly what I mean! Of course you've had an effect on me. I'm not always right about everything. I just shout louder than you do.'

'Mina, do you realize how much money you've saved me in psychiatrist fees?'

Mina gave her a hug. 'What are friends for?'

Mina was away for the weekend on a shoot when Lokis broke in to the apartment and made his way up the stairs into Susie's bedroom. She came out of the shower, wet and dripping, her hair plastered against her head, but to him it didn't matter. He wanted to fuck her and he wanted to fuck her now. It had been so long since he'd touched her, she wouldn't let him near her, wouldn't answer his calls, slammed the door in his face, and she needed to be punished. Bitch, goddess, whore — his mind was turning over every agonizing humiliation. Stripping the towel from her hands before she could utter a sound, he threw her on to the bed and kissed her hard, forcing her mouth open, his fingers pressing into her flesh, feeling her struggle against him, thrusting his tongue between her teeth, running his hand up and down her body, reclaiming possession. Holding her hands away from him, he bit at her neck, her breasts, grinding his hips against her bare

460

skin, the snaps of his shirt scraping against her nipples, the zipper of his jeans catching in her pubic hair.

After her initial shock, Susie fought back, twisting and turning, trying to get away from him. When it only seemed to excite him more, she stopped fighting. She hated him for doing this to her, but she knew what he was really after. Power. Lost power. Holding her down with one hand, Lokis sprang the snaps on his shirt and pulled his jeans down. He threw himself on her, shoving her legs apart, driving into her, pinning her to the bed, pulling out and slamming into her again, over and over. His eyes were wild and she could hear his breath rasping in his throat. She turned her head away and closed her eyes.

God, she was gorgeous, lying there under him, Lokis thought, feeling the magnetic pull of the familiar. Her body seemed harder than he remembered, hip bones digging into him, but his own pain felt good. He wanted her to feel it too, to feel herself the pain she had made him feel, get through to her, make her cry, make her beg for mercy. As he slammed into her over and over again, his mind screamed out silently, Hurt! Hurt! Take it! Take it! You deserve it! And he was winning this round. He could feel her arms come around him, her fingers slipping between his buttocks. He tried to escape them, didn't want to come yet, not yet, wanted to make it last, but he couldn't stop, he was going to explode, feeling himself grow larger within her, trying to hold off, can't, can't, and with a long low groan, the life drained out of him. He lay there panting across her body. She lay very still underneath him. 'You made me come,' he panted finally, moving off her.

'And not a moment too soon.' Susie abruptly pulled away from him. Her face was white. 'Do you realize I could charge you with rape? For what you just did to me?'

461

'What?' He hadn't come back to earth yet.

'Rape. You just raped me.' She watched the flush of exertion recede from his face.

'What are you talking about?' He struggled up on to his elbow, trying to understand what she was saying. Her voice seemed to be coming from far away.

'Marital rape. It's fairly new on the books, but it *is* a crime.' Susie got off the bed, grabbed the towel, and started rubbing her still damp hair.

'I don't understand.'

'The Rideout case. John and Greta Rideout. Unlawful sexual intercourse without permission. That's what you just committed.'

'But I'm your husband.' Lokis looked at her with utter bewilderment. 'What about marital rights?'

'Doesn't matter if we're married.' Susie returned his gaze steadily. 'Rape is rape.'

'But you gave your permission.'

'When?'

'Well you must have.' His heart was hammering and he could feel beads of sweat leap out on his forehead. 'At least you went along with it'

'Did I?' She looked him straight in the eye.

'Well, I mean, you didn't exactly resist.'

'How could I? You're bigger than I am. And stronger. Isn't that the point? Wasn't that what you were trying to prove?'

'Prove? I wasn't trying to *prove* anything. I just wanted to touch you, to win you back somehow . . .' He broke off helplessly.

'How? By overpowering me? By showing me who's boss?'

'No, Jesus, no! Why do you twist everything I say to make me the enemy? I didn't rape you! Sex is a natural force!'

'Yes, it's natural. But it's still a form of aggression.

462

Like other unnatural ways of handling aggression. War. Torture. And rape.'

'Where did you learn that garbage? The Club? Dyke paradise? A bunch of bitches sitting around bitching about men?'

'Rape is not a sexual act. It's an act of violence.'

'All right, all right, all right! I get the picture. You listen to your lesbo friends if you want to, and you play the victim, but I'm telling you that was no rape. You went along with it.'

'I went along with it because I had no choice. Our motives for the act were different. You fucked me' — watching him wince — 'yes, that's the word, you fucked me to establish control. I let you fuck me to set myself free.'

His face darkened with rage. 'Well, you're not free. That goddamned club. And I actually was crazy enough to invest in it. Fifty thousand bucks! I should never have given you the money to join in the first place. I should never have given you the money for the business either. Remember that? I paid for all this. $10,000 to join The Club? $65,000 to open your store? $125,000 it cost me to turn you from a wife into a ball-breaker.'

Susie started to laugh. She reached for her purse. 'Watch me!' she said. 'You once did this for me. Now I'm doing it for you.' She wrote him a cheque. Handing it to him, she said, 'There you go. $250,000. That's a one-hundred-per-cent return on your initial investment. Thanks for the loan. Your money was well spent. We're even now. Now I'm giving you exactly two minutes to put your clothes on and get out of my life. If you'll excuse me, I'm going to take another shower.' Still laughing, she turned on her heel and went into the bathroom, slamming the door.

Six weeks later, when she missed her period, she stopped

463

laughing. The joke was on her. After all those years of trying to conceive a child in love, one had now been conceived in hate. Through force. She could already feel the life lodged inside her and she wanted to hit her stomach. Outwardly she raged at Lokis but inwardly she raged at herself. How could she have allowed this to happen? It was her fault. She should have fought him harder. She didn't want a child. Not now. Not like this. Not when she was free for the first time in her life. If she told Lokis she was carrying his child, he would never let her go.

Mina was ecstatic. 'It's great! It's what you've always wanted! Now take that cigarette out of your mouth! You can't smoke if you're pregnant. Bad for the baby.'

'I know, it's what I've always wanted, but not like this. How can I possibly have his baby?'

'But ever since I met you you've been crazy to have a kid.'

'That feeling's gone. That's what I'm telling you. I feel nothing about what's growing inside me. Nothing except frightened and unprepared. It's taken me thirty years to learn to take care of myself. And there's the business. I don't need any added responsibilities right now. I can't handle it.'

'I'll help you. Look, I'd love to have a little baby running around here. We can raise her together. I can photograph you at every.stage of your pregnancy. We can write a book about the joys of single motherhood.'

'I don't want to be a single mother! I don't want to raise a child without a man. It's too hard. Oh Mina, what if it turned out to be deformed or retarded or something?'

'You're only thirty-three.'

'Almost thirty-four.'

'So what? You know, Susie, you really are obsessed with age. Plenty of women even into their forties have

464

perfectly healthy babies. There's not going to be anything
wrong with this baby.'

'But what if there was?'

'This is what you've always wanted. It's time to grow
up, Susie.'

'No, no,' her voice sounded shrill and tiny even in her
own ears. 'I can't handle it. I just can't handle it!'

'So you're going to have an abortion.'

'I don't know. We're talking about twenty years of my
life, you know. I'd be over fifty by the time it's . . . in
college.'

'If you really want an abortion, you don't have to go
to the hospital. Or a clinic,' Mina said quietly. 'You can
have one at The Club.'

'What?'

'It's part of the private retreat services. I know, because
a friend of mine, Clare Holt, had an abortion done there
last fall. Go and talk to Gwen. Get her advice. At least
she'll be objective. I'm not. I admit it. I'd love to see a
little baby toddling around here. I believe in a woman's
right to own her own body and all that and I know it's
your decision and only yours, but Susie . . .'

'Yes?'

'Be sure that your decision is the right one.'

As always, Gwen listened intently to all that Susie had
to say, letting her spill everything out. Then she started
to speak, weighing all the arguments, exploring all the
options and then finally voicing the one fear that Susie
hadn't even realized she had. 'You're afraid that if you
have this baby it will send you right back into the arms
of your husband.'

'Yes you're right.' Susie was astonished at her
perception. 'It was so tough making the decision to leave
Lokis. I just know I wouldn't have the courage to stand
behind it if I continued with the pregnancy.'

'Why? It shouldn't make a difference. If you feel that it will, it will; but it shouldn't.'

'You don't understand, Gwen. It's like there's this life-raft. In the middle of the ocean. Only one person can be saved. There's only room for one on the raft. And goddamnit, the survivor is going to be me!' Susie got up and rushed out of the office, brushing past Merilee who was on her way in to see Gwen.

'What was that all about?' Merilee asked.

'Please don't repeat this to anyone. Susie just told me in strictest confidence that she's pregnant and she wants to have an abortion. You saw how upset she was.'

'Gwen, you can trust me. I won't breathe a word of it.' Merilee turned away to hide her smile. Interesting. Very interesting. This was extremely useful information. She would bide her time, hold on to it for a while, until she figured out just the right moment to tell Lokis that his ex-wife was planning to get rid of his baby.

# Twenty-one

How dare they? Sara was fairly quivering with anger. How dare they try to edge her out as co-anchor and replace her with a twenty-seven-year-old bimbo, a former Miss Kentucky? She should never have left the security of CNN for the cut-throat competition of the majors.

She'd known there was bound to be trouble when Jack Melville was brought in as a senior vice-president. A new broom always wants to sweep clean. She had sensed even more trouble when Dahlia Lee was brought on board as a 'back-up' newscaster. Sara didn't need a back-up; she'd never missed a broadcast in her life. Oh yes, she'd known someone was about to get dumped but she hadn't expected it to be her, she'd expected it to be the senior anchor, her male colleague, Peter Harrison. He could barely get it up to read the news these days and during most of his interviews had to be fed a constant stream of information through his earpiece in order to ask even one intelligent question. So why weren't they dumping him? Because the rule in television news was a middle-aged male anchor and a younger, female co-anchor. As far as they were concerned, Sara was approaching middle age. God, it wasn't fair. She hadn't even turned forty yet and she looked maybe thirty-two at the most.

Old. They thought she was too old. Of course, none of them had the guts to say so to her face. At the moment, they weren't saying any thing at all except to drop a few veiled hints.

Hadn't Dahlia taken to the tough prime-time news biz like a duck to water? Sara could only nod and smile in agreement, knowing full well that what they were really admiring were Dahlia's silicon tits, luxuriant hair extensions, and radiant smile of undoubtedly white bonded teeth. In fact, the ex-beauty queen owed both her former state title and her present career to one Dr Marty Silverman who had been on the panel of county judges and who, like a modern-day Frankenstein, had remade her into the monument to womanhood she was today.

Dahlia was supposed to appeal to the under-thirty set. Dahlia with her gentle manner and soft-spoken style who was not only happily married but with twin boys, no less, apparently able to keep it all together, marriage, family, and career.

Never mind that her journalistic credentials didn't come close to Sara's at that age. These days the networks appeared to be more interested in what Linda Ellerbee called 'Twinkies' than they were in real journalists with experience in the big issues. The public had fallen in love with Dahlia Lee and she had appeared, with her big-bruiser husband and a twin under each arm, on every magazine cover from *Newsweek* to *Good Housekeeping*.

To make things even worse for Sara, Dahlia Lee was black. Not truly dark-skinned, more café au lait, with neat little Caucasian features, but definitely black and proud of it. In fact, she never shut up about it, and it was partly what had got her the job in the first place. The pressure was on the networks to hire visible minorities, members of 'our ethnic communities'.

The irony of this situation was not lost on Sara. She could hardly declare herself black at this stage of the game. She would laugh if she didn't feel a hell of a lot more like crying. She had changed her name, changed her persona, wiped out her background as if it had never existed. At night, when she walked into her own

468

apartment and shut the door on the outside world, even then she was not truly herself. The apartment was decorated in the style of someone named Sara Town. Who the hell was Sara Town?

The tabloids were having a field day, keeping an eye on the new ménage à trois of Sara, Peter, and Dahlia. If two was uneasy company, three was definitely a crowd, One of them would have to go and probably very soon. Of course Peter was revelling in the controversy. Secure in his own position, he appeared to have two gorgeous women dancing attention on him in grand style. And, boy, did that bimbo Dahlia know how to suck up, picking out new ties for Peter in colours that would work better on camera, baking pecan muffins for the crew and giving make-up tips to the female production assistants. It was enough to make Sara puke, but the main thing Dahlia had going for her was her air of innocence and sincerity.

And much as Sara hated to admit it, Dahlia probably *was* sincere. She had been a straight 'A' student at the University of Kentucky and a winner of the Humana Award for achievement in broadcasting. Things appeared to have come relatively easy to Dahlia Lee, despite her being black, whereas it had been a long hard struggle for Sara Town.

The tabloids and the talk-show hosts were monitoring the situation, too. They were full of praise for the network bosses who had given such a high-paying position to a young black female journalist. These days Sara was afraid to turn on the television or to pick up a newspaper for fear there would be another screaming headline about how her position as queen of the press hill was rocky as she was in danger of being shoved off the mountain.

Through all of the shit, it was vital that she maintain at least a superficial civility with both Peter and Dahlia, not always an easy thing to do. She and Dahlia were constantly being asked by photographers to hug each other or shake hands to prove there were 'no hard feelings'. What a laugh. Nothing would make Sara happier than to find Dahlia dead, face down in her own vomit.

How could they do this to her? Everybody knew that Dahlia Lee was just a bit of fluff and that Peter Harrison was merely along for the ride. Surely Sara wasn't in any real danger. She couldn't be.

She knew the powers that be, the male executives, considered her a threat to them. After all, she wasn't some beauty queen bimbo who would put up and shut up. But what the hell was she going to do? Thanks to Michael Taylor's negotiating skills, she was making more money than she'd ever made in her life. If she behaved like a good little girl, they might channel her into another area, but at least they probably wouldn't cut her yearly income. Was the money worth such humiliation? It was the waiting for the other shoe to drop that was driving her crazy. It was ruining her life. She couldn't eat. She couldn't sleep. Even sex didn't work any more.

Michael had spent the night with her last night and she had awakened to feel his erection pushing against her. Her lips curved into a cynical smile. Even in his sleep, he stood at attention for her. How sweet. Idly she ran her hand down the smooth chest, circling the small pouting nipples, watching them contact at her touch.

In the beginning, Michael's youthful body had been a marvel of engineering, but lately her world-weary fingers had begun to detect the beginnings of a slight paunch, a gradual softening of the body, a subtle blurring of the edges. His forehead had been as smooth as a china plate when she first signed with him; now it displayed signs of turning into the Magna Carta by the time he was her age. It was the booze and cigarettes. Destroyed the Vitamin C. Pretty soon Michael would have to start exchanging his cases of J and B for cases of Oil of Ulay.

Still there was one part of him that remained unchanged. It was rather nice to have your own personal erector set. Mind you, it had little to do with her. An alcoholic, urea-filled, early morning hard-on was not much to write home about. She rolled away from him and reached for the glass of mineral water she always kept on the night table during marathon sex sessions. She always seemed to gulp air when she came. She took a long drink.

Michael slept heavily beside her, smelling of nicotine and stale beer. What the hell was she doing here with this overgrown Pac-Man addict in her bed? Now that she was in danger of losing it all, she was afraid, so afraid. She looked down at the sodden lump lying next to her, one hand clutching the pillow, the other clinging to her silk teddy. The least he could do was wake up and fuck her.

She gave him a nudge with her knee. Nothing. Gently at first, then harder, she poked him, digging her fingernails into the flesh of his stomach. She blew in his ear, she bit him on the neck, she tickled him under his arms. Sighing heavily, he pushed her away and shifted to the other side of the bed.

Slipping down towards the foot of the bed, she took him into her mouth. Just a tiny bit at first, licking carefully, fingers holding him at the base, then mouth sliding up and down the shaft, applying gentle suction, feeling him jump in her hand, throb between her fingers. Michael stirred, his hips twitching convulsively, his eyes still closed, the rest of his body passive. She shifted her zone of attack, taking her mouth off him, biting the insides of his thighs, squeezing his buttocks. Michael sleepily moved his cock in the direction of her mouth and she took it again, her hand grasping him, pumping him, but his eyes remained closed. Why the hell didn't he wake up? Like a human hoover, she sucked his cock into her mouth, creating a vacuum, letting him slip almost all the

471

way out and then catching him by surprise, drawing him again as far as she could take him. His eyes were squeezed shut, his breathing remained unchanged, but his hips were moving like a piston. Was he asleep or just faking it? With all the delicacy of a pure-bred bluepoint Siamese, Sara sank her teeth into him — a surprise attack that caused him to let out a bloodcurdling yell as the hot liquid flew out of him. His eyes snapped open.

'Jesus, Sara!' he cried, pulling himself away, 'What are you trying to do, castrate me?'

'Just trying to get your attention, darling,' Sara snuggled up against him.

'Well, that's a hell of a way to do it!' Michael examined himself worriedly, for visible signs of damage, fully awake now.

'Oh come on, I didn't bite you very hard. It was just a little love bite.' She stroked the side of his thigh and kissed him lovingly on the elbow.

'Some love bite.' He pushed her hand away. 'Don't you realize that's the basis of every male's morbid fear of fellatio?'

'Every male's? What do you mean?'

'Entrusting the most tender part of the male body to the possible danger of a female's jaws. Jesus, I think you did some permanent damage there. I'll never play the violin again.' Sara reached for him, but he slapped her away. 'Hands off!'

'My turn then.' Sara pulled her nightie up to her waist, but Michael's eyes were already closing in the hopes of holding off the hangover agony for at least another hour. 'Come on, love,' she whispered.

'Gotta sleep now,' Michael mumbled into his pillow, 'Got a screening first thing in the morning.'

'Oh for Christ's sake.' She whipped off her nightgown, climbed over Michael, and sat own on his head.

Like a dog galvanized by the scent, Michael began to

act, sending electric currents charging through his body and into hers. A she moaned and writhed above him, his mouth turning her to liquid fire, she thought about how useful he had been to her. He had been worth every penny she paid him as an agent. Now she was about to give him a little nocturnal commission. As far as Sara was concerned, soixante-neuf was where you separated the men from the boys. Some were too dainty, bringing you to the edge but no further. Others thrashed about, slurping and sliding hopelessly. And then there were those who took the bit between their teeth, as it were, and worried it like a dog with a bone. Hysterically hopeless, all of them, but it was no laughing matter when you were dying to get off. Her own climax interrupted her thoughts as she bucked and tossed and then came to a shuddering standstill like the old ride-the-horsie-for-a-dime machines at JC Penney.

She sighed and rolled off Michael, got out of bed and went over to the dresser for some Kleenex. Glancing in the mirror she saw that she was crying, soundlessly, tears streaming down her face. There was an aching, gut-wrenching fear in the pit of her stomach. The overwhelming emptiness of her life seemed to rise up and surround her. She blew her nose and slipped back into bed. 'Michael,' she said softly, sliding down next to him and wrapping her arms around him. But she could tell from his shallow, even breathing that he was already asleep again. When she woke in the morning, he had left for work. There was no sign of him except the faint odour of cigarette smoke that clung to the pillow.

Sara sighed. The waiting was killing her. Had the network made up its mind about her future? Or were they waiting to see how the public might feel about her imminent departure? Certainly she was popular, all the polls reflected that, and the viewing public was known for resisting change. She felt like saying to them, why fix it if it ain't broke? But the trouble was she couldn't really say anything to them; she had to pretend that everything was just fine. The ball was in their court and they knew it.

The phone rang, a tiny electronic purr that immediately set her teeth on edge.

'Hello,' she snapped.

'Hi, it's Michael.'

'Look, forget it. I don't want to see you tonight. I'm not in the mood.'

'This call's not personal,' Michael said quickly. 'It's business.'

Sara felt her stomach turn over. 'Have you heard anything definite from the bosses?'

'No. But in the meantime, we have had an offer from CNN.'

'Forget it. That's where I came from. It would be a step down to go back there.' She almost hung up on him when he continued quickly.

'Wait a minute! It's a terrific offer! They want to create a brand new prime-time news magazine show for you. You know, something to give *60 Minutes* and *Prime Time Live* a run for their money? Working title *In Depth*. An hour-long weekly show built completely around you!'

'No co-anchor?'

'Just you. They think you can carry it all by yourself.'

'Damn straight I can.' Suddenly she was alive again. She tried to speak calmly. 'What are they offering in terms of money?'

'Are you sitting down?' Michael could hardly control the excitement — and greed — in his voice. 'A million and a quarter. I have a feeling I can drive them up to a mil and a half.'

Sara whistled softly. 'Nobody's worth that.'

'You are baby.'

'Not even me. Margaret Thatcher doesn't make that and she runs an entire country.'

'Take it while you can. I intend to buy myself a new Porsche.'

Sara hung up the phone and laughed out loud. Tomorrow she was going to march straight into Jack Melville's office and tell him she was quitting. She could hardly wait to see the look on his pockmarked face. Let Peter and Dahlia have each other; she had bigger fish to fry. Her own show! She felt light-headed, the burden of the last two months suddenly lifted miraculously from her shoulders. Maybe she was a little bruised and battered but, like the streetsmart alley cat, she was indomitable. She'd come close to using up every one of her nine lives but once again Sara Town had landed on her feet.

# Twenty-two

Luigi del Bello and Stephen Andrews were relaxing in Lou's private office. Gwen had a working office with her desk and computer but she also had a salon for more informal business meetings, so Lou had insisted upon having his own 'salon'. It was a room that could only be accessed with his personal code. 'It's not that I'm trying to keep you out,' he told Gwen and Merilee, 'but The Club is for women. You can basically go anywhere you want, while there are certain areas that are off limits to me. I need my privacy, too, a place where I can be on my own. Of course you're welcome any time. If the door's locked, just buzz me and I'll open up.'

Lou's private office was wood-panelled and tastefully decorated in an elegant, masculine style. Except for a large desk whose top concealed his built-in personal computer terminal, the room, with its large leather sofa and glass-topped table, looked more like a living-room than an office. Its best attributes were in hiding: press the right panel and the fully stocked bar swung out; press another panel and a king-sized Murphy bed dropped out of the wall. Press yet another panel and it revealed his private cachet of social drugs. Lou ensured that he was surrounded by all the comforts of home.

Stephen moved to the bar to freshen his drink. He felt safe and secure here, away from the prying eyes of the world. 'Thanks for talking to Gwen,' he said, pouring himself a shot of absinthe. The lethal liquorice-flavoured liqueur was illegal in North America but trust Lou to be able to get his hands on it from somewhere. 'Having The Club behind me is going to make a big difference to the campaign.'

'It was nothing,' Lou said in Italian, stretching out his legs and kicking off his Guccis. 'You scratch my back, I'll scratch yours. It's good for you, it's good for The Club, and it's also very good for the boss lady. Getting involved in your campaign is just what she needs. She doesn't have many outside interests.'

He made it sound easy, but actually it had taken a lot of talking to convince Gwen. She and Lou weren't as close as they used to be, maybe because she was spending a lot of time with Merilee. She didn't seem to trust him as much as she once did and she wasn't sure about Stephen Andrews either. He appeared to be well-versed in women's issues and his voting record was OK, but could he be counted on to stay on side with those issues when and if he was elected? Lou had assured her he could.

'I need her support,' Stephen added unnecessarily.

'Well you've got it. Just keep toeing that feminist line.' Lou laid out a couple of lines of coke on the glass-topped table. 'You have to try this stuff. High grade. Pure Colombian. Not like some of that shit that's cut with too much mannite. You snort that, you spend your whole time in the john. Goes right through you.'

'Sure, sure in a minute. But I don't regard it as a feminist line. Women really are becoming an important part of the power base in this country. The Club represents a lot of the most powerful ones. They have a lot of clout.'

'You can say that again.' Lou ripped a page out of a back issue of *Penthouse* and neatly folded it, isolating the apparently helium-filled mammaries of the Pet of the Month.

478

'With The Club behind me, I'll have female visibility in the campaign, which will give me even more credibility with women voters.'

'*Bene*.' Lou rolled the pet's breasts into a careful cone and delicately inhaled a line into each nostril. 'So how's it going with *la bella signorina* Hughes?' he asked.

'Great. You know there's something so purifying about sleeping with a virgin, conquering a territory that's completely unknown. There's so much Laura has to learn and so much I can teach her.'

'Funny, I would have thought your tastes lay in a different direction,' Lou said, his snake's eyes sweeping over him.

Stephen laughed and rolled up the pet's spread shot to snort the other two lines. He enjoyed the nostril-numbing sensation. He felt as if the top of his head were about to fly off. 'You're right, Lou, this blow is wild! What a rush!'

'Or should I say,' Lou continued, 'that from what you've shared with me of your sexual history, you prefer something a little more exotic?'

Luigi's tone was light and easy, but Stephen was suddenly aware of how much of his own body his silk dress shirt and double pleated linen trousers revealed. He crossed his legs. 'What do you mean?' he asked, unable to look away from Lou's small, glittering eyes.

'Something . . . *come si dice* . . . closer to the edge?'

'Hell, I've done everything there is to be done,' Stephen said with attempted bravado. 'I'm jaded. There's nothing left to be explored.'

'Can you really be sure of that?' Lou was leaning forward now, his eyes boring into Stephen's own.

'What do you mean?' Stephen repeated, finding it difficult to breathe. The physical presence of the man sitting beside him was suddenly overpowering. Luigi was not conventionally handsome but he dressed very well and

479

he had a male presence that was compelling. His hair was thick and curly, just beginning to grey, and the chest hair curling around the casually unbuttoned chamois sport shirt was wiry and plentiful. He had a beautifully shaped head, a sensual mouth, and a strong nose. Suddenly Stephen was riveted to him.

'I'm sure you've heard I like it both ways.' Lou's look assessed him with open provocation and complete enjoyment. As long as the prize was within reach, and he was pretty sure it was, he was willing to wait. He stretched his arm across the back of the leather sofa and touched Stephen lightly on the shoulder. He knew he would have to tread softly. A good sex partner he could locate any time but a good friend and business contact was something to hold on to. And yet, there was something so deliciously attractive about a straight man going gay. They wanted it so desperately. Since it was outside their norm, they felt guilty about it and the guiltier they got, the hotter they got. 'You are a beautiful specimen Stephen,' Lou said in a deep, quiet voice. 'A beautiful male animal, *sai*?'

Stephen's face burned and his throat went dry. He felt himself trembling slightly as he studied Lou's soft, practised mouth and imagined slipping himself inside it. It was important, he knew, that he stay in control.

Lou took Stephen's hand and moved it slowly up his own thigh. 'You see?' he asked. 'You see what you do to me?'

Stephen pulled his hand away but he couldn't take his eyes off the erection straining against the buttons of Lou's trousers. He, Stephen, had caused that. What a sense of power it gave him to turn another man on. He hesitated and then decided. Why limit himself? He reached over and took Lou's hand, returning his intense gaze boldly for the fist time. The current that passed between them surprised and jolted them both.

'I don't know if I'm ready for this,' Stephen said quietly.

Lou smiled ever so slightly. 'Why don't we try it and find out?'

'All right,' Stephen whispered hoarsely. 'But not here.'

Merilee caught Lou and Stephen just as they were leaving Lou's private office. 'Lou baby, you've just got to help! I've just wiped out the entire program from my computer!'

'You couldn't have.' Lou stopped while Stephen paused nervously in the doorway. He looked torn between escaping and staring in fascination at the fluffy-haired apparition in pink 'How?'

'Well, I had just finished programming this month's events schedule and I meant to copy it on to a floppy so I could put it in my file, you know?' She held up a small diskette. 'And then I realized I didn't have any pre-formatted disks so I got a blank one from the office.'

'*Si, si,*' Lou said impatiently, sensing that his prey was preparing to bolt.

'So I put in the new disk and I typed in "format" and it said "to format the C drive, punch any key." Well, I didn't know what to do because I wasn't tryin' to format the hard drive, I was just trying to do the A drive for the disk, so I hit "escape" and of course "escape" is a key. And everything went blank. The hard drive's completely gone and now I can't do anything with my machine until I get the whole DOS system back in there.'

'Merilee, Stephen and I are just heading out for a very important meeting,' Lou said, trying to conceal the urgency in his voice. 'I don't have time to put it in now, *sai*?'

'Oh, I know, honey, and I'm not askin' you to. You can do it tomorrow, but in the meantime, could you let me use your computer? If don't get this spreadsheet done within the next hour, Gwen is gonna kill me.'

'I'm sorry, *cara*, but I'm locking my office up now. This meeting could run into the evening; I don't know if I'll be back. Why don't you go into the members' computer room and use one of the terminals there?'

'They're all booked for the whole evening.' Merilee looked ready to cry.

'Then use the one in Gwen's office.'

'I can't. She's on her computer and I don't want to bother her. I don't want her to know I did such a dumb stupid-ass thing. I just want to finish what I was working on and get the machine fixed tomorrow.'

'Look, Lou, if we're going to have this meeting, we've got to get out of here now.' Stephen turned abruptly and headed down the hall.

'All right, all right, you can use my computer. Just make sure the door to my private office is closed tight when you leave.'

'Oh, thank you, baby doll! You're an angel!' She managed to give him a quick kiss before he hurried off down the hall after Stephen.

Merilee closed the door to Lou's private office and leaned against it, shaking with silent laughter. What an idiot he was! She looked around the room. It was all familiar to her. They had made love a few times on that leather couch; Lou liked the smell of leather. She knew about the Murphy bed; they'd made love on that, too. Now she was looking for something bigger than the private bar and the coke paraphernalia. She had a feeling Lou's secret was locked away in his computer.

His computer was programmed to access all the other computers in the building, and he'd put a lock on his own machine so that other people couldn't get into his. There had to be a secret access code. She lifted the top of the desk and pulled out the computer. As she waited for the machine to boot up, she tried to think of possible passwords Lou might have chosen for his most personal files. The words came up o the screen, 'Open which file?'

She typed variations on his name. Nothing. She tried them backwards. 'Cannot find file' was the response. Suddenly she remembered Lou saying to her, 'I am defined by my sexuality.' She typed in all the synonyms for 'homosexual' she could think of, without success. And then she tried *finocchio*. Bull's eye! Suddenly the screen was full of strange files and documents. 10-11-3 am – drop – St Andrews by the Sea – Lobster. 1-12-8 pm – drop – Montreal – Emmenthal. There were pages and pages of entries and they all seemed to have something to do with food. She didn't know what any of it meant, but she knew she had stumbled on to a gold mine.

Luigi del Bello was a relative amateur in the increasingly professional field of drug-dealing. Cocaine had become a worldwide industry, but there was always room for the little corner-store business, a place for the hustler, and Lou had always been a hustler. Like a lot of other kids in the late sixties, he had sold grass. He was busted once, for possession. Never for dealing. In those days if you hadn't been busted for possession at least once, you were treading water way out of the mainstream.

Running Carpaccio's, he'd stayed pretty clean. But cocaine was a drug of mystique and glamour, the social drug of choice for movie stars and rock groups; it was part of making the scene and very hard to resist. It made him feel powerful, brilliant, in charge of all his faculties and those faculties were even sharper than usual. Just before Gwen had approached him about The Club, Lou flew down to Bogota where he fell hard for the joys of the brown boys and the thrill of the lady in white. He scored a contact for pure Colombian coffee and also for erythroxylon coca.

He started out in a small-time way, as an occasional user, and a supplier for lovers, close friends, and eventually favoured Club members. He maintained a connection with the Italian brotherhood who kept him supplied as long as he was dealing in small amounts. Sometimes he cut the stuff himself with just a bit of baby laxative to smooth it along and make a little extra on the side. But the pressure to keep up with the growth of The Club and Gwen's continual plans to expand had pushed him into a corner until he had no choice but to move into the big time. He'd never crossed a border himself any way but clean; he had never had to. The brotherhood came up with the most ingenious methods to keep his clients supplied.

The mob moved it in through Miami. The mules were single parents, sometimes men, but usually unwed mothers. A woman carrying a baby, a diaper-changing bag complete with disposable diapers, zinc ointment, and baby powder was never searched. They were paid fifteen hundred flat to walk it across the border, plus a free vacation in South America or a visit to the famous baby clinic in Key West.

It had been even easier, and much safer because there were fewer variables, to have it shipped in with the high-grade coffee The Club was so famous for. A kilo of coke could easily get lost in a large shipment of coffee beans. His cousin Giuseppe remained a safe contact in the food import business; they knew they could count on him to keep his mouth shut.

Then a runner was caught. The police were checking every bag of coffee. The brotherhood told Lou they would have to lie low for a while and wait.

But Lou couldn't wait. Up to this point, he had basically been a distributor. Now he wanted to move

484

himself up the chain, even if it meant bringing stuff in on his own without protection. He was looking for a safer connection and he found it — in Canada. There were miles of unprotected entry points along the US—Canadian border. The Colombians could fly into an airstrip in New Brunswick and make the drop there, provided Lou could find a way to get it across the border into Maine and down to New York. Of course Lou could find a way. And if it worked, it would mean he would eliminate the middle man and be the main supplier. And there was a chance he could score big.

He had a small load shipped in along with crates of lobster. It was easy. He was elated. Next he tried packing it in heavy, wax-lined cardboard boxes of Malpecque oysters from Prince Edward Island and the highly prized Bras d'or oysters from Cape Breton. He made a deal with a commercial company who canned oyster stew to recycle the empty shells to his supplier. His supplier filled the shells with coke, sealed them with wax, packed them up and loaded them along with the other boxes of fresh oysters into a refrigerated truck bound for New York. Again, there were no repercussions. When the customs officials came aboard the truck, they wouldn't dream of ruining the product by opening the oysters and, noting that the order was always the same, they eventually just waved the truck on through.

The Bras d'or special was a big hit with Club members who were willing to pay several times the going street price for the drug of their choice to avoid the risk of buying it on the street. Cheap Crack with all its connotations of ghetto crack houses and rat-infested slums was not for them. They wanted the real thing and they were willing to pay top bucks for it.

It was the perfect solution for Lou's financial problems. Now he could build that weekend place on Fire Island, take the odd vacation in the Florida Keys or

Thailand, invest in a new car. And of course some of the revenue he would simply plough straight back into The Club.

It was vital that the brotherhood know nothing about his arrangements. As far as they were concerned their job was to bring it in and Lou's job was to distribute. For the moment, they believed their connection had dried up, but if they learned that Lou had found a way to bring it in and cut them out of the deal he would be in big trouble.

It was vital that Gwen know nothing about this either, of course. He was greatly indebted to her and he wanted to do everything he could to make her happy, everything possible to fulfil her dreams, everything within his power to keep The Club alive. After all, it was The Club that had made all this possible.

# *Twenty-three*

Los Angeles, California. Miriam and Tabitha flew to LA
for the Golden Globe Awards. She had won both the New
York Critics' and the LA Critics' prizes for *Paloma* so
chances were looking good for this one, too. As they
landed at LAX they were bracing themselves for the usual
hassle of claiming their luggage and locating the studio
car and driver as they came through the arrivals gate,
when Miriam was suddenly surrounded by a barrage of
photographers, all calling out, 'Miriam. Hey, Miriam,
over here.' 'Miriam. Look this way, Miriam.' 'Why are
they calling me by my first name?' she asked, amazed
by all the attention. Nothing like this had happened on
their trips to Boston or Toronto.

'To get you to look straight into the camera. Some of
these guys are official press but a lot of them are just
paparazzi. They'll try and sell their photos to rags like
the *Star Weekly* or the *National Enquirer*; they can get
a lot of money for the right picture.'

Miriam started to laugh uncontrollably. '*The National
Enquirer*! My God, now I really feel like a star!'

'Honey, you *are* a star. You'd better get used to it,'
Tabby said very seriously. 'Your life is about to change
for ever.'

In the sea of people waiting to greet her, Miriam
recognized one familiar face. 'David' she cried, throwing
her arms around him. She hadn't seen him for over a
year, not since his wife had died. They hugged each other

hard and then pulled away, aware that flashbulbs were popping all around them. 'You look incredible!' Miriam could hardly believe her eyes. David, plump, pale, serious little David was gone and in his place stood a slim, tanned handsome man with expertly styled thick dark hair and a dazzling smile. 'You're gorgeous! And what happened to your little rimmy glasses?'

'Contact lenses,' he said, blushing. The warm brown eyes and sweetly sensual mouth were still the same. 'And OK, I admit it, I've actually been working out. Out here, something called muscle definition is very highly prized.'

'Southern California obviously agrees with you! You look as if you belong here!'

'Oh, please don't say that! I still fancy myself a true eastern intellectual snob. I'd hate to think I've fallen completely for Paradise.'

'God, it's so good to see you. I've missed you so much.' And she couldn't help it, she just had to hug him again, hard. How's Tamiko?'

'Tammy's beautiful I'm dying for you to meet her. She's at daycare right now. Look, hope you don't mind' − he grabbed her carry-on bag and swung it over his shoulder in one easy motion − 'but I've taken the liberty of dismissing the studio car and driver. I know you don't have anything definite scheduled until the *LA Times* interview tonight at Spago at six and I thought, if it's OK with you, we could just drive around a bit, maybe have brunch somewhere? It's still early. If you're not too tired from the trip. I'd really love to spend some time with you.'

'Miriam looked at Tabitha who said quickly, 'Sounds like a great idea. I'll grab a cab to the Beverly Hills Hotel and unpack our stuff. David's right, you're meeting Kevin Allman of the *Times*, but that's not until dinner time. You really don't need to prepare for it. Kevin's very bright, young, personable. Word is he loves the film and he is eager to meet you.'

'OK,' Miriam gave Tabby a grateful kiss. 'That'll give you a chance get some rest. You've got to look after that baby.'

'Are you kidding? I'm going to check us in, have a quick swim and hit Rodeo Drive. See you later, Mim.' Tabby disappeared into the crowd.

'I'm all yours,' Miriam told David, and they headed for the parking lot.

'What do you think of the car?' he asked as they sped along the San Diego Freeway towards Santa Monica. 'It's a Jaguar VS J12. I bought it with my advance money from *Paloma*.'

'I love the colour,' Miriam said, running her hand over the buttery soft leather upholstery. 'I never imagined you having a red car. Or a cellular phone. It's pretty flashy. But if you're really going to buy into the whole Southern California materialistic obsession, why don't you have a Mercedes or a BMW or a Porsche?' She was amused. Crouched over the wheel of the shiny red convertible, his hair blowing in the wind, he looked like a kid with a new toy.

'No, no, I'm not that far gone. I could never drive a German car. I feel guilty enough spending this kind of money on a car. It makes me feel a little better to know that at least the money isn't going to the Germans.' They turned north on to the Santa Monica freeway.

'I can't get over how great the weather is for December. In New York, it's grey and bleak. No snow yet, although it keeps threatening. I've been away from California for so long, I'd forgotten how gorgeous the weather is.'

'Yep. The weather is everything here. It's practically the only topic of conversation. I mean, it's not as if you can say there are a lot of first-class minds here. There aren't. Nobody would value them if there were.

489

'I looked at this terrific apartment. Perfect layout. Lots of room for Tamiko and me. Except that there was no place to put my bookshelves. And then I realized most of the places I was looking at had no space for my bookshelves. Nobody out here needs them because nobody in LA reads. It's awful to say it, but most of the clichés about California are true.'

'I believe you. That's why I left it.' Miriam looked at a blonde bimbo on the back of a motorcycle as they passed her. She was wearing tight fluorescent green bicycle shorts and white boots, her sun-bleached hair streaming out behind her.

'You go to a party out here and nobody ever says, "How are you?" It's "Who are you?" And "What business are you in?" "How much do you make?" "Are you single?" and, if you're female, "Are you still young enough to bear my children?" I have a good friend, writing for a sitcom, interesting woman, intelligent. The other night I asked her, "What's your assessment of the situation in Lebanon?" And she said, "Oh, David, it would take too long to discuss that, really," and then she launched into an hour-and-a-half explanation of who's screwing whom and who's suing whom at the network. It's all superficial. I miss New York a lot.'

'Maybe so. But I've never seen you look better.'

Well, I had to do something. There's so much emphasis on looks here. Even if you're a writer. Everywhere you look there are ads for plastic surgery and eating disorders. Eat till you puke and then let us liposuction your thighs. Californians seem to be in a love-hate relationship with the body. Youth culture to the max. Beautiful People who look young and act younger. It's like living in a gigantic summer camp for overprivileged kids.'

'Yeah, I know what you mean.' They passed a hot pink jeep driven by another blonde who was far too old to be wearing huge, flower-shaped sunglasses and a pink

490

mini skirt and halter top. Two fluffy white Yorkshire terriers wearing matching pink bows sat on the front seat beside her. 'New York must be the last city in North America where age and experience still count for something the way they do in Europe.'

'God, I miss that city! In New York people stay up all night, drinking and talking about ideas. Here they all go to bed early, drink Perrier, and talk about people.'

'I don't think you hate it as much as you say. I just can't get over how wonderful you look,' she repeated.

'Stop saying that. You're starting to embarrass me. You look pretty wonderful yourself. I don't think I've ever seen you wearing jeans before.' He glanced over admiringly at her tight pale blue jeans, white silk shirt, Mexican jacket, and turquoise jewellery. 'Your hair is lovely, braided like that.'

'Thanks. The studio is encouraging me to dress more "ethnic" because of *Paloma*. Tabby and I call this look "Navajo chic". 'I've got a great dress for the Golden Globes. Spanish embroidered silk. You'll love it.'

'Am I your date for these awards?'

'Stephen's flying out. I don't know how long he'll stay, though. We never see each other these days.'

'How are things going between you two?'

'OK,' she answered guardedly. 'Look at that' — she pointed out a giant taco shape along the edge of the freeway, with vivid yellow, green and red for the cheese, lettuce and tomato. 'The Taco That Ate LA — Is that a restaurant?'

'Yeah, that's what they call programmatic design. Buildings shaped to look like the thing they sell. You want to eat a taco, you got to eat it in a restaurant that looks like a taco. Just in case you forget what you're eating, I guess.'

The Santa Monica Freeway dumped them on to the Pacific Coast Highway and for the first time the ocean came into view, large and blue and glittering in the bright sunlight. 'Oh, wow,' Miriam exclaimed, 'I'd forgotten how spectacular the ocean is! The scenery, the weather – no wonder they make movies out here.'

'That's the problem with Californians; they all think they're in a movie.'

'So where are you taking me to eat?'

'A place called The Inn of the Seventh Ray. They do a great brunch and it's fun because it's run by New Agers.'

'I'm not exactly sure what New Age thinking is,' Miriam said. 'All I know is Shirley MacLaine, Wyndham Hill, and something to do with the crystals and power.'

'It's geared around a convergence of the planets where everything gets lined up more closely than has happened in the past and is supposed to result in a spiritual cataclysm.'

'I think I read about that. Didn't everybody go to Peru for a big sort of spiritual be-in and then nothing happened?'

'Apparently it happened but God decided to be kind and give us another chance for harmonious sychronicity.'

'Oh good, that's a relief.' They both laughed and Miriam realized how good it felt to share a laugh with a friend.

David reached over and snapped on the radio. 'Hear, listen to the soundtrack for southern California. It's a New Age radio station.' The creamy voice of an announcer said, 'This is 97.4. Catch the wave', and Miriam heard the strains of flute and harp that created a wave of sound and colour.

'It's actually quite soothing,' she said, 'and it really does convey the image of water bubbling along or light shining through crystals. It's very fluid.'

'Wait till you've heard three cuts. It all sounds the same.' They both listened in silence to the tinkling music

as the car turned off the highway on to the Topanga
Canyon Drive. Miriam gasped at the jagged beauty of
the canyon. There was a long-haired man dressed
completely in white, sitting cross-legged on the side of
the road, facing the green and gold mountain across the
gorge, saluting the sun in some kind of silent prayer.
Miriam thought how far away the almost surrealistic
scene was from the traffic-congestion and negative energy
of New York City. How easy it would be to lose one's
sense of reality here. The Inn of the Seventh Ray was
nestled in a cluster of hills, surrounded by Mediterranean
bush, eucalyptus trees, and hanging ferns, overlooking
a rippling brook.

'This place is sheer fantasy,' Miriam whispered, as the
gorgeous blonde hostess in a purple caftan checked their
reservation.

'I know. It's rumoured to have been Aimee Semple
McPherson's mountain retreat in the 1930s.'

'What's with the purple?' Miriam asked. There were
purple tablecloths covering the tree-trunk tables, purple
ribbons strung through the bushes, and amethyst and
pink balloons hung everywhere. Even a fountain pouted
violet-tinted water over the purple flowers that trembled,
floating, in it. Of course, all the waitresses were wearing
purple, too.

'I'm not exactly sure. I think it has something to do
with the angelic vibration of the violet ray.' Seeing her
face, he said, 'Listen, I promise you, the food is great.'

Their waitress, yet another blonde, wearing lavender
gauze harem pants and enormous earrings hanging down
past her shoulders, seated them at one of the individual
terraced stone patios, handed them menus, and then sort
of floated away. 'Did you see her earrings?' Miriam said.
'They're miniature men. That woman is wearing men in
her ears.'

'Welcome to LA,' David studied the menu. 'Listen to

493

this. Entrées are listed "in order of their esoteric vibrational value." "The food is prepared by our dedicated staff with the vibration of the violet flame for your personal gain and transportation to a higher plane." '

' "It may cost your pocketbook a penny more," Miriam read, "but by raising your body's Light vibration, this way of living may ultimately prove less expensive." I think I've figured this out. It's hippiedom joins yuppiedom for the purpose of making money. Usually religion asks you to give up self; New Age seems to be asking you to give up everything but self.'

The waitress drifted back to take their order, blonde hair so long she could sit on it. 'Would you like some olliberry wine to start?'

'La la berry?' Miriam couldn't believe her ears.

'No, olliberry,' the waitress breathed, wetting lips already slick with lip gloss.

'Could you spell that?'

The waitress looked faintly worried. 'Um . . . OK . . . I'll try. It's . . . um . . . got an l and a b, oh I don't really know.'

'That's OK,' David said kindly. 'We'll have the wine. I'm going to order the artichoke, queen of light, and white fire tofu, and the lady will have the salad bar and the cinnamon rolls rolled with Sunday's early morning light.'

By the time the waitress wafted off again, Miriam was giggling so hard that David had to kick her gently under the table. 'If she didn't get mail, she'd forget her own name,' she managed to choke out.

'You have to remember that theirs is a TV generation,' David said. 'They grew up without the written word. Prose is too linear for them.'

'So how come they're all blonde? Since I got off the plane, I've seen nothing but blondes. The whole city seems to be peopled by the Master Race. Hitler would have loved LA.'

'See those women with the little bodies and big hair dos?' David pointed out two at the next table, a golden blonde wearing a white chiffon toga with black leather boots, and a platinum blonde in a red and white polka-dot mini suit with matching polka-dot ankle socks. 'They're what we call AMWs.'

'What's an AMW?'

David tossed his head, shaking back an imaginary mane of blonde hair. 'Actress, model, whatever.'

Miriam laughed so hard she nearly fell off her chair. The waitress drifted back to place an enormous platter of brown rice salad, mushroom salad, spinach pie, salmon mousse, tabbouleh, and fresh fruit in front of her, with a wicker basket filled with freshly baked cinnamon buns, each the size of a dinner plate. Miriam dove in. She always felt comfortable eating with David because he loved food as much as she did and never bugged her about her weight.

'So how does it feel to be a star?' David plucked a leaf from his artichoke and sank his teeth into the thick green flesh.

'I'm trying hard to keep my priorities straight,' Miriam said. 'Film is such a high-tech industry, there's so much at stake, it's very money-oriented. I'm used to theatre, which seems more people-oriented. Film is such a cold business. I'm just not sure that making movies is all that important, you know? However, I do want the artistic freedom this kind of stardom can bring. I want to be able to pick and choose what I do and who I work with. Now maybe I'll get the chance to try directing, for example. All of that is wonderful, but being treated like a star, that's really hard to adjust to. All the publicity, the hype, gives people the sense that I am somehow important. But I'm not any different than I was last year at this time.

I'm sorry,' she stopped abruptly. 'Am I talking too much?'

'It's OK, it's understandable. Suddenly everybody wants a piece of you,' David said sympathetically.

'Exactly. Anybody who has ever come into contact with me is after me to speak at synagogues, churches, the Kiwanis Club, to open supermarkets, launch ships. They don't want *me*. They just want somebody famous. It's crazy.'

'How's Stephen handling all of this?'

'Well, with him heading into a campaign, it's even worse because it's double publicity. His team of publicists is constantly calling my team of publicists, pressuring me to attend political functions, show up for a few minutes and have my picture taken with him. Then I can leave. Now I know what Stephen's been feeling all these years, only now it's doubled for both of us. He's happy for me, but he wants to use me for his own advancement. I don't blame him. I'm willing to have him use me if it will help. But at the same time, I know he resents the fact that a lot of the voters are turning out just to get a look at me. They aren't really interested in listening to him.'

'Well, sure. A movie star beats a politician any day.'

'But I never set out to be a movie star. I wanted to be an actress. Now producers who wouldn't even take my calls before hail me as a wonderful actress. I always *was* a wonderful actress! I've been better than I am in *Paloma*.'

'I doubt that. Just ask the writer.' David reached across the table and kissed her hand. 'Part of your appeal, Mim, is that audiences can identify with you. Even though Paloma is heroic, they feel that they could have done what she did. That makes them proud to be human beings. You are playing an ordinary woman who is placed in an extraordinary situation and therefore becomes extraordinary. You're touching some very human chords — love of country, desire to protect your children, trying to save your lover from death. The audience feels they know you personally.'

'That's exactly what I mean. People come up to me all the time and start babbling away in Spanish. I have to remind them I'm not Spanish, I'm Jewish. You know the way Paloma cooks the chicken in her kitchen, the way she stuffs the inside of the bird with lemon and garlic and rubs lemon peel all over the skin? I can't tell you how many people come up to me and say, "I cook chicken just the way you do with lemon and garlic." Sometimes I want to scream at them, "It's not me, it's the character, it's Paloma!" And it's not even Paloma. The props people arranged it for me. I walked on to the set. The director told me what to do and I did it. I'm part of the audiences' families now.'

'And that gives you a certain kind of power,' David said intensely. 'And you can't abdicate that responsibility. You can only try to use it to effect some good.'

'I don't know if I can handle all this, David.'

'Well, look on the bright side. If you don't win the Golden Globe, then you may not get an Oscar nomination. And if you don't win an Oscar, all this attention will be gone just as suddenly as it came.'

'Gee, thanks!' She threw her napkin at him.

'However, my feeling is that you are going to win, so if I were you, I'd get ready to accept more responsibility. So good luck getting through the next few days.'

The next few days were such a whirlwind of activity that Miriam had little time to enjoy her stay at the Beverly Hills Hotel. The massive pink edifice, surrounded by palm trees and dating back to the thirties — where Howard Hughes had kept Jean Peters ensconced — had always been a favourite of hers. The studio car and driver arrived promptly at eight o'clock every morning to take

497

Miriam and Tabitha to their first breakfast interview — breakfast meetings seemed to be very popular in LA — and the round of publicity action didn't stop until well into the evening. Miriam had let it be known she was willing to do virtually anything to help sell *Paloma* and the studio kept her hopping. She was officially photographed having dinner at Nicky Blair's and by the paparazzi lying in wait for her outside Morton's. She spoke at a luncheon for the Variety Club and hosted a fundraising cocktail party for the Cedar Sinai Women's Guild. She did the *Tonight Show* and Johnny Carson treated her like royalty. Her folks came down from Fresno and it was great to see them, but other than that her time in California was pure business.

The studio had paid for a series of ads in the trade papers announcing Miriam's Golden Globe nomination, and there were items planted in the gossip columns as well. Of course it was impossible for the media to stay away from her connection with Stephen Andrews. 'Can we expect to see a Oscar winner in the White House?' teased the Click page in the *LA Herald Examiner*, and George Christy of the *Hollywood Reporter* asked her if she would give up her career if Stephen was elected President.

Miriam had expected to have to be seen at nightclubs and late night parties, but the studio publicist, Shelley Arnstein, informed her that was only for the Brat Pack. 'The adults have to get up early. And why waste two hours of precious time hanging out at a club when you could be actively networking?'

So Miriam met with the heads of two large studios about future film projects. Once again she was approached by a major network boss about doing a television series. Back in New York, working for scale at the Manhattan Theater Club, she couldn't have believed that one day she'd turn down a role on a series that would net her fifty grand a week, but here she was saying thanks but no thanks, she was going to pursue feature films for a while and see where that led her for a while. She was near exhaustion although still breathless with anticipation by the time the Golden Globe Awards were held at Century City. *Entertainment Tonight* had picked her to follow during the day leading up to the awards. They were at her hotel room early in the morning before she had even had her coffee or put her make-up on and they trailed her until she sat down in the plush velvet seat next to Stephen and he kissed her to wish her luck. David sat on her other side and she held hands with them all the way through the awards ceremony until her name was called. The entire room rose en masse, applauding her, winner in the best actress category.

'This practically assures you an Oscar nomination,' Tabitha whispered as Miriam was flooded with congratulatory well-wishers at the awards party afterwards. She thought her heart was going to burst with pride and happiness.

But once again Stephen publicly congratulated her in front of the cameras and then slipped away to grab a plane back to Washington. David wasn't staying for the party; he wanted to get home in time to give Tammy a late night tuck-in, but he had invited Miriam to stay in town for the weekend and come to a Shabbat dinner at his house on Friday night. Once again she was left alone to savour her triumph.

David's house was off the Pacific Coast Highway near Point Dune and looked right out over the ocean. 'How can you possibly afford a place like this?' Miriam exclaimed as he took her out on to the deck to show her the spectacular view.

'When Kyoko died, I became a workaholic. Well, among other things. Suffice it to say that I'll be financially secure for quite some time to come, a rather

unusual situation for a struggling young New York writer
to be in. Hello, sweetie.' He looked up and smiled as the
nanny brought his little daughter out to greet them.
'Miriam, this is Alma and Tammy.'

'*Buenos noches*' Alma greeted her, holding an exquisite
little girl of about two.

'Tammy speaks three languages,' David said proudly,
'English, Spanish, and Japanese — although I don't
know how long she'll remember the Japanese. I'm trying
to keep up with her because I don't want her to forget
her mother. Tammy, can you say hello to Mim?'

Enormous almond-shaped eyes peered over Alma's
shoulder. Miriam said, 'Hello, Tammy. Your daddy
showed me a picture of you and I've been really wanting
to meet you.'

The little girl took her thumb out of her mouth.
'You've got princess hair,' she whispered, reaching out
to clutch one of he long rippling strands.

'That's right,' David said. 'The prince could climb right
up all that hair and get to Rapunzel pretty quickly.'

'Wouldn't that hurt?'

'Maybe a little bit,' Miriam said, 'but if Rapunzel
wanted to see the prince really badly, I bet it would be
worth it.'

'Besides, this princess has tough hair,' David said,
giving her hair a sharp tug.

'Tough hair, that's funny!' Tammy repeated
delightedly and they all laughed. 'Mim, do you want to
see my new kitten?'

'I'd love to.'

'Great idea,' David said. 'Tammy, you take Mim to
see your kitten and Alma can help me finish up dinner.
It's almost sundown.' Alma slid the child down to the
floor and Tammy held out her hand to Miriam. They
went off to the nursery to play with Wheezer, a fat little
bundle of orange fur with huge paws which meant,

Miriam explained, that he would probably grow up to be a very big cat. Watching the little girl put doll clothes on the squirming kitten, chatting away partly to Miriam and partly to herself, she felt a thrill of joy and even a proprietary sense of pride. My friend David produced this wonderful little being, she thought. This is David's daughter. She wondered whether she and Stephen would ever have a child of their own, and then she turned her attention back to Tammy. The two of them played happily together until Alma called them in to dinner.

# Twenty-four

The sunset turned the sky a fiery orange and deep purplish pink over the sea. As soon as it was sundown, David asked Miriam to light the shabbas candles. As she leaned over to touch the lit match to the candles, she was suddenly a little girl back in Fresno watching her mother going through the very same ritual and her father, a yarmulke on his head, preparing to say the brochah. It had been such a long time since she'd done any of this or even thought about what it all meant. She and Stephen never talked about their religious beliefs. Besides, his family was Episcopalian, although he rarely went to church.

The shabbas candles cast a warm glow over the four of them around the table. David said kiddush over the wine and then he blessed the bread, two large loaves of fresh challah. Miriam joined him in the brochah, pleased that the treasured words came back to her.

'Why are there two breads, Daddy?' Tamiko asked, who enjoyed ripping hunks of bread from the huge braid.

'When the Jews were in the desert, you remember that God sent down manna from heaven so that they could eat. No one is supposed to work on the sabbath, not even to gather manna, so the day before he sent down two loads of manna. The two loaves of bread are in memory of the two loads of manna.'

'Loaves and loads,' Tammy giggled. 'Daddy, what's a manna?'

'Fluffy and white,' Miriam said, 'like little bread snowflakes coming down out of the sky. But you've never seen snow, have you, Tammy?'

'Yes, I have. At Mama-san's.'

'At her grandmother's, in Vancouver,' David explained.

Alma put little plates of gefilte fish down in front of them. Miriam looked at the little black-haired girl affectionately. Her father was Jewish, her grandmother Japanese, and her nanny Mexican-American. 'Wonderful gefilte fish,' she murmured.

'*Gracias*,' Alma said. 'I'm glad you like it.'

'You made it?'

'She grated the horseradish too,' David broke in. 'It's a lot easier than when I was growing up. My mother used to pound the whitefish for hours. Alma uses a Cuisinart, Some traditions deserve to be changed. And I'm glad you brought dry wine instead of the sweet stuff which has, I'm sure, a sugar count of fifty-two.'

'There was lots of kosher wine to choose from,' Miriam said. 'I was surprised.'

'California Jews know their wines. What do you think of the challah?'

'It's very fresh. Intricately braided.'

'I made it,' David said proudly. 'And the kreplach soup. But the roast chicken and the chulent are Alma's.'

'*Si*. I put beans and jalepenos in with the lentils and bulgar,' Alma offered. 'Then it's Jewish chilli.'

They all laughed and Miriam thought again how lucky Tammy was to be part of this unusual family, sharing tastes and exchanging customs. She was growing up completely surrounded by love.

After dinner, Tammy came to Miriam in her nightie to say goodnight. 'I like you,' she said gravely, hugging Miriam.

'Glad you approve.' Feeling the soft little arms go

around her neck and the whisper of a kiss on her cheek, Miriam felt a pang. Stephen didn't seem to want even to talk about the possibility of children these days. Had they waited too long? She honestly didn't know.

David and Alma took Tammy off to bed and Miriam took her wine glass out on to the deck, to look at the night sky and watch the black waves depositing their white foam on to the sandy shore. There were so many questions she wanted to ask David, so many things she wanted to tell him about herself, but the rhythmic sound of the ocean lulled her into a contented peace. She was always going to want more. It was part of her nature to keep reaching out, to look ahead to the future. Right now, however, it was enough to be right here in this wonderful place at this moment, feeling the cool sea breeze, hearing the water and the last gulls at sunset.

David came back from tucking Tammy in bed for the night.

'She's perfection, David, she really is,' Miriam said.

'Yeah, I know. At least I've done one thing right in my life.'

Alma had slipped off discreetly to her suite in the basement. The two of them sat together on the deck watching the stars rise in the sky and the twinkling lights of the small boats out on the sea. David stretched out on the canvas sofa and Miriam sat opposite him, curled up in a rattan chair. The balmy air softly blew through the Oriental wind chimes hanging above them.

'So tell me,' she said, slowly sipping the last of the Carmel cabernet sauvignon from the black-stemmed glass, 'How are you really? You seem to be in good shape but Kyoko's death must have been very hard on you.'

'Well, if you want to hear the whole rotten truth it's been quite a journey. I'm happy to say I've come out the other side, but it wasn't easy. I was a hermit for about six months. Then I just went crazy. I sent Tammy to her grandmother in Vancouver and I really went wild. Eight months of mindless numbing sex, lots of coke, I'm afraid, daily nosebleeds, the whole Hollywood cliché. I gave myself over to being selfish, stupid, and bad. After all, I'd been good all through Kyoko's illness and her death. I'd made a pact with God that if he saved her, I'd never do anything bad again. When she died, I thought, "Fuck you, God. What's the point? I might as well be bad." '

'A perfectly natural reaction,' Miriam said quietly. 'I have to ask you, though, were you careful? In terms of the sex, I mean?'

'Oh yes. I was never crazy enough to swim the rapids unprotected. But I was hooked on the excitement of casual sex and I knew I could get caught in it for ever. Waking up in bed with some strange woman, thinking this is a mistake, I don't want to be here, and yet not being able to stop. I've always loved women, I love everything about them. I'd had a couple of films made and the advance word on *Paloma* was already pretty hot, so I never had trouble finding willing partners.'

'I'll bet you didn't,' Miriam murmured. She sensed this was the first time David had discussed this with anyone.

'I was very good at making myself what I call "QA" – quietly available. I found that if you send out vibes of "I'm on the make, I want to get laid", it's death, but if you do nothing but wait, pretty soon they all come to you. It makes me sick to think about it now, but sex was the only thing that could numb the pain.'

'There's nothing wrong with that if it works.'

David sighed. 'It worked for a while and then it stopped working. I hit bottom. I was no longer responsible. I didn't have to carry the ball any more and I just floated for a time. Then, at a certain point, I found myself wanting a deeper seriousness, a real satisfaction, more of what I had had with Kyoko. I missed Tammy but I couldn't let her be here while I was screwing around, so I just stopped, I've been celibate for quite some time now. It feels fine. My hand and I have become best friends.'

'I know what you mean,' Miriam giggled. 'Stephen's away a lot of the time.'

'I've been doing a lot of thinking and reading about male-female relationships. The amount of violence perpetrated by men against women is staggering; the inventiveness of the violence is overwhelming. I don't want to be part of that in any way, shape, or form.'

'Oh David, you're not. You're the kindest, gentlest, funniest man I know, unique and strong. An exceptional, extraordinary human being.'

'Well, if that's true, and I thank you for the compliment, the uniqueness and strength have to come from somewhere. I know for me, it comes from raising a child. Tammy literally saved me. It's charting the progress of another human being, this radiant little person who positively glows with life, a brain and a heart that devours everything I can give her. She can only be who she is, with no preconceived notions, because her consciousness is not fully developed yet. She's so eager to learn and I'm learning right along with her. It's like being born into this world all over again.'

'Is it helping your writing or does it take time away from the focus you need for your work?'

'No, no, family and kids can open up the creative process,' David said with sudden passion. 'I'm actually able to write more, better, than I could before. It's just flowing out of me. You learn to exercise your spiritual muscles for a change. We're so damned self-absorbed out here. The entire entertainment industry dictates that the people I work with and write for are the most self-absorbed of all. But a child is a constant reminder of what is basic, what is real. Having Tammy has made me look away from myself, to another life.'

'Oh, I envy you,' Miriam said involuntarily. 'I envy you having a child and I'm so afraid I'll never have one.'

'What's wrong, Mim?' David looked at her with concern. 'You've got lots of time still.'

'No, I don't know, oh, everything's wrong.' Miriam found herself starting to cry. 'I don't think Stephen loves me any more. I don't know what we have between us, but it doesn't feel like love, it feels like war.' She paused to try to gather herself together, looking blankly out to sea. 'We're locked in this never-ending struggle and I'm so afraid I'm going to lose. I don't know what to do.' The tears were streaming down her face now, all vestiges of pride gone completely.

David held out his arms to her. 'Come over here and let me give you a hug.'

She ignored the momentary flash of warning that went through her mind, and the next minute he had pulled her down on to his lap and was holding her in his arms. Gently he kissed the tears away, moving from her eyelids along her cheek to her mouth, and she knew it was too late to stop it. They had both been waiting for this for a long time. Her hands were in his hair and she pressed herself tight against him, feeling the warmth of his body flow into hers, comforting her, soothing her. She opened her mouth and let his tongue slide into it and suddenly comfort changed instantly into desire. He was kissing her hungrily, avidly, holding on to her tightly as if he were afraid she might bolt at any minute. She wanted to tell him that she was here, he could have her. They kissed for a long time, deep, searching kisses, and when his hand finally found her breast it seemed so right. She could feel her nipple through the fine cotton of her navy blue shirt straining against his touch. She heard his breath catch as he cupped her full breast in his hand. She sighed as he caressed her more and more urgently. With infinite delicacy, he lifted the thin gauze shirt over her head and

508

she felt the ocean breeze whisper over her. She moved her hand between his legs to free him into the night air, and then neither of them could wait any longer and he was inside her and they were moving together as if they had known each other all their lives.

When she opened her eyes again, the stars were brilliant in the sky above them and she gasped at the wonder and beauty of them. David stood up and took her hand. 'I need more of you,' he said. 'Please . . . come with me.' He led her into the bedroom where the moonlight streamed in through the tall windows, bathing the room in an unearthly silvery glow. The thick roar of the ocean followed them.

This isn't happening, Miriam thought. This is David, my friend. She could still hear the roar of the ocean in her ears. They lay down on the bed together, skin to skin, and as soon as he touched her, the electricity flashed through her again, as if they had not just made love. He stroked her gently, exploring every inch of her body, as if reading her by Braille. She felt as if his hands were actually under her skin, brushing every nerve end and setting it on fire. His mouth came down over her breast and encircled it with flame, and then his mouth moved down her body to a circle of even more exquisite pleasure. She gave herself over to him until the circles joined and ignited in one gigantic burst.

'I love you,' he said softly, as he kissed the inside of her thighs and then spread her legs wide apart. 'I've always loved you.' And she knew it was the truth. He was touching her with infinite love. 'I love you,' he whispered as he came into her. 'This is my love inside you' — he plunged deeper and, 'This is love, love, love,' as he plunged into her over and over again, the sweet sensation building until she cried out that she loved him, too, because in that moment she did.

\*     \*     \*

When she awoke the next morning, the smell of freshly ground coffee drew her to the kitchen where she found David wearing only a pair of red jogging shorts, his muscular body shining in the sun that was pouring in from the glass doors to the deck. She watched his strong, sensitive hands moving quickly and deftly as he cracked several brown eggs into a blue pottery bowl and began to beat them expertly. She felt another sudden jolt of desire as she remembered how expertly those sensitive fingers had moved delicately over every inch of her last night.

God, how could she have allowed that to happen? Once could be called a spur-of-the-moment indulgence. Twice was definitely a more serious mistake, although even that was understandable, given the emotional history between them. But with total abandon she had allowed her best friend, David, to make love to her all night long.

His face as he looked up to greet her was radiant. She said, 'Good morning,' in a loud and cheery voice, hoping to convey in those two words that last night had been a momentary lapse in judgement that was unlikely to be repeated.

'Hello, gorgeous,' he said, pouring the egg mixture into a copper frying pan. 'I thought I should let you get at least one hour of sleep. I've already been for a run. It's a glorious morning. What time is your flight?' He handed her a glass of freshly squeezed orange juice.

'Noon.' She turned away from him and took a sip, trying to compose herself.

'Good, then you've got time for breakfast. I'll drive you to the airport. I've already called Tabitha at the hotel and asked her to bring your things. Gives us a little more time to spend together.'

'Where's Tammy?'

'She's gone home with Alma for the day. She lives in the country with a couple of goats and a lot of chickens.

510

Tammy's crazy about animals. Of course, I hope she'll grow up to be an actress, but at the moment it looks more likely she'll turn out to be a vet.'

'I'm sorry.' Miriam was disappointed. 'I wanted to say goodbye to her.'

'Just as well you didn't. Tammy's not great with goodbyes. She tends to cry when anything valuable is taken away from her. Probably because of her mother's death. So, how does scrambled eggs with peppers and onions, fresh blueberries, and matzo-meal pancakes sound to you?'

'Great.'

They ate out on the deck, chatting noncommittally, trying to keep conversation light. David pushed his chair away from the table and held out his hand. 'Let's go for a swim, just a quick one.'

'No, no, I didn't bring a suit.'

'So what? It's still early. There's nobody on the beach for miles around. Neighbours are still asleep.' Seeing her hesitation, 'We've seen each other already. I know every part of you intimately now, so what's the big deal? Come on.'

He grabbed her hand and they raced down the wooden steps, leaving their clothing in a pile on the sand behind them. In the water, they laughed and played like naughty children, splashing each other, tickling and biting and then he was kissing her and it was happening again. She wrapped her legs around his waist and let him thrust into her again and again until they both shouted at the top of their lungs with joy.

'You know, you're awfully good at that Miriam teased him on the way to the airport as she slipped her hand inside his thigh. She was high on sex and punch-drunk with happiness. 'I had no idea you were such an expert lover.'

'Enthusiasm counts for a lot,' David said, keeping his eyes fixed on the freeway.

'We've wasted some very valuable time over the years.'

'What do you mean?'

'I mean is this going to be a Same-Time-Next-Year kind of affair where we meet every eight months or so?'

'What about Stephen?' David asked. His face was expressionless.

The name jerked her abruptly back to reality. 'I don't know,' she faltered. 'I'm not sure. I've never been unfaithful to him. Not in fifteen years. But I don't want to give you up . . .'

'I love you, Miriam. I meant every word I said last night. But I can't share you. If you come to me again that way, it must be because you're going to stay with me. I won't touch you again unless you're mine.'

'Are you sure you mean that?'

'Yes. I mean it. I'll always be your best friend. You can count on me for anything, you know that. But I don't want to be your lover again unless it's for ever.'

Miriam's eyes filled with tears. When she looked over at David, she saw his eyes were wet, too. They drove in silence the rest of the way to the airport. At the security gate, Tabitha was waiting for them. She went on through while David gazed into Miriam's eyes searchingly and then kissed her goodbye, a long, soul-searching kiss. Then he gently moved her away from him. He pressed a piece of paper into her hand, rolled her fingers tightly over it, and kissed her fist. 'These are all my phone numbers,' he told her, 'work, home, car. You can reach me at any time. Night or day. Call if you need me.' He stopped, embarrassed, as his eyes filled with tears again. 'Don't mind me,' he said. 'I'm afraid I'm just like Tamiko. I always cry when anything valuable is taken away from me.'

\*     \*     \*

512

On the plane, Tabitha lowered their tray tables for lunch. 'You done good, kid,' she said. 'On to the Oscars.'

'Yes,' Miriam said. The Awards seemed meaningless to her now. Her thoughts were on the ground, back at Point Dume, on the deck, in the ocean. She sighed and poured the contents of a miniature bottle of gin into her glass of tonic.

'Did you have a good time in LA?' Tabby asked. 'I think I've been very discreet, but I am dying to know.'

'I had a wonderful time. A magnificent time. The best time I've had in a long time. But oh, Tabby, I'm so confused.'

Tabby placed her hand over Miriam's. 'I know, honey. You just can't predict the way things are going to turn out. I'm afraid you just have to look upon it as all part of life's rich pageant.'

# Twenty-five

'I don't want to wait any longer,' Gwen said to Lou and Merilee. 'I intend to move ahead and open a branch of The Club in LA. London is pushing for a branch, too, and there's a piece of property in the Sloane Square area that might be great. After New York and Tokyo, London is the leading financial centre of the world, but I don't want to proceed with a deal until we've done more thorough market research. Despite the country's having a female prime minister, Britain's women's movement is about ten years behind ours. Mrs Thatcher may be female, but she ain't no feminist. In fact, my sources tell me things are worse for women right now. They're not in positions of power, they are not holding high-paying jobs, and the bulk of the money is not in their hands. But that could be changing, so let's keep our eye on the situation. I think we should keep exploring the options, checking things out. I mean, I'm determined to have a London branch at some point in the future . . .'

'Me too,' Merilee chimed in, busily scribbling shorthand notes on her steno pad. Gwen had this habit of turning an informal business meeting into a lecture on world trade. Time to lighten up! 'I've only been in London once, but I'd sure love to live there. I'm a sucker for an English accent. I had this limey lover who could make me come just with the sound of his voice. He us to call me at work and . . .'

Gwen cleared her throat and looked at Lou. 'My

concern is that there's not enough money in the English market to support a branch of The Club at the moment. When the money's to be made, that's when we'll make our move, right Lou?' No response. She tapped her gold-plated pen on the table. 'Do you agree about the London branch, Lou?' He looked down at his drink and said nothing. 'Now, as far as LA is concerned,' Gwen continued, 'we've got to act quickly. We've found the perfect property in LA. It's in Westwood, surrounded on three sides by money.'

'Right,' Merilee leapt in excitedly, 'You've got Bel Air, Beverly Hills, and Brentwood. Now you don't have the self-made working women and top executives there like we got in New York, but there's plenty of money out there and plenty of women who have it. Especially female stars moving into the area of directing, producing, even becoming studio heads. Not to mention "Hollywood Wives". When you're talkin' about the three Bs, you're talkin' about big bucks. I've seen the property myself. It's prime real estate. We'll be lucky to get it.'

'My point exactly,' Gwen said forcefully. Lou still said nothing, slowly continuing to stir the ice cubes in his Scotch glass with the tip of his Cross pen. 'Crown Trust informs me that Donald Trump has his eye on the very same property and they are expecting him to make a counter-bid. They want a guarantee from us by the end of this week that the deal will go through. We've got to move right away. Are we all agreed?'

'Absolutely,' Merilee said. 'We know the market in LA. It's not like London where there's a whole lot of other variables and major risk involved. I say the time is right. Let's move on LA now.'

Gwen smiled at her. She could always count on Merilee's support and enthusiasm. She turned to Lou again. 'Lou?'

He sighed. 'Look, I don't want to be the wet blanket here,' he said hesitantly, 'but I'm not sure the time is right for LA. I don't know if we're in a position to go ahead with this deal. We've still got a lot to learn.'

'This doesn't sound like you, Lou. What was it you said to me almost ten years ago when we were starting The Club? "Risk now, learn later. Seize the opportunity and do it before someone else does." '

'Yeah, I know, but The Club definitely is a success now. Merilee's lifetime membership scheme has really filled the coffers. We're making money, we've got financial security, which hasn't been all that easy to achieve, you may remember. We don't want to run the risk of over-extending ourselves.'

'Why would we? We've got the right property, we've got the right organization, we've already assembled the investors. What's particularly gratifying this time around is that the members of The Club are willing to invest and take a chance on the LA branch. We've proved we can do it.'

Merilee looked up from her steno pad. 'Susie Krumins is in for a pile of money, of course she can afford to take a risk but there's Lacey Talbot, Sally Traynor, Liz Jordan, Miriam Newman, and quite a few others too. The members of the advisory board are totally behind my plans for expansion. They all want a piece of the action.'

'And why not? The Club has been such a success in New York, it's bound to go well in LA. That is, if we all believe in the project and get behind it.' She looked sternly at Lou. 'I don't understand why you're dragging your feet on this one, Lou.'

'*Mamma mia*!' Lou exploded. 'Have you forgotten what happened the last time we allowed ourselves to be over-extended? I lost my restaurant, a family business for over thirty years. Have you forgotten that I lost my papa?

517

How much do we have to sacrifice for your precious Club?'

'No,' Gwen said quietly. 'Of course I haven't forgotten. We both know what personal sacrifices we made the first time around. But it's different now, I'm sure of it. We're on solid ground here in New York. I want a national profile. Eventually I want us to be international. Damnit, Lou, I thought you were in for the long haul. You've been assuring me for months that the money was in place for this deal. Now is it or isn't it?'

'All right, all right.' His voice rose in pitch with his agitation. 'I didn't want to have to tell you this, but one of our major investors has pulled out. We're short a piece of the pie.'

'How big a piece?' Gwen asked with deadly calm. She was sitting motionless in one of Lou's black leather armchairs, prim in a navy and white suit, legs crossed.

'About a million.'

'So we'll take a loan from the bank.'

'No!' Lou cried. 'No loans. Any bank we go to, even our regular bank, will want a full audit before they'll guarantee this kind of money.'

'So what's wrong with that?' Her mouth hardened.

Lou felt like a butterfly pinned to the wall. 'Nothing, nothing, it's just that all that takes time we don't have and . . . look, I just don't want to be into the bank again. I told you, we're already over-extended.'

'What the hell is wrong with you two?' Gwen threw her pen across the room. 'The Club is a business. And business is all about taking risks. Of course the bank will want a full audit. So who cares? We've got nothing to hide.'

'No, of course not,' Merilee said sharply. 'But maybe Lou is right. Another bank loan could jeopardize all the financial security we've worked so hard to build up. It

518

would be better to find another investor. Someone we can trust.'

Gwen stood up from her chair swiftly. 'Then find another investor. Fast. I want to close on that property and clinch the deal by the end of this week. Do I make myself clear?' And she swept out of Lou's office. Merilee gave a little shrug, grabbed her pad, and followed her out.

Lou closed the door and stood there shaking. He absent-mindedly smoothed the front of his double-breasted grey wool jacket as he paced slowly to his desk. He was in too deep here, way over his head. On the surface, 37 Middlesex appeared to be a raging success. But its net worth was not what Gwen thought it was. Only he knew that there was virtually no margin of profit in the business, partly because their expenses were astronomical and partly because he had been skimming off the top, just a little, every now and then. He maintained an expensive lifestyle — the house on Fire Island, the trips to Mykonos, the beachfront property in Key West, the boat, the new car.

Of course he had been counting on the drug deals to bankroll further expansion of The Club, but he was no longer dealing with his favourite poule as his supplier or a simple campesino-turned-small-time profiteer. He was involved with the big-time drug bosses, the ruthless Medellin cartel. There was no telling what the *mujers de violencia* might do. And he didn't know how to get out of it.

The US market was almost saturated now. Prices had dropped, which meant that more people were buying at the same time so that he had to sell more to make the same amount of money. There were a lot of high-risk activities going on down at The Club that Gwen might overlook or even condone in order to keep The Club going, but he knew drugs was something she would never sanction, never in a million years.

Now that the United States and Colombia had joined forces against the drug dealers, Lou could feel the trap closing in on him. And now Gwen was pressuring him to find more capital. Christ! He didn't know where else to look. There was only one person left to whom he could go.

His affair with Stephen was in full swing. Miriam was engaged in her whirlwind publicity tour for *Paloma*. It had been well received at the Festival of Festivals in Toronto and had won a special prize at Cannes. With her away so much, whatever free time Stephen had in New York, he was free to spend with Lou. It had been a delight for Lou, introducing Stephen to the many and varied pleasures of his erotic knowledge, including *l'amour grecque*.

'The words "do what you want with me" fill me with the most perverse joy,' he said to Stephen. 'That is my entry to heaven. Through the back door, of course.' Coke always made him talk nonstop; he loved the sound of his own voice.

Stephen hung on to his every word. 'But isn't it frightening the first time?'

'Of course, my friend, but that is part of the joy. And you must be slow and careful.'

'But do they like it?'

'If they trust you, they learn to like it. But you must convince them that they are "*normale*". That it is normal. If you are not careful, they will use it against you. Like all so-called perversions, one day they throw it in your face. Men can usually handle it or they will not ask for it, but with women, you must be more careful. If you are a serious student of eroticism, you will categorize every woman you meet in love: 1. She talks well. 2. She fucks well. 3. She gives great head. 4. She's willing to take it up the ass. In my book of love, you get the most points for number four, *ecco*?'

'Which do you prefer, men or women?'

That was a hard question for Luigi to answer and it was one that every lover eventually asked him. Making love to a man was like making love to himself. He loved women, but at the same time they frightened him. No matter how many he had, women remained unfamiliar to him. He feared their hysteria and he feared their power. Lou had matured early and by the time he reached adolescence, mainstream sex had palled on him.

'The usual games bore me. Will she, won't she: it's just a power play. When you're young, copping a feel is the ultimate. Then the screw, it comes next. Each taboo stripped away, bit by bit, becomes less of a high. Getting your cock sucked, well, half the thrill is having someone at your feet on their knees. The subservience of sex I thrive on it, it makes me live. But eventually even that wanes. You need more, you look for something − *come si dice* − closer to the edge. If I am with a boring lover, I want to hurt him. Or her. I want to wake them up, bring them to the precipice, push them off, and watch them fall. The more resistance I get, the more exciting is the ultimate fall, *sai*?'

'But the pain?' Stephen could hardly control his shock and excitement.

'There is a fine line between pleasure and pain,' Lou smiled. 'Have you not read *The Story of O*? With some very special people you both realize you can do anything. It is a common bond that tips the balance of power, i.e. if you do this for me, I will become your slave.'

At this point Stephen would do anything for Lou. Now it was time for Lou to call in the chips.

He picked up the phone and dialled his number. 'I need your help,' he said as soon as Stephen answered and he explained the squeeze he was in. 'The Club has been supportive of you. Remember I talked Gwen into becoming involved with your campaign. I need this

521

favour from you. You've got to get me the money now. All I need is one last piece of the puzzle in order to complete the package.'

'How much do you need?' Stephen's voice sounded uncharacteristically cool.

'We're short roughly a million. I've got nowhere else to get it, I swear to you, Stephen. Believe me, I hate asking you to do this.' He could feel the sweat trickling down the back of his neck. God, he really did hate doing this.

Stephen gave a long, low whistle. 'That's a lot of money. I can't come up with bucks like that. Besides, I need every penny I can get my hands on for the campaign.'

'I think you owe me this.'

There was a pause. 'And just what do you mean by that?'

'Nothing in particular,' Lou said evenly. 'But I need the money by the end of this week. Somehow I have a feeling you'll be able to get it for me.'

Lou's soft, measured tone chilled the other's blood. He would have to get the money somehow.

The only possible solution that came to mind was the CAFF. The Central American Freedom Fund had been set up by a group of private citizens who called themselves the Central American Freedom Foundation. Now that it was illegal for Congress to aid the contras directly, similar private funds had sprung up all over the country. Stephen had become involved in CAFF through Stanley Hughes. The group's plan was to monitor the contras, hold frequent talks with them, and continue to raise funds from private sources until the contras were in a position to receive them. At the moment, the contras were lying low, regrouping, and formulating a new plan of action, while CAFF amassed a fortune earmarked for them.

It would be easy, well relatively easy, for Stephen to

borrow a million. As the fund's treasurer, he was one of two cheque-signing authorities. The president of the organization, Malcolm Millican, was a wealthy businessman with links to Central America. He didn't live in Washington and was often out of the country altogether, so he and Stephen had each signed three blank cheques apiece, just in case an emergency situation arose and cash was needed quickly, The Executive Committee of CAFF had no meetings scheduled until three months from now, at which point Stephen's treasurer's report would be required. Three months was a good long time away.

All of this raced through his mind while Lou assured him that he would be able to repay the loan almost immediately. It seemed a reasonable solution, provided there were no hitches. Damn Lou for backing him into a corner like this.

Stephen cleared his throat. He could hear Lou waiting nervously at the other end of the line. 'I think I might be able to manage it,' he said finally. 'But you'll have to get the money back to me as soon as you can.'

'No problem,' Lou said quickly. 'We've got a piece of property in Boston we can sell off, not in time for the LA deal, of course, but soon enough to repay your very generous loan.'

'All right,' Stephen said curtly, 'I'll have it for you by Thursday.'

Lou hung up the phone and wiped his dripping forehead. He regretted the ever-widening web but he knew he could count on Stephen. He was well aware of how easily owing money to a lover could kill good sex. Still, certain sacrifices had to be made in order to keep the main game plan in effect. He hurried down the hall to tell Gwen the good news.

'Good for you,' Gwen said as she broke out a split of Moët & Chandon in celebration. 'I knew you could find another investor. I just didn't think you'd be able to do it so quickly.'

'I cannot stand still when a lady accuses me of dragging my feet.' Lou took a healthy sip of the cool, bubbling liquid. He could almost instantly feel his anxiety being supplanted by euphoria. Of course everything would work out all right. He had never failed Gwen before and he didn't intend to start now.

'I want to celebrate this deal.' Gwen was moving around the room in ecstatic circles. 'We'll announce the opening of the LA branch with a gala here in New York. Let's aim for three months from now. And I want to renovate The Club completely in the meantime.'

Lou felt his euphoria vanish as quickly as it had seeped in. 'You're crazy! There's no way we can afford that.'

'Of course we can. We'll sell off that property in Boston. We've been looking for a buyer; it shouldn't take us too long to find one. I'm not interested in Boston at the moment. What I'm interested in is LA. Use the Boston property to pay for the renovations.'

'No, I don't want to do that.' Lou couldn't control the panic in his voice. 'I keep telling you. We need some security.'

Gwen swung around to face him, her face hard. 'Do it,' she said. Lou nodded silently and left her office, leaving his champagne glass on her desk, hardly touched.

She sighed and leaned her head back in the leather swivel chair. She couldn't understand what was going on with Lou these days. She hated to be sharp with him, she still counted him as one of her best friends, but the time for action was now and she didn't like the way he was hanging back. There was a gentle tap on her door. Good, it was probably Lou come to say that of course she was right, he was just a little chicken, no problem, he'd move right ahead. But when the door opened Mina van Houghton, by now the official photographer for 37

Middlesex, stuck her head in the doorway. 'Hi, can I come in?'

'Sure.' Gwen smiled with genuine warmth. She was very fond of Mina although they didn't get together all that often any more except for business purposes. Mina's radiant smile and warm manner never failed to lift her spirits. She missed the early days of The Club when she and Mina had sat around Susie Krumins' kitchen table giving Susie advice on how to start her small business.

So much had changed since then. Mina was considered one of the top freelance photographers in the city now; her work was given frequent showings at some of the most prestigious galleries in New York. An enormous coffee-table book of her prize-winning photographs had been published last Christmas and she was moving into the area of film as well.

And Gwen? Well, Gwen had 37 Middlesex, The Club, which seemed to demand every minute of her attention, night and day. She wasn't sure she wanted to think about just how much she herself had changed.

'Are you OK?'

'Yes, sorry. Just remembering how much fun it was giving Susie lessons in the high art of big business. I miss it.'

'Yeah, that was great. Boy, Susie doesn't need our help now, does she?'

'You can say that again,' Gwen snorted. The two women both laughed and their eyes met for a long moment. Gwen was touched by the concern she recognized in Mina's eyes.

Mina blushed and looked away. Clearing her throat briefly she said, 'I . . . I came in to show you the layout for the new brochure.' She put the mock-up on the desk.

Gwen leafed through it quickly. 'This looks terrific, Mina, but I have to tell you it may soon be out of date.' Excitedly, she explained her plans for the renovations and the gala to her. 'I've been feeling for some time that The Club is just too dark. I want to open it up a bit. Get some light in here. I'm thinking tropical. Lots of white walls and pink with touches of bright, bright colour, masses of flowers, woven wall hangings, some ceramic maybe. What do you think?' Mina looked startled as though she hadn't heard everything Gwen had just said. 'So what do you think?' she repeated.

'Sounds sort of Cal-Caribbean. That's great. New York is so dark. Sometimes I really feel we're living like gerbils in a sci-fi computer maze. We're all running blindly around looking for an opening of light. Your idea sounds marvellous.'

'Yeah, if I can make it all happen.' Gwen sighed.

'You look tired,' Mina said sympathetically. She moved behind Gwen and began to massage her neck lightly.

'I am.' Gwen gave herself up to her relaxing touch.

'So what do you do for fun these days?'

'Fun?'

'You sound as if that's a foreign concept to you,' Mina laughed. And then she reddened slightly as she said, 'I miss you, Gwen. I really do. I don't know why I'm even saying that. I mean, we see each other a lot. But our lives are so . . .' — she stopped, suddenly confused — 'so full of business, I guess.'

Gwen straightened up and circled her head a couple of times. 'Thanks. That feels a lot better.' She smiled at Mina and was surprised to see her redden again. She'd always counted on her as a loyal friend, if not a close one, but sometimes Mina seemed nervous around her. Right now she was moving around the room as if she couldn't bring herself to light anywhere.

'I was just thinking,' Mina said in a whispery little voice, 'that . . . well . . . maybe we could have dinner some time . . . you know, just the two of us, somewhere, preferably . . .'

526

'Outside The Club,' Gwen finished.

'Right. With a strictly enforced rule. No talking about business.'

'That's the best offer I've had in a long time.' Gwen smiled at her. 'I'd like that very much. Once I get the gala set up, perhaps. I'm going crazy with it.'

Mina took a deep breath. 'Look, I know you're a very private person, Gwen, and I respect that, in fact, it's one of the things I admire most about you, but if you ever need a friend to talk to . . . and I don't mean to give advice to you or organize life choices, I mean really talk to . . . please call me. I'm a good listener.'

'Thanks,' Gwen said with some surprise. 'How's Susie?'

'She's OK. It was a tough decision to make. You know, about the pregnancy.' Mina looked down at the mock-up on Gwen's desk and gave a little cough. 'Um . . . Susie and I live together but she's not . . . we're not, you know, involved.' She suddenly stopped, flustered. She looked up at Gwen and said firmly, 'So, listen, are we on for dinner?'

'Yes.' The mixture of joy and doubt on Mina's face startled her. 'I mean it, I promise. Just let me get through the gala.'

'Sure. Right. Great.' Mina flashed her another of her wistful, dazzling smiles, gathered up the brochure and disappeared out of the door.

Gwen looked after her, puzzled. She could use a real friend right about now. But the walls that had surrounded Gwen's personal life had been inviolable for too long. There was no time to think of that now; she needed to concentrate on LA and London. She looked at the latest issue of *Vanity Fair* on her desk. The face of Sara Town smirked back at her. Sara was back in New York now. It was too early to predict the success of *In Depth* but there was no doubt that the critics already had their knives

527

out and finely sharpened. Sara had always had a lot of enemies. Gwen wondered fleetingly if she had ever managed to make any real friends.

Sara picked up her own copy of *Vanity Fair* and threw it across the room. The caption on the cover said: 'They're Paying Her a Fortune, But Has Sara Town's Luck Finally Run Out?' The intro to the article read: 'Ask Sara Town what motivates her and she will say, "Drive, ambition, the desire to be the best I can be." But the real answer is revenge.'

Great. This was just what she needed: a full-blown hatchet job just at the moment that the entire country was holding their combined breath to see if *In Depth* was going to bomb. She had acquired a thick skin in this business, but this time, if she failed, it wouldn't be in private. At least twenty million people would know about it. And she would have no one but herself to blame. She had insisted on doing the show by herself, without a co-host.

It didn't help that the network had slotted her in on Friday evenings opposite the hottest prime-time sit-com. Was even the network setting her up to fail? No, crazy, that was pure paranoia. They were counting on her powers to woo the viewers over to *In Depth*. The whole thrust of their ad campaign was geared to her seductive quality. Both the print and electronic promos had the same theme: 'Who would you most like to spend this Friday night with? Get into bed with Sara Town. Sara is saving one whole hour just for you.' It was so suggestive it was almost pornographic. Never mind that the show was built around celebrity profiles and that she and her staff of researchers were busting their buns to find just the right celebrities to profile. What was going to make or break the show was Sara and whether or not the public was still as much in love with her as ever.

Well, fuck the critics. As far as she could see, the public still adored her. *In Depth* was climbing slowly but surely in the ratings. She certainly had enough personal contacts to give the show the most exciting guests possible. Right now she was after Senator Stephen Andrews and God knows her contact with him was personal enough. She'd show them all. There was no way they were going to back her into a corner, pressure her the way they did Jessica Savitch until she was strung out on drugs and dead at forty.

She wandered to the corner of the room and retrieved the magazine from the floor. At least no one could say she looked less than fabulous on that cover. Oh, the network bosses might grumble a little that the black off-the-shoulder dress was a touch too revealing, but Sara knew the readers would love it. In any case, she was a survivor.

# Twenty-six

Miriam dreams that Stephen was making love to her, slowly, silently. She can feel his hardened cock pressing into her back, she can feel his hand reaching around her to cup her breast tenderly. The warm breath close to her ear, the gentle kisses at the corner of her neck and shoulder, stroking her softly, fingers lost in the heavy weight of her hair. She feels her nipples hardening like rough-cut diamonds. He toys with them, precious jewels, ever circling, rubbing them between thumb and forefinger. She feels the familiar pull between her legs, the magic spiralling downwards. In her dream she is asleep, too. Or pretending to be asleep. She wants him to wake her with his love. From behind, he slides his fingers beween her legs, gently, insistently, stroking from back to front, circling, opening, widening, probing. She cannot hear whispering. She cannot even hear him catch his breath. Slowly he turns her face towards his and with his fingers he forms her lips into an O, reshaping her mouth, thrusting his tongue in and out, insistently, rhythmically. Symbolic. Erotic. He is kissing her with deep, dizzying kisses, while his hand continues to strum her, lower, lower. She is quivering, shimmering, poised on the edge of exquisite sensation.

The gentle hands grow gradually stronger, gripping her buttocks, digging into her flesh, hurting her. She fights to get away, but he holds her down with one hand, pinning her under him. She struggles, then feels a sharp, jagged pain across her back. She opens her mouth to scream but no sound comes out. She screams and screams but the dream completely muffles the sound. She tries to turn her head to look at him, imploring him with her eyes, begging him to stop. He holds her by the neck with his teeth, like an animal, like a dog. He lifts her ass towards him, his fingernails still raking her, and her body tenses for the ultimate attack. He parts her and she feels the hard stab. She is twisting and turning under him but he holds her fast as the pain rips through her, violating her . . . not there, please, no . . .

Miriam woke in a sweat, shaking, her teeth chattering with cold. Where was she? Oh yes, the little *pied-à-terre* that she and Stephen had lived in when they were first together. They'd kept it as a second apartment, a place to get away, out of the public eye. Reporters had been hanging around her for days now.

The official announcement of the Academy Award nominations was going to be made that morning and Gwen had arranged for a group of friends to be with her at The Club to watch the live satellite transmission from LA. It would be an interesting media angle for Miriam and of course good publicity for The Club. The Academy held a news conference at 5 a.m. LA time, which meant it would hit the early-morning new shows around eight o'clock New York time. Miriam had to be dressed and made-up early so that *Entertainment Tonight* could cover the breakfast party as her friends watched the television around her in the hopes of celebrating a nomination with her. What time was it now? She searched in vain for her watch.

She shivered. The dream clung to her like an unpleasant echo from some unlived past. How could she dream such a thing? Whatever faults he had, whatever was wrong between them, Stephen would never hurt her physically. Her own guilt had triggered the nightmare, obviously.

532

Did she secretly believe she needed to be punished? No, that was crazy, too. She shivered again. It really was cold in here. She missed the oversized goose-down duvet she and Stephen had on their other bed.

There was a trunk at the foot of the bed that she remembered usually held some extra linen. Slinging on her red silk robe, chilly in the early morning air as she got out of bed, she knelt and opened the trunk. There was no blanket. Just an odd collection of paraphernalia. At first she didn't know what she was looking at. The knotted leather riding crop. The black leather mask and boots. The candles and the pool of congealed melted wax. What in God's name was this stuff and what was it doing here? There was a pile of magazines. She selected one and leafed through it, then slammed it closed. In an envelope in one corner was a stack of colour Polaroids. As if hypnotized she picked it up. What she saw revolted her. The spike-heeled boot on the face. The foot to the groin. And then, her heart skipped a beat as she saw but didn't believe what she saw. Stephen. She looked again, her heart beginning to pound wildly. My God, it was *Stephen*. Stephen bound and gagged. Stephen handcuffed to the bed. And the man in the photos with him was Luigi del Bello.

Waves of nausea hit her. Spilling the photos to the floor, she lurched blindly toward the bathroom, dropped on to the cold tiled floor on her knees in a sweat, retching into the toilet, tears stinging her eyes. After a long time the nausea gradually ebbed and there was nothing left in her to come up. She lay huddled there, shivering, the horrifying images flashing before her in succession again and again. Who was this man she had shared the last fifteen years of her life with? She didn't know him at all.

She pulled herself up to a standing position. She caught sight of herself in the mirror and was surprised to see that other than the red eyes and pale face, she looked the same as ever, her luxuriant hair floating over her shoulders. She looked normal. Normal. What did that mean? Nothing. It was all relative. What was normal for Stephen now? And what did this say about them? She felt the bile rising in her again and she turned away to take a deep breath. She carefully made her way back into the bedroom and with trembling fingers picked up the photos again. She pulled several from the middle of the packet and hastily stuffed the others back down towards the bottom of the trunk, closing the lid. Then she sat on the bed, clutching the photos without seeing them.

Dear God, he needed help. She would get him help. She must talk with him as soon as possible. But he was out of town until the evening of the gala. She'd go crazy if she didn't find out the truth about this before then. Lou. She would confront Lou. There had to be an explanation, it was a joke, it was a mistake, Stephen couldn't have known what he was doing . . .

Her mind raced round and round in circles and her head pounded, echoing the massive pounding on the door. Then it swung open and she faced a barrage of cameras. She was totally bewildered until she realized the press had tracked her down. It was then that she learned that she had been nominated for an Academy Award for Best Actress for *Paloma*.

She had no time now to deal with what she had just found. And she couldn't deal with it anyway. She greeted her pursuers graciously, smiling and prepared to face the day.

# *Twenty-seven*

Gwen's brownstone. Gwen climbed into bed alone, as usual, with an apple and a good book. Even though the book was *In Search of Excellence* and the apple was a highly polished Australian pippin that had cost her two bucks at the local Korean grocery, she knew her nightly routine was a cliché. She had three breakfast meetings tomorrow morning, one at seven, one at eight and one at a quarter to nine; she had to meet with her lawyers at ten, finalize the catering contract with Susie Krumins at noon, and spend all afternoon in a rehearsal of the entertainment for the gala.

It was two o'clock in the morning now and she had to be up by six at the latest. If she was lucky she'd be able to get four hours sleep, but lately she hadn't been able to sleep much, and when she did drift off she was plagued by nightmares. In her dreams, the renovations were complete, The Club was more magnificent than ever, its handsome oak doors wide open, chamber music playing — but its long halls and spacious rooms were completely empty. Clustered outside the front door, faceless women of all shapes and sizes crouched, cradling undernourished babies. As Gwen tried to enter the building the women blocked her way, clutching at her skirt, trying to shove their children into her arms, their mouths open, expressions desperate. Sometimes she dreamed she was running up the street, The Club before her, just out of reach. When she finally put her hand on the cool brass, it disintegrated, the door gave way, and the walls of the building came crashing down around her. The nightmare had recurred often enough that she was reluctant to fall asleep now.

She reached for her mug, picking the brown scum off the Ovaltine and blew on it to cool it. It was hard to find Ovaltine in New York; it appeared to be a Canadian-British tradition. Merilee teased her about her addiction to it, but Gwen refused to resort to sleeping pills.

At last she turned out the light and settled under the covers. Her mind continued to flick nervously over the problems of the day, replaying the current crises at The Club. Somebody had been stealing underwear from the change-room again, not just the lacy chemises and teddies but the one-hundred-per-cent cotton briefs with the loose-weave crotch that some of the members liked to wear. While the Great Books Club met in meeting room A and Merilee's co-ed aerobics thumped on in the workout studio, Cheryl Tops had slit her wrists in the Jacuzzi. Cheryl, an out-of-work actress with a sulky face and over-sized breast implants, had bled all over the pink marble steps and into the whirlpool. She was going to be fine, but hers was the third suicide attempt at The Club this year. What was the attraction of committing suicide at The Club? Less chance of actually going through with it maybe, and a bigger audience left behind to grieve if you did succeed. Just outside The Club, a member had been mugged recently. And this was supposed to be one of the safest areas of New York.

Everything was becoming increasingly dangerous, Gwen told herself. Coffee caused cancer, but there was no point in switching to decaffeinated coffee because 'they', whoever they were, had decided the decaffeination process also caused cancer. An apple a day no longer kept the doctor away because of what the fruit was sprayed with. Syringes were washing up on the shores of New York. Water was no longer safe to drink or to bathe in. If you wore a tampon you were taking your life into your hands. Now there was a warning from the Surgeon General on every box of tampons. Life was full of such toxic shocks. The Club was supposed to provide a haven from all that. Why did she feel danger creeping in under the doors?

This kind of thinking was getting her absolutely nowhere. She sat up, snapped on the bedside lamp, and looked at the digital clock. It was nearly three. She dialled Merilee's number. Merilee never minded being awakened and she always answered her phone, unlike Gwen who would put her phone on the answering service for days at a time if she didn't want to be disturbed. She let it ring ten times and hung up. On impulse she dialled Lou's number and let it ring ten times, but he didn't answer either. Wearily she replaced the receiver, stuck her earplugs in her ears, pulled her sleep mask down over her eyes and tried, once again, to go to sleep.

Sara's apartment in the World Trade Center. Sara's cry of exhilaration still reverberated around the room. She lay there panting. There was nothing like good sex to focus her thoughts. Michael's breathing slowed and he raised his head to look at her.

Sara groaned inwardly. This was the part she hated. The après-sex chat. She could see it in his eyes, he was going to start talking and she would have to listen to his myriad problems: the unhappy love affairs (and they were all unhappy), his broken teenage marriage, the illegitimate twins he'd fathered in San Diego. Who the hell cared? Sure enough, he rolled off her, lit a cigarette and said, 'You know something, Sara? I've been thinking. I'm sort of drifting, I need a real relationship, some focus in my life, you know?' Sara reached for the Perrier water beside the bed. Maybe if she didn't respond, he'd go back to sleep. 'What we have is really special . . .'

'Let's get one thing straight, Michael,' Sara cut in sharply, 'I like your dick and I like your mind, but your emotional needs don't interest me.'

'What do you mean?' Michael sat up to look at her. 'You pissed off with me or what?'

'I'm getting to know you too well.' She reached over and took a drag from his cigarette. She was trying to give up smoking but so far with limited success.

'I wish I could say the same about you. I feel as if I don't know you at all. You never tell me anything.'

'I don't want to tell you anything. That's the point. I don't want to have to waste time having dinner with you or holding your hand or picking out your ties. I just want to go to bed with you. As frequently as possible.'

'Well, that' s all I want from you.' Michael looked hurt and bewildered, rubbing his eyes like a sleepy child.

'No, it isn't. You want love. Every pore of you is screaming out, Love me, love me. You're one big massive need.'

'What's wrong with that?'

'Love is the last thing I want. Our drives are completely different. You want love; I want lust. Pure, uncomplicated lust. You're good at sex, Michael; you perform extremely well. You could probably love very well, too, but I simply don't need it.'

'I wasn't asking you to marry me,' he mumbled sulkily.

'Good. Any woman who marries you better come armed with a sugar tit and a year's supply of Pampers.'

'Jesus, you're a cold-hearted bitch!' Michael pulled the sheet over himself. 'Why don't you just admit you're bored with me?'

'All right.' Sara smiled at the familiar refrain. 'I am bored with you. You're becoming predictable, my love,

538

and that is the eighth deadly sin.' She picked up her watch from the bedside table. 'Now I can give you fifteen more minutes of my time. Would you like to make love again?'

But Michael was already pulling on his clothes. 'Are you crazy? You kick me in the balls and then you expect me to perform for you?'

'Why not?' Sara stretched out lazy on the oversized bed.

'Forget it. This relationship is finished. From now on, it's strictly business.'

'You'll change your mind.'

'No I won't.' Michael slammed out of the door.

But she knew he would. They always came back to her. No man ever left Sara Town until she was ready to let him go. Still that old fear feeling was back in the pit of her stomach. Why? *In Depth* was consistently in the top ten now, even beating out *Sixty Minutes*, so why was she unsatisfied? More, she wanted more. Quickly she picked up the telephone and dialled a number.

'Hello, Stephen?' she said. 'I know it's late, but I need to see you. Right away.'

Stephen and Miriam's apartment. Stephen hung up the phone and turned to face Lou. 'I've got to go out for a bit.'

'Who was that?'

'Sara Town.'

'I thought you were out of that relationship.'

'I am. This is business. She's doing an *In Depth* profile on me.'

'At this hour? You better watch yourself, *cara*. Sara Town is the mouth that ate New York. If you want to sell your soul to the devil, you may have to give your prick to Lilith. She is, *come si dice*, rapacious.'

'I don't need advice from you, Lou.' Stephen's voice

was icy cold. 'What I need is money. It's been three months and you still haven't come through.'

'I told you, my major sources have dried up.' Lou couldn't stop sweating. 'The Boston land went to pay for the renovations. That's what's holding everything up. I'm just beginning to see my way clear. You've got to give me another week.'

'You don't understand.' Stephen was starting to feel frantic himself. 'I haven't *got* a week. My back is against the wall. CAFF wants an accounting. Some liberal Democrats are about to introduce a bill into Congress that limits the use of private funds to the contras. They're going to be pushing for full disclosure of the books and in the meantime I've got to show the members of my organization exactly what is in our fund at present, what money has been spent, and exactly where it has gone. I've got to have that million right now.'

'Look, we're friends, Stephen. I promise you, I'll come through.'

Friends. Stephen looked at him with revulsion. He hated Lou now and he hated himself for getting involved with him. He'd become hooked on a highly dangerous thrill that had shifted from desire into compulsion, each release bringing only a brief satisfaction, a momentary peace before the need was there again. Somehow, through it all, he'd felt invincible, as though nothing could hurt him. He knew now he'd made a grievous error of judgement.

Senator Hughes had warned him about being seen too often in public with Lou unaccompanied by Gwyneth Roberts. Of course, the older man had no knowledge of the relationship between Stephen and Lou; he was merely concerned about appearances. What would he do if knew the truth? It was all beginning to catch up with him. Between the lofty ideals of his public career and the depths of depravity of his private life lay a no-man's-land

540

that even Stephen himself could not reconcile.

He was rumoured to be the front-runner when and if he declared himself officially in the race. Once he did, he would be subject to even greater scrutiny from the press. Journalists would be looking for Stephen Andrews' 'fatal flaw'. He remembered Gary Hart's example very well. He couldn't let that happen to him.

It was too late for Miriam to save him this time. She was too close to the world that was destroying him. He needed someone young and unformed, someone whose private life was still above reproach, someone who could get him back on the straight and narrow and give him new faith in himself. Right now, he believed more than anything that the only person who could save him from himself was Laura Hughes.

'I'll get the money for you, I promise.' Lou's voice brought him back to reality.

'When?'

'I'll have it for you the night of the gala.'

Lou's apartment. The phone rang ten times and Merilee just let it ring. 'It could be one of Lou's lovers calling, in which case it would be unwise for her to answer the phone, or it might be Lou himself, in which case Merilee didn't want him to hear her voice at the other end of the line. She wanted to surprise him, let him find her in his studio draped decorously on his huge waterbed wearing a fur coat, long white socks and nothing else. Her collection of knee socks was bigger than the rest of her entire wardrobe but, thanks to Bob Guccione and his Vaseline-covered lens photos of Penthouse Pets, most men considered her knee socks a turn-on. She'd seen the fur coat bit in *Midnight Cowboy* years ago. It had taken her almost that long to amass the cash to buy a fur; now she was looking forward to fulfilling the fantasy.

Since breaking up with Lokis, her current source of

good sex was Lou again. She had expected Lokis to be grateful to her for telling her about Susie's plan to have an abortion. Instead he'd broken down and cried and said he didn't want to see her any more. She would have to rely on Lou until she found her next quarry. She glanced at the bedside digital clock. Three in the morning? Where the hell was he? Wrapping her coat tightly around her, she rocked back and forth. There was the thud of heavy bodies against the studio door, drunken whispering and suppressed giggling. The door swung open and Lou stumbled into the room, follow by a rough-looking young blond man, drunk as a skunk, with one arm around Lou's shoulders, the other gripping Lou's crotch. The guy looked seedy, like a hooker from Times Square.

'I didn't expect to find you here.' Lou looked a bit sheepish, his voice ascending and then descending in scale. Suddenly his eyes lit up and he turned to the man behind him, 'Hey, baby, what would you say to a threesome? Shall we give Goldilocks another bear?'

The hooker nodded slowly, his eyes bright and vacant. Merilee felt the fury rising within her. He hadn't even ask her what she wanted. All right, she would do it; she would give him the time of his life. And then she'd make pay. She didn't know how yet, but she would find a way. Majestically she rose to her feet, balancing carefully on the bed undulating beneath her. Opening her fur coat wide, she said, 'Come on in, guys, the water's fine.'

Sara's apartment. 'I'm sorry, Sara,' Stephen gently extricated himself from her welcoming embrace. 'Things can't be quite the way they used to be between us. There have been some major changes in my life. I'm turning over a new leaf. It's not official yet, but I'm secretly engaged to be married.'

'Don't tell me you've finally decided to make an honest

woman out of Miriam Newman?' Sara managed to maintain a note of amused detachment in her voice.

'It's not Miriam. That's why I'm keeping a low profile on this thing right now. Miriam and I are going to go our separate ways. Too many separations, too much career pressure — it just wasn't working out. I think she's planning to base herself on the coast. No, I intend to marry Laura Hughes.'

'Senator Hughes's daughter? Well, well, well.' Sara's left eyebrow shot up in surprise. 'That's a smart political move, but I can see why you want to wait a bit — at least until the Oscars are over.'

'Exactly. It's vital that I get the attention off Miriam and back on to me at just the right time, I'll wait till Mim is relocated in LA. Then Laura and I can announce our plans.'

'I can't believe, given your track record, that you intend to be entirely faithful for the rest of your life.'

'Actually I do. I've resisted marriage for a long time, but now that I've made the decision, I intend to do everything I can to make it work.'

Sara shrugged. 'Fair enough. I do have another proposal to make to you, however, and perhaps it will be better if there are no strings attached.'

'Go ahead. Shoot.'

Sara looked him straight in the eye. 'I believe in you, Stephen. I believe you can win the nomination. I also believe you can be elected president. I want to work with you to make sure that it happens.'

Stephen was somewhat taken aback. 'But you're so high-profile! You represent a major network! You can't be seen to be supporting either party or a particular candidate.'

'I know,' Sara agreed quickly, 'but I can work behind the scenes for your campaign. I've got a lot of influence where it counts most, both here and in Washington, and

I want to use it to help you. My motives are not completely altruistic, I admit. Quite frankly, I'm looking to get out of television. I want something more. Eventually, I'd like to be in politics myself. This is all in the future, I realize, but if you are elected, I want you to consider me for some sort of position.'

Stephen stared at her, dumbfounded. The woman was out of her mind. With her history of drugs and sex, there was no way he wanted her near him. Ever again. That's what he had to make clear to her tonight before he left here, and without hurting her feelings. Sara was far too powerful for him to risk alienating her in any way.

He cleared his throat and tried to smile at her. 'I have tremendous respect as well as a good deal of fondness for you, Sara, as I'm sure you know. But Gwyneth Roberts has already agreed to lend her support to my bid for the presidency. I am grateful to have the full backing of The Club.'

Gwyneth Roberts. The name drove little stabs into Sara's gut. 'What are you doing involving Gwyneth Roberts and The Club in your campaign? It may get you the female vote, but it could cost you the male one, not to mention those women who think The Club is designed to exclude them and make them feel like the great unwashed.'

'Those women aren't going to support my position anyway, I'm after the financially successful women, the women who already wield some power in this country and would like to wield more.'

'I still think you're making a mistake linking yourself to The Club. It could prove a political liability. I have reason to believe that place is about to blow sky-high. I'm on the trail right now of some very shady dealings at The Club, and I'm not just talking minor indiscretions either.'

544

'Of what kind?' Stephen could feel himself starting to sweat.

'Sex and drugs.' Sara tried to sound casual. 'The illegal kind. Gwyneth Roberts presents a clean surface, but there's definitely more there than meets the eye. I think she's one hell of a manipulative bitch.'

'You're twice as manipulative as Gwen. Don't be offended,' he added hastily. 'I respect you for it. It's the way I operate, too, but I do think it might make it difficult for us to work together.'

'What about our past history?' Sara said seductively. 'Doesn't that me anything to you?'

'Of course it does, but I feel I need new people around me now,' Stephen said, hoping his tone sounded reasonable. 'A clean slate. I'm sure you understand.'

'No I don't. I think you owe it to me.'

Goddamnit, he didn't want to hear that again. He owed it to Sara. He owed it to Lou. He owed it to Miriam. 'Look, Sara,' he said firmly, 'I can't guarantee you a job just because you screwed me. That's what this is all about, isn't it?'

'No, Stephen, it's not.' Sara spoke more calmly now that she had him on the defensive. 'I care about the American people. I don't want to see you screw them. You've marketed and sold an image of yourself as honorary mascot of the women's movement. My job is to find out if you live up to that image.'

'For Christ's sake, of course I live up to it.' Stephen exploded.

'I personally know that you haven't.'

'There isn't a public figure in North America who hasn't dallied around a bit. It didn't cost Kennedy any votes. There have even been rumours about George Bush. The public doesn't expect a politician to be a saint any more.'

'No, but they still don't expect him to be a satyr either.'

'So what are you going to do, Sara, expose my sordid past on camera and embarrass yourself into the bargain? I'm a single man; do you really think your viewers are going to care that I've poked a few babes in my time?'

'No, but they might find drugs a little harder to deal with, especially since you are the chairman of the Presidential Action Committee for the war on drugs.'

'Drugs? What are you talking about?' The hair stood up on the back of his neck at the same time as his mouth went dry.

'Why don't we watch a little video that I've been saving especially to share with you?' Sara shoved the cassette into her VCR and punched the buttons.

He watched in horror as his own image came up on the screen, spread-eagled on the bed, tied to its four posts with strips of leather. A naked woman knelt over him, giving him what appeared to be, from the look on his face, a highly expert blow job. On the table next to the bed, in full view of the camera, were at least eight lines of cocaine waiting for them. It was unmistakably, undeniably him. It revolted him to see himself like some kind of tortured animal, the veins in his neck standing out, the muscles of his face contorted with ecstasy as he reached his final tormented release.

He watched in silence, overwhelmed. He was so close to getting everything in life that he wanted. How could he have allowed himself to be sidetracked like this?

Sara snapped off the machine. 'Well?'

'You're willing to invade my privacy and yours,' Stephen said quietly, 'for some sort of perverted sense of revenge? Exploit both of us and engineer your own downfall in the process? I can't believe you would do that.'

'Believe it.' Sara stood before him, her eyes bright. 'It

546

might be difficult to prove the woman in the video is me. She could be any dark-haired woman. It's rather hard to tell, isn't it?'

It was true. Bent over him, her long dark hair completely hid her face. He could feel the forces of evil closing in around him. He would have to think quickly. 'How many of our little encounters did you preserve like this?'

'Just this one. But it's more than enough to get the point across, don't you agree?'

'Give me that you bitch.' He lunged at her as she sprang away from him, heading for the door. He beat her to her escape, blocking her way, and backed her up on to the bed where the two of them fell, scrabbling for the tape. Cursing under his breath, he tried to hold her down but she fought and clawed at him like a tiger. At last he knocked the cassette out of her hand. They both leapt after it, Stephen grabbing it first and darting into the kitchen with Sara right behind him. She tripped him and sent him sprawling, the tape bouncing away from him. Sara ran after it, but Stephen was on her, covering her hand with his, and they grappled until he managed to subdue her and drag her into the kitchen. With his free hand he slammed the drawers open and shut, searching for a knife, rifling through the flatware and implements until he found a pair of shears. With the cord of her satin bathrobe he tied her to one of the cane-backed chairs and slammed the case of the cassette against the counter edge until it snapped in half.

'You bastard' — Sara fairy spit the words out as he unwound the reams of tape — 'you can't destroy that.'

'Watch me,' he said, slicing the tape into ribbons. 'What did you plan to do — get me on air, set me up, and then shoot me down?'

'I never intended to use it.'

'The hell you didn't.' Stephen hacked away at the yards

of tape ferociously. 'You want some sort of hold over me, don't you?'

'I've *got* a hold over you.'

'Not any more.' Stephen grabbed most of the pile of curling strands and, turning the water on in the sink full force, he ran the tape into the garburator. Then, panting and red-faced, he leaned over her and spoke directly into her face, 'That's the end of it, Sara. All of it. You understand?' And he walked out of the apartment, closing the door behind him.

'It's not the end,' Sara whispered. 'Not by a long shot.' And she turned her attention to loosening her bonds.

Gwen's brownstone. Gwen tossed and turned. She just couldn't get to sleep. Sara. Was it Sara that was keeping her awake? The knowledge that she would be coming face to face with her for the first time in years, at the gala? Crazy. That was crazy. So long ago. Blood under the bridge by now. It had to be. And yet she knew there was a part of her that longed to prove to Sara just how successful she had become, to show off the magnificent structure she had built virtually on her own, The Club. She was suddenly flooded with self-doubt. She couldn't shake the feeling that the idealistic motives that had led her into the women's movement in the first place and later to create The Club were no longer part of her agenda. Her idealism had somehow slipped away not only from her but from even the most committed women. They were no longer united and they needed that particular strength more than ever now that the pendulum seemed to be swinging the other way and feminism was no longer in fashion. Women were in danger of losing what they had only just barely achieved. That meant that women who had made it to the top felt threatened by those who were still trying to get there.

She knew she was guilty of this herself. She was fighting

to protect her territory. There were rumours of other women's clubs starting up in New York and she feared competition. That's why the LA deal was so important. LA first and then on to London. Surely Lou could see that? Why the hell was he dragging his feet on all this? Merilee had been dropping veiled hints about his behaviour, but she was acting just as strangely herself. It seemed she couldn't trust either of them these days.

If she could just get through the gala. Everything was riding on the gala. The gala would show everybody that The Club was still original, still the best of them all.

# Part III

*Return to the Gala*

# One

Sara held Gwen firmly by the arm and the two women
stood looking at each other. Below them, in the foyer,
the swell of the party continued, but everything seemed
to fade away as they came face to face. They were both
visibly shaken by the events of the past hour. Sara had
wasted no time in drawing the battle lines. Her frankly
hostile approach in the television interview had confirmed
that. Her insinuations that The Club was on shaky ground
with a history of shady business practices. Her veiled
threats about Gwen's personal life. Everything was
guaranteed to throw Gwen off her guard. Yet somehow
Sara seemed to be even less in control of her feelings.

And then the confrontation with Lokis Krumins in
front of Sara. Susie had taken Lokis down the stairs and
out of the front door. Lou had disappeared. Merilee was
nowhere to be seen. Gwen and Sara stood facing each
other, alone for the first time in almost twenty years.
Twenty years of leading separate lives, lives in which
neither one of them had ever felt completely free of the
other.

They saw the obvious surface changes in each other.
They were both undeniably older. There were shadows
under Sara's amber eyes and fine lines around Gwen's
firm mouth. Sara was still startlingly beautiful, her thick
hair still dark and rich, the fine eyebrows etched just as
sharply, the magnificent eyes luminous above her strong,
smooth cheekbones, but the eagerness and expectation

that had once made them sparkle had dimmed, the restlessness replaced by a bitterness and hostility that was both sad and frightening. Still she looked as elegant as ever and vaguely restless, like an exotic cat in her black mini skirt.

Gwen appeared taller than Sara remembered her, with a confidence and poise that emanated not only from her expensive haircut and designer clothes, but from an inner calm that was reflected in her steady gaze at Sara. She looked sophisticated. Serene.

Sara broke the silence between them. 'Mr Krumins seems to blame you and The Club for just about everything wrong with his life. The kind of hate you engender in men, it's really quite interesting, don't you think?'

'It's an isolated incident, Sara,' Gwen said. 'Don't blow it all out of proportion. I'm an easy target these days, that's all.'

Sara smiled. 'I'm surprised you don't receive daily threats on your life. You're quite the paper tiger now, aren't you? There must be a number of people who'd like to punch a few holes in you. You never could learn to keep your mouth shut.'

'I could easily say the same for you. You were, after all, my most important role model.' Gwen held her gaze steady. She'd dreaded this moment for such a long time and now that it was finally here none of it seemed to matter any more. 'There's no point in hating me now, Sara. The truth of the matter is, I've changed. If anything, I would suspect that you and I have grown rather alike.'

Sara's eyes narrowed. 'Oh no, Gwenny-Penny, we're still worlds apart. The only reason you wanted to start an exclusive club was so that you would have somewhere to belong. You've always been on the outside looking in. Apart from The Club, you have no life of your own. I

554

know. I've kept track of your career. You haven't changed at all.'

'I'm still a private person, if that's what you mean.' Gwen smiled, her auburn hair gleaming under the light of the chandelier. 'I live by my own rules. I should think that you, more than anyone I've ever known, would understand my need for that.'

'How do you feel about the fact that after all these years, despite your so-called success, despite the money you've made, you're still alone?'

'You sound exactly like my mother.' Gwen tried to smile again, but Sara still refused to respond. 'You don't really mean alone. What you mean is unattached. I don't have one person to share my life with, that's true. Maybe it's because I've seen too many women make the mistake of defining themselves only through love. From what I remember of you, you made that particular mistake yourself at least once. Have you changed?'

Sara brushed the question aside. 'What I want to know is, have you shared your bed with a man since you lost your virginity to my fiancé?'

'You've been in and out of far more beds than I have, Sara,' Gwen said quietly. 'There's no contest there. But what have you got to show for it?'

'You've screwed more people in business than I ever did in bed.' Sara's face was twisted with anger and bitterness. 'You may fool these dessicated dykes at The Club into thinking you're some socio-psychological guru who can offer them power and happiness with a high-priced lifestyle, but you're the last person who could actually help them. You love playing God, don't you? You're so involved with controlling the lives and feelings of everyone around you that you don't even really see them, so busy directing your own life that you've never learned how to live it. You were a scared little country mouse when I knew you and underneath this big city-woman facade, you're still scared. Of your own shadow. Of your sexuality. Tell me, have you finally come to terms with what you really are?'

'I hope so,' Gwen said simply. 'And I sincerely hope you have, too.' But it was obvious Sara hadn't. She was still carrying a tremendous amount of anger. Gwen herself felt no anger, only relief that she was no longer under this woman's spell. 'Look Sara, we're both ambitious. We both wanted to get to the top and we both have. It's time to celebrate our success. Can't you simply wish me well? As I wish you?'

'No,' Sara said fiercely, 'I can't.'

'Then I'm truly sorry for you.' She turned to go, but Sara gripped her arm.

'You think you're on a roll right now, don't you,' Sara hissed. 'You're a big success and nothing can hurt you. Well, let me tell you, old friend, you are riding for one hell of a fall.' Sara pinned Gwen against the door of her own office. 'The foundations of The Club are rotten and I intend to prove it. Publicly. A word of warning to you, dear. You may think you have your foot firmly placed over this can of worms, but when they turn, they'll turn on you.'

'And a word of warning to you, Sara.' Gwen slid away and gracefully stepped through the door. 'You'd better watch yourself. You're getting too big for your britches.'

Sara was surprised to find herself trembling. The confrontation had unleashed long-hidden feelings in her, feelings she'd managed to hold in check for years. Suddenly she was angry and jealous and hurt all over again. Why? What had she expected from all this? Somehow to bring Gwen to her knees in front of her, begging for her forgiveness? Even if she had done that, what would it have accomplished? Was there nothing that would make her life right?

556

She was actually shaking. She needed a cigarette. She opened her purse to dig one out and her fingers touched the padded envelope that Miriam Newman had thrust at her just before the television interview. She might as well take a look at what Miriam considered valuable information on her soon-to-be-lost love. She drew out a set of Polaroid pictures and quickly thumbed through them, her brain beginning to race. The photographs in her hands were hot enough to burn her fingers. They shocked even her jaded sensibilities. Miriam must be mad as hell to have given her these. They were pure gold. And exactly what she needed.

Now the question was, should she confront Stephen tonight? Her revenge was going to be absolutely delicious however she played it. She had a feeling Stephen might be prepared to negotiate.

Thoughtfully she slipped the photos back into their envelope. There was always the chance that Miriam might change her mind and ask her to return them. She headed for the main entrance. She would give this hidden treasure to Joe Garcia, the security guard, to be locked up in visitors' valuables.

Slipping into her office, Gwen closed the door firmly on Sara. She was surprised to find that she'd stopped shaking and felt quite calm. Whatever connection there'd been between them was severed for good. She was stronger. She had exorcised a ghost and she could feel it slide from her shoulders like a cloak of anxiety, leaving only lightness and relief.

She poured herself a stiff Scotch from her private bar and sat down at her desk. Gwen picked up the phone and buzzed the front desk, asking the receptionist to find Merilee in the party and send her up to Gwen's office. She took a drink, hoping for a few quiet moments to work through what had just happened, but almost immediately there was a knock at the door. Merilee came in. As she opened the door, the noise from the party pounded behind her; the minute she closed it, the sound was cut off completely. Gwen was glad she had had her office soundproofed like an isolation chamber during the recent renovations. She needed to talk to Merilee in strictest confidence where nobody could disturb them. Merilee had betrayed her, Gwen was sure of that. She wanted to know how far she had done so.

Across the desk, Merilee sat in quiet terror, watching Gwen's face for any indication of emotion. She looked unusually demure, her hands in her lap. Gwen looked at her searchingly and Merilee's heart turned over. This woman loves me, she thought. I know it. She doesn't want to lose me. I'm the only friend she's got.

'You've got some explaining to do,' Gwen said quietly. 'It was you who told Lokis Krumins about Susie's plans to have an abortion. You're the only person who could have told him. It was a confidence that I — foolishly — shared with you. You swore that information would never leave this room.' Merilee said nothing. 'What happened? Answer me!' Gwen slammed her hand down on the top of her desk and Merilee jumped.

All of a sudden Merilee was back in eighth grade. She looked at Gwen defiantly and thought, You trying to scare me into confessing something here? Forget it, lady. I stand up real good under pressure. I'll tell you exactly what I want you to know and not one pissant bit more. Gwen was staring at her, waiting for an answer. Merilee forced her eyes to fill with tears. 'Oh Gwen, don't. Don't look at me that way. You couldn't feel any worse about this than I do. It's all my fault, I admit it. But it was for a good cause, I swear.'

'What good cause?' Gwen unceremoniously shoved a box of Kleenex across the desk toward her.

'Merilee meekly took one and wiped her eyes. 'I know

558

I shouldn't have opened my big mouth to Lokis, but I was only trying to help the poor guy. I wanted to be like you.'

'Like me?'

'You're so good at fixin' other people's lives. And they love you for it. I just felt honoured he would ask me to help.'

'Lokis Krumins asked you for help? Why?'

'It's kind of a complicated story. You sure . . .?'

'Tell me.'

'Well, he just burst into tears one day. Right after one of my aerobics classes. Susie was out the door the minute the hour was up and he ran after her, but he couldn't catch her, so he just sat down on the studio floor and started to cry. I offered to buy him a drink. I didn't know what else to do. He just sat there in the bar crying in his beer.'

'Because Susie had left him?'

'Well, that's what I thought at first, but he finally told me that he was afraid he was sterile and wouldn't ever be able to have kids. He said he and Susie had been trying everything since they got married but nothing seemed to work. He felt he couldn't call himself a man any longer and maybe that was why Susie had left him, because he couldn't make her pregnant. I know I shouldn't have gotten involved with their private business. I felt just sick about it.'

'Merilee, you can't play God with other people's lives' − but the minute Gwen said it she realized that was exactly what Sara had accused her of just moments ago. 'Why *did* you get involved?'

'I don't know. I guess I just wanted somebody to depend on me. I wanted to advise him the way you would.' Gwen shivered. Could Sara be right after all? 'I was flattered that Lokis would share such a personal problem with me. He seemed confused about his male

559

identity. I just wanted to reassure him, so I told him he couldn't possibly be sterile because I knew that Susie was pregnant and then . . .' She faltered.

'You told him Susie was intending to terminate the pregnancy.'

'Yeah, I'm afraid I did.'

'Then why didn't you tell him Susie changed her mind, that she was still pregnant after all?'

'I was going to but by then I had stopped . . .'

'Sleeping with him,' Gwen finished.

'I wasn't . . .'

Gwen interrupted her. 'He said you seduced him and I believe he meant that literally. He accused us both of trying to destroy his marriage.'

'Hell, I never even started seein' Lokis until he and Susie had already split! I felt sorry for him, that's all. Basically it was what you'd call a mercy fuck.' A week ago that would have elicited at least a chuckle from Gwen. Now she didn't crack a smile. 'I knew it was wrong, but, shoot, Gwen, even you've got to admit that a lot of husbands are havin' a pretty rough time these days. Their wives don't pay them no mind, so they're all pretty frustrated. Hey, you should be pleased with me' — she winked conspiratorially — 'I keep our members happy by keeping their hubbies occupied.'

'Do you mean what I think you mean?' Gwen stared at her, her eyes enormous.

'Oh come on, don't give me that hot-potato shit-eatin' look. We've known each other too long for that. I want things to be the way they used to be between you and me. Totally honest, you know? We make a great business team and we have a lot of fun.'

'I can't believe what you've just confessed to me.' Gwen's words slammed into Merilee's face. 'You've been using The Club to pimp for yourself? You've been screwing around, on a regular basis, with Club members'

560

husbands? I'm sorry, Merilee, you've given me no alternative but to fire you.'

Terror gripped Merilee. 'Wait a minute. If you're going to fire someone around here, why not fire Lou? He's the one who should go. And leave you and me to get this Club back on target.' Surely Gwen couldn't be prepared to let her personal assistant and best friend walk out of her life and her business without a second chance. 'Fire Lou. He's the one responsible for letting The Club go over the edge.'

'I'm planning to send Lou to England,' Gwen said firmly, 'to run the London branch. When and if we manage to get it open.'

The London branch. That was supposed to be her job, her reward for putting up with all this shit. She exploded: 'So I laid a few horny husbands, so what? I never put The Club's financial security in jeopardy like Lou is doing right this minute under your very nose! The Club could go into receivership at a moment's notice. We could *all* be brought up on criminal charges!'

'What on earth are you talking about?'

'How do you think your little tugboat stays afloat these days? Because of your brilliant managerial skills and creative counselling? Not on your ass.' The words were spilling out of her, but she didn't care. Miss High-and-Mighty deserved it. 'It's because the members know they can get whatever they want whenever they want it right inside these four walls. What do you think the "special privileges" private retreat area is all about?'

'What do you mean?'

'Lou's been double-dealing on you, sugar and I do mean dealing.'

'I don't understand . . .' Feeling faint, Gwen put one hand to the gold-link necklace at her throat.

'Try twenty years to life if he gets caught. Try the police raiding The Club and closing it down. Slapping you with a charge of aiding and abetting a small-time, big-bucks coke dealer.'

'Drugs!'

'You got it! Mostly cocaine. He's been moving several kilos a month, supplying a lot of our members and God knows who else. The Mafia's involved, too. I'm pretty sure of it.'

'I don't believe you.'

'Where do you think he got the money for the renovations? We're in a recession, honey. Who's tossin' money around to redecorate a ladies' health spa? But there's always plenty of money to get laid or to get high. People are willing to pay top dollar for what they really want and, hey Lou's got the perfect cover – The Club.'

'How long has this been going on?' Gwen could hardly get the words out.

'The heavy dealin's been a couple of years. Started small, but grew real big. You pretty much gave him a free hand. You made him business manager. You allowed him to set up his own computer system. It's all there in a secret programme. I cracked the code.'

'How can you be sure of all this?' Gwen whispered.

Merilee smiled. 'Let's just say that Lou and I are close. Very close. Oh, there's a lot I could tell you about our Lou.'

'You're lying.' Gwen was having trouble breathing and there was a roaring in her ears.

'I don't know why you're mad at *me*. I've followed your ass at close range doin' your dirty work for you. Hell, I've even wiped it for you! You wanted a spy and you got one. Now I bring you the results and it's all "hush my mouf, I don't believe you, you must be lyin' " . . .'

Gwen was out of her chair and at the door in a flash. 'Get out. Pack your things and clear out your office. I want you out of here. You're fired.'

Merilee's face reflected her panic. 'You can't fire me.

I know too much about this place. I can make things hot for you . . .'

'Listen to me, Merilee, and you listen hard. You don't know jack-shit. I never really bought the whole southern-flower act you were peddling around here but I always assumed it hid a real you that was better than the image, not something infinitely worse. You want to soil your own pasture, that's your lookout, but you start spreading the muck over the rest of us and you are out, my dear friend, out on your ear.'

Merilee strolled over to her and slipped an arm around her waist. 'More than friends, wouldn't you say? We've never spoken about it, but we both know it's there. Please let me try . . .'

Gwen stood frozen to the spot. 'Get away from me,' she said, her voice deathly still.

'I love you, Gwen, I really do. I know I could learn to love you any way you want, if you'll only give me the chance . . .' Her mouth was close to Gwen's ear as she stroked Gwen's hair with her other hand.

'Goddamnit, let go of me!' Gwen struggled to get free, and as Merilee tried to hold on to her, she grabbed Merilee's neck with both hands, choking her until she couldn't breathe. With a gasp, Merilee shoved herself back with every ounce of strength that she had, so forcefully that Gwen was thrown against the file cabinet. Merilee watched in horror as she struck her head on the red metal and collapsed. She lay there, quiet and still.

Merilee's stomach began to heave. She's not moving at all! I've killed her, she thought, God in heaven, I didn't mean to, but I've killed her! She bent down and tried to shake Gwen into consciousness, gently at first and then more urgently, speaking her name. She looked around helplessly. She had killed Gwyneth Roberts right here in her own office. What in hell was she going to do now?

She had to get out. As quickly as possible. She bolted

from the room, slamming the office door heavily behind her. Nobody noticed her rejoin the gala. The party was still going strong. She made her way through the crowd of glittering, laughing guests, scurried down the stairs, and headed for the front door.

And then she stopped halfway down. If you leave now, Lou will know there's something wrong. You're always the last one to leave a party. You always hang in there until the bitter end. Until Joe Garcia makes his rounds and locks everything up. Oh God, Joe's going to find her in the office. He'll find the body and he'll know . . . what? Nothing. How could anybody know that Gwen had just fired her? Certainly Gwen wasn't going to tell them. The worst thing Merilee could do right now would be to leave The Club. She had to hang in there, act like her usual self, make the rounds, have a few drinks, stay cool. Pulling herself together and straightening the bodice of her dress, Merilee made her way into the bar and loudly ordered a double bourbon on the rocks.

# *Two*

Stephen Andrews was desperate to find Luigi del Bello.
He had to get that million dollars back into the Central
American Freedom Fund. He couldn't hold off the
accounting for CAFF any longer. The liberal Democrats
in Congress were screaming for full disclosure of the
books and even Stanley Hughes was beginning to question
Stephen's reluctance to produce them. Stephen's excuse
had been that his co-signer, Malcolm Millican, was still
out of the country, but he was expected in Washington
the day after tomorrow. Everything had to be back in
place within the next thirty-six hours or the shit would
really hit the fan.

Lou had been avoiding him all evening. Passing by the
security lock-up near the main entrance, he saw Sara
Town handing a Manila envelope to Joe Garcia to put
away for safekeeping. Jesus, the last person he wanted
to run into tonight was Sara. He ducked and went the
other way.

He found Lou in the waterfall lounge, holding court
with his usual circle of sycopohantic friends. God, how
that whole scene disgusted Stephen now. This time, as
soon as Lou saw him, he excused himself and came over
to him. He was carrying an expensive-looking leather
briefcase.

'Do you have what you promised me?' Stephen said,
hearing his own voice tighten. He was probably sweating,
too. He wished he could handle this transaction more

565

smoothly, but at the moment all he wanted was to get it over with as soon as possible, get out of The Club, return to the safety of his own home, and completely erase the last three months of his life.

'Right here.' Lou handed over the leather briefcase and a small envelope containing the key. 'It's all there, I promise you.'

'Thank God.' Stephen could feel his whole body instantly relax.

'Sorry there was a bit of a delay. Big score tonight,' Lous said quietly. 'I had a lot riding on this . . .'

'Don't tell me any more,' Stephen cut him off. 'I don't want to know about it. I can't afford to know about it.' He was sick of the whole intrigue. What had once seemed dangerously exciting now just seemed dangerous. How could he ever have put his body, his reputation, his life, into this man's hands? He must have been out of his mind.

'Are you sure?' Lou's eyes glittered. 'We've got a lot to celebrate. Don't you think it might be particularly interesting to celebrate together?' He reached for Stephen's arm, but Stephen pulled away.

'Are you crazy? Don't you understand? We're finished. I'm through with all of it. I can't see you again.'

Lou shrugged. 'Up to you, of course. I never overstay my welcome. But just so you know, I'll be in my private office later tonight.'

'It's over,' Stephen whispered hoarsely. 'Go fuck yourself, Lou.'

'I want to go home, Stephen.' Miriam appeared suddenly at their side. 'Would you get our coats, please? Now.'

'Fine.' Stephen turned to go, but Lou caught his arm.

'If you should change your mind . . .' He let the rest of the sentence trail off as Miriam stepped between them. For a moment there was a charged silence.

566

'Let him go,' she said firmly, her face white. 'You've held on to him long enough. You're a sick man, Lou. It's time to let go.'

Lou relaxed his grip instantly. 'As you see it,' he said smoothly. 'Hope you enjoyed the party. Goodnight.' And he returned to his friends.

In the car, Miriam broke down. 'I know,' she said. 'I know about you and Lou.'

'I have no idea what you're talking about,' Stephen said with a sinking feeling, glancing at her as she looked for a Kleenex in her evening bag. The look on her face told him all he needed to know. There was no point in denying anything.

'I found the pictures in our downtown apartment. In the trunk at the foot of the bed. Disgusting pictures, pictures of you and Lou . . .' She couldn't bring herself to finish the sentence. 'Stephen, you've kept so much from me. You've lied to me at every turn; you've manipulated me into thinking everything that was wrong with us was my fault.'

'I know. I just couldn't tell you the truth. I'm sorry.'

'Stephen, what has happened to you? I don't know you at all any more.'

'I don't know myself.' He barely managed to choke the words out. He looked completely stricken.

'Stephen, why didn't you tell me you were going to marry Laura Hughes? Why did you lie to me tonight? How could you keep something like that from me?'

'I didn't want to hurt you.' Then: 'How did you find out?'

'Sara Town. I had to learn about the future of my relationship with you from a network news anchor! Our private, personal business! Do you have any idea how much more it hurt to find that out from a stranger, someone you barely know?'

'I know her,' Stephen said dully. 'She's part of this whole fucking mess.'

Miriam immediately knew just what he meant by that. Her stomach turned. 'Can you tell me what's wrong?' she asked hopelessly. It was too late now to salvage anything. Too much had already been lost.

'Everything. I can't bear to tell you all of it; you'll despise me once you know.' Stephen's face was a mask of despair. His entire world seemed to be shattering around him and he felt powerless to stop it. He had no idea how to hold on. 'I've betrayed you in so many ways . . . if it's any consolation to you, I've betrayed myself even more. Mim, my life is so far off track I don't know how to get it back on again. Sara Town is a highly dangerous woman. As long as she's alive, I may never be safe again. She knows too much, she . . .'

'Oh God, Stephen! I gave those photographs to Sara!'

'You *what?*' The colour drained from Stephen's face. He wheeled off the road and jammed on the brakes.

'I'd been holding on to them, hoping that somehow it was all a mistake, a joke, something . . . I don't know. I thought maybe we could talk about it, I could help you. . . . Then tonight when Sara told me about you and Laura, I was so angry, so hurt, I just handed the photographs over to her. In an envelope.'

'You mean she has them with her *now*? At The Club?'

'Yes.'

'Christ! Did you tell her what they were?'

'No, I said they were baby pictures, background information for the *In Depth* profile.'

'Then she may not have looked at them yet. With the gala going on, maybe she hasn't looked at them. I've got to go back. I've got to find her and get them back.' The words came tumbling out of his mouth. 'Please, dear

568

God, don't let her have looked at them. This could finish it for me, Miriam.'

'I know,' she said softly.

They pulled up in front of the apartment. 'Look, you stay here,' Stephen said urgently. 'Wait for me. Please. I'll be back, I promise. We have to talk.'

'All right.' In a state of shock, Miriam slowly got out of the car. She turned to look at Stephen and for no more than an instant their eyes met in a searing moment of shared pain.

'Miriam,' he said in a voice barely above a whisper. 'I'm so sorry.'

'I know,' she said. 'Me, too.' And he sped away.

The party seemed to be winding down at last. Guests were streaming out of the front door, still laughing, talking, heading for their cars. Stephen fought his way through them. She was not on the main floor. He headed upstairs, praying she had not already left. No, there she was, outside the sauna, talking to that slimy agent of hers, Michael Taylor.

'Sara! I need to talk to you.'

She turned and smiled, 'Ah, the elusive Mr Andrews. I was wondering where you'd got to. You're looking very handsome tonight.'

He couldn't tell from her tone whether she had opened the packet or not. Putting on a social smile he gave her a quick kiss on the cheek and said, 'And you look sensational, as always. Earlier this evening Miriam gave you something by mistake. She needs it back, if you don't mind. It actually belongs to someone else.'

'Oh, there's no mistake,' Sara said calmly. 'The package was definitely meant for me. Miriam gave it to me. Very helpful of her, I thought. There's some pretty interesting stuff in there.'

'I really need it back, Sara.' He fought to control

569

himself. 'It's vital information and it needs to be put in a safe place.' It was so difficult to do this in front of her damned agent. Why didn't she send him away?

'Not to worry, Stephen. It's in a very secure place and that's where it's going to stay. Until we strike a deal. I assume you're now in a position to re-negotiate? Shall we say lunch, next week? I'll call you.'

'No, I need it now.' He no longer tried to conceal the desperation in his voice. 'Give it to me, Sara. Please.'

'You heard the lady, pal.' Michael Taylor stepped forward. 'She's busy now. She'll talk to you next week. Now why don't you move out and shake a few hands before all the party guests go home?'

Stephen shifted from one foot to another. He couldn't cause a scene, not with the people who were still left standing around them, people who obviously recognized him. Muttering a powerful expletive under his breath, he turned and ran three steps at a time down the stairs.

'What was that all about?' Michael wanted to know.

'Oh nothing,' Sara smiled. 'Let's just say I've won a little personal victory. And now I'm ready to go home.'

'Hey, wait a minute. Not so fast. You promised me something this evening and I intend you to keep that promise.' He leered at her. 'It's my turn, baby.'

'For God's sake, Michael, I can give you that at home.'

'Why not here?' He jerked his head slightly toward the sauna.

'You're crazy!' But then again, why not? It gave her a perverse little thrill to think about making it in The Club right under Gwen's nose. 'OK, but I've got to get something first. You go on in and wait for me. Get the sauna steamed up for me, baby. I'll be right back.' She gave him a long kiss to hold him and then sauntered slowly down the stairs, knowing that he was watching her every move.

\* \* \*

Stephen Andrews was heading for the door when he recognized Joe Garcia standing in front of the visitors' lock-up. He suddenly remembered Sara handing a large envelope to the security guard earlier that evening.

'Evening, Joe,' he said. 'Miss Town, you know, the reporter from *In Depth*?' The beefy guard nodded. 'She just asked me to get something for her out of visitors' valuables. An envelope she gave you, oh, maybe an hour ago.'

'Sure, Senator, I remember.' The paunchy guard grinned at him. 'You got the claims ticket on you?'

'Gee' – Stephen made a show of searching his empty pockets – 'no, I don't. I guess she forgot to hand it to me. I don't really need it, do I?'

''Fraid so. No tickee, no washee.'

'But she specifically asked me to get it for her.' He tried to keep his voice pleasant. 'I hate to disappoint the lady.'

'Sorry. That's the rules.'

'You know who I am, don't you?'

'Sure. Who doesn't?' He grinned again.

God, the man was a fucking moron. 'You don't trust me?' Stephen could hear his voice rising.

'Ain't a matter of trust. It's a matter of rules. I can't give you nothin' out of visitors' valuables unless you got a slip for it. Whyn't you go on back upstairs and get the claim check offa Miss Town? And tell her if she doesn't claim it before the party's over, it'll automatically be put in lock-up in Mr del Bello's outer office and she'll have to get it tomorrow. Anything that hasn't been claimed before I make my rounds, I just take it on upstairs to his office. It's a real hassle to get it outa there.'

'Look, *amigo*,' Stephen said, pulling a hundred-dollar bill from his wallet. 'Why don't you just slip it to me now and save us all the hassle. I'd really appreciate it.'

A look of suspicion passed over Joe's stolid face. 'I

don't accept no bribes to break the rules here. Ms Gwen, she pays me just fine.'

'Of course she does,' Stephen agreed, hastily stuffing the money back in his wallet. 'I didn't mean to offend you.'

The security guard nodded again. 'Well, we're fixin' to close up here, Senator. The party's over. I'll ask you to leave by the front door.'

'Certainly. Wonderful party.' Stephen grabbed the guard's hand and shook it firmly, then headed for the door.

'Goodnight, Senator.' The security guard held the heavy brass doors open for him and watched him exit.

'Goodnight, Joe.' Stephen found himself out on the street. Damn. There was nothing he could do except wait for Sara. She had to come out of The Club eventually and the pictures would undoubtedly come with her. There was no way she would leave them at The Club; they were much too precious for that, and he knew she was not a member. No, once she left for the night (God, what the hell was keeping her in there when the party was virtually over?), she would bring them with her. He'd get them from her then even if he had to beat the shit out of that agent of hers in the process.

He asked the parking attendant to bring the Mercedes around for him. The street was now fairly clear. He would sit in his car, across the street and watch for her to emerge from The Club.

Susie helped Lokis climb into her chauffeur-driven car and they headed downtown to Tribeca. As the car pulled up in front of his loft apartment, Lokis put his arms around her. 'Come in with me, please,' he begged, 'just for a little while. I won't keep you long, I promise, but I have to talk to you.'

'OK,' she sighed, 'but I really can't stay. I've got

572

an early morning meeting at Bloomingdale's.'

'You mean you landed that deal you've been after?'

'Looks like it. We're just going to settle the details tomorrow.'

'That's terrific, honey! Things are really going great for you, aren't they?'

'In some ways,' Susie said softly as she led him up the stairs and through his front door.

'Yeah, I know what you mean.' He looked at her through bleary eyes as she helped him into bed. 'Susie, I can't believe you're still pregnant. It's like a miracle ot me. We're going to have a baby.'

'This doesn't change a thing,' Susie warned him.

'Maybe not about us,' Lokis agreed, 'although I'm going to fight to change your mind about that. But a baby makes a big difference to me. God, I feel like such a complete asshole. I'm sorry for everything. Sorry for causing a scene back there at The Club. Sorry for the way I've hurt you. I'm not asking you to forgive me. I just wish we could start over.'

They looked at each other.

'Well, we can't.'

'How did we get here? What happened to us?'

'I don't know.' Susie felt just as bewildered as he did.

'You must know that I love you. I can't imagine loving anybody else the way I love you. I mean, we've pretty well loved each other for all of our adult lives.'

'I've never loved anyone else the way I loved you either, but ultimately that's not enough.'

'How could we blow something that good?' He was crying now. 'I mean it, I never meant to hurt you. I'd do anything to make it up to you.'

'Good intentions aren't enough any more,' Susie said firmly, although it was hard to stay firm in the face of his tears. 'You can't go through life acting like a peacock.'

573

'I know that. I was just so jealous of you. Every minute of the day I wondered where you were, what you were doing, who you were doing it with; it was driving me crazy. And I was jealous of your success, I admit it. I just couldn't handle it. I don't know, maybe I love you too much.'

'You've got real problems, Lokis, you've got to realize that. It's not about love, it's about control, it's about power. You've got to take responsibility for your own life.'

'People can change,' he said softly.

'I know. I have.'

'Yes, you have,' he looked at her admiringly. 'And as much as I hate to admit it, it's for the better.'

'It means a lot to me to hear you acknowledge that.' For the first time that evening, Susie smiled at him.

'Are you going to cut me out of your life altogether now? Will you keep me from seeing the baby?'

'No. I think you should be involved. But don't look for anything else from this. I'm enjoying being on my own.'

'We could be a real family. Please . . . think about it.'

'I don't know. . . .'

'People can change,' he said again.

'Get some rest now.' She leaned over and kissed him on the cheek.

Susie turned off the lights as she closed the apartment door behind her. She looked up at the night sky with its thick haze. She was glad she had asked her chauffeur to wait for her. She really didn't feel like hailing a cab. Wearily she climbed into the back seat. It would feel good to get home, take a hot bath, and climb into bed with her portfolio, and go over her strategy for tomorrow's meeting.

Her portfolio! Damnit, it was still at The Club. She had left it in the visitors' lock-up. In the excitement of

574

the confrontation with Lokis and Gwen and Merilee, she'd forgotten all about it. There was no way she could make that meeting at Bloomingdale's in the morning without it.

She knocked on the bulletproof glass and told her chauffeur to take her back to The Club.

Merilee was still passed out in the bar. The gala was over. All the guests had gone home and The Club was dark and still. Joe Garcia, making the rounds, came into the bar and shook his head when he saw her there. Ms Houston was always the last to leave the party. Sometimes she didn't leave at all but spent the night in the bar. He'd found her there the next morning plenty of times. He leaned over and shook her gently to try and wake her up. He hated to see a lady like this. Ms Houston was just trash. He shook her again.

'It's OK, Joe. You can just leave her there,' Lou said out of the darkness. He had stopped to grab a bottle of Calvados from the bar. He appreciated a good brandy late at night. 'I'll keep an eye on her. I'm heading upstairs to do some late-night book-keeping. I can look in on her later.'

'OK, Mr del Bello. I gotta start locking up.'

'Goodnight, Joe.'

''Night, Mr del Bello. Don't work too hard.' The guard ambled out of the bar, the gun at his side thwacking against his khaki-covered thigh.

Lou glanced at the sleeping Merilee, stretched out on one of the red velvet banquettes. For a brief moment he considered waking her up for a little late-night party. But she was snoring quite heavily. She certainly knew how to tie one on. What the hell. Might as well let her sleep it off. As long as she was awake before Gwen arrived first thing in the morning.

Well, if sex was out of the question, there were other,

more solitary pleasures he could turn to. He turned out the lights and headed for the supply-room. Given the events of the past twenty-four hours, he felt he deserved a very special reward.

Bodine Johnson, newscaster for Channel 7 *Late Beat News*, was locked in the little powder-room on the second floor of The Club.

She had been there since the party ended an hour ago and she intended to stay there until she was absolutely sure that everyone had gone. Call it a private little stakeout. Investigative journalism. Once she'd determined that everybody was gone from the building, she was going to do some snooping around.

Her hands were closed tightly around her evening purse, which contained the can of baby powder Sara had tossed to her earlier that night in the washroom. It made her laugh to think that a big-time muckraking reporter like Sara Town had missed such incriminating evidence about The Club. A baby-powder tin filled to the brim with pure cocaine, sitting out in plain view in the washroom! What a stroke of luck!

Now it was up to her to dig up the rest of the dirt and she had no doubt she could do it. Provided she had enough time and provided nobody caught her.

She checked her watch. It was already two o'clock in the morning. She had heard nothing outside the powder-room door for over an hour. She would wait fifteen minutes more and then make her move. Talk about privileged information. This could lead her to the exclusive she had been hoping for.

Lou unlocked the door to the storeroom that contained his private stock, his own personal Shoppers Drug Mart. It always gave him a thrill of danger to go into it, even though he knew it was relatively safe.

Except for Merilee who was passed out in the bar. And even that was safe. Lou knew that when she was in that state, she wouldn't wake up if a wall fell on her.

Of course there was Joe Garcia. Right about now Joe would be finishing his rounds. But that was safe, too, because Joe had a routine and Lou was very familiar with it. He always took the elevator straight up to the top floor and then walked down the stairs, checking each floor on the way down. He moved slowly and carefully, letting the light from his torch fall over every inch of The Club.

It was easy to avoid Joe. Provided you knew the routine.

Stephen Andrews knew Joe's routine almost as well as Lou did. From the late nights the two of them had spent together at The Club, when they would lock themselves in and listen to Joe pass by. Stephen knew how long it would take him to get from the top floor all the way down to his post just inside the main entrance. He knew that Joe took his time, but would it be enough time to enable Stephen to break into the visitors' lock-up? He was going to have to risk it. He'd been watching the front door for an hour and a half with no sign of Sara. She had to be still inside The Club and if she was in there, so were the photos.

Lou had taken the photographs for fun, he said. Setting the camera on a tripod so they could both be in the picture. Kinky Polaroids. The thought of those photographs in Sara's possession was driving Stephen crazy. Why hadn't he burned them right away? He should have destroyed them. He'd been meaning to get rid of them, but he thought they were perfectly safe in the trunk of the foot of the bed in the downtown flat. Miriam hadn't gone there in years. He'd been out of town when she decided to spend the night there. He had only himself to blame for what had happened. He hated to think of

577

how she must have felt when she found them. Sick, revolted. She must hate him now. He wouldn't blame her if she did. Oh God . . . Just when he'd been feeling safe, when he'd managed to get the money back, when he'd thought he was completely off the hook . . .

He couldn't wait any longer. He would have to go into The Club and somehow find the photos.

He slid the locked briefcase containing the money under the driver's seat. He opened the glove compartment and riffled quickly through the contents, until he found the gold Club card.

He got out of the car and locked it. Then he opened the trunk and removed a tyre iron. He gave a quick, surreptitious look around the streets to see if anyone was watching and then realized — what the hell — this was New York.

With an air of infinite confidence, he carried the tyre iron up to the main entrance of The Club. He inserted the gold card into the magnetized slot and the heavy doors of The Club obligingly swung open to admit him.

Miriam arrived just in time to see Stephen disappear into The Club. After waiting over an hour for him to come home, she was practically frantic with worry and guilt and anger. How could she have placed Stephen's entire future in such jeopardy by giving the photographs to Sara? If she went back to The Club herself, maybe she could persuade Sara to return the envelope to her. Nothing was worth the agony of sitting in the apartment and waiting. She ran out, got into the BMW, and drove as quickly as she could back to The Club.

She pulled up behind the Mercedes just as Stephen was heading up the stairs to the front door. She watched him slide the card into the slot and slip inside the doors. How had he managed to get a programmed card? Probably

578

Luigi del Bello had given it to him in order to facilitate their late night rendezvous. She felt sick again.

From her vantage point The Club looked completely dark. She wanted to follow Stephen but she was afraid to leave the car.

Suddenly a light went on in one of the upper floors. Past Gwen's office, past Merilee's office, down the hall to . . .

Stephen must have ended up in Lou's private office. The pain flooded through her. Lies. He had told her nothing but lies. Bastard!

She resolved not to leave until he came out. She would wait for him if it took all night.

In the sanctity of his private office, Lou reverently unwrapped the relics of his own personal white mass and laid them on the polished top of his desk.

The pure crystalline white powder. The host. The sacrament.

The gleaming mirror.

The bunsen burner. The holy chalice. Its blue flame the blow of an especially divine spirit.

The sight of these objects of devotion set him a-quiver in expectation of the high that he knew so well.

Carefully, methodically, he rinsed the glass bowl of his pipe and wiped it clean with a soft white cloth. He enjoyed every step of the ritual. He revelled in the sensuality of the experience. The preparation excited him almost more than the high itself.

Stephen slammed the metal door of the locker shut in utter frustration. There were two wallets, both expensive leather and both monogrammed, obviously forgotten by guests at the gala. There was a set of diamond cuff links. One emerald earring with a broken clasp. A large portfolio containing a detailed proposal for a line of chocolates. Chocolates! No Manila envelope. No photographs. Damnit all to hell!

He wished that he could pound on the door in rage and frustration. With the aid of a cigarette lighter he'd searched every inch of the locker, taking it apart and putting it back together again. There were no photographs. He wanted to scream. He was breaking out in a cold sweat, his breath coming in rapid gasps. He felt as if he was about to faint. This couldn't be happening to him. Jesus, if he didn't get his hands on those photos pretty damn quick . . . Christ! He ordered himself to stay calm.

He racked his brain for ideas. Lou had told him he would be in his private office tonight. Everything seemed dark but maybe there was a chance that he was still upstairs. He headed for the elevator. No, wait. Joe Garcia might hear it going up. Better take the stairs. Stephen snapped off his lighter and began to climb the stairs in the darkness, the lighter pressing comfortingly against him in his hip pocket.


With the expertise of a Cordon Bleu chef, Lou broke down the white crystals, separating the powder. He liked the purity of freebasing, the thirty-second rush followed by two minutes of euphoria.

Straight into the brain.

He mixed the powder with ether, heating the base in the bowl of his pipe with a butane torch, inhaling the concentrated fumes from the glass bubble. The hit was always instantaneous, the rush powerful. Travelling faster than the speed of light, up, up, soaring, floating. Coming sharply into focus. Then the blessed freeze, the icy cold numbness, the deadening of all sensation in his face. And then the crashing down, down, falling too fast and too far, nothing to break the fall, struggling to stay up but slipping under.

The only cure for down was up again. With shaking

hands, Lou relit the torch and moved it closer underneath the glass bowl of the pipe.

There is a flash of red, a blinding white light, followed by a thick, smoky haze that chokes him instantly. His chest constricting, an excruciating tightness, closing off all air, he gasps for breath, the ever-tightening band around his head closing it off, the blood vessels in his brain dancing to their own music. The sound of shattering glass and the sudden piercing pain in his left eye. He sees stars. He sees red. As a great shudder rocks the room, he is shoved against the wall, the pain in his eye — jagged, moving — zigzagging to meet the pain in his chest. He holds himself rigid against the ultimate authority of impending death, but with the next explosion he feels his heart burst, breaking through the bounds of his chest. He cries out again and again in pain and fear, and as he lifts his arms upwards in agonized prayer to the Madonna, the ceiling rushes down to meet him

The explosion rocked The Club. Miriam was paralysed with shock as the building lit up. She watched flames racing across the top floor of the building in long fingers, stroking its edges, greedy tongues licking away at the foundation. The whole upper right corner of the building was on fire. Lou's private office! With Stephen trapped inside! No, oh God, no! He couldn't die! Dear God, don't let him die! Right in front of her eyes, the flames suddenly doubled in size and ferocity.

Without thinking she found herself running up the steps to the front doors, tears streaming down her face, her heart slamming against her chest. She turned back around just in time to see a small crowd of people beginning to gather. She tried to scream to them to go for help, but no sound came out. Nearly hysterical, she jammed her card into the slot and plunged straight into the burning building.

Even on the first floor, the heat was intense and almost overpowering. In the hall, the heat rose up and caught her like a blast from a furnace. However, the smoke in the air was worse. Half gulping it in, half holding her breath, Miriam started up the staircase, grasping the banister. On the next level up, the heat surrounded her, the black acrid air threatening to suffocate her. She couldn't tell where it was coming from. She called out Stephen's name, choking and coughing as she went. There was no answer. There was a door in front of her. When she grabbed the door knob, the heat from the metal seared her hand, and the door gave way. Terrified she instinctively walked straight into a black cloud.

# *Epilogue*

As the haze of the smoke lifted, Gwyneth Roberts stood on the sidewalk at the front of the crowd held back by the cordon. She was staring at the rubble that had been 37 Middlesex, now a charred, hollow shell. Fragmented, empty, bleak. And only an overwhelming reminder of the emptiness at the centre of her life. Furniture, fittings, the original art on the walls, the computer system and all the records had been lost. The unofficial estimated damage to the building was already in the millions; the damage to her own life was immeasurable. She was sweating. She was drowning. She was hurtling downwards. But she didn't feel anything. If only she could cry, she needed desperately to cry, but the tears wouldn't come. The loss was still too great, too fresh. Maybe she was still in shock. Dry-eyed, she had watched everything she had worked so hard for, all she had fought for, her whole life, literally going up in smoke. The luck dragon on her back was finally gone for good.

When she came to after the fight with Merilee, she didn't immediately know where she was. She lay still on the office floor, waiting for the room to come into focus. She concentrated on forcing herself to breathe deeply and on trying to remember exactly what had happened. Oh yes, it was the night of the gala. She'd had a fight with Merilee. Merilee had hit her or pushed her and she'd fallen. Her head. Her head was pounding, she was a little dizzy and there was a lump over her right eye the size of a golf ball. She didn't seem to be bleeding much. She didn't feel nauseated. She couldn't be too badly hurt. Tentatively, she ran her hands over her body. No, nothing was broken. Even her white silk dress seemed to be fine.

Slowly and tentatively, holding on to the edge of the file cabinet, she climbed to her feet and, leaning on her desk, took a few more deep breaths. The dizziness began to subside. She made her way to the bar and poured herself a stiff Scotch. She drank it straight down and immediately poured herself another. There; her hands had stopped shaking. The Scotch was working. She was beginning to feel a lot better. In fact, she was perfectly fine. Where the hell was everybody? She opened the door. Silence and darkness greeted her. The gala was obviously over. And more than anything now, she wanted to be home too, in her own bed, with this night behind her. Maybe she should call a cab? But no, what for? She felt absolutely OK. She'd take the car.

Once in the driver's seat, she realized she should not have attempted to drive herself. Her hands were trembling on the steering wheel, the dizziness had returned, she felt as if she were going to throw up. And she was weaving all over the road. She pulled over to the side of the street, got out and, leaving the car parked in a metered spot, hailed a cab. She asked the driver to take her to the emergency department at Lenox Hill. Leaning back in the seat, exhausted, she put her hands over her mouth, as the lurching in her stomach began to mimic the lurching of the cab as it careered through the city streets.

They were two blocks from the hospital when a scratchy, barely decipherable but urgent announcement from the dispatcher came over the cab radio: 'Mondo fire in midtown area. Looks to be lower Sixties. East side. Lexington and Third. Traffic's backed up real bad. They've got the whole area barricaded. There's fire trucks and cops all over the place, so plan your routes accordingly.'

Oh God. The dizziness and nausea left her immediately. With terror in her heart, she ordered the driver to turn right around and take her back to 37 Middlesex.

'You crazy, lady? You heard what the guy said. Nobody can get near there. The whole area's blocked off. You'd be taking your life in your hands.'

'Get me as close as you can, then. Please. I'll pay you triple the fare. Just get me there.' Her heart was pounding wildly. Her head was completely clear, the dizziness gone, and fear had taken over. It was almost as if she had been expecting some kind of a disaster, that this was what all her nightmares and fears had been leading up to. 37 Middlesex was in danger. All she could do now was to pray she wouldn't get there too late.

'OK, lady, whatever you say. It's your funeral.' With a piercing squeal of the brakes, the cabbie pulled a U-turn and headed back to The Club.

And now that she was here, standing in front of what was left of The Club, it was indeed a funeral, for she was witnessing a death. The death of everything her life had been leading up to until this moment.

Strange. She felt oddly detached. As though this were happening to someone else. A thick haze still covered everything. The firemen were directing their hoses over smouldering patches in the ruins. All around her, the rumours were flying. It was arson. An act of violence. Yes, the fire was deliberately set. But it was to collect on the insurance. No, the fire was definitely an accident. Grease in the dining-room kitchen? Somebody smoking in the sauna?

The police had told her quite a lot and yet it still seemed they didn't know very much. Or maybe she was just too

585

upset really to hear what they were saying. They thought the fire had started in Lou's office. A couple of hours after the party. They suspected a bomb. Of course it would take a good fire analyst and a full investigation to determine that for sure. Gwen didn't know what to believe and Lou wasn't around to ask. He was fighting for his life in intensive care at New York Hospital.

It was so hard to take it all in. To Gwen it proved only that her strange dreams and premonitions had been right all along. Somewhere, somehow, The Club had gone off course, as programmed to self-destruct. She was filled with anger and bitterness and remorse. She would have to sort through all those feelings later. Right now she gave herself up to the pain of overwhelming loss. Rebuilding The Club, even if such a thing were possible, would be a long and costly process, even with the insurance. By the time she got back on her feet again, she would have lost valuable ground to all the vultures lying in wait to take over her territory. What did this mean in terms of her plans for LA? For London? Gone, all gone. Looking at the wreckage of 37 Middlesex, wet, scorched, its very foundations eaten away, it was almost as if The Club had never existed at all.

The fire had been out for some time now, but the crowd of the curious remained. Traffic was backed up for blocks, and more and more people continued to gather behind the barricades. What were all of them doing here? Were they here to gloat over her anguish? Gwen wanted to shout at them all to go away and leave her alone to grieve privately. This was her personal loss. It had nothing to do with them.

Bodine Johnson, wearing a yellow fireman's slicker and holding a microphone was conducting a virtual press conference on the site of the fire, surrounded by a Channel 7 *Late Beat News* camera crew and several sound technicians.

586

The sympathy in people's eyes was almost too much to bear. She turned to make her way to the back of the crowd and found Mina van Houghton running towards her. Without saying a word, Mina opened her arms and Gwen fell into the circle of her embrace.

Bodine Johnson knew she was damned lucky to be alive. Aside from singed eyebrows and sore lungs, she was miraculously none the worse for wear. She'd taken a risk tonight, a dumb risk. She could have been killed hiding out inside 37 Middlesex. Acting like some third-rate detective, sneaking around, putting her own personal physical safety in jeopardy . . . shit, she must have been crazy. Still, it had certainly proved to be worth it. Somewhere along the way she had lost the powder can full of coke, but she hadn't exactly come away empty-handed. She'd managed to get an eye-witness, first-hand account of the fire from a very important political figure, Senator Stephen Andrews.

Once the fire workers brought her out of the burning building and she told them she was perfectly fine, the first thing she did was beep the Channel Seven news crew to tell them to drag their asses out of bed and get down here as fast as they could. She was about to get an exclusive interview with Stephen Andrews, the hero of the hour. The Republican presidential hopeful had bravely gone into the burning building and managed to save the lives of CTA agent Michael Taylor, and America's favourite network news star, Sara Town of *In Depth*. What a story! The press were going to have a field day with this one. And she, Bodine Johnson, was right here to cover the event before anyone else from the press had arrived on the scene. She had her precious exclusive.

Pushing her way through the crowd, Susie found Mina standing in front of the remains of The Club with her

587

arms around Gwen. She was holding her tightly, as if
shielding her, as if the smoky ruins of The Club that lay
before them were even more frightening than the fire
itself. Susie realized that of course, for Gwen, they were.
How could she ever rebuild from this tragedy? Susie
hugged Gwen hard and told her over and over again how
sorry she was, but Gwen hardly responded. Obviously
she was still in shock.

'How did you get here?' Susie asked Mina. 'How did
you hear about the fire?'

'Lokis phoned our place looking for you. He heard it
on the news just after you left him. He's probably on
his way down here, too.'

'Do they know how the fire started?

Gwen stepped back with a wan smile. Then she looked
back at the scene, the flashing red lights and the crackle
of the fire and police radios.

Mina shook her head. 'The police think it was arson,
but nobody's really sure. Witnesses say they heard an
explosion before they saw the flames, so it could have
been a bomb.'

'Oh my God! Was anyone still in the building? Was
anyone hurt?'

'Quite a few, considering the gala had been over for
hours. The fire started in Luigi's office, they think. Lou
had a heart attack, apparently, but he's still alive. They've
taken him to the hospital.'

'Is he . . .' Susie lowered her voice, 'is he going to pull
through?'

'Think so. Sara Town was trapped inside, too. Along
with Michael Taylor.'

'Michael!'

'He's OK,' Mina said. 'Stephen Andrews managed to
get them both out. He's quite the hero of the day,
Michael's been taken to hospital, too, for minor burns.
He'll be fine. You know him. He was so tanked up, I'm

sure he didn't feel a thing. Sara's being treated on the spot for smoke inhalation but she seems to be fine. And Stephen Andrews is in great shape, as you can see.' Mina nodded in the direction of Bodine where Stephen was standing in front of his car, surrounded by a myriad of attentive reporters and cameramen jostling for position. More were arriving on the scene.

'What were they all doing in The Club after hours?' Susie asked.

'Who knows? A little private celebrating, I guess. A post-party party.'

'Jesus! Anybody else hurt?'

'The security guard's dead. Joe got trapped in one of the stair wells while he was making his rounds. Oh, and' – Mina reached out to take Susie's hands – 'Merilee Houston's gone, too.'

'Merilee? Dead? Oh, no!' Susie couldn't believe it. She'd always figured Merilee to be one of life's survivors. Once the affair with Lokis happened, she and Merilee had stopped being friends, but she knew the blame for her marriage break-up didn't lie solely with Merilee. She and Lokis had had problems long before Merilee came along. She shivered. 'God, nobody deserves to die like this!'

'Yeah, I know. They found her in the bar. She must have passed out after the party and nobody knew she was there. She was dead by the time the firemen got to her.'

'God, how awful.' The eyes of the two women met. It could so easily have been one of them. 'How's Miriam?'

Susie noticed the actress standing slightly apart from them on the other side of Gwen. She was standing stock still, her arms wrapped around herself, holding her fur coat closed. She was staring in front of her, tears rolling unheeded down her cheeks.

'I don't know. She was here when I arrived. We both

589

saw Stephen lift Sara out of one of the top floor windows. I got a couple of great shots of that' — she patted her camera case fondly — ' "Politician saves media star." I'm sure I'll be able to sell it to one of the wire services, either UP or AP. It was a pretty spectacular sight. That should help to get him elected. He's a hero tonight, no doubt about it. America's going to love him for this. Miriam must be very proud.'

The fire workers who had got Miriam out of the building were urging her to go to the hospital for a check-up but she couldn't seem to tear herself away. She tried to piece together the events of the past few hours. She had gone into the fire to save Stephen, but in the end he had saved himself. She realized he'd become very good at doing that. And, even more important, good at saving his precious image.

She glanced over at him as he held forth, surrounded by members of the press, hanging on his every word. He was in his element now, standing tall and handsome, his blond hair becomingly rumpled, his face and clothes artistically smudged. He was leading a mini press conference at the fire site, giving each reporter a perfect fifteen-second sound bite and trying to make sure that his best side was turned to every clicking camera. He didn't need her now. Perhaps he had never really needed her at all.

No, she mustn't think that. He'd shown tremendous courage tonight. After all, he had saved two people from almost certain death. That took a physical bravery she hadn't known he possessed. She had never thought of him as courageous. Strong and powerful, yes; manipulative, of course, but never brave. He had actually risked his life for someone else. And, thank God, he himself had made it out alive. She knew he had been near the edge of an emotional precipice for some time now, even if she hadn't been able to acknowledge it to him or to herself. It was time now for her to face the fact that, as much as she loved him, she hadn't been able to save him and bring him back to her. Whatever future he might now have, it would not be with her. That part of her life was over. So why was she crying? She still had a lot to look forward to. She was a hair's breadth away from winning an Oscar. She had a chance for a new life.

And after all, someone was waiting for her, someone who loved her as much as she had once loved Stephen. David. It might be nice to be the person who was loved for a change. Well and truly loved, even cherished.

And Stephen? Oh, she hated to admit it, but he would be all right. Stephen would manage just fine without her. She glanced over at him, holding court in the crowd of reporters and, for just a moment, their eyes met. Then a camera flashed and Stephen turned away again.

There's no doubt now, Stephen thought, elated, I am on my way to the White House. The fire had been a bizarre stroke of good luck. He had the money back and the photographs had been destroyed in the fire. He was off the hook, home free, the anguish of the last few months now just a bad dream. Tonight he was a hero in the eyes of all America. He'd risked his own life to save the life of another person, a celebrity, Sara Town. How the press would lionize him now! He had saved one of their own. He saw Sara Town coming towards him and gracefully, magnanimously, he held out his arms to welcome her into the circle of reporters.

A hero, Sara thought bitterly as the crowd of reporters and cameramen parted like the Red Sea, allowing Stephen to put his arm around her as flashbulbs went off all around them. Stephen Andrews was a hero. She felt weak and shaky, nauseated. The smell of smoke was everywhere — in her hair, in her clothes; she could even taste it in her mouth, acrid and dry like ashes. The press would rush to elevate Stephen Andrews to sainthood now.

Only she knew the truth about him, the 'saint' headed for the White House. And she still had the photographs in her purse. She had had them in her possession all the time Stephen was carrying her out. What a laugh! And what a quandary the events of this evening had put her in. She could use them to destroy his chances. But how could she use them? After all, he had saved her life. In a way, that gave him the ultimate power. For the first time in her career, Sara accepted the fact that she was looking at a moral dilemma. What was she going to do? At this point, she did not know.

Stephen leaned over and kissed her warmly on the cheek, angling her head towards the bulk of the cameras. Hell, the game wasn't over yet. She bared her teeth for the cameras. She had plenty of time to make up her mind.

Miriam saw them kiss. God, what hypocrites. The two of them really deserved each other. They weren't worth crying about. God, she must look like shit. And with all these cameras around. She blew her nose, wiped her face, and moved closer to Mina and Susie.

'It's so weird. A bomb!' Susie was exclaiming. 'Who would want to bomb 37 Middlesex?'

'The police think there may be a link with organized crime.'

'What?' Miriam was amazed. 'You mean like the mob?'

'Well, there were always rumours, you must have heard them, that Lou's connected to Sicilian Mafia. Apparently the police have had him under surveillance. They suspect he was involved in a major drug operation.'

'What do you mean "major"? I'd heard that you could

get drugs at The Club, but I thought they were just for social use, nothing big.'

'We're talking big here,' Mina went on. 'Major shipments of coke direct from the south. The police think it's possible that he was trying to cut the syndicate out of the deal and they put out a contract on him.'

'So they bombed The Club. God, that's incredible,' Susie whispered. 'How did you find all this out?'

Mina grinned for the first time since arriving on the scene. 'I've got a friend on the force. Remember when I did that spread on the NYPD Ball? Julio would do anything for me. He says it's going to be tough to prove anything now. The fire has destroyed just about everything.'

'How's Gwen handling all of this?' Miriam said softly.

'She's pretty much still in shock.' Mina moved to put her arms back around Gwen, and Susie and Miriam came in close around her. 'I'm not sure she's aware of all of this.'

Actually Gwen is beginning to resurface. She feels herself fighting her way up through waves of despair as the welcome tears finally fill her eyes. It feels so good to cry at last, ultimately to let go. She puts her head on Mina's shoulder and cries like a baby. Mina holds her close, saying nothing, but rocking her gently, until she has cried herself out. Slowly, somewhere deep within her, Gwen is beginning to focus, to see things with a new clarity. As though she'd been sick for a long time, but could now feel the virus departing her body, the gaps closing behind it, leaving her with the chance of becoming whole again.

She'd lost control of The Club. 37 Middlesex had become something she'd never intended it to be. A symbol of a decade of greed. Like a spoiled, self-centred, selfish child, The Club had demanded too much, too soon, chafing at its boundaries, pushing aside its founding principles like so much confining baggage. What had happened to those early glorious ideals? Too many compromises had been made. Too many variables, too many strings pulling in different directions to hold it together any more.

And she cannot lay all the blame for that on Lou either. She should have been more aware of what was going on around her. How could she have turned such a blind eye to the 'special privileges' areas? Because as long as the money kept rolling in, she hadn't wanted to know. Her public self had taken over her private self and come close to destroying it. She'd stood by and watched the rich get richer and the poor get poorer and she hadn't done anything about it. Hell, she'd contributed to it, capitalized on it. She'd created a fantasy. Ultimately that's all The Club was, a fantasy. Maybe her eyes had been so tightly shut in order to hold on to the fantasy that it took an apocalyptic, cataclysmic event to wake her up to the fact that it was time to move on.

The eighties at 37 Middlesex had been like a gigantic party that had gone on just that little bit too long, with a hangover that, in the cold, hard light of day, brought with it sickening ramifications. She knew nothing of the drugs. She shudders even thinking that such an allegation could be true. But if it is true, she can only hope and pray that, as Mina keeps assuring her, there will be nothing left to link them to her or The Club. That all the demons, real and imaginary, can be laid to rest.

There are still a lot of unanswered questions here, not only about the fate of 37 Middlesex but about her own fate as well. Maybe it's time for her actively to pursue those answers. Not knowing exactly how she is going to do that doesn't even seem frightening. In fact, it's almost exhilarating. She is perhaps halfway through her life, but it's not over. Not by a long shot. She senses some of her old optimism creeping in; she can almost feel the old luck dragon struggling to climb back up on her back. The power of her imagination, the strength of her vision, was what built The Club in the first place. And that she will never lose. What she wants now, more than anything, is a chance to start over again. Not from where she once started, not from what The Club had become, but something brand new. Something good and worthwhile.

In the early morning cold, Gwen shivers. Miriam and Susie and Mina surround her. In the safety of their arms, she can feel the pain begin to recede. She's been alone for such a long time. It feels good to be held, to let someone else be strong and allow herself to be comforted. She will not have to survive on her own. She feels the strength of the other women supporting her, enclosing her in a circle of warmth.

Miriam, Susie, Mina, and Gwen. Pale with the first suggestion of morning, the light surrounding them defines the scene, sharp and strong with a strange clarity. Gwen relaxes within the circle of arms embracing her. She feels, for the first time in her adult life, that she has finally come home.